I0787986

THE UNDERWORLD SAGA, BOOKS 1-3

THANATOS, CHALLENGE OF HADES,
A NEW GODDESS

Eva Pohler

Copyright © 2021 by Eva Pohler.

All rights reserved. No part of this publication may be reproduced, distributed or transmitted in any form or by any means, including photocopying, recording, or other electronic or mechanical methods, without the prior written permission of the publisher, except in the case of brief quotations embodied in critical reviews and certain other noncommercial uses permitted by copyright law. For permission requests, write to the publisher, addressed "Attention: Permissions Coordinator," at the address below.

Eva Pohler Books
20011 Park Ranch
San Antonio, Texas 78259
www.evapohler.com

Publisher's Note: This is a work of fiction. Names, characters, places, and incidents are a product of the author's imagination. Locales and public names are sometimes used for atmospheric purposes. Any resemblance to actual people, living or dead, or to businesses, companies, events, institutions, or locales is completely coincidental.

Book Layout ©2017 BookDesignTemplates.com

Book Cover Design by B Rose Designz

The Underworld Saga: Books 1-3/ Eva Pohler. – Anniversary Edition
ISBN 978-1-958390-32-0

For Zack Newcomb, whose support helped to make this happen.

MAP OF THE UNDERWORLD
The Gates of Horn
The Gates of Ivory
The Fields of Asphodel
The Titan Pit
The Fate's Abode
Hypno's Abode
Thanatos's Abode
The Abode of the Furies
The Elysian Fields
Phlegethon
Hydra's Sinkhole
The Palace of Hades & Persephone
Tartarus
Erebus
Charon's Abode
Garage & Stables
The Seer's Pit
Cocytus
House of Judgement
Styx
Lethe
Acheron
N
W
E
S

Contents

BOOK ONE

Thanatos

Chapter One: The Drowning

Therese Mills peeled the white gloves off her sweaty hands as soon as she and her parents were in the car. Now that her mother's thing was over, she could finally get home and out of this blue dress. It was like being in a straitjacket.

Anything for Mom, of course.

What the...

A man glared at her through her backseat window. She jumped up, sat back, blinked. The man vanished, but when she blinked again, she could still see the eerie face behind her lids: the scruffy black beard and dark, haunting eyes.

"Thanks again for making tonight so special," her mother, apparently not seeing the man, said from the passenger seat as her father started the engine. "You two being there meant a lot to me."

"Did you see that man?" Therese peered through her window for the face.

"What?" Her mother also looked. "What man?"

"What man, Therese?" her father asked.

"Never mind."

Therese did not find it unusual that her mother hadn't noticed the man. Although her mother was a brilliant scientist, she wasn't the most observant person.

Just last spring after all the snow had finally melted around their house in the Colorado mountains, and Therese and her mother had been able to enjoy their wooden deck with the melted lake spread out in front of them and the forest rising up the mountains behind them, Therese had spotted the wild horse and foal she had seen just before winter. They both had reddish brown coats with a white stripe between their eyes, the foal nestled beside its mother's legs, staring intently at Therese without moving. The animals stood beneath one of two magnificent elm trees ten feet from their back door—the tree her mother said had gotten the Dutch elm disease. Therese relaxed with her mother at the wooden table on the deck, each of them with a mug of coffee in the bright Sunday morning. Her mother had the paper but wasn't reading it. She had that look on her face when she was thinking of a scientific formula or method that she planned to try in her lab. Therese stared again at the horse and didn't move. She whispered, "Mom."

Her mother hadn't heard.

"Mom, the wild horses," she whispered again.

Therese looked from the beautiful creatures to her mother, who sat staring in space, transfixed, like a person hypnotized.

"Mom, are you deaf?" she blurted out, and then she heard the horses flee back up the mountain into the tall pines. She caught a glimpse of the foal's reddish-brown rump, and that was that.

As Therese strapped on her seatbelt, she also considered the possibility that she had only imagined the man in the window. She was, after all, prone to use her imagination and fully capable of making daydreams as real as reality, as she had, just now, with her memory of the horses.

Her phone vibrated. A text from Jen read, "Heat sheets r n call me when u get home." Awesome, she thought. Therese was anxious to see who would share her heat in tomorrow's championship meet. She hoped she would be swimming breaststroke in the top heat against Lacey Holzmann from Pagosa Springs. She wanted to beat her this time.

She searched outside her window for the scruffy face but saw only a line of headlights as others, like they, exited the parking lot of the concert hall. Maybe she had only imagined the man. It was getting dark. The mountains across campus were barely visible as dusk turned into night.

"We're both so proud of you, Honey," Therese's dad said from behind the wheel.

Therese probably got her imaginative talent from her father, who was a successful crime fiction writer. As soon as his first book made the New York Times bestsellers list, he moved his family out into their big log cabin in the San Juan Mountains.

Therese saw her father eyeing her in the rearview mirror. "Aren't we, sweetie pie?"

She wondered at her father's need to praise her mother all the time. Didn't her mother already know she was brilliant and that her husband and daughter looked up to her? "Absolutely. You're awesome, Mom."

Therese's phone vibrated again. A text from Paul read, "Wat r u waring?"

She cringed and murmured, "Oooh. How gross." She couldn't believe he had got her number. He had been stalking her around campus just before school let out for the summer.

Before she had a chance to delete the text, Therese heard the rear window behind her head explode. "What the…" Glass shards pricked at her neck and bare shoulders. The car swerved left and right. She looked back to see the window behind her busted. The line of headlights had dispersed into chaos, horns blasting, people shouting.

"What the hell was that?" her father yelled. "Oh my God! Linda! Linda!"

"Dad, what's wrong? Is Mom…"

Another explosion rang out, and something zipped just past Therese's head.

"Therese? Are you okay? Get down!"

"What's happening? What's going on?" Therese cowered in the back seat as a third explosion sounded, this time near the windshield. Therese could barely breathe. She gasped for air, her heart about to explode.

"Stay down! Someone's shooting at us!" her father shouted.

The car swerved, slowed, and turned. The smell of burned rubber permeated the air. Therese's head whipped back as her father gunned the accelerator. Her fingers trembled so wildly that she was barely able to punch the correct numbers on her phone. She messed up twice and had to start over. Finally she pressed them in slow motion: 911. It seemed an eternity before a woman answered on the other end.

"Nine-one-one, is this an emergency?"

"Someone's shooting at us! You've got to help us. We're leaving Fort Lewis College. Dad, where are we?"

"Heading toward Huck Finn Pond."

"Huck Finn Pond!" Therese screamed into the phone as the car swerved, her seatbelt digging into her hip. Then she noticed the blood dripping down the back of her mother's neck and onto her mother's silk scarf. "Oh, my God! Mom? Mom, are you okay?"

"She'll be okay, Therese!" her father shouted.

"Oh my God! I think my mom's been shot! You've got to do something! You've got to help us!"

A crushing sound shot through the car, and Therese felt herself jolted hard to the right. She hit her head on the window and dropped the cell phone. When she bent over and tried to pick it up, the back end of the car lurched upward like a seesaw, and her head hit the back of her mother's seat in front of her. She sat up and saw they were sailing through the air over the lake. The front end of the car hit the water, causing her head to flop forward and back. She heard the air hissing through the airbags as they inflated in the front end. She was so stunned, she couldn't speak. She watched in silent shock as water crept into the front end of the car, up to her father's neck, the untied bowtie of his tuxedo floating around him. The front airbags pressed against her father's cheek, her mother's face. Water spilled over the front seat and onto the floorboard in back where she sat elevated higher than her parents.

She unfastened her seatbelt and leaned over and looked down at her mother in horror. A bullet had put a hole in the back of her neck, and blood rushed from it. Her head lay against the airbag turned to one side, toward Therese's father. Her eyes were open and she was gasping for air, but blood was pouring from her mouth and choking her.

"Mom! Oh my God! Mom!" Therese's teeth chattered uncontrollably as her mother strained to look at her. She reached down and caressed her mother's hair. "Mom! Oh my God!"

She realized her father had been shouting her name for several seconds. "Listen to me, Therese! Therese! Try to open your window. Therese! Try to get out of the car!"

His voice sounded like it did when he was cheering her on from the deck of the pool at her swim meets. "Keep going, Therese! You're looking good! Kick! Pull!"

Except now it was tinged with desperation.

"I'm not leaving without you and Mom! I'm scared! Dad, please! Can't you get out?" Her teeth continued to chatter.

The water level rose to his mouth. He shook his head. "I'm stuck!" He shouted through the water. His eyes widened as the water crept to his nose. He was drowning right in front of her.

"Dad! Dad!"

In a state of frenzy, he turned from side to side, only the top of his head visible.

Therese watched in silent shock.

She looked at her mother. Her mother's eyes met hers briefly, then closed as the water washed over all but her red hair. Unlike her father, her mother didn't move, but simply relinquished herself to the water. Her hair danced like seaweed, like long veins of blood. Therese became aware of the coldness of the water that had been sucking her down. Its cold fingers crept up to her shoulders. Her white gloves floated beside her, pointing at her. You! Do something!

She took a deep breath and went underwater toward her father. She couldn't see in the dark, so she pushed against the airbag and felt around for the harness. The belt was undone, but the steering shaft was crushed across her father's lap. She pulled with all her might on the steering wheel. It didn't move. She tried to puncture the airbag but without luck. Then she yanked on her father's lifeless arm. She couldn't lift him from the seat.

Another memory shot through her mind: She was pulling her father's arm, coaxing him from his recliner. "Come see the deer," she was saying. She was small—maybe six. "Come on, Dad. Come see." He had laughed and made a comment about her chipmunk cheeks and dimples, that he'd do anything to see those dimples. She pulled at his arm and he laughed and climbed out of his chair to follow her outside.

But now she could not get her father to follow her.

She felt her mother's hand and flinched. She found it again. It was as cold as the water and as limp as a dead fish. She hugged her mother, held on to her for dear life till her brain hurt and she needed air.

Therese popped back up near the top of the car for air, but there was none. She hitched her body up and hit her head on the roof of the car. She then noticed a bright light shine on her through her backseat window. She thought she saw someone swimming toward her. She heard another crash and a surge of water, but she needed air! Panic overtook her like a wild beast, and she opened her eyes as far as they would open, writhed her body against every molecule in reach, and strained her mouth wide open. Her lungs filled with burning water, the cold water burning her like fire. She gagged on the water, gagged, kicked, went wild with fear, and then stopped and gave in to the darkness.

Chapter Two: Thanatos

Humans didn't realize how lucky they were, Than thought as he took the woman's hand. At least, if they were mostly good, they could live a brief life with some kinds of freedoms and then spend eternity in a dreamlike trance, unaware of the monotony around them.

"Just this way," he said to the woman and the man as they floundered above the abyss, disoriented, like all of them were at this stage of the journey.

"What about Therese?" the woman asked. "Where's Therese?"

Than sighed. He couldn't imagine the pain they almost always showed on their faces. He couldn't imagine it because he had never felt it. At least it was temporary. The Lethe, the river of forgetfulness that flowed from the Acheron, would soon ease that pain, so long as these two souls were destined to the Fields of Elysium. The judges would soon decide.

"It's not too much further," Than murmured. "Come along."

"But what about our daughter?" the man asked.

The three of them now hovered up to the muddy bank where Charon waited on his raft. Than brought them down and allowed some of the water to wash up against their feet. It would help fog their memory until they reached the Lethe.

"Oh, that's cold," the woman said softly. "But it feels nice."

"Very nice," the man agreed.

Than gave a curt nod. "Time to board."

Charon nodded back as he dug his slender pole into the mud to hold the raft steady. He rarely spoke, with his nearly bald head, long, white mustache, and pale, cracked skin, and seemed more a cog in the wheel than any of them, churning on and on, back and forth, up the river and down, in an endless cycle. Than supposed Charon's existence was still worse than his own. At least Than got to travel the world. Charon saw the same sights day in and day out. His life never varied.

Than put a hand on the shoulder of each of the passengers, knowing it would comfort them. Yes, he thought again, humans were lucky. A brief, exciting life trumped a dull eternity. As his father always said, nothing ever changed. A few details might, but the big picture always remained the same. Than realized that none of the gods was really all that different from Sisyphus who, each day, must face his rock.

But what if things could change? Than wondered, not for the first time. He sighed and once again shook his head and waited as the raft approached the gate.

Chapter Three: Sleep

Therese opened her eyes and found herself standing on a cool, muddy bank. Fog curled around her, and through it she could see water in front of her, and it flowed in a narrow gorge between two ominous granite mountains. "Mom! Dad!" Her screams were stifled by the thick fog. "Mom! Dad!" She looked around the empty bank. Her bare feet sunk into the itchy mud. Where were her shoes? Her white gloves were back on her hands, her gown perfectly dry, and her hair back up in its fat clip. Tall blades of grass as high as her knees grew in tufts along the shore. Mosquitoes swarmed over one area of the water. Three large boulders leaned in a cluster on the left side of the shore against the base of a steep, massive wall of rock. How did she get here?

She waded into the icy lake. The cold water crept up her thighs. She couldn't see Huck Finn Bridge. Nothing looked familiar, but she had to find her parents. Isn't this where they went under in the car? She dove into the freezing water.

Long, snakelike tendrils of hydrilla weeds grabbed and scratched at her ankles. She flinched, kicking her legs all about.

"She's moving," a familiar voice above her said.

"Therese?"

She resurfaced. "Who said that?" Her voice was only a whisper, though she tried to speak loudly. It was hard for her to move her mouth. "Who, who said that?"

When no answer came, she dove back into the icy lake. "Mom! Dad!" Why was she looking for them? Her memory went fuzzy. "Mom? Dad?" She could talk underwater as though she were talking through air. She could breathe without water entering her mouth. How strange, she thought to herself. She felt as though she had turned into some kind of mer-creature. The lake transformed into a beautiful world of colorful coral, tropical fish, and sunken treasure chests.

She swam back to the muddy shore. "I must be dreaming." She walked over to the three boulders and sat on one of them. "Or I'm dead." She pulled off the wet gloves and tossed them on the ground.

Therese jumped into the air and swam a breaststroke through the fog, like she always did to test if she was dreaming. She went up above the curling, iridescent moisture where she could see the twinkling stars. Therese turned somersaults, forward and backward, dolphin-kicked a loop-de-loop, and then floated on her back. "Yep. I'm either dreaming or I'm dead."

She made the fog disappear, so she could see all around her. She reached up and touched a sparkling star, turned it into a diamond ring, and put it on her finger. Then she plucked her flute out of the air and played a Handel sonata. The flute felt comfortable in her hands, the cool, shiny metal beneath her fingers. The tones flowed smoothly as she blew, moving from one fingering to the next with perfect fluidity.

"I've never seen anyone like you," a voice came beside her.

Therese stopped playing. She hadn't willed him, as she had willed other guys to appear in dreams past, but she was glad he was there floating in the night sky alongside her. His thick golden hair covered his ears and fell on his forehead almost into his eyes. His eyes were blue, his skin fair, and his lips moist and peach. They parted into a smile.

"Are you checking me out?" he asked.

Therese blushed. "This is my dream, isn't it? Or am I dead?"

"You're not dead."

"So I'm dreaming, then. I can do whatever I want." She tossed the flute and willed her parents to appear, and they did.

"Mom! Dad!" She flew across the sky and into their arms. They were still in their formal wear. Her mother's neck, face, and scarf were perfectly clean, and she smelled like Haiku, her favorite fragrance. Her father smelled like musk, like the deodorant he always wore. Unlike Therese, her parents wore their shoes. Therese decided she should have her new shoes back, so she willed them to appear on her feet.

"Fascinating," the boy said. He wore a white, opened shirt, and his tight abs gleamed in the moonlight. White loose pants covered his legs, and he wore brown sandals on his feet.

Therese willed his shirt off, and the shirt disappeared.

The boy laughed. "You have so much control. Very few people are lucid dreamers, and I've never known anyone like you."

Therese turned to her parents. "I thought you were dead."

"Silly girl. Of course not," her mother scolded. "Give me a kiss."

She kissed her mother's cheek. It felt warm and soft and fully alive.

"Who's your friend?" her father asked.

Now that Therese had been comforted by her parents, she could let them go for a while. "I'll be home later. 'Kay?"

"Not too late," her father said.

Therese willed him to take it back.

"Whenever you get home is fine," he said.

Her parents vanished, causing a vague sense of panic to quell her excitement over the boy, but she pushed the panic down, reminding herself this was just a dream. She turned to the sexy guy, still shirtless, beside her. "So what's your name?"

"I have many. Most people call me Hip, short for Hypnos."

Okay, that's strange. Whatever. "Hip. I'm Therese."

"Are we going to make out now, or what?" He took her in his arms. "Is this a projection, or your real image?"

Therese had willed many sexy guys to appear in her dreams and have romances with her, but even there, she had kissed and made out with them on her own terms, and in the awake, real world, kissing was still a faraway anticipation. The eager look in the boy's face made her wary.

She pushed him back. "Why are you in such a hurry?" She looked over her body. She decided to make her boobs bigger. She smiled down at the soft, round flesh protruding from the top of her blue formal gown. Nice cleavage, she thought. "How's that?"

He threw his head back and guffawed. Then he shook his head, regaining his composure, and said, "I liked them better before."

"You've got to be kidding." She blushed and deflated herself. "It's my dream, not yours, but okay."

"No kidding. And I like your dimples. You've got a cute round face and full lips. I wouldn't mind kissing them."

Another voice sounded above her. "Therese?"

"Who is that? Who keeps calling me?"

A vague inkling of a car in a lake threatened to impose itself into memory, but Therese turned back to the boy and took in his beauty, forgetting all else.

Hip said, "They're trying to wake you up. But I'm not ready for you to go yet. You're such a nice diversion."

"How old are you?" She turned and floated on her back and looked down her body at him where he hovered near her shoes.

"Ancient."

"You look eighteen. I'm seventeen. I'll be a junior this year."

Down below, she noticed a raft floating across what she now saw was a river. There were four people on it, but she couldn't make out who they were. She swam the breaststroke through the air toward the water to get a better view. Her teeth felt loose. They started to crumble. She willed her teeth back into her mouth and licked them to be sure they were set correctly. Satisfied, she smiled.

Hip was fast behind her. "You're so incredible. People usually wake up when their teeth fall out."

She saw an old man standing on the raft dragging a long paddle through the water. Alongside him stood two familiar people and one other she didn't know. "It's my mom and dad. Hey, wait up." She flew above them, but they didn't seem to notice her.

The old man and the other passenger, whom she could now see was another guy, as cute as Hip, looked up at her. He looked sad and serious, like the silent moody type. His eyes were blue, and his hair was nearly black. He's so awesomely beautiful, she thought. He wore loose white pants and an opened white shirt like Hip had worn earlier, and, as with Hip, she willed the shirt to disappear. The boy looked startled, but her parents didn't react. They stood expressionless on the raft.

Hip laughed at the other boy's bewilderment. "That's my brother, Thanatos. Everyone calls him Than. I'm pretty sure that's a first for him."

"He looks a lot like you."

"We're twins, but not identical. I got the sense of humor, the easygoing disposition, and the charm with all the ladies. He got, well, not a whole lot, actually. I suppose he's trustworthy. My father says dependable and responsible, but those are pretty boring qualities, if you ask me. I sometimes feel sorry for him."

"What's he doing with my parents?"

"He's taking them to the Underworld, where all the dead go."

"My parents aren't dead." Again, the vague inkling threatened to return to memory, but Therese shook her head. She willed herself back home in her own cozy bed with her dog, Clifford, curled beside her. Hip was not with her.

"Time to wake up," she said to Clifford.

The brown and white fox terrier licked her cheek.

Therese tossed back her comforter and climbed out of the bed, the warm, wooden floor familiar beneath her feet. She dropped some hamster food into Puffy's hamster cage and turned on the lamp over her Russian tortoise's tank.

"Good morning, Jewels," Therese said.

The tortoise winked at her.

Therese headed downstairs. Clifford bounded behind her, as usual. Her parents were in the kitchen sitting at the granite bar drinking coffee and reading the paper, as on any Saturday morning.

They were still in their pajamas, but she was in her blue formal gown. She replaced the gown with a nightshirt. Poof: There, better.

"Good morning," she said to her parents.

She went through the screened front porch and out into what she was expecting to be the sunny morning on their wooden deck in the mountains but was instead the night sky over the foggy river. Hip greeted her.

"Nice outfit."

"So this really is just a dream," she said. "None of it's real."

"What makes a dream any less real?" he challenged.

"Hip, let her go!" the boy from below on the raft warned. "They need to revive her or she's going to die!"

"Therese?" a voice came from somewhere above.

Than flew up and pulled Therese away from Hip. "Let her go, brother. You're endangering her life."

Therese felt weak and she tried to wriggle free but nearly fell from the air.

Than held her up. "You shouldn't be here," he whispered, close to her ear. He sent a shiver down her spine, but his breath was sweet.

She didn't like the direction this dream was going. In the dreams in which she was about to die, she usually bolted into the air and changed the events into something happy. Although she couldn't find the strength to jump up and twirl around, she did manage to throw her arms around the good-looking boy holding onto her. She could make the dream into a new romance. "My dream," she managed to say as she clung to him. She put her lips against his lips. "You're...so...lovely."

"Whoa, brother," Hip said. "Today's full of all kinds of firsts for you, man."

Than seemed shocked. He looked at her like she was an alien. "You can't do this," he said, but he didn't push her away. His eyes closed, he sighed, and, almost reluctantly, it seemed, he put his strong arms around Therese, who felt weaker. She could feel his mouth near her forehead. A sound came from his throat, something like a groan.

She liked being in his arms. "You're...so...lovely," she murmured, growing weaker and weaker.

"Take her back." Than seemed to be fighting an inner battle. "I'm to take her parents, but not her. It's not her time."

Therese willed herself up. "My parents? Where are you taking them?"

Than looked into her questioning eyes. He looked as though he wanted to kiss her. She wanted to kiss him, too. His face moved closer. She nearly lost her breath. But her parents! She flew from his arms and down to the raft.

"Charon, don't board her!" Than growled, fast on her heels. "She's not to go across."

"Mom! Dad!"

Her parents didn't seem to hear her.

"This is my dream, dammit. Look at me!"

Her parents turned toward her. "Therese?"

Than gave Therese a look of astonishment. "How did you do that?"

Therese flew down to her parents.

Strong arms went around her and pulled her away from the raft. The brothers were on either side of her. She was fighting a futile battle. The brothers were much too strong for her to break free from them.

Than smiled. "You're right. She's a powerful soul. I've never known someone to follow loved ones down this far."

"You're forgetting Orpheus and Hercules," Hip pointed out.

"But they were demigods." Than's hands tightened their grip on Therese. Hip started to say something, but Than interrupted, "And Odysseus was sent down, so he doesn't count, either." Hip opened his mouth, but as before, Than was too quick with his retort, "And Aeneas had a guide and a golden bough, unlike this girl who came all on her own with no bribes."

Hip finally got his say, "I told you this girl was powerful. You're making my case, brother." He pulled Therese closer to him. "I want to keep her."

Therese wondered if they could possibly be talking about her. Powerful? She was anything but, as her inability to break free from them proved.

Than frowned. "If you try, she'll die, and then what fascinates you about her will be lost."

"Therese?" the voice from above called.

"Let her go!" Than implored.

Hip moved his lips to Therese's ear. "Seek me out in your dreams. I want to find you again. Look for me. Call for me."

Chapter Four: A Warning

Still jarred by his brother's foolish risk, Than waited in the poppies, until he fell asleep, and then he sought out Hip in the dream world.

Than knew exactly what Hip would be doing when he found him.

"I'll get you, my pretty! And your little dog, too!" Hip's voice rang out over the abyss.

"Maybe not exactly," Than thought, rolling his eyes at his brother's projection of a little green woman in a pointed black cap. "Hey, witch!"

Hip turned in surprise and spoke in the voice of an old hag. "What are you doing here? I'm kind of in the middle of something."

Than looked at the pretty girl cowering in fear before his brother. Then he asked his brother, still in his witch form, "Since when has this been your style? What happened to lover boy?"

"Now come on, brother," Hip said. "I've been doing this for over a millennium. Shows how often you come to see me."

"What exactly is this?" Than asked. "I don't think that particular character has been around for over a millennium."

"Details, details," Hip said. "I'm talking strategy here, not the details."

"Scare them to death?"

"Never to death, brother. Then you'd get them. I just scare them enough to want a protector." Hip changed his witchy projection back to himself and spoke in his own voice. "There, there, Melody. I'll save you from that nasty witch."

The girl ran into Hip's arms.

Hip gave Than a smirk and a wink. "Works every time," he said over the girl's head.

Hip's mouth fell on the girl's. "Nice," Hip said in between kisses.

Than remembered the feeling of Therese's arms around him, her lips pressed against his.

Hip read his thoughts before Than could block him. As twins, they had a special insight into one another's minds.

"Aha!" Hip laughed, tossing the girl to the side. "That's why you're here. All these centuries you have chastised me, looked down on me for making the most of my lot by having a little fun with the girls, a little harmless fun…"

"Not always harmless," Than murmured.

Melody faded into the background.

"And here you are now, wanting some tail now that you've had a small taste. What a hypocrite!"

"Tail? Is that what you so irreverently call human beings? They're not playthings."

"Oh? Says who?" Hip folded his arms at his chest. "Get off your high horse."

"They're our responsibility, not our amusement."

"They are both, Than. That's your problem. You take everything too seriously. You need to learn to have a little fun."

"Switch jobs with me for a day and then tell me how that's possible!"

"Broken record, bro'! That's what you are! A scratched disc. I didn't choose our lots. All I can say is, you need to make the most of yours, and you don't."

Than moved closer to Hip, putting his face inches from his brother's. "And you need to be more careful. You almost killed that girl before her time."

"You're just mad that I get to go to her now, and you don't."

"Leave her alone, Hip. I mean it. She's been through a hard time, losing her parents."

Hip moved his face so close to Than's, that they almost touched. "That's exactly why she needs me, to help divert the pain. And believe me, bro', I'll show her a good time."

Than shoved his brother out of his face.

Hip flew back to retaliate, but then didn't. He smiled, took a relaxed stance. "Lighten up. I'll leave her alone."

"Good." Than backed off, about to leave, about to wake in the field of poppies.

"I've never seen you like this before," Hip teased. "If I didn't know better, I'd think you like this girl, Therese."

Than ignored him and opened his eyes. Another death beckoned him to China. But as he met the old man to lead him to Charon's raft, his mind went back to the red-haired girl who had kissed him.

Chapter Five: Figments and the Underworld

She's waking up! Sheila! She's waking up!"

"Tell Dr. Burton her patient is waking up."

Therese grabbed the plastic tubing in her mouth and yanked. It scratched her throat, and tears welled in her eyes. Hands in latex gloves guided the tubing out and away. Therese gagged, heaved a dry heave. The latex-gloved hands held out a cup.

"Take a sip of water."

Therese put her parched lips to the cup and sipped. Her neck hurt when she lifted her head, so she lay back again. She blinked and looked up, squinting against the bright lights. She cleared her throat. The crud was still there. She cleared again. Took another sip. Ow, my neck.

"Therese, can you hear me?" It was her Aunt Carol, her mother's sister from San Antonio. What had happened to the brothers? They were right here, so close to her. How could they vanish like that? Carol kissed Therese on the forehead. "Oh, sweetheart!" Therese felt a flutter of kisses sweep over her cheeks. "Oh, Therese! I'm so glad you're finally awake!"

Why would Carol be here without her parents? "Where's Mom and Dad?"

Carol took her hand and squeezed it. "First tell me how you feel. The nurse needs to know."

She looked around the room. Machines beeped beside her. An I.V. ran through a needle in her hand. A nurse stood beside her aunt.

"My neck hurts." Then she added. "I'm so cold."

Carol pulled the covers up around Therese. "Can we get her another blanket, Sheila?" Carol said to the nurse.

Sheila left the bed and opened a nearby cabinet.

"Anything else hurt?" Sheila asked.

"I don't think so." Therese cleared her throat again. "Where's Mom and Dad?"

Another woman entered the room in a white coat.

Carol said, "Oh, Doctor, I'm so glad you're here."

She nodded hello and took a small flashlight from her front pocket. "Hi there, Therese. I'm Dr. Burton."

"Where are my parents?"

Sheila unfolded a thin white cotton blanket and added it to the heap of covers already atop Therese. Although the three persons in the room, including her aunt, looked at her with the kindest eyes, she had a sudden feeling of dread dragging her down like a heavy weight into a sea of gloom.

"Your parents didn't make it, Therese," Carol said, squeezing her hand. "They died in the crash. I'm so sorry."

Therese's mouth dropped open. Despite the dread and the inkling memory she had suppressed, she was utterly surprised. "But I just saw them. They were right there with me, hugging me, kissing me. I saw them plain as day!" Then, against her will, she remembered the shooting, the car plunging into the lake, and her parents drowning in front of her. She saw her father writhing in the water and her mother's yielding face. She felt panic gripping at her chest. She was all alone. Her mother and her father were gone. A silent scream of terror rose in her throat, but she pushed it down.

She wanted to be a little girl again sitting in her father's lap, curled in her mother's arms. She wanted to be a tiny thing making sand castles with her parents at the Great Sand Dunes, canoeing and kayaking on the lake and down the river, making snow people and snow animals in front of their house. She wanted to feel the warmth of her father on a summer evening standing on their deck around their house with binoculars turned toward the mountains beyond the reservoir in front of their house. She wanted to bake brownies with her mother one more time. She didn't need to lick the bowl; she didn't need to eat a bite; she just wanted her mother there telling her what to do with the big wooden spoon and array of ingredients. She just wanted to hear her mother's voice one more time. She wanted to be a baby again, safe and swaddled, and listening to her mother's sweet lullabies:

Sweet Therese, my precious girl; you're my love, my life, my world.

Then she remembered the boys, the brothers, and her parents on the raft with the old man. It had been a dream, hadn't it? But at least she could be with them there. She wanted to be with them any way she could. She closed her eyes and tried to go back to the dream.

"Therese, try to stay awake," the doctor said, shining the flashlight in her eyes as she held open each lid, one at a time. "I need to check your reflexes." The doctor tapped an instrument against Therese's elbow, then her knee, her foot.

No, she thought. I want to die. I want to go be with my parents. She closed her eyes again.

Sheila strapped a band around Therese's upper arm. The band expanded and squeezed Therese's arm, hurting her, forcing her awake again.

"Where are my mom and dad?"

Carol gave the doctor a look of concern and then stroked the bangs from Therese's eyes. "Oh, sweetheart. They didn't make it. They're in a better place."

Her aunt's hair was red and straight like her mother's, but shorter, in a stylish bob, the front ends slightly longer than the back. Her eyes were the same blue as her mother's and her eyebrows had the same arch. Even their slender noses looked alike. Therese was grateful Carol was with her. She loved her aunt like a big sister and had relished every Christmas and spring break and summer vacation they had ever spent together either in San Antonio or here in Durango. She held her aunt's hand and allowed the flood of tears to pour from her eyes. "But Carol, where are they? I mean their bodies. Are they in the lake?" The sobs shook her. She thought she might be sick.

The band released its pressure on her arm.

"Her vitals are normal," Sheila informed the doctor.

"Oh, thank God!" Carol cried. She squeezed Therese's hand.

"Tell Lieutenant Hobson he can come tomorrow," the doctor told Sheila. "Let's give her today to rest."

"Yes, Doctor," the nurse left the room.

Carol caressed Therese's forehead. "You've been in a coma for a week. We've already buried your parents."

Therese tried to understand what her aunt had just said.

"I'll check on her again later." The doctor excused herself.

Therese turned to Carol. "A week?"

Carol nodded. "I've been staying at your house. Puffy, Jewels, and Clifford are fine."

"It's really been a whole week? I missed the championship meet?" As if that really mattered now.

She briefly wondered if her swim team had won, but then indifference set in. It no longer mattered anyway. Her parents were dead. Nothing mattered anymore. She closed her eyes and tried again to find her parents in her dream.

Therese quickly realized she was wearing nothing but a t-shirt. No shorts, no undies, no socks and shoes—as if socks and shoes mattered when she was wearing no shorts and undies. She pulled the t-shirt over her hips and sat, crisscross, in the middle of the gymnasium floor. The entire sophomore class soon noticed her. They stopped playing basketball on the half court. They piled into the stands, all pointing, staring, and laughing at Therese sitting there in the center of the gym floor with her shirt pulled over her naked bottom. Soon the entire student body, all 1, 352 students, sat in the stands laughing.

Even Vicki Stern, the new girl Therese had befriended because she felt sorry for her, pointed and laughed.

To complicate matters, Puffy, Therese's hamster, was loose and running across the floor.

"Get Puffy!" Therese cried out. "Save him! He could get hurt!"

No one, not even Jen, came to her aid.

"Wait a minute," Therese whispered. "I'm not a sophomore anymore. It's summer. And I would never forget to put on shorts and undies. This must be a dream." She willed herself into a pair of jeans. To be sure it was a dream, she jumped into the air and swam the breaststroke toward the ceiling. She swooped down, picked up Puffy, and soared back into the air. She kissed her hamster on the head. "Where do you think you're going, mister?"

She dove down to the gym floor, made an announcement over the microphone that everyone was to return to class, and looked across the room for Jen. "There you are. Ready to drive me home?"

Jen drove her truck toward Therese's house, toward the outskirts of Durango. They rode over the Animus River and into the San Juan Mountains.

Therese tried to remember the important thing she was supposed to do. Didn't it have something to do with finding her parents, or someone who could help her find her parents?

Without transition, she found herself in the back seat of Jen's pickup with the steering wheel in her hand. She was trying to see from the back, but was having trouble. She strained her neck as she approached an intersection flanked by tall pines. She turned to the left. The road looked as though it was winding in impossible dimensions. The steering wheel came loose and the pickup swerved out of control.

"What are you doing?" Jen asked.

Therese let go of the broken steering wheel, jumped out of the window with Puffy in her hands, and dolphin-kicked up to the clouds over Durango. "I'm taking control again. I call the shots in my dream. Which reminds me: I need to find Hip." Therese kissed Puffy and told him to go home like a good little hamster. "Feed Jewels and Clifford," she told him.

Puffy gave her a thumb's up and said, "No problemo." Then poof: Puffy disappeared.

Therese waved goodbye to Jen.

Jen's Toyota pickup sailed away, just like Chitty-chitty-bang-bang, the flying car from her favorite childhood movie.

Now off to find Hip, Therese thought. She flew the breaststroke over the tall pines and cypresses of the mountains near her home. "Hip! Hip! Where are you?"

"Over here!"

She couldn't see him, so she ran toward the sound of his voice. She was running down a long corridor with white floors and white walls and lots of closed doors. This must be a hospital, she thought. She ran faster, sure Hip was ahead, his golden hair just visible as he turned a corner. She turned the corner expecting to see him, but he wasn't there.

"Hip!"

No answer.

She kept running down the winding hallway. Now down a flight of steps. She could just see the golden hair as the figure rounded the landing to the next flight of stairs. Then she cried, "Hip! Enough of this!" and she stopped dead in her tracks.

The hospital setting faded away, and she was floating over the foggy river between the massive granite rocks of the gorge.

Hip floated in front of her. "You're amazing." He took her in his arms and kissed her lips. "I'm so impressed." He kissed her again. "Most people just keep on running. They don't even know why, and they never think to stop."

"You've got lipstick on your cheek," Therese said, pushing him away. "Have you been kissing another girl?"

Hip sighed. "Look, this may be your dream, but I'm the sleep guide." The lipstick disappeared. "I usually get my way when I appear in people's dreams, and I say we make out, no questions asked. Got it?"

He went for her, but she slipped past him and dolphin-kicked several feet away. "Then you're with the wrong girl."

Hip looked amused. "No. You're different. I like that."

Therese wondered in what way she was different. She was probably the most flat-chested girl going into tenth grade, her thighs were losing the gap between them and curving out past her hips, her nose could use the hands of a good plastic surgeon, and she was prone to daydream, which drove her teachers crazy. Despite her popularity as a fun person, the only boys who ever liked her—aside from Paul who was downright strange—were the ones she conjured up in her dreams, but she hadn't conjured up Hip, had she?

"Tell you what," Therese said. "I'll let you kiss me again if you answer a few of my questions first."

"Deal. Shoot."

"Where did your brother take my parents?"

"To the Underworld, where all the dead go. Your parents made it to the Elysian Fields—kind of a paradise. I've seen them. They're happy. But they can never leave that place now."

"Then how come I've been able to will them here?" Therese made her parents appear.

"Hey, sweetie pie," her father kissed her head. He was wearing a t-shirt and his favorite jeans with holes in the knees.

"How was band practice?" her mother asked, wearing a pair of sweats that did nothing to diminish her beauty.

Why can't I look like that? Therese thought. "I didn't go," Therese replied.

"What? Why not?" her mom asked.

"They're just figments," Hip interrupted.

Therese and her parents looked at Hip.

"What do you mean?" Therese asked.

Hip crossed his arms and leaned back. "Your parents' souls have passed on to the Underworld, and once Cerberus, my dad's three-headed dog, lets them in, he won't let them out. The images of your parents here are figments. Figments are nymph-like creatures that reflect the dreamer's unconscious images. They have no reflection of their own in a mirror, so you can always test it out if you're not sure. Watch this." Hip pulled a hand-held mirror from out of the sky and held it up to Therese's parents. The mirror was blank where the reflection of her parents should have been. "See? No reflection." Then he shouted, "Figments, I command you to show yourselves!"

Therese's parents turned into eel-like creatures with scales and long, winding bodies. They curled around the air and then zipped away, giggling.

Therese hung her head.

Hip moved his arms around her waist. "Don't I get my kiss now, or do you have other questions?"

"How can I get my parents back?"

"You can't. Only two other people in history have ever tried to retrieve a loved one from the Underworld, and both attempts turned out badly. Besides, that's my brother's area of expertise, not mine."

"Can you take me to your brother?"

He snickered and shook his head. "No one ever wants to find Death."

"Your brother is Death?"

"Most call him Than."

"He was Death?"

"Look, I can give you a bird's eye tour of the Underworld. I can even show you your parents from above. But I can't actually take you into the Underworld proper while you're alive. The other day when you met my brother, you were very near to dying. That's the only way a person can come into contact with him."

"That's so sad," Therese said.

"What do you mean?"

"Doesn't he have any friends?"

Hip shrugged. "Our sisters, I guess."

Therese bit her lip. "Well, I guess we can start with the tour."

Hip moved in close to her again. "First I get my kiss." He pressed his lips against hers. His breath was like mint. She closed her eyes and brushed her lips across his.

"Nice," he said. "Let's do that again."

Therese pulled back. "First the tour."

Hip took her hand and led her down to the river. A few feet away she could see the old man on the raft, his long white mustache, slight and slumped shoulders, and red peasant robe visible through the fog. He used his stick to pull away from the bank with two other passengers, one whom she recognized.

"That old man is Charon," Hip said. "He ferries the souls across the Acheron River where it meets the Styx River at the gates to the Underworld. My brother retrieves the souls from the world of the living and accompanies them until they're settled in."

"Than!" Therese called.

He looked up at her, astonished.

"She wants a tour," Hip explained.

Hip didn't wait for his brother's reply. He took Therese's hand and pulled her past the raft, down the river to where it entered a dark cave. Sitting near the mouth of the cave was a creature about six feet tall, black as night, with a sweeping dragon tail, and three ferocious heads resembling those of a French bulldog: tall batlike ears, pug upturned noses, large frowning mouths with slight under-bites exposing white sharp teeth, and plenty of loose skin and wrinkles around the three necks. The eyes on the heads looked red and unfriendly, but Therese had never met an animal she hadn't tried to befriend.

"That's Cerberus," Hip said. "He guards the gate." A massive iron gate, maybe a hundred feet above the water, and who knew how many feet below, stood just past Cerberus tightly fastened. "Only the gods can go in and out, so I can't take you through, but I can show you what's down there by making the upper part of the caverns transparent."

"Gods? You and your brother are gods?"

Hip gave her a smug grin. "That's correct. Hades, the god of the Underworld, the gatekeeper, is our father, despite some misguided myths you people have about our origins."

"I've heard of Hades, but I've never heard of you and your brother," Therese stated matter-of-factly, which seemed to offend Hip.

He grabbed her arm in a tight grip. "Come on."

"Wait," Therese insisted when Hip pulled her onward. "Can I say hello to Cerberus?"

Hip's mouth dropped open. "You actually want to?"

"Yeah. Why not?" She let go of Hip's hand and floated closer to the creature. "Hello there, Cerberus. Are you a friendly thing? May I pet you?"

The three-headed dog leaned toward her and wagged its dragon tail.

"I wouldn't do that if I were you," Hip warned as he caught up to her. "He can be pretty vicious. And he's always suspicious about being tricked, especially after what happened with Orpheus and Hercules."

Therese wanted to ask about Orpheus and Hercules, but Cerberus now bared his teeth and uttered a low growl from all three heads.

"Why did you have to mention them? Look what you've done!"

"Come on." Hip pulled Therese past the creature, above the enormous gate, and over the mouth of the cave. "There's a lot more to see."

They flew over rocky terrain with the night sky above them and the stars and crescent moon piercing through the fog now and then. Beneath them, the layers of rock vanished, and Therese could see several large chambers attached by tunnels through which five different rivers flowed. One of the rivers was alight with flames, illuminating the many chambers.

Hip explained that the first chamber, just passed Cerberus, was the room of judgment, where three judges worked together to determine whether a soul was worthy of the Elysian Fields. If a soul was found to be unworthy, the judges would then determine which punishment in Tartarus would be most fitting. Some of these punishments were terrible, like that for Tantalus, who stood in water up to his neck but could never drink and saw fruit above his head but could never grasp it. Others were laborious, but not too unlike the world of the living, like Sisyphus, who was doomed to roll a huge rock uphill all day only to watch it roll to the bottom of the hill where he must start again. Some souls were doomed to remain in Tartarus for all eternity, Hip explained; but others, after their debts were paid, could travel over to the Elysian Fields. Tartarus was narrow and long like a great hall, just past the room of judgment. It seemed to stretch endlessly in two directions further than Therese could see.

Hip then pointed out Erebus, a chamber just after Tartarus and much deeper, though also smaller in circumference, perhaps fifty feet wide at most. He explained that victims of terrible crimes were often sent there through the Lethe, the river of forgetfulness, to forget the heinous crimes that tortured them in life. Mostly abused children and women, suicides, and prisoners of war went there before they were eventually led up and out into the Elysian Fields. Therese could see people below in the dim light lying in their clothes in a shallow pool of water as though sunbathing.

The fields were vast and amazing, covered in beautiful flowers of white, pink, and purple. There were trees and something like sunshine, but more of a purplish-pink veil of light that added beauty to all it touched. The Lethe River met its banks, and spread in small streams marbling through the fields, which meant that the souls who frolicked there had only the vaguest recollection of a previous life. Therese could see hundreds of souls all doing different things. Some read or slumbered under trees, others danced or swam or ate at huge tables covered with massive amounts of food. Others played sports like golf and tennis. A few children flew kites. Hip explained that the kites, the trees, the food, and the books and things were merely shared illusions, part of an ongoing dream for the dead. The Elysian Fields, like Tartarus, seemed to stretch infinitely in two directions, the boundaries invisible to her eyes.

She squinted at a couple sitting on the bank with their feet dangling in the river. They were her parents.

"Can I speak to them?" she asked Hip.

"They won't hear you from up here," he answered. "And we can't go down to them below. Besides, chances are they won't remember you."

Therese couldn't bear the thought of her own parents forgetting her. She burst into tears. "Take me to your brother, so he can tell me what I need to do to get my parents out of here."

"I haven't even showed you my parents' palace. It's the most fascinating place of all."

She saw the old boatman docked at the gate just past Cerberus. She flew down to find Than.

"Therese, wait!" Hip warned. "If you follow the raft in, you can't come out. You'll die, and then there's certainly no way to save your parents."

She stopped and looked back at Hip.

This is only a dream, isn't it, she thought. There's nothing real about any of this.

"Therese! Wake up!"

"Wait!" Hip called. "What about my kiss?"

Chapter Six: Distractions

Than left Charon and headed to Mexico to escort the souls of three teenagers who had died in an earthquake. He would be making several more trips there over the next few days as the frail human bodies gradually expired. He had disintegrated and dispatched himself to four other locations--Turkey, Japan, Iraq, and Egypt. It was a busy day, busier than usual, and because of the disintegration, he found it a little more difficult to keep his mind on his duties.

Therese had come back, had called out his name. He knew she wanted her parents, like so many of the survivors whose family members he carried away. Than had learned to block those futile prayers, "Spare my sister," "Bring my child back to me," "Let my husband be alive when we find him," and so forth. He had blocked them because there was nothing he could do about them. Therese's prayers were no different. He could not help her.

Yet, he couldn't forget the feel of her soulful arms around him, the sensations of her warm lips against his, and the scent of her sweet breath. No one—human or god—had ever touched him like that. His mother must have when he was a baby, but he had no memory of it. If Therese's spirit were capable of making him feel so much sensual pleasure, how much more pleasurable could she make him feel in the flesh?

Only now did he become aware of what he had been missing.

He disintegrated and dispatched another part of himself to the poppy field beside Hip's rooms. Than wanted to re-enter the dream world and talk some more to his brother, even on this busiest of days.

Chapter Seven: Visitors

Therese blinked her eyes as Carol leaned over her saying, "Wake up, sweetheart. The lieutenant is here."

Carol smelled like her mother. She smelled like Haiku perfume and Jergen's lotion.

A memory of her aunt teaching her to blow into the flute distracted her for a moment. They had given one another manicures and pedicures, and when the polish had dried, Therese had asked to try the flute, which Carol had played in high school years before. She had the scent of Haiku and Jergen's even then.

"Therese?"

"I'm still in the hospital? What day is it?" Therese tried to sit up. Her neck was stiff, but slightly better. She rubbed it and noticed the IV was still attached to her hand.

"It's Tuesday morning. You woke up from your coma yesterday," Carol said. "There's a tray of breakfast for you here. Are you hungry? You slept through yesterday's dinner."

Therese looked across the room at a short, round man with gray hair and razor stubble. He wore a policeman's uniform and looked to be in his late fifties.

"Maybe I'll eat something later."

"Hi there, Therese." The lieutenant approached her bed. The smell of body odor wafted above her head. "How are you feeling?"

"My neck is stiff, but I'm okay." She pulled the covers up around her.

"Good. I'm glad to hear that." He scratched the stubble on his chin. "Look, I know what happened to you was pretty scary. I'm really sorry it happened. But I want you to know that I'm going to do everything I can to find out who did this, okay?"

Therese nodded as the tears welled in her eyes.

"I'm Lieutenant Hobson with the Durango Police Department." Beads of sweat forming on his forehead dripped around his temples as if he had run all the way to the hospital.

"Hi."

"What can you tell me about what happened? What do you remember?"

She told them what she could, and then cleared her throat, her mouth suddenly dry, her chest tight. "I couldn't save them."

Carol stroked Therese's arm. "It's not your fault, sweetheart."

Therese grabbed Carol's arm. Panic overtook her as it had beneath the water trapped in her mother's car. Her throat burned, like it had when the water rushed through her lungs and she had hit at every space around her. "Tell me I'm dreaming!" Therese wailed. "Tell me I'm going to wake up and it will all be over!"

Carol kissed her cheek and started crying. "I wish I could."

The lieutenant took a small notepad and pen from his front shirt pocket and gave Therese a moment to recover. Then he cleared his throat and said, "Can you remember anything else?"

The face. It popped into her head and startled her as much as it had the night her parents were killed. "I might have been imagining this, but right before the shooting, I thought I saw a gruff-looking face outside my car window. It was a man."

"A man's face? Can you tell me what he looked like?"

"His skin was dark."

"Black?"

"No."

"Native American?"

"No, oh, I don't know. He had dark brown eyes, black hair, kind of short, like yours, and a scruffy beard."

"How old would you say he was?"

"I don't know. Not too old. Younger than my dad."

"Would you describe him as heavy-set, thin, tall, short?"

"I just saw his face. I don't know."

"Do you think you can remember enough details about his face to work with an artist from my department?"

"I can try."

"Anything else you can remember? Anything at all?"

"Right before I went out, I saw a bright light and someone swimming toward me."

The lieutenant nodded. "Yeah, that would have been the rescue crew. They went in and pulled you out of the car."

"Oh." She wondered if they got her parents out then, too.

"Therese, do you know if either of your parents had any enemies?"

"What? You mean you don't think this was just some random school shooting? An angry student gone postal? Like Columbine?"

"That's a possibility, Therese," the lieutenant said. "But your car seems to have been the primary target. Other people suffered some minor injuries when the perpetrator drove recklessly through the parking lot, but your car was the only one shot at."

The hair on her neck stood up and she felt her heart go wild. She could hardly breathe. She never imagined someone would want to murder her parents.

"Do you know if your parents had ever received any threatening phone calls, emails, or letters?"

"No, sir. I don't know of anything like that. My dad got letters and emails from his readers, but they were fans, not enemies. My mom's students all loved her. Both of my parents were well liked by everybody, I think. I can't imagine why anyone would want them, want them…" She lost her voice and broke into sobs again. "I'm sorry."

The lieutenant closed his notepad and stuffed it back into his front shirt pocket. Then he added his ballpoint pen. "Thanks, Therese. I'll follow up with you again soon. I'll have an artist meet with you for that description later today, while your memory is fresh."

A panicky feeling threatened to surge through Therese again. "Lieutenant Hobson?"

"Yes?"

"What do you know so far? Who do you think did this?"

"I shouldn't discuss the case with you, Therese. You just focus on getting better."

"That's not fair." Therese's voice was desperate. "I have a right to know. They were my parents."

"Get some rest, and I'll come back and tell you something when I know more. Maybe your description of the face will give us the lead we need." The lieutenant reached out and took her hand, shook it, patted it, and said, "You take care, now. Call me if you think of anything else."

"Okay." She wiped the tears streaming down the sides of her face.

The lieutenant handed his card to Carol.

"Thank you, Lieutenant," Carol said.

Just as the lieutenant walked out of the hospital room, Therese's three best friends—Jen, Ray, and Todd—walked inside carrying balloons and a toy stuffed animal lemur.

"She's really awake!" Jen cried, rushing in and grabbing Therese's hand.

"Hi guys," Carol said. "Therese? Are you sure you're ready for company?"

"Yes, I'm sure. I need some cheering up."

"Well, if you're really sure…"

"I'm sure."

"Then I'm going downstairs for a bit. Enjoy your visit."

Once Carol left the room, Ray said, "Todd wanted to get you the lemur. You should have seen him moaning and groaning in the shop if either one of us picked up anything else. So if you don't like it, blame him." Ray was tall, chubby, and Native American.

"I love it. He's cute."

"His hands have Velcro," Todd said. "You can wear him around your neck, like this." Todd put the lemur's long, skinny black arms around his neck and attached them. "You can wear him here in front," he moved the monkey to his back, "or back here. It's quite a fashion statement." Todd was tall and thin with sandy-blonde hair and a face full of acne.

"Just what everyone wants, Todd," Ray said. "A monkey on their back."

Therese and Jen laughed.

"I like him guys," Therese said. "Let me have him." She was glad they hadn't said anything about her parents. For a little while, she wanted to pretend everything was normal again.

Todd handed the lemur over. "He's going to miss me. He wants me to come visit."

Therese smiled. "I guess I can allow visitations."

"When I called yesterday, your aunt said your neck has been hurting. Are you any better today?" Jen asked as she tied the balloons to the railing at the foot of the hospital bed.

"Some. Still stiff." Then she thought, please don't say anything about my parents. "How did we do at the championship meet?"

"Pagosa Springs won by thirteen points," Jen said. "We came in second. Bayfield got third."

"Did Lacey swim breaststroke in the first heat?"

"Yeah. She got first. You would have beaten her though, I just know it," Jen reassured her.

"Maybe. I guess we'll never know."

"There's always next summer," Todd said. "Hey, listen. I finished rebuilding the engine for my truck."

"The fifty-seven Chevy?" Therese asked. "Are you serious?"

"You should see it," Ray cut in. "He painted it yellow, of all the colors in the universe."

"I like yellow," Therese said.

"It looks awesome," Jen added. "Todd's going to take us for a ride as soon as you get out."

"Hey," Todd said, coming close to her, his face taking on a more serious expression. "I haven't told you yet how sorry I am about your parents. I know you already know it, but I wanted to say it, you know?"

"I know." Therese clenched her jaw as she fought off tears. She supposed she couldn't go on pretending, and it was nice to know he cared.

"Me, too," Ray murmured. "What he said."

"Me, too," Jen said, taking Therese's hand.

"Thanks guys."

Her three friends stood there now in awkward silence, brushing away tears they didn't want one another to see. Luckily, Carol eventually returned and asked the visitors how they were doing, shifting the focus from Therese. She lay there in the bed wiping more tears from her face.

Her friends chatted with her and her aunt for a few more minutes, and then they said their goodbyes. Therese put the lemur's long, furry arms around her stiff neck and closed her eyes.

Carol said, "Your lunch is here. You never ate your breakfast. Do you think you can eat something now?"

"I think so."

A different nurse was standing over Therese with a tray. She moved a few things on the rolling bedside table and set it down. "Today we have a turkey sandwich, vegetable soup, fruit cup, and chocolate pudding."

"Thanks," Therese said.

The nurse studied the machines near Therese's bed. "Everything looks in order. My name's Letty. Just call if you need anything. How's your neck?"

"Better. Still a bit stiff."

"I can give you something for the pain."

"Okay."

"I'll bring it in a while, give you time to eat." Letty left the room.

Carol gave Therese an update about her pets while Therese ate. They chatted about school and Therese's friends. Therese really didn't feel like talking, but she could see it made Carol feel better. The food tasted good. She hadn't realized how hungry she was. Not long after she finished her pudding cup, Letty returned with the medication.

"Thank you," Therese said.

"You're welcome, mija." The nurse removed the empty tray and left the room.

Carol must have noticed the tears welling in Therese's eyes, for she leaned over the bed and took Therese's hand. "You know, when your grandpa died, even though we knew it was coming, it was so hard. It felt like a part of me died with him. And then when your grandma died two years ago…gosh, I can't even believe it's already been two years. Then all I had left were you and your mother. Now that my big sister's gone, well, Therese, you're all the family I have left."

Therese sucked in her lips as she watched the tears slide down her aunt's cheeks. "And you're all I have left."

"I'm coming to live with you, Therese. I've already moved out of my San Antonio apartment. I hope that's what you want."

Therese hadn't thought that far ahead. She was still trying to get used to the idea that her parents were, that her parents had….she couldn't even think the idea through in her mind.

"I mean, I could take you with me to San Antonio, but you have your life here, and I can live anywhere. Since I work from home, my boss has no problem with me coming to Durango. Now that grandma's gone, there's really nothing keeping me there."

"What about Richard? And I'm sure you have friends."

"Richard and I will work something out. We've dated long distance before. Absence makes the heart grow fonder, you know." Carol gave Therese a smile.

"I do love my house," Therese murmured.

"I do, too," Carol said.

"I guess we can see how things go, right?"

"Oh, sure. We don't have to decide anything today." Carol kissed Therese's cheek. "You know, I've always been so grateful for you in my life. I don't know when or if I'll ever have children, and having you for my niece has kind of fulfilled that maternal part of me. I know I can't replace your mother—and I don't want to—but I want you to know I will be there for you. I'm not just a babysitter. I'm not just a temporary fix. I'm here for you for the long haul, through thick and thin, and the works. Okay?"

Therese nodded, more tears piling up in the corners of her eyes again.

"Now, sweetheart, I can ask them to bring me one of those hideaway beds and sleep here with you tonight if you want me to. I've been staying at the house because of Clifford, but he can go a night without me if you want me to stay here now that you're staying awake for longer periods of time."

"No," Therese said. "I'd be worried about Clifford. Go ahead and go home. I'm just gonna go right back to sleep."

"Good. You need the rest," Carol said.

Therese sighed, nodded.

Carol nodded too. "I'll come back this evening to check on you again. Go to sleep."

"Okay. Thanks."

Carol kissed her forehead and stroked her hair. Then she crossed the room and waved one more time before disappearing through the door.

Therese sat in her ninth grade AP English classroom with the rest of her classmates taking a multiple choice exam, but none of the questions made sense. They seemed written in a different language. Therese pressed her pencil into the bubble next to "E. None of the above," but the lead on her pencil broke. She raised her hand. Mrs. Spencer stood with her back to the class writing something on the dry erase board and didn't notice.

"Excuse me," Therese said.

When Mrs. Spencer turned around, Therese saw she wasn't Mrs. Spencer at all. Her eyes were red, her ears pointed, and when she opened her mouth to ask, "Yes?" blood dripped from her lips.

She's a zombie, Therese thought, frozen in her chair.

She looked around the room. They were all zombies.

That's when she knew she was dreaming.

"I need to find Hip," Therese reminded herself, so she took off flying from the school, looking for the Underworld.

Then her parents appeared in front of her, and she couldn't resist stopping midair and looking at them. Could they possibly be her real parents?

"Mom? Dad?"

They smiled and held out their arms. She ran to them and felt their warm embrace. Then another zombie appeared and ruined the delusion. Therese willed it to disappear.

"You're just figments, aren't you?" she asked her parents softly, stepping away from them just a bit, but not too far.

Her mom and dad shrugged.

"Tell me you're real!" Therese commanded.

"We're real?" her father laughed. "What are you talking about? Of course we're real."

The zombie English teacher approached, scolding Therese, "You didn't finish the test, young lady!"

Reluctantly and full of sadness, Therese said, "Figments, I command you to show yourselves."

Her parents and the evil teacher transformed into eels, giggled, and flew away, leaving Therese hovering in the air alone in the middle of nothingness.

"Hip!" she shouted at the top of her lungs, full of anger. "Hip! I need you!"

The handsome twin appeared. "You called?" he had a smirk on his face.

"I want to rescue my parents from the Underworld, and I want you to help me."

"Impossible," he said. "And you owe me a kiss.

He moved against her and touched his lips to hers. She froze, waiting.

"Aw, what kind of kiss was that?"

"If you're not going to help me, go away."

"You've got a lot of nerve, giving commands to a god. I could kill you, you know."

She looked him dead in the eye. "Do it."

He rolled his eyes. "My brother would cause trouble for me." He backed off and shook his head. "He's obsessed with you, Therese. He can't stop thinking about you. He thinks he's in love with you. He's trying to work out some kind of deal with our father."

"What are you talking about?"

"Than? My twin brother? The one you threw yourself at saying, 'You're so lovely. You're so lovely!' Ring a bell?" He crossed his arms and sulked.

"You mean the god of death?" she asked with some hesitation. This was sounding a little crazy. Maybe this wasn't Hip. Maybe he was a figment. "Figment! I command you to show yourself!"

Hip rolled his eyes again and said, "Give it a rest. I never should have taught you that."

"Hip, please tell me what you're trying to say."

"My brother's coming for you."

"What? The god of death is coming for me?"

Pound, pound, pound!

"What was that?" Therese asked.

"No! Don't wake up! I want a real kiss this time!"

Pound, pound, pound!

"Hello?" a woman's voice called out.

Therese opened her eyes and saw an ultra-thin woman with chocolate skin and blonde hair and outlandishly colorful clothing enter the hospital room. She carried a sketch pad.

"Therese?"

Therese gave her a nod and then winced from the pain. Her neck was better but still tender.

"I'm Margo Brewster. Lieutenant Hobson sent me over to sketch a suspect."

"Oh, yeah."

"How you feelin'?" The artist sat down in the chair next to the bed and opened her pad to a blank page. She pulled a pencil from behind her ear, which was studded with rings.

"Okay."

"Well, I'm so sorry you're here and can't imagine what things are like for you, but I'm here to help, okay?" A little diamond shone on the side of one nostril.

"Okay." Therese described the face she had seen in her car window as best as she could, fighting the tears without success.

The artist would show her the drawing in progress, and ask, "Eyes like this? No, how 'bout more like this? Okay." And then, "So, okay, more of a pointed jaw, like this?"

Eventually they came up with something that Therese thought looked eerily like the man she saw before the shooting began. Chills ran down her spine. "That's him. Wow, you're really good."

Letty came in and checked on Therese, took her temperature, checked the machines, and asked how she was feeling. "Do you need more medicine for your pain, mija?"

"Yes, please."

Letty left the room.

Margo Brewster was nice, but Therese was glad when she left and Letty gave her the pills, and she could close her eyes again and go to sleep.

When she found herself running through the hospital, Therese was immediately suspicious. She stopped at the end of a hallway and walked into a room. Todd, Ray, and Jen lounged around on living room furniture laughing at something on the television.

"Hey," Todd said. "Look who finally made it."

Therese sensed something behind her, outside of the door in the hallway. It felt bad, dangerous, frightening. She sprung to the door and pushed it closed, but it didn't have a lock. In fact, the door didn't even fit properly in the door frame, as it was bordered by a one-inch gap all the way around. Even the hinges seemed loose. Whatever was out there would have no problem getting inside.

Therese quickly recognized that she wasn't in a hospital room, but in her grandmother's house back in San Antonio. Strangely, she recalled that her grandparents had both passed away—her grandfather several years ago and her grandmother in more recent years. So she wondered now how she could be standing in their living room trying to keep their front door from being busted open.

A bright light spilled through the one-inch gap around the door.

"What is that?" Jen asked.

"I have a bad feeling about this," Todd added.

"Very good, Obi Wan Kenobi," Ray sneered.

"Wait a minute!" Therese burst out. "This can't really be happening." She jumped into the air and turned a somersault. Then she turned to her friends. "Figments, I command you to show yourselves!"

Three scaly, eel-like creatures flew about in a tizzy, giggling wildly.

Then the door crashed in and the bright light illuminated the room. The three figments rushed out through the opening and into the light. Out of the light a figure emerged.

"Figment, I command you to show yourself!" Therese said.

"None but my father commands me." The figure stepped within inches of her. He was tall and muscular and wore a fierce look on his beautiful face.

It was Than.

Therese dropped with weakness to her grandmother's old green carpeting, which still smelled like wet dog. Than rushed to her side and helped her to sit up. She leaned against him. Her grandmother's blue merle Australian Shepherd, who had died the same year as her grandmother, strolled over to Therese and licked her cheek.

"Hello, Blue," Therese said to the dog in a faint, weak voice.

"I don't have much time, so listen," Than said. "I came to tell you three things."

Therese felt inexplicably drawn to him. "Am I dying?"

"Not if I can help it," he replied. "Now shut up and listen to me."

His cold, hard glare suddenly frightened her, so she kept her mouth shut, her eyes wide.

"First, I've asked the Furies to seek you out. Look for them in the waking world of the living. They can help you solve your parents' murder."

"Who or what is a Fury?" She felt faint.

"I'll let them explain. You could die if I don't hurry. Let me speak."

She gave him a weak nod.

"Second, don't let my brother keep teasing you. He respects your powers but not you, and I don't like it."

Therese managed a smile. "Jealous?" She would never be so bold outside of her dreams.

"Absolutely." He looked deeply into her eyes, his face close to hers.

"Do you want to kiss me?" The air left her body and her mouth flooded with moisture.

"Absolutely."

She closed her eyes and leaned in.

"Listen," he said, swallowing hard. "I haven't stopped thinking about you since that day you kissed me, and that brings me to the third thing I want to say. Thank you for your affection. Know that I stay away, not because I want to, but because if I don't, you'll die."

Therese found it hard to breathe. "Don't go," she barely managed to say. "I want to die. I want to be with my parents. And then you and I could, we could spend some time getting to know each other." She was really faint now, on the verge of collapse.

He leaned close and took a breath of her scent. Then he clenched his jaw. "You're not the same when you die. You lose your free will, and that's what is so attractive about you. It's what sets you apart from the others. You have a strong will."

Therese gasped for air and none came.

Than vanished.

Therese heard a loud beeping sound next to her ear. She gasped and gasped, and finally her lungs opened up and the air rushed in, burning her chest. Someone rushed up beside her.

"Mija!" the nurse shrieked. "You okay?"

Therese lay on the hospital bed. Was she awake? "Figment, I command you to show yourself!" she said to the Letty.

The nurse bent her brows. "Mija, what are you talking about?"

"Oh. I thought I was dreaming." Okay, Therese thought. I'm not saying that ever again.

Letty looked at the oxygen monitor. "Well, what is wrong with this thing? It was beeping like crazy just a second ago, but now it looks fine." She checked the probe taped to Therese's big toe. "Maybe it's come loose. Well, it looks alright. You feel alright?"

Therese nodded. "I'm fine."

"Well, alright then. Call me if you need me. I'll be back in a little while with your dinner tray." The nurse left the room.

Chapter Eight: A Deal with the Gatekeeper

Why should I do this?" Hades asked from his jewel encrusted throne. The one beside him was empty because Persephone was gone in the summertime. Her absence made Than's father irritable. This wasn't the best time to ask for favors.

In fact, the cavernous room of golden walls inlaid with precious stones was usually brimming with bustle as Persephone and Hecate discussed the affairs of the Upperworld and of Mount Olympus. With his mother and her assistant gone, the chamber echoed with the silence of slinking shadows caused by sleeping bats that barely moved and would not fly till nightfall. The nearly vacant castle had not even ghosts to move the air, for all the souls were in their proper places, and even the formidable form of Hades could not fill the room. Hades, who now slouched and picked at his beard, would, in a few months' time, with the first chill of autumn, sit erect and commanding and proud like a peacock before his mate. Despondence, however, was his only companion until then.

Than spoke with confidence. "Because I can help the Furies find the killer and bring him to justice."

"They can do it without you. So I say again, why should I do this?" Hades's voice was not ignited. He sounded bored and unmoved. "You know it's impossible for Hypnos to disintegrate between two duties. He'd have to take your place."

Than grasped for ideas. "Hermes at one time conducted the dead."

"He's busy with other duties now. He can't possibly take on your job."

"Humans can go without dreams for a few weeks while Hip escorts the souls."

"Why, Thanatos? Dreams are more important than you seem to realize. Humans need dreams to work through the range of experiences and emotions they deal with during their waking hours. Without dreams, they'd shut down, die early deaths, and that's not how I want to build my kingdom. I want honorable souls. Just souls. The unjust ones can usually learn to be honorable with a series of behavior modification courses, courtesy of your sisters."

"And Sisyphus? Tantalus?"

"Serve to amuse."

"Amuse, Father? Are you amused by their suffering?"

"When it's deserved. I find it both amusing and satisfying."

Than caught on to a glimmer of hope. Hades was known for saying that life wasn't fair, but death was. Over the centuries, Hades had made it his utmost goal to level justice at every soul that crossed his path, complaining that Zeus showed favoritism and that most of humankind suffered for it. "You are just, Father, and it is for this reason you should let me go to earth as a mortal and force my brother to take my place escorting the dead. You know that, of the two of us, my brother got the better lot."

"So it is with me and my brothers. Do you think I chose the Under-world?" He moved his hand above him through the air as if to dismiss the splendid emeralds and diamonds and rubies around him. The golden palace would be a pleasure from which any lesser god would willingly rule, but the open skies and the expansive seas were superior in the eyes of Than's father. "Don't you think I'd prefer the sky or the waters? You must learn to accept your calling. Believe me, you'll be much better off."

"But you have mom, at least for half of the year. Hip has the company of hundreds, thousands of girls. I can think of no other god, save Charon, who is expected to live a lonely existence without end, and even he finds companionship from time to time in Cerberus, who's like a puppy to him. Why shouldn't I have a chance to find a queen? You have the power to grant me this request. You have the authority to make my lot more equal to that of the other gods of my rank. You should do this because you are just and because you can."

At that moment, Hermes entered the room. "Excuse me, Lord Hades. Should I come back later?"

"No. We're finished for now. What do you have?"

"Hello, Than."

Than gave a nod to his cousin but was in no mood for light conversation.

Hermes turned back to Hades. "A message from Poseidon regarding the small colony of white abalone beneath the coast of California. As you may know, the white abalone are headed for extinction, and because this particular colony is underground, Poseidon wants to be sure you stand beside him on his conservation efforts."

"Of course. He knows I support diversity. How dull of him to send you all this way."

"Something's brewing, my lord," Hermes said. "I think he fears your alliance won't last."

"Do you have wind of it?"

"I know nothing yet. I'll report back when I know something."

"Yes. Do that." Hades rubbed at his temple.

Than moved closer to his father as Hermes left the room. "I'm sorry to have burdened you further with my request. I know you have a lot of business to manage."

"You may think I don't care about your happiness, son, but I do, and in this matter, you are right. You deserve a chance to find a queen, and I do have the power to grant you this chance. So be it. You have forty days and no more."

Than's mouth fell open. "Thank you, Father."

"Wait. There is something she must do. Remember, nothing in this world is free."

Chapter Nine: Back Home

Even though Therese felt pretty sure the saga in her dreams was imaginary, she couldn't stop herself from getting on the Internet as soon as Carol brought her home from the hospital two days later. She had to use her laptop, though, which was slower than her parents' computer, because that computer had been taken by the police for their investigation.

Her neck had finally loosened up, and she could walk around without much pain. She could even run up the stairs to her room. She should have played around with Clifford, her little brown and white fox terrier, who was obviously starved for her affection. She should have let Jewels climb up her chest to nestle against her neck as she did most evenings while Therese read a good book. She should have taken Puffy from his cage and allowed him to scamper around in her hair, which she fanned out for him over the bed like a curtain, her arms carefully hovering over him lest he scurry out of reach. The chipmunks were in need of sunflower seeds, the deer their corn, and the wild horses the apples she tossed out behind her house. But Therese put off all these things, usually so important to her, to log on and surf the net for information about the Underworld.

A part of her knew her obsession with her dreams was a distraction. Her brain didn't want to think about what her house would feel like without her parents in it. Her brain didn't want her to go downstairs and into the kitchen on Saturday morning and find only Carol sitting with the paper at the granite countertop. As much as she loved Carol, Therese's brain wanted more.

She googled "Underworld mythology" and was surprised by all the links that appeared on her search results page. She clicked on the first link: "Hades, brother of Zeus and Poseidon, was the king of the Underworld, which he ruled with his bride Persephone, whom he kidnapped and made his queen. Guarded by Cerberus, a three-headed dog, the Underworld was underground and separated from the land of the living by five rivers, one of which was the Acheron, across which the dead were ferried."

Therese sat bewildered as she read articles describing many of the features about which she had dreamed. Not all the sources agreed on the details, but there were enough commonalities about them and her "tour" that made her hair stand on end: Charon, the old boatman; Tartarus and the Elysian Fields; Lethe, the river of forgetfulness; Sisyphus and his huge rock. Maybe she had read this stuff somewhere before?

A particular passage soon caught her eye: "Thanatos, also known as Orcus and Mors, was the god of Death. The son of Night and twin brother of Hypnos (Sleep), he was believed to be a beautiful young man but, because of his ghastly task, was very unpopular with both man and gods."

Therese's heart pounded in her chest. She felt she might be sick. Surely she had read this stuff before? Of course she had, she thought, taking a deep breath and slowly releasing it.

One article depicted Hades and his sons as evil demons. Therese shuddered. Then she clicked on another link. An image of the Grim Reaper, also named Death, tall and hooded with a gruesome face, long, thin hands, one of which held a scythe, made Therese flinch.

Clifford must have sensed her anxiety, because he jumped on the bed beside her, shook his stubby tail, and looked pleadingly into her eyes.

"You want to go outside?" she asked.

He immediately pranced around her room, full of eager excitement, running through the cluster of balloons that were beginning to sag. Puffy hopped onto his wheel and ran with enthusiasm, even though he usually waited to exercise at night. Even Jewels poked her head over the side of her plastic tank to peek at the activity around her.

Therese carefully took her tortoise into her hands and placed her against her chest. "You can come another time, Jewels." She stroked the shell and then put the tortoise back on its log in the tank with the hot lamp shining.

As she and Clifford went down the stairs—he like a speeding bullet and she a little more slowly than usual—panic gripped Therese's heart. She had almost forgotten. She had almost expected her parents to be downstairs reading or watching TV. She stopped on the bottom step and looked past the kitchen to the empty living room. Where was Carol?

Therese went to the deck outside, followed by Clifford. Carol sat at the wooden table talking on the phone, her body turned toward the reservoir side, away from the giant elms in back. The sun was just over the lake, heading toward its rest behind the mountains on the other side. The sky was a clear blue, and though it was still a long time till dusk, some of the animals were making themselves visible. There were always the birds hopping from tree to tree, twittering anxiously about this and that. But now there were also the chipmunks scampering around, and across from them, two deer plucked grass beneath the trees.

"Of course, Lieutenant," Carol said. "We'll be there." Carol pushed the end button on the portable phone. "No cell reception out here, I guess." She waved the receiver. "It's been a long time since I've been land-locked."

"We're lucky we get good Internet service out here. We had to use dial up until just a few months ago."

"Ugh."

"Did the lieutenant have any news?"

"They want us to come for a line up tomorrow, to see if you can identify the man whose face you saw, you know."

"They think they got the killer? Already?"

Carol tilted her head to the side. "The man you saw may not be the killer. They think they got him, though. His picture was in their system. They went to his apartment and brought him in for questioning and have enough to detain him overnight. He could be the killer. They don't know yet."

"Oh." Clifford lifted his paws to Therese's jean-clad shins. "Okay, boy. Let's go."

"Where are you going?"

"Just for a walk through the woods where Clifford likes to do his business. We'll be right back."

Therese realized as she led Clifford off the back steps of the wrap-around deck that Carol probably would have liked an invitation to join them, but Therese didn't want human company just yet. She wanted to retreat like she always did to the mountain forest with her dog and the wild animals for company.

Clifford frolicked around in front of her, sniffing this tree and that, as she headed up the mountain through the pines, aspens, and cypresses. A cardinal swept down and landed five feet away on a cypress branch. Therese inspected the feeder on the elm by the back deck. Empty. If she wanted to watch the birds through the kitchen window while washing dishes, she'd need to refill it. She looked more closely at the elm. One of its branches had turned completely yellow. Her mother had told her it had Dutch elm disease and the tree would slowly die if they didn't cut off the dead branch and treat the roots, but her parents hadn't had a chance to do anything about it. They kept saying later this summer…

She headed back up the trail after Clifford. She stepped over little round pellets, evidence that more deer had been visiting.

The national forest climbed behind her property for miles, and she rarely ran into another person on her walks. Only five homes stretched the expanse between Lemon Reservoir and the national forest, and the homes were more than half a mile apart. On the end lot on their northern side with twenty-five acres of private ranch land was Jen's house. It was three quarters of a mile down the dirt road that separated the houses from the reservoir, and Jen's mother ran the trail rides up through the forest in spring and summer, so, occasionally, Therese could hear them calling out commands to their animals. Usually the woods were quiet, like they were now.

Up ahead, Clifford started growling and barking. Therese caught up with him where he stood crouching in the woods.

"What is it, Clifford? Do you see a deer? You think you're so vicious, don't you, boy? But you and I know the truth."

Therese glimpsed a sudden movement ten feet away that was nothing like a deer. It seemed larger, like a bear, but human. "Who's there?"

Clifford's growl grew more intense, and he bared his teeth, backing away toward Therese.

Could a stranger be roaming around the forest?

Or worse, could her parents' killer be after her?

"Come on, Clifford! Let's get out of here!" Therese ran, but the dog stayed planted, baring his teeth and growling viciously.

"Clifford, come!" Therese's heart beat wildly, her throat felt dry, and her body numbed.

Still Clifford growled.

Therese ran over to Clifford and swept him up in her arms. Then, in her peripheral vision, she saw the figure move, closer this time.

"Therese!" It was a woman's voice, but it did not belong to her aunt.

Therese held on to Clifford and scrambled down the trail to her house, her head and neck throbbing with pain. Her foot caught on an aspen root, and she fell to the ground, hurting her knee and the palms of both hands. Clifford leapt from her arms as she fell, and he bounded back up the trail.

"No, Clifford!" She sprung to her feet and followed her dog. "Come back here, boy! Please! Come!"

From the corner of her eyes, she saw the figure move between two trees. Clifford yelped and ran down the trail, back to the house. Before Therese turned to follow him, she saw a woman wearing a short brown leather skirt and brown knee-high boots. She had pale skin and blonde rogue curls falling from a high bun. Therese thought she saw a bird perched on the woman's shoulder, but she couldn't be sure, because Therese had turned around so quickly and ran so fast that she couldn't be sure of what she had seen. She knew it was a woman, and that was all. A woman who had said her name.

"Call the lieutenant! Call 911!" Therese cried to her aunt, who still sat on the wooden table looking out toward the reservoir. "But come inside! Lock the doors!"

"Therese?" Carol jumped up. "What's wrong?"

"Come inside! Now!"

It seemed to take Carol forever and a day to follow Therese in through the kitchen door, but when she did, Therese slammed it shut, locked it, and turned the dead bolt, which was not easy because they hardly ever used it. Therese then ran to the front door and did the same. "Check the downstairs windows!" Therese yelled. "All of them!"

"What is going on, Therese! Tell me what happened!"

Why couldn't grownups ever just do what kids asked of them without asking a million questions? "Please, Carol! I saw someone out there. She looked really weird. And she called my name."

Carol went to the bedrooms to check the locks on the windows, but not without saying, "Calm down, honey. It's probably nothing. Maybe a neighbor you didn't recognize?"

Therese finished checking the last window and then found her aunt in the guest bedroom. She pointed a finger at her aunt and shouted, "You either think I'm paranoid or you're acting brave because you think you need to for my benefit! Well, I think I have a right to be paranoid. And if you're just acting brave, don't."

She left the room and sat on the sofa, which faced the kitchen, and stared at the back door. Clifford jumped into her lap.

"Therese, I'm sorry." Carol crossed the room and sat on the other end of the sofa.

"I know my own neighborhood," Therese said, still worked up.

"You're right. I'll call the lieutenant. I'm a little scared now, too."

It was dusk when the lieutenant arrived with another officer in tow. They came inside, accepted glasses of iced tea, and listened to Therese's account of what happened earlier in the woods.

The lieutenant said, "To be on the safe side, I'll post an officer on guard for a week or so to keep an eye on the place. Officer Morgan here will stay tonight. I'll see you both in the morning for the line up. Let Officer Morgan know if you hear or see anything the least bit suspicious to you, okay?"

"We will," Carol said, following the lieutenant to the door. "Thank you so much."

Officer Morgan slept on a cot on the back deck, so Therese felt a little more at ease, even though she couldn't take Clifford out to pee without him barking up a storm.

At night, when it was time to go to sleep, she was glad the officer was there below her on the deck outside. She lay there with Clifford and first thought of the fear. The woman had looked so strange. Even her voice was strange. Then Therese thought of the despair, and she fought off the panicky feeling until it won and she sobbed and sobbed until she finally fell asleep.

Therese was riding on a carousel at a carnival on a painted horse rising up and down to accordion music when Hip appeared and said, "My brother is coming for you."

"But he said he'd kill me if he came to me," Therese said.

"Only when he's acting as the guide for the dead. He's getting our father to make me take over that loathsome job. I'm not looking forward to it, and I guess I have you to thank for it."

"I don't get it. You're going to be the new guide for the dead?"

"Just temporarily, so Than can come for you."

"And then what?"

Hip shrugged. "I think he wants you to become his queen of the dead." Then he said, "Why don't you become my queen instead?"

Therese laughed. "You're not the marrying kind, Hip. I can see that."

The next morning after breakfast, Carol drove Therese to the Durango Police Department. Lieutenant Hobson met them at the front desk and escorted them into a dimly lit room that smelled like her father's cigars. Through a window on one wall, they could see six men being led into an adjacent room. Each wore a number around his neck. Two of the men were tall and the others closer to average size. One had a big belly. All six men had dark skin and beards, though the beards were of varying lengths and tidiness. Therese recognized the face she had seen the day of the shooting. Seeing him sent shivers all down her spine and made the hair on the back of her neck stand on end. She could barely breathe. There was no question in her mind. He was there the night of the shooting.

Had he killed her parents? She looked at him with hatred and fear as tears slid down her cheeks. Had he been responsible for ruining her life forever? She wanted to break through the glass and strangle him. "Number four," she finally said with confidence. "Definitely number four."

"You're sure?" the lieutenant asked.

"Positive."

The lieutenant spoke into a machine and said, "Thanks. You can lead them out now."

As the men turned to follow the officer out of the small chamber, Therese saw a reflection in the window of a woman standing behind her. The reflection appeared out of nowhere and looked exactly like the woman in the woods from the day before—the woman who called her name. There was definitely a large bird perched on the shoulder of the woman in the reflection, and the woman was smiling and nodding, apparently at Therese. Therese quickly turned, gasping, but there was no one behind her.

"What's wrong?" Carol asked, standing beside her.

"What? Oh, nothing. Can we go home now?"

Chapter Ten: Setting Up

Late at night, Than listened for her voice among the multitude praying to him. So many voices all at once, "Please don't take my son! He's all I have!" and "Don't let the cancer take her. Help her to recover." As if he had a choice. People are born, they live, and they die, and there was little the gods could do to alter their experiences. In many ways, Than thought, the gods were the slaves of humans, each with a duty to help maintain the world and to keep all of its creation in balance. The gods served the world and its inhabitants, not the other way around.

At last he heard her voice echoing above the mountains of Colorado. He flew to her and listened.

"I hope my parents feel no pain," Therese whispered, and her voice lifted up to him and into the clouds like sweet, soft music, like something his mother might have once sung to him. "I hope my dream was true, and they really are in the beautiful Elysian Fields, perfectly happy."

Than looked down upon Therese where she sat on her bed with her little dog. "I miss them, Clifford," she said out loud. "I miss them so much!" She hugged her dog and sobbed.

A knock at her bedroom door brought her beautiful face up again. "Yes?"

"Can I come in?" A woman, a redhead, too, stood behind the door.

As Therese and the other woman spoke, Than wondered if he were acting too hastily in his decision to pursue Therese. She was, after all, the one and only girl he had ever met alive. Once he changed into mortal form, he could meet other girls and make a more informed decision. What was so special about Therese? As soon as he had asked himself the question, he answered it: she was the only soul in the centuries of his existence to have willed herself to the outskirts of the Underworld and to get close enough to him to touch him. This alone set her apart. Also.

she hadn't come to him in a proud, arrogant, threatening way. She hadn't realized she had left the dream world and was close to dying herself. She had believed herself to be the author of her own dream, and in that dream, she wanted her parents alive. Who wouldn't? If she had exerted her will and demonstrated strength, she had done so in ignorance. She had not set out to challenge him.

She hadn't come like Sisyphus to bind him so humans could not die. She hadn't come like Hercules to steal Cerberus. She had not come like Orpheus first to persuade with song and then to defy a broken agreement.

She had come, put her arms around him, and told him he was lovely—so lovely—and she had kissed him. Who in the history of time had ever done that to Death?

And the deal with Hades required Therese to do something that not just any mortal could do. He wasn't sure that even Therese could do it.

Plus, he had only forty days. Why had his father chosen forty days? To Than, this seemed an arbitrary number. Why not one hundred? Why not twenty? At any rate, forty days seemed hardly enough time to make a selection among the billions of girls on earth. No, unless Therese was less than she seemed, he would spend his time courting her. He would not do like his father had his mother and take her unwillingly. Than had seen how her resentment had poisoned her relationship with his father. He wanted to win Therese's heart.

From the conversation below him, he came to understand that the woman was Therese's aunt, Carol, and this woman was now encouraging Therese to visit her friend, Jen. Than soon learned where Jen lived, and so he turned his attention to her, to see if he could use her in his efforts to meet Therese in the flesh.

When he found her, he was surprised to hear her praying to him. Most mortals prayed to a different god, unless they or someone they loved were dying or already dead. But this young woman was asking for death?

"Everything would be easier for everyone else if you just took me. Then he could come back, and they'd all be happy."

Than saw a way to befriend Therese. He would first study Jen and her family.

Chapter Eleven: Invitations

A few weeks passed since Therese had identified the man she saw the day of the shooting, and, after mostly lying around in bed and spending time with her pets, she finally returned to the woods with Clifford. She didn't go as far as usual, and Carol stood on the back deck watching her in full view. The police were no longer standing guard at the house, and Therese could finally take Clifford out to do his business without a leash and without him barking and growling and driving her mad. The wild animals, which had not come around while the officers were here, returned to eat the sunflower seeds Therese sprinkled across the deck and railing.

Jen had called several days ago and had begged Therese to come and groom the horses with her, and Therese decided today she felt like going.

Carol turned on to the gravelly drive leading up to Jen's house. Clifford leaned his head out of Therese's open window, his tongue hanging happily from his mouth, his stubby tail wagging. Clifford loved to come to Jen's and run around the ranch, though he wasn't allowed in the pen. He knew Jen's family and their horses, and they knew him, and so everyone got along just fine. Therese loved to come too. She looked at the big log cabin, similar to her own, on the right of the property, and the barn and pen to the left. On the opposite side of the pen from the house, two pastures spread out to the north at the base of the mountains. A stream cut across the entire property behind the house and pen, and through the center of the pastures. Tied to the base of the front wooden steps of the house was a lone goat, which bleated as Jen opened the front door and skipped down the five steps to the ground.

Jen's blonde hair was pulled up in a high ponytail, and she wore a white tank top and old blue jeans and boots. Therese felt a wave of jealousy at Jen's beauty but shrugged it off as soon as Jen called to her in her friendly voice, "Hey there! You're finally here!"

When Therese opened her car door, Clifford sprang out to meet Jen. The goat bleated its objections, and Clifford cowered away from it.

"Hey there, boy!" Jen pet Clifford when he greeted her with his front paws on her legs. Then Clifford ambled down to his favorite hangout: the stream at the back of the property, which was full of trout.

Therese turned to Carol. "Thanks for the ride."

"Sure. Call me if you want a ride home. First I'm running into Durango to get a few more groceries, but I'll be back in a couple of hours."

Therese stepped out of the car, but before she closed the door, Carol asked, "You sure you don't want me to run you by the cemetery later? You still haven't visited your parents' graves. It's been over a month since we buried them."

"I'm sure. I'm not ready to do that yet." She wished her aunt wouldn't have brought this up now. She'd been close to happy and excited, but now she was filled with dread.

"Okay. Bye, sweetheart."

Therese closed the car door and turned to her friend. "It's nice to be out of the house. Thanks for inviting me."

"Hey, listen. My mom was wondering if you want a job. The two brothers she hired this spring had a death in the family. She hired a new temp a week ago, but she still needs one more hand, just until she can find someone more permanent. Up to it?"

Therese shrugged. It would be a lot of hard work, which could be both good and bad. "Would she need me every day?"

"Pretty much. She pays ten an hour." Jen led her across the gravel drive past the barn toward the partially sheltered pen where the dozen horses hung out.

"I don't know. If she can't find anyone else, maybe." Then to Clifford, who had come back to check on her, she said, "No boy, not in the pen. You know better."

"Please say yes. We could hang out."

"How early in the morning?"

"Okay, you wouldn't have to do the early morning stuff."

They reached the pen and the General greeted her with a sniff. He stretched his long gray neck over the fence for what he knew would be a soft stroke. He was the biggest of the horses, a huge gray gelding. Jen and her brothers sometimes called him the elephant. "Hey, General," Therese said, rubbing the side of his face.

"We bring the horses in at nine for grooming before they start their first trail ride of the day. My brothers and the new handler are in there finishing up now. We'll need help with the grooming and tack so they're ready to go by eleven. You could leave after that."

"So nine to eleven? That's not bad. Let me think about it." She could use some of her own mad money, and twenty dollars a day for just a couple of hours of her time seemed like a good deal, and a good distraction. She loved grooming the horses.

Jen added, "After my mom's trail rides, we exercise them hard before dinner, when we turn them out to pasture again till dark. We could use another rider then, too, from like four to five. Not necessarily every day. Just when you can."

One of Jen's two brothers appeared in the middle of the pen from behind the shelter. He was the tallest and oldest of the Holt kids and had blond hair like his sister, which he kept short around his face like a bowl. He graduated last May and would be attending college in the fall. "Hey, Therese."

"Hi Pete."

"Oh, hey, Therese!" the other brother, who would be a freshman this year, called as he popped up from behind a horse. He wore the same blond bowl on his head as his brother, but the freckles that peppered his cheeks were more prominent.

"Hi Bobby."

"Sorry about your parents," Pete, the older one, said.

"Yeah. Thanks." She bit the inside of her bottom lip.

Then Bobby asked, "Hey, have you met Than?"

Another boy, slightly taller than Pete with dark wavy hair and a bigger build, stepped out of the shelter and into the middle of the pen and the horses.

It was the Than from her dreams.

Jen must have noticed the look on her friend's face, because she asked, "Do you guys know each other?"

"You look familiar." Than strolled up to the fence in his blue jeans and tight white t-shirt.

"No, I don't think we've met," Therese said. It couldn't be. It just couldn't be him. But how many people had she known named Than? Her knees felt like they might buckle.

Than extended his hand. "Well, then, it's a pleasure to finally meet you, Therese. I've heard a lot about you, thanks to Bobby here."

Bobby's face turned crimson as she gave the new guy her hand, and she couldn't pull it away fast enough. Than seemed to be laughing at her behind his smile, enjoying her pain and confusion and Bobby's embarrassment. She decided she did not like him.

"It's nice to meet you, too," she lied.

Jen opened the gate of the pen. "We're half way done with the grooming."

"Can I groom Sugar?" Therese asked.

"Than's finishing her up now," Pete said. "Can you take Hershey?"

Without warning, Clifford ran through the gate and leapt into Than's arms. He licked Than all over his face. The General spooked back, causing a domino effect as two other horses, Ace and Chestnut, reared and snorted. Fear gripped Therese as she recognized the danger. But Than tossed Clifford to Therese, grabbed the General's mane, and whispered something in his ear. The General settled, which calmed the other horses, and Therese finally released her breath.

"Bad boy! Go back to the stream! Go catch a fish!" she scolded Clifford, turning him out of the pen. She said to Jen, "I'm so sorry. I don't know what came over him. He should know better than that." Then she looked up at Than with suspicion and awe. Why had Clifford run to him? And how had he settled the horses so quickly?

"Wow, Than," Jen said. "How did you do that?"

Than shrugged and said he had a way with horses, but Therese still felt as though he were laughing at her, as though the threat of danger had been her fault because she couldn't control her dog, and she had needed Than to save the day. She took up a brush and went over to Hershey, a mare whose coat, as the name implied, was like chocolaty brown silk.

"Hey girl," Therese said in a soothing voice. "Did you miss me?" Therese could feel Than's eyes on her, but she tried her best to ignore him. He was too sexy for her, anyway, and much too arrogant and self-assured. Jen had probably already staked her claim on him, and she was probably more his type, so naturally beautiful. As Therese brushed through Hershey's coat, she wondered if it had been a mere coincidence that Than looked like the Than in her dreams. Or, maybe he didn't, and somehow she was now imposing the image of him on her memory.

Therese bent over to brush Hershey's belly, and her rear-end bumped against Than, who was passing behind her. She popped upright, the blood rushing to her face, and muttered, "Excuse me." He said nothing, but when she snatched a glance his way, she could see he looked pleased with himself.

Had her subconscious somehow sensed she would be meeting him? Had it been a prophetic vision? And if so, what had it meant?

After they finished grooming and saddling the horses, Jen's mom came out of the barn where she had been working to formally offer Therese the job and to thank her for accepting it. She was surprised to hear Therese wouldn't be coming at dawn to help with the barn and pen cleaning, but Jen quickly explained that she planned to work every morning instead of splitting the chores with her brothers. Jen's surreptitious glance toward Than confirmed Therese's suspicion that Jen was interested in him, and this explained Jen's sudden eagerness to work more. Mrs. Holt seemed pleased with the arrangement, since she paid Jen less than ten an hour.

Jen invited Therese to stay for lunch when her mom and Pete took the first riders on the trail. "We're just having frozen pizzas," Jen explained, "but it would be fun to chat."

Clifford was splashing around in the stream behind Jen's house chasing trout he would never catch, but perfectly entertained, nevertheless. Luckily, he was too preoccupied to bother the riders walking up the drive toward the pen. "Sure," Therese said.

Jen surprised Therese by asking Than if he wanted to stay, too.

"Maybe next time," he said. "I promised my sisters I'd eat with them today."

He waved goodbye as he left, on foot, down the gravel drive, where cars were now parked in a line, and south up the dirt road toward Therese's house. Therese and Jen both watched him until he was out of sight. Even a few of the trail riders waiting to mount stole glances at him.

Then Jen said, "Is he drop-dead gorgeous, or what?"

Therese shrugged.

"How can you take such a casual attitude toward his splendid good looks? Does this mean I don't have to fight you for him?"

"What about Matthew?" Therese referred to the boy Jen had been with most of their sophomore year.

"He hasn't called much this summer. I think he's lost interest."

"Maybe he's just busy or on vacation."

Jen asked again, "So you're not interested?"

They walked up the steps toward the front door, Bobby close behind. "He's all yours," Therese said, though, as soon as the words came out, she felt nauseous.

"Well, I won't hold my breath," Jen said. "He was checking you out the whole time we were grooming in the pen. I think he prefers you."

Bobby squeezed by Jen and went down the hall. "I'm outta here."

Jen laughed at her brother.

"That's impossible," Therese said when they were alone. "I mean, God, look at you."

"Oh, shut up. You always talk yourself down. I would kill for your curly hair and pouty lips."

"You can get a perm and botox—not that you need it. I wish I had your boobs."

"You've got boobs!"

"Nubs." She cupped her hands around her half-lemons and looked enviously at Jen's full oranges.

"Cute nubs. And some people develop later than others. Plus, there's always implants," Jen laughed.

"Yeah, right." Therese rolled her eyes and took a seat at the kitchen table. "So, where's Than going? Did he really walk here?" Just saying the name sent a shiver down her spine.

Jen grabbed some paper plates from the pantry and put three around the table, though just now Bobby was watching television in the other room. "He and his sisters are renting the Melner cabin for the summer."

"The Melner cabin?" It was about a half-mile south up the road from Therese's house, the third of the five houses across from the reservoir. The Melner's had turned their home into a vacation getaway, and although Therese was used to different people staying there throughout the year, she found it upsetting that Than was one of them. She recalled the image of the Grim Reaper on her computer screen and shuddered. It was just a coincidence, she reminded herself.

"Yeah, you guys are neighbors," Jen giggled.

"If his family can afford the cabin, why's he working for your mom this week?"

"For the same reasons you are, I guess." The oven started beeping—it was hot now—so Jen put the frozen pizza directly on the center rack. "He said that he enjoyed working with horses and that he wanted to get in touch with nature." She laughed. "I'm part of nature. He can get in touch with me."

Therese laughed with her. It felt good being with her friend like this. Jen could be bossy and stubborn, but she was so worth it.

Jen closed the oven door and asked, "Diet Coke?"

"Sounds great." She took the ice-cold can from her friend and popped open the tab. The cold pop felt good going down her throat. The grooming had worked up a thirst. "So where's he from?"

"He said he's from down south. At first he said 'down under,' and we thought he meant Australia, even though he doesn't have the accent. But he said he meant down south, from Texas. From what we gathered, he used to work on a ferry."

Therese choked on the Diet Coke and broke into a fit of coughing.

"You okay?" Jen asked, patting Therese on the back.

Therese eventually nodded. "Wrong pipe," she explained when she could.

Carol dropped Therese and Clifford at the Holt ranch again the next morning. Carol had been thrilled about Therese's new job, saying it was just what she needed to get her mind off…things. Therese was partly glad that she would be out of Carol's hair this week and keeping herself entertained with her best friend and the horses, but she was also partly annoyed by Than's appearance, especially since the more she thought about it, the more she was sure he looked exactly like the Than in her dreams.

"Come on, boy!" she called to Clifford, as she climbed from the car. Then she said to Carol, "I'll call if I need a ride."

As Therese walked up the gravelly drive with Clifford stopping to pee on every tree, she thought more about her discoveries last night.

When she couldn't sleep, she had gone on the Internet and googled "the Furies." One article had this to say: "The Furies are three sisters: Alecto (The Unceasing), Megaera (The Avenger of Jealousy and Hatred), and Tisiphone (The Avenger of Murder). They are the goddesses of revenge, sometimes called the daughters of the Night. They haunt criminals until they go insane and die. The Furies are untiring and persistent in their pursuit. They are impartial and indifferent, merely carrying out their duty. They continue to torment wrongdoers even after death. In some traditions, they are the daughters of Hades and Persephone, rulers of the Underworld, and their brothers are Hypnos (Sleep) and Thanatos (Death). The Furies are known for tormenting sinners under the command of Hades and for pursuing criminals on Earth until their victims have been rightfully avenged."

In her dream weeks ago, Than had said he was sending the Furies to the waking world of the living to help her solve her parents' murder. Therese now shuddered at the prospect.

Of course, it had only been a silly dream, something her subconscious must have conjured up based on this mythology she must have read a long time ago and had forgotten all about.

As she approached Jen's house, Clifford turned around back down the gravelly drive and took off across the dirt road toward the reservoir. Boulders and short aspens made a kind of barrier between the road and the water until the road reached Jen's house. Across from the Holts' was a big field of tall grass, and out in the middle of the grass this morning was a lone figure. Clifford was running toward it.

"Come back, Clifford!" Therese followed her dog into the grass. She was stunned when she saw Than, soaked from head to toe, walking toward her with his clothes bundled in his hands. All he was wearing were his wet white boxers and boots.

"Good Morning, Therese," he said when he got closer.

She couldn't avoid looking at his golden body—his golden naked body, for the wet boxers didn't leave much to the imagination. His skin wasn't what you would call tan, but it seemed to almost glow.

"How are you today?" Than asked.

She could tell he was amused by her reaction, which she hadn't been able to disguise. Her eyes were about to pop out of her head.

"Fine," she said, turning away. "Come on, Clifford."

"That water felt so good," Than said. "Do you go swimming in the lake often?"

Not often enough, she thought. She'd only been a few times this summer, and that was before…her life had changed. "Not often."

"That's too bad. I'd go every day if I could. I had no idea how beautiful everything is up here, how nice the sunshine feels, the water, the cool mountain air when the wind blows. I love listening to the birds, too. I think I've found seven different species in this forest alone." He caught up to her now and walked beside her.

"They don't have those things down in Texas?"

"What? Oh, well not like this."

Therese noticed that Clifford walked beside Than, putting Than between them. Clifford never took to strangers this quickly. "Come on, Clifford," she said again, a little jealous that he wasn't trotting alongside her instead of him. "Don't you have barn and pen duty this morning?" Therese asked Than with a touch of hostility as they reached the dirt road and headed toward the gravel drive.

"We finished. I worked up a sweat and thought I'd come cool off a bit before grooming the horses. You should join me tomorrow. Come a little earlier."

He stopped on the gravel drive to put on his shirt. Therese took the opportunity to study his tight ruffle of abs but looked away as soon as his head was visible again. Then he knocked off his boots and climbed into his jeans. Therese didn't know whether she should stand there and wait for him or keep walking toward the pen, so she walked on, but at a slow pace.

"Come on, boy!" she said to Clifford.

Clifford decided to wait for Than, but, in no time, both boy and dog had caught up to her as she reached for the gate to the pen. "No, Clifford," she warned.

"Mornin' Therese," Bobby called brightly from behind the yellowish-brown horse named Ace.

"Hey, Bobby." Therese quickly closed the gate behind Than. "Go play, boy," she said to Clifford. "Where's Jen?"

"She'll be out in a minute," Mrs. Holt called from the shelter. "She's on the phone. Mornin' Therese."

Therese stepped under the aluminum structure. "Mornin', Mrs. Holt. Who do you need me to start on?"

Jen's mother had her gray-blonde hair cut short, like her sons, in a bowl around her leathery freckled face. She was beautiful once, but she stopped caring about her skin in the elements, and the sun had taken its toll. Plus, she smoked and looked slightly underweight, and the lines in her face were deep. "Bobby said you prefer Sugar."

Therese liked all the horses, but Sugar, the white mare, never resisted Therese's requests. The General, Chestnut, Rambo, and Rusty were the most stubborn of the herd, all constantly vying for the upper ranks in the pecking order, and Therese didn't like having to hit or kick or growl at the animals to get their cooperation. Sugar, Ace, and Dumbo had mild dispositions and seemed indifferent to rank and status. Therese took up a brush and said in a gentle, even tone, "Hi, Sugar, girl. You already look so pretty today." She took the brush to Sugar's withers. "You're not nearly as dirty as Hershey was yesterday."

Bobby laughed, "That's because she's a lazy girl. She just stands around and sleeps all mornin', don't you, girl."

Therese noticed Than was just a few feet away from her, eyeing her with a smug look on his face. What had she done to give him the impression she was interested in him? She was confused by how confident he seemed to be that he had some kind of an effect on her. Well, she'd have to show him. He didn't need to know that he did have an effect on her, that his very presence had suddenly made her more self-conscious than she could ever remember being, but she could very well control herself and make Than think otherwise. She wanted to wipe that all-too-confident grin right off his face, even though his dark wavy hair, now wet and clinging to his beautiful face, set off the crystal blue of his eyes. She took a deep breath and focused on the animal. Sugar soothed her; the contact with the warm mare and the look of her friendly eyes made a feeling of peace wash over Therese. "You're such a good girl, even if you are lazy."

"Ace, on the other hand, is a roller, aren't you boy?" Bobby said to the yellowish-brown horse. "If you could get one more weed stuck in your coat, I'd be surprised."

"Oh, come on now," Mrs. Holt said. "You're being too hard on Sugar. She's not lazy. She and Satellite groom each other, don't you, Satellite. That's why you're so clean."

Satellite was pure white and seemed to have a bond with Sugar. Therese often noticed them standing head to tail flicking away the flies and licking off the grass and dirt from one another's coats.

"Where's Pete?" Therese asked.

"He's practicing today," Mrs. Holt said. "His band is performing at the Wildhorse Saloon in Durango tomorrow evening."

"That's awesome!" Therese knew Pete dreamed of making it big with his music and that, as much as he loved horses, he probably wouldn't come back to work on the ranch after college. "I bet he's about to pop."

"He's pretty excited," Bobby said.

"We're all going after supper," Mrs. Holt said. "You're welcome to come with us." Then she added, "You, too, Than."

"Thanks, Mrs. Holt," Than said. "That sounds very entertaining."

Before Therese could reply, she heard Jen greeting Clifford on her way to the pen. "Good boy!" she was saying. "You go catch a fish! Catch a fish!" Then she came in through the gate and came up beside Therese. "Hey. How's it going?"

"Okay," Therese lied. She couldn't very well say she'd cried herself to sleep because she missed her parents so terribly and that she'd felt restless the whole night long. She couldn't say what she had discovered about the Furies and how suspicious she felt about Than showing up here not long after her strange dreams. "What's up?"

Jen grabbed a brush and started working on Annie, a red mare who happened to be on the other side of Than from Therese. "We're all going to the Wildhorse Saloon tomorrow night. You have to come with us. Ray and Todd might go, too."

"Ray and Todd are going?" Therese perked up. She loved hanging out with them. They always managed to make her laugh.

"Yeah, I was just on the phone with Todd. Pete's band is performing."

"That's what your mom said." Although Therese didn't like the idea of being there with Than and his arrogance, she could use a good dose of company from her friends, a distraction from all the anguish and longing and dread, especially at night, when she had more time to think. She patted Sugar's front leg for the hoof. Therese picked out a small pebble wedged against the shoe.

"So are you going?" Than asked.

He looked Therese directly in the eyes, all signs of smugness gone. Therese's mouth opened with surprise. He really seemed to like her. Therese shot a glance at Jen and from the look on her face realized she had drawn the same conclusion. "Um, I'll ask my aunt."

Mrs. Holt said, "Pete would be glad if you could make it. Tell your aunt to call me if she has any questions."

"Yes, m'am, I will." Therese squatted down to work on Sugar's legs.

"Oh, and I have a favor to ask, Therese," Mrs. Holt said. "Could you help us ride later today before supper? With Pete gone, we could use the extra hand."

Therese frowned. Riding made her nervous. She hated kicking and shouting the commands. But she didn't want to let down Mrs. Holt. "I'm sure my aunt won't mind. She's working anyway."

"Great," Mrs. Holt said. "Sure do appreciate it. We already exercised Sugar yesterday, but Dumbo's a gentle ride. You can ride him."

Therese finished grooming Sugar, a little knot forming in her stomach now over having to ride later today. She rode last summer a few times because Jen had pleaded with her and then stooped to bribing, but a year is a long time. "Who should I work on now?" Therese asked.

Mrs. Holt told her to groom Dumbo, so they could get better acquainted.

"Stay clean, Sugar." Therese petted the horse's cheek and neck. "You look so pretty. Yes, you do."

Therese spotted Dumbo on the other side of Jen, behind Annie. Dumbo was the youngest of the males and the new stallion, added to the group after Benji was put down last summer. His ears were slightly bigger than those of the other horses, hence his name. Just now they were pointed forward and his muzzle was extended toward Therese and sniffing at her with curiosity like Clifford sometimes did with visitors. "Hi there, Dumbo. Remember me? I'm Therese." She took the brush to Dumbo's withers and pet his neck with her other hand. "You're a handsome boy, and from the look of you, you're a roller like Ace, aren't you?" She started pulling weeds and stickers from his thick mane.

Bobby snickered. "You should see 'em at night before we bring 'em in. He and Ace are like puppies the way they roll around in the grass and chase each other across the pasture."

"I bet that's fun to watch," Than put in. "I'd like to see that some time."

"You're welcome to come and watch the horses any evening," Mrs. Holt said. "Just stay outside the fence. If they see you in with them, they'll get upset. They like their routine."

"Maybe I'll come by this evening," Than said.

"Come just before dusk," Bobby said. "That's when all the fun starts." Then Bobby added. "Therese, you should come too."

"I'll have to see how I feel after riding. I haven't done it in so long, I may be sore."

Mrs. Holt let out a loud guffaw that made Therese jump. "No sugar. You won't be sore tonight. You'll feel it in the mornin'."

Therese looked at Dumbo's eyes, and he looked back at her with a knowing smile, as if to say, "You'll be alright." Therese rubbed his face and put her cheek against his. Dumbo nuzzled up to her and softly whinnied.

"He likes you," Bobby said.

After Therese helped saddle the horses for the first trail ride of the day, Jen asked if she wanted to stay again for lunch. They were standing near the gravel drive beneath the shade of a cluster of cypresses as the cars were pulling up—the first riders of the day.

Therese's eyes were on her dog, who noticed the cars and was coming up from the stream to investigate. "Come here, Clifford! Come, now!" He bounded over to her like a good boy. She picked him up to avoid conflict. Then she turned to Jen. "Thanks for the invitation, but I better get some rest at home if I'm coming back this afternoon. What time does your mom need me? Four?"

"Yeah. You're really only riding for about half an hour, but by the time you remove the tack and turn 'em out, an hour's gone by before you know it." Then Jen added, "Don't feel like you have to do it if you're not up to it. I don't mind riding an extra hour tonight. I don't think my mom knows how nervous you get."

"Thanks, Jen, but I'll give it a try. I'll call you if I chicken out. Can I use your phone to call my aunt? She won't let me walk."

Than came up from behind her. "Would she mind if I walked you home?"

She shrugged. "I guess that would be okay." She tried to seem indifferent, but her heart was pounding so loudly that she worried he might be able to hear it. She knew she should call and ask permission, but she knew the answer would likely be no, and she wanted to walk with him. They said goodbye to the Holts and headed down the drive toward the dirt road. Clifford wriggled in her arms and then settled.

"You have a gift with animals," Than said, stroking Clifford. "I like to watch you interact with them."

"Thanks," she said, unable to prevent herself from giving him a genuine smile. Being an animal lover was probably the thing she liked most about herself. "You're pretty good with animals, too. Clifford has never taken to a stranger the way he has with you, like yesterday when he jumped in your arms."

"I don't get to spend much time around animals." They stepped out onto the dirt road between the houses and the lake, so Therese let Clifford down as Than continued. "I wish it were otherwise. The horses and the birds and even your little dog have brought me a lot of pleasure these past two days."

Therese didn't know what to say. All of this was so unexpected. She had taken Than to be arrogant and maybe even selfish, but he sounded sincere. "I couldn't live without animals," she said.

Than frowned. Then he turned to her and said, "Being around people has been a pleasant change, too. I tend to be a loner, except for my sisters' company."

"That's too bad. But you can always change."

He sighed, gave her a sad smile, and shook his head. "Some things never change."

She wondered what he meant, but she was afraid to pry, so she looked across the reservoir to the mountains on the other side. The sun was almost at high noon, and everything sparkled under its brilliant light.

"I never get tired of this view," Therese said. "I feel so lucky to live here." Then she thought of who else used to live here, and the tears welled. Panic gripped her heart, but she took a deep breath and let it out slowly. She wasn't going to cry.

"I know you must miss them," Than said softly. "Bobby told me. I wish I could say I know how you feel."

"Are your parents staying in the Melner cabin with you?" Therese wanted to change the subject.

"No. My dad had to work and my mom is visiting my grandmother."

They were silent for a while, both looking out over the lake and at Clifford stopping again to pee on every other tree. When they reached Therese's gravel driveway, they slowed down and came to a stop. "What does your dad do?"

He stuck his hands in his pockets and let out a deep breath. "Hmm. Well, my dad, he manages a large operation, and my mom helps him during parts of the year. It's difficult to explain."

"So he never gets to get away?"

"Never. In fact, this is my very first trip away from home, and I had to beg and make promises." He laughed. "My dad's a good guy. Please don't misunderstand. But he's got a huge responsibility, and, well, it's difficult for him to be flexible."

Therese noticed Clifford had gone on ahead of her toward the house. "Well, I'm glad you got to come out here. It's beautiful country and the Holts are an awesome family. And the horses are so incredible."

"I'm glad, too." He took a step closer to her. "I'm glad I got to meet you."

Therese felt the blood rush to her face, and she looked down, shuffling around the gravel of her driveway with her sneaker. "Thanks. I'm glad I got to meet you, too." She looked up to see him grinning down at her.

"So I guess I'll see you later this afternoon, when it's time to exercise the horses."

"Yeah." She wanted to add, "Unless I chicken out," but she didn't.

"See you later." He turned and headed toward the Melner cabin.

She watched him walk away, enjoying the view.

Chapter Twelve: Mortal Sensations

Being human certainly had its advantages, Than thought as he walked away from Therese toward his cabin. For one thing, he never realized how much more humans than gods experience the world. As often as he had been all over the planet, he had never felt the sun on his back. He had never experienced the cold water of a lake or river running through his fingers. He had never heard the beautiful music of the birds. Than realized his primal senses were more finely-tuned when in mortal form, while his mind was more finely tuned when in godly form. In other words, he had never felt so much in all his life.

He wondered if the lower one went in the animal kingdom, the more this was true. Did horses feel more than humans? Beetles more than horses?

He stopped before a pine tree and pressed his nose close to its tickling branches. He breathed in the fresh, astringent scent with immeasurable pleasure. The path was alight with voices of insects, birds, and rodents, like an orchestra unaware of its audience and so unlike the quiet desolation of the Underworld. Even as Than travelled across the globe for souls day in and day out, he had not heard these insect sounds or felt the freshness of this air or basked in the heat of this sun. Before turning up the gravelly drive to his log cabin, he went to the reservoir once again to kick off his boots and dip his feet into the cool water. In the Underworld, he was surrounded by rivers but in none of them could he indulge his senses like he could now as a man.

Therese had baffled him. Earlier in the pen, she shouted prayers at him that had made it hard for him to keep a straight face. She had said, "What are you looking at? You think you're so sexy? So what if you are? Quit looking at me like that! You're a jerk, aren't you?"

It had amazed him how quickly these prayers that she unwittingly hurled at him changed as the afternoon went on. By the next day, by time he was walking her home, she directed other thoughts his way, "Who are you? Why do you like me? How can someone like you be interested in someone like me?"

He couldn't read her thoughts, but prayers that she sent his way were crystal clear, even if she did not know he heard them.

When he reached his cabin, he found it empty. Meg and Tizzie were rarely there, always busy hunting. Apparently they had a new lead in the case and would be gone for a while. Than felt a little guilty, now, as he thought of their constant work. His sisters enjoyed their job, but did they ever get a break? Who was he to have this extended vacation where he could revel in the sensual pleasures the earth had to offer?

Than sat on the sofa and immediately felt his brother's appearance.

Hip appeared on the opposite end of the sofa. "I was just wondering the same thing myself, brother," Hip said.

"I have no sympathy for you, lover boy."

"I don't blame you. Your job sucks. The past three weeks have been absolutely odious. I wonder how you've suffered through the past centuries without complaining before now."

Than shrugged. "It's not so bad as you make it out, Hip. There's satisfaction in bringing an end to earthly pain and suffering, which is almost always present at death. Don't you think?"

"Absolutely not. It's perfectly depressing. Not a bright spot anywhere to be found. I came to beg you to give me a day's reprieve, just a day, so I can have a little fun in the dream world, just to tide me over these next horrible days to come."

Than frowned. "I suppose I can find a day to do it. Let me think on it and get back with you." Than didn't want to risk the possibility of his father shortening his visit because of a complaining brother.

"Have I told you lately that I love you, bro'?" Hip jumped up and smiled.

Chapter Thirteen: News

Carol looked up from the couch where she had been working on her laptop as soon as Therese and Clifford entered the house. "Oh, good. You're home. Hungry?"

Carol must have assumed one of the Holts had given her a ride, and Therese didn't say otherwise. "Not yet."

"Well, the lieutenant is coming by for a bit, so I guess we can wait till after his visit to have lunch."

Therese plopped onto the couch beside Carol and then winced. She kept forgetting about her neck. It felt good most of the time, but plopping on couches reminded her that her neck was still a little sore, and today's exercise probably made it a little more so. "Why is he coming?"

"He said he had some news and wanted to discuss it with us. He'll be here in about twenty minutes or so."

"I'll go shower and change."

Later, Therese opened the door and let the lieutenant inside. He was sweating again, and she wondered if he had a health problem.

"Did that man kill my parents?" she asked.

"Sweetheart, let the lieutenant come in and sit down."

"I don't blame her," Lieutenant Hobson said as he crossed the room. "I'd want answers, too, if I were her." He took the seat Carol offered him beside the fireplace.

"Can I get you something to drink? Iced tea? Lemonade?" Carol asked.

"Iced tea sounds nice. No sugar, please. I'm diabetic."

Therese sat on the sofa across from the lieutenant and waited until Carol returned with his drink. Once Carol was beside her on the couch, Therese asked, "What news do you have for us?"

"Well, I've established a couple of possible motives. Your father's most recent novel was based on a crime committed by a felon released a month ago from the federal prison in Three Rivers, Texas. My team has been tracking this man's whereabouts, and, as soon as we've located him, we'll bring him in for questioning."

"What about the man in the line up?" Therese asked.

"Another motive involves your mother's work. She was being honored at the university for her role in leading a team of students close to finding an antidote for the mutated anthrax toxin C. Maybe there are folks out there who wanted to slow down its discovery."

Therese's mouth dropped open. Her head started spinning and she closed her eyes.

"We've questioned a lot of people from the university and have pretty much ruled out disgruntled students and colleagues."

Therese opened her eyes. "What about the man in the lineup?" she said again.

"Sweetheart, be patient," Carol said. "He's getting to that."

"Yes. He's confessed to the shooting."

"Oh my gosh!" Therese cried. "He really did it!" She couldn't believe she had seen the killer before he committed his gruesome deed. Maybe if she had gotten her parents to see him, maybe she could have somehow prevented, maybe…" She broke into tears. She felt panicky and so alone. She wanted her mother and father!

"The shooter claims he was working for someone else," the lieutenant said, "and that's as far as we've gotten. We don't know who this other person is or why he was after your parents. But we know we've got the shooter, and we're in the process of offering him a deal to talk." The lieutenant finished his tea and set the glass down on the end table beside the chair. "That's all I have for now, but I wanted to tell you in person. I'll call as soon as we break this guy."

Therese shuddered. That man had killed her parents. She couldn't get his deranged face out of her mind. She shuddered again as the tears streamed down her cheeks. "I'm going upstairs," she said, before the lieutenant had left.

Sometime later, Carol came upstairs into Therese's room. "I'm so sorry you have to go through all this," Carol said gently, sitting beside her on the bed.

Therese didn't reply.

Carol stroked Therese's hair. "Can I fix you something to eat?"

"Maybe in a little bit."

"Richard's coming tomorrow night to stay with us through the weekend," Carol said, obviously trying to lighten the mood. "It'll be nice to have a man around."

"He's coming tomorrow night?"

Carol frowned. "I hope that's okay. What's wrong?"

"Nothing." Therese patted Clifford, who lay on the bed beside her. "I'm glad he's coming and everything. It's just that the Holts invited me to the Wildhorse Saloon tomorrow night. Pete's band is playing. Pete is Jen's older brother."

"That sounds like fun. Rich and I could join you after I pick him up from the airport."

"Oh, that would be so great. I need to get out of here, you know? You really want to go?"

"Sure!"

"Awesome," she said this softly, unable to show enthusiasm, but she really was glad they would all be going out. "I'll call Jen."

"I'll go fix a salad. Come down when you're ready." Carol left the room.

Therese sat up and reached for the phone on her nightstand. Jewels poked her head up from her log with a piece of spinach hanging from her mouth.

"You're still eating?" Therese teased, wiping a tear from her cheek. "Is it good?"

Jewels answered with a loud crunch.

Therese looked over at Puffy, who was asleep in the little tower on the top of his plastic house. She could just make him out through the bedding he had carried up there. She would need to clean out his cage soon. She dialed Jen's number. Jen was pleased with the news. Therese didn't mention anything about the lieutenant's visit nor did she mention the panicky feeling that had gripped her heart.

Carol called up the stairs to let Therese know the salad was ready, but Therese wasn't hungry. She had just finished cleaning out Puffy and Jewels's houses, which always messed with her appetite.

"Do you mind if I play my flute?" Therese called down. She hadn't played since before…everything changed.

"Of course not, sweetheart. You go right ahead."

Before she could get out her instrument, the phone rang, so she picked it up, and found it was Vicki Stern calling.

"Hi Vicki."

"What's going on?"

"I'm getting ready to practice my flute. What's going on with you?"

"Nothing."

Therese waited for Vicki to say why she was calling, hoping it wasn't to share her regrets, and when she didn't, Therese asked, "Have you seen any movies lately?"

"Nope. Want to go with me tomorrow night?"

Therese cringed. "I'm sorry. I'm going to…I have other plans. We're going to the Wildhorse Saloon, if you want to meet us. A whole bunch of us will be there."

"Hmm. I don't really like crowds. What about Thursday?"

"I'll check with my aunt and call you back. Okay?"

"Okay."

"Bye then."

"Bye."

Therese slid the black instrument case and fold-up music stand from beneath her bed, set up the stand, and got her sheet music out from a desk drawer. What did she feel like playing? She had received a one in a

UIL solo and ensemble contest last spring playing a Handel sonata. She took it out now and put it on the music stand. Then she assembled the three pieces of her silver flute. She hadn't played in so long, and she realized now as she blew the air across the mouth piece how much she had been missing it. Playing relaxed her, fulfilled her, and brought her pleasure. She launched into the sonata full of emotions.

She hadn't played very far into the song when she started crying. She wasn't sobbing and shaking as she had done each night since she woke from the coma. Instead, the tears simply fell down her face, like water dripping from a broken faucet. She could no longer see the sheet music, but she didn't need to. She played the song by memory, moving her fingers quickly and effectively, a trill here, an eight-note rise there, and a whole note pause. She bent her brows and threw her heart into the song. She sang in her mind to the rising melodic scale: They are still with me, in my heart and in my soul. They are a part of me forever.

She kept repeating the words in time with the melody: They are a part of me forever.

A movement in the woods outside her second-story window caught her attention. She stopped playing and went to the window. At first she didn't see anything, so she almost went back to sit on her bed and continue playing, but as she was about to turn away, she caught a flash of white and blue.

"Oh my God, it's Than," she said to herself. "What's he doing out there?"

As if he had heard her, he looked up and waved. He looked huge, even beside the giant diseased elm.

She opened the window. "Hey, Than. What are you doing?"

He walked down the side of the mountain toward the back of her house and looked up. "I was taking a walk when I heard music. I came this way to find out where it was coming from. It's beautiful. Is it coming from you?"

She blushed and nodded. "Hold on a minute, and I'll come down." Then she turned to Clifford, who sat curled on her pillow on the bed. "That's not your pillow, boy. Why do you always have to lie down on my pillow? Yours is right there beside you! And you have another over there on the floor! You greedy boy." Then she laughed, suddenly joyful, and petted him. "You want to go outside?"

Clifford leapt from the bed, scattering the limp, pathetic balloons, and headed downstairs. Therese followed with her flute, anxious to show off her talent to Than.

Carol looked up from the granite counter as Therese came down the stairs. She was eating her salad. "Who is that guy?" she asked. She must have seen him through the kitchen window.

"He's staying in the Melner cabin. I met him at the Holts'. He's working for them this week, too."

"He looks like a god," Carol said. "How old is he?"

Therese shivered at her aunt's choice of words, pushing down the memories of her dreams. "Eighteen, I think. I'm not sure."

Carol looked as though she was about to say more, but she took another bite of her salad instead.

Therese went out the back kitchen door and onto the deck to meet him. "So you can hear me all the way at the Melner cabin? That's embarrassing. I thought having the window closed would keep the sound from carrying."

Clifford put his paws up on Than's shins.

"Hi, Clifford," Than said, patting the dog. Then he answered Therese. "I was actually closer to your place than mine. I don't really know if you can hear it all the way at the cabin. But I hope so. I haven't heard music like that in a long, long time, which is crazy because both of my parents are big fans of music." Then he asked, "Will you play some more for me?"

Now she was shaking. She had planned to show off, but now that it came down to it, she didn't know if she could control the movements of her fingers. They shook much more than they had at the UIL contest last spring. "Um, I don't know."

"Please?"

His crystal blue eyes were just too persuasive for her to say no, so she led him to the side of the house to the wooden table and offered him a chair. She sat across from him, with her back to the side of the house, took a deep breath, and played. Everything came out all wrong. Then she took a deep breath, tried to forget his presence, turned to face the reservoir, and played again. Automatically, her mind picked up the words where she had left off: They are with me, in my heart and soul. They are part of me forever.

When she had finished the complete sonata without having made a single error, she looked up at him and smiled.

He clapped his hands. "I loved it. You put so much of yourself into the music. It's almost like you're voice is singing in place of the flute, or as if the flute were an extension of yourself."

"Thanks." She didn't know what else to say. She was much too nervous to think beyond playing for him. A chipmunk ran up onto the deck and saved her from an awkward silence. "SShh," she whispered, and pointed to the little furry animal just behind one of the other four chairs at the table.

Than's smile at the sight of the animal took her breath away. What a gorgeous smile.

Therese scooped a few sunflower seeds from the clay pot on the table and dropped them on the deck. The chipmunk froze for a few seconds, and then he went for the seeds. Therese looked up at Than and watched him while he watched the chipmunk. His smile could kill.

She shuddered at her own choice of words.

Clifford came bounding onto the deck from the forest and scared the chipmunk away.

"Bad boy!" Therese scolded. "Time for you to go inside."

"No, let him stay. It's not his fault. He's just following his natural instincts, doing his job."

"Yeah, I guess you're right." To Clifford she said, "I'm sorry boy. You can stay outside." Then she said, "Actually, we could all go inside. I could introduce you to my aunt. Do you want anything to eat or drink?"

"No, that's okay. I don't want to bother you. I just wanted to hear you play."

"It's no bother. Really." She mentally crossed her fingers for luck. She wanted him to stay. Stay, she willed. Stay.

"Well, if you're sure."

She smiled. "Come in. My aunt's just inside having lunch." Therese led Than to the front of the house, through the screened front porch, and inside the living room.

Carol seemed pleased Therese brought Than in to meet her, and she immediately offered to make him a salad just like hers. Therese insisted her aunt sit down. "I know how to make salad," she said. So Therese chopped up some spinach, green leaf lettuce, bok choy, white cabbage, green onion, and a few radishes. Then she sprinkled on some toasted sesame seeds, Chinese noodles, and Ginger dressing. She divided it up into two bowls and gave one to Than where he sat beside her aunt at the countertop. Therese stood up and ate at the bar across from them.

She enjoyed watching his face after he took his first bite. She could tell he liked it.

"I've never tasted anything like this salad before," he said. "It's delicious."

Therese watched him take great pleasure in every bite. "It's so easy," she said. "It's not like I made you a five course meal."

"Oh, offer him a drink, sweetheart," Carol said.

"Sorry." Therese opened a cabinet behind her and took out two glasses. "What do we have?"

"There's iced tea in the fridge. Than, do you like iced tea?"

"I've never tried it, but I'd love to have some."

Therese knew they had iced tea in Texas. What was with this guy? Did his parents keep him in a cave or something? The memory of her dream popped into her head, so she pushed it back out with a shudder. Silly, silly dream.

Carol and Therese both chuckled as they watched Than try the tea.

He frowned and licked his lips.

"You don't like it?" Therese asked.

"It's bitter."

Carol crossed the room. "Try some sugar." She brought the sugar canister over and put a couple of teaspoons in his glass, mixed it, brought the spoon out. "Try it now."

Therese put her hand over her mouth to hide the huge grin she couldn't stop from forming on her face. He obviously liked tea with sugar. He drank down half the glass in one gulp.

"I think I like sugar," he said. Then he gulped down the rest of the glass.

Chapter Fourteen: Therese's Prayers

Than realized as he put down the glass of tea on the kitchen bar that Therese was praying to him again. Sometimes it was difficult for him to discern whether she was praying or speaking out loud, for when he was this close to her, as he was now, with her face less than two feet away, he could hear the voice and the prayers with the same pitch, clarity, and volume; whereas, from a far distance the prayers were clearer to him than speech. He also knew that she wasn't aware that her prayers to him were heard, for she hadn't yet accepted the fact of who he was. The human mind interested him in this way, in its ability to play tricks on its owner. As far as Than knew, gods were unable to achieve such feats of self deceit as humans.

Her prayers to him this afternoon, so different from earlier, went something like this, "You are such a breath of fresh air to me after all that's happened. I hope you stay around a while. I hope I get to know you. You are so cute, Than. So cute and so sweet. What crystal blue eyes you have. What muscles. And the way you fill out your jeans, oh! Never mind! Stop it, Therese! Oh, don't look at me like that."

Than had to work hard not to react to the words she did not say out loud, but just now he found himself blushing and wanting badly to press his lips to hers like she had done to him that night they met.

He didn't want to leave, especially with her silent pleading, but he had to give a few hours to helping his sisters track down the killer—after all, that was his selling point to his father in getting permission to come up here. He couldn't neglect that duty.

"Thanks for the lunch," he said. "It was delicious."

"You're welcome any time," Carol said.

Than stood up from the bar stool as Therese took his empty bowl and glass and put them in the sink behind her.

Therese said, "I'm going for a walk with Clifford. If you're not doing anything, you could come along." Then she prayed, "Please say yes."

Than stepped around the bar and looked through the window to follow Therese's gaze. Her back was to him as she stood at the sink. He wondered what she was looking at. Then he heard her pray, "Save that tree. Don't let it die." He saw she was looking at an Elm, one of two that towered behind the house.

"Is that tree special to you?" he asked, again forgetting that she had made her request silently.

She turned to look at him in surprise. "What? Oh, yes. It's got the Dutch Elm disease. My parents were going to try to save it. I guess I'd hate to see it die… too."

Than awkwardly patted her shoulder where he had touched countless souls before on their journey down the river, but her warm skin and the tension between them made him uneasy. He looked out the window at the tree. He said, "I wish I could join you for your walk, but I have to go help my sisters with something. I'll see you this evening, though, okay?"

"Darn," she prayed in her head. "But I like that you help your family."

He almost made the mistake of responding to this silent statement. "Thanks…again for the lunch, and for playing your flute for me," he corrected himself. "I'll see you later."

Her hair smelled so fresh and her body felt so warm beside him, that he had a hard time pulling himself away from her company to the dreaded deed of hunting with the Furies.

Chapter Fifteen: Another Tragedy

She pulled on her oldest pair of Justin Ropers, glossed her lips, and headed down the stairs, her hair loose and flying behind her. The smell of her peach shampoo made her feel fresh. She ran her fingers through her curls. Her dad used to say how he loved her hair and that it was the perfect combination of Therese's mother's red hair and his own mother's curly hair.

"Sorry, Clifford," she said to him at the front door. "You have to stay this time. You're not allowed on the pasture."

Carol was typing furiously on her laptop while she sat on the living room sofa. "I'll drive you," Carol said, jumping up. "I'm not ready for you to walk alone yet, especially if Clifford's not going."

Than appeared at the door to the screened porch. "Hi there. I was wondering if you want to walk up to the Holts' together."

Therese turned back to her aunt. "That okay?"

Carol hesitated, then smiled. "I guess so. Just call me when you get there."

The sun had fallen behind a thin layer of clouds. It usually rained for a few minutes every afternoon, often with thunder and lightning, and Therese wondered now as she and Than turned onto the dirt road from her gravel driveway if it would today. She hoped not. She was nervous enough about riding without adding rain into the mix.

Than hadn't changed from his tight white t-shirt and jeans, but he looked refreshed and clean and, even under the cloud cover, brilliant.

"Thanks again for the salad and the recipe," he said. "I told my sister Tizzie about it. She might go into Durango tomorrow for the ingredients and try to make it herself."

"Be sure to tell her to buy you some tea bags and sugar," Therese said. "You seemed to like that a lot, too."

"Yes. Especially the sugar."

He asked why Clifford wasn't with her, and she explained that he'd want to follow them into the pasture and how that was dangerous for the horses. "Small dogs tend to spook horses. They can handle the big dogs, but because horses have a lot of blind spots, the littler animals tend to freak them out."

"I see," he said, apparently attempting a pun.

Therese shook her head and chuckled. "That was really bad."

"You're right. It was." He chuckled too.

Although she had initially thought him to be arrogant and selfish, she found him easy to talk to as they made their way down the road. He asked her about her hobbies and she talked a bit about swim team and band and the times she liked to spend in the forest with the animals. When she asked about him, he shrugged.

"I've realized these past few days how little I know myself," he said cryptically.

When they reached the ranch, Mrs. Holt, Bobby, and Jen were already in the pen saddling up five of the horses.

"Hey, guys," Bobby greeted them. "Think it's gonna pour?"

"I hope not." Therese put on her long-sleeved shirt.

"Don't worry," Jen said. "The horses love the rain. It won't bother them or anything."

"It'll just make them stinky," Mrs. Holt said. "Somethin' we have to look forward to come mornin'."

"Oh, I'm supposed to call my aunt." Therese turned toward the house.

"Use the phone in the barn," Mrs. Holt said.

Therese found the dusty, old-fashioned dial phone mounted to the wall and called her aunt to let her know she had made it safely. Then she returned to the pen with the others.

They led their horses from the gate on the pasture side of the pen, on the opposite side from the barn and the house, and Bobby closed and secured the gate. Hershey and Ace put their heads over the fence and brayed their objections. They wanted to come, too.

Than turned and said something to the two horses that Therese could not hear. She inwardly laughed. He liked talking to them as much as she did. Despite his inability to describe himself, she was learning a lot about him. He loved the outdoors, especially the water, and he loved animals. She looked forward to learning a few more things.

Therese approached Dumbo, and he nuzzled against her. She put her hand out for him to sniff. He caressed her hand with his mouth and then nuzzled her palm. She stroked his face, whispering, "Thanks. I needed that."

As soon as Therese mounted Dumbo, the nervous anxiety made her chest feel tight. Jen must have noticed, because she came up beside her and said, "Just follow me. You've got nothing to worry about."

Jen started at a walk, and without Therese having to say "Go," or squeeze Dumbo's sides, the horse followed. Therese relaxed. Maybe this would be easier than she had thought.

"You're doing good, boy," Therese said as she stroked Dumbo's neck. She watched Jen moving gracefully ahead of her on Sassy, as though she and her horse were one fluid organism. Jen made it look so easy.

Than came up beside her on Midnight. "You okay?"

"So far so good." She gave him a brave smile. She could do this.

Bobby and Mrs. Holt had already gone on ahead across the stream where it narrowed and up where the pasture began on an incline up the mountain. Jen now took Sassy up to a trot, and, without warning, Dumbo followed suit. Therese held on to the saddle horn and hugged Dumbo with her thighs. She managed not to shriek, but her heart was beating a million miles an hour as the adrenaline pumped through her. Than and Midnight were soon beside her again.

"This is fun, don't you think?" he asked.

Therese was bouncing hard on Dumbo, so she stiffened her legs against the stirrups and pulled her bottom up, practically in a standing position. "As long as Dumbo follows Sassy, I'm alright." She didn't admit it was like riding a scary rollercoaster.

Drops of rain began to fall and a sudden streak of light illuminated the clouds above them.

Great, Therese thought. Just what I need.

A moment later, the roar of thunder followed.

Jen and Sassy approached the stream, so Jen slowed down to a walk. Dumbo slowed, and Midnight beside him. They took turns jumping across the narrowest part and then joined Bobby and Mrs. Holt in the trees on the other side. They kept the horses at a walk as they followed the trail through the trees near the fence line. The trees offered some protection from the rain, but not much. Another streak of light shot across the sky, and the thunder followed. Therese wondered how the horses would react if the thunder got loud and if they were safer in the trees or if they should head back across the stream to the open part of the pasture, but she didn't say anything, sure Mrs. Holt would know best. She couldn't help but feel even more nervous, though.

They walked the horses through the trees, weaving up and down, occasionally having to jump across a low dip or fallen log. Therese focused on talking with Dumbo, to ease her nerves and to let Dumbo get to know her.

"You're doing great, Dumbo. You're such a good boy." Therese stroked his mane, which was now clean of all sticker burs and weeds thanks to her hard work this morning. "Wait." She said to him when Jen paused up ahead. "Wait." She gently pulled the reins and released, and Dumbo obeyed.

They jumped over a steep incline, one at a time, and then weaved back down through the trees back in the direction of the stream. Here again Therese asked Dumbo to wait his turn to cross the stream, and he did. Then Mrs. Holt took Rambo back up to a trot. Bobby and the General were fast behind. Jen followed with Sassy, then Therese on Dumbo, and Than and Midnight brought up the rear. From the trot, the horses in front moved to a canter. When Dumbo took off to catch up with the others, Therese felt the adrenaline surge through her. This was the scariest part. They galloped at high speed across the open pasture with the rain hitting her in the face. Lightening continued to streak the sky and the thunder to crash. Therese wanted to squeeze her eyes shut, but she was too afraid that Dumbo would scrape her leg along the fence or take her beneath tree branches that would whack her in the face. She heard Than say something to her, but she couldn't speak; she had to concentrate on holding onto the saddle horn, her legs rigid against the stirrups.

Mrs. Holt reached the fence line and turned Rambo south and followed the fence toward the dirt road in front of the house. They all followed Rambo and turned with the fence line, now parallel to the dirt road, still at a full canter. As they reached the pen where they had started, Mrs. Holt took Rambo down to a trot, but kept going, back up toward the stream. The rest of them followed. When she reached the stream, Mrs. Holt slowed Rambo down to a walk and led him along the stream to where it grew about six feet wide. She stopped him and told him to drink. Bobby brought the General beside her and did the same. Dumbo followed Sassy to the other side of Rambo from the General. Midnight came up beside Therese, and all the horses had their fill of water.

The stream in front of them danced with each raindrop. Therese saw several trout diving under rocks in the shallow water away from the muzzles of the horses. Clifford would have a field day here. She was glad for this chance to catch her breath. She looked up at Than and was surprised to see his face turned up to the rain, his eyes closed, and a smile lingering on his lips. His dark, wavy hair blew in the wind and caressed his strong jaw line. She longed to reach out and touch him.

Mrs. Holt led Rambo away from the stream back toward the open pasture. Jen and Bobby followed. Dumbo and Midnight continued to drink, and Than seemed oblivious to the departure of the others, his face still turned up to meet the rain. Therese just sat and watched him.

Than opened his eyes when thunder crashed again. He looked over at Therese, and they shared a smile of embarrassment. He noticed the others had gone several yards away to the open pasture, so he said, "Come on Midnight," and he gently pulled her reins to one side to lead her away.

Therese mimicked Than. "Come on, Dumbo." But Dumbo stubbornly refused to come. He pulled up a tuft of grass that had been growing near the stream to feed. "Come on, Boy!" Therese said a little more forcefully. Instead, Dumbo walked further up along the stream and fed on more stalks of grass. "Great." Therese glanced back at the others. Than was waiting for her about twenty yards away, but the others were already cantering along the fence line again.

Meanwhile, Dumbo refused to listen. "Come on, Dumbo!" Therese gently touched the stirrups against his sides. He went further up the stream, pulling long tufts of yellow grass. Before Therese knew what was happening, Dumbo reared up and down, over and over, braying loudly. She screamed in horror, "Whoa, Dumbo! Whoa, boy!" His back right hoof slid on the bank and into the stream; she could hear the rocks slipping, the hoof sliding, and then the leg belted beneath him, and he fell sideways toward the stream. Therese screamed in terror and pushed both feet against the stirrups, and she managed to stay on top of Dumbo as he rolled into the water on his side. She pulled her right foot loose and pushed with her left to avoid falling under the horse. She fell on the opposite side of him, on the bank among rocks and grass, on her left side. She rolled when she fell and came to a stop at Than's feet. Her elbow and hip hurt, not to mention her neck, and she was terrified for Dumbo.

"Are you okay?" Than knelt beside her with wide eyes.

She sat up, dazed. Then she looked into the stream. Dumbo hadn't moved from his side in the water. His head was lifted toward the sky, and he was whining with pain. "Dumbo!" Therese jumped to her feet and went to the horse. "Oh, no! Oh my God! Than, I think he's really hurt!"

Than held Therese back, and as she tried to pull away she saw a snake hissing in the grass at his feet. He grabbed the snake behind its head with one hand, and then he flung it nearly a hundred yards down the stream away from them.

Therese was in too much shock to wonder how he could throw it so far. "That snake must have been what spooked him," Therese said. "It's okay boy!" She couldn't take his loud cries. She felt so helpless.

Soon Mrs. Holt and the others returned.

"Oh no!" Jen cried from on top of Sassy.

"What happened?" Mrs. Holt dismounted Rambo. She quickly went into the stream and squatted in the water next to Dumbo to assess his injuries while Therese and Than told the story. Therese was in tears before they had finished. Than put his hand on her shoulder.

"Are you hurt, Therese?" Mrs. Holt asked.

Therese shook her head. "I'm fine." Then she said, "I'm so sorry, Mrs. Holt. I'm so, sorry! Do you think he's going to be okay?"

"Bobby, go to the barn and call Dr. Gilbert. Ask him if he can come right away. Tell him it's an emergency. The rest of you take the other horses back to the pen and remove their tack. Then turn all the horses out to the second pasture. Jen, lead Therese on Rambo. I'll stay here with Dumbo."

Bobby took off on the General across the field.

"Is it bad?" Therese asked.

"We'll know more once the vet takes a look at him," Mrs. Holt replied.

Another crash of thunder cracked overhead as the sad party obeyed Mrs. Holt's orders. Therese couldn't stop crying. On top of her worry over Dumbo, she was scared to death to ride Rambo, even though Jen held a lead and would be in complete control.

"Try not to worry," Than said as he helped her mount the huge horse.

After they had returned to the pen and removed the tack from the horses, Jen went to turn them all out to the second pasture while Than led Therese, still in tears and beside herself, toward the house. Bobby got them clean towels. The thunder shower had passed, but they were soaked. They went inside to wait for the vet. Therese called Carol to tell her what happened and why she'd be late, and Carol made her promise over and over that she was telling the truth about not being hurt.

"I really am okay," she said into the phone. "At least, physically." Then the sobs came over her again in another wave. Than put his arm around her where they sat on a wooden bench in the entryway with towels draped over their shoulders. "I'll call you when I'm ready to come home."

After a while, Jen ran inside to say the vet was here, and so Bobby, Therese, and Than jogged behind her out across the first pasture where Dumbo lay in the water, no longer whining, totally exhausted, but still on his side. Mrs. Holt was soaked with her hand on Dumbo's cheek as the vet, shin-deep in water and using a flashlight, did his best to examine his patient.

As the group of teens got closer, Dr. Gilbert was telling Mrs. Holt that he was giving Dumbo a sedative and pain killer solution so that he could more safely maneuver around the animal. The water was shallow enough so he wouldn't drown. Therese watched in horror as the vet stuck the giant needle into Dumbo's neck. Dumbo flinched, but within seconds closed his eyes and lay still. The vet propped Dumbo's head up on a rock to keep it out of the water.

Bobby wrapped a dry towel around his mother's shoulders and convinced her to come out of the stream. Therese looked into Mrs. Holt's anguished face and said again how sorry she was.

Mrs. Holt gave Therese a big hug and said, "Please don't feel for a minute that this is any fault of yours. This could have happened to any rider."

But it happened to me, Therese thought.

The group stood on the banks of the stream watching as the vet conducted his exam. Therese became aware—vaguely at first and then more acutely—that Than had his arm protectively around her shoulders again. Jen came up and put her arm around Therese's waist from the other side. Bobby stood close to his mother with a hand on her back.

Eventually, the vet stood up and walked over to them. "It's not good," he said. "Maybe the kids should go inside."

Mrs. Holt looked at Therese. "Than, would you please take Therese back to the house? The others can stay."

"Please, Mrs. Holt. I want to stay, too."

Mrs. Holt hesitated. Then she looked at the vet and nodded. "It's okay, Dr. Gilbert. Go ahead."

"Well, Dumbo has two broken legs, his right front and his left hind. His left hind leg is broken in two places, and I think a couple of ribs may be cracked as well."

"Oh no," Bobby groaned.

"What do you recommend we do about it?" Mrs. Holt asked.

"I hate to say it, Steph, but I think we're gonna have to put him down."

"No!" Therese yelled.

Everyone looked at her, Than tightening his hold around her shoulders.

"Stay calm for the others," he said softly in her ear.

"What's the alternative?" Mrs. Holt asked.

"A slow and painful death," the vet replied. "He'll never recover."

A blanket of dread and grief wrapped itself around Therese. This couldn't be happening, she thought. She covered her mouth with her hand.

Mrs. Holt walked back out into the stream beside Dumbo. She kissed his still and quiet cheek. "Alright, kids. Time to go back to the house. I'll stay here with Dr. Gilbert. Than and Therese, it's business as usual in the mornin', okay?"

Therese slowly nodded. That would be hard to do.

When the four teenagers got back to the house, Than asked Therese if he could walk her home, and she said yes, glad for the company. She could have called her aunt, which would have been a good choice since she was wet and cold and really upset, but she wanted to be with Than. He had become quite good at comforting her.

She hugged Jen and Bobby before she and Than headed home, apologizing over and over for something she knew wasn't her fault but had nevertheless left her with a horrible feeling of dread. She and Than were quiet most of the way. Dusk was falling, and the deer had come out in the tall grass across the road. Therese watched them with blank eyes.

Than broke their silence. "That's the first time I've seen firsthand what happens when a person or animal dies. I've never seen how hard it is for those they leave behind."

Therese's thoughts went from Dumbo to her parents. She clenched her jaw to stay back the tears. "Very hard," she muttered.

"I really am sorry, Therese," his voice was low and husky. He stopped and took her hand. "I'm so sorry people and animals have to die. I wish there were another way."

He seemed more upset than she had realized, as on the verge of punching something, and she wanted badly to fling herself into his arms and let them each wash away the other's pain, but she checked herself. "Thanks."

He released her hand and walked her up to her front screened porch. "Will you come early tomorrow for a swim?" he asked.

"I don't think so."

"You need to do something to heal the pain," he said.

"You see your first death, and now you're an expert," she snapped, and then immediately regretted it. "I'm sorry."

"It's okay. See you in the morning."

Therese went inside to find Carol wrapped in a blanket on the living room couch watching a movie. "You alright?" Carol asked.

"I'm tired. I'm going to bed."

"Are you sure? You don't want to talk about it?"

"I'm sure."

Clifford jumped from the couch beside Carol and followed Therese up the stairs. She turned off Jewel's lamp and told her good night. Puffy was in his wheel already at work. Therese climbed out of her soggy clothes and went to her bathroom to take a long hot shower. Clifford stood outside the shower curtain waiting, as though he sensed she was upset and needed a friend.

Once she was dry and in her nightshirt, Therese cuddled with Clifford on her bed. She felt bad for snapping at Than when he was only trying to help. She was also worried he might not like her anymore. Why did she have to be so rude? She took the stringy stuffed animal toy lemur from where it hung on the headboard post and wrapped it around her neck. She couldn't stop her mind from replaying the tragedy with Dumbo over and over. Her mind went from the tragic events on the pasture to those at Huck Finn Pond. Therese closed her eyes, wishing she could die, too.

Before she had fallen completely asleep, she felt a presence other than her pets in her room, and her eyes snapped open. The moonlight washing into her room wasn't bright, and she could see no one. She could have sworn she felt someone standing over her bed looking down at her, about to touch her face. She stopped breathing to listen, but after seeing and hearing nothing more but Puffy running in his wheel, she closed her eyes and told herself it must have been a dream.

Chapter Sixteen: Doubts and Confliction

After leaving Therese safely at her door, Than went to her room and, in invisible mode, conversed with the hamster and the tortoise.

"I love her," he said in each of their tongues. "And she's hurt. Please comfort her. Can you please?"

"If she picks me up!" The hamster said, as he ran round and round. "Good human! Good human! I've known others, and she's good! If she picks me up, I'll lick her with my tongue!"

Than turned to the tortoise, which now said, "She's loving and tender. So gentle and loyal. I try as best as I can to let her know I love her, too."

A noise came, and then Therese entered. Than softly thanked the animals, and listened as the tortoise said a bit more. Then Than took his leave.

He soared down past the abyss, past Cerberus and the gate and down to his father's chamber in such a state of fury that the bats swirled down from their perch and made their escape into the cold night earlier than was usual. Although Hades must have foreseen his son's arrival, he still showed surprise at his son's rage, the son whom he was used to seeing as the more temperate of his two boys. A tinge of guilt ran through Than as he told himself to show more control.

His sister Alecto stood in the shadows beside their father. Her fire-red hair stood up in a Mohawk and contrasted with her deep black, beautiful eyes. A choker of black stones adorned her neck and similar stones served as buttons in her leather jacket and tight leather pants and high-heeled boots.

"Thanatos?" Hades asked. "Alecto was just apprising me of her progress in a number of the Furies' pursuits, including the killer of your girlfriend's parents. But something tells me you are not here for a report."

"Have you found him?" he asked his sister.

She shook her head.

"Why are you here?" Hades asked Than.

Than tried to think how to put his sorrow and his shame and his desperation into words, but no words seemed to fit the caged and raw emotion he had never before felt. Finally, seeing his father was in a patient mood, Than swallowed and said, with more control and less rage than he felt, "I used to envy the humans their short lives. Their deaths make their lives more meaningful."

"You no longer think it now?"

"I still think it, Father. Death is better than immortality, a yoke only we gods must bear."

"I can't see your thoughts, son. You must speak them."

"Death is good for those who die, but not for those left behind. Why haven't I understood before tonight the depth of that pain? If a horse could raise so much anguish in my mortal heart, I can only imagine what the loss of a parent or child would do. Father, I've ignored countless prayers from billions of souls because I felt there was nothing I could do; but I'm a god. Surely there is something?"

Hades looked down his thin nose at Than. He scratched at his beard and, Than could see, stifled a smile.

"Are you laughing at me?" Than said, moving dangerously close to his father.

Alecto stepped back, further into the shadows.

"Not at you. At the whole cosmos."

"What is that supposed to mean?" Than asked.

"Son, nothing is free. Everything comes with a cost. As you have said, the mortal creatures of the world, at least the good ones, are fortunate that their lives end and their souls spend the rest of eternity in near oblivion; unlike we who must endure our mundane tasks forever. You said yourself that the brevity of their conscious lives makes their journey more meaningful than ours. We are like caged hamsters in a wheel, spinning, spinning, spinning. Humans have but one spin, one go, one bright moment and then the flame goes out.

"The advantage of mortality is clear to us, but not to them, and that is why those left behind suffer. They miss the company of their loved ones, but it is the feeling that the deceased no longer exist that hurts the most. This is the cost mortals must pay. Let me put it to you this way: Mortality is better than immortality, but only the immortal have the ability to see this, and there lies both the irony and the cost of human happiness."

Than shook his head. "So there really is nothing then? Nothing we can do to ease that cost?"

"If there is a way we gods can ease that burden, it is by inspiring this understanding into the human heart. I don't know if it is possible, though. They have such limited minds."

Than sat at the foot of his father's throne on the hard, cold rock awash with defeat.

Hades asked, "A horse's death has brought you to me in fits?"

Than looked up, ashamed. "Hip winked at me as he took the soul of the creature, completely ignorant of the pain we were feeling. How many times have I been so calloused as that?"

"Never. You and your brother are very unlike each other, as I am to mine."

"It wasn't the horse's death that hurt so much as the pain I could feel in the humans left behind. That and the overwhelming feeling of helplessness. And also the rage that I, a god, could do nothing."

Hades smiled. "I am familiar with the feeling. I suppose it is good that gods are humbled now and then."

Than said nothing.

"How goes it with the girl?" Hades asked.

Than, used to being honest for so many centuries, could not find it in his heart to lie. He glanced at Alecto, unsure if he wanted her to hear, but went on and said, "I love her, but I'm having second thoughts about teaching her to love me."

Hades lifted a brow. "You find her unworthy?"

"No. Just the opposite."

"I find that insulting and despicable. Don't weary me this way."

Than stood up. "You don't understand me because I can hardly explain myself. What I'm trying to say is that she loves the Upperworld and its inhabitants more than most humans, and I worry I would make her into a despondent wife down here."

"There is no other kind of wife down here," Hades said. "Remember that."

Chapter Seventeen: The Wildhorse Saloon

Therese woke up sore Wednesday morning. She climbed out of bed, stiff and in pain. She replayed the events of the previous evening over in her head and shuddered. Maybe she should stay home. She picked up the phone and called Jen.

"My mom warned me you would call," Jen said on the phone. "But she says it's really important that you come this morning. You'll heal a lot faster if you do. Moping around all day will make it worse. My mom had to threaten Bobby for the same reason."

"But I'm in pain," Therese objected. "I hadn't gone riding in a year. And I fell down and hurt myself, remember?"

"We can't make you come," Jen said, "but my mom will be very disappointed and really upset. It's your choice. Don't forget we still have the Wildhorse Saloon tonight. I've gotta go."

Therese groaned. She couldn't have the entire Holt family angry with her, especially when she still felt guilty over what had happened. She kept thinking if only she had been in better control of Dumbo, things might have happened differently. Reluctantly, she threw on some clothes and sneakers and headed downstairs. She shared some breakfast with her aunt before they and Clifford climbed into Carol's car. She kept her eyes out for Than as she absently made two braids in her hair, but didn't see him along the dirt road. When they reached the tall grass across from the Holts' house, she craned her neck to see if he might be swimming. His golden figure glided through the water. After she climbed from the car and thanked her aunt, she followed Clifford across the field to the lake where Than was swimming.

"Come in," he said when he saw her watching him from the bank where his clothes sat piled in a heap. "It feels great." His eyes sparkled in the sunlight, and his wet hair and body glistened.

Sometimes a weird feeling that he was merely a product of her imagination made her long to touch him to make sure he was real. "I didn't wear a suit." She was relieved he wasn't mad about the way she had snapped at him yesterday. "But maybe another time."

He swam toward the shore and stood up where the water grew shallow. His skin glowed as the sun behind her sprayed its rays across his wet body. Therese turned away from his beauty. Sadness still hung over her.

"You okay?" he asked.

"I'm sorry I snapped at you yesterday." Her voice cracked.

"No apology necessary."

She waited for him while he climbed into his clothes. She tried not to steal glances at him, but she failed miserably. Clifford came up to Than for some affection.

"Hi, Clifford." Than patted the dog's head. Then he turned to Therese. "Ready?"

They walked across the tall grass and dirt road to the gravel drive leading to the Holt house. Than asked her a few more questions, like what was Clifford like as a puppy and she as a little girl. He laughed when she told him about the time she lost Jewels in the woods and had actually called 911 and the person on the phone thought Therese was talking about a younger sister.

"I got in a lot of trouble for that," she said. She looked over at him and took in his grin. It unnerved her, but she managed to ask, "Have you ever gotten into trouble?"

"Never," he said.

"Never ever?"

"Nope. I've always been good. My brother, on the other hand, well, that's another story."

"You have a brother?"

"A twin. But we're not identical. I got the good looks, the sense of humor, and the charm. He got the more devilish qualities."

Although Than was laughing, like he was only joking, Therese froze in her tracks.

"What's wrong?" he asked.

She'd heard something like that before. A chill moved down her back. "Um, nothing." She shook her head, reminding herself that what she was about to suspect was entirely impossible, but as she looked at Than through the corner of her eye, she could have sworn he was laughing at her.

Jen and Bobby were coming from the house at the same time Than and Therese approached the pen. Mrs. Holt was already in the pen working on the General.

"Mornin', Than. Mornin', Therese," Mrs. Holt said.

"Mornin', Mrs. Holt," they replied.

"Than, you go ahead and get started on Rambo. Therese, Sugar's waiting for you."

Jen and Than entered the pen and shared their good mornings all around. Jen said she had just gotten off the phone with Ray who said he and Todd would definitely be joining them at the Wildhorse Saloon tonight to hear Pete's performance. No one mentioned anything about what had happened the night before.

Mrs. Holt drove up in her Suburban at seven o'clock Wednesday evening. Therese climbed down the front wooden steps and entered on the passenger side. Bobby sat in the passenger seat wearing his cowboy hat and a short-sleeved Western shirt. He smelled like soap and had a huge grin on his freckled face as Therese climbed into the seat behind him. Jen laughed as soon as she saw what Therese was wearing because they wore almost the same thing: same dark blue shade of boot-cut jeans, same red Justin Roper boots, and nearly identical white blouses, except that Therese's had a round neckline whereas Jen's had a v. Both wore their long hair down, and although Jen's was straight blonde and

Therese's was curly red, they fell to the same length, to the center of their backs.

"We do this all the time," Jen said.

"It's almost eerie." Therese grinned.

"Are you wearing Oscar De La Renta, too?" Jen asked.

Therese shook her head. "No, it's, um, it's called Haiku. It's what my mom wore. I've been wearing it a lot lately."

The two girls looked away from one another.

"It smells nice," Mrs. Holt offered.

Therese's heart skipped a beat when she referred to her mother, but now that they were pulling up the gravel drive to the Melner cabin, it sped up considerably, more than making up for the skipped beat.

Jen explained, "Than and one of his sisters are riding with us. His other sister had plans."

Mrs. Holt's reaction expressed Therese's same sentiments when she said, "Lordy, Lordy, look at those two."

Than's sister wore a tight black leather mini-skirt, black go-go boots, and a red silk blouse with spaghetti straps. Her blonde curls were wound together in a thick bun on her head, a few strands spilling out of the bun down to the nape of her neck in a wild cascade. Her lips matched the red in the blouse. The rest of her rather fierce face seemed void of makeup. Her skin glowed like her brother's, but hers was fairer, almost white.

Like the white witch from Narnia, Therese thought.

Even in that conspicuous outfit, Than's sister could not outshine her brother. His clean dark wavy hair gleamed with golden highlights in the evening sun and danced against his strong jaw line. His pale blue cotton polo seemed to match the crystal in his eyes, and together with his white trousers, emphasized the golden hues of his magnificent skin. His brown boots and matching belt were the same shade as his hair. Therese climbed out of her seat and into the back to make room for them.

Before Jen could do the same, Than said, "Jen, why don't you stay there with my sister. I'll climb in back. I don't mind at all."

Jen's face looked like a mixture of giddiness and jealousy.

Then Than said, "Everybody, this is my sister, Meg."

They took turns introducing themselves to Than's sister, who was courteous if not friendly. "A pleasure," she said.

Therese could barely breathe in the third seat next to the golden boy. She almost thought, "Golden god," but then her memory of the dreams and the fear of insanity made her shrug that word out of her mind. It made more sense to her that she had felt him coming, that she had had some kind of prophetic dream about a new crush, than that she could have been communicating with gods.

He gave her a friendly smile, and this made Therese shiver with excitement.

"You look and smell so nice," he whispered.

"So do you," Therese replied, unable to think of anything original with her heart going a million miles an hour against her rib cage.

Meg turned around in her seat and gave him a disapproving glare. Than looked away from Meg and from Therese to stare out of the window.

Meg's face looked vaguely familiar to Therese: Her pale skin and unruly blonde hair and dark red lips. "Oh my God!"

Everyone turned to look at Therese.

"Is something wrong?" Mrs. Holt glanced at her from the rearview mirror.

"No. No, nothing's wrong." She bit the inside of her bottom lip, not wanting to utter her thoughts. Than's sister looked uncannily similar to the strange looking woman in the forest who had called her name and frightened poor Clifford a few weeks ago. How embarrassing if she had simply been frightened by a guest at the Melner cabin. On the other hand, how would Meg have known Therese's name?

But hadn't she also seen her reflection in the glass at the police department? No. Of course not.

Than said, "The sun looks so beautiful when it drops behind those mountains across the lake. The pines seem to twinkle."

Bobby chuckled and shook his head. "I've never heard that one. Twinkling pines, huh?"

Jen snickered.

Than glanced at Therese, and she gave him another smile. She didn't like the way Bobby and Jen had laughed at him. "I know exactly what you mean," she whispered. "I never get tired of sunsets here."

Meg, who spoke without turning, startled Therese with her loud condemning voice, "If you've seen one, you've seen them all. They never vary."

Jen glanced back at Therese to give her the "What's with her?" look. Than caught it too and chuckled.

The drive to the dance hall from Lemon Reservoir Dam took a little less than twenty minutes down winding country roads flanked by tall trees. Therese felt Than looking at her when he wasn't watching the scenery through his window. She liked the attention and was beginning to allow herself to believe he really could like her. Normally, this would be enough to make her nervous, but compounded with that were her insane and persistent suspicions about his connection to her bizarre dreams.

As they pulled into the parking lot, pretty bare since it was still early and a Wednesday night, Therese asked Jen, "Todd and Ray are still coming, aren't they?"

"Yeah, they said they were. Oh, look! They're in Todd's truck!"

The bright yellow fifty-seven Chevy pickup towered over the other vehicles from its heightened position on a lift kit including giant mag tires with thirty-inch rims. Jen and Therese piled out of the suburban and rushed over to meet their friends.

"Come on," Therese called to the others. "You guys have got to see this!"

"Hello, down there!" Todd shouted through his window as the truck bounded into a parking space. He rolled up his window when he came to a stop.

"Oh my God!" Therese and Jen giggled, shaking their heads in disbelief.

Bobby and Than came up behind with Mrs. Holt and Meg bringing up the rear.

Therese laughed as she watched the long and lanky Todd jump more than a meter to the ground from the monster truck.

"Of all the colors in the universe," Ray said laughing. He came around the cab to join the group gathered on the driver's side. "I kept expecting the truck to transform into a giant robot."

"It's awesome!" Therese exclaimed. "I mean, wow, Todd!"

"You don't think it's a little extravagant?" Jen asked. "It's a bit big."

Therese gave Jen a warning look. Don't hurt his feelings, her look said.

"That's kind of the idea," Ray said. Then he added, "Think he's compensating?"

Todd slapped Ray on the back. "Thanks a lot, Ray. Don't forget I'm your ride home."

Therese noticed the second and third looks Ray and Todd gave to the newest members of their group. Jen introduced them, and then they all went inside the saloon. Everyone but Mrs. Holt had to wear a special red bracelet made for minors. Therese was relieved to learn that Than wasn't twenty-one. She wondered how old he was. She thought maybe eighteen. She thought she might get up the nerve to ask him tonight.

Pete's band was still setting up equipment on the stage, so the music that carried throughout the dance hall was a prerecorded mix of songs usually played over the radio. Just now, Lady GaGa's voice had Jen jumping up and down.

"I love this song! Let's go dance!" Jen pinched Therese's hand and pulled her toward the dance floor.

Therese grabbed Ray's hand and shouted, "Help! You guys have to come, too!"

Ray and Todd made it to the edge of the dance floor but refused to go any further. Only a few others were dancing, as the place was pretty empty. Jen pulled Therese onto the floor, and Therese, not wanting to disappoint her friend, cheerfully made a fool out of herself as she bounced her hips and swayed her shoulders to the music. She stole a quick glance at Than to confirm he was watching. She could feel him laughing at her, but his eyes seemed pleased, like he was admiring her.

Jen sang with the song, waving her arms in the air.

Pete flashed them a smile when he noticed them on the floor. He gave Therese a thumb's up, so she mimicked it back to him. As embarrassed as she was to be one of the few people dancing, she also, and unexpectedly, felt free. Just a few weeks ago, she wouldn't have thought it possible to smile and have fun. She knew it was temporary—that tonight in the quiet of her bedroom—well, not complete quiet, for Puffy would be exercising in his wheel—she would not be able to avoid the flood of memories that would fill her with dread and bring that panicky feeling gripping at her chest. She wouldn't think of that now!

"P-p-p-poker face!" she cried. She could do this. She could go on pretending that everything was fine and she was free.

Therese stayed out on the dance floor with Jen for one more song, and then the two of them joined the others at the bar where they all got pops. Therese was relieved for the sake of Pete and his band by the arrival of more and more patrons as the hour grew later. By eight o'clock, there was a decent crowd, and swirls of cigarette smoke began to fill the air, Mrs. Holt contributing her fair share of it. The sheer number of bodies on the dance floor brought the place alive.

Therese was glad when Pete's smooth voice penetrated the dance hall from the sound system in perfect harmony with his background singers. She watched with delight as he plucked the strings of his guitar without missing a note, looking handsome in his white cowboy hat and starched denim shirt and jeans. The microphone was perched on a stand, and Pete swayed behind it, strumming the guitar. He winked at her, which made her smile. He had always been the big brother she never had, and she wanted everything to be just right for him tonight. His voice rang out to an old Mac Davis song her father used to sing, "Oh Lord It's Hard To Be Humble."

Therese pushed down the memories of her father to think instead of Than. The song described him to a tee. He was perfect in every way.

Her thoughts were interrupted when Todd was at her side asking to dance.

"Sure," she said and took his hand as she followed him to the dance floor.

Waltzes were the easiest dance to follow, in Therese's opinion, and Todd was a strong lead. He twirled her around the dance floor, giving her that fake feeling of freedom again. She smiled when she saw Bobby and Jen join them and the other couples moving across the floor with the smoke and the laughter and Pete's smooth voice. She glanced back at Than, and a thrill moved through her entire body when she saw he was looking back at her.

When the song ended, Todd asked for another dance—a polka to "The Yellow Rose of Texas"—and Therese loved to polka, so she gratefully accepted. Round and round they went, flying across the floor. Todd was good at this too. As he turned her once again, she noticed Carol and Richard standing next to Mrs. Holt. Carol had tears in her eyes and a huge smile, obviously relieved to see Therese could still have fun in a world where her parents no longer existed. Carol's tears sobered Therese, though she knew her aunt would be utterly grieved by that knowledge, so she bravely smiled and gave a quick wave before Todd pulled her around again. When the song ended, Todd ushered her off the dance floor to join their friends.

"Thanks, Todd. Come here so I can introduce you to my aunt and her boyfriend."

Therese introduced Carol and Richard to the group, though they had met the Holts briefly last Christmas, and Carol had met them one other time years ago, before Jen's father had left. Richard stood a foot taller than her aunt, about six-four, the same height as Than, and his chocolate complexion and dark brown eyes shimmered in the sparkling light thrown off by the disco globe above them.

"An investigative journalist?" Mrs. Holt asked as she shook Richard's hand. "How interesting. Political or criminal?"

"Mostly political, but a bit of both."

After the introductions and Richard's attempt to field Mrs. Holt's barrage of questions about the war and the president and Homeland Security, Richard pulled Carol out onto the wooden floor to dance the Texas Two-Step to a George Strait song, Pete's voice easily matching the inflections of the original.

"Jen, ready?" Todd asked.

"Let's go," Jen beamed.

Therese was aware of Than when he stepped beside her to watch the band and the dancers.

"Can you teach me to do that?" he asked.

"What? Dance?" her mouth dropped open. Was this god—no, not god—was this really hot guy asking her to teach him to dance?

"Yes."

She could feel the blood rush to her face as a nervous giggle popped from her throat. "Um, I don't know. I guess so. Have you ever Country-Western danced before?"

"Never. I've never danced, period." He bent his brows and looked troubled. "These past few days I've come to realize how much I've missed out on while living down, down in the south."

She scrutinized his lovely face. She knew people danced in Texas, but she didn't mention it. He looked like an angel flung down from

Heaven. His soft frown moved her. "Sure. I can teach you, but maybe we should go outside and practice before we try it on the dance floor. We wouldn't want to get run over out in the crowd."

She told Mrs. Holt what they were doing before leading Than outside, but not before noticing the glare Meg cast them as they left.

"I don't think your sister likes me," Therese said once they stepped from the smoke-filled dance hall and out into the cool night air. Stars twinkled down on them from the clear sky, and the full moon illuminated the otherwise dark parking lot. The gravel crunched beneath their boots. Somewhere, far off in the distance, a dog was barking.

"It's not you," he said.

She studied his face. "Then what?"

"She's worried about me forming attachments. We can't stay long."

Therese cleared her throat as she looked for a spot on the edge of the parking lot. "When do you leave?"

"My father gave us forty days. He was quite firm about that."

It was approaching the end of July. "So how long do you have left?"

"We've got about two weeks."

She had only two more weeks to spend with him? "Are you going to school in the fall?" she asked.

"Back to work."

"Down south?"

"Yes."

"What do you do for your father's business?"

He sighed. "It's complicated."

Therese stopped in the open space at the end of the lot and squared herself in front of Than. He was so tall. He towered over her. She felt a little shaky. She decided not to pry.

The dog's barking seemed to grow louder, and the two of them looked in the direction of its barking and giggled.

"He sounds scarier than Cerberus," Than said.

The hair stood up on the back of Therese's neck and she froze. "What did you just say?"

"I said teach me to dance already. We've been out here for ages."

She knew that wasn't what he had said, but she decided to dismiss it. Maybe he was a fan of Greek mythology.

"I'm going to teach you the waltz first because it's the easiest. You can basically march in place, one foot and then the other, and not miss a step. You don't have to spin around until you get the hang of it. Here, put your hand on my waist." His warm hand on her body made her tingle with pleasure. She put one hand on his shoulder and took his free hand with the other. "If a girl is a good follower, she will put her fingers against the backside of your shoulder like this and her thumb against the front side of your shoulder like this." His shoulder was thick with muscle. She couldn't prevent her fingers from trembling slightly. "That way she can feel if you're going to lead her backward or forward. She can also tell what you're going to do by the pressure you put on her other hand with your hand, and here, too, at her waist. You have to use your hands, along with your body, to talk to her, to tell her what to do."

"So I'm supposed to tell you what to do with my body, and you're supposed to follow?" he asked with a wry smile.

She broke into a grin. "Are we still talking about dancing?"

He lifted his chin and laughed. Then he looked at her. "I like you so much."

She bit her lip and looked down. He'd just told her he was leaving. Why let her heart get broken in two? "Okay, so the steps are in counts of threes, but like I said, it's like marching: one two three, one two three."

He tried it out and she followed, but he paused when he should have kept going, causing her to crash into his chest.

She righted herself. "Sorry."

"My fault." He swallowed hard. "Let's try that again."

"Ow!" She pulled her foot out from underneath his boot. "It's okay."

"Are you hurt?" His face was full of concern.

She couldn't feel anything with his face so close to hers. He could have chopped off her leg, and she wouldn't have known it standing here looking into his crystal blue eyes, his mouth so close to hers. "I'm okay. But I forgot to explain that the guy should always start with his left foot."

After a smoother start, he seemed a natural leader: firm, but sensitive to her movements. He moved her across the parking lot effortlessly now, the gravel crunching beneath them and that dog in the distance incessantly barking.

"You're very good," she said. "The best leaders don't try to master their partners. It's like a cooperation of wills."

"I like that," he said. "A cooperation of wills. I like that a lot."

He picked up on the movement quickly and after a few minutes tried to mimic what he had seen Todd doing with her on the dance floor earlier.

"Wow, you're a fast learner."

"You're a good teacher." He twirled her around.

"What are you doing in Colorado, besides working with horses? I mean, why'd you come?"

"I'm waiting for you to recognize me."

Her mouth dropped open and a shudder worked its way down her spine. She stopped dancing, pulling herself away from him. She took several steps back. "But we just met two days ago."

He frowned and looked at the ground. "Have you really already forgotten? Don't you remember putting your arms around me and," his voice faltered, but he swallowed and found it again, "giving me my first kiss?"

She stopped breathing.

"I haven't forgotten," he added, looking into her eyes. "I will remember it for all eternity."

She shook her head and took several steps backward. "Do you have me confused with someone else? Or are you making stuff up? I'm sure I would have remembered that. I haven't even had my first kiss."

"If we had more time, I'd take things slowly. I don't have you confused with anyone, and I'm not making stuff up. You kissed me in your dream that night I took your parents' souls."

She staggered back against a parked car, nearly falling. Her entire body trembled with fear. The hair on her neck stood on end. She found it difficult to speak. "And now you've come to take me, too?" She swallowed hard. "Good. I want to go."

He took a step closer. "I've come to help you avenge their murder."

"But, but the lieutenant has already…"

He stood only inches away from her. "He wasn't the master mind. The real villain is still out there."

She pushed herself up with the help of the parked car. She knew that. But how did he? Her knees were weak, and she could barely stand. "I don't care about the real villain. I want to be with my parents. Take me, too." She stumbled forward and into Than's arms. "Take me to them," she said again.

He kissed the top of her hair. "I told you, you wouldn't be the same if I did."

"I don't care," she whispered breathlessly.

"That's not why I'm here."

"Therese?" It was Jen calling for her through the dark parking lot. "Therese? Than? Are you guys out here?"

Than steadied Therese onto her feet. "Are you okay?"

She gave a near-hysterical laugh. "No! I'm not okay. I'm losing my mind."

"Therese?" Jen's voice was closer now. "Oh, there you are. Sorry. I didn't mean to interrupt. Pete's about to play his last song of the night."

Therese turned to her friend and tried to hide her misery. "Already?"

"Yeah. It's almost ten. The place shuts down early on weeknights."

Therese nodded. "Of course I want to hear it. That's why we came." She took a step forward, but her knees buckled, and she fell on the ground.

"Geez, are you alright?" Jen asked.

"Um, yeah. Just tired,'" she replied as Than helped her to her feet. "Still a little sore from yesterday."

He kept his hand around her waist as he led her back to the Wildhorse Saloon. Once inside, their group gave them suspicious looks as she and Than joined them on the side of the dance floor, but no look was more scrutinizing than Meg's.

Pete's smooth voice soothed Therese as it carried through the building.

"It's a waltz," Than whispered in her ear. "Can we try it? Please?"

At first she shook her head. She could barely walk. How could he expect her to dance? But when she looked up into his pleading eyes, she couldn't resist him. "Okay."

Therese could feel the stares of everyone in their group as Than took her in his steady arms and practically carried her across the dance floor to Anne Murray's beautiful song, a wedding song, she thought. It was called, "Can I Have this Dance for the rest of My Life?"

He was leaving in two weeks, but just as she had in the ride over here, she felt herself falling for this sensitive, beautiful guy who claimed to be a god. She was crazy, or maybe he was, or maybe both of them shared an insane delusion between them.

By the end of the song, though, she felt better and could actually return Than's smile. She clapped along with the others to congratulate Pete, but then, before leaving the floor and rejoining the others, she whispered to Than, "This can't be real, can it?"

He whispered back, his breath hot but somehow managing to send chills down her scalp and neck, "Give yourself time to process it. I'll see you in the morning."

He walked her over to her aunt and the rest of the group to say their goodbyes. Therese rode in the backseat of her aunt's red Toyota Corolla and stared out the window at the darkness around her. She tried to push off into the sky to turn somersaults, but she remained planted beneath the seatbelt. It hadn't been a dream. It hadn't been a dream at all.

Chapter Eighteen: Hunting with Alecto

After the dance, Than hovered with Alecto, both of them invisible in the air conditioned air above a man at a desk in a small room at the back of a shoe store in Indianapolis. The shoe store was closed for the night, so there were only two others in the shop, taking inventory of their stock. The man Than and Alecto knew as Steve McAdams had short brown hair and a suit that was old and too small with a slight brown stain on its lapel. He was about forty and the ring on his pudgy finger signaled that he was married. He was filling out forms with a ball point pen that bled black ink on the side of his hand.

The two gods materialized outside his door and knocked.

"Yeah?" the man called. "I'm busy. What is it?"

The two gods entered. "Federal agents." They flashed badges. "We have a few questions."

"And what is this about?" He sat up, flustered, tossing the pen on the desk.

"Do you recognize this man?" Alecto showed him a picture of Kaveh Grahib, the man that had shot Therese's mother and caused the death of both of her parents.

Steve McAdams shook his head. "No. Who is he?"

"Think carefully," Alecto said in a threatening voice. "Be sure before you reply."

"His name is Kaveh Grahib," Than said. "Ever heard of him?"

The man looked at Than and then back at Alecto, whose eyes were narrowed and appeared to be shooting invisible darts into the man's skull.

"No," Steve McAdams said. "Why? Should I?"

Alecto walked across the room and put both hands on the desk, leaning her face toward the man's within a foot of his. He leaned back as far as he could in his chair.

"I swear I don't know him."

The room began to shake, and hot steam jets shot up from the Lethe River through the floor on each side of the man's chair.

"What the…?" the man flinched and cowered further back in his chair.

Pouring up from the two jets were swarms of black snakes, hissing and darting their tongues as they quickly curled their way up from the floor, onto the legs of the man, and up to his wrists and neck.

"Ah! Ah! What's happening? What the hell is happening?"

"Think carefully," Alecto said again. "Are you sure you do not know of this man?"

"Help!" the man screamed, but Than knew his cries were futile, for Alecto had already immobilized the two others in the store with her acrid steam from the Lethe, putting them in a funk they would not recall.

The steam enveloped the man.

"I swear I don't know him!"

Alecto stood up and turned to Than. "He's not the one."

Immediately the snakes rushed back down from the man back into the holes in the floor from whence they came. The man fell in a stupor on his desk covered with the foul steam. The jets stopped and the steam began to dissipate. Than and Alecto left the man, but not through the door.

Chapter Nineteen: Questions and Answers

After a warm shower, Therese lay in her nightshirt in bed with Clifford curled up beside her near her waist. Than said to give herself time to process what he had told her outside the Wildhorse Saloon, but how does one process such information? He's the god of death? His sisters are the Furies? They've come to Earth to avenge her parents' murders?

She couldn't sleep, so she took the remote from her nightstand and turned on the television tucked in a small armoire beside her desk. Puffy stopped in his wheel to see what the bright lights were all about. "Sorry," she said to him. "I know it's late." Puffy liked to work in silence and darkness.

Puffy continued on his wheel as she flipped through the channels and finally settled on an old George Lopez episode she had already seen. She tried to distract herself with the humor before her, but her eyes left the television to stare at the light reflecting on the ceiling. This whole business with Than as the god of death couldn't be real, could it? Had she lost her mind? The death of her parents had taken a toll on her sanity, right? She'd become a deranged lunatic.

The hair on the back of her neck stood on end. Clifford's ears pricked up. Therese was vaguely aware that Puffy had frozen, like a chipmunk in the middle of the road. She and Clifford jumped to their feet at the same instant. Standing across the room in the same pale blue polo and jeans he had worn earlier was Than, the supposed god of death.

Clifford sat back down on his haunches and wagged his stub of a tail.

She didn't move. "How did you get in?"

Than gave her a wry smile. "I'm a god."

"Why are you here? Did you decide to take me after all?" She was suddenly not so certain she was ready to go.

"I came to check on you. I was worried." He moved toward the bed. The smell of cigarette smoke and alcohol lingered in his clothes from the dance hall. "Mind if I sit down for a while?"

Laughter roared on the television, but Therese wasn't laughing. "I guess not. Go ahead."

He sat at the foot of her bed, and she returned to the headboard against her pillows by Clifford. She tucked her feet closer to her body to avoid touching him.

"I knew you wouldn't be able to sleep and that you'd have questions, so I decided to come to see if I could help put your mind at ease. I know this is hard for you."

"You have no idea. How could you?"

His mouth tightened into a frown. "I suppose you're right. I can't know how you feel."

"How can you be here, anyway? Don't you have a job to do? Is nobody dying while you're here handling horses?" Her voice had a touch of hostility in it. Then she remembered Dumbo. "Why couldn't you do anything to save Dumbo?"

He gave her a weak smile. "So I was right. You do have questions."

"And you haven't answered any of them," she said sharply.

"There was nothing I could do about the horse. I'm sorry. I don't kill living things; I merely guide their souls after they die. I have nothing to do with the timing."

"Couldn't you pull some strings?"

"No." He cleared his throat. "As to your other question, I made a deal with my dad. I told him if he'd make my brother, Hip, take my place as the guide for the dead, I would come to Earth and help my sisters find your parents' murderer and avenge their deaths. He gave me a time limit because while Hip is doing my job, humans have restless nights without dreams, and Zeus won't tolerate that for long."

That explained why she hadn't been able to reenter the dream lately. "But why would your father care about avenging my parents' death?"

Than shifted by lifting one bent leg partly on the bed and turning to face her, his back to the television. "My father is a just god and his priority is justice for the souls in his care. When humans fail to find justice for the dead, he and my sisters step in. The lieutenant needs help finding the person who orchestrated your parents' death. My sisters, Tizzie and Meg, are working on the case. I plan to help as well, but first I wanted to get to know you."

"Why?"

He moved closer to her on the bed, sending her heart into arrhythmia. "Don't laugh, okay?"

Laugh at a god? she thought. Yeah, right. "I won't."

"My mother may have given me some affection when I was young, but I don't remember it. The other gods on Mount Olympus rarely visit the Underworld. They only come if they want a favor. They know my job is necessary, and I suppose they're glad it's me doing it and not them, especially Hermes who did it before me, but that doesn't stop them from looking down at me with contempt. And the humans I encounter have already died. They have no love for me.

"But that night I took your parents and you came close to dying yourself, that night you swept down from the sky from out of nowhere and took me into your arms, that night you kissed me, well, that night changed me."

Therese pulled her knees into her chest with her covers around her. Than moved closer, his face inches from hers. She couldn't tell if she was frightened or aroused. Maybe she was both.

His mouth seemed to twitch with anxiety. "Before that night, I didn't know what I was missing, but once you showed me what affection was like, I needed more. So, to be honest, my true motive in coming to Earth was to seek you out."

Therese couldn't speak. She didn't know what to say. She sat there, stunned.

"I knew I wouldn't kill you—at least, I didn't think I would. As I've said before, you wouldn't be the same. I don't think I'd like having a wife with little personality and no freedom."

"Wife?" Therese whispered.

"Just listen," he said. "After that day your parents died, I went to my father to see what it would take to make you a god. As a god, you would retain your personality and free will and could live with me in the Underworld unchanged. I reminded my father how he got my mother, Persephone. Are you familiar with that story?"

Therese shook her head. "Vaguely. I don't recall." She still hadn't gotten past the word "wife."

Than pulled off one of his boots. "Do you mind?"

Like she would deny a god. "Make yourself comfortable," she murmured.

He pulled off his other boot and then brought both legs straight in front of him on the bed, crossed, stretched over the tan and white comforter nearly to her headboard. Therese shifted over to give him more room, still unable to believe. He didn't sound like a god. Shouldn't a god speak differently? In her mind she said, "You sound so human."

"We've been around humans for centuries. Why wouldn't gods sound like humans?"

Her eyes shot up to his. He could hear her?

He crossed his arms at his chest. "My mom, Persephone, is the daughter of the goddess of the harvest known as Demeter. Technically, she's Zeus's sister. The genealogy of the gods is…complicated. Anyway, one day Persephone was walking along with some friends when she was drawn by a cluster of white daffodils. Persephone was picking the daffodils near a cliff edge separated from her friends when my father came riding by in his chariot and swept her up without stopping. He plunged the chariot over the cliff edge into this giant chasm in the earth and took her down with him to the Underworld where he made her marry him and become his wife."

"That's so cruel." She pulled her legs closer to her chest, hugging them with her arms. "Your dad sounds like a jerk." Did she just say that out loud? To a god? She sucked on her lips. Keep your mouth shut, she said to herself.

"Hades thought if she could just get to know him, she would fall in love with him. See, like me, he had little contact with the other gods, and all the humans he knew were already dead. He was lonely."

"I don't think that justifies…"

"I know," he snapped.

Therese's eyes widened. Shut up, she said to herself again.

"My grandmother, Demeter, looked all over for Persephone, but no one would tell her the truth because they feared my father. She even disguised herself and came to Earth and lived for a while with a human family, but her misery made the Earth barren, and people and animals were beginning to die along with the vegetation. So my father's brother, Zeus, decided to take the matter into his own hands and force my father to let Persephone go. By that time, Persephone had grown fond of Hades, but she missed her mother and was anxious to see her. Before Persephone left, my father offered her a pomegranate seed, which is one of the most powerful foods you can eat, as a farewell blessing. She graciously took his offering without knowing it was another trap. By taking his food, Persephone was obligated to return."

Therese shuddered, still convinced Hades was a jerk.

"Zeus, trying to please everyone, commanded Persephone to live with Hades in the Underworld as his queen for six months out of every year, and the rest of time she could spend on Mount Olympus with her mother, Demeter. That's why humans have to deal with fall and winter every year: For six months, Demeter sinks into depression and mourns the loss of her daughter. Most of the vegetation dies. Demeter never gets over losing my mom."

Therese thought of her own parents down in the Underworld, permanently. At least Demeter had the six months each year. Therese would take that deal. She had nothing. She released her knees and sat up crisscrossing her legs. Clifford crawled over into her lap. "What does your mother's story have to do with me? My parents are already down there. My aunt wasn't expecting to have to finish raising me. It would be better for everyone if I died, too."

Than moved along the foot of the bed so that he was lying on his side propped on an elbow, his head resting in his hand. "You know that's not true." He gave her a gentle smile. "Your aunt, your friends, and your pets would all miss you."

"They'd get over it." She pet Clifford as tears came into her eyes and spilled down her cheeks.

Than reached across the bed and wiped the tears from her face and then lay back on his side. "My brother told me I should come to Earth and have my way with as many girls as I wanted, to sow my wild oats, he said; but that's not my style. There's only one girl I'm interested in."

Therese's heart sped up. "You can't really mean me?"

He smiled, apparently amused. "Why not?"

"I'm the first girl you've met. How can you be so sure there isn't someone better? And you hardly know me. And I'm, I'm nothing compared to many girls I know." She couldn't believe she had blurted all that out. She felt her face flush red.

"Earlier I said the humans I come into contact with are dead, but I have still seen the living from afar. I have travelled all over the earth and have seen all kinds of people. You are the sweetest, most natural, most vibrant person I have ever observed." He reached across the bed and touched her hand.

"That's impossible," she whispered.

He laughed out loud. "Jen's right. You're way too hard on yourself."

Her eyebrows flew up. Had he listened in on their conversations?

"And you seem to have no clue about your natural abilities."

"Abilities?"

He laughed again. "The way you communicate with animals, the way you read people's thoughts, the way you naturally know what to say to make others at ease. You are so full of life and aware of the nature around you. Ironically, you are the exact opposite of the dead I ferry. And that makes you utterly attractive to me in every way." He leaned in and touched his lips to her cheek. She felt her heart beat erratically and her lungs fill with air which she couldn't release.

He sat back and smiled shyly at her, and then he frowned with doubt, but she didn't know what to say. "So, anyway, I reminded my father of his own loneliness before finding my mother and asked him to consider making you a god. He said there is a way."

"What is it?" Therese asked with enthusiasm. "Please tell me. I want to know."

His face turned bitter. "It's not worth doing just to see your parents. I'm telling you, they aren't the same. They probably won't remember you."

She slid on her knees and then lay down on the bed across from him, mimicking his position propped on her elbow. Clifford moved between them. Therese and Than both pet Clifford as she struggled to put into words what she was feeling. "That's not my only reason," she finally said in a soft voice. "I want to be with you, too."

He looked up at her with surprise, but he didn't seem convinced. "I know you liked me before, but now that you know who I am, you still want to be around me?"

Therese gave him a shy nod.

"I was under the impression you despised me, like everyone else." His face was full of anguish.

"No. I don't. I was just frightened."

"I don't believe you," he said.

She stopped petting Clifford to take his hand. It felt big and moist and warm in hers.

He gently squeezed her hand and closed his eyes. "That feels so nice." Then he jumped from the bed. "Your aunt is coming. I better go. Come early tomorrow."

He vanished into thin air just as Carol knocked on the bedroom door.

"Can I come in?" Carol asked.

Therese was momentarily jarred. "Um, yes. Come in," she finally said.

Carol poked her head in the room. "Richard and I are going to bed. I just wanted to say goodnight. I had a good time tonight, and I hope you did, too."

Therese managed a smile for her aunt's sake. "I did. I really did."

"Good. I'll see you in the morning." Carol closed the door behind her.

Therese sat up on her bed hoping Than would reappear. When a half hour passed and he still hadn't come, she turned off the television and tried her best to go to sleep.

Early Thursday morning after toast and eggs, Carol and Richard dropped Therese off in front of the Holts' place.

"Have fun in Durango," Therese said as she climbed from the car. A feeling of guilt for leaving Clifford alone in the house made Therese frown, but she knew he'd find ways to entertain himself.

The sun peeked over the forest behind Jen's. The road was mostly in shade and the morning air was cool, maybe too cool for swimming, she thought. Instead of heading up the drive to the Holts', she walked across the dirt road and through the grassy field in search of Than. She wore her bathing suit beneath her shorts and tank top in case she felt brave enough to swim with him.

When she reached the lake, she looked for him. She even called his name. A mother duck and her ducklings scurried away from the bank, but there was no sign of Than. Disappointed, she turned away from the water and headed across the tall grass to Jen's.

She wondered what Than had meant when he had said there was a way to make her a god. She still couldn't believe he had come to Earth to seek her out. Maybe he had been changed by her affection, but affection could be found from many sources. She still felt like he was settling when he could have someone better.

When Therese approached the pen, she found it empty of people. Ace came to the fence and stretched his yellow-brown neck out to her. "Where is everybody, Ace?"

"You're early," Pete called from the barn. "Than and I are just finishing up in here." He appeared at the barn door, shirtless. Therese stole a cursory glance over his well-formed chest. "Jen, Bobby, and my mom went inside for a short break." He gave her a big smile as she moved closer.

"You were awesome last night," she said. "I'm so excited for you."

He gave her a sweaty hug that smelled of earth and hay. "You're a sweetheart for saying that."

Than appeared at the door, tense, as though Pete's embrace upset him. He also wore no shirt, and she could immediately see there was no comparison. How could you compare a mere man to a god? "Hey, Therese," he said with reserve in his voice.

"Hi, Than." She felt shy. "I looked for you at the lake."

"I was just about to head over there," he said, brightening. "I need to cool off after all that barn work."

"That's a great idea," Pete said to Than. "Mind if I join you?"

"Not at all, Pete."

Therese could see the disappointment in Than's face, and she herself felt let down. She was anxious to find out how she could become a god. "I'll just come along and watch you guys from the bank. I'm not hot enough to get in that cold water yet."

"Believe me, you're hot enough," Pete teased.

Therese felt her face flush red and could make no reply.

Pete mussed her hair.

She walked between the two tall boys across the dirt road and the field of grass. As they walked, Pete talked about his hopes for his band. It was difficult for her to hear what he said. She wasn't used to being pinned between two gorgeous guys—one a god, no less. She tried to keep her breath steady as they approached the water and the two boys stripped off their boots and jeans. Pete's boxers were gray, and Than wore white again.

She laughed when the two boys decided to make a race of it as they jumped out into the deeper part and swam freestyle till they were out in the middle. She smiled with delight as they dunked each other, playing like bear cubs vying for fish.

"Come in!" Than shouted during a reprieve from their game. "It feels great."

"Maybe later!" she shouted back. "After I work up a sweat!"

They swam back to the shallows and stood up, water dripping down their glistening bodies—the one thick and glowing, the other almost as tall, tan, and well-formed by human standards. Therese looked away. It was just too much to take in.

The boys climbed into their jeans and boots and the three of them headed back to the pen to begin their work on the horses. Thoughts of Dumbo sobered Therese as she took a brush to Sugar.

"Hey pretty girl," she said to Sugar.

Jen, Bobby, and Mrs. Holt soon joined them from the house.

"Hi Therese!" Jen noticed Than and Pete were both soaked and shirtless. "Go for a swim, guys?" She took a brush to Sassy.

Pete laughed from behind the General. "Yeah. Than here nearly drowned me." He must have recalled the fact that Therese's parents' drowned, because she caught a glimpse of his face behind the horse as he turned red and said no more.

Therese shuddered, but Than was soon there to distract her. "I sure had fun at the Wildhorse Saloon last night. I wouldn't mind going again sometime."

Bobby piped up. "Me, too. That was a blast. Hey, Mom. Can we go again tomorrow night?" Bobby held the brush midair, above Chestnut's back, waiting for his mother's answer.

"I don't know, Bobby," Mrs. Holt replied as she dug something from Rusty's hoof. "It gets pretty crowded on Friday nights."

"Oh, come on, Mom," Jen joined in. "Pete could take us if you don't want to go. Couldn't you Pete?"

"Sure. I don't mind."

"Maybe so," Mrs. Holt said without committing to anything. But both Jen and Bobby exchanged smiles. They knew "maybe so" meant "yes."

When Jen finished with Sassy, she came over to Therese and said in a confidential voice, "Matthew called late last night and invited me to lunch today. I'm a little nervous."

Therese stood up. "Are you excited? I mean, are you glad he called?"

"Yeah. It was like we hadn't stopped talking all this time. He said he had pictures to show me. He just got back from Alaska. I'm pissed that he didn't call before he left, though." She picked Sassy's hair from the brush.

"Language," Mrs. Holt warned.

"Sorry, Mom," Jen said.

Therese continued their conversation in a whisper. "Maybe he'll explain why. He wouldn't have called last night if he weren't still interested." Therese patted on Sugar's leg for the hoof. Therese inspected the shoe while she waited for Jen's reply.

Jen shrugged. "You really think so?"

"Yes, I do."

"I'm meeting him at Hondo's for chicken fried steak. I'm dropping Bobby at Gamestop to get him off my back. He's been bugging me to take him all week. Matthew offered to come pick me up, but since Bobby wanted to go to town...anyway, that's why I'm meeting him." Jen went over to Annie, the red mare, and started brushing her back. "What did you get into, girl?"

Jen and Bobby went inside to wash up after the last horse was saddled and ready for the first trail ride. Pete and Mrs. Holt started helping the riders mount their horses, one at a time. Than and Therese waved their goodbyes and headed home. Than stopped her on the dirt road in front of Jen's house.

"Are we going swimming?" he asked with a smile.

Therese grinned back. "I'm up for it if you are. But only if you promise to answer a few more questions."

"I was planning on it anyway. Let's go." He took her hand in his and walked with her across the field.

Therese felt giddy with excitement. His big warm hand surrounding hers made her shiver with delight. Their arms brushed every so often, sending tingles of pleasure down her skin. She became even more excited when they reached the bank of the reservoir and Than kicked off his boots and jeans. She pulled off her tank top with shaky arms and stepped out of her shorts. She left her sneakers on so her feet wouldn't get hurt on the rocks on the bottom of the lake.

She stood there, embarrassed, in her two-piece bathing suit while he looked over her body. She felt good about her flat stomach and curvy hips, but, even though Jen said she was crazy, she didn't like her blossoming thighs and the lemon halves she had for boobs.

Than walked up to her in his white boxers and, with one finger, pulled up the strap that had fallen from her shoulder. "You're so beautiful," he said in a soft voice. Then, without any warning, he took her waist in his hands and carried her into the water.

She screamed with pleasure. "It's like ice!"

"Nice, isn't it?" He took her out where she couldn't stand and then released her waist to tread water.

She treaded beside him. "You said you'd answer my questions first, you cheater!" She splashed water against his face.

"Cheater? You didn't specify the order!"

He splashed her back, and it felt like a tidal wave had washed over her. She sputtered and gagged on the water that had unexpectedly entered her mouth. Her hair flattened in her face.

"Sorry about that," he laughed.

She had the feeling he wasn't sorry at all. She shivered with the cold of the water but managed to stick out her tongue at him in mock anger.

He put his hands on her waist again and towed her to shallower water, where she could stand, the gentle waves clearing her chin. The water came up to his nipples, and she could see from the look of them that he was cold, too.

"I don't need your help," she teased. "I'm an awesome swimmer."

"Is that right?"

"Wanna race?"

He laughed. "Let me get this straight. You are challenging a god to a race?"

"You raced with Pete."

"That wasn't a real race. I wouldn't dare show my true speed and give myself away."

She narrowed her eyes. "Show me. I want to see."

"Others might be watching."

"Please?"

He laughed. "Who could resist you anything?" He dove under and swam freestyle in a flash of white to the other side of the reservoir and back before she had counted to ten.

She opened her mouth with surprise. "Oh my God!"

"You can call me Than," he said slyly.

She splashed him again. "Time to pay up. What did your father tell you when you asked him how to make me a god?"

His face grew somber. "Do you have to ruin the fun?"

"You promised."

"Fine. He said if you personally avenge your parents' death, if you take the life of the one responsible so that he or she can be properly punished in the Underworld, he will make you a god."

She narrowed her eyes again. "So if I avenge the death of my parents, I can become like you?"

He frowned. "But it's a bad idea. I thought about it all night. I don't want you to do it."

"You're kidding, right? Who wouldn't want to be a god?"

"Not just any god, Therese. A god of the Underworld. Even my mother can only handle it six months out of the year. Hades isn't offering you the same bargain."

"I don't care. I told you. I want to be with you." Then she shivered. "Unless you've changed your mind." Maybe he didn't want to be with her, now that he had a chance to know her and to see that there are other, more beautiful, fish in the sea.

He put his arms around her waist and put his face inches from hers. She felt light headed and weak kneed. "You've got it all wrong," he said. "Once I thought more about the way you were with nature and the animals, I realized you belonged among the living. Therese, the Underworld would be a dull place for someone like you. There aren't any animals except the delusions created by the psyches of the dead. You said yourself you couldn't live without animals. The souls of dead animals are like those of dead humans—without freedom and full of delusions."

Even though she could barely control her arms because of the trembling, she put them around his neck and pressed her body against his, so warm compared to the ice cold water. "It should be my decision."

He licked his lips and looked at her mouth. "Then you've got a lot to think about." He gave her a playful smile and then picked her up in his hands and tossed her high across the water.

She had a feeling as she flew above the water, squealing like a pig, that he hadn't used his full strength. She plunged into the water as though she had been on a high slide in a water park. She swam underwater back to him, and when she returned to the surface, she dipped her head back to pull her hair from her face, looked right into his eyes, and said, with her own playful smile, "You're gonna pay for that."

She dove under water and pulled his legs out from under him, but when his head went under, he merely looked at her and laughed. He could breathe underwater and talk underwater. She shook her head at him, folded her arms to show she was pouting, and resurfaced.

"What's wrong?" he laughed as he came up to meet her face.

"You've got to have a weakness. It's not fair otherwise. Achilles had his heels."

He pulled her into his arms and she gladly yielded into his warm embrace. "I do have a weakness now."

She didn't need to ask what he meant, even though she couldn't believe it was true. How could such a remarkable being feel so strongly about her?

He walked with her to the bank and said, "Wait here. I'll be right back." She blinked and he was gone.

"Than?" She felt totally unnerved. It was creepy, surreal. He had been standing right in front of her and now he was gone. She suddenly felt the need to sit down, but before she could move, Than reappeared, and he was holding a quilt in his hands.

Her mouth dropped open as she watched him spread the blanket out a few feet from the bank in the tall grass.

"What did you just do?" she asked.

He grinned and shook his head. "Give me a break, Therese. You don't expect much from the gods, do you." It wasn't a question.

"Um, I've just never personally known one. I'm trying to adjust. Excuse my human ignorance." She hadn't meant that to come out as mean as it sounded.

"I'm sorry," he said. He had fixed the blanket neatly across the grass, and now he reached over to her and took her hand. "I need to be patient. I'm so unused to the company of living mortals." He pulled her close and kissed her cheek. "Why don't we dry off in the sun before heading home?"

She lay down on her back beside him. Both of them turned their faces up to the sun, eyes closed. He held her hand, and she couldn't decide which was warmer: he or the golden orb above them.

"Tell me about your parents," he asked suddenly.

His question took her by surprise. She was almost always thinking about her parents, longing for them, but over the past several minutes they hadn't crossed her mind. "What do you want to know?"

"What was your mom like? Tell me about her first. Was she like you?"

Therese gave a short laugh. "She was nothing like me. She loved solving problems, you know, problems in science and discovering answers to things. Ironically, she was afraid of unreasonable things, like heights, planes, and elevators. She hated escalators, too. She was even a little afraid of the water, I think, and I love the water. I feel the most at home there. I sometimes think if I had a previous life, I must have been a dolphin. My mom and nature didn't get along. I sometimes got the feeling that as a scientist she was trying to conquer nature by understanding it. She was scared of spiders and snakes, I'm talking about ones that aren't even poisonous. A lizard would have her in hysterics." Therese laughed. "Dad and I used to have a lot of fun with that."

"What was your dad like?"

"He was more like me. We used to go on hikes. Nearly every evening we'd sit on our deck with our binoculars and study the wildlife across the reservoir. My dad was a writer, so sometimes months would go by and I'd hardly see him, but then he'd finish a book and we'd have months together before he'd start on another. The thing I liked most about my dad was that he was the best practical joker I've ever known, and luckily my mom, and not me, was his most common victim. But I think she liked being victimized in a strange kind of way. He always made us laugh. My dad and I were often in collusion together against my mom, but she never minded. She even seemed to like it."

The memories swept over Therese and she nearly forgot where she was and what she was doing as she relived brief moments with her parents. She giggled when she remembered the time she and her dad got her mom with the plastic rat they had planted beneath the kitchen sink.

Than squeezed her hand and brought her back, and she looked at him with gratitude. "This is the first time I've gone down memory lane with any kind of joy since the shooting. You have a way of keeping me happy and on the bright side of things."

He returned her warm smile. "I'm glad. You already know what you do to me."

"No I don't. What is that exactly?"

He closed his eyes and turned his face back to the sun. She watched him, studied every line and feature of his golden face and chest as he spoke. "You make me feel human, in a very good way."

"What do you mean?"

"Humans often envy the gods because of our power, but the truth is we have far more responsibilities than freedoms. We have duties, obligations we can't neglect without significantly affecting the world—the whole world and the life on it. My entire life has been about serving. I have been a dutiful son to my father. This is the first time in my ancient history that I have ever done something solely for me, and it feels great. It makes me realize that I need to strike a balance, more like my brother, who has always managed to find time for both work and play."

Therese laughed. "That's an understatement. I'm not sure he works nearly as much as he plays."

"You're wrong. Dreams are more important than most humans realize. Hip plays around a lot, but he also works hard to make sure people are inspired, fulfilled, provoked, challenged, comforted. It's a big responsibility."

Therese was quiet while she let that information sink in. She hadn't thought of Hip as rendering an important service. She had only seen him as a playboy. "It sounds like you love your brother."

"I do. I love all the members in my family."

She turned on her side and put her free hand—the hand he wasn't holding—on his heart. She wondered if it beat like a human heart. She could feel it thumping in a regular, humanlike rhythm beneath his chest, and it picked up speed as she moved her hand across his skin.

"I don't want this afternoon to end. I hope my aunt's not worried."

"She and her boyfriend have lost track of time sightseeing in Durango."

"That's so weird that you know that."

He laughed softly.

"Do you really have to leave so soon?" she asked.

"Yes, I do."

"But what if we don't find the person behind the shooting? What if I can't avenge my parent's murderer in time?"

He opened his eyes and looked at her. "Would that make you sad?"

She nodded. She never liked someone so much and couldn't imagine it ending so soon. "I want more time with you. I'm just getting to know you. Can't you use your powers to freeze time for everyone else or something?"

He chuckled and his body moved beneath her hand.

"What's so funny?"

"You freak out when I disappear and reappear, but you expect me to stop time."

She laughed, too. "But why can't you? You're a god."

"Like I said, we have more responsibilities than freedoms. I doubt even Zeus could pull that one off."

From high above, a streak of light flew from the sky and struck a boulder not twenty feet from where they lay, sending sparks and smoke and a loud crack in all directions in the echoing valley. The boulder was split in half and was as black as coal.

"Holy crap!" Therese cried, falling against Than. "What was that?"

"Oops. My apologies," he muttered, but it didn't sound like he was talking to her. "I made someone angry."

"That scared me to death. Does that happen often?"

"No. Never to me. But this is an exceptional time in my life."

Therese now realized she had flattened her body against Than, on top of him from the waist up. He wrapped his arms around her and held her against him. Heat surged through her. She reached her lips to his.

His mouth was warm and wet. A tingling sensation surged through her and she could hear nothing but her heart thudding in her ears.

He said softly, "If I could stop time for you, I would."

In her mind, she said, "I'd rather die than be parted from you," and then he looked at her with shock, as though he had heard her thoughts.

"What?" she asked, mortified by the possibility that he could read her mind.

He leaned his head back and closed his eyes. "I can't stand the thought of causing you pain."

"Then don't." Her words sounded hostile.

He opened his eyes again and looked at her. "Should I go away before your feelings…"

"No!"

He cracked a smile. "Does this mean you've decided?"

She couldn't help but return his smile despite the conflicting emotions coursing through her. "First, I want to meet your sisters."

Chapter Twenty: Hunting with Tizzie

Than and Tizze flew above hundreds of humans in an airport terminal in San Diego. Some sat at tables inside small cafes and sandwich shops. Others sat crammed together near gates. Still others walked quickly through the corridors dragging their bags on wheels behind them. The man they knew as Steve McAdams had short, blond hair and blue eyes and sat sharply dressed in a crisp white shirt, unbuttoned at the neck, black trousers, and shiny black shoes. He sat looking at a cell phone with another man, about the same age, mid-thirties, also sharply dressed but with dark, curly hair and glasses. Both men held their heads together looking at the phone and laughing.

"This should be fun," Tizzie said to Than as they landed before the men and made themselves visible.

Tizzie stood in her tight black leather pants and silver halter top and tall black boots. She spread out her arms and legs and closed her eyes and smiled. The men looked up at her and then looked at Than and then looked at each other, perplexed. Tizzie opened her eyes and smiled at the men as dozens of wolves appeared in the terminal around them.

The humans were shocked and stopped what they were doing and backed into areas away from the hounds, and as the hounds lifted their heads into the air and howled their loud, screeching, blood-curdling cries, the humans dropped whatever they were holding and cupped both hands to their ears.

The two men before Tizzie also dropped the phone and cupped their ears, tears streaming from their eyes.

"Hear me, Steve McAdams?" Tizzie said coolly, barely perceptible to Than over the howls of the hounds.

The flustered, frightened man nodded.

"Do you know this man, Kaveh Grahib?" She made an image appear in the air over her head, an image of him in his jail cell slumped on a cot, staring into space.

Steven McAdams shook his head.

Tizzie beckoned one of her hounds to her side and then he bared his fangs at the man as he uttered a threatening growl.

"Be truthful, Steven," Tizzie warned. "I do not like men who lie."

Steven McAdams looked at the growling hound and then back up at Tizzie, still cupping his ears and streaming tears. "I don't know him!" he shouted but could be heard by none save the two gods.

Tizzie lifted her arms higher in the air, and at once the howling stopped. The humans stared blankly as the wolves descended upon the humans in a rush and a flash, licking each one with a forgetting serum before vanishing into thin air. Than and Tizzie also vanished as Than heard her voice mutter with profound disappointment, "He's not the one."

Chapter Twenty-One: The Furies

Therese was glad when she came home Thursday afternoon to find herself alone—except for the company of her pets—because she could hardly contain her excitement. She couldn't wait to have more of her questions answered, to find out what the Furies were like, and to spend more time with Than.

The phone rang just after she had stripped down for a shower, but she picked it up in case it was Carol, or better, Than. It was Vicki Stern.

"So can you go to the movies tonight?"

Therese had completely forgotten her promise to call Vicki back. "I'm sorry. I've actually got plans again. I was invited to have supper with another friend."

"But I asked you first, Therese."

"This is a family thing that came up. I'm sorry. My aunt's in town and…"

"You just said it was a friend."

"A friend of the family. Hey, let's shoot for next week, okay?"

"Okay."

"Bye now."

"Bye."

"Ugh," Therese said to herself. What was she going to do with that girl?

After her shower, she threw on a comfy t-shirt and shorts and went downstairs to make a batch of brownies to take to tonight's dinner. She hummed as she poured the chocolate batter into a pan and popped the pan in the preheated oven. Although she was humming "Poker Face," it dawned on her that she wasn't faking this new feeling of liberty as she had on the dance floor. Something about Than's presence and his apparent love for her had freed her from the dark depression that had threatened to overtake her. She still wanted to go to the Underworld, but now she could do it without dying. She could be with her parents and the sweetest, sexiest guy she had ever met.

Things hadn't turned out so badly for her after all.

As she made herself a peanut butter and jelly sandwich, she wondered if she truly loved Than. There was no doubt that she was enamored with him, no doubt that she crushed on him harder than anyone she had ever met, no doubt that she longed to be with him every second he was away from her. But could she really say she loved him when she barely knew him? And if her answer was yes, as crazy as that would sound, did she love him enough to spend all of eternity with him?

She took her plate and glass of milk with her upstairs so she could log on to her laptop to learn more about Thanatos and the Furies. She found a passage from an ancient poet named Hesiod who described Than and his brother this way:

And there the children of dark Night have their dwellings, Sleep and Death, awful gods. The glowing Sun never looks upon them with his beams, neither as he goes up into heaven, nor as he comes down from heaven. And the former of them roams peacefully over the earth and the sea's broad back and is kindly to men; but the other has a heart of iron, and his spirit within him is pitiless as bronze: whomsoever of men he has once seized he holds fast: and he is hateful even to the deathless gods.

A new doubt worked its way into Therese's head as she processed the description. Could Than be deceiving her only to show his true self once she's his wife and it's too late for her to change her mind? Was he like his father, Hades, willing to trick her into becoming his queen of death?

Impossible, she thought.

She came across three different images depicting him. One showed him wielding a sword, wearing a shaggy beard and head of curly black hair. His ugly face looked fierce, unrelenting, and cruel. The second image was one she had seen that day she had come home from the hospital: the Grim Reaper, thin like a skeleton, cloaked in black, bearing a deadly scythe. The third image still wasn't her Than, but was closer to how she viewed him: a winged boy, like Cupid, maybe sixteen or seventeen years old, with a sweet air about him.

Therese knew these were all human interpretations of him and not factual renditions, but, nevertheless, uncertainty about his identity gripped her heart and made her anxious. Her anxiety increased when she read that the Furies had wreaths of snakes in their hair and blood dripping from their eyes and were horrible to behold. Meg had been beautiful. Had she somehow disguised herself?

After more reading, the oven timer beeped, so she went downstairs to take the brownies out and let them cool on the stove top. What a strange circumstance she found herself in: baking brownies for a handful of gods from the Underworld.

The ringing of the telephone startled her from where she had been standing in the kitchen deep in thought. She hoped it wasn't Vicki. She picked up the phone. "Hello?"

It was Carol calling to check on her, which gave Therese the opportunity to tell her about her supper plans. Carol seemed relieved, for she and Richard had lost track of time and now wouldn't need to rush back home. Therese hung up and went upstairs to her closet to figure out what to wear. Nothing in her wardrobe seemed good enough for a dinner with gods.

Standing there in the small walk-in closet, she thought of her mother. Normally, she would ask her what she should wear, for her mother seemed to know the latest style, maybe because she worked around college kids every day. Mom could be oblivious to so many things around her, but she had seemed to always notice fashion.

Therese went back downstairs to the master bedroom. Across the hall from it was a guest bedroom, where Carol was staying. Neither Carol nor Therese was ready to disturb the master bedroom. Therese had taken the bottle of Haiku perfume but had touched nothing else.

Now as she stood there, perfectly alone, she went to her parents' bed and lay down on her belly with her face in her mother's pillow, taking in her scent. She took her dad's pillow and practically inhaled it. His scent washed over her along with a current of tears. She pulled back the covers and crawled beneath them and wrapped herself in their smells. She closed her eyes, willing herself to dream, but there was nothing. After about twenty minutes, she climbed from the bed, not troubling to make it up again, and went into her parents' closet where their scents were even stronger. She gingerly touched their garments. Would she ever wear something of her mother's without falling apart? Could she dare part with her father's clothes by giving them to charity?

She left the closet and went to her mother's dresser. She opened the tiny drawers of her wooden jewelry box, a gift from Therese's father before Therese was born. She took a diamond necklace from one of the drawers and held it up to her throat, gazing at her reflection in the dresser mirror. Twelve round stones linked together on a delicate golden chain made a beautiful choker around her neck. Maybe one of these days she would find an occasion to wear it. Maybe she would take it with her when she became the goddess of death.

She laughed nervously. "I have lost my mind," she whispered.

Therese tucked the necklace back into its drawer, closed the drawer, and went back upstairs. She was surprised to find Clifford had not come down with her but had chosen to stay on her bed. She hadn't given much thought to how much he probably missed her parents, too. She now shuddered at the thought of leaving him and Jewels and Puffy forever.

Therese returned to her own closet again. She finally chose a short red skirt and tight white, short-sleeved sweater that she thought made her boobs look bigger. She slipped on her white wedge sandals and looked over herself in the mirror. She picked up her hair to see which looked better—down or up—and decided to stick with it down, the way her father liked it.

Her heart felt tight as she wondered if she should have told someone the truth about her hosts tonight. What if they killed her and took her down to the Underworld before she could say goodbye? What would her aunt and the Holts think if Therese never returned? Should she leave a note just in case?

I'm being paranoid, she thought. Than would never hurt me.

Therese went to the kitchen to cut up the brownies and put them on a platter. She folded plastic wrap across them to keep away bugs during her walk through the forest to the Melner cabin. She looked like a normal girl headed toward a normal neighborhood potluck, or something; not a possibly deranged girl with illusions of eating with gods.

She put the platter down on the counter and swept her dog up in her arms. "I love you, Clifford. Be a good boy. I'll be home soon."

Than gave Therese a bashful smile when he answered the door in his khaki shorts and a short-sleeved denim shirt. She was glad she had come. She didn't care what happened to her. She wanted to be with him.

"What is this?" he asked of the platter she handed him.

"Brownies. Have you ever tasted some?"

"You obviously aren't talking about nymphs." He looked confused.

Therese threw back her head and laughed. "Chocolate and sugar. They're for dessert."

He gave her a sheepish grin as he led her through the living area and into the kitchen. He sat the brownies down on the kitchen bar. "Thanks. I can't wait to taste them."

The Melner cabin was similar to her house in that the living room and kitchen were open to one another. But in the Melner cabin, the stairs started near the front entrance instead of the back. At the back of the house, off of the kitchen, where Therese's stairs would be, a door led to a dining room. A huge bay window opened to the forest climbing the mountain behind the house. Therese could see a flagstone patio and grill outside.

Than's two sisters were already gathered waiting for her with the table set. They stood up when she entered, their round eyes shining with the light of the crystal chandelier hanging over the center of the beautiful table scape.

Therese recognized Meg even though her thick blonde curls were loosed from their usual bun and spilling out down the length of her back. Her beautiful face was without makeup, and Therese now realized that her lips were naturally deep red. Meg wore the black go-go boots from the night before with a short black fitted dress. Unlike last night, she wore red ruby studs in her ears, matching stones in rings on her fingers, and one enormous blood-red ruby pendant around her neck. She looked fiercely beautiful.

A little much for a dinner at home, though, Therese thought.

The other sister—Tizzie, Therese presumed—had equally long, thick hair, but hers was jet black, and her curls were individual serpentine ringlets, as though she had curled her hair and then not brushed it out. Her face was darker complexioned, and her eyes were black like her hair. She had dark eyebrows with a delicate arch and deep red lips. She also wore no makeup and yet possessed an eerie kind of beauty. Tizzie wore tight black leather pants, black stiletto heels, and a silver halter top that tied around her neck, leaving her dark back bare. Shimmery emeralds hung from her ears, and smaller ones linked in several loose, jangling bracelets around both wrists.

Therese felt she had underdressed.

Than pulled out a chair from the table. "Please, sit down."

When Therese sat, the Furies sat, too.

"Therese, these are my sisters. You've met Megaera, or Meg for short."

Meg gave a courteous, but distant, nod.

"This is Tisiphone. Everyone calls her Tizzie," Than said.

"Welcome to our table," Tizzie spoke without smiling. "Our brother told us you wanted to meet us. I must say you are the very first human to ever make such a request."

Meg's sneer sent a shiver down Therese's back.

"Thanks for having me," Therese managed to say. "Everything looks delicious, and the table spread is absolutely beautiful."

"What nice manners," Tizzie commented.

Meg added. "We've been known to punish those without them."

Than cleared his throat. "Why don't we eat?"

Therese saw that the salad was like the one she had made for Than. Along with the salad was a bowl of vegetable soup and a plate with fried potato patties.

"We're vegetarians," Than explained. "I hope you like the food."

Therese took a sip of the soup with her spoon. "Mmm. Delicious. I tend to be vegetarian myself—not strictly, but usually." She cut a piece of the potato patty with her fork and gave it a taste. It melted in her mouth. "Oh my goodness. So this is what gods eat?"

Than said, "We usually eat ambrosia and nectar, but when in Rome…"

Therese smiled. "Oh yes. Right." She was terrified now of appearing impolite. She continued to eat in silence.

After several minutes of cutting and scraping and drinking and chewing, Meg prompted her, "Than says you have questions."

Therese stammered, "I, I hope you won't think it rude of me."

Tizzie said, almost demanded, her arched brows raised with curiosity, "What do you want to know?"

Therese wasn't sure where to begin. "Maybe you could tell me what you've learned so far about my parents' killer."

This question apparently pleased both sisters, for they gave her lascivious smiles.

Tizzie spoke, "Every night I go and torment the man who pulled the trigger that shot the bullet into your mother's neck"

Therese shuddered.

"That is why I could not go dancing last night," Tizzie added.

Well, of course, Therese thought. That sounded perfectly normal. She couldn't go dancing because she was too busy tormenting a man in jail.

Tizzie continued, "This man's name is Kaveh Grahib. He lies in his cell while I fill him with anguish and dread and terror. I whisper in his ear to tell me the details of the plotter. I climb on top of him and let my snakes slither on his clammy skin. Blood drips from my eyes when he resists, and my legs squeeze him until he cannot breathe. So far, I have only a name, but it won't be long before I track the plotter down."

Therese's appetite left her, and she sat chilled and afraid. "What is the name he gave you?"

Tizzie looked at Than, and Than nodded, so she said, "Steven McAdams. I know he is American, but that is all. Tonight I will find out more." She gave her lusty smile.

Meg scowled at Therese. "It's rude not to finish your plate."

Therese took a sip of the soup and tried her best to finish the rest.

"Maybe we should change the subject," Than suggested. "Why don't you two tell her what it's like living in the dark abyss that is the Underworld. She'd like to be better informed before making the decision I discussed with you."

"It's actually quite fun on days when I go to Tartarus and torment the evildoers for their sins on Earth," Meg said.

Therese shivered and let out a just-audible moan.

Than's smile faded. "Listen, Therese, my sisters may take satisfaction in their work, but they, unlike the souls they torment, are not evil." Then he bent his brow at Meg, "Could you tone it down a little?"

Tizzie smirked. "Well, I have to admit, I enjoy my job. Than's right: It is very satisfying. But I also like the precious stones our father has mined from deep underground. He gives them to us as gifts when we are especially swift with his just payment." She lifted one of her arms to jangle the emerald bracelets.

Than frowned. "Now let's not go in the opposite direction with extremes, Tizzie. I don't want her to be terrified, but I also don't want her under any delusions of grandeur. The Underworld is a loathsome place, even if there are a few perks. There aren't any animal companions or beautiful plants. No sunrises and sunsets. Everything is cold and lifeless."

"That's not so," Tizzie objected. "Cerberus is there, who can be quite entertaining when provoked, and so are Swift and Sure, Father's two black stallions that pull his chariot. They look fierce with their red eyes and huge bodies, but they are sweet when they are eating pomegranate seeds from my hand. And as far as real plants, you're forgetting the poppies around Hypnos's abode—albeit, they make you want to go straight to sleep."

"And don't forget the asphodel along the Elysian Fields," Meg added. "Those fragrant white flowers are real even if everything else there isn't. And the rivers are real, and they're really quite beautiful and serene when neither I nor my sisters are using them as weapons of torture." The edges of her lips twisted up into a half smile.

Therese narrowed her eyes at Than. "Your sisters don't make the Underworld sound nearly as bad as you do." Then she frowned. *Maybe he doesn't want me after all.*

As if he had read her mind, he took her hand in his and gave it a warm squeeze. "I would love for you to come with me, but I want you to be sure. I want you to know what you're getting into."

So he's not like his father, she thought. *He's not going to trick me like Hades did Persephone.*

"And Cerberus can be kind if you bring him cakes," Tizzie offered. "Though Alecto never should have given that information to Orpheus."

"You have to admit, dear sister, how fun it was to see him torn to pieces," Meg snickered.

"Not for me. I saw no justice in it."

Meg spoke though grit teeth. "It was his due dessert for how he tricked us all."

Therese asked them to tell her the story of Orpheus, so Tizzie began.

"First you must know that the very first musicians were gods. Though Athena didn't play, she invented the flute. Hermes made the lyre and gave it to Apollo, and when he plays, we all lose our thoughts to his beautiful music. Hermes also invented a shepherd's pipe, which he plays himself, quite well, actually, when he's not running errands or going on adventures with Zeus; and Pan, Hermes's little goat-footed son, made a pipe of reeds that sings the songs of nightingales when he blows through it.

"The Muses play no instrument, but their voices are the loveliest of any I have heard in my long existence. I tell you all of this because despite the superiority of the gods to humans in all ways, there was one demigod—part human and part god—who nearly equaled the gods in musical talent, and that, of course, was Orpheus.

"Wherever Orpheus played his lyre and sang his sweet voice, the animals—even the rocks—followed. Every nymph of the woods where he travelled was in love with him, but he had interest for none until his eyes fell on Eurydice. She, like the others, could not resist his song, and she loved him immediately. They were married in the woods among all those who loved them, but right after the wedding, when Eurydice went walking through a meadow with her bridesmaids, she was bitten by a viper and instantly killed.

"They say even the rocks wept. Orpheus's grief was impossible to endure. He hastened to the Underworld, set on charming everyone there with his song. Our sister Alecto was the first one to be moved by his beautiful voice and the melody emanating from his lyre. She gave him cakes to feed to Cerberus. Once through the gates, his music charmed the judges next, and then Meg and me, the tormenters in Tartarus. For the first time, I think, we wept with tears. Sisyphus got to sit down on his rock, and Tantalus forgot his hunger and thirst. Our father Hades and our mother Persephone came from their chambers to hear the melodious sounds.

"Orpheus sang a song about the bud being plucked before its bloom and his wish to borrow, not take, his love for a little while. Iron tears fell down my father's face, and my mother kissed his softened cheek. They beckoned Than to bring forth Eurydice but gave Orpheus this condition: He could not look back at his love until they were through the gates of the Underworld and across the Acheron."

Meg took up the story here, "Orpheus had little faith, it seemed. Eurydice was behind him, followed by our brother, as they climbed through the caverns above the river. As Orpheus passed Cerberus and jumped onto Charon's waiting ferry, he looked back, extending his hand, and in that moment, my brother, under my father's strict command, pulled Eurydice back down into the darkness."

Therese shuddered and glanced at Than, whose mouth was turned down in a frown.

Meg jeered, "Orpheus did not keep his end of the bargain, and he should have gone on back with the fact of his failure; however, in a desperate rage equal to Zeus, he tried to force his way back into the Underworld. When his entrance was refused, he finally gave up and wandered off until a band of Maenads—women frenzied with the wine of Dionysus—found him and tore him limb from limb, flinging his severed head into the river."

Therese looked away from Meg's awful smile. She felt sorry for Orpheus, suspecting he hadn't meant to betray his deal with Hades.

Than spoke up here, "I found his soul and took him directly to Eurydice, and they are there now together, though as I've told you, they aren't quite the same as when they were alive."

The change of subject had done nothing to bring back Therese's appetite, but she chewed on the potato patties lest she appear rude. She forced the food down with the glass of tea, which she tasted now for the first time. She nearly choked. It was sugary sweet, just the way Than apparently liked it. The corners of her mouth curved up into a smile when she recalled the way he had relished his sweet tea at her house two days ago.

The sugar reminded her of the brownies. "Oh, Than, the brownies. Should I get them and serve them to you and your sisters?"

The girls exchanged confused looks.

"She's not referring to nymphs," Than explained. "Her brownies are something called chocolate." He stood up from his chair. "I'll get them."

Both girls produced their lustful smiles. Apparently they were familiar with chocolate.

Than brought the platter to the table and passed it around. Therese watched him take his first bite of the chewy, fudgy square. He closed his eyes and uttered something like a moan. "Oh, my," he said once he'd swallowed. He took another bite. "I can't believe I've lived so many centuries without chocolate."

"And we're always so busy," Tizzie said, still smiling. "We rarely take the time on Earth to enjoy its pleasures."

"Well, well, well," Meg said after finishing her square. "I think Therese has discovered a bribing tool. If you ever have a request for me, bring me chocolate." She took another square and shoved it whole into her dark red mouth.

After Than ate a third brownie, he pushed his plate away from him and took Therese's hand in his. "So, Therese, will you go with me to-morrow night to the Wildhorse Saloon and teach me more about danc-ing?"

"On one condition," she said, with a bargainer's smile that would have made Hades proud. "I want to meet your parents."

The three siblings looked at one another with astonishment.

Then Than said, "Maybe if you offer to play your flute for them, they'll come."

"Music and chocolate," Meg said. "A killer combination."

"No pun intended," Tizzie laughed.

Chapter Twenty-Two: The Wildhorse Saloon Revisited

Therese felt strange Friday evening squished in the backseat of her aunt's old red Toyota Corolla between two gods, Than and Meg, on their way to the Wildhorse Saloon to meet the Holt kids, Ray, and Todd. Richard kept stealing glances behind him at the eccentric beauty beside her, dressed as she was in a red leather short suit, black go-go boots, and her blood-red rubies on her earlobes and around her neck. Although Therese had been proud of how she looked in her olive cotton camisole and her Levi boot-cut jeans, she now felt totally eclipsed.

Tizzie had promised to meet them later after her tormenting obligation. Therese imagined her hovered over her victim with a swarm of snakes dropping from her head. Would the blood still be dripping from her eyes when she arrived at the saloon? Therese shuddered.

"Are you okay?" Than whispered close to her ear. His warm breath sent chills across her scalp and down the nape of her neck. Because her red curls were up tonight in a high ponytail, she could feel Than's warm breath caressing her neck as he spoke. "Are you cold?"

"I'm fine," she said. "Just a little nervous."

"Do I make you nervous?" he whispered.

She made a little nod, but then breathed, "In a good way."

He gave her a broad smile, showing his perfect white teeth, and took her hand in his. Therese quivered with desire.

"Can you drive a little faster?" Meg asked coldly.

Carol looked at her in the rearview mirror. "I'm going the speed limit."

Meg rolled her eyes. "Great."

Therese wondered how Meg could get away with punishing people for forgetting their manners and be so rude herself. "I'm sorry we don't have more room," Therese offered.

"It's quite alright." Meg's voice was not kind.

"That's not what's getting on her nerves," Than whispered. "She's jealous of how smitten I am with you."

"Than," Meg threatened. "There's no need to speak rudely of others."

Richard gave another uncomfortable glance back at Therese's companions.

When they arrived at the Wildhorse Saloon close to eight o'clock, Todd's giant yellow truck stood out as a beacon in the parking lot, but neither Pete's truck nor Mrs. Holt's Suburban was among the three dozen other vehicles. Therese texted Todd while she led the group inside the dance hall, a wave of cigarette smoke accosting her like a stifling blanket. She tried to hold back the cough gagging her throat. Ten or so couples danced a fast polka around the wooden dance floor in front of the empty stage where Pete's band had performed two nights ago. More people gathered around the two bars—one on either side of the hall—and two or three older men, sitting on stools alone, looked drunk. Todd and Ray turned from where they stood in line at one of the bars and waved, their red minor bracelets dancing around their wrists. Therese waved back and led her group across the dance hall toward them.

After their initial hellos and some talk about Todd's truck and when Therese would get her ride—since she had missed the maiden voyage—they stood around awkwardly sipping their straws and watching the dancers on the floor across the room. One of the older men who had been sitting alone and apparently drunk approached Meg and asked for a dance. Therese was surprised when Meg consented, but Meg's mocking expression made her wonder about the Fury's motive.

The new song was a waltz, and Therese could feel Than turning toward her to ask, but before he had his words out, Todd grabbed her hand and said, "Let's go!"

Therese gave Than a look of apology as she allowed Todd to pull her out onto the floor. He glided her easily around and around with his thin but strong frame, and soon Therese was having fun and laughing out loud, especially at Todd who was now telling her all about his family's trip to California and the strange people they met there. He gave a glance at Meg as they passed her and her drunken partner and said, "Though we have a few strange folks right here in Durango."

He wanted to know more about Meg and Than. Although Therese was just a bit tempted to tell the truth—Than was the god of death and his sister was one of three tormenting avengers known as the Furies— she decided to hold her tongue, shrug, and say, "They're guests at the Melner cabin. I don't know much about them." She knew she wasn't telling him anything he didn't already know.

"Be careful with this guy," Todd said. "I have a bad feeling about him."

"Okay, Obi Wan Kenobi." She laughed.

She wondered exactly what it could be that gave Todd this negative impression of Than. Had Todd sensed something different about him?

When the song ended, he asked for another dance, but she thanked him and said she was thirsty, maybe later, so they joined the others and finished their pops.

About that time, Pete, Bobby, Jen, and Matthew appeared. Therese thought Jen and Matthew looked like they were back on, the hot item they had been for most of their sophomore year. She couldn't help but suspect that Matthew had wanted his summer free, in case someone new came along, perhaps while he vacationed in Alaska, but now that school was only a few weeks away, he'd reclaimed her. She didn't particularly care for his behavior, but she was glad Jen looked happy.

As Jen introduced Matthew to those in the group he had not yet met, Pete turned with a look of excitement to Therese. "This is an old Bob Wills song! Let's go swing. How 'bout it?"

Therese couldn't say no. She loved the Western Swing, and Pete was a great dancer. She also loved the idea of showing off for Than.

Pete pulled her around the floor with authority, easily leading her away from him, to him, away from him, and back to him. He swung her under his arm and around his back and picked her up in the air like she was a rag doll.

As soon as the song was over, she excused herself and ran straight to the restroom. Jen followed closely behind. Luckily there wasn't a line.

Once they were out of the stalls and washing their hands at the sink, Therese asked, "You've forgiven Matthew?"

"Yeah," Jen smiled guiltily. Her hair was in a ponytail tonight, too. It was like they could read each other's minds. "He said he didn't mean to get back with me, but he just couldn't force himself to stay away."

Therese's forehead wrinkled with doubt, not because her friend wasn't beautiful and sweet and capable of making it hard for boys to stay away from her, but because she tended to be too gullible when it came to Matthew.

Jen asked, "So what's with you and Than? Do you guys like each other?"

Therese couldn't stop the smile from crossing her face. "I don't know. I think so."

"Has he kissed you?"

Therese watched herself blush in the mirror. "Yes. And he had me over for supper last night."

"And you didn't tell me? How did it go?" Jen dried her hands on a paper towel and then dropped the towel in the trash can.

Therese told her friend a few of the details.

Jen sighed. "Sounds like he really likes you." Then she added, "Don't tell Pete I told you this, but I think he's jealous."

"You mean Bobby."

"No. Pete."

Therese's mouth dropped open as she stared at her friend's reflection beside her in the mirror. "No way. Did Pete say something?"

"No, but I know my brother."

"You're imagining things. Pete's like a big brother to me."

"Whatever you say."

When they rejoined the group, Carol and Richard were out on the dance floor and, much to Therese's astonishment, so were Bobby and Meg. Ray was telling Than a story, but Than seemed to be only half listening as he kept his eyes on Therese. Before she could make it to Than's side to hear what Ray was saying, Todd grabbed her arm and said, "Let's go. I love this song."

Therese glanced at Than over her shoulder, but he had politely turned to listen to Ray.

Matthew and Jen joined them on the floor. It was a Texas Two Step to a George Strait song.

As soon as it was over, Pete took Therese from Todd for a polka. She felt the sweat dripping down her face, the small ringlets of her hair that hadn't made it into her ponytail sticking to the nape of her neck. Her hands were slippery in Pete's dry hands, but he held fast to her as he swung her around, closer, she now realized, than he had before.

As she danced round and round with Pete, Therese wondered if there could be even a smidgen of truth in Jen's assessment of her brother. Pete smiled at her, laughing when they barely missed running into another couple, or when Therese nearly lost her balance and he had to catch her. Yet his smiles and laughter seemed no different to her tonight than they had any other day. Had there always been something there, just beneath the surface? If Than hadn't stepped into her life, Jen's revelation would have excited Therese. She had hero-worshiped Pete all her life—she'd liked the kind of music he liked, played the sports he played, watched the shows he watched. He was gorgeous, just like his sister, his blond bowl-cut hair framing a strong face and blue eyes. But it had all been a sister-brotherly love, hadn't it?

She tried to see Than, but the Friday night crowd had thickened, and he was lost in the swarm of bodies and smoke. When the song ended, Therese thanked Pete and went looking for Than, but before she could reach him, Bobby snagged her hand and asked for a dance. This was a Texas Two-Step, Bobby's specialty, for he hadn't yet developed the same level of skills in the polka, swing, or waltz as his older brother and Todd possessed.

The song ended, and a new one played throughout the hall. Therese felt a tap on her shoulder, and she turned midstride to find Than there smiling at her. "A waltz. Shall we?"

"Yes." She smiled back, a thrill coming over her. Then she thanked Bobby, who went straight to Meg.

Alan Jackson's voice brought a lump to Therese's throat as Than took her in his arms and with near-expert control led her in the slow waltz.

As if Than knew what she was thinking, he said, close to her ear, his warm breath sending chills across her cheek and bare neck, "This song describes my feelings exactly. I was worried I wouldn't get my turn with you. I'm glad it came on this song."

She leaned her head against his chest and closed her eyes, unable to look at his sweet longing. It seemed too surreal. All of it. Was she still in a coma, and all this was a dream? Could she jump into the air and turn somersaults?

Before she had time to answer her own questions, Meg and Tizzie rushed to their side and began talking fervently in Than's ears. Therese was unable to hear what they were saying.

"How long?" he asked, his brow bent with worry.

"There's no time to lose," Tizzie answered.

The group moved from the dance floor, Therese all the while wondering what was going on. "What's the matter?" she asked when they stopped between the bar and the exit.

Tizzie answered, "I made your parents' killer talk, but we don't have time to explain. You stay here."

"Where are you going?" Therese was horrified.

"Back to your house," Than explained. "McAdams has men there waiting for you."

"They're waiting for your aunt, too," Meg added coolly.

"Clifford! My pets!" Therese felt sick. "Oh, please let them be okay!"

"We're on our way now," Than assured her. "We'll come back and let you know when you can return home."

"Take me!"

"It's too dangerous," he said. "Stay here with your friends, where it's safe."

She followed them through the exit and out to the parking lot. She forgot about god travel and expected them to take a car, but when they went to the dark part of the lot and simply vanished, she sighed, and a feeling of helplessness washed over her.

Therese knew she should listen to Than and his sisters and stay put, but she was in agony over what might be happening to her pets, especially Clifford, who would have been barking like crazy at the intruders' approach. Would they have killed her very best friend? She couldn't wait here for who knew how long. She had to go see for herself. But she didn't want to endanger Carol and Richard by asking them to drive her home. They would go into her house and directly into danger. The Holts wouldn't have room for her if they came in Pete's truck, plus Matthew and Jen were having too much fun. Unless she revealed the true reason she wanted to go, she wouldn't have their cooperation.

Maybe Todd would take her! He would be bored by now, with Jen dancing exclusively with Matthew and with Therese unavailable. Todd was too shy to approach girls he didn't know. She could ask him to drop her off and to not even bother to drive up the long gravelly driveway to her house. He would be safe, she hoped.

She ran back inside the dance hall, stopped in the entrance, and turned her head from side to side. The crowd was too thick to spot him, even though he was tall. She texted him as she picked her way through the crowd and the noise, feeling more and more desperate. In her haste, she accidentally knocked into someone's drink, and some of it spilled on her shirt. She weaved through the bodies and smoke, a wave of panic threatening to overtake her. Then she saw Ray.

She practically ran to him. "Where's Todd?"

"Bathroom. Why? What's wrong?" Her face must have looked bad, because Ray, usually quick to joke around, showed sudden concern.

"I don't feel well. I was going to see if he'd take me home. He promised me a ride in his truck sometime. I thought maybe tonight. I don't want to ruin my aunt's good time. Maybe you'd like to come, too? Y'all can come right back."

"Sounds good to me. I'm bored anyway. But I don't know about Todd. He loves this place. Where are your new friends?"

"They had to leave."

A flicker of understanding and suspicion crossed Ray's face. "And they wouldn't give you a ride? Some friends."

"It was a family emergency. That's why I don't feel well. I'm worried about them."

"What happened?"

"I don't really know. They were in too much of a hurry to explain."

"Maybe there was no emergency."

She shook her head. "It was too obvious. They were so upset."

Todd joined them then, and Therese turned and explained everything she had told Ray to him. Would he take her?

"I don't know. You want me to take you for a ride in my pride and joy? That's tough. Hmm." A smile illuminated his face. "Do I want to show off my new stereo? Hmm. This is a hard one."

She gave him a pleading smile.

Todd shrugged. "Alright. Let's go."

"Great!" Relief came but still could not outdo the approaching panic. "Thank you so much! I'll be right back. I have to tell Carol."

Therese found Carol and Richard on the dance floor and was about to tell them the same story she had told Ray and Todd when she realized Carol would insist on taking her home if Therese were upset, so she stopped, mid-sentence and said, "I've been dying to take a ride in Todd's new truck. He's ready to leave, though. Can he take me now to get a shake from McDonald's and then on home? Than and Meg already got a ride. Their sister came and got them."

Carol's face lit up even brighter than Todd's had, probably because she was relieved to see Therese having fun with friends. "Of course. We'll be home right behind you."

"Don't rush," Therese said. "We'll hang out at McDonald's for a while before heading home."

"Sounds great!" Carol said.

Therese felt awful about the lie as she ran through the crowd back to Todd and Ray without even bothering to explain to any of the Holts. She was in too much of a hurry to leave so she could check on her pets and her house and see what was going on. She would text Jen on the way. She was tempted to call 911 as she picked through the crowd but decided the Furies and the god of death could handle the situation better than humans. Once she found Todd and Ray, they left the dance hall, climbed into Todd's ostentatiously high truck with her in the middle in the bench seat, and took off.

Todd turned on the stereo, and Therese oooed and awed over the sound, the feel of the ride, the restoration to the dash, the paint job, and anything else she could think of to show her gratitude and hide her anxiety as they drove through the winding country roads to her house. The height from their perspective did lend a strange sense of power despite the panic threatening to burst inside her. More than anything now, she wanted to be a god so she could better protect those she loved.

Chapter Twenty-Three: Meg's Falcon

Than waited above the abyss as, first, Alecto sprang up from the granite below with a wild look of hatred, made more horrific by the blood dripping from her beautiful, dark eyes. Next came Tizzie with a shrill cry of outrage, echoed by the howl of the great hound on whose back the Fury was straddled. Finally, up came Meg with a large falcon on her shoulder, its toothed beak dripping with blood from a recent kill.

They left the abyss and quickly emerged inside Therese's house, where the dog Clifford lay dying on the floor.

Than hastened to the dog's side and grunted, knowing what the dog's death would mean for Therese. He disintegrated and dispatched himself straightaway to Aphrodite at Mount Olympus to beg for her help.

The other Than remained with his sisters to catch and torment the men who were waiting in the shadows to ambush Therese and her aunt.

There were four of them, for Than could easily sense their presence--one for each of them, he thought, smiling. He finally understood the pleasure his sisters took in their duties. He couldn't wait to strangle the man he had heard talking about Therese.

The man had said, "So young and pretty," as he had looked at a photo of her on her dresser. "I wonder if she's a virgin. I can't wait to pinch her pretty flesh." Than had shuddered with rage and clenched his teeth at hearing those words from the man's filthy mouth.

Alecto brought the first scrawny, little human up by the neck from the master bedroom where he had been filling his pockets with jewelry, including a diamond necklace now falling from his flailing hand. Meg came up from the basement with a hairy blonde whose blue eyes now opened wide with fright, the whites of his eyes like perfect circles. He was the only fair-skinned man among them. The others were brown skinned, like Grahib.

Tizzie held her man from the back, putting her beautiful face against the side of his face and allowing the snakes that were once her hair to curl around him from behind. Than found his man in Therese's room holding the tortoise, so he had to be careful. In invisible mode, he extracted the animal from the human and then bound his hands behind his back with a leather belt. He brought his man to the main living room, where his sisters and their prey had gathered.

He watched with profound satisfaction as Meg took her falcon from her shoulder onto her finger and ordered him, "Do it!"

The falcon went up to the man that Tizzie held entwined by her snake hair, which hissed at the man and flicked its many tongues. The falcon took his toothed beak and viciously pecked one of the man's eyeballs repeatedly in the socket as the man screamed and writhed with pain. Blood poured from the gory socket when the falcon fluttered away and back to the shoulder of his mistress. The other men moaned and cried out as fiercely as the victim.

"The location of McAdams!" Alecto commanded. The man in her possession floundered and writhed.

"Please!" the man begged. "I don't know anything. Let me go!"

Meg gave another command to her falcon, which flew directly to Alecto's prisoner, and as the whites grew larger in the scrawny man's eyes, the falcon pecked one of the eyes to bits, which poured out in bloody tears down his cheek. He screamed and cried and flailed his body against Alecto's strong hold.

The falcon returned to Meg's shoulder, his beak dripping.

"We're dead either way!" the blond in Meg's possession cried. "Have mercy on me and I'll tell you where McAdams is. But don't let your bird near me, or I'll never speak!"

Meg gave the command to her falcon, which went before the blond who had just spoken and then carved out his eye with his beak.

Meg said, "Never issue ultimatums to a Fury."

"Hell 101," Tizzie said with cruel sarcasm.

Alecto laughed a rueful laugh.

Than did not share in the pleasure of his sisters as he had expected he would. He turned and looked at the frail man he held, bound at the wrists by his leather belt. "Do not tempt my sisters with arrogant words or foolish silence. Tell them where they can find McAdams. Maybe they will have mercy on you, and maybe they won't."

"There's a warehouse," the man said with heavy breaths. "In San Antonio, Texas. He has an office there on a street called Nakoma. There's a sign called 'Dougal's' on the door. The building is close to the airport. That's all I know. I swear!"

Chapter Twenty-Four: Thwarted Attack

When Todd pulled onto the gravelly drive of Therese's home, Therese said, "Stop here. You don't have to go all the way up to the house."

"Don't be silly," Todd said.

"Seriously!" she cried with full panic. "I need to walk. I'm, I need some fresh air after all that smoke."

Todd turned off the engine. "Fine. We'll walk with you, won't we Ray."

Ray shrugged. "I don't care, but I have a feeling Therese doesn't want us to."

She met Ray's gaze. "I'm just a little worried, that's all. I've had a great time with you guys, as always. Please don't be offended."

Ray shrugged again, "Who's offended?"

Todd opened his door and jumped out. "Give me your hand," he said.

As she stepped onto the huge tire, Therese listened to the quiet night air, wondering if the gods were here, or the murderers waiting for her. She took Todd's hand and jumped. "Thanks," she said softly. "And thanks for the ride. I owe you big time."

"Big time," he teased. "I'll collect. Don't you worry." He climbed back in to his truck. "Night."

"Night." She watched him back up, the crackle of pebbles spitting out from beneath his huge tires, and pull away. When she could no longer see his taillights, her knees shook.

She stepped quietly up the drive toward her house. There were no lights on—not even the porch light. She wondered whether she should take the stairs up to the front screened porch or enter through the back as she crept slowly up the drive, her heart thudding in her chest.

A sound from the dark forest behind her house startled her. She sucked in a breath and froze, just like the chipmunks on her deck always did whenever they became aware of her. Like they, Therese stood perfectly still, waiting. The dying branch of the elm was just visible in the moonlight, and it pointed at her like an omen: You, Therese Mills!

The fact that Clifford was not alarmed by her presence or the presence of the thing in the woods filled her with terror. He would be barking by now. He would smell her scent. He would be aware of the other thing, too.

She decided to move toward the front door, away from the woods. She slid her key from her front jean pocket and had it ready to gouge someone's eye if needed. She took a step up. The wooden board beneath her foot creaked. Otherwise, the house was silent and still.

On tiptoes, she slipped through the screened porch to the front door. Before she could put her key in the lock, she found the door ajar. She pushed it in, gently, hesitantly. She stood there in the crack of the door, vigilant. Except for the dim light of the moon washing in through a skylight above her, the living room and kitchen behind it were bathed in a curtain of darkness. The hallway to her right, leading to the two bedrooms, was in shadows, but Therese could now hear a vague sound—like someone breathing—coming from it. Her own heart pounded so loudly, and her own breath moved through her so quickly, she found it difficult to trust her hearing.

She swallowed hard and reached for a lamp, but it failed to illuminate the room. She remembered then that the bulb had burned out and hadn't been replaced since…since before everything had happened. She took a few steps into the room to find the light switch. A low whine, barely above a whisper, came from the hallway. Therese froze like a statue.

When the whine came again, Therese recognized it, and she flew for the switch. The room was showered with light. "Clifford?" She ran to the hall. Lying on the wooden floor on his side, not moving, but still breathing, was her dog. She rushed beside him on the floor. "Clifford!" He didn't move. She used her hand to feel around his body, but she couldn't find any injuries. There was no blood, but he could barely open his eyes, and his tongue was hanging from his mouth like he was dying.

"No!" she screamed, forgetting all else. She buried her face against his fur and sobbed uncontrollably now. Clifford was her best friend. She couldn't take any more loss. This was too much for one person. She would be so alone. Did Hades have a vendetta against her? She cried for her parents. She cried for Dumbo. She cried for Clifford who looked as though he were leaving her now as well. "No, boy. Hang in there. Please don't leave me." Then with a desperate wail that would have put Orpheus to shame, she shouted, "Than! Thanatos! Thaaaannaaaatossss!"

Her eyes caught sight of something silver gleaming on the small console table to her left. Whether it had already been there or had appeared after her loud cry, she did not know. On the table lay a syringe full of blue liquid with a pink square piece of paper attached that read, "For Clifford." Therese snatched up the syringe, looked closely at it, and knew what she was supposed to do. She looked over Clifford's body for a place to stab him, and, not sure of herself, but hopeful, nonetheless, thrust the needle into Clifford's haunch and pressed the medicine through the needle. He didn't move, barely flinched, and his breaths were labored. She watched him closely, waiting, hoping to see a change.

She sat there with him for what seemed like an eternity, when she noticed his breathing slow down to normal. He brought his tongue into his mouth and swallowed. After another minute, he tried to pull himself up. Though he failed, she knew whatever the blue liquid had been in the syringe was working. Tears of joy streamed down her cheeks. She kissed Clifford on the side of his face.

In another ten minutes, he rolled up to his feet, wagged his stubby tail, and licked her face. Then he ran to his bowl of water in the kitchen and lapped up the liquid till the bowl was dry.

Now that she knew her dog would live, Therese began to wonder what had happened. Surely if the killers were still in the house, or nearby in the woods, Clifford would be barking by now. She ran to the front door and closed and locked it, just in case. She checked the backdoor, too. Maybe whatever had hurt Clifford had desensitized him. She took the broom from the kitchen closet and held it like a weapon. Then, cautiously, she went upstairs to check on her other pets. Clifford followed.

Luckily Jewels was basking in the light beneath her lamp, untouched. Therese turned off the lamp, stroked her shell, and checked her water, which was still clean. Puffy was just now grooming himself after his long daytime nap. Therese's bedroom appeared inviolate until she turned toward her bed and noticed something lying in the middle of it.

It appeared to be a long silver robe made of fine silk. A note was pinned to its sleeve—a square piece of pink paper just like the one that had been attached to the syringe, and the same writing said, "For Therese." Whoever had left the syringe for Clifford had left this fine robe for her. She touched the robe, cautiously in case it was some kind of trick, and then picked it up in her hands when nothing terrible happened. Should she put it on?

Before she could decide what to do with the robe, she was suddenly aware she was no longer alone. The hairs on the back of her neck stood on end. Clifford, too, froze in his place. She was afraid to turn around, but when she saw Clifford's stubby tail wag back and forth, she knew it must be Than.

"Therese!"

She dropped the robe on her bed, turned to him, and nearly hit him with the broom.

"Whoa!"

"Sorry!" She dropped the broom and ran into his arms. "I was so afraid!"

His arms wrapped around her waist and pulled her close to his warm body. "You were supposed to wait at the saloon."

She buried her face in his chest. "I'm sorry. I couldn't stand waiting behind." She didn't want to let go. She never wanted to move from this warm, thrilling place that brought her comfort.

He lifted her chin with a finger. "I'm just glad you're safe. When I didn't find you there, I…well, then I heard you calling. I'm just glad you're okay."

She wanted him to kiss her. She thought he might when he leaned in, but then he took her hand and led her to the bed to sit down. The wide gap between them brought her back to her senses. "What happened?" She pulled Clifford into her lap when he followed them onto the bed. "Please tell me everything. Who left the medicine for Clifford?"

"I'll tell you everything. First get comfortable. It's a long story."

They sat side by side with their backs against the fabric headboard. Therese moved a little closer to Than so that her shoulder pressed against his arm. She stroked Clifford, where he curled up in her lap.

"Tizzie learned from Grahib that tonight McAdams planned to kill you," Than said. "Grahib didn't know how many would come but said their plan was to ambush you and your aunt here in the house. Apparently, they didn't know about Richard visiting." Than swallowed hard and hesitated. Then he grit his teeth. "Grahib told Tizzie the men were promised that they could have their way with you and your aunt."

Therese gasped, her mouth wide open.

"Then they were to kill you and burn down the house. Make it look like an accident." He clenched his jaw.

Therese took his hand, unclenched his fist, and rubbed it between both of her hands. His words frightened her, but his obvious feelings for her exalted her. "So what happened when you left me? Did you come here?"

He nodded. "The men beat us here. There were four of them. They had already poisoned Clifford. I thought he would die. I knew it would be the last straw for you. So I went to Mount Olympus to beg Aphrodite for her help. I reminded her how I tried to help Orpheus to be reunited with his true love, Eurydice. I also told her how I helped Theseus and Hercules, favorites of hers, and also Odysseus during the Trojan War. I told her our story, from the beginning when you first embraced me in your coma, and of the deal my father made with me to make you my wife. She agreed to help. I returned to the Underworld to help my sisters punish the men who came here to use and kill you, and she came here to bring you the antidote. She wouldn't administer it herself, though. She said she doesn't have the stomach for it."

Therese jumped up off the bed full of incredulity. "Aphrodite, the goddess of love, was here, in my house?"

Than smiled. "So you've heard of her, huh?"

"Who hasn't?"

"That answer will bring a smile to her face." He laughed. "So I was very relieved to see Clifford wagging his tail when I arrived. I didn't know how it would all turn out."

"Thank you for saving my dog." She threw her arms around his neck. Then she sprang up, jittery and blushing, to pick up the robe she had dropped at the foot of the bed. "I think she left this for me, too. But I don't know what I'm supposed to do with it."

Than looked at the robe as Therese held it up to him. "It's a traveling robe." His mouth turned into a broad smile. "I can't believe it. Obviously you have found great favor with Aphrodite. This is a rare gift."

Therese hugged it to herself. "Oh my gosh. I can't believe I have a gift from a goddess, and from the most beautiful goddess, too."

Than laughed. "She's certainly happy to hear that, I bet, but you might want to be careful not to offend others who might be watching over you."

Therese pushed her arms through the sleeves of the robe. "It's so soft." She looked at herself in her dresser mirror. "I love it. How do I thank her?"

"I'm sure she's watching you now. But you could think of something to show your gratitude."

"Yes. I'll think of something." She sat back on the bed beside Than, still wearing the robe. Clifford moved back on her lap.

"It's magic, you know," Than said, stroking her hand. "The traveling robe enables a mortal to travel like gods."

"What do you mean? Like disappear?"

"Travel quickly from one point to another without having to travel the full line. This robe will allow you to do the same, though I don't recommend that you try it alone since you don't yet know what you're doing."

Her mouth dropped open. "I will be able to vanish and appear just like you?"

"While wearing the robe, yes."

"Can you show me?"

"Now?"

She eagerly nodded her head. "Just a quick trip, maybe to your place and back?"

He jumped up off the bed. "Your aunt and her boyfriend are pulling up the drive. Go talk with them. Don't let on what's happened. And when you've come up for bed, I'll be waiting for you. We'll take a quick trip to my cabin and back, as you wish."

She gave him a smile and clapped her hands with excitement. Clifford jumped off the bed and ran around the room. "Thanks!"

"Till then." He disappeared.

"Wait! Than?"

He reappeared. "Yes?"

"Am I still in any danger? Will McAdams send more men to try and kill me?"

He walked across the room and took her in his arms. "He may send men, but now you have the attention of more than one god. We are watching over you. Don't worry."

She closed her eyes and sighed. When she opened them, he was gone.

In the next moment, her aunt was knocking at the door. "Therese? You awake?"

Therese pulled off the robe and gingerly laid it on her bed. "Yeah. I was just coming downstairs."

She and Clifford followed Carol down the stairs to the living room where Richard sat watching the late news.

"Did you have a good time with your friends?" Carol asked as she sat on the sofa next to Richard.

Therese and Clifford curled up together on a chair beside the empty fireplace. "Yes. Todd's truck is so awesome. I was a little scared at first, up so high, but once I got used to it, it was really cool." Then she asked, "Did you guys have fun dancing?"

Carol and Richard exchanged smiles. "A blast," Carol said. "I can't believe we've gone dancing twice in one week!" She patted Richard's thigh.

Richard laughed. "Yeah, hopefully I'm paid up for a while."

Carol punched him in the shoulder. "You hush!"

Therese smiled. "Thanks for driving. Did Jen get my text? She never replied."

Carol nodded. "She and her boyfriend seemed not to mind. Pete, seemed disappointed. They left before we did."

Therese wondered again over what Jen had said in the restroom of the Wildhorse Saloon, but before she could think much about it, something on the television caught her attention.

"Late breaking news," the anchor person said from the television. "A La Plata County inmate known as Kaveh Grahib was strangled and killed tonight behind bars by an unknown perpetrator. Grahib was arraigned several weeks ago as a suspect for the murder of a Durango couple, Linda and Gerald Mills, which took place near Fort Lewis College five weeks ago. Investigators have no leads but are looking into this case."

"Oh my God," Therese said gaping.

"I'm calling the lieutenant." Carol stood from the couch.

Richard took her hand. "It's after midnight."

"I don't care. This concerns us." Carol crossed the room to the phone at the kitchen bar, took up the business card lying next to it, and dialed the lieutenant's number. "Lieutenant Hobson, this is Carol Stuart. Would you please call me as soon as possible? We just heard about what happened to Kaveh Grahib, and we're concerned. Thanks."

As soon as she hung up the phone, it rang.

"Hello?" Carol said. "Uh-huh. Is that good or bad?" Carol paused. "Okay, thanks." Carol hung up the phone and looked across the kitchen at Therese. "The lieutenant said he's sending out another officer to guard the house and that we should play it safe for a while. So, Therese, no more walking, even with Than. Got it?"

Therese nodded.

Carol sat back down on the couch beside Richard, who wrapped his arm around her and kissed her cheek.

"Don't worry," Richard said. "I'll stick around until the police know you're absolutely safe."

Therese was grateful that Richard could offer her aunt some peace of mind. She knew that gods were watching over her aunt and him, and although that didn't erase the fear looming over her, it diminished it and made it bearable.

"I'm going to bed," Therese said to them. "See you in the morning."

"Are you working again tomorrow?" Carol asked.

"Through Sunday," Therese replied. "Sunday is my last day, I think."

"Good night," Richard said. "Just call us or come down if you need anything."

"Thanks," Therese said, and then she and Clifford went upstairs to her room.

As promised, Than was waiting for them, stretched out on her bed with his eyes closed. She wanted to cross over the room and climb on top of his perfect body. She was studying him when he opened his eyes and gave her his brilliant smile.

"Sleepy?" she asked.

"A little."

"Did you hear what's happened?" She climbed on the bed next to him.

He sighed. "My sisters just returned from the Underworld. Grahib's in Tartarus now. McAdams had him killed for talking. He found out about tonight's failed attack."

"I'm scared," Therese said, and though it was true to some extent, she knew she should be a lot more frightened than she was. It was hard to be frightened when she felt so safe with Than.

He took her hand and kissed the inside of her palm. "I won't let anything happen to you. Now let's get your mind off of this. Are you ready to travel with me?"

"Yes." She got up and put on the silver silk robe. "What do I do?"

"Just hold my hand. This will feel a little weird." He stood beside her and took her hand. "Ready?"

"Ready."

Everything around her was bright—so bright she closed her eyes. Her body felt as if she were wrapped in tight plastic wrap. She couldn't move and could barely breathe, and the air seemed thick and impenetrable around her. She wasn't hot or cold, but the pressure was great, as it is when ascending in an airplane, and her ears popped. All of this happened within a few seconds. Then she felt the cool plastic wrap disintegrate, and she could breathe. She opened her eyes to find herself in the living room of the Melner cabin, and sitting on the cozy furniture were Than's two sisters and someone else—a glowing man with golden winged shoes on his feet. He looked up at Therese with astonishment.

"You shouldn't have brought her here," he said to Than.

Chapter Twenty-Five: Hermes, the Messenger

Than stepped forward. "I didn't know you were here, Cousin Hermes." Hermes stood and took Than's hand. "What has caused you to grace our presence?"

Therese noticed that Hermes was older looking and not as tall as Than, though his hair was the same dark brown, but curly rather than wavy, in tight knots around his head. His beard looked much the same as his hair. His pale red robes hung to his knees, and a wide gold belt secured the robes at his waist. The belt matched the golden shoes and the helmet lying beside him on the arm of the chair. He wouldn't blend with humans as well as the others without changing his wardrobe. "I bring grave news from Mount Olympus."

"How grave?" Than asked.

Meg frowned. "You may as well sit down, Than." She pointed to a chair, her diamond bracelets jangling. Her usual black go-go boots had been replaced by brown sandals, and her white silk pantsuit gave her a less intimidating look.

"First return the girl," Hermes suggested.

"This concerns her, too," Tizzie, in green silk and her emerald set, offered. "She should stay."

Therese could not imagine how any news from Mount Olympus, grave or otherwise, would have anything to do with her.

"Very well," Hermes replied. "Please come have a seat. Tonight will be long and grave for us all."

Before sitting down, Therese asked, "Shall I make us a pot of coffee?" She offered because she needed a cup herself, and she suspected the Melner cabin was well stocked.

Than squeezed her hand. "That sounds nice. Thank you."

So he'd heard of coffee, but not tea, Therese noted. Or maybe he just didn't want to bother with asking what coffee was. Hermes seemed anxious to talk.

Than and Hermes sat down while Therese crossed over to the kitchen, which was open to the living room, so she could still hear Hermes speaking as she rummaged through cabinets looking for coffee and filters.

"Zeus sent me to warn you that Ares is supporting this man, McAdams."

Therese froze like a statue.

Hermes continued, "He hopes to protect the potency of the biological weapon McAdams has already sold to numerous foreign coups. Ares's ultimate goal is to build a strong power in the Middle East to enable a third world war. He wants to see the U.S. fall."

Therese shuddered as she scooped the coffee grains into the filter. So they had been after her mother.

Than groaned. "No wonder."

"That's not all, brother," Meg said sardonically. "Listen."

Hermes said, "In an effort to keep you from winning over the girl, who might someday be a threat to him if made a goddess, Ares went to Cupid and convinced him to shoot his arrow into a mortal man who had a chance of wooing the girl away from you. The man has been struck, and his love is growing more and more devout every day."

Than shifted on the couch. "What's the mortal's name?"

Hermes replied, "Peter Holt."

Therese dropped the spoon on the kitchen floor, splattering coffee grains everywhere. She looked for a broom as Hermes continued.

"Aphrodite is sick over this, and so is Cupid now that he knows about Ares's intentions, but there's nothing they can do to prevent the mortal from loving the girl. However, both have sworn allegiance to you against Ares, and as we speak, Aphrodite is securing the support of

Apollo. You know how Ares feels about Aphrodite. Angry isn't strong enough to describe how he's feeling now."

Tizzie said, "Even so, Shining Apollo will be a useful ally."

"You speak as though there's a war," Than said.

"You haven't yet heard all, brother," Meg warned.

"In response to this move of Aphrodite's," Hermes said, "Ares went to Poseidon to seek his aid."

Therese finished cleaning up the coffee grounds, fitted the filter in the coffee maker, and added the pot of water. When she returned to the living room to take her spot beside Than on the couch, she noticed the worry in his face.

"Poseidon has agreed to stand by Ares," Hermes said. "Fortunately for you, Artemis has already pledged her allegiance to the girl."

"Her name is Therese," Than said. "So Artemis sides with Aphrodite? That's highly unusual. Those sisters of yours are typically at odds."

"Yes," Hermes agreed. "But Artemis is pleased with Therese's love for the animals and the forest. It makes no difference to her what Aphrodite chooses; Artemis wants to help the girl."

Therese's mouth dropped open. She couldn't believe she had attracted the attention of so many gods. She felt afraid and excited at once.

"Hades stands with us, of course," Tizzie added.

"At least for now," Hermes interjected. "He's miffed about his son making a choice that offends Ares. He wishes you would reconsider, but he will stand by his promise."

Than grimaced. "I will not reconsider. Only Therese's choice to remain a mortal can keep her from becoming my bride."

Therese felt faint. Than's love inflamed her, but the whole god and marriage situation was overwhelming.

Tizzie said, "But even with Hades on our side, Ares has a formidable threat against us. Along with Poseidon, Ares has his three daughters—the Amazons—and his wife, Enyo, and their children."

"Not to mention McAdams and his other men," Meg said.

"What about your father?" Than asked Hermes.

"Zeus and the others are still undecided. Hera will likely align herself against Aphrodite, but that is merely speculation." Then Hermes added, "This is the biggest rift between the gods since the Vietnam War. I can only imagine how it will end."

"What do you recommend, Hermes?" Than asked in a husky voice.

Hermes shook his head. "For now, I do not know. I wish to discuss some possibilities tonight. Ares is an evil, blood-lusting ass of a war-god, and I and my father despise him, but I fear for all who oppose him."

Therese got up to check on the coffee, and although the pot was only half full, she poured the four gods and herself a cup. Recalling Than and his sisters' love of sugar, she added generous, heaping teaspoons to each of the cups except her own. She put all five cups on a tray and served them. "It's hot," she said. "Be careful."

"Mmm," Meg purred. "Delicious. You can add coffee to your new list of bribes for me. Coffee and chocolate will get you what you want from me."

Tizzie added, "Don't forget a concert to boot."

"Thank you for the coffee," Hermes said to Therese. "And what is this I hear about a concert? Do you play a musical instrument?"

Therese blushed. "The flute." She hoped she wouldn't now be asked to perform. She had just learned an evil god helped to kill her parents and was behind tonight's attempt to kill her—not to mention the fact that Cupid unwittingly locked Pete's heart on hers, which started a chain reaction among the gods, the largest rift since the Vietnam War!

"The flute! That will please Athena. She invented it, you know, though some folks credit me with it. Perhaps some music would calm us after all this talk of strife and discord," Hermes said. "If you will play your flute, I will harmonize upon my pipe."

Therese was about to point out that her flute had been left behind when it dawned on her how easily that problem could be remedied now that she had her traveling robe. The last thing she wanted to do was disappoint a god, especially one who could easily change his allegiance. Maybe if she played with him, and played well, she would win his heart. She looked at Than, "Shall we pop back over to my place to get my flute?"

He gave her his brilliant smile and stroked her hair. "Aren't you too upset to play?"

Of course, she was, but she wasn't stupid. "Not for this company."

"That's a good girl," Hermes said.

Hermes smile cheered her. She stood up, took Than's hand, and together they traveled to her room where Clifford jumped from her bed and yelped with surprise.

"It's okay, Clifford," she said in a soft voice so Carol and Richard wouldn't hear. She slid her case and music stand from beneath her bed, grabbed some sheet music from her desk, and took Than's hand. "I'm ready," she said. Then to her dog, she said, "Be a good boy, Clifford. I'll be back."

Although the pressure made it hard to breathe for a few seconds, the trip to her house and back was otherwise effortless with the robe and Than's guidance. Her feet nearly fell out from beneath her both times she landed, but, fortunately Than was there beside her, with his arm around her waist, ready to catch her.

Therese played on her flute with Hermes on his pipe for a solid hour, which seemed a worthy investment since he said more than twice how much he liked her. And after, the four gods shared many stories about their lives, especially in the Underworld. Therese finally heard the complete story of Hercules and understood from Than's contributions and his reactions to the others that his opinion of Hercules was very low.

"His emotions got the best of him," Than complained. "He never stopped to use his head."

Meg laughed, "I'm not sure his head would have done him much good."

"Now there's a wonder," Hermes said. "Perhaps it's a testament to the values of humankind that such a one like Hercules, with no apparent intelligence, would be considered the greatest hero among the Greeks."

Tizzie added, "His temper got the best of him. Even I know the importance of temperance."

"He killed his wife and sons while enraged," Meg said. "Normally Tizzie would persecute such a heinous crime, but Hercules wanted to be tormented. He begged us to make him suffer. So Apollo told his oracle to send Hercules to a king he knew would come up with a just punishment. So the king commanded Hercules to complete twelve harsh labors."

"Hercules wasn't very smart," Hermes said, "but he was resourceful. First he had to kill a lion that no weapon could injure, and he solved that problem by using his own hands to choke the beast. Then he had to kill the Hydra, which had nine heads that would only grow back multiplied each time Hercules hacked one off. He eventually seared the necks as he chopped them to keep the heads from growing back."

"Iolaus brought him the iron," Than said. "Hercules didn't think of that on his own."

"He spent a year catching Artemis's sacred stag," Hermes continued. "Then he spent another year capturing a great boar from Mount Erymanthus. Let's see, after that he had to clean the Augean stables in a single day, which he did by shifting the flow of the river."

"But most of his labors required no cleverness," Than said. "Just brute force."

"True," Hermes agreed. "He had to drive away the birds plaguing the people of Stymphalus, fetch the savage bull Poseidon gave to Minos, and round up the man-eating mares of Thrace. What else? Oh, yes, bring back the girdle of Hippolyta, the queen of the Amazons. You've got to wonder why Apollo didn't intervene with that one."

"Now that right there is an example of what I mean when I say Hercules allowed his emotions to get the best of him," Than said. "He acted rashly, without reason. After all the help Hippolyta gave, he assumed she was responsible for the Amazon attack stirred up by Hera. He killed her without even offering her a chance to explain."

"We should have been granted access to him then," Meg snarled.

"But Hermes has told of nine. There were three more," Tizzie said. "He had to bring back the cattle of Geryon, who was a three-bodied monster, and then he ran into trouble with Atlas when he had to fetch the Golden Apples of Hesperides."

"But the hardest labor of all," Hermes said, "was the last. Hercules went to the Underworld and captured Cerberus, with Hades's permission. Poor Cerberus had to find his own way back."

"That's not when Hercules most offended me, even though he tied me up until I told him of Hades's permission," Than said. "I was there when he took Cerberus, and he wasn't cruel to the poor beast. I made sure of it. It was much later, after the Fates made their deal with his friend Admetus, that he angered me."

"What happened?" Therese asked.

Hermes shook his head. "When Hercules heard that his friend's wife had died, he rushed to the Underworld to retrieve her. If only he would have waited for more explanation."

"What do you mean?" Therese asked. "What explanation?"

Hermes said, "Long before, the Fates had hinted to Admetus that his life was about to end, and Admetus begged them to let him live. They said they would if he found another to take his place. Admetus asked everyone he knew, including his elderly parents, but no one wanted to die for him, until he asked his wife. So his wife took his place and went with Than to the Underworld."

Than grimaced. "I should have stopped Hercules when he came for her years later, but he was such an arrogant ass. I took pleasure in watching him put his foot in his mouth. When he came to me and pushed me aside, I was ready for him this time and could have easily taken him, but I knew that as soon as he delivered the woman to Admetus, Admetus would die, and Hercules would realize what he had done."

"That's not Disney," Therese mumbled.

Than had heard. "What?"

"Nothing," Therese didn't want to attempt to explain the Disney story of Hercules.

Than shook his head. "What man asks his wife to die in his place? That's plain cowardice."

Something clicked for Therese just then. Than was just, not cruel. Her admiration for him multiplied like the heads on the hydra.

"What?" he asked after she had looked at him for many seconds.

"Nothing," she smiled. In her mind, she said, "I'm falling in love with you."

He gave her a huge grin, as though he had heard her thoughts.

It was four in the morning when Therese and Than returned to Therese's bedroom. Now she was utterly exhausted, and Than had just a little over an hour to rest before getting up and heading to the Holt ranch for pen and barn duty.

Than waited with Clifford curled in his lap on top of her bed comforter while she changed clothes in her bathroom. When she returned to her bed in her nightshirt, Than pulled back the bedcovers for her. Her heart skipped a beat with anticipation. She crawled in between the sheets and lay back on her pillow. She looked up at him expectantly, suspecting he wrestled with his own desire, for she could see it in his face. Kiss me, she said in her mind. Oh, please, Than. Kiss me.

He pulled the covers over her body and up to her neck and tucked her in so that she was under and he over the comforter. He leaned down close to her face and brushed a few strands of hair from her eyes. "Your skin is so soft." He rolled onto his stomach and propped himself on his elbows and touched his fingers to her cheek. He ran a finger along her lips.

Therese closed her eyes as the longing swept through her. Please, Than. Kiss me.

He moved closer to her so that when he spoke, she could feel his breath on her skin. "You feel so good beneath my fingertips."

Her breaths came rapidly, and she felt like she was flying.

He whispered, "I've never touched someone as much as I've touched you." He smoothed her hair away from her face. "I've never longed for anything as much as I long for you."

Kiss me, she said in her mind. Please, Than. Kiss me.

"But I'm afraid," he whispered.

She opened her eyes. "Of what?"

"I'll take more of you than you're ready to give," he said breathlessly.

"I'm ready," she sighed, but she was frightened and excited and nearly out of breath.

His breaths were as rapid as hers, his brow bent in agony. "I might not have the strength to let you choose. If I kiss you now, if I take you now, I want it to be forever, but it's too soon, too soon for you to decide. I don't want to be like my father was with my mother."

"I want you," she breathed. "So you see, it won't be like that."

"Forever?"

She nodded. "Please kiss me."

He swallowed hard and then ever so gently touched his lips to hers.

She closed her eyes and was soaring now, spinning, her heart going wild. She touched her hands to his face and held him to her. Something electric passed between them. Oh, Than, she thought. I want to be with you forever!

He lifted his face.

She opened her eyes, and they shared a smile.

"You feel nice," he said. "But I want to give you more time. I want you to be absolutely sure. A week isn't long enough for such a decision." He kissed her lips once more and then stood up from the bed. "I'll see you tomorrow."

And before she could beg him to stay, he disappeared.

Chapter Twenty-Six: Tortured Than

Than returned to his chambers in the Underworld wishing he could be more like his father and sisters. They seemed less moved than he by feelings of compassion. They saw right and wrong, and they acted on justice.

"I'm weak. My father would find these thoughts pathetic."

If he could be more like the rest of his family, he would not be tormented now, tortured by the wrestling emotions, human emotions, disturbing every atom of his being. If he could be more like them, he would bring Therese down straight away without another thought the moment McAdams was found and brought to justice.

But he couldn't do it. He wanted to be sure she would be happy, and it seemed more and more plain to him that she could never find joy in such a dismally dark and lifeless place as his home.

He studied his rooms, looking at them as though for the first time, contemplating what Therese would think of them. The entrance was rather imposing, but he had to have Hephaestus make the jutting iron bars, like a giant jaw with jagged teeth, to keep away the constant threats by demigods. How often had Than had to listen to their arrogant claims to immortality as he guided their souls to Charon? "My father will punish you for this!" "Hermes will have your head!" "Zeus will never let you get away with this!" They spoke as though Than had any choice in the matter.

And of course, there were the powerful human souls who made themselves rich and famous, and when their threats failed to move Than, they resorted to bribery. "I can give you all the gold you desire." As if Than needed gold! The Underworld was full of it, and Than could have as much as he desired, if he desired it. But Than found gold to be worthless, overrated, and not the most comfortable material for adorning his home.

Of course, there were also the desperate souls, not necessarily powerful, but cunning, who every few centuries would find a way back to Than's door after the judges had proclaimed their sentence but before reaching their final destination. None of them succeeded in binding Than except Sisyphus and Hercules, but they had tried. The iron jaws at his entrance were made after Hercules's stunt, and since then, Than no longer had to deal with unexpected intruders.

But once one passed the intimidating entrance, the first chamber was quite pleasing. The dome shape of the rock walls provided a beautiful symmetry to everything in the room, from the leather club chairs by the cozy fireplace to the marble cabinets where he kept his goblets and wine and dishes that had been given to him by various gods, including the best wine from Dionysus. Along the opposite wall across from the fireplace flowed the Phlegethon with its bright flames illuminating all the rooms. Several instruments made for him by Hermes, Athena, and Apollo hung above the flames, and in the middle of the room were a table and two chairs. The second chair was rarely used, so seldom did he have visitors. But the occasional visitor from Mount Olympus, such as Aphrodite and her son, Cupid, Hera, Hermes, and his grandmother, Demeter, though they came for favors or information, would always find this chamber comfortable and welcoming, even if it did lack sunlight and wind. The flames from the Phlegethon produced no heat, and underground rock kept the room consistently cool, and although the humidity could be stifling at times, the running waterfall in the next chamber, where he slept, usually kept the air fresh and circulating.

From this front chamber, he entered his bed quarters, where the trickling waterfall helped him to sleep every so often when he needed rest. Unlike humans, he did not sleep every day, and not regularly, just when he needed to, perhaps once a month or less. The water fell from a high point in the dome-shaped room and cascaded over a series of rock shelves where Than kept a collection of shells given to him over the centuries by various people, such as Aphrodite, two different sea nymphs, the Maenads, and once, even Poseidon. A thick and living stalagmite growing in the center of the room served as a table for other possessions, such as the clock given to him by his father and made of precious stones, a tablet of Cyprus and a golden quill given to him by his mother, a moon rock from Hecate, and a pair of slippers that his brother made for him of lamb's wool. Leaning against it was a quiver with a dozen arrows made of bone.

Over his bed hung a steel sword in a golden sheath, made by Hephaestus, a bow given to him by Artemis, and a shield given to him by Zeus. His bed was round and made of a silk-lined mattress stuffed with goose feathers and draped with finely woven and magical linen, a gift from Athena.

His rooms were quite comfortable for him, but he doubted Therese would think so. There was no natural light and no living things, only the underground elements of stone and water. How could she ever come to love this place after living in her log cabin in the mountains of Colorado where the birds sang freely, the sunrises and sunsets painted the wide blue skies daily, and the green, lush trees towered in forests that rustled with all manner of life?

Chapter Twenty-Seven: Persistent Pete

Saturday morning, after taking hot coffee to the officer stationed on their back deck, Carol drove Therese the half mile down the road to Jen's house, and, as usual, Clifford went, too. As Therese stood on the gravel drive waving goodbye to her aunt, she noticed Than and Pete walking toward her across the grassy field in their jeans and boots with water glistening down their bare chests and their wet hair clinging to their heads. They were talking to one another and laughing. Therese watched them in awe, thinking to herself that life could really suck, but it could be really sweet, too.

Clifford ran across the road to greet the two boys, and that's when they looked up and spotted her.

Pete jogged across the road and gave her a wet hug. "Cold, huh? Wake you up, sleepy head!"

Therese bit her lip. Cupid's arrow seemed to be working. "Thanks a lot, Pete. You just wait."

He laughed and walked on to the pen.

Than came up with a dubious smile. "Hey."

"Hey." She could feel her entire face transform into a huge grin. He just had that effect on her.

Before she could say anything more, Jen screamed twice from behind the house, and Clifford took off toward her. With lightning speed, Than ran past Therese. By the time Therese caught up to them, Pete was there, too, and Jen was screaming, "Kill it! Kill it!"

Clifford barked ferociously.

On the ground several feet away from them lay a brownish snake with a yellow stripe down its back and white stripes down its sides. It was about three feet long, thin, stretched rather than coiled, and very still.

"I think it's already dead," Pete said. "Calm down, sis. It's just a garter snake. It's not poisonous."

"I don't care!" Jen shrieked. "Kill it! It's gross! It scared the crap out of me!"

Pete grabbed a shovel from the nearby shed.

"Wait!" Therese said. "Don't kill it if it's not poisonous." She went up to the snake and touched it. Although it barely moved, it was still alive. "It's hurt." She stroked its back. "Clifford, stop. It's okay."

Clifford stopped barking and watched her anxiously. She could feel Clifford's anxiety as he paced and whined.

"It's okay, boy," Therese said again.

"What are you doing?" Jen objected. "Quit touching it!"

Therese picked up the snake gingerly with both hands. She was afraid she might further injure it if she didn't handle it carefully. "If we leave it here, it will die. It needs food and protection from predators."

Jen looked furious. "Therese, we don't save snakes. We kill them. Remember what happened to Dumbo?"

"Yes, I remember!" Therese snapped. "How can you say that?" She held back the desire to push Jen down to the ground, and she clenched her jaw in anger. She already felt burdened with guilt over what happened to the horse. How could her friend say such a thing?

"Now girls," Pete said.

"Me? How can you want to save that, that thing?" Jen shouted.

"Jen, it can't help what it is," Therese said. "And it's not hurting anyone now."

"So what are you going to do with it?" Pete asked.

"Do you have a box I can have?"

"I'm sure I can find one somewhere around here. For now, you can put the snake in the bed of my truck."

"Maybe we could put a wet towel down." Therese walked with Pete toward the garage where his truck was parked next to Jen's and the Suburban. "And maybe we could leave the garage door open?"

"Sure." Pete walked close beside her.

"I don't believe this!" Jen complained. "It's a damn snake!"

"Language," Mrs. Holt said coming out of the house.

"But, Mom. This is crazy. Therese is saving a slimy ol' snake. I wanted Pete to kill it."

"I wanna see," Bobby chirped.

Therese couldn't hear them anymore once she was inside the garage with Pete.

"I'll run inside and get a wet towel," Pete said.

When he returned with the towel, he spread it out on the bed and then helped her to lift the snake onto it. The truck and garage were hot, which was good for the snake. It wouldn't get too cold on the wet towel. Therese stroked the snake several times while saying, "Thanks, Pete. Thanks for your help."

He moved closer to her and put his hand on her shoulder, and the close proximity of his bare chest made her shiver. He kissed the top of her head. "I don't know anyone like you, Therese Mills."

Just then Bobby burst in. "Where's the snake?"

"I'll go get a box," Pete mumbled.

Later, when they were grooming the horses, Than seemed distant. Therese was still angry at Jen for the Dumbo comment, and so she looked to the horse to soothe and comfort her as she brushed. "You're such a sweet thing," she cooed to Sugar. "Does that feel good?" Therese looked into the horse's eye and stroked her cheek. "You're so easy. Always so clean."

"And lazy," Bobby added.

Therese was grateful for Bobby, because he was the only one who seemed oblivious to the tension between the humans in the pen. If he had known how angry the two girls were at one another, he wouldn't have kept on talking in the otherwise silent company.

"Therese, did Jen tell you she and Matthew are going on a date tonight, just the two of them?" Bobby asked.

Therese shook her head.

"They're going to see a movie," he said. "But I doubt they'll be watching it."

"Shut up, Bobby," Jen said.

"Well, excuse me."

Therese finished Sugar and asked, "Who now, Mrs. Holt?"

"Why don't you take Annie?"

"I'm doing Annie," Jen griped.

"Chestnut, then," Mrs. Holt said.

Than walked Therese home with Clifford ambling behind as the trail riders showed up. Therese was supposed to call her aunt for a ride, but she felt safe with Than and wanted to be with him as much as she could. Her aunt would be cross, but she'd get over it. Therese carried the garter snake in a medium-sized cardboard box with the wet towel Pete got for her. Than still seemed distant. Maybe he thought she was stupid for wanting to save the snake. Maybe the enchantment was wearing off.

Unable to bear the silence for another second, she asked, "Do you think I'm crazy?"

He stopped in the road and turned to face her, his dark brown hair full of golden highlights from the sun. "What? Why would I think that?"

She kept walking, so he followed alongside her. "You know. The snake thing."

Hi voice was husky. "No. I don't think you're crazy."

"Then what's wrong? You're so quiet."

He let out a deep breath. "I'm having…doubts."

Her throat tightened. "Oh." Her heart beat so hard that she could hear it in her ears. She knew his attention had been too good to be true. She should have known it couldn't last. Tears pricked her eyes.

Maybe he had been in love with love, and she just happened to be the first girl to come along. Maybe now that he had spent some time on

Earth, he realized he should put more thought into such an important decision. Maybe he concluded that Therese wasn't right for him after all.

By the time they approached her gravelly drive, tears were streaming down her cheeks, and because she was carrying the box, there was nothing she could do to hide them. She tried wiping her cheeks on her shoulders, but she couldn't quite reach. She couldn't look at him. She was so embarrassed and full of despair that she just wanted to get to her room where she could cry in peace.

"Thanks for walking me home." She turned away from him and practically ran to the house.

Once inside, she went past Carol to the stairs. "I'm tired. I'm going to lie down for a while."

"You walked home?"

"Than was with me."

"Therese, please don't take chances like that. Does Than carry a gun? Is he a police officer? He's just another kid. You have to take this seriously. Understand? If the lieutenant thinks we're in enough danger to post a guard here, you shouldn't be walking!"

"I'm sorry." She really was sorry. If she had called her aunt, she might have avoided hearing about Than's doubts.

Then Carol added, "Pete just called. He wants you to call him back."

"Okay. Thanks."

"What's in the box?"

"It's a snake. It's not poisonous. It's hurt."

"Are you crying?"

"No. I'm fine. I just need to be alone."

She expected Carol to say something more but was relieved when she didn't. She went upstairs to her room, put the box on the desk next to Jewel's tank, and let the tears come raining down.

How could he have doubts?

Before she could kick off her shoes, the phone rang.

"Hello?"

"Oh, good. You're home." It was Pete.

Disappointment flooded through her. She had hoped it was Than calling to apologize, to explain why he had been so quiet, to tell her he wanted to be with her forever. "Hi. What's up?"

"I talked Jen into letting us tag along with her and Matthew tonight, to the movies. Sound good?"

"Um, I don't know." Was he asking her out, or was this a group thing? And should she encourage him if Cupid's arrow was really at work? On the other hand, if Than had changed his mind about her, maybe Pete could be a helpful diversion from the horrible pain in her heart.

Pete added, "Don't be mad at Jen. She was just freaked out. She's terrified of snakes and thinks that garter will eventually find its way back here when you let it go."

"If it lives. I'm not so sure it'll make it." Then she said, "Hey, aren't you supposed to be on the trail ride?"

"Bobby went. I have the next one. So, do you wanna go tonight?"

Should she? What else was she going to do now that Than was dumping her? Mope around all night? She knew if she didn't do something to distract her she'd sink down into that deep dark place she inhabited in the few weeks after…her life had changed. "That sounds good. Let me check with my aunt and I'll call you back."

After she hung up the phone, she collapsed on her bed and sobbed some more. Clifford jumped up next to her and licked her face.

"Thanks, boy," she said, her voice breaking up with weeping.

"Why are you crying?" came a woman's voice which Therese did not recognize.

Therese froze. Clifford stopped licking but didn't bark. Slowly, she turned to see an amazingly majestic woman with glowing pale skin and long black hair standing in the room across from her. She wore a white short gown, golden boots, and a golden helmet. Beneath the helmet, her amazing blue-gray eyes stared directly at Therese.

"Who are you?" Therese gasped, wondering if she should get down on her knees.

The woman smiled. "I will answer your question if you answer mine. Why are you crying?"

Therese decided to be perfectly honest. "Um. For one thing, both my parents recently died."

"Go on."

"Then a horse I was riding was injured and had to be…put down."

"Yes?"

"And now a boy I thought really liked me has changed his mind."

"I see." The woman took off her helmet. "And now I will answer your question. My name is Pallas Athena. I am the daughter of Zeus. He is my one and only beloved parent, and, presently, he is upset, like you. But his tears become showers and his rage thunderbolts."

Therese could barely breathe. She didn't move. "Is he upset because of me?" she asked in a small voice.

Athena narrowed her eyes. "Do you think so highly of yourself that you could be the cause of his sorrow, his rage?"

Therese covered her mouth and shook her head. When she could, she said, "No, m'am. Hermes said…"

"Hermes has spoken to you?" Athena hissed.

Therese wished she could disappear. "He didn't seek me out. We, we met by accident." In a desperate voice, she added, "Look, if you want to kill me, please just go ahead." Then she put her arms around Clifford and thought better of it. Who would care for her pets?

"I didn't come to kill you, but to test you." Athena's voice was no longer harsh. "I came disguised as a serpent, and you took pity on me when others wished me dead. I see you have a kind and compassionate heart, and you are worth saving. Unlike Ares and Poseidon who stand with McAdams, and Aphrodite and Apollo who stand with Thanatos, I, like Artemis, stand with you. However, both of us wish you to reconsider your desire to become the wife of Thanatos. He is a good and kind and noble god, but his ghastly life is not the kind of life for someone like you who loves all living things. Furthermore, to marry a god carries many risks, as the males are usually unfaithful. When my brother Apollo wished to marry a maiden named Daphne, she would rather be changed into a laurel and spend eternity as a tree because she feared the warring among jealous female divinities. Think before you act."

Therese at first was stunned, her eyes wide. Daphne would rather be a tree? Forever? She swallowed and cleared her throat and picked at her sleeve. "Thank you, Pallas Athena. I don't know what to say, except that I don't think it's an issue anymore, my going with Thanatos. He's, he's changed his mind."

"Good. That is as it should be." And with that, Pallas Athena vanished.

Therese sat still and bewildered for several minutes after the goddess left. When the shock of the visit finally wore off, she checked in the cardboard box to be sure the snake wasn't still there and the entire event a bizarre hallucination. But the snake was gone, and in its place was a golden heart-shaped locket. She reached into the box and took it in her hand. The locket was secured to a delicate gold chain. She opened the locket. Inside, she found an inscription in slanting, flowing letters that read: "The most common way people give up their power is by believing they have none."

Therese closed the locket and clutched it to her heart. She opened the locket and read the inscription again. Why had Athena given her this message?

Therese put the locket on her dresser and went to her bathroom to take a hot shower. The water running down her tense body calmed her after the strange events of the day. Although the gift from Athena made her happy, the overall disappointment she felt from Than's behavior today was like a suffocating blanket that could not be lifted away nor washed off with the heat of this shower. Once more, tears streamed down her face. She wondered how a person could never run out of tears.

Afterward she changed into a t-shirt and cotton shorts and, with her hair still wet, climbed beneath her covers to take a nap. Clifford followed her and curled up near her hip. The lack of sleep during Hermes's visit had caught up with her, so despite the despair, the dread, and the awe, once she closed her eyes, it wasn't long before she fell asleep.

Now she was in the Melner cabin looking for the restroom. "Restroom?" she asked Hermes.

He pointed to a toilet in the middle of the living room.

From where they sat around her on the living room furniture, Meg sneered and Tizzie shrugged.

"Go ahead," Than said from behind.

Therese's bladder was about to burst, so, very quickly, she crossed the room to the toilet, but with all the eyes on her, she could not bring herself to pull down her jeans and go.

"Never mind," she said. "I'm late for school."

She grabbed her backpack, sitting by the front door, and ran out to the dirt road just as the school bus drove by toward the dam.

"No!" she shouted from the middle of the road after it had gone right past her.

Then she heard another bus coming and saw its dim headlights emerging from the Holt place, so she waved her hands to flag it down, but it sped past without noticing her.

She bit her lip, and her teeth moved, like they were loose. She touched a front tooth with her finger, and the tooth fell out. Then she smiled. "This must be a dream."

She put the tooth back in place, ditched the backpack, and sailed through the air.

"Yep. It's a dream. I can do whatever I want."

She flew back to the Melner cabin and went up to Than. She was furious with him but feeling desperate. He had been the medicine that would help her get over losing her parents. If he abandoned her now, she would be left with nothing but her grief. She couldn't take that.

"I'm going to make you change your mind," she promised him. "I'm going to make you love me again." She took his face in her hands and planted a passionate kiss on his lips right there in front of Meg, Tizzie, and Hermes.

"Figments, show yourselves!" a voice came from behind her.

Than, his sisters, and Hermes vanished, and in their place were four scaly eels, whirring through the air and giggling. They flew out of the windows and the open front door.

Therese turned to see Hip standing behind her. He was tall and well-built like his brother, but his hair was blond and his blue eyes deeper set. He wore white trousers and a white open shirt.

"You still owe me a kiss," he said. "A real kiss. That last one didn't count."

She frowned. "Aren't you supposed to be guiding the dead?"

"My brother returned to give me a brief reprieve. Zeus would have eventually commanded it." He took a few steps closer to her. "My kiss? For the tour? Remember?"

"Oh yeah." She closed her eyes and puckered her lips. When he didn't kiss her, she opened her eyes to find him sulking. "What's wrong?"

"That's not how you kissed that figment you thought was my brother. I want you to kiss me like you kissed it."

Her eyes widened. Then she narrowed them. "That wasn't part of the deal. You said a kiss. You didn't say what kind." She sighed. "Besides, I don't think I have it in me to kiss anyone right now with your brother no longer in love with me and then there's Pete forced by Cupid's arrow to love me against his will."

"What? Gods can't force people to do anything. Humans have free will—while they're alive, anyway. Cupid's arrow can only enhance and make compelling a feeling that was already there."

"Really?" This cheered her, to know that Pete had already felt something for her before the gods interfered, that he wasn't being forced against his will to like her.

"Now can I have my kiss?"

She was a little uplifted by this news, so she put her arms around him and planted a grateful, albeit not passionate, kiss on his mouth.

"That's better." He grinned.

"Will you answer one more question?" She gave him a flirtatious smile.

"You know the fee." He put his face close to hers.

"Why did Than change his mind about me?"

Hip's smile turned into a scowl. "How am I supposed to know? Can't you ask me a question I can answer?"

"Okay, okay. Calm down. Maybe you can answer this: When will Than return to Earth?"

"Tomorrow. Though why should you care if he's changed his mind? Forget him, Therese. You can have me." He held his arms, spread wide, palms up, with a sweet but devilish grin.

"Like I said, I have a feeling you're not a one-girl kind of guy."

He threw back his head with a loud guffaw. "You know me too well. Now give me my kiss."

As she leaned in to meet his lips, she heard a loud crash and snapped awake. She sat up in her bed and looked around. She was alone with her pets. It was thundering and raining outside. Was the storm caused by Zeus's rage and sorrow?

She looked at her clock. Six o'clock! She had slept for six hours? She still hadn't called back Pete. She ran downstairs to get permission from Carol to go to the movies, and then returned upstairs to call the Holts.

"Sorry about earlier," Jen said on the phone.

"Me, too."

It was still thundering and pouring down rain when Pete and Jen drove up the drive in Pete's truck to pick her up. She huddled beneath the umbrella feeling her curly hair get frizzier with each step she took toward the vehicle. She was glad she had decided to wear it pulled back at the nape of her neck in a wide, thick barrette. At least the frizzies would stay out of her face.

Pete opened the passenger side for her and helped her in the front seat. Jen sat in back. So maybe this was a date after all.

"Where's Bobby?" Therese asked as she fastened her seat belt.

"He spent all his money on a new gaming station," Jen said. "Plus, I didn't really want him to come. He's so immature."

"Is Matthew meeting us there?"

"We're picking him up," Pete said. "That's why Jen's sitting in back. She doesn't want you anywhere near him."

"Shut up, Pete," Jen punched his arm.

"Yeah, right," Therese said. "Like she's got anything to worry about."

"How's the snake?" Pete asked.

Therese thought fast. "Good. I'm going to find it a home. There's a snake farm in Pagosa Springs."

"Good idea," Jen said. Then she leaned forward. "Hey, is that a new necklace?"

Therese fingered the locket at her throat. "Um, yeah. Sort of. Well, it was my mom's." Like she could really tell them a goddess named Pallas Athena transformed from a garter snake and gave it to her.

"Oh." Jen sat back. "It's really pretty."

Pete glanced at her throat. "It looks nice on you."

"Thanks."

They were silent now as Pete drove through the winding country roads with the rain beating down on the truck. Therese was glad to be with her friends, but she missed Than and still despaired over his change of heart. She knew she should stop thinking about him altogether, but she couldn't no matter how hard she tried. She peered across the bench seat at Pete looking as handsome as ever, but even his charm and good looks could not help her forget Than. It was too late. She was in love and feeling rather desperate.

Guilt flooded over Therese when she recalled she was supposed to be going to the movies with Vicki. She needed to remember to call her tomorrow to make arrangements before her feelings were totally hurt.

During the movie, Jen and Therese sat beside one another with the boys on either end. She mostly whispered to Jen, but about halfway through the film, Pete put his arm around Therese, and she stiffened. She tried to relax, to remind herself that he was her friend and this could be comfortable, but it felt totally wrong. After several minutes, she excused herself to use the restroom. Jen came with her.

"What am I going to do about Pete?" Therese asked her when they were at the sink washing their hands. "I think he likes me."

"And you don't like him?" Jen crossed her arms and lifted an eyebrow, which disappeared behind her straight blonde bangs.

"I like him a lot. But I think I'm in love with Than."

Jen slipped a tube of lipstick from the front pocket of her jeans. "Than's leaving soon. Long distance relationships suck. You should let it go." She pressed the lipstick to her lips.

"And Pete's going to college. What's the difference?"

Jen held the lipstick out to Therese.

"Thanks." Now it was her turn to apply the makeup.

"He's not going after all. He decided to stay and help mom with the horses and work gigs with his band."

"That's stupid." Therese handed over the tube and rinsed her hands again.

"He doesn't think so. And neither does Mom. She's glad he's staying."

Therese dried her hands and said nothing.

"Give Pete a chance," Jen said in a pleading voice. "Just think. If you two got married one day, we'd be sisters."

"This isn't about us."

One of the stalls on the end burst open, and out walked Gina Rizzo wearing tight jeans, rhinestone boots and matching belt, and big silver earrings. Her blonde hair was twisted up in a clip and spilling down the back of her head. "Hey, guys. What's this I hear about Pete and Therese? Are you two dating now? I thought that was you I saw in front of me in line. I can't wait to tell Maddy and Katie."

"We're not dating," Therese said.

"Sure you're not." She washed her hands at the sink and ripped off a piece of paper toweling. "Later, girls."

Apparently it didn't matter if your parents died. The school bitch would show no mercy.

After the movie, a lame comedy with a disappointing ending, they stepped out of the theater to find the rain had stopped and the night sky was clear and full of twinkling stars. The air was cool, so Therese zipped the front of her jacket.

"Cold?" Pete asked. He put an arm around her as he walked her to his truck.

"Let's go dancing," Matthew said from behind. "Want to?"

"Yeah," Jen said. "Great idea, Matthew. What do you guys think?"

"Sounds good to me." Pete pointed his clicker at the truck to unlock the doors. "Therese?"

"I don't know. I'm kind of tired."

"But you napped for six hours!" Jen reminded her.

Therese climbed into the truck. "I know, but I think I might be coming down with something. I don't feel that great."

Pete patted her leg from behind the wheel. "That's okay, then. Let's go home. And hey, Mom doesn't do trail rides on Sunday, so why don't you sleep in tomorrow? I'll cover your grooming for you since you're not feeling well."

"Come on, Therese," Jen said. "Don't ruin it for the rest of us. You're just upset about Than."

Therese flashed her a fierce look. "Shut up, Jen."

Pete's smile faded as he turned the key in the ignition. "Drop it, Jen."

Chapter Twenty-Eight: Back to the Dead

Than could no longer put off giving his brother a reprieve from guiding the dead, for he could feel tension building somewhere, either among the humans or the gods or both, and so, since he wasn't sure, anyway, how he should proceed with Therese, he decided this day would be as good as any to return to his duties.

Hip appeared to Than where he hovered over the deep granite abyss that seemed to have no end to the darkness below. "Thanks, bro'," Hip said, too anxious to stop and chat. He flew on by and went straight to the poppies and into the realm of the dreamers.

Than hadn't been there for a full second when he sensed the souls of many ready to be guided. He disintegrated into five and dispatched to three different regions of the world.

One of the souls in his custody proved to be a small old woman kneeling in her garden bed. Her body lay in a heap in the grass with a spade in her gloved hand and a plant with its root ball exposed, as though she were about to plant it before she died, and her hand had clutched it and stiffened. The foliage on the plant, which Than did not know, since he knew nothing about such things, was withering, dying along with its caretaker. Much to his astonishment, as the woman's soul climbed from the heap in the grass and turned toward him, bewildered as all souls of the dead were, she held in one hand a projection of the withered plant. Never before in the history of his existence had he seen a plant-like soul accompany a human. Plenty of animals, billions of them, and at times even insects, had come with him to Charon to be taken over to the other side and, unlike the humans who must be judged, guided straight into the waters of the Lethe and its everlasting oblivion. Cats and dogs and other pets sometimes came with their hu-mans when they died together, and the animals were allowed to go with their humans to the Elysian Fields; but never had Than seen a plant-like soul, and so he stood a moment, transfixed.

"Who are you?" the woman finally asked.

"Death," he answered, as he always did. "Your time has come. Take my hand."

"But I hadn't finished yet," she said. "My garden's nearly done. Look. I have one more to plant. Can you wait?"

The answer was always no, though because of the circumstances, Than hesitated before saying so. "Don't worry," he said in a calming voice, and together they hovered over the land toward the abyss, and as they flew, she spoke to him as so many others had before her.

"How will my husband manage without me? He's disabled. He can't care for himself. Who will cook for him? What will he do?"

"Someone will take over your duties. Someone always does."

"I didn't get to say good-bye. He'll be so shocked. He might even go into cardiac arrest."

"And then he can join you. Come this way."

As they approached Charon and his raft, Charon also noticed the plant and furrowed his brow. "What's this?" he asked.

The woman looked at the plant in her hand. "This? It's Lily of the Nile. I didn't get to finish planting it. I was just about to. May I go back and finish?"

Charon shook his head.

"Have you seen this before?" Than asked. He allowed the woman's feet to touch the bank of the river, knowing it would calm her.

"Yes," Charon said as Than and the woman boarded the raft. "But not often. It happened twice in Hermes's time."

"Do plants have souls?" Than asked.

"That is a question for your father, Thanatos," Charon replied.

Than disintegrated and dispatched another of himself to Hades's palace, where he found his father engaged with Hermes.

The two gods looked agitated, and when they felt Than enter the chamber, they stopped talking and turned their faces toward him.

"Is something wrong?" Than asked.

"Always," Hades said, "But I was about to ask you the same question."

"It can wait, if you're busy," Than replied.

"Out with it, son."

"All right then. " He swallowed, feeling foolish now and embarrassed. "Do plants have souls?"

Hades narrowed his eyes. "The gods are about to break into war and you come here asking about plants?"

"I said it could wait, Father. You insisted. And the gods are always on the brink of war. Questions are meant to be asked and, when they can be, answered."

Hades sat up on his throne and looked down his thin nose at Than. A hint of a smile tugged at the corners of his mouth. Then he said, "Bravo. Yes, Thanatos. How right you are."

"So? Charon told me Hermes has seen something resembling a plant soul twice. I saw one just now. What does this mean?"

Hermes started to speak, and then stopped, looked at Hades, and waited.

Hades plucked at his beard, deep in thought. "Some do," he said. "Plants have been evolving since as long as I can remember, and some have gone beyond simple sensory reflexes, such as turning to face the sun to make food. Some seem to be infused with a primitive consciousness, like those of many insects, and when it is coupled with a deep bond with a sentient being, a kind of symbiosis seems to be awakened between the sentient being and the plant being. Plant souls have never come here of their own accord, but in the company of a caring human soul, they have on the three rare occasions you have mentioned. I suspect we shall see more of this in the centuries to come."

Than felt a flicker of happiness and a lightness of spirit as he pondered the ramifications of his father's words. He said, "I want the woman's Lily of the Nile for my rooms. Is that possible? She won't remember it once she reaches the streams of the Lethe. I want to change the circumstances of my dwelling by infusing it with more life. Can I keep the plant?"

Hades shrugged. "It makes no difference to me."

Another thought occurred to Than. "If I can maintain a plant soul in my rooms, what of animal souls? We have Cerberus and your steeds, Swift and Sure, but they were immortal from their birth, so I never considered adding other animals as companions down here. If I can have the Lily of the Nile without any consequences to you and to the rest of the world, why not a dog or a hamster?"

Hermes fell to the floor overcome with laughter. Hades soon laughed along with him. Than stood with his mouth agape.

"What's so funny?"

"Never in a million centuries," Hades managed to say in between laughs, "would I have ever imagined that one of my sons would come to me asking if he could have a pet!"

"How human of you!" Hermes added, holding onto his belly.

Than felt his face flush, but he stood his ground. "And your answer then I presume is yes?"

Hades nodded but could not speak, for when he looked at Hermes rolling on the floor, he broke out in another fit of laughing.

Than had other questions for his father, very serious and private ones, but he knew he would have to wait till Hermes left to ask them.

Chapter Twenty-Nine: Than's Apology

Therese was walking between her parents as they crossed the Royal Gorge Bridge, over a thousand feet above the raging Arkansas River, when she heard someone behind them call her name.

It was Gina Rizzo, and with Gina were about twenty scraggily men wearing turbans and carrying swords.

"Get them!" Gina shouted.

Therese and her parents started to run, but Therese slipped, lost her balance, and fell over the side of the bridge. Her parents reached their hands out to her from on top of the bridge, but it was too late. Therese was free falling a thousand feet toward the bottom.

She could make out various shapes in the solid granite formations all around her as she fell closer and closer to the raging river below. One group of rocks resembled a giant hand, like that of a god. That triggered an idea in Therese's mind.

I'm dreaming.

She stopped herself midair and sailed up through the gorge. She turned several somersaults in the air to be sure. Yes! She was relieved to discover she would not crash to her death against rocks or in the raging river, but even more than that, she was glad to have a means to find Than. First she would seek out Hip.

She stuck a fist out and flew out of the gorge. She hadn't gotten very far when Hip appeared.

"Nobody establishes lucidity during a free fall," he said, flying beside her. "You are spectacular to watch. What a treat."

"Why thank you. I'm glad you find me so entertaining. But I need your help. I want you to take me to Than."

"I can't do that."

She put her hands on her hips. "Why not?"

"You'll die."

"Just for a second. Just long enough to give him a message. Then you can pull me away."

He crossed his arms in front of his chest and grumbled, "Sorry. It's impossible. Got to go."

Hip vanished from her sight.

Therese decided to try another route. "Thaaaaannaaaatos! Thaaaaaaannaaaaaatos!" She would keep screaming his name until he came to her. "Thaaaaaannaaaaatos!"

The sound of her own voice woke her. "Thanatos," she mumbled, not quite the yell she envisioned in her dream. Clifford sprang to his paws and looked at her, wagging his nub of a tail. "Sorry, boy," she said. "It was just a dream."

She looked at her clock. "Ten? I slept till ten o'clock?" She sat up in her bed and rubbed her neck. It was hot this morning, and the sun coming through the trees and in her windows was unusually bright. She crawled from her covers and went to her bathroom, trying to recall the details of her dream. She knew she had been looking for Than and hadn't been able to find him. Hip refused to help her. Maybe Than had warned Hip to keep her away from him. After brushing her teeth, she came back to her room and turned on Jewel's lamp.

"Good morning, sunshine," she said in a friendly voice to her tortoise, who hadn't yet opened her eyes.

"Good morning," a voice answered. It was Than's.

She turned to the window, thinking he was on the ground below, but he wasn't. He was in the room with her. He wore the white trousers and white shirt from her earliest dreams, before he had come to Earth.

"I heard you calling me." He fidgeted with the hem of his white open shirt. "Sorry it took so long. I was waiting for Hip to relieve me."

She resisted the urge to run into his arms. He was bathed in sunlight, and his dark wavy hair looked soft to the touch. "Why did you leave?"

He scratched his chin. "I needed to give the humans a break from their dreamless nights."

She ran her fingers through her messy hair. "I wish, I wish you would have told me you were going." She rubbed beneath her eyes, hoping there weren't mascara rings.

"I'm sorry." He crossed the room and pushed a strand of her hair that must have been poking straight up over to the side.

A wave of heat surged through her. She couldn't meet his eyes. "Than, I know you've changed your mind about me. But I just want you to know, I want you to know that I haven't changed mine."

He lifted her chin. His blue eyes were bright in the sunlight. "What makes you think I've changed my mind about you?"

"You, you said you had doubts," she stammered.

His face broke into a grin. "About taking you as my wife, but not about how I feel."

"What's the difference?"

He stepped back and fell into a chair beneath her window. Clifford jumped into his lap, and Than pet him. "I've made such a mess of your life. You had an ordinary human life, and now I've pulled you into a war between gods. Not to mention the fact that you adore life and would probably despise the Underworld."

She stepped closer to him. "Go lie down, Clifford." Clifford sulked over to his pillow in the corner beneath her other window. She looked at Than, trying to muster up courage. Finally she blurted, "I don't care about all of that. God, Than, I just want to be with you. Can't you see that? Why can't that be all that matters?"

He stood up and took her in his arms.

"Just tell me the truth," she demanded. "Do you love me or not?" Tears threatened to spill down her cheeks.

He returned the intensity of her gaze. "I do," he said in a husky voice. Then he covered her mouth with his and gave her a deep, lusty kiss. "I do love you," he said again.

A hunger like she'd never known took possession of her, and she wrapped her arms around his neck. A feverish, burning sensation flamed through her skin. Her heart either pounded frantically or stopped altogether; she could no longer tell. She grabbed fistfuls of his soft dark hair and pressed her body against him. Her knees trembled. She held on for dear life.

He took her up in his arms and carried her to her bed just as she was about to fall. He laid her down on her back and knelt on the floor beside her. She took his face in her hands and kissed him.

"I love you, too," she said in between kisses. "You're all I think about." She kissed him again. "I don't want to live without you." Then she said, "And if you leave me again, I swear I'll kill myself to be with you."

He stopped and lifted his face to look into her eyes. "Don't say that, Therese. Promise me you'll never do that to yourself."

"No."

"If you love me, promise me."

"If you love me, don't make me promise."

"Then there's only one thing to do."

"What?" Fear pricked her skin.

Than grinned. "Introduce you to my parents."

He covered her lips with his and she laughed with joy. She laughed so hard, she couldn't stop. Clifford pranced around the room.

"I'm sorry," she said, still laughing, almost hysterical now. "I'm so sorry."

He laughed at her and plopped beside her on the bed. "Don't apologize. I love to hear you laugh. I rarely hear laughter."

He blushed, and she wondered why, but instead of asking, she broke into another fit of laughter.

"I can't stop. I can't breathe."

"I seem to have that effect on people lately."

His hand at her waist sobered her, and she caught her breath. "You make me so happy. I like you so much."

He rolled to his back. "I've never been happier." Then he sat up. "Hey, I have an idea." He had a curiously sneaky expression on his face.

"What?"

"Let's travel the world together today. Let's start with Paris. I've heard it's the most romantic city."

She sat up with her mouth hanging open. "Are you serious? Paris?"

"And London, and Tokyo, and Honolulu, and Cairo, and all the places I've been to but never visited properly."

"What will I tell my aunt?"

"The truth. Tell her you're spending the day with me."

With her traveling robe from Aphrodite and her golden locket from Pallas Athena, Therese held on to Than's hand in front of the Melner cabin and closed her eyes against the bright light. The invisible plastic wrapped itself around her, and she held her breath, but soon the pressure was gone and she could open her eyes.

First they arrived in Paris, in the Louvre for just a minute and held hands while they gazed at the Mona Lisa, where a fashionably dressed woman complimented her robe and wanted the name of the designer. Therese grinned at Than and explained it was a gift; she didn't know. Although it was lunchtime in Durango, the sun was just about to set here.

"How about a cruise?" Than asked.

"How will we pay?"

Than pulled out a wallet from his trouser pocket. "My father gave me this before I left. It's magical. The paper bills become the currency of whatever country I am in at the time. See?" He pulled out the bills and showed her they were euros.

They boarded a private dinner cruise near the Eiffel Tower and sat outside on deck in the cool evening. A light breeze blew from the Seine, and the soft sound of violins lingered in the air. While the sun sank behind the Eiffel Tower, they ate omelets and soup.

While they ate, Therese asked Than a few questions about what it was like to be a god.

"Can you hear people's thoughts?" she asked, taking a sip of her Diet Coke.

"Only when a person prays directly to me."

"Does that happen often?"

"Yes, but people pray to me under the false assumption that I have anything to do with the timing of their or their loved one's death, so I tune them out. It just makes me sad." He looked into her eyes and smiled. "But your prayers to me are different." He winked. "Finally, instead of begging me to postpone my visit, or pleading for me to take them swiftly to avoid the agonizing pain, somebody actually wants me just for me, for my company. You can't know how exhilarating that is."

Color rushed to her face. "Wait a minute. Do you hear me every time I speak to you in my mind?"

A huge grin crossed his face.

"The other night..." she dropped off.

"When you begged me to kiss you?" he teased. "And when you complimented my butt?"

She licked her lips. "Okay, I'm going to have to be more careful."

"Don't."

She tried to recall other times she might have said things to him in her mind. Color rushed to her face, but what did it matter? He knew how she felt. Why should she hide her feelings from him?

When they had finished eating, Than said, "Let's go see another sunset, this time in London. We have to hurry. The sun's about to set."

They leaned on the rail of London Bridge looking out over the Thames as the setting sun cast its golden hues across the water. A crisp breeze carrying the smell of rain blew into their faces. A shower was on its way. Sure enough, within ten minutes, it began to drizzle, but they stayed to enjoy it.

Therese asked another question. "Can you make yourself invisible and eavesdrop on what others are saying?"

"Yes." He looked down as color came across his face.

"You look guilty. Have you ever done that before?"

He shrugged and the corners of his mouth turned up. "Maybe."

"Have you ever eavesdropped on me?"

"Once or twice perhaps."

She punched his arm. "Tell me everything, Than. I mean it! I want to know!"

The rain came down a little harder now, sending chills down Therese's back.

"Let's get out of this rain first." Than put both arms around her.

They took a taxi past Buckingham Palace, and drove around until the rain stopped. Then they strolled through St. James Park as the sky turned into night. "Please tell me?" Therese asked now that there were no other people around them.

"Let's pop over to Tokyo first. It's late morning there."

They took another cab over Rainbow Bridge and gazed at the cityscape, the sun just coming up from the east.

"That's Tokyo Tower, I believe." Than pointed to the tallest tower in the city.

"Yes, sir," the cab driver said. "The tallest one there. Also known as the Sky Tree Tower."

"It's beautiful," Therese said. "Now let's go someplace where we can talk."

"How about Cairo for dessert?"

"I better call my aunt," Therese said, getting out her cell.

The cab driver gave them an astonished glance in the rearview mirror. "That may take a day of travel, sir."

"Just drop us at the nearest museum," Than said.

Although by Durango time, the hour was late, approaching ten o'clock at night, it was sunrise in Cairo. They looked out over the Pyramids of Giza and gazed for a long while at the magnificent Sphinx, with its lion body and human head, before heading to a restaurant for dessert, or what was to the other tourists' breakfast. On their way to the Lakeside Café, they strolled through Al-Azhar Park and caught a glimpse of the mosques and the Citadel. The café itself was a cluster of white pavilions floating on a lake with citrus groves visible through the screens. They ordered coffee and Baqlawa, which the waiter had explained was made of many layers of paper-thin dough with a filling of crushed nuts and sugar between the layers. Once the waiter left to fill their order, Therese asked her question again.

"So tell me. When did you eavesdrop on me?"

Than rolled his eyes. "You aren't going to forget about this, are you?"

"You promised."

The waiter returned with their coffee.

"Thanks," Therese said.

Once the waiter left again, she said, "So?"

"Okay. Remember the first day you came to work for the Holts, and you had lunch with Jen?"

"No way! You were listening?" She tried to recall what she had said. Jen had liked him then, too. She shrieked and covered her mouth. She had talked about her boobs!

He laughed at her, like he knew what she was thinking.

"When else?"

"I may have listened in on a few of your conversations both times we went to the Wildhorse Saloon."

"Oh my God!"

"Like I said. You can call me Than."

She slapped his arm. "Quit saying that!"

"I just wanted to be sure you weren't already in love with someone else. So many guys asked you to dance. I worried you were in love with them all."

She threw her head back and laughed.

"I might not have been wrong about Pete, though. I heard you went out with him last night." Than frowned.

Their dessert arrived.

"What's this called again?" Therese asked the waiter.

"Baqlawa."

"Mmm, it looks good," Therese said. "Thank you." When the waiter left, she said, "Were you there with us at the movie theater?" She dug her fork into the pastry and took a bite. "Oh my gosh, this is so good."

"I'm glad you like it." He took a bite. "Mmm. You're right. It's delicious."

"So were you at the theater?"

"No. I had to work. But just before I left, I heard Pete call and ask you to go, and you said you'd ask your aunt."

"You were there? In my room?"

Than blushed. "Are you angry with me?"

"I'm only angry that you didn't make yourself visible and kiss me, especially when you saw me crying."

"Yeah. It was hard not to take you in my arms."

"I'm angry that you didn't."

"I'm sorry."

She sipped her coffee. "The waiter probably thinks we're crazy eating this for breakfast."

"I doubt it. He's probably used to international travelers. Plus, people do sometimes eat it for breakfast here."

Therese smiled. She never would have referred to herself as an international traveler, but she supposed that's what she was today. "So then you saw my visit with Pallas Athena? And you know about my locket?"

"No. She gave you a gift?" He looked flabbergasted.

"There's an inscription." She opened the locket and tucked in her chin so she could read it. "The most common way people give up their power is by believing they have none." She closed the locket and lifted her chin. "I guess she wants me to believe in myself more." Then she added, "Too bad you weren't there. It was really awesome."

"Yeah, I left as soon as she transformed from the snake." He swallowed a sip of his sweet iced tea, loaded with extra sugar. "I didn't want to anger her. She would have sensed my presence."

"Did you know she was the snake all along?" She loaded her fork.

"Not at first. I sensed her later, when we were walking home from the Holts', which is part of the reason I didn't go into depth with you about how I was feeling. I didn't want her to overhear."

"Oh. That makes sense now. But you scared me, you know. I was so hurt."

He looked penitent. "I'm sorry. I really was thinking of you and all that you would sacrifice." He kissed the tip of her nose and asked, "Can I make it up to you with a sunset cruise in Honolulu?"

She wiped some crumbs from her nose, which he had put there with his kiss. "The sun is setting in Honolulu?"

"Yes. If we hurry, we won't miss it."

She gave him her biggest smile. "That could work."

The wind lifted her hair from her back before she opened her eyes and found herself on a catamaran holding Than's hand with the sun setting in the distance behind the Honolulu cityscape. A tourist beside her jumped and muttered, "Excuse me. I didn't see you there," and Therese stifled a giggle. God travel was amazing.

The catamaran sailed along Waikiki Beach. The ocean glistened with an orange hue, and three dolphins leapt from the water with the volcanoes spread out on the horizon behind them. According to Than, Diamond Head, its vast silhouette resembling the profile of a tuna, was the largest of the volcanoes.

She quickly called her aunt—it would be later in Durango—and told her she was next door at the Melner cabin and Than would walk her over in a half hour, when the movie he and his sisters had rented was over. She hated to lie, but who could pass up a third sunset in one day?

Over a loud speaker came a series of clicks and long and short tones, and the captain of the vessel explained that a hydrophone enabled them to hear the dolphins speaking to one another underwater.

Therese couldn't believe she could hear them so clearly. "Wow. I wish I could understand what they're saying."

"They're excited about the boat," Than said. "They get bored easily, and racing the cruise ships gives them something to do."

She smirked. "That's one theory."

"It's no theory, Therese."

She looked at him with her mouth dropped open.

He laughed and turned to watch the dolphins.

In a low voice, she asked, "You can understand what the dolphins are saying?"

He answered softly, so the other mortals couldn't hear, "Gods can understand all languages, including animal languages."

She couldn't speak for a minute. She had to let that sink in.

He put his face close to hers and pushed her windblown hair from her eyes. He spoke softly, again, tenderly, "That's how I knew about the snake that night with Dumbo."

"What a wonderful gift," she murmured. She looked at him intently. "That just makes me more certain of my decision."

He covered her lips with his.

Outside of her house in the dark night at half past midnight, while clouds obscured the stars and the moon, Therese and Than walked up the gravelly drive. Therese didn't want the day to end. It had been so perfect. "When will I see you again?" she asked as they approached the steps to the front of her house.

"Tonight, if you want, after you visit a while with your aunt and her boyfriend. I suspect they waited up for you. I could wait for you in your room."

Therese heaved a deep breath, desire prickling her skin. Would he touch her again the way she longed to be touched? He must have sensed the mood washing over her, because he pulled her body close to his, nearly crushing her against him, and let out a sigh.

"Mmm," she purred. "That sounds good. I'll be right up."

He gave her a sideways grin. "Talk with your aunt first."

"Right. Good idea."

Than walked her in and Therese found that Carol and Richard had, indeed, waited up for them, and she wondered if he had other powers, like seeing the future. Luckily, her aunt said she was glad Therese was having fun. They spoke briefly before Than said goodnight to Carol and Richard and then left through the front door. Therese followed him back out through the screened front porch. "Later," she whispered with a smile.

"That's a promise," he whispered back. He pecked her cheek and vanished.

Therese sighed and crossed back into the living room, taking her favorite chair by the empty fireplace. Clifford jumped in her lap. She wondered if he had anything to say to her. She'd have to ask Than later.

"Hi boy. Did you miss me?" she asked her dog.

He panted and wagged his tail.

She laughed. "I'll take that as a yes."

"Did you have fun today?" Carol asked from beside Richard on the sofa. Carol's legs were curled up beneath her, and she and Richard shared a quilt. They had the television turned on to a movie.

"One of the best days of my life," Therese said. "I wouldn't have thought it possible a month ago."

Carol and Richard exchanged looks of amusement, but then Carol said, "Be careful, Therese. You're at that age when a person gets her first broken heart."

"I'm not worried," Therese said with a sly smile.

"We might also want to discuss a curfew. Eleven o'clock sounds more reasonable than after midnight for a seventeen-year-old."

Therese sighed.

Carol and Richard asked more about her day, and Therese made up stories about sightseeing in Durango. She turned her Parisian cruise into white-water-rafting and her London-Bridge-gazing into a lift over Purgatory Mountain Resort.

"Oh, what good ideas," Carol said. "Richard and I should have come along. He's never done those things."

"You and I can go tomorrow, then," Richard said. "You can take a day off, can't you?"

"I don't want to leave Therese here alone all day."

"I won't be alone," Therese pointed to the back deck. "The officer will be here. Plus, Than and I are going to…" an idea hit her. "Than said he'd help me sort through mom and dad's clothes and things. I've decided to donate most of them to charity so someone can get use out of them."

Carol got up and crossed the room. "That's a great idea, sweetheart." She kissed Therese's cheek. "Oh, I'm so glad to hear you're ready for that."

"Maybe you want to go through mom's stuff?"

"I took one sweater I gave her a few years back." Carol returned to the couch. "I don't really want anything else, I don't think. And you should keep her jewelry and pass it on to your daughter one day."

"I guess you're right. But I won't keep all of it. So let me know if there's something you want."

"Maybe one ring to remember her by—the opal ring my mom gave her as a graduation present."

"Sure." Therese couldn't wait another minute to meet Than upstairs in her room, so she faked a yawn, said she was sleepy, wished them good night, and used every ounce of self-control to resist running up the stairs.

Chapter Thirty: Hope

Than popped down to his rooms to wash and change into some fresh clothes and then popped back up to Therese's room to wait. He felt lighter in spirit and more joyful in heart than ever in his life. Never had he imagined that Death could find a companion willing to spend eternity by his side. Lonely and desolate he had felt, though he had found some satisfaction in knowing he was bringing an end to pain and suffering, offering peace to tormented souls, and ushering in justice to the evil ones. As much as his duties had sometimes pleased him, never had they made him feel this good. Surely nothing could compare to the feeling that one is loved by and devoted to another.

He imagined now how he would alter his rooms to bring pleasure to his new bride. He would fill them with the souls of animals and plants. He glanced over at Puffy, the hamster, and Jewels, the tortoise. He could hear Clifford downstairs with the humans. He would be waiting for them and would bring them directly to his chambers. Perhaps Clifford should come down with Therese. That would make the transition easier for her, and the dog would be happier to remain with the soul his had so rigidly imprinted upon. Puffy's time was near, Than sensed, but Jewels would live another fifty or more years; nevertheless, when the time came, he would bring her soul to Therese.

And there would be music! Than would encourage Therese to play her flute in his parents' palace. Hermes and Apollo would be invited to join her. The Underworld will become a better place with her presence.

And they would swim together. He had never before thought to glide through even one of the many waters of the Underworld. Each river played a part in helping the souls of the dead to deal with their afterlife. The Acheron was a transit river on which Charon moved his ferry. The Lethe helped the souls to forget. The Cocytus provided a place for souls to wait when the judges could not reach a proper decision; it was a kind of holding place, like the human concept of purgatory. The Phlegethon was full of fire, though it didn't burn or produce heat, and helped bring light to the darkness that would otherwise envelop them. The Styx was a sacred river on which the gods made their oaths. Than had always seen the rivers as practical functions in his duties and not features to be enjoyed. Because his godly form was less sensually perceptive than his mortal form, it just hadn't occurred to him. But now that he could feel, really feel the world around him, he would remember these feelings and use them to further enjoy his surroundings down there. And he would help Therese enjoy them, too. They would play together in the Styx, which ran right by his rooms.

He would spend the rest of eternity thinking of ways to please his wife.

Chapter Thirty-One: A Lot to Sort Out

Than was waiting for Therese on the chair beneath her window. He had changed into a comfortable t-shirt and loose, cotton trousers. He smelled clean, and his hair was wet.

"That's not fair." Therese leaned over and took in his scent, touched his hair. "You took a shower."

He gave her a devilish grin. "We have all night. Go ahead and shower, if you want."

As anxious as she was to be in his arms again, she wanted to smell good, too, and after all their travels, she could use some refreshing. "I won't be long. Oh, and while I'm in there, I want to try something."

He stood up and gave her a look of surprise. "What?" He shifted his weight from one foot to the other and clasped his hands together like a juror about to read the verdict.

She could tell then that he was as inexperienced as she. Of course, he had never been with anyone, she thought. He said she was the first to ever touch him, to ever kiss him. "Relax and wait here. I'm going to try to pray to you, to see if you can hear me."

"Oh." He seemed a little relieved, but disappointed, too, as he unclasped his hands and fell back into the chair.

She turned on the shower and undressed as she waited for the water to get warm. Once inside with the curtain closed, and as she shampooed her hair, she whispered, "Than, I hope you can hear me. I figured out how I can thank Aphrodite and Pallas Athena for their gifts. We'll have to go to Greece, though. I hope that's okay. I want to donate my parents' clothes to charities that support their temples or their memories or something. I'll have to do a little research to get the specifics straight." She rinsed her hair and babbled on, hoping he could hear. She soaped down her body and rinsed herself, all very quickly and eagerly, and turned off the water. "Anyway, my aunt and her boyfriend will be gone tomorrow. I told them you were going to help me go through my parents' clothes. You should have seen my aunt. She seemed really glad."

She took her nightshirt from the hook on the back of her bathroom door and slipped it on along with a pair of fresh undies. Then she opened the door to her bedroom. "Did you get that?"

He smiled at her from the chair. "Every word. No one has ever prayed to me like that before."

She crossed the room and sat on his lap, appearing more confident than she felt, for she still found it hard to believe that this handsome god was her boyfriend. "Do you like my idea?"

"As a matter of fact, yes. There's a group in Acropolis devoted to memorializing Athena and supporting her values of peace and justice. They clothe the poor. There's another group on the Cyprus Island that raises money to hold an annual festival in Aphrodite's honor. They would take your donations as well. The goddesses are going to love you for this."

She played with his wet hair and kissed his forehead. "I'm glad you like my idea. So can we go to Greece tomorrow?"

"Absolutely. And that gives me an idea as well." He gave her a playful look.

She narrowed her eyes. "What are you smiling about?"

"While we're in Greece, we can go to Mount Olympus and maybe persuade my parents to meet you. My mom should already be there, so it would just be a matter of convincing my dad to leave the Underworld."

She frowned.

"What's wrong?"

"I'm a little nervous. You're my first boyfriend. I've never had to meet the parents of a boyfriend before, and, well, meeting yours sounds a bit, I don't know, daunting."

"Don't worry." He kissed her neck. "You'll do fine. Maybe we'll take your flute along."

Like the notion of performing for the gods of the Underworld was supposed to make her less worried. "And chocolate?"

He laughed. "Yeah. And chocolate."

She kissed his cheek and sighed. "I want to know more about you," she said.

"Like what?"

"What's an average day like for you as the guide for the dead? I mean, do a lot of people die in one day?"

"On average, and only considering the past ten years, about a hundred thousand people and maybe twice that amount of animals."

Therese frowned. "Per day?"

He nodded.

She looked down at the floor, her mouth suddenly dry.

"What?"

"That's so sad. What do they mostly die of?"

"Hunger."

"That seems so…preventable."

"Yeah."

She continued to gaze at the floor.

"Is there something else bothering you?"

"This is going to sound so selfish."

"Tell me. I want to know."

"Well, how would you ever have time for me?" She blushed. "Sorry. That sounds so, selfish and immature. But, I mean, think about it. When would we ever be together? It sounds like you have to work nonstop."

He laughed. "Now don't freak out, okay?"

"What do you mean?"

"I can be in several places at once."

Her mouth dropped open. "I don't understand. How is that possible? I mean, are you somewhere else right now?"

"Right now you have my undivided attention, but when I'm acting as the death guide, I can be at many places at the same time."

"That's hard to grasp. So there's like a whole bunch of your clones running around?"

He shook his head. "No, no, not clones. In each instance, it's me, only me, and completely me, and not an imitation of some sort. I disintegrate into many selves. Right now I am integrated into one."

"I still can't picture it."

"You know how you can be on your computer, on the phone, and listening to music at the same time? You might also be petting Clifford, eating a snack, and glancing out the window."

Therese nodded. "So?"

"Well, I can do a million more things at the same time as a human, even though I have one brain that is aware of the million things I'm doing and the million places I am at."

"Okay, I think I'm beginning to understand. But then why can't you be with me and be the guide for the dead at the same time? Why did Hip have to take over for you?"

He moved a strand of hair from her face and pushed it behind her ear. "Because as the death guide, I would endanger your life. As long as one part of me is acting in that capacity, no human could survive my company."

"Oh." She thought about that for a moment. "Then why can't you do Hip's job and be with me?"

"Because then you'd fall asleep around me."

She laughed. "That's hard to imagine." She touched his cheek. "So is there anything you can do while you're with me?"

He cracked a smile. "Oh, I can think of something."

She laughed and lightly slapped his chest. "I mean somewhere else!"

"No. As long as I'm in my mortal form, I can't disintegrate. I have to shift into my godly form."

Her eyes opened wide. "This isn't your usual form?"

He shook his head. "No. I'm brighter. Too bright for your eyes. Any more questions?" He leaned in.

She closed her eyes and shook her head.

He kissed her neck again, enkindling her quickly and unexpectedly. Her body felt like it was inflamed, the heat rising within her and flooding all of her senses. She ran her fingers through his soft, wet hair and met his lips with hers. He dazzled her, overwhelmed her, made her want to soar across the sky. Their slow, romantic kisses turned into feverish, passionate ones, and he lifted her up and carried her to the bed. He gently laid her down on her bed without moving his mouth from hers. He moved on top of her, his body hot and hard against hers. She clung to his hair, keeping his face next her hers.

"Mmm," she moaned.

He pulled away and collapsed beside her on his back.

She turned on her side to face him. "What's wrong?"

"I'm afraid I won't be able to stop," he said breathlessly.

"Oh." Then, with her heart speeding up even more in her chest, she whispered, "That's okay."

He looked at her with a mixture of shock and desire. She was afraid but overcome. He kissed her, fervently, and she felt like she would overflow with passion. Then he stopped and collapsed on his back again.

"You're killing me," she said with frustration.

He laughed. "I'm sorry, Therese. But there's something you don't know."

"Oh no. You're already married."

He broke into a boisterous laugh. "Oops. That was too loud. I hope Carol and Richard didn't hear that." He covered his mouth with his hand and they both sat there, listening for the other humans in the house.

After a few minutes of silence, Therese said, "Tell me what's wrong."

He turned on his side to face her, propping himself up on an elbow. "I talked to my dad a little yesterday about…things. You have to know that every time a god has ever made love to a human, it has always, invariably, ended in pregnancy."

Understanding washed over her, along with disappointment. "Oh."

"Human forms of birth control are powerless against the seed of gods."

She giggled at that. It struck her as funny. Not that she had any birth control anyway.

"What?" he demanded.

"Nothing. That just sounded kind of hilarious."

"But it's true. And you're not ready to have a baby."

She bit her lip. "No. You're right. I'm not."

He sat up. "I should go."

She grabbed his arm. "No. Please don't go. Stay. Sleep here with me."

He grinned. "You want to drive me crazy, huh?"

She giggled again. "No." Then she was somber. "I just don't like being away from you."

He lay back down beside her and stroked her hair. "Okay. I'll give it a try. Maybe if you talk to me, you can distract me from what it is I really want."

She giggled once more and then called to Clifford, who had been curled up in the corner on his pillow. "Come here, boy."

He jumped on the bed between them.

"Can you translate?" she asked Than.

"He's just glad you're finally paying attention to him again. He was whining a minute ago, full of jealousy."

She pet Clifford. "I already knew that."

"I know," Than said. "You can read animals really well. That's what I meant when I said you had a gift. Your conversations with the horses in the pen made sense both ways. The horses love you, especially Sugar." Then he said, "By the way, Jewels is wondering when you're going to remember to turn off her lamp. She's tired and wants to go to sleep, but she's too warm."

Therese jumped up. "Oh my God!" She snapped off the lamp. "I'm sorry, Jewels! Is that better?"

"She's sighing with relief," Than said.

"You should have said something earlier."

"I was distracted." He gave her a lusty smile, and she nearly lost herself again.

Therese flopped back down on the bed beside Than and Clifford. "What about Puffy? Has he said anything lately?"

"He wishes we'd shut up and go to sleep so he can have peace and quiet while he works. He's miffed, but he'll tolerate it. He really likes you and is glad you're finally home. He'd just rather you go to sleep."

"He said all that?"

"Here and there, throughout the evening. I had to finally tune him out."

"Why don't I hear anything?"

"He speaks on a different frequency. Most animals do."

She turned off the lamp on her nightstand and made the room dark. "That's for Puffy, of course," she whispered.

"Of course."

She climbed beneath the covers. "Coming in?"

He cleared his throat. "Um, I think I'll sleep above the covers."

She moved around beneath the sheet until she was comfortable lying against his chest. She made Clifford lie down on the other side of her so she could be against Than.

"He's jealous again," Than said.

"I know. He'll live." She nestled against Than's chest. "Are you sleepy?"

"A little."

"Gods do sleep, don't they?"

He stroked her hair. "Yes, just not as much as humans. You go to sleep, though. Don't worry about me. We have a big day tomorrow if we're going to Greece."

She kissed his chest and closed her eyes.

Therese awoke after a dreamless night to the bright sunshine coming through her bedroom windows. It took a minute for her to remember that Than was supposed to be there, that he had been beside her when she had fallen asleep. Clifford gave her a cursory glance as she sat up and wondered where Than was. Do gods use the restroom?

"Than?" she called softly as she climbed from the bed. He wasn't in the bathroom.

The clock on the night stand said it was 9:30. She wondered if Carol and Richard had left for their day of sightseeing. Only one way to find out. She and Clifford went downstairs to see if they were alone, except for the officer she knew would be on the deck.

"Oh good, you're awake," Carol said as she emptied a half-eaten bowel of cereal into the sink. She was dressed in jeans and a button-down blouse, her red hair pulled back in a short ponytail, make up perfect. "I was hoping to see you before we left. You sure you don't want to come along?"

"I'm sure. He'll watch out for me." She pointed to the kitchen window through which they could see the police officer sitting with a pastry and coffee, his feet propped on a cooler. Then Richard walked in from the guest bedroom. "Hey, Richard."

"Hey." He sat at the granite bar and opened the newspaper in the same spot her dad had always sat. He too was dressed and ready to go.

Therese sucked in her lips and sighed. "No, I really want to do this. I've decided donating mom and dad's things to charity might give me some…I don't know…closure." She put the leash on Clifford. "I'll take him to the front to do his business. Come on, boy."

Carol kissed Therese's cheek as she passed and then took Richard's empty cereal bowl to the sink. "Call me on my cell if you need anything." Then she asked, "You won't be alone, right? I mean, except for him." She nodded her head toward the officer.

"No. Than's coming to help."

"Okay. Don't hesitate to call 911 if anything suspicious happens. Even a police officer may need help. Promise?"

"Promise."

As soon as she came back inside with Clifford, and after Carol and Richard had left, Therese poured herself a bowl of cereal and said out loud, "Than, where are you? Will you please come back?" She was startled by his instant appearance by her side. "Geez, you scared the crap out of me."

He gave her a smirk. "Sorry."

"Why did you leave? I thought you were staying the night." She ate some of the cereal while she waited for his explanation.

He took her face in his hands. "You look so cute first thing in the morning." He kissed the top of her head.

"How would you know? You weren't there." She couldn't hide the slight hostility in her voice.

"Was too. I didn't leave you till dawn. I wanted a quick shower and a moment with my sisters. They had news."

Clifford put his paws on Than's jean-clad shins.

"Hey, boy. Good morning to you, too," Than said, patting the dog.

"So, what was the news?" Therese stood to rinse the bowl in the sink. "Want some?"

"No thanks. I already ate." Then he said, "The news is complicated and I'm not sure…"

She left the bowl in the sink, turned, and pressed herself against him. "Tell me. I want to know."

He toyed with her mussed up hair, straightening it, smiling. "You're so cute, and you've been so happy. I hate to…ruin that."

She wrapped her arms around his waist. "As long as I'm with you, I'll be happy."

The doorbell made her jump. "Who could that be? I'm not dressed."

Hold on. He vanished and then instantly reappeared. "It's Pete Holt."

She sighed. "Oh God. Will you get it while I run up and get dressed?"

"He won't like that."

"Too bad."

She dashed up the stairs and quickly changed into a knit top and matching short skirt. She brushed her hair out, glossed her lips, and hustled back down.

Pete lingered at the front door, a wide space between him and Than. He wore jeans and boots and no shirt and was sweaty and grimy, as though he had just finished cleaning the barn. "Hey, Therese." Pete's voice was sobered, nearly grave.

"Hey, Pete."

"Sorry to barge in…"

"Don't apologize."

"My mom sent me to deliver your earnings. She would have given them to you yesterday, but…Hey, are you feeling better?" He glanced at Than and back at her.

"Yeah, thanks." She gave him a hesitant nod. "And thanks again for covering for me. I hope it wasn't too much of a drag."

"Not at all." He gave Than another glance.

They all three shared a moment of awkward silence without looking at one another.

Therese finally said, "Well, hey, thanks for coming by."

"Oh, sure. Here's the money." He held up a white envelope. "I don't want to get your house dirty."

She crossed over to him and took the money. "Thanks."

"I'll give you a call later. And hey, Mom says you're welcome to come visit any time if you get bored and want to, I don't know, hang out while we work the horses."

"Thanks. Sounds good."

She followed him through the screened porch, where Pete turned to her and muttered, "Are you two going out or something?"

Therese blushed. "Um, or something, I guess."

He glanced once more in Than's direction. "Bye, then."

"Bye. Thanks again."

She felt sorry for him as she watched him leave. When he was in his truck, she waved once more before going back inside. Than was waiting for her. He, too, appeared sobered.

"You could have a good life with Pete." He said this without looking at her. "He'd make you happy, and you wouldn't have to leave. You could live among the living. You could see sunrises and sunsets. He could give you everything I can't give you."

She stood in the living room across from him. "Don't. Please." She could see the diseased elm through the kitchen window and a sudden urge to chop down the dying branch overcame her, but she pushed it down, thinking she was losing her mind. She couldn't chop it down.

He met her eyes but said nothing.

"Is that what you want?" The hostility from earlier crept back in her voice.

"This is about you, about what's best for you."

"Then quit talking like that." She stormed off to her parents' room. In her mind, she thought, "If you can hear me, Than, please follow me. Please come in behind me and put your arms around me and tell me you will never say such a thing again."

She stood there just inside her parents' room waiting. Seconds later, he swept in behind her with his arms around her waist and clasped across her stomach.

"I'm sorry," he whispered.

She turned in his arms and kissed him, closed her eyes, and touched his neck with her hands. "Me too." Then she played with his shirt and asked meekly, "Are we still going to Greece today?"

"If you wish."

"Then we better get busy. Why don't you tell me what your sisters learned about McAdams while I start bagging some of these clothes?" She went into the closet and grabbed four or five hangers with clothes and laid them on the bed. Before Than had begun his story, she said, "Oh. I remember the last time my dad wore this shirt." She swiped the tears away as they fell unexpectedly down her face.

"Maybe you're not ready for this."

She rubbed her eyes with the backs of her hands. "I want to do this."

Than sat on a chair in the corner of the room and talked as Therese created piles of her parents' possessions and then bagged them in giant black yard bags she found beneath the kitchen sink. While she worked, Than explained that McAdams was the CEO of a corrupt pharmaceutical company in Texas that bought counterfeit drugs at cheap prices from a manufacturer in Pakistan and sold them to customers at regular market prices. McAdams then split the profits with the Pakistani manufacturer, who was also able to provide forged approval certificates, valid samples for occasional testing by regulatory agencies, and pay-offs to agents when needed. The manufacturer had connections with various foreign rebels and so was able, through McAdams, to develop and sell the mutant anthrax to them. Than explained that when McAdams got wind of her mother's research at Fort Lewis College, he ordered her execution because he feared he wouldn't get paid if his customers heard that an antidote was being developed.

Then she asked, "But why would McAdams still want me dead?"

Than stood up and put his hands on Therese's shoulders. "His men weren't after you that night. They were after your aunt."

Chapter Thirty-Two: Tagalong

What do you mean they were after my aunt? What has she got to do with any of this?" Therese asked, her face twisted up to his with confusion.

"Maybe you better sit down." Than wished he could shield her from this news.

"Okay," she murmured and sat on the edge of her parents' bed.

He stood in front of her. "Your aunt works for a pharmaceutical company, right?"

"Uh-huh."

"A few months ago she attended a professional conference in Dallas. She went to lunch with a group of attendees, all salespeople like herself, and they got to talking about where they were all from, about their families, and things. Carol mentioned how proud she was of her sister, a professor at Fort Lewis College, who was going to be honored this summer for her outstanding work. Someone asked what work. Carol talked about the antidote for the mutated anthrax. One among the group worked for McAdams."

Therese's mouth dropped open, and she sat stunned for several minutes. She looked as though she had lost the gift of speech.

Than touched her shoulder. "Therese?"

"So that's how he found out about my mom?"

Than nodded.

"Carol can't ever know this." Therese stood up and twisted her shirt in her hands. "This would absolutely kill my aunt. We can't let her know. Oh my God." She paced around the room. "Oh my God."

"She doesn't have to know." He could hardly keep up with the combination of silent and spoken prayers.

"Please don't let her know," she either said or prayed. "Please protect her, forever. I can't stand this."

Therese continued to pace. "But is McAdams still after her? I mean, is my aunt in danger?"

"I and many gods promise to protect her." Then, gingerly, Than explained, "McAdams murdered his informer, the one who lunched with your aunt, James Barber. He's in Tartarus now. That's how Tizzie discovered the connection. She got him to talk. Tizzie thinks McAdams is afraid that if the media show pictures of his informer once someone realizes Barber's missing, your aunt will recognize him and remember having lunch with him, and that she might eventually put it all together."

"Oh no."

"But Aphrodite and Cupid are with her and Richard today. They won't let anything happen to her. And even with Ares trying to thwart their every move, Tizzie and Meg are close to finding McAdams. Barber said McAdams is meeting with his Pakistani manufacturer today. Tizzie and Meg and I will be waiting for him. It won't be long now."

Than could hear Therese's prayers, for she directed them to him. She was explaining to him that it was one thing when Therese thought that McAdams and his men were after her; but it was another thing entirely to learn the bad guys were after her aunt. Since the death of her parents, Therese hadn't been too afraid of dying. She wasn't going to commit suicide, but if death happened on its own, that wouldn't be so bad. That had been her attitude. She hadn't tried to be careful. She hadn't stayed up nights worrying about her safety. If she couldn't fall asleep, it was because she missed her parents and longed to be with them, not because she was afraid to die. "I want to be with you, so death is no longer scary," she prayed. But now that her aunt's life was in danger, now that her aunt was the target, Therese was overcome with fear and a deep desire to seek out McAdams and put a stop to him.

"Help me avenge the death of my parents," she said suddenly, and now he could see she was speaking, not praying. "Help me kill McAdams and protect my aunt. I don't want to wait another minute."

He put his arms around her rigid body. "Calm down," he whispered. "I'll help you. But calm down. I don't like to see you so upset."

She relaxed a little in his arms and put her head against his chest.

"Listen," he said softly. "Let's finish sorting through your parents' things and take the donations to the goddesses' charities in Greece. We want to make sure we have them on our side before we get you involved. You'll need their protection as well as mine. Maybe there's something you can do for Artemis as well, since she has also vowed to stand by you."

"I've already thought of something." She looked up at him. "I want to donate my earnings from Mrs. Holt to a wildlife preserve."

Than was full of admiration for her. "Excellent. She'll like that."

They spent the rest of the day sorting and bagging Therese's parents' clothes, shoes, accessories, and a select assortment of books, magazines, and jewelry. Often Therese would stop, hold something up, look at it and remember. Tears would flow down her face like a waterfall, but she'd slap them away and keep going, and Than felt lost and helpless, unable to comfort her. They took only one break, for a short lunch of egg salad sandwiches Therese made for them, and by the time they were satisfied, they had ten large garbage bags and four cardboard boxes ready to donate, and it was seven o'clock in the evening.

"We'll have to go to Greece in the morning," Than said. "I promised my sisters I'd help them now. I'm already a little late."

"Can I come?"

He cringed at the thought of his sweet Therese seeing the hideousness of the Furies, the blood pouring from Tizzie's eyes, the vicious snakes, the fierce falcon, the howling hounds; but, he supposed she would have to see these things eventually if she were to follow him to the Underworld and live there with him.

Therese quickly added, "I hate being on the sidelines all the time. This is about me and my family and I want to help." She clutched the locket from Athena, which she wore around her neck, and he sensed the determination to wield her own kind of power.

He looked at her, still considering.

"Unless I'd be a liability," she said.

"You're not too tired?"

She shook her head. "Please?"

"Do not leave my side, got it?"

She nodded, smiling, and prayerfully thanking him. Out loud, she said, "Got it."

"And wear Aphrodite's robe just in case we get separated."

They went upstairs to her room, where she found and put on the robe.

"If we do get separated, concentrate on your room, on this spot, with all your might. The robe will help you get back here."

"Okay."

He could feel her trembling beside him and could see her shaking as she put her arms through the sleeves. "Try it out first on your own. Think of your kitchen. Concentrate really hard on the spot in front of the kitchen sink."

Therese closed her eyes. She prayed to him the entire time, explaining that she felt a pressure against her body, like plastic wrap enclosing her, and then, a second later, he watched her open her eyes where she was standing, or stumbling rather, in front of the kitchen sink. She grabbed onto the counter to get her balance.

"I did it!" she shouted.

The police officer sitting out on her deck turned from where he had been eating his sandwich, his feet propped up on his cooler. He looked at Therese through the window. She gave him a wave to let him know everything was okay.

Than, who had been waiting for her, said, "Okay, here we go. But hold tight to my hand and don't let go unless I tell you."

"I promise." Then she said, "I better tell Officer Gomez I'm leaving."

"Good idea, but hurry. We're late as it is."

She quickly poured some lemonade into a glass and took it out to the officer. She practically ran back into the kitchen, anxious to get started on their journey.

"Where are we going?" she asked, taking his hand.

"Peshawar. A city in Pakistan."

Chapter Thirty-Three: Artemis's Gifts

Therese closed her eyes against the bright light, and held her breath as the invisible plastic wrapped itself around her. When she opened her eyes, they were standing in the early morning sun in an abandoned alley. The foul smell of urine and rotting food accosted her. She gagged.

She followed Than, stepping over rubbish and weaving through garbage cans to a dusty window in the back of a metal building. Like Than, she peered inside, but it was difficult to see anything.

"My sisters must be around here somewhere." He closed his eyes and appeared to be in deep concentration. Then he opened them and said, "This way."

"So you can communicate with your sisters telepathically, like ESP?" Therese asked as she rushed beside him.

"ESP?"

"Extrasensory perception."

"Telepathy is not an 'extra' sense for a god. Just as I hear your prayers directed to me, they can hear mine and I theirs, though the sounds can get distorted." Then he said, "Turn here."

A pack of skinny dogs, crouched around a half-eaten carcass, looked up at them and were about to bark when Than said, "Silence." The dogs obeyed and went back to what they had been doing.

Than led Therese around the side of the building from which they could see a road and a jeep approaching. Than flattened against the building, pulling Therese beside him. "They're meeting us here."

"The people in the jeep?"

"No."

Before he said more, Meg and Tizzie appeared before them. They too pressed their backs against the building, out of site of the jeep, which had stopped now. Therese could hear men talking and the jeep doors slamming shut. Then she heard laughter. The laughing stopped at the sound of another vehicle approaching.

A man Therese could not see spoke in a harsh voice. The only word she recognized was, "McAdams."

Meg signaled the others to follow her to the back of the building, back to the heaps of rubbish and garbage cans. The dogs looked up as the group passed by and then the animals returned to their carcass.

The gods and one human huddled behind the building where Tizzie said, "I've found a place in the building where Therese can hide while we use invisibility to get McAdams."

Meg snarled, "I can't believe you brought her, Than. You know Ares is against us. You've endangered her life, our mission…"

"Enough," Than said. "This is her battle, too. I'll stay beside her but will help if you need me."

Than held tightly to Therese's hand and the bright light surrounded them. They reappeared behind a metal pallet stacked high with cardboard boxes. Through the boxes, Therese could see three men gathered in the middle of a large room full of machines and assembly lines that at the time were not running. Two of the men were dark-skinned and holding weapons, but the thin, bald, white man trembling before them must be McAdams.

"May I remind you that you work for me!" McAdams shouted. "We stand to make a lot of money together, and you can't do it without me. Damn it, you cowards, put away your weapons!"

"What happened to Grahib?" one of the darker men demanded.

"McAdams had him killed," the other said. "He had his own informer killed, too. We can't trust him."

"But I have your money. If you kill me, you won't get paid," McAdams said. "Those other men betrayed us. I only kill betrayers. You are good men who have served me well. I can still get you the women I promised, the red-head and her virgin niece. Trust me. Money and women. What could be better?"

"Security," one of the men replied.

Than nodded, and whispered, "I know. We need him alive."

The one man said to the other, "Let's just do it. Do it now!"

They pointed their weapons at McAdams and pulled their triggers. A loud roar echoed throughout the building as Therese watched in terror. She was shocked to see McAdams standing unharmed, but then Tizzie appeared before him. She spit the bullets into her hand and gave the men an arrogant smile. Blood spilled from her eyes and snakes coiled and hissed in her hair. The two men turned on their heels to hide, one of which came to the very spot where Therese and Than were huddled.

"Go now," Than said urgently. "Go back to your room. Concentrate. Now!"

Therese shut her eyes and focused on her bedroom, but then an image of her grandmother's green carpeting in her old house in San Antonio entered her mind, and before Therese knew what was happening, she found herself standing in her grandmother's old living room in San Antonio. Everything smelled new, and the furniture had all been removed.

"Oh, hello," a woman's voice came across the room. "I'm sorry, but the open house ended over an hour ago."

"I'm, um, so sorry," Therese said. "I'll, um, just show myself out."

"Are you okay? Did you come with your parents?"

"I'm fine. My parents are waiting for me outside."

She went through the front door and recognized her grandmother's old street just visible in the dusk. The woman from her grandmother's house stepped onto the front porch and watched as Therese hurried down the sidewalk. She walked a little way further and found a cluster of trees, but before she could god-travel, a scrawny old man approached her.

"Hey, girlie, you got any spare change for a starvin' man?"

Therese turned and ran down the darkening street. She wasn't sure where to turn. Tears welled in her eyes as she rounded a corner and saw a park up ahead which vaguely looked familiar. Two teenagers were snogging on a bench, but Therese crept behind some bushes and deeper into trees where she closed her eyes.

She tried to focus on her bedroom. A strong image of Clifford waiting for her on her bed made it easier this time. She was so afraid and wanted Clifford! She hadn't been much help on this journey. How stupid she had been to think she could help the Furies! The invisible plastic wrapped itself around her, she held her breath, still focusing on Clifford on her bed, and when she opened her eyes, she found herself standing on her bed looking down at her dog wagging his tail at her.

She went downstairs and was surprised that Carol and Richard weren't home yet. Officer Gomez still sat out on the back deck, so she felt fairly safe. After letting the officer know she was home, she put Clifford on a leash and took him outside in the front to do his business. Then she came inside and grabbed a cookie from the countertop, nearly eating it whole.

Therese looked at all the bags and boxes lined up on the floor of her parents' bedroom and wondered how they would transport them all to Greece. She was too tired to think long on it, though, and before she realized it, she had curled up on her parents' bed beneath their covers, trying to smell their scents and trying to erase from her mind the scene that had transpired before her in Peshawar. Clifford sat in the corner of the room. He had never been allowed up on her parents' bed, and even though he probably knew her parents were gone, he couldn't bring himself to break the rule.

She was nearly asleep when the phone rang. She answered the one on her parents' bedside table. It was Gina Rizzo. Gina had never called before.

"What's up, Gina?" Her voice was deep with sleep.

"I just wondered if you heard the news about your friend Vicki."

Therese sat up. "Uh-uh."

"Oh. Well her mother committed suicide yesterday. She slit her wrists with a razor blade and bled to death in the master bathroom. Vicki was home when it happened. Isn't that terrible?"

Gina's voice sounded more excited than sad, and that eerie excitement drove Therese to anger.

"I've gotta go," Therese said. She hung up the phone and left her parents' room and was sick in the kitchen sink.

Through the window, she caught sight of the diseased elm tree illuminated by the moonlight. Then, in something like a blind rage, she ran down the stairs to the unfinished basement, another project her parents had planned to one day complete. She went past the washer and dryer and stack of dirty laundry. She grabbed an axe and went through the basement to the garage, which opened to the side of the house. She squeezed by her father's Chevy truck, pulled out a ladder, and dragged it uphill to the diseased elm tree.

"What are you doing?" Officer Gomez asked.

"Fixing that tree!" Then she went back for the axe. She practically dragged it out of the garage door and up the hill.

"You're going to hurt yourself. Why don't you wait until someone can help you?"

Ignoring the officer, she climbed up the ladder and stretched herself out as tall as she could and hammered the blade of the heavy axe against the dying branch. It barely made a scratch, but she brought that axe up and she struck the branch again, despite the police officer's protests. She was going to save this dying tree. She was sick of watching the disease slowly suck the life from it, and she was going to put a stop to it once and for all. She struck the branch again and again, nearly toppling over once, till it hurt her arm to keep raising the axe, and then she did it several more times. She broke through the bark, but she could see that she had been right all along. She could not chop down the dying branch. She could not save the tree. She dropped the axe, climbed down from the ladder, collapsed on the dirt, and cried.

And then it began to rain.

The officer went to the overhang to get out of the rain and didn't seem to know what to say.

Clifford barked at him from the back door. She could see Clifford looking at her through the glass pane. He was probably worried she had lost her mind. He should be, she thought.

She pulled herself up, leaving the axe to rust in the rain, the ladder to stand like an unfinished promise beside the elm she could not save. She looked over at the other elm a few yards away. Her mother had said that if they did not stop the disease from getting the one tree, it would eventually spread to its twin. It seemed wrong that two such magnificent living structures should be the victims of a life-sucking fungus to be left withering skeletons that would eventually break, crumble, and decompose and then disappear from sight altogether, as though they had never existed.

"It's okay, boy!" she hollered to her dog, who had started to whine, but before she left the tree, she caught sight of something shimmering in the adjacent cypress.

She walked in the rain toward the shimmering tree, blinking her eyes several times and rubbing them. The forest was dark on this side of the house where the moonbeams couldn't reach. And maybe the rain was blurring her vision. But, no. Even with her eyes rubbed dry, the tree shimmered. Therese backed away now, frightened.

"Come inside!" Officer Gomez called out.

"Do not be afraid," the tree said. "I am Artemis, goddess of the wood, and I will not harm you."

Therese held very still, not sure if she should speak. She swallowed hard and waited.

"I am pleased with your stewardship of the forest and the animals that abound in it. You have won my heart."

Therese couldn't make out an image of the goddess, just the shimmering tree. "Thank you. I'm grateful."

"Like Aphrodite and Athena, I have gifts for you, but mine are far better than theirs. Aphrodite may have saved your dog from death, but I have given him immortality."

Therese sucked in air. Did she just say that her best friend Clifford would never die? "Oh, thank you! Thank you so much!" She glanced at Clifford still looking at her through the back door. His tongue hung happily from his mouth as the stubby tail wagged back and forth. He seemed to understand what had happened to him. He would be able to go with her now and live in the Underworld! "I don't know what to say." Tears pricked her eyes.

"Therese!" Officer Gomez called again. "What are you doing out there? Come inside!"

"Wait," Artemis commanded. "There's another. Whereas Aphrodite gave you a traveling robe, I now give to you a beautiful crown. It is made of the finest pearls and diamonds, and when placed upon your head, will make you invisible to mortal eyes. It is waiting for you on your bedroom bureau."

Therese put her hands to her cheeks. "I can't thank you enough."

"Don't forget your promise to me, Therese. The wildlife preserve. I am counting on your offering."

"Yes, m'am. I'm pleased to give it."

"Is there anything else you would ask of me?"

"No, m'am it's just..." Therese faltered.

"What is it?"

"My friend Vicki. She's all I can think about right now. Her mother committed suicide yesterday. If I can ask something of you, I ask you to please watch over her and help her, if you would."

Before Therese had finished her sentence, the cypress no longer shimmered and the rain no longer fell, and Therese had the feeling the goddess was no longer there.

The crunching sound of gravel made her aware of Carol and Richard pulling up the drive in Carol's little red Toyota Corolla. Carol waved to her before driving into the garage beside Therese's father's pickup. Therese wondered whether it was her request of the goddess or the appearance of her aunt and uncle that had made her disappear.

A few minutes later, Carol and Richard came through the back door, Clifford scrambling out ahead of them to growl at Officer Gomez, standing beneath the overhang of the house. Carol and Richard looked across the deck to where Therese stood beside the elm, the axe, and the ladder, still flabbergasted by Artemis's visit and the news of her gifts.

"What have you been doing?" Richard asked.

"Um, I was trying to save this tree from the Dutch elm disease. Mom and Dad were going to chop off that dying branch and treat the roots, but…well, I couldn't do it."

"You should have told me," Richard said. "I'll take care of that for you."

"Sweetheart, you're soaked and your backside is covered in mud. And you could have hurt yourself."

They went inside, including Officer Gomez, who moved to the screened front porch to avoid the rain, which had started falling again. After a shower and change of clothes, Therese came back down to hear about her aunt's day while Carol made spaghetti and Richard sat on the sofa with the news turned down low. Therese showed Carol the bags and boxes she had lined up in her parents' room, and Carol was amazed by all she and Than had accomplished. Therese told her about taking the things to charities tomorrow—though she failed to mention they were located in Greece.

Therese also mustered up the strength to tell Carol about Gina's phone call and the terrible thing that had happened to Vicki. Tears streamed from Therese's eyes when she admitted to her aunt that she had been blowing Vicki off, especially the night they were supposed to go to the movies.

"I should call her, shouldn't I?" Therese asked. "I should invite her to come over sometime soon, don't you think?"

Carol put an arm around Therese, while she stirred the pasta boiling in the pot.

"Don't be too hard on yourself. Things haven't been perfect around here, either." Then she added, "But maybe it would be nice to invite her to do something."

Therese nodded. "Maybe I'll go give her a call."

Upstairs in her room, before she made the call, Therese noticed the crown inconspicuously tucked on a blue silk scarf on one end of her dresser behind her CD player. She hadn't noticed it before when she had come up to shower and change, and with the arrival of her aunt and the appearances she had at first tried to keep up, she had forgotten the goddess's gift. Now she took the crown in her hands and studied it.

A gold base with embedded diamonds was topped by a scalloped band of gold studded with smaller diamonds. Between the scallops hung teardrop pearls from a third, thinner golden band shaped in five large scallops along the front of the crown, and at the crest of each scallop was a single large diamond. The largest of them was set in the top center scallop. Therese had never seen anything like this jeweled crown in all her life.

She watched herself in the mirror above her dresser as she placed the crown on her head. She gasped when her reflection disappeared. Frightened, she instantly removed the crown and sighed with relief when she could once again see herself gazing back from the glass.

With a mixture of trepidation and excitement, she returned the crown to her head and watched her reflection vanish. She decided to test to see if she really were invisible to mortal eyes, so she went downstairs to the kitchen and waited to see if she would be noticed.

The pasta had been drained and three plates of spaghetti sat cooling at the granite bar, but Carol and Richard sat together at the sofa speaking in muted tones. Therese crossed the kitchen so she could hear what they were saying.

"So are you going to tell her tonight then?" Richard asked.

"I think so. Do you think she's ready?"

"You know her better than I do. It's your call."

"I might know her, but I have no idea what's good for her. I wish I were better prepared. What a responsibility. And you're still sure it's the right thing to do?"

"Positive. It would be best for all of us," Richard said.

Therese couldn't figure out what they meant, but a part of her worried they were talking about Carol giving her up. She had suspected becoming Therese's guardian would be too hard for her aunt, leaving her life in Texas, her independence. Maybe they planned to give Therese to an orphanage, or foster care, or a halfway house for abandoned youth. She knew she was being ridiculous, but, what if? Her heart sped up as she waited to learn more details, but they stopped talking to listen to the news, and then Carol got up to pour glasses of iced tea. It wouldn't matter for long, anyway, she told herself. Therese intended to become a god. Carol wouldn't need to worry anymore.

Therese backed up to the stairwell, and as she tiptoed away, she heard Carol say, "I'll wait and tell her tomorrow. She's worried about her friend tonight."

That's right. Vicki. Therese went upstairs and took off the crown and called Vicki, reminding herself that there were others besides herself to think of. She sat on her bed next to Clifford and took up her phone.

A man with a tired sounding voice answered. "Hello?"

"May I speak to Vicki please?"

"Sure."

Vicki's voice sounded tired, too. "Hello?"

Tears came to Therese's eyes as she told her how sorry she was to hear about her mom. "I know what it's like to lose a parent," she muttered. "I'm sorry this happened to you."

"Yeah. Me too."

"We should go somewhere and do something and get our minds off…things."

"We have a lot of family in town for the funeral and everything. Maybe next week."

Therese wondered if she would still be human then. "Okay, but let's not wait too long."

As Therese hung up the phone, Carol called for her to come eat, so she went downstairs unable to stop herself from worrying about Vicki and how tired she and her father had sounded. She also wondered anxiously about what it could be that Carol and Richard had wanted to tell her.

After supper, Therese scuttled off to her room where Clifford was waiting for her. She still couldn't believe he was immortal. She hugged him and told him they would be together forever—if the Furies and Than could help her successfully catch McAdams. If only there had been a way to make her parents immortal, too. They could all be together—one big happy family.

Therese lay down on her bed and closed her eyes. She was anxious for Than to return. "Than," she whispered. "Than, come over."

When he didn't appear, she grabbed her laptop from her desk, sat back on the bed, and turned the computer on. She googled wildlife preserves in Colorado, found the Perins Peak State Wildlife Area west of Durango, located the website, and made an electronic contribution using her debit card in the amount she earned this summer. She would deposit the cash to make up the difference in her account later.

"Are you coming, Than?" she whispered again.

The phone rang, so she picked it up to find Jen on the other line.

"I'm sorry about the other night," Jen said. "I was rude."

"It's okay. I'm sorry, too. I was being selfish."

Jen's voice had the same tired sound Vicki's had had earlier. "Did you hear about Vicki?"

"Yeah. I talked to her earlier."

Then, out of the blue it seemed, Jen said, "My dad came home today."

Therese sat there on her bed in shock.

"You still there?"

"I'm here. Oh my gosh. Is everything okay I mean, are you glad?"

"Not really."

"Oh no. Do you want to come over?"

"Can't tonight. Unless I run away. If I run away, can I hide out in your basement for a while?"

"Jen, I'm coming over there."

"Don't. Just wait. I'll call again later, or tomorrow." Jen hung up before Therese could say anything more.

Therese hung up the phone and flapped her hands like she'd just washed them and there were no paper towels. "Oh my God." Then, in her mind, she screamed for Than.

His sudden appearance startled her. She leaned back in the bed with her hand on her mouth.

"I can't stay," he said, panting in his white trousers and open white shirt. "We're on a chase. The men from Peshawar. Can you hold on another hour or so?"

She saw the frantic look in his eyes and nodded. He vanished.

After saying goodnight to Carol and Richard, Therese went to her dresser and put on the crown, witnessing her own image disappear from the mirror. Then she slipped down the stairs and out the back door to Jen's.

Chapter Thirty-Four: Battle Rising

As soon as Therese was gone, Than clutched the hair on the heads of two men who had come to hide from his sister in the back of the warehouse in Peshawar. One of them stumbled and looked up in shock while the other shut his eyes as though waiting to be shot. Than pulled them to the center of the warehouse for their interrogation where Meg waited with her falcon.

McAdams was bound by Tizzie's serpent hair. The snakes twined around his neck and arms, hissing and flicking their tongues, dripping with the blood from his sister's eyes.

Alecto uttered a laugh of hysteria as she closed in on McAdams.

Before the gods could take the mortals' souls to the Underworld for further persecution in Tartarus, a flash of light washed over the building and the loud crack of a whip, as harsh as thunder, made Than flinch.

In the middle of the room stood Ares, accompanied by his twin sons, Phobos, also known as Panic, and Deimos, also known as Fear.

The Furies screamed a shrill, blood-curling shriek and disappeared, leaving Than alone to face the other gods.

"Hades wants these men!" Than said, standing his ground. "They belong to him!"

"You can have those two, but McAdams comes with me to Mount Olympus where I shall seek council with Zeus. Follow me if you wish."

Ares, his sons, and the mortal McAdams disappeared, leaving Than and his two terrified prisoners.

Chapter Thirty-Five: The Holts

The sun was setting behind the mountains across the lake, and a cool wind blew through the trees as Therese made her way down her gravelly drive to the dirt road leading to the Holts' place. She could hear her sneakers crunching against the pebbles and dirt, so she was invisible but not soundproof.

The horses were still out to pasture when she crept up the drive to the house where the one goat was tied to the rail by the front steps bleating like a child who hadn't been fed. A branch danced in the wind and scraped against the logs of the house, but, other than the bleating goat and the scraping tree, all was quiet.

Therese snuck to the back of the house and peered through the open window. She could see Mrs. Holt standing in the middle of the kitchen with her arms crossed, and then her hand moved to her mouth and stuck a fingernail between her teeth. She leaned against the kitchen sink like she was tired but too tense to sit down. Her bowl-shaped blonde-gray hair looked greasy, and the wrinkles in her face deeper than ever. Suddenly she walked across the kitchen, opened a cabinet, and took down a pack of cigarettes. She took the last from the pack and ditched the empty box in the trash. Her hands shook as she lit the end of the cigarette and sucked.

Bobby's voice cried, "But he's reformed now! He went to therapy! He said so himself!"

Therese couldn't see Bobby. She saw Pete leaning against the mantle of the fireplace. He wore a pair of ragged jeans and boots. His tight gray t-shirt was too short, like it belonged to Bobby and he had put in on by accident. He looked tired but tense, and as he ran his hand through his hair, Therese had the feeling he'd been doing that motion all evening. "I just don't know," Pete said. "Mom, how do we know it won't happen again?"

Now she saw Bobby standing by the front door entryway with his hands open, like he was begging everyone to listen to him. He had a look of anguish and desperation, and again he said, "He went to therapy, Pete! He won't do it again!"

That's when she heard Mr. Holt say, "Y'all just think about it. Sleep on it. I'll come again tomorrow, see what y'all think. I'll go on back to the hotel now. Where's Jen?"

"She won't come out," Mrs. Holt said without looking up from the kitchen floor. "Just leave her be."

Then Therese saw Mr. Holt get up from wherever he had been sitting toward the back of their living room and walk to the entryway. He looked thin and old, and he didn't stand up straight. His gray hair made a shaggy ring around a glossy bald spot on top of his head. Bobby threw his arms around him before he had made it to the door.

"I've missed you, Daddy," Bobby cried. "I want you to stay. I know you can do it. I believe in you."

Mr. Holt hugged his son. He held the embrace for nearly a whole minute, his thin bowed figure looking slight beside his younger son. He said through tears, "I love you, Bobby. I love all my kids." Then he walked out without turning back to Pete or Mrs. Holt.

Mrs. Holt continued to lean against the kitchen sink and suck on her cigarette. Pete held himself up by the mantle. Bobby paced back and forth near the front door, seeming to fight an urge to run out and chase down his father. After several minutes of this, Mrs. Holt cried out, "Jen, come on out. He's gone now."

Therese watched Jen come down the stairs and walk straight into her mother's arms. Her eyes were red and swollen, her face pale, and her hair sticking out in all directions. She sobbed as she spoke. "I'm scared, Mom. Seeing him made it all come back. I thought I could handle it, but I can't."

Mrs. Holt held her cigarette away from her daughter with one hand and patted Jen's back with the other.

"He's reformed, Jen!" Bobby cried. "He hasn't had a drink in over a year. He only did those things when he was drunk."

"Leave her alone, Bobby," Pete muttered. "It didn't happen to you."

"It's her fault he left in the first place!" Bobby shouted. "If she'd only forgiven him!"

"That's enough!" Mrs. Holt snarled. "It's not her fault."

"And it's Pete's fault for telling!" Bobby cried.

"That's enough, Bobby!" Mrs. Holt snarled again, like a cornered animal.

"Mom," Jen said in small, shaky voice. "I think it's going to have to be him or me, and what I want to know is, who would you choose?"

"You, baby doll, every time," Mrs. Holt smoothed Jen's hair with a jittery hand. Then she lifted Jen's chin and asked, "But what I want to know is this: Doesn't everyone deserve a second chance? Can we just give it this one try?" Mrs. Holt put the trembling cigarette to her lips and sucked.

Jen looked like she was wilting, like she was a flower that would never stand straight in the vase again.

Therese sat outside of Jen's house in a wrought iron chair and watched the sun set behind the mountains across the lake. She wanted to knock on the door and talk to Jen, but she was afraid. She didn't know if Jen would feel like talking. So she sat there watching the sun sink behind the mountains, the hawks swoop back to their nests, and the deer come out of the trees. While she sat looking around, she thought how cruel and beautiful, how sweet and ugly, the world could be. She missed her parents, but was glad to have Than; she was sorry for Jen that her dad had returned, but was glad for Bobby; she was sad for Vicki, but was glad her mother had found a way out of whatever pain life had brought her. Vicki's mom would go down to Erebus and forget everything and spend the rest of eternity in the Elysian Fields living whatever delusions of grandeur her soul desired. In Cairo, the sun was getting ready to rise over the Great Sphinx, and a new day would be dawning for Egypt, while here the sun was barely visible, and now, altogether gone behind the mountains.

"Let's bring those horses in before dark," Mrs. Holt said coming out of the house.

Therese froze. No one seemed to notice her. She watched the four forlorn figures make their way out to pasture.

While they were gone, she removed the crown and waited for Jen to get back. She had an idea. She knew what she should do.

"Artemis, if you can hear me, I hope you won't be offended by what I'm about to do."

Jen was the last of the Holts to make it back to the house, and none of them spoke a word till they spotted Therese sitting in that wrought iron chair on the side of the house, the bleating goat eyeing her from around the corner.

Pete was the first to spot her, and his face lit up like lighter fluid. "Therese! What a nice surprise." He fell into the chair beside her. The smile on his face couldn't erase the lines of worry or make him look less tired, but it was a small improvement.

"Hey, Pete."

The others caught up, one at a time, like they'd been walking in their own private worlds.

"Hey, Bobby," Therese said.

"Hey, Therese." Bobby kept walking into the house.

Mrs. Holt was next, and then came Jen, barely moving, like every step hurt.

"What's that you have in your hands?" Mrs. Holt stood, slight and bent, in front of her.

"Part of an old costume," Therese said. "I wanted to show it to Jen."

"It looks so real," Mrs. Holt said. "May I?"

She extended her leathery hands out for it, and Therese felt a panic coming on. What if Mrs. Holt put it on her head and everyone saw its effect? But what could Therese do, tell the poor woman no, you can't hold my crown?

Therese gave it to Mrs. Holt. Her heart thudded so loudly she thought for once the goat's bleating would be drowned out.

Mrs. Holt turned it around in her hands as Jen looked over her mother's shoulder. "It's so beautiful. It looks so…authentic. That must be some costume you have." Mrs. Holt handed it back, and Therese inwardly sighed with relief.

"Hey, Jen. Can I come up and visit with you awhile?"

Jen looked at her mother.

"Fine with me," her mother said.

Pete followed her into the house. When she glanced back at him, he smiled at her. He didn't seem to mind she was here to see Jen. He was just glad she was here.

Upstairs in Jen's bedroom, Therese kicked off her shoes and sat on the bedspread crisscross with the crown in her lap. Jen sat against a pile of pillows stacked by the headboard. Jen's eyes were still swollen and her face pale, and Therese noticed she had a sore on the corner of her mouth.

"I have something to show you," Therese said, her hands trembling a little. "Don't freak out, okay?"

"I can't promise anything."

"Listen, before I show you, let me explain. This is a special gift. I know this is going to sound crazy, but it has a special power. I'm not giving this to you, but I want to loan it to you."

"Therese, you're making it hard not to freak out. What are you talking about?"

Therese licked her lips. "First you have to promise me, I mean swear on our friendship and all you hold sacred, that you will never tell another soul about this."

"Okay, I'm officially freaked now."

"I'm serious."

"Me, too."

Therese sighed. "Don't be scared. I promise I wouldn't give you any-thing that could hurt you."

"Okay. I promise to keep your secret."

Therese's heart sped up as she lifted the crown toward her head. "Just watch what happens. And don't scream, okay?"

Jen nodded.

Therese put the crown on her head.

"Jesus! What the heck?"

"Sssh. Not too loud, Jen. I don't want your whole family running in here."

"Oh my God!" Jen jumped off the bed and backed into the corner of her room. "Okay, I'm really, really freaked. Where are you?" Jen acci-dentally bumped a stack off books off her table, then lost her balance and fell on the floor beside the strewn books. "Where are you?"

"I'm still here." Therese removed the crown from her head. "You want to try?"

Jen blinked. "This can't be happening." She carefully stood back up, her whole body trembling.

"Go on. Take it to your mirror and watch what happens."

With trembling hands, Jen took the crown from Therese and walked over to her mirror and placed the crown on her head.

"Holy crap!" Jen removed the crown. Then she returned it to her head. "Oh my holy crap!"

"Your crap ain't holy, Jen."

The two girls laughed, only one of them visible.

Jen took the crown off and turned to Therese. "Where'd you get this?"

"I can't tell. It's a secret."

Jen kept putting the crown on and off her head and watching her re-flection disappear and reappear several more times. "I still can't believe it. I must be dreaming."

"I want to loan this to you because I was thinking…" she struggled to find the right words, "I was thinking that if your dad moves back home, you could wear this crown when you feel like disappearing."

Jen took the crown from her head and turned and looked at Therese, then her eyes gradually moved upward toward the ceiling, like she was figuring math. A smile curled onto her face and her eyes grew wide. Tears welled. She crossed the room and threw her arms around Therese. "I love you." Then she went back to the mirror, stood up a little straighter, and tried on the crown one more time.

The wind had picked up when Therese left the Holts' and walked down their property to the dirt road. Pete had offered to drive her—had practically begged—but Therese had said she wanted to walk, so Mrs. Holt had given her a flashlight and made her promise to call when she got there. Carol would freak if she knew, but of course Carol didn't know that the bad guys weren't after Therese. And without her invisibility crown, Therese would have to be extra careful when she reentered the house.

"Hold on, Therese!" Pete's voice called from the end of his gravelly drive. "Wait up a minute."

Therese stopped and shined her light on the ground in front of Pete, so he could see. He looked tall and muscular when he wasn't standing next to Than.

He came up close beside her, and the scent of him was strangely comforting. "Ooh, that wind is something, huh? A northern must be blowing in. Hey, you cold?"

"I'm okay." She was cold, and although it would feel good if he put his arm around her, it wouldn't be good for him. She should be discouraging him.

"You look pretty tonight. That a new shirt?"

She smoothed down the front of her purple knit top. "I've had it a while. Thanks." Then she looked at his shirt. "That Bobby's?"

"What? Oh, yeah. I'm behind on my laundry." Even in the darkness, Therese could see his face color.

"You do your own laundry? That's impressive," she teased.

"Yep. My mother is a slave driver." Then his voice softened. "Not really. She just wants us all to know how to take care of ourselves."

Therese nodded. "That's good."

"Hey, so how's Than? Seen him lately?"

Therese's heart contracted a little harder as she looked at Pete, and she felt sorry for him. She didn't want to add any more pain to his suffering. With his dad coming back and Bobby's anguish and Jen's trepidation, she knew Pete was hurting. She wished she could help. She felt guilty that she couldn't. "I saw Than earlier. He's, um, he's running an errand for his parents today." Never had that line seemed so literal.

Pete nodded. "I see." Then he asked, "He's leaving soon, right?"

Therese looked at the dirt road beneath their feet. "Yeah, I think so. In another week or so."

Then Pete dug the toe of his boot into the dirt and said, "I guess you heard about my dad."

Therese saw the pain in his face, his need for human affection and understanding, and she wanted to help. "Oh, Pete. I'm so sorry about all that. I wish I could…"

He put his arms around her and held her tight. "You're a sweetheart for saying that, but there's nothing anybody can do." With his face in her hair, he breathed in deeply, like he was taking in her scent, and then he released her with his breath. "It was good to see you again. Come by more often, okay?"

She felt guilty for feeling good in his arms. She had always liked Pete. If Than hadn't come into her life, he would have been a natural partner for her. "I will." Then she watched him turn and head back up the drive. She sighed and headed home.

Therese was glad she had been able to help Jen, but she knew the situation around the Holt family would be tense for a while, maybe even forever. She didn't know exactly what it was Mr. Holt had done to his daughter when he was drunk, but her imagination made her shudder. Bobby had said that Pete was the one who had told, so that meant Jen hadn't. Therese now wondered how long Jen had kept silent. She also wondered how miserable it had made Pete to rat out his own father in order to protect his sister.

A low roar, like a train, came from the lake. Therese shined the small circle of light across the grassy field toward the reservoir. By the light from the stars and the half moon in the sky, she saw deer running away from the water, across the dirt road, and up the mountains behind the houses. The roar grew louder, like the train was upon her. Now chipmunks scurried across the road, and the ground beneath her trembled. An earthquake? She looked all around her as panic set in. She wanted to run like the animals, but her feet were like bricks, and so she stood there, waiting.

Then she had this thought: Maybe Artemis was angry that Therese had loaned her gift to Jen.

"Pete?" She shined her light toward the Holts' driveway, but Pete was no longer in sight. She ran toward the driveway. "Pete?" Nothing.

She ran toward her house, the ground quaking beneath her feet. The dirt road cracked.

"Than!" Therese called. But before she could cry out his name again, a giant wall of cold water washed over her. It entered her mouth before she had gotten air. She lost her footing and dropped the flashlight. Underwater, she couldn't see. Her body tumbled and turned, and her hair whipped and clung to her face. She frantically tried to gain control by swimming, but she didn't know which way was up or down. Something like a tree branch scraped against her midriff, cutting the skin. She swam away from the force pulling her, but she couldn't even tell if she was making progress, and she needed air and couldn't find it.

Water entered her mouth and her throat burned and scratched, like sandpaper on fire, hard and hot and scraping everything it touched. She writhed in the water, as her father had the night he died.

All of a sudden she saw her parents drowning in front of her: her father turning his head side to side in a wild frenzy and her mother silently yielding to the terrible depths that took her. Therese called to Than in her mind as the darkness overpowered her, and she lost consciousness.

Chapter Thirty-Six: Ambush

At the gates of Mount Olympus, Than and his sisters had amassed an army to recapture McAdams from Ares and his sons. Than's heart thudded with fierce determination, for he knew that if Therese could not avenge her parents' death upon McAdams, she would never be his bride.

As soon as the Furies had left Peshawar, they had flown straight to their cousin Hermes, who had further solicited help from Demeter, Persephone, and Hecate.

But their greatest ally was Aphrodite, who stood in all her beauty, waiting for Ares, who loved her.

She was also the mother of Phobos and Deimos, who obeyed her.

When the god of war appeared at the gates with his sons and the prisoner, ready for battle, he was caught off guard by the beautiful sight of his one true love.

"Go, boys," Aphrodite said. "This is between Ares and me."

Phobos and Deimos vanished.

"Will you betray me?" Ares said gently.

"What you do is wrong, my love," Aphrodite said.

"No. What you do is wrong. Don't interfere. Humans can never rise to greatness without the challenges of the gods! Now stand back and let me through, you coddlers!"

Ares made to charge, but at once, Than and his sisters and his mother and grandmother, along with Hermes and Hecate, descended upon him in a cloud of determination and will, and it took every one of them to bind back the arms of the god of war and recapture McAdams.

Ares roared and pulled free and jumped up into the sky above them and laughed. "Take him. I have a better prisoner."

At that moment, Than heard Therese's cries from below. With bitter hatred, he narrowed his eyes at the god of war and shouted, "What have you done?"

"You'll soon discover." Ares disappeared.

Chapter Thirty-Seven: Poseidon

Therese awoke on a cold hard rock in the middle of a vast, unending ocean. She and her rock were the only things she could see for miles. She was cold and wet. Her shorts and shirt stuck to her like glue, her sneakers were filled with water, and she shivered uncontrollably. Was she dreaming?

She stood up on the rock to see if she could fly, but her feet barely lifted from the ground, she lost her balance, and she fell backward into the cold, salty water. She resurfaced, spitting mouthfuls of the yucky salt water, and clambered onto the rock. Now she was even colder, and her teeth chattered, and she shivered even more than she had before.

In her mind, she cried for Than, and she asked what had happened. She asked him where she was and would he please, please, please come and take her home. She clutched the golden locket around her neck thinking she was the least powerful creature in the world right now.

Five feet away, a man emerged, waist high, from the water. His sun-bleached hair clung to his head and neck, and his sun-bleached beard dripped nearly down to his bare chest. He appeared to be about fifty. His eyes were the blue-green color of the sea and his lips sun-burnt red and his skin bronze. His nostrils flared with anger as he lifted his trident from the water, about to speak.

Therese could guess now who he was.

"I could kill you this instant!" he roared like thunder.

His voice had startled her, and she clutched the locket around her neck, but then she took a breath and calmed herself down.

Although she preferred to go to the Underworld as a god, she wasn't as afraid of death as she had once been, before her parents were killed. *Before my parents were killed.* She had actually allowed herself to think the words she hadn't been able to think in over a month? *My parents* were killed. It was a small victory, but it made her feel like maybe she wasn't the very least powerful person in the world.

Poseidon raised his trident even higher, above his head.

Therese closed her eyes and waited. She couldn't believe that Poseidon was her enemy, because of all the gods she had ever read about, he had been her favorite. As a swimmer and lover of ocean life, she had always thought of him as an imaginary guardian, certainly not the foe facing her now. She had chosen him for her sixth-grade mythology project.

In her mind, she was talking to him without realizing it. "You were my friend," she thought. "I've always looked up to you and aspired to be like you. I love the sea and marine life. I love to swim through water. It makes me feel so free. I used to think that if I had a past life, I must have been a dolphin, and my dream has been to go to Sea World in San Antonio and swim with dolphins. And I remember reading that you gave the horse to humankind. I love horses and help take care of my friend's horses. We lost Dumbo last week. It was so sad, and I'll miss him, but I'm thankful to have known him, and I'm thankful that you brought humans and horses together. How can you, of all the gods, be my enemy? It seems unnatural. You're my idol.

"But I guess if I'm going to die now, it's fitting that it is in water. That's where my parents died, and maybe I should have died with them. I realize now Dumbo also died in water. That's strange. Anyway, I started this life in water, in my mother's womb, and now I'll end it in water. That's almost poetic.

"I do wish I could say goodbye to my aunt. I wish I could find Clifford and bring him with me. I wish I could say goodbye to Puffy and Jewels and my human friends. I wish I could see Vicki and help her deal with her mother's suicide. I wish I could be there to watch over Jen when her dad moves home. I wish I could spend eternity with Than as his wife."

Oh, Than! She thought of his perfect face and his strong body and the soft touch of his hands. She recalled the pleasure he had taken with his face turned up to the rain, his body moving effortlessly through the cool water of the lake, his expression of delight as he tasted her salad, the sugared iced tea, the brownies, and the other foods he had tried for the first time. She remembered their first waltz and his eagerness to learn. And she thought of the joy they took together in watching three sunsets and a sunrise in a single day. She longed to be in his arms, safe in his warm embrace.

She stood there shivering on the rock waiting for Poseidon to kill her. Why hadn't he done it yet? She opened her eyes.

Poseidon's expression had changed. His nostrils no longer flared, and he lowered his trident back into the sea, his arms hanging limp beside him.

"I do not wish to be your enemy," he said in a voice that wasn't gentle, but wasn't harsh.

I don't understand, she said to him in her mind.

"I am obliged to Ares," Poseidon said. "I swore an oath on the river Styx."

Oh. So she would die in water like her parents. "Are you going to kill me?"

"No. I'm to deliver you to Mount Olympus."

Therese should have been frightened by this, but she was elated.

"Before we go, I want to give you a gift, to prove I bear no personal animosity toward you." He waved his trident in the air, and a herd of dolphins sprang from the water and surrounded her rock with their heads above the surface and their eyes on her. She wished she had Than's power of understanding animal languages as they clicked their greetings to her. There must have been a dozen of them, with their mouths open in a perpetual grin, clicking their hellos.

"Hello," she said shyly. Then to Poseidon, she said, "What a wonderful gift. Thank you for giving me the chance to see the dolphins up close." She wished she could touch one, but she didn't want to ask and appear ungrateful.

Poseidon laughed. "I appreciate your gratitude and humility," he said, still laughing. "But my gift is better still. Would you care to ride on a dolphin's back across the sea to Greece?"

"Would I!" she shouted with glee. And to think she had just wanted to touch one. She would ride one, like they did at Sea World, something she had read about on the Internet a few years ago. "Yes! Thank you very much! What? Do I dive in?"

Poseidon laughed again, and now that he no longer had a stern face, he appeared quite beautiful. "I've never seen a happier prisoner. Yes. Dive into the water."

Therese was so excited that she dove in and swam the dolphin kick between the rock and the circle of dolphins. She added her butterfly arms so she could catch breaths of air in between her strokes, and then she swam up to the closest dolphin.

"You're a skilled swimmer," Poseidon noted. "It pleases me to see humans move so naturally in the water. I wish more were able. It bothers me that so many don't even know how to swim. The Earth is mostly water, you know."

She treaded water, her teeth chattering with the cold. "Y-y-yes. Th-thank you. Is th-there a p-p-articular d-d-dolphin I sh-should r-ride?"

"Arion there will take you. He's named for one of my sons."

The dolphin dipped his head to her in greeting.

Excited, thrilled, and totally overjoyed, Therese climbed onto the dolphin's back. His skin was slick and rubbery and hard to grasp. Her bare legs kept sliding off. She wished she had worn jeans instead of shorts.

"Hold onto his dorsal fin," Poseidon said, moving closer. "I will wrap a golden net around you and Arion's body. The net will keep you attached should you slip. It will allow you to stay underwater for long periods of time. It will also keep you warm." He raised his trident, and the net, like a fisherman's net but golden, encircled her and Arion.

The warmth instantly soothed her, and a low moan escaped her lips. The relief from the chilling cold was itself a gift. Her muscles relaxed, she took in larger breaths, and she could actually enjoy the feeling of sitting on the dolphin's back. She hugged him, circled her legs around him, kissed his wet rubbery skin, and said to Arion, "Thank you in advance. This is one of the most amazing moments of my life."

Several other dolphins swam up to her and rubbed their bodies against her. She extended her fingers through one of the openings between the weave in the net and stroked them. They clicked sounds of affection, and in reply, Therese said, "This is heaven."

"Are you ready?" Poseidon asked.

She was scared and excited all at once, and she was as ready as she would ever be. The golden net was surprisingly light and flexible. She lifted her head from the dolphin's back to face Poseidon. "Yes sir."

"We'll stop at my palace at the bottom of the sea first. It is a halfway point between this rock and Mount Olympus. Do you know where we are?"

Therese shook her head.

"The Aegean Sea. My palace is at the bottom, you see. I want to fetch my chariot. I prefer to travel over land on it. It makes for an exhilarating ride." He raised his trident. "To my palace!"

With that, Arion and the company of dolphins sprang into the air and dove down into the water with Poseidon in the lead. She could see him in front of her, swimming like a dolphin, his hair and beard flowing from his head and his green sarong flowing from his waist. He wore leather sandals that extended from his feet like flippers.

Below them the ocean world came into view. Her eyesight was improved, though she wasn't sure how. Was it the golden net that allowed her to see so many details of this spectacular vision? Fingers of purple, blue, and gold waved to them, and fish of many shapes, colors, and sizes darted this way and that, some in large schools, and others, like the huge groupers suspended near the bottom, alone. Occasionally, she caught sight of a barracuda or a shark, but most of the sea life was nonthreatening. Sea anemones and coral decorated the ocean floor where the sunbeams barely hit. Oh, she could just make out a cluster of starfish. And, ah! Look at those jellyfish! And there! A manatee! The most curious to Therese were the sea horses and their curly tails.

As they swam closer to the ocean floor, she was able to see other forms of marine life burrowing in the sand and rocks. Sting rays there! Hermit crabs! A lobster! And over there, eels, like the figments in her dreams!

Arion dodged a rock formation full of shadows and fluttered over another city of coral. Then he turned sideways as they passed through a rocky tunnel in a matter of seconds. Past the tunnel was a deep drop in the ocean floor—so deep Therese could see nothing beyond the darkness.

Into the darkness they plunged.

Although the golden net kept Therese warm, she could feel a drop in temperature as they plunged deeper and deeper into the darkness. She held on to Arion, wondering for the first time if Poseidon planned to keep her as an underwater prisoner so that she would never see the light of day again.

Then she realized this is how it would be when she was the queen of death in the Underworld: dark, gloomy, airless. A shudder made its way down her spine, and she pressed her face against Arion's back.

"I'm scared," she thought.

A new vision presented itself to her. Bright golden lights came from the bottom of the ocean, illuminating an amazing transparent structure. Its walls seemed to be formed from clear crystals, and it made her think of an aquarium. This must be Poseidon's palace. Without entering, she could see many figures inside of it—merfolk with tails and other, more human-like, people sitting among the furniture, eating at tables on golden chairs, and lounging on beds clustered in curtains of seaweed growing up from the ocean floor. At the back of the palace, the walls were no longer transparent and were made of something like shell, perhaps mother-of-pearl. Poseidon disappeared behind the shell wall as she waited on Arion's back, and before she had a chance to scan over the other figures a second time, a flash of white bolted toward her.

Three white stallions the color of sea foam and wearing harnesses of gold halted before her, hurling a current of water all about her. Then Poseidon appeared. "Let go of the dolphin," he commanded, after which he unwrapped the golden net from Arion and secured the net around her.

As Arion swam away, Therese cried to him, "Thank you!" and surprisingly, she could hear herself perfectly underwater. Then she turned to Poseidon. "That ride was spectacular. Thank you so much!"

"You're welcome. And I apologize in advance for what I'm about to do."

Despite the ominous sense of foreboding she felt after Poseidon's words, she asked cheerfully, "What are your horses' names?"

"Riptide, Seaquake, and Crest."

"May I pet them?"

He nodded, so she reached her fingers through a hole in the weave of her net and touched the flank of each horse. "Hello," she said softly. "How are you? You are all so beautiful."

Poseidon led her into his golden chariot, and before she had even sat on the bench behind his large, standing body, they took off in sudden lightning speed.

Up from the depths of the ocean they went, and then they were riding along the surface of the sea as though they were in a boat and not a golden chariot being pulled by horses. The wind whipped against Therese's face, and she squinted against it. For the first time since she had awakened, she could see land. Within minutes, they rushed onto a deserted beach and dodged past rocks and trees. When they neared a city, they rose above it, flying in the air. Therese peered down at the buildings and streets and cars and people below. She wondered if the people could see them flying over Greece. She looked ahead once again as a cluster of mountain peaks came into view. A light fog covered the highest of these, and the sunbeams against the fog created a majestic hue, a circle of light, like an enormous halo.

Mount Olympus, Therese thought as she gasped at the beautiful sight. And she hoped already there and waiting for her would be Than.

Chapter Thirty-Eight: Mount Olympus

Poseidon stopped the chariot before a giant wall of clouds at the top of Mount Olympus. Nothing but white stretched up and into the sky. Poseidon said, "Spring, Summer, Winter, and Fall, open the gates of Olympus so I, Poseidon, may enter with my prisoner."

A loud roar carried through the air, and a tunnel of cold wind lifted in front of them, startling Therese. At its center was a single rain cloud. As the wind settled and the rain cloud emptied its contents right before their eyes and then dissipated, the giant wall of clouds opened, and Poseidon drew the chariot forward. The wall of clouds closed behind them, and, in front of them, at the center of a golden-paved plaza, was a round fountain spraying water into the blue sky from the spout of a golden whale. At the top of this fountain, where the water arched and fell into a pool bordered with golden bricks, was a rainbow. Therese looked on with amazement.

Behind this fountain was a giant palace of white stone and ornate columns. To the right and left of the palace were separate buildings, as tall, but not as wide or deep. Poseidon guided the chariot to the right of the fountain to one of these separate buildings. The golden doors were latched open, revealing two golden chariots parked on either side with a space in between, into where Poseidon now backed his chariot.

"It looks like Hades beat us here," the god of the sea mumbled. "And Zeus's chariot has a new ding. Wonder where that came from, and if he knows of it."

A beautiful young man with long thick eyelashes and golden curls stepped forward to unbridle the horses.

After he had the chariot free of the animals, Poseidon said, "I'll take them to the stables myself, Cupid. I think my prisoner would enjoy the tour."

Cupid gave a subtle bow and disappeared.

So that was Cupid. She wondered if Cupid knew that she knew he had pierced Pete's heart.

Poseidon kept the golden net around Therese as he helped her from his chariot. She noticed the sandals on his feet had retracted so they no longer formed flippers for swimming. With the three stallions tied to leads, Poseidon led her and Riptide, Seaquake, and Crest across the golden-paved plaza, passing the center fountain, to the other building separate from the palace. It was the same size as the chariot shed and had the same type of golden doors latched open at the entry. As the god of the sea led his horses into the building, which Therese now recognized as stables, Therese caught sight of Than standing among a group of people at the back stall near two black horses.

"Therese!" Than said, rushing to her side.

She had barely time to blink from the moment she saw him, and now he was putting his arms around her with the golden fishermen's net between them. Her hair had dried during the journey, and it curled wildly from having dried in the beating wind. Than put his fingers through an opening in the weave to touch her hair and hold it between two fingers.

"I'm glad to see you safe," he said softly.

Her heart warmed at the sight of him, and she longed to wrap her arms around him, but the net prevented her. She gazed into his eyes and whispered, "I missed you."

"I missed you, too," he whispered back. "I'm sorry it's come to this, but I promise to protect you."

From the direction of the black horses came another man, tall like Than, but older-looking, with the same dark hair, but eyes as black as coal, and a short beard. Like Than and the other gods, he was beautiful. He walked over to Therese with an air of authority. "So, son, I finally meet your sweetheart," he said.

This was Hades, Than's father. "How do you do?" she said.

"Better than you, apparently," he replied.

"This wasn't what we had in mind," Than murmured. "She wanted to play her flute for you, feed you chocolate. This has gone all wrong."

"Better to meet like this than not at all," Therese said bravely.

"Oh boy, an optimist," Hades said with sarcasm.

Therese's face flushed. She could see the red color rise all the way to the tip of her nose.

"And sensitive to boot," he spoke again.

"Dad, can you lighten up?" Than kept his arm on Therese.

The god of the Underworld turned his attention to the god of the sea who lingered near the stall where the latter boarded his white horses. "Poseidon."

"Hades."

They each gave the other a civil nod.

During this exchange, Therese noticed Meg and Tizzie standing with their prisoner in the back of the stable. The third sister was there as well. She had fire-red hair that stood up in a Mohawk, deep black eyes, and a choker of black stones around her neck. All three Furies wore tall black heeled boots and short skirts. Tizzie wore her emeralds and Meg her rubies, and their hair was down and wild. A large bird sat perched on Meg's shoulder, and a wolf stood beside Tizzie.

The man in the middle of them she recognized as McAdams. Therese's eyes grew wide, and hot tears flooded them as she faced the mastermind behind her parents' death. She would kill him. She would make him pay. Though now, as she looked at him—short, thin, bald, with spectacles and wearing a suit that looked too big—he seemed terrified, pathetic, and about to pee in his pants.

"We will take the prisoner to court," the redheaded Alecto, said, and then the Furies and their prisoner disappeared.

"Poseidon," Than sneered his greeting.

"Thanatos." Poseidon gave him a tired nod. "I will entrust my lovely prisoner to you for now. You cannot break the spell of the golden net, so I have no fear of losing her, especially here among so many." And with that, Poseidon vanished.

"Don't be mad at him," Therese whispered. "He was kind to me."

Than scowled. "Some kindness. Don't you realize what he's done?"

She shook her head. "No. Oh my God, what?"

Hades turned toward the back of the stables. "Cupid, make sure my black stallions get the same amount of oats as Poseidon and Zeus's beasts. I won't tolerate special treatment, understand?"

Cupid appeared in front of him and gave a slight bow. "As always."

"I'll see you at court," Hades said to Than and Therese, and then he disappeared.

"So what's Poseidon done?" Therese asked.

"Come on," Than said. "They're all waiting for us."

Therese trembled with fear as they entered the golden-paved plaza and walked past the fountain to seven steps, each a different color of the rainbow, starting with red and ending with violet. Her new fears made it difficult for her to appreciate the two giant columns flanking the entryway, and, just inside, the magnificent foyer. But her eyes opened wide, and she did not fail to notice as she stepped into a large rectangular assembly hall open to the clear blue sky, from which nearly solid beams of sunshine shot down to form a bright canopy above them.

Therese looked down from the sky to the white marble floor as she followed Than past Hades into the hall. Hades stood just inside with the Furies and their prisoner nearby. As Than and Therese passed them, a golden chair ascended from the floor, and Hades sat on it. It was apparently his throne. He sat opposite the long hall from two gods whom Therese presumed were Zeus and his queen, Hera.

"Should I kneel or something?" Therese asked Than, staying close beside him.

"No. I'll introduce you to each god, one by one," Than whispered. "Just give a subtle bow. Don't go deep. They despise groveling." Then Than spoke in a surprisingly loud and confident voice. "Gods and goddesses of the court, with your permission, it is my pleasure to introduce you to Therese Mills."

Zeus gave a nod. "Please bring her before each of us, beginning with Aphrodite to your left."

"Therese, I present you to Aphrodite, the goddess of love," Than said.

Still wrapped in the golden fishermen's net, Therese stood before Aphrodite and gave her a bow. The goddess of love was the most beautiful of all gathered there. Her hour-glass figure was accentuated by the white, form-fitting gown that ended just above her delicate sandaled feet. Without speaking, Therese met her crystal blue eyes and mouthed, "Thank you." Before now, Therese hadn't been able to properly thank the goddess for curing Clifford and leaving her the traveling robe. Aphrodite flipped her blond hair from her creamy bare shoulder and gave Therese a smile of pleasure, then dipped her head in polite greeting.

Than continued. "To Aphrodite's left is the goddess of the woods, Artemis."

Therese took four steps and faced the goddess on her throne. Also beautiful, her eyes and her gown were deep green, like the color of pine needles, and her brown hair was fastened into a knot on her head, a few stray hairs caressing her neck. Therese gave her subtle bow and again mouthed, "Thank you." Artemis bowed in return.

To Artemis's left was a double throne, and on it sat a mother and daughter, very similar in appearance, with golden brown eyes and hair the color of corn. Their hair was long and straight, as were their gowns of pale pastels. Than introduced them as his grandmother, Demeter, goddess of the harvest, and his mother, Persephone, queen of the Underworld.

"She's lovely," Persephone said.

To their left sat a red-haired, brown-eyed goddess whose gown reminded Therese of Alice in Wonderland in that it was blue with a white apron. Than introduced her as Hestia, goddess of the hearth, Zeus's unmarried sister.

To the left of Hestia and to the right of Zeus sat gray-eyed, black-haired Athena, whom Therese immediately recognized. Therese clutched the locket at her throat, and as she had done with Aphrodite and Artemis, mouthed, "Thank you," before she bowed to the goddess.

Zeus and Hera sat together on a double throne at the center back of the great hall, and though all the thrones were ornamental in design, theirs stood out because of the golden birds perched behind them. Behind Zeus perched a golden ruby-eyed eagle, and behind Hera three golden finches. Both gods gave their subtle bow after Therese gave hers.

Therese detected a hint of snarl in Than's voice as he introduced red-haired Ares, the god of war, who, along with McAdams, was responsible for her parents' death. Ares showed no anger or emotion as he gave his bow at his introduction. He was as beautiful as the other gods and as civil and polite.

Therese recognized Hermes, who winked at her when he was introduced, producing a broad smile across her face. Her smile lingered when she faced Poseidon next, for despite the fact that he was the god who had captured her, she would be forever grateful for the dolphin ride across the sea.

Beside Poseidon, across the hall from his twin sister Artemis, sat the most beautiful god of all the males. Than introduced him as Apollo, god of truth, of music, and of healing. He held his lyre upon his lap. His eyes were the same evergreen as his sister's, and his hair was the same golden brown. Next to Apollo, and directly across from Aphrodite, was Aphrodite's husband, Hephaestus, the god of the forge, who appeared opposite to Apollo in every way. Whereas Apollo looked young, Hephaestus seemed old; where Apollo looked strong and erect, Hephaestus appeared bowed and misshapen. His hands were gnarled and calloused, his black hair streaked with gray, and his black eyes lined with dark circles and bags beneath them. He was the only god among them not beautiful. Therese gave her bow, and he his.

The Furies moved away from their father, pulling their prisoner to the center of the hall, so that Than and Therese could stand before Hades. Although he had already introduced them in the stables, Than formally presented her here before the other gods.

Hades gave a deeper bow than the others and surprised Therese by saying, "It is a pleasure to meet you, Therese. I speak on behalf of all the gods when I welcome you to our court. I am only sorry that it could not be under better circumstances." He gave Therese a pleasant smile, and his coal black eyes sparkled in the sunlight.

Zeus cleared his throat. "Thank you, Hades. Thanatos, bring the prisoner to the center of the hall beside the Furies and the other prisoner." He then addressed the others "I believe all present are aware of the situation at hand. The Furies want to avenge the death of two souls by punishing their killer, Steven McAdams. Ares and Poseidon have captured Therese Mills in attempt to negotiate for McAdams's release. The girl for the man. We shall first hear from Ares, then Hades, and finally, Poseidon. If other Olympians have opinions, we will hear them, but remember that only the Olympian gods may speak in a court hearing unless I say otherwise. We will then come to our decision and pronounce our judgment. Ponder this: should Hades take both, one, or neither mortal soul before us?"

Therese gasped. None of the outcomes would allow her to avenge her parents' death and become a god. If Hades took McAdams's soul, Than's deal with his father would become impossible to carry out. You can't kill a soul. And if McAdams were granted his freedom by this court, how would she find and kill him on her own? Wouldn't the gods have to honor the judgment of the court? Wouldn't that mean Than and his sisters would be prohibited from helping her? She looked at Than, and he met her eyes with sympathetic understanding.

"No," she said in her mind to all of the gods around her. "I can't let this happen." She clutched her golden locket and waited.

Ares stood before his throne. "I do not deny the clear discrepancy between these two prisoners. One is vile, contemptible, though he has served me well; the other, kind and good. But sometimes good people must be sacrificed for the greater good. You all know as well as I that human power must be spread through many countries, and one among them has become too strong. It is no secret that I believe the fall of the United States will set this imbalance straight. McAdams, the prisoner who was not introduced and who cowers there in the middle like a pathetic toad, must be spared the torments of hell because in his crimes he served me. To make my demands more appealing, Poseidon and I have taken as our prisoner the object of Thanatos's desire. We will free her upon the release of McAdams and with an oath upon the river Styx to never enact that punishment upon him." Ares returned to his throne.

Therese felt herself go limp. Than's hand was fast around her waist. Ares was a persuasive speaker. She felt all hope was lost. She could never become a god and spend eternity with Than if the gods agreed with Ares. She had to be permitted to avenge her parents' death.

Hades now stood and took a few steps toward the middle of the hall. "Since when has Ares cared about the fate of his human instruments? He's not here to protect McAdams. His real purpose is less noble. He knows that my son, Thanatos, struck a bargain with me. I swore on the river Styx to make his sweetheart a god if she personally avenged the death of her parents. Ares fears the conflict that might ensue, the leverage he may lose among us, if the daughter of his victims were to become like him. In fact, he would rather see me take both souls now and damn McAdams to a fate worse than that of Tantalus than see Therese Mills become a god. My daughters, the Furies, have learned that this cowering toad, as Ares has so perfectly described him, has been manufacturing and selling fake medicines to humans. Think of all those other souls in my care who have died because they did not have their proper drugs. If justice is our concern today, then choose justice. I urge you all to free the girl and watch her avenge the death of her parents and the death of those not represented here today."

Therese perked up with renewed hope. She felt a new respect for Than's father, and, in her mind, she prayed to him, "Thank you, Hades. That was an awesome speech."

As he took his seat upon his throne, Hades met her eyes and gave her a subtle nod.

Zeus cleared his throat. "Poseidon?"

All eyes turned to the god of the sea who now stood before his throne. "I have nothing to add. I defer my turn to my cohort, Ares." Poseidon sat back down.

Ares stood and said, "I see the merit in Hades's speech."

Therese's mouth dropped open in surprise. She looked up into Than's eyes, but he seemed wary.

Ares continued. "Hades agreed to make the girl a god, and his condition was that she should avenge the death of her parents. But I ask you, would that be accomplished by allowing her to simply walk up to him, imprisoned, and slit his throat? Haven't the Furies already done the hardest part of the avenging? They have worked day and night tracking his whereabouts, and they have taken him captive. What role has the girl played in any of that? And so she walks up and cuts his throat and that merits her to be here among us gods? Any pathetic wight could do the same."

"What do you propose?" Zeus asked.

Therese's face fell. She looked again at Than and met his worried eyes. This was not going well at all.

"I propose," Ares started, "that we place the two of them in a contained arena with invisible walls far from civilizations; that we allow them each the same weapons—a sword and shield—equitable in all ways; that the gods may watch and make suggestions, but not intervene;

and that these two humans fight to the death. The victor lives and is set free; the loser goes straight to the Underworld, a soul among the dead."

"That's barbaric!" Aphrodite cried.

"Unfathomable!" Apollo shouted.

"Fair!" Hades said. "But I say let the girl choose between these three: first, set them both free to live and find their fates without interference from the gods; or, second, have me take both souls to the Underworld, neither made a god nor given his just punishment; or, last, fight the battle to the death, as Ares has suggested. If the girl chooses the latter and wins, she becomes a god."

"Agreed!" Ares snapped, eagerly it seemed to Therese.

Than gave Therese a hint of a smile, but she could not return it. Maybe he assumed she would choose the first and live a safe, and perhaps long, life. But it would be a life without him, for her chances of finding McAdams and killing him on her own were so remote as to be insignificant. Maybe he assumed she would choose the second and go peacefully with him to the Underworld a dead, unfree, soul. She doubted he thought she would choose the third.

"What?" he whispered.

She shook her head.

Zeus then said, "So, Therese, which do you choose?"

She walked to the center of the hall and looked around at each of the gods, settling her gaze on Ares. "If I choose the third—"

"What?" Than shouted. He ran to her side. "Don't even consider it! Therese! Listen to me. McAdams will kill you. He's small, but stronger than you. You might suffer abominable---"

"Let the girl speak," Ares said.

Therese bit her lip. "If I choose the third, to fight McAdams to the death, which I have a feeling is the choice you most prefer, will you swear on the river Styx to protect my aunt and all my loved ones until they die their natural deaths?"

"You have my word," Ares said with obvious satisfaction.

She met Than's pleading eyes. "No, Therese," he begged. "Don't do this. Choose the first. I'll find a way to come back for you."

If she chose the first, McAdams would be forever hunting her and her aunt. She didn't want to live a life in fear. Plus, there would be little hope of killing McAdams without the Furies' help, which meant life without Than.

If she chose the second, she would die a painless death and join her parents in the Underworld, but there would be no chance of a happily-ever-after with Than since her personality and freedom would be gone.

If she were to choose the third and die at McAdams's hand, she would join her parents in the Underworld. And if she were to succeed in killing him, she would become a god and be with Than forever. Plus Ares would guarantee the safety of her loved ones regardless of the outcome. With the third choice, she couldn't lose.

Her heart hammered in her chest. "I choose the third," she said. "I choose to fight."

Artemis and Athena lifted their fists simultaneously and shouted, with smiling faces, "Yes!"

Aphrodite covered her face with her hands and wept.

Ares smiled triumphantly.

The others looked wary, even afraid for her.

Chapter Thirty-Nine: More Gifts

Then let us proceed," Zeus commanded, lifting his arms.

"Wait!" Than objected. "Permission to speak, Lord Zeus."

"Permission granted."

"Both of the prisoners are exhausted and hungry. Ares will see a better fight if he permits them one more meal and night of rest." He looked at the other gods and then back at Therese, unable to believe that it had come to this.

"Hear, hear!" several shouted all at once.

"Agreed!" Ares said. "The battle should begin in twelve hours. That will give Hephaestus plenty of time to wield two equal weapons and two equal shields all made from the same metal."

"But before we adjourn," Hades said, "I need clarification. Ares said the gods may watch and make suggestions but not intervene. Specifics, please."

Everyone turned to Ares. "Yes. We need specifics," Ares agreed. "We shall be an audience like that in the Roman coliseum of old. We can watch from our thrones and shout our suggestions and encouragement. But no gifts shall we give them! No magic help at all! We may encourage and offer guidance, but the humans must fight without magic. Are all agreed? Are these rules specific enough?"

"Hear, hear!" several exclaimed.

"Agreed!" Hades said above them all. "Now remove the net from your prisoner!"

As soon as the golden net vanished, Therese flung her arms around Than. "I'm so sorry!"

He held her tight and dipped his head to kiss her shoulder, feeling that this would be the last, the very last chance he would have to hold her as she truly was, as a full and complete being. He felt tears stinging his eyes and desperation gripping his heart. He had come so close to finding love and happiness for all eternity. So close. He would have been better to never have met her. Then he wouldn't now be possessed by such pain and anguish.

"Why are you sorry? I'm the one who got you into this disaster!" He held her more tightly. "You chose to fight to be with me. If gods could die, I would die right now of grief."

"You have a lot of confidence in me," Therese said.

Aphrodite's weeping continued to sound throughout the hall.

"I'm sorry," Than replied. "I shouldn't be so pessimistic. Of course, you have a chance of winning."

"It's slim, but it's there," she murmured.

Others had gathered around them, so she lifted her face from Than's and separated her body from his. He felt he would cry.

Poseidon spoke first. "You may sleep in my chambers, Therese. I prefer my palace beneath the sea." He gave her a friendly smile and touched her shoulder in a fatherly way.

"That's so nice of you," she said meekly.

"And I will weave you fresh sheets from silk," Athena said. "They will help you sleep." Athena fingered the locket around Therese's neck. "Like this gift, they are not magical, only comfortable and soothing. I will have them ready in an hour."

It brought Than great pleasure to see the goddess's support of Therese.

"I'm so grateful," Therese said.

"And I will serve you a delicious, filling meal," Hestia said, with eyes that were pools of chocolate. "Just come to the banquet hall when you are ready to eat."

"Thank you," Therese said to Hestia, whose red hair reminded Than of Therese's.

To Than, she said, without speaking, "I'm so sorry. She's so lovely."

"And you shall use my pillow," Artemis offered to Therese. "It is made of the softest goose feathers." Artemis's evergreen eyes against her fair skin stood out like the first leaves do in the melting spring snow.

"That sounds lovely," Therese said. "Thanks so much."

To Than's mind, Artemis communicated, "She is strong. Stay hopeful."

"And I will play my lyre in my chamber beside yours," Apollo said to Therese. "You will hear the soft lullaby through the walls."

Than was overwhelmed by the support of so many. Apollo was a great ally, and Than would remember this.

"That would be comforting," Therese said in her sweet voice.

Apollo's mind was full of sympathy for Than, "Hold her while you can."

"And I shall harmonize on my pipe," Hermes said, "from the chamber on the other side."

Hermes winked at her, like a kind uncle, and Than felt himself moved by his generosity.

"Thank you so much," she said. "I'm truly grateful."

Aphrodite wiped her beautiful eyes and said, "And I will lend you my silk eye mask. It will keep light away and soothe your tired eyes."

Therese said, "Oh, I will definitely need that. Thank you."

To Than, Aphrodite silently communicated, "I am full of the greatest sorrow."

"And before you sleep," Persephone said to Therese, "my mother and I shall bathe you in warm mineral water to relax your tired bones."

Both mother and daughter, with their long hair of corn and their deep chestnut eyes, put a hand on Therese's shoulders, and Than saw the family they might have made.

"That sounds so nice. I don't know how to thank you enough."

Hades took his wife in his arms and kissed her cheek. "Lovely idea, my love."

Persephone gave her husband a smile.

Demeter asked Therese, "Would you prefer to bathe before or after you eat?"

"After, please. I have a feeling I will want to go immediately to bed after such a treat, though I'm not sure I'll be able to eat."

McAdams stood alone except for Ares, who spoke to him in quiet tones, and Than noticed Therese was looking at him with astonishingly kind eyes.

"You don't feel sorry for the murderer, do you?" he asked softly.

"Of course not. But this doesn't seem fair, the gods giving me attention. When I kill him, I don't want Ares to have any room to contest my win."

Hades put a hand on Therese's shoulder. "The prisoner reaps the harvest of the evil character he has sown. If none help him but Ares, McAdams can only blame himself. He has free will. Ares never forced him to do his evil deeds."

Therese nodded.

"I must return to my kingdom," Hades said. "I'll see you in the morning."

"Thank you."

"I must go as well," Poseidon said. "But I, too, will return tomorrow."

"Goodbye and thanks again."

Than stood with her in the great hall as the gods made their exit. He was grateful for a little more time, but the anguish was almost unbearable. He took her face in his hands and gently put his lips to hers as tears welled in his eyes and fell down his cheeks.

Chapter Forty: The Last Supper

Than led Therese into the banquet hall where an oblong table of gold with twelve matching ornate chairs stretched the expanse of the room. Unlike the assembly hall, this room did not open to the sky, and the white ceiling was trimmed in golden crown molding on which was painted a continuous grapevine. In the center of the ceiling hung an enormous gold and crystal chandelier, with five gradated layers of circular curtains made of teardrop crystals. Than pulled out a chair for Therese, and they sat together on the farthest end of the table, where Hestia now entered from another door to bring them plates of food.

"Mortals are not allowed to eat the food of gods," Hestia said, "but I hope you will find this meal of vegetables and rice the next best thing." Hestia laid out the food along with a basket of rolls and a cup of butter as Therese thanked her over and over. Hestia returned with cups of wine. "This will help you sleep."

Therese ate even though she wasn't hungry. She knew she needed to keep her strength. She was so nervous that she couldn't really taste the food. The wine, though, tasted strong and she couldn't decide if she liked it, but she forced the entire glass down. She wanted to sleep.

As she ate with one hand, she held Than's hand with the other. She couldn't touch him enough. This might be their last night together. As a soul in the Underworld without freedom and personality, she would no longer be attractive to him, and, because of the River of Forgetfulness, she would likely no longer appreciate him. Although she was frightened, she ate for strength, and she tried to savor every bite, every moment of this last meal, this final night.

"I will be there watching over you," Than said. "I will be the one shouting the loudest."

She gave him a brave smile. "Just think, tomorrow I may be a god like you, and we can begin our life of eternity together."

He smiled back. "You're right to think positive." He stroked her hair and kissed the hand he held with his.

Therese frowned.

"What?" Than touched the lines on her forehead. "What happened to your positive thoughts?"

"I'm worried about my aunt. I wish I could get a message to her. She'll be wondering where I am, freaking out, probably assuming the bad guys have captured me."

"I've already thought of that." He gave her a wry smile.

"What? What did you do?"

"I called Jen and asked her to call your aunt and tell her you were spending the night with her. I told Jen that you and I wanted to spend as much time together as possible before I leave. Jen was glad to do it."

"Jen thinks I'm staying with you at the Melner cabin?"

He nodded.

"She probably thinks we're, I mean, I bet she suspects we…"

"What?" He gave her a flirtatious smile.

Therese's appetite returned, and she popped part of a roll into her mouth.

Before they had finished their meal, Zeus entered the banquet hall and approached the end of the table where the two of them sat. Therese worried she was sitting in his seat and started to get up from her chair, but Than, holding her hand, kept her down.

Zeus wore a robe of gold silk, and a golden crown adorned his head. His brown hair was cropped short, but, despite his beauty, his beard appeared unruly, reminding her of a brown version of the beard of Santa Clause. "I have a gift for you, too," he said. "You are a brave mortal, one of the bravest to cross my path. If you wish, once you have eaten your fill, it would be my pleasure if Thanatos would accompany you on a ride of my most treasured steed, Pegasus."

Therese squealed with delight. "Oh my God! That would be so awesome! Really? We can ride Pegasus? Oh, Than, let's go! I can't eat another bite!"

Zeus's laughter thundered through the room as Hestia came in to clear the plates and glasses. Therese thanked Hestia once again, and then she and Than followed Zeus to the stables.

Pegasus's coat was so white that it glowed like the headlight of a car, and Therese couldn't look directly at it. Squinting, she reached her hand to stroke his flanks.

"Unlike the other gods, he can't shift into a form that would benefit your eyes. His brightness, though, isn't as bright as ours, so you can handle it, right?"

"Yes, if I squint." She stroked his mane.

"He's saying how good that feels," Than translated. "Apparently he hasn't been petted in a while."

This made Therese that much more determined to give him a good brushing. She asked for a brush, and, to her surprise, Cupid appeared with a golden one. She took it, thanked him, and he disappeared.

"He's practically purring," Than said as she brushed Pegasus. "But don't exhaust yourself. You have a big day tomorrow."

"Such a kind and giving heart," Zeus muttered. "It's too bad. Well, I'm off. See you tomorrow. Thanatos, I trust you to bring Pegasus back in one piece."

"Yes, sir," Than replied.

As soon as they were alone, Than took Therese in his arms and pressed his warm lips to hers, then to her cheeks, and then her neck. A sigh escaped her, and then a moan, as desire swept through her. But Than stopped and looked at her. "I know how badly you want to take this ride on Pegasus, so finish brushing, and let's go. But hurry. I'm jealous of the pleasure you're giving him."

Therese giggled and arched one of her brows.

Because Pegasus wore no saddle and tack, Than helped Therese mount his white bare back just behind his wings. Than then climbed behind her and asked Pegasus to give them a tour of the skies above the mountain range. Although Therese was excited, she recalled what happened the last time she rode a horse, and she filled with anxiety. This is different, she told herself. Pegasus is immortal and he knows what to do. I don't have to control him.

At Than's request, Pegasus went into a canter across the golden-paved plaza and then, just as Therese thought they would crash into the chariot shed, he lifted up into the sky.

Than explained that the sun always shone above Olympus, but Pegasus would take them over and outside of the wall of clouds so they could see the stars and moon and natural landscape.

The rush over the wall of clouds brought a scream of exhilaration from Therese's lips. Then suddenly the day was night and the stars, so close and numerous, illuminated the mountaintops below. Than pointed out Mytikas, the highest peak, and pointed to the city of Macedonia, its bright lights illuminating the dark night, and the small village of Litohoro, where little lines of smoke rose from rooftop chimneys. Therese felt a sinking feeling in her chest at the view of all those homes in the village, because it made her think of her home and how, no matter what happened on the battlefield tomorrow, she would never see it again.

Than sensed this change in her mood. "Are you ready to go back?"

She nodded and held on as Pegasus plunged back over the wall of clouds to the palace of the gods.

Once Pegasus had been returned to the stables and thanked again and again by Therese, Than led Therese back up the rainbow steps into the palace walls. He took her past the foyer and into the assembly hall, where Hades's throne had vanished back into the marble floor, or perhaps all the way down to the Underworld, Therese didn't know which. Than explained that each of the gods possessed a private chamber behind his or her throne, and he led her now past Poseidon's throne to the chamber door. When he opened it, they saw Demeter and Persephone sitting in chairs. Persephone held glass bottles filled with colorful liquids, and Demeter held two white towels draped over one arm.

"We've drawn your bath," Persephone said, standing from the chair.

Demeter also stood. "It's this way, in Poseidon's spa."

"I'll meet you back here in a while," Than said. Then he kissed her cheek and vanished.

The walls of Poseidon's chamber were lined with pale blue silk curtains gathered in pleats as if to simulate the sea. His canopy bed lay in the center of the room, and white gauze, like foam from the sea, hung from the canopy down in piles on the floor. The bed coverings were also white and looked to be made of silk. Green tassels, like seaweed, skirted the bed.

"Athena just dressed the bed with her new sheets," Persephone said. The goddess was small, petite, and not quite what Therese expected the Queen of the Underworld to look like.

"Artemis left her pillow there for you," Demeter added. She was only a few inches taller than her daughter and also petite. For the goddess of earth, or agriculture, Therese had expected a mountain of a woman.

Persephone pulled back one curtain of gauze to expose the pillow. "And Aphrodite placed her eye mask on top of Artemis's pillow." The white silk object looked like a luxurious comfort on this solemn, dreadful night.

As Demeter opened the door to Poseidon's spa, she said, "Hera came by, too, and left a nightgown for you to wear. She said it will protect you from any god wishing to force his way on you tonight. Although it's magical, you can change out of it in the morning so as not to break any of the rules of your battle. It only works while worn."

Therese hadn't thought of that. She couldn't imagine one of these noble gods—except maybe Ares—trying such an ignoble act. Then she recalled Athena's story about Daphne, the maiden with whom her brother Apollo once desired and how she would rather be a tree than face the wrath of jealous female divinities. Apparently some male gods had problems with fidelity.

Persephone took Therese's hand and led her into the spa.

The spa was amazing. She wondered as she gazed at the huge tub if all the gods had such elaborate baths or if the one belonging to the god of the sea was special. The tub was shaped like an open clam. The bottom shell was filled with water, and the top shell was a mirror. Persephone emptied one of the colorful liquids into the water, creating a mound of foamy bubbles that glinted with the light thrown off by the many candles lit throughout the otherwise darkened room.

"We'll leave while you undress and climb beneath the bubbles," Persephone said. "We want to give you some time to yourself, but we'll return in a little while to wash your hair and to give you a facial and hand massage."

Therese's brow flew up. "Are you serious? I'm getting a facial and massage by goddesses? Oh my. Thank you sooooo much!" She couldn't believe it. Then she realized why she was getting such special treatment. They all expected her to lose, and they felt sorry for her.

She clutched the locket around her neck and wished she were home in her own bed, in her own bathroom.

Then she thought of Than and her love for him strengthened her. She would show them.

After undressing and using the other facilities—so gods do use the restroom!—Therese climbed into the clam-shaped tub and moaned with pleasure at the warm and soothing water. She was able to stretch her body straight, and a soft waterproof pillow, also shaped like an open clam, but turned on its side, held her head in place.

Now that she was alone, her thoughts went to the impending battle, and the fears took possession of her. She gnawed on the inside of her lip as she tried to relax. She could have chosen the first option and be in her own bed right now. She'd have Clifford curled beside her, Puffy running in his wheel across the room, and Jewels poking her head above the plastic walls of her little house. Therese's aunt would be downstairs, her best friend would be down the road, and Pete would be there to comfort her, to love her, and to make her happy.

But McAdams might come after her aunt.

And her parents wouldn't be there.

And she wanted Than.

She wasn't sure how she had gotten to this point where she felt like she couldn't live without Than. She wondered if Cupid had pierced her heart or if this was her own doing. But, regardless of who was to blame, she loved him, and she could not imagine life without him.

She closed her eyes and prayed, "Than, come back for just a minute. Give me a quick kiss, and then leave before your mom and grandma return. Please, oh please, come back."

When she opened her eyes, he was there beside the tub sitting on a marble bench shaped like a fish. His hair was wet, and he had changed from the open white shirt and trousers to a pale blue of similar design. The blue in the cloth brought out the crystal blue of his eyes, which sparkled with the reflection of the candlelight.

He leaned over the water, slowly, taking in the view of her, though her body was covered by bubbles—perhaps it was just the idea that she was naked—and ever so slowly, too slowly, oh please don't make me wait, he touched his lips to hers and swept her mouth, her cheek, her chin, her neck with the warmth and moisture of his mouth and tongue. She fought the urge to pull him down into the bath with her as she took fistfuls of his wet hair and kept his face to hers. When she pressed her mouth more firmly to his, he vanished, her hands suspended in empty air, and Persephone and Demeter entered the room.

Talk about frustration.

But her frustration was soon replaced by pleasure as Persephone took Therese's long hair and bundled it in her hands, working through a freshly scented shampoo.

"Is that oranges I smell?" Therese muttered like one drugged.

"Mm-hmm," Persephone softly replied.

Persephone massaged her scalp, sending chills down Therese's neck and back. Then Demeter was at her right hand massaging lotion into the palm, between the fingers, along the back of the hand and wrist.

"Oh my god-desses," she moaned.

The other hand received the same treatment as Persephone rinsed the shampoo and now lathered in a conditioner, more scents of citrus wafting through the room. Again Persephone massaged her scalp, and Demeter continued to knead her palm, squeeze her fingers.

"I will let the conditioner sit in your hair a few minutes while I apply the exfoliating mask to your face," Persephone explained.

Now Persephone was massaging Therese's forehead, temples, cheekbones, jaw.

"Oh," Therese sighed.

Demeter placed Therese's left hand back in the tub and Persephone finished applying the mask.

"When the mask feels dry, wash it off and rinse your hair," Persephone instructed her.

"You'll find your towels on the bench to your right," Demeter said. "And the gown from Hera is hanging on the back of the door."

Another woman entered the room and said to Persephone, "Thanatos wishes to speak with you, my lady."

"Thank you, Hecate." Persephone turned back to Therese. "Good luck to you, sweet girl."

"Thanks so much," Therese managed to say. Tears pricked her eyes. Perhaps she had already died and gone to heaven!

The three figures vanished from the room and left Therese alone.

After a few moments, Therese dried and put on the white silk gown from Hera and extinguished the candles the goddesses had lit. Then she left the spa and went to the large canopy bed in the middle of Poseidon's chamber where a small bedside lamp in the shape of a mermaid had been left on for her. She pulled back a fluffy down comforter and silk white top sheet, moved the eye mask from the goose feather pillow, and climbed inside the bed and pulled the covers over her. Her whole body relaxed. Every muscle, every bone, every neuron firing at the synapse seemed to respond to the most comfortable bed and sheets and pillow she had ever slept on. She put the eye mask aside for now and prayed for Than to return.

He was there beside her in an instant, and a good thing, too, for she had nearly fallen asleep. He lay above the covers and she below, like the last time they spent the night together. He stroked her wet hair.

"You smell so good," he said. "And you feel so soft."

She reached her arms up and took his face in her hands. "This may be our last night together," she whispered. "So I want you to…"

"Shhh," he whispered, putting a finger to her lips. "Don't talk like that. What happened to being positive? I know what you want, and believe me, I want it too, but I won't give it to you tonight. You have to wait, to fight for it." He kissed her, and kissed her, and then he groaned, "So you better win."

She kissed him back, ran her fingers through his now dry hair, and took pleasure in his caresses. They caressed one another for several more minutes, neither really wanting to stop, but both knowing it would be better in the end. Then she put on Aphrodite's eye mask and snuggled against his chest just as the most beautiful music she had ever heard began to sound through the walls. Apollo played the lyre and Hermes the pipe, and the beautiful melodies lifted her spirits again and carried her to heights of optimism that gave her the feeling, as Than lay there stroking her hair, that nothing could stop her now.

Soon after, she fell asleep.

Chapter Forty-One: The Battlefield

In the morning, Than gave Therese a pair of jeans, a shirt, clean undies, and pair of socks he had brought her from her house.

"You went through my underwear drawer?" she asked.

He gave her a wry smile.

"How are my pets?"

"Your aunt and her boyfriend are taking good care of them."

Luckily her sneakers had dried overnight. After she changed, Than led her to the assembly hall where the gods and goddesses were just now coming in from either their chambers behind their thrones or the banquet hall or, in the case of Poseidon and Hades, the chariot shed.

Once the gods and goddesses were seated, Hephaestus presented McAdams and Therese with the golden sword and shield he had wrought and forged for them. Ares belted the sheathed sword around McAdams's waist while Than did the same for Therese. Therese pulled the blade from the sheath. It was surprisingly light.

Than stood close by and whispered, "Be careful with that thing. I can't be killed, but I can still feel pain."

She gave a nervous giggle and returned the sword to its sheath, watching McAdams with a wary eye.

Than grabbed her hand and pulled her closer, so that they were breast to breast. "Speaking of pain, if McAdams, you know… I won't let you suffer. I'll take your soul, and I'll take you straight to your parents."

She swallowed hard and gave him a frightened nod. Then he kissed her once more before taking his seat beside his father.

McAdams had dark circles beneath his eyes and bags that would put those of Hephaestus to shame. He looked pale, almost languid, and Therese actually felt a little sorry for him. She wondered where he had passed the night and what comforts Ares, and perhaps other gods, did or did not provide.

Then she remembered how she had watched her parents die, and anger rose within her. She would kill him.

"We all know the rules," Zeus announced. "So let us begin."

Therese nearly jumped from her sneakers when the assembly hall vanished and in its place was a clearing surrounded by woods. Pines, cypresses, elms, hemlocks—all trees Therese recognized. Beyond the clearing, the sun at high noon pierced through the canopy of leaves onto a deer here, a squirrel there. Cardinals, sparrows, jays, and other birds whose names she did not know flittered from tree to tree, just like they did in the bird atrium at the San Antonio Zoo. Ants burrowed in the dirt around her feet, and white limestone rocks, pink granite rocks, and other kinds, too, were partly buried in the earth, partly exposed.

The thrones had disappeared, but the gods and goddesses sat on tree stumps in the clearing in the same formation in which they had gathered at the hall on Mount Olympus. For all Therese knew, they had never left the court, and all of this nature around them was a vast illusion.

Suddenly with a roaring thunder, the ground beneath them lifted up, like the floor of an elevator, and both Therese and McAdams stumbled and fell with the trembling earth. The clearing rose at least thirty feet so that the gods could look down upon the forest surrounding them below, like the reverse of a coliseum in that what was once the battlefield in the center had become the audience seating, and what was usually the audience seating was an outer circular battlefield. But unlike the audience of a coliseum, this battlefield was ripe with life and natural structures. Behind Zeus, mountains of pink granite jutted up from the forest below, exceeding in height the level of the gods' platform. Beyond Poseidon, Therese could make out a river bordered by forest. A stream ran from the pink granite mountains, into the river, and then circled around Apollo and Hephaestus and plunged into a roaring fall to a deeper canyon behind Hades. The water pooled into a smaller body of water at the bottom of the deeper canyon. Another stream ran into a waterfall behind Aphrodite, but the trees were so thick on that side of the forest, that

Therese could not see through them. Among the trees behind Demeter, however, she thought she saw fruit. If her plan was to outrun and hide from McAdams, this would be a long battle, and fruit would be necessary to keep going. Otherwise, she and her enemy wouldn't need to kill one another. They would starve to death.

Therese and McAdams stood up on opposite sides of the platform staring at one another with fear and anger. Therese wasn't sure what to do, and McAdams appeared as indecisive. All of the gods sat around them on their tree stumps, waiting. Aphrodite's face was stained with tears.

Than, still close by, spoke in a low voice. "My best advice is to avoid hand to hand combat."

"Then how will I kill him?" Therese muttered without taking her eyes off McAdams.

"Set traps, if possible, and keep far away from him. You're in better shape and can probably outrun him, but he's stronger." Than could not keep the desperation from his voice. "Please be careful."

Therese kept her eyes on McAdams as she backed away from him towards what had now become a cliff edge behind the tree-stump thrones of the gods. A person would certainly die if he or she fell from the platform and into the canyon woods surrounding them below. But the rocky ledges could be navigated the thirty or so feet to the bottom, and it seemed to Therese there could be caves in the canyon walls. She decided she should descend behind Demeter and collect whatever fruit she could carry, and then run for a hiding place until she could think of another plan.

McAdams charged at her, however, and gave her no choice but to climb down the cliff edge behind Hades. Therese threw her shield down and it plunged, then slid, and finally came to a stop near the bottom of the deeper canyon at least a hundred feet below. She turned and clung to the rock wall, quickly finding her footing as she scaled down the side.

She looked up and saw McAdams standing above her. He wasn't climbing down after her…yet.

"Oh, Than, I should have run to the trees!" she said in her mind, praying frantically, even though she knew he could not help her. "My plan was to collect food and stay on the run till he got weak. But look at me clinging to these walls! This is stupid! What am I doing? I'm going to kill myself slipping on these stupid rocks, and he'll win by default! I've already dropped my shield!"

"Your plan is sound!" Than called after her. "You can still do it!"

Then it dawned on Therese, something she hadn't thought of before! She could speak to the gods through prayer, and they could answer her! She would have to call them by name so Ares would not hear. Ares would inform McAdams. But the other gods, the ones she knew were on her side, she would speak to them!

She increased her pace down the canyon wall and lowered herself to the bottom. Her shield lay below in the deeper canyon, but she decided she would be faster without it. Since her goal was to avoid hand to hand combat, why be burdened with it when her hands could be free?

She ran along the base of the upper canyon wall toward the thick forest behind Demeter. In her mind, she said, "I'm thinking I should collect food, Than. And then hide. Do you agree?"

"Yes!" he shouted.

Then another thought hit her. She would ask the gods questions that could be answered with yes or no, so as to prevent McAdams from overhearing her plans.

"Artemis, Athena, Aphrodite," she said in her mind as she ran. "If you can hear me, shout out my name, so I know."

"Therese!" Artemis cried.

"Therese!" Athena echoed.

"Therese, my dear!" Aphrodite sang.

Therese looked up and saw McAdams had not descended to the forest. He stood there hovering over the cliff edge watching her. She wondered what he was doing. Perhaps he had the same plan of waiting until she wore herself out.

"Demeter, Persephone, Hades," Therese prayed as she disentangled herself from the thick undergrowth, twigs snapping beneath her feet. "Say 'yes' if you can hear me."

"Yes!" Demeter cried.

"Oh, yes!" Persephone said.

"Smart girl!" Hades hollered. "Yes!"

Therese was filled with a renewed hope as she picked her way through the branches of trees and shrubs, some stiff like spears, others flexible like snakes, toward the fruit trees. The woods were now so thick, that she could no longer see McAdams. "Than, has McAdams climbed down from the platform?"

"No!" Than shouted.

So maybe he did plan for her to wear herself out. She found a narrow stream and sighed with relief. The woods had become so thick that only little spots of sunlight pierced through the canopy of leaves above her, and she couldn't tell which way she was going, but the stream would now be her guide. Layers and layers of rotting leaves covered the ground beneath her, and she had to be careful to step over the occasional fallen branch or decaying log.

Another idea struck her.

"Than and Artemis, should I attempt to make spears from these fallen branches?" she prayed. "Just say yes or no. If it would be a waste of time say no."

"Yes!" Artemis said.

"Ask me another question!" Than cried.

Ask another question? What question? She stared at the sticks.

"You want me to use the sticks for something else?" A thorn bush scratched her arm. "Ow," she muttered.

"Yes!" Than shouted. "Recall what I said earlier!"

"Is McAdams still up there?"

"Yes!"

What had Than said earlier? He had said to avoid hand to hand combat, to run, and…to set traps! "You want me to use the sticks to set traps?"

"Yes!" Than answered.

"But I have no idea how to do that!" She groaned as she bent over and picked through the sticks on the ground, looking for strong ones.

She saw several bruised apples among the sticks and leaves, most of them rotten, but when she looked up, she could see ripe ones on the branches within her reach.

"I should pick fruit, Than, Artemis, and Athena, but carrying it now will hold me back. I should store it someplace. I should find somewhere to hide, to store my food and my weapons. I could booby-trap it!"

"Yes!" all three voices rang out.

Therese pulled off her shirt and bundled fruit inside of it. She found nuts on the ground and further up the stream, grapevines. She plucked as many grapes as she could fit into the makeshift bundle, gathered up the edges, and carried it in one hand and her collection of sticks in the other.

Think, she told herself, standing in her bra and jeans with her bundle draped over her back. Originally, she had planned to climb the granite rocks jutting up above Zeus, but only because she thought a lookout was necessary. Now that she had figured out she could use prayer to keep tabs on the whereabouts of McAdams, she wouldn't need the lookout. She would need to hide, and she would want to make it as hard as possible for McAdams to get to her.

She stood there, thinking. "Is McAdams still up there?" she prayed to Than.

"Yes!" he shouted. "But hurry! Don't waste time!"

He wanted her to set traps, but she didn't know how to do that. Think, Therese! Okay, McAdams would eventually need food if she managed to stay away from him long enough, so he would come here, to this part of the woods. This would be a good place to try and trap him, or at least weaken him with an injury. But how?

She shuddered. She was not cut out for this. Strategically planning how to hurt and kill someone went against her grain. Remember your parents, she told herself. Remember the last time you saw them!

She forced herself to visualize her father writhing in frenzy as the water washed over him, suffocating him. She forced herself to see her mother, bleeding at the neck, blood pouring from her mouth as she yielded to her death. She clutched the golden locket around her neck. I can do this!

Than said not to waste time, so maybe she should start sharpening the sticks until another idea came to her mind. She followed the stream out of the thicket where the undergrowth thinned out and looked for a place to sit and work. She saw a fallen log up ahead that would serve as a bench. On her way to the log, the ground dropped below her and she fell flat on her chest, dropping her bundle, apples flying everywhere. She had landed in a hole about two feet deep and four feet wide.

"Ow! She scrambled to her feet. "Oh, damn!" Leaves stuck to her skin and fell in her bra as she gathered the apples, leaving the nuts and most of the grapes, which had fallen beneath the rotting leaves. She heaped the apples back onto her shirt, bundling it back up. Luckily they still looked good, no bruises. Her knee, on the other hand, would definitely have a bruise. It had been stabbed by a sharp rock. At least her jeans had protected her skin.

A flash of inspiration.

She could use this hole to set a trap, and she could look for similar places in the ground. She would sharpen sticks at both ends, drive them into the bottom of these holes, and cover them with dead leaves.

"Than!" she said in her mind. "I've got it!" She told him her plan.

"Yes!" he shouted. "But hurry!"

"Is McAdams still there?"

"Not for long!" Than yelled.

"What is he doing? Oh, wait, you can't answer that. Is he watching me?"

"No!"

"Is he making plans?"

"Yes! Yes, hurry!"

Now Therese was filled with worry over what McAdams might be doing up on the platform. She took her collection of sticks to the large fallen log, sat down, and unsheathed her sword. The sword was too long to whittle the wood, so she drove the blade into the ground and used it like a cheese grater, rubbing first one end and then the other of each stick against the blade. The sword was so sharp that it didn't take her long to produce a large mound of sticks sharpened at both ends. Now she needed to find a big rock so she could drive each stick into the ground.

She ran around the fallen log looking for a rock. There has to be a rock in these woods! Panic threatened to overtake her as she dug through the layers of leaves and came up with nothing, over and over. Then she remembered where she had hurt her knee in the bottom of the hole and looked there. Yes, sharp on top but smooth on the bottom where it was wedged into the ground, it was the size of a large brick. She dug it from the earth and went back for her sticks. She had made the sticks a little more than a foot long and now she hammered them into the ground, a foot apart, so that they stuck up about eight inches from the bottom of the hole. Once she had impaled the bottom of the hole with the sharp, jutting weapons, she grabbed armfuls of dead leaves and hid the trap.

Then she picked her way back to the fruit trees to gather a few oranges, this time looking more closely at the ground for small dips where she could set more traps.

"Therese!" Than cried.

"Is McAdams climbing down?"

"Yes!"

"Is he coming after me?"

"No!"

"Where's he going? Is he headed for the rocks behind Zeus?" That's where she would have gone, for the lookout.

"Yes!"

"He hopes he'll see me better from there," she muttered.

"Exactly!"

"He's waiting for me to wear myself out, and then he plans to come for me!"

"Exactly!" Than's voice sounded desperate.

Therese trembled wildly. "I'll set more traps. Shout if he heads this way."

"I will!"

A movement in the wood caught her eye, and she froze, waited. She took a slow step and looked beyond the tree where she had seen the flash of something brownish. Now she saw it was a wild horse there with her in the wood. At first, she smiled, comforted by the vision. Then she thought of the traps. The animals!

Again in her mind, she asked, "Than! Artemis! The animals! What if they hurt themselves on my traps? Can you warn them somehow?"

"No!" Artemis called out.

"Ares!" Than shouted.

Ares? "Ares will understand where the traps are."

"Yes."

"But how can we warn the animals?"

"Your scent!" Artemis cried.

"They'll avoid the traps because of my scent?" She found herself whispering rather than praying in her head.

"That will be our message! To avoid your scent!" Artemis shouted.

Therese looked at the horse. It made her feel less alone. She took an apple from her bundle and held it out. The horse's nostrils flared, but it didn't move toward her or away. Therese tossed the apple toward the tree. The horse trotted away.

Of course. The apple carried her scent. He had already been warned.

She spent at least two hours sharpening sticks, driving them into holes, and covering the holes with leaves, but she began to fear she might be wasting her time. What if McAdams never came this way? What if he killed her before he got hungry? She was wearing herself out. Was this worth it?

Then she slapped her forehead. Maybe she should have tried to mount the horse. She might have had a better chance against McAdams if she came at him from above on horseback.

Too late now.

She should set more traps, but she should seek a path he was sure to cross.

She gathered more fruit—oranges and pomegranates, and stuffed them in her shirt, but they wouldn't all fit. Then she had the idea of tying the hem of the shirt in a knot and stuffing the fruit inside the shirt rather than gathering the edges all around. More fruit would fit this way. She wanted to collect as much food as she could because with all her traps out here, she didn't want to have to come back this way and risk injuring herself in one of them. That would be ironic, she thought.

As she tore her way through the woods back toward the deeper canyon, she stopped whenever she found a good dip in the ground to set up another trap. She'd set down her bundle and the big rock she used for hammering, sharpen a dozen more sticks at both ends on her blade, and then stake the sticks firmly in the ground before hiding them with fallen leaves. The further she got from the thickest part of the woods, however, the fewer dead leaves were there on the ground. She realized as she followed the stream back down to the rocky canyon behind Hades that she would have to think of a different way to set traps on this side of the battlefield.

"Therese!" Than shouted.

She prayed, "Is he following me?"

"Hide!"

She looked up and realized she had now come into view of those on the side of the platform closest to her. She could see Than, Hades, and Aphrodite directly overhead. She had to remember to stay out of Ares's view. She clambered against the canyon wall and hid beneath the cliff edge above her.

"Is McAdams following me?" she asked Than.

"Just now!"

"He's just now leaving the rocks behind Zeus?"

"Yes!"

"Is he headed toward the woods or the lake?"

When he didn't answer, she said, "I mean, is he headed toward the woods?"

"Yes!"

"Good. Maybe he'll come across at least one of my traps. I think I have twelve or thirteen all around the fruit trees. But I need to think of something else down here in the canyon. There's nothing here but rocks."

"Yes!"

"What? I didn't ask anything." She thought back on what she had said. "Rocks? I should make traps with rocks?"

"Yes!"

But how? she thought. How could she use rocks to make a trap? The sticks went into hidden holes waiting for McAdams to happen by. They probably wouldn't kill him, but he could get cut up really bad. But falling on rocks? What could she do with the rocks? Could she sharpen them? Chip them into sharp wedges? No. The rocks could fall on him. How could she make it so the rocks could fall on him? She could throw them at him. She could gather a stockpile and keep them near her hideout so that when he came for her she could launch...

Wait! Launch?

She had to work without being seen by Ares, and she had to work fast. She crept along the base of the cliff edge scanning for possibilities. She looked down into the deeper canyon below where her shield lay useless to her and out across to the other side about a fifty yards away. Think, Therese! Think!

Then, like a bullet, it hit her.

The waterfall!

Chapter Forty-Two: The Battle

Therese filled with hope and enthusiasm when it dawned on her that she could scuttle along this canyon wall beneath the cliff edge and make her way to the roaring fall behind Hephaestus without being seen. She prayed to Than to let him know her plan.

She would find a place behind the falls to stash her food and store her rocks, which she started collecting in her arms now. She would find a lower place, visible to Ares, to set up a decoy camp. Then, when McAdams came to the decoy, she would launch her rocks at him. The rocks probably wouldn't kill him, but as with the traps in the thick part of the woods by the fruit trees, they would injure him and slow him down, hopefully enough for her to defeat him with her sword.

"Good!" Than shouted.

A blood-curdling wail rang out across the canyon and caused Therese to freeze. "Was that McAdams?"

"Yes!"

"Did he find one of my traps?"

"I think so! I can't see him!" Than called out.

Whether McAdams injured himself in one of her traps or in some other way, he was nevertheless injured, and this added to Therese's overall optimism as she scrambled beneath the cliff edge with her arms full of rocks the size of softballs. The noise of the falls thundered as she neared them and the spray hit her bare skin and chilled her, a relief after the sweat she had worked up from building her traps in Demeter's woods.

"How long till nightfall?" she asked Than in her mind. It seemed like hours had passed, and yet the sun still bore down on them high in the sky. "Wait a minute. We never left Olympus, did we? The sun always shines, right?"

If Than answered her, she could no longer hear him this close to the crashing falls. She hadn't thought of that! How would she make it without him?

Unlike Than and the other gods, she had no powers of telepathy and could not be sure if voices in her head were inspirations or delusions. She almost turned back. In fact, she changed her mind five or six times and nearly wore herself out beneath the cliff edge with indecision. At last she decided it was her best chance of survival to go on with her plan. "I can't hear you anymore," she prayed. "But I've decided to go on anyway."

She reached the falls and found a hidden grotto behind the roaring water, but if McAdams came this way to her decoy camp, she would have no advantage for attack. Although there were many little nooks and crevices back here that she could climb onto, she would be open, visible, and vulnerable to his retaliation. She dropped her rocks in a heap, set down her fruit, and looked around.

At the furthest lip of the grotto on the outer edge of the falls, she found a nook way up high that just might work. If McAdams came through the grotto, she would see him, and she would be above him, with gravity on her side. She would also be hidden until he reached the point where she stood now. It also seemed, from down here, anyway, that she might have a view of the deeper canyon in case he came that route. The trick would be hauling the rocks and fruit up the steep wall nearly twenty feet to the nook. First she would try it empty-handed to see if it was possible.

Now that she couldn't hear Than, she felt really anxious that McAdams could be coming around the corner for her at any moment, and this anxiety caused her to tremble more profoundly than she had before. The trembling made climbing up the nearly vertical wall very difficult. She used her fingers to find places in the wall to grip, and she fished around with her feet for footholds to support her weight. One false step meant falling to her death at the bottom of the canyon.

Dirt from the canyon wall got into her mouth and crunched in her teeth when she clenched them. She ran her tongue around her teeth, trying to wash it out, and she spit and gagged. She reached for another rock, keeping her mouth closed this time, breathing through her nose. A fingernail broke at the tip as she clung to another ledge, but that was the least of her worries.

Thankfully, there were plenty of strong footholds within reach of one another. When she made it to the nook, she found it was actually a cave that tunneled back into darkness. While she was glad to have all this room to store her things and move around, the unknown darkness added to her anxiety. Stop it, Therese! McAdams was the only threat worth fearing right now, she reminded herself. She walked over to the furthest edge and saw that she could indeed see most of the lower canyon from here. This just might work. There were even a few loose boulders she could move, though barely and straining with all her might. Maybe if she scooted them to the edge and found something to give her leverage, she could launch them from the nook. She needed a branch or heavy stick, but there were none around. Would her sword work, or would the rock break it? She unsheathed the sword and tested it, gently at first. The blade gave. It was too flexible. She'd have to find something else. She returned the sword to its sheath.

The sheath! It was light, but it was solid and firm. She unbelted it from her waist and tested it out. It would work! This could be her saving grace! She looked around for other such boulders and found four more loose enough and light enough for her to drag to the edge of her cave.

She re-belted her sword and sheath and climbed back down, quickly but carefully, to carry up her bundle of fruit between her teeth. Then she took the empty shirt back down and filled it with six of the softball-sized rocks. Any more than that might throw off her balance too much or be too heavy and slip between her teeth. She'd have to make a third trip down for the remaining six. She hesitated. If McAdams spotted her, she'd lose the element of surprise. Was it worth getting the remaining rocks? She decided to go for it.

Climbing up with the bundle between her teeth was not easy. She held on by the back molars, where her jaw was stronger. She couldn't swallow properly, so she let the drool drip down her chin. Most of it was absorbed by her shirt. The rocks pressed against her neck and chest as she pulled herself up the wall. Her neck was sore from both the weight of the rocks and the position in which she had to hold her head in order to clear the rocks with her body. But her shirt wasn't big enough to tie around her back or neck and still hold her bundle.

Now she had twelve softball-sized rocks she could throw at him and seven watermelon-sized boulders she could launch at him with her sheath. It was time to set up her decoy camp, and she'd have to move quickly since McAdams could be gaining on her at any time and she would not hear Than's warning. She gathered up three apples and put them in her shirt to take with her.

Oh! Another idea struck her. She couldn't hear Than, but maybe she would be able to hear several gods if they all shouted at once. She concentrated on all of them but Ares. She couldn't risk giving away her position to him. "If you can hear me, please oh please scream yes as loud as you can when I get to the count of three. One, two, three!"

Faint, but audible, she heard the whisper of a yes.

Awesome!

Again, with great concentration, she focused on all of the Olympian gods except for Ares. "If you think McAdams is still in the forest, when I count to three, please scream yes. One, two, three!"

Again, faint, but audible, like a breeze across the canyon, she heard the gods say, "Yes."

Awesome! That meant she had time to set up her decoy camp. She cautiously but quickly scrambled down the wall from her cave back to the grotto floor behind the falls. Then she scaled further down beneath the grotto to the deeper canyon floor, all the while being careful to keep herself hidden behind the falls to avoid Ares's watchful eyes. She hadn't heard him communicating with McAdams so far, but that didn't mean he wasn't doing so now that McAdams was down in the woods.

During her decent down the wall, she sought cliff edges, nooks, anything that might offer passage past the falls where she could be visible across the canyon from the platform and the lower edge of the forest. She needed to be seen in her decoy camp, but her entrance and exit to it should be hidden. She was getting nervous that this wasn't going to work. Maybe she should head back to her real camp and simply wait.

But she had come this far, and this was the perfect plan if she could make it work.

"If you can see McAdams, on my count of three, please say yes. One, two, three!"

"Yes!"

Oh, no! She was expecting a no. If they could see him, where was he? "If he has made it to the edge of the deeper canyon, please say yes on my count of three. One, two, three!"

"Yes!"

Oh my God! "Is he near the larger of the two falls? One, two, three!"

"No."

She felt some relief, but she couldn't see it in her hands, for they trembled so badly now, she could barely grab hold of the canyon wall. She climbed down a few more feet and found another nook. It tunneled beneath the cliff edge above it, into the wall of the canyon, about five feet or more and extended out past the falls. If she were to follow it to its length, she would become visible. It was now or never if she was going to set up this decoy camp. With shaking limbs and chattering teeth, she edged her way out and looked across the canyon at the gods.

A memory of touring Mesa Verde, the ancient cliff dwellings in southwest Colorado, with her parents three years ago swept through her mind.

"Than, if you can see me, wave! I want Ares to see me, and McAdams, too!"

Than waved. She waved back and blew him a kiss. Then she saw McAdams across the canyon at the smaller fall below Aphrodite. He was without his jacket and tie, and his white shirt was stained with blood and dirt. His black pants were torn and also stained, and as he moved forward, he walked with a limp. Unlike her, he held his shield, but this, too, was smeared with blood and dirt. Either he had fallen or at least one of her traps had worked!

Still, as she looked at him, trembling like her, fumbling along the rocky quay at the top of Aphrodite's smaller waterfall, perhaps closer to death than she originally thought, she found it hard to feel joy. Therese! Remember what he did to your parents! Remember what you have to do to be with Than! The anger at her parents' brutal, painful murder and the hopeful expectations of living eternally at Than's side renewed her determination. Either McAdams would die, or she would die trying!

She opened her bundle and took out an apple. Standing in sight of McAdams, she bit the apple and retreated back into the cave, leaving her shirt and the other two apples visible. Then she worried she was being too obvious in her attempts to lure him. She ran back to the edge and snatched her bundle and dragged it back out of sight. She went to the edge one more time and limped around, trying to look weaker than she was, and then she got down on her knees as though in supplication to the gods, and prayed, "Than, I'm not really injured. I am trying to appear weaker than I am to lure McAdams here. This is my decoy camp. I have another set up for attack." She noticed how badly she trembled now that she was trying to hold still. She kept praying, "I love you, Than. I can tell the end is near. No matter what happens, after this I will be with you always, either as a god like you, or a soul among the dead like my parents. If you can hear me, please wave to me one more time."

She watched him lift his arm up to her and wipe his eyes with the other hand. She wished she could see the details of his face, but he was too far away. She looked over at McAdams. He was drinking from the top of the smaller falls. Now he washed his face. She couldn't see the details, but the overall smear of red was horrible.

He deserves this, she reminded herself.

She took several bites of the apple and looked up again at Than. The other gods had crowded around him, probably realizing that this canyon was where their game would end. Surprisingly, she felt ravenous, and ate her apple down to the core. Then, looking once more at the bowed figure of McAdams, she tossed the core to the canyon floor to lie beside her shield, and she retreated to the back of the cave and out of sight of all.

From the back of the cave, she tunneled toward her real camp behind the roaring falls. She climbed back up to the grotto with her bundle between her teeth, and then rested there a moment, wondering which direction McAdams was going now. After ten or fifteen minutes, she climbed the rest of the way to her upper chamber where she had stored her food and rocks. She was still hungry, so she bit into another apple while she waited.

She couldn't see McAdams, but she could see the lower canyon if he tried to cross it. She doubted he would attempt it since he was apparently injured. More than likely, he would come the way she had, behind the falls, and so she mostly looked down in that direction. She had her sheath unbelted and her sword on the cave floor close by. She rested the sheath over a rock to form a lever and tucked the sheath beneath one of the watermelon-sized boulders ready to launch it at McAdams when he came.

While she waited for signs of McAdams, she ate another apple and an orange. She was thirsty, and the juice quenched that thirst. She had planned to save more of the food in case McAdams dragged this battle out over the course of days, but once she had started eating, she had found it too hard to stop. Her food supplies were diminishing, and this filled her with new anxiety.

But she couldn't stop herself from eating another apple.

On top of having only a few pieces of fruit left after her binging, she was getting sleepy. She wasn't sure how many hours had passed, since the sun hadn't moved from its position at high noon in the sky, but boy, oh boy, could she use some sleep! She knew, of course, that McAdams would find and kill her in her sleep and that closing her eyes for even a moment was out of the question.

The adrenaline that had rushed through her body earlier when she had heard the gods warning her of McAdams's pursuit had waned somewhat when she saw him, bloody and limping and trembling. And now that she was full and resting in this somewhat safe cave, the adrenaline seemed to have gone out of her body completely.

Think of your parents! But even her attempts to force the images of her dying parents into her head could not pull her from this sudden fatigue and sleepiness. She would not share this with Than. She had been about to pray, "I'm sleepy," to him, but now she realized it would only make him that more fraught with anxiety. No, she would bear this burden alone. She stood up and paced around the cave, like an animal in a zoo.

A movement in the lower canyon caught her attention. She couldn't believe her eyes. McAdams had climbed down into the lower canyon and had picked up her shield. What would he do with it? Wait. He tossed it aside. He was looking for something. What? He picked up the apple core she had tossed and was ravaging it like a starved animal. He had it eaten in an instant, seeds and stem and all, and then he looked around, trembling and pathetic.

He went to the small reservoir at the lowest point of the deeper canyon, the pool to which both falls spilled into, and drank. This body of water wasn't nearly as large as the one behind Poseidon—only about ten feet at the widest point—and Therese guessed it must empty into the ground and spring out again somewhere else. Then she remembered this was Mount Olympus, and all this was an illusion. The water didn't have to flow anywhere. It could just disappear.

McAdams continued to look around, over his shoulder, as though he feared he were the one being pursued. This thought made Therese giggle slightly. So he was afraid of her? He thought she was coming for him?

From her height she could probably hit him with one of the softball-sized rocks, but her chances of missing him were high, and she would give away her location. Plus, he looked so pathetic, like a lame animal, and until he outright attacked her, she might not have it in her to further injure him. But then how long would this battle drag on? How long would she have to hang out here in this dark cave waiting for him to come for her? Shouldn't she just end it now if she could? Launch her rocks and try to crush him to death? Wouldn't she starve to death otherwise?

"Should I attack?"

"Yes!" the barely audible answer came.

She watched McAdams scramble along the canyon floor toward her decoy camp. Perhaps he wouldn't drag this battle out after all. He seemed anxious now, almost lustful. He climbed the wall of the cliff edge furthest from the gods directly beneath her decoy camp. It was time to launch her attack. It was now or never.

Therese took a deep breath and, as she exhaled, she emitted a loud grunt, which she knew no one could hear because of the falls. But as she grunted, she took up a softball-sized rock and threw it at him. She missed, but without thinking, she threw again and again and again, until all twelve softball-sized rocks were gone, and she hit him more than once. He cowered beneath her with his arms over his head, sliding down to the canyon floor. She lunged against her sheath and launched the first watermelon-sized boulder. It dropped a foot or two away from where he crouched, so quickly, before he could move, she launched the next, and bam! It hit its target. He fell over onto the canyon floor, grasping his left shoulder, where the boulder had hit, and moaned. She couldn't hear him but she could see his mouth moving. Now she moved her lever to another boulder and launched it directly on his chest. It hit him and then bounced and rolled away, breaking into smaller pieces. Although she couldn't hear his wails, she could see his face, and she could see he was in terrible pain and agony. Shuddering at what she had done, but not allowing herself to think on it, she launched another boulder and hit her mark again.

McAdams rolled over onto his hands and knees and crawled away from her. Blood poured from his shoulder, which he continued to hold with his right hand. He scrambled away, out of her reach but not her sight, and he sat against the canyon wall, breathing rapidly.

It was time for her to go to him. She belted on the golden sheath and found her sword on the cave floor. She returned the blade to its sheath and prepared to descend. You can do this, she told herself. Then to the gods, even to Ares, she said, "I'm going to end this."

Although she dreaded what had to be done, the feeling of imminent victory lifted her spirits as she climbed down from her cave to the grotto below. McAdams was no longer in view from here, but once she worked her way out past the falls, scaling down toward the deeper canyon, she could see him again sitting and slumped against the rocks.

"You killed my mom and dad!" she shouted as she got closer. "I had to watch them die! Your gunman shot my mom in the neck! My father drove off a bridge trying to dodge the gunman's bullets, and he and my mother drowned right before my eyes!"

McAdams's eyes were wide and his breathing rapid. She was within ten feet of him. She drew her sword. It was dirty from use, but it would still do the trick.

"Please don't kill me," McAdams begged in a shaky voice.

"Kill him!" Hades shouted. "Do it now and be a god among us!"

"Kill him!" the gods shouted.

She looked up at them gathered above her, and even Ares had a look of lust on his face.

She looked back at McAdams lying there quivering, bleeding, tears welling in his eyes. She looked for a place to stick him. Should she slit his throat? Stab his heart?

She shuddered as she raised the blade, still not sure where to pierce him.

"Kill him now!" Hades yelled. "Slit his throat! Think of what he did to your parents!"

Therese gritted her teeth and raised the blade higher, shaking and breathing so rapidly. This was it! This was it! Do it!

"Wait!" she screamed. "Isn't this enough? To prove I could kill him? Can't you make me a god without me having to follow through?"

"No!" Hades shouted. "A deal is a deal! He deserves death, and so much more! Kill him!"

Again she looked at him, trembling worse than she. Tears fell from his eyes. He had wet himself. What had she become? He looked at her like she was the monster, she the villain. Was she? Had she become as bad as he?

What was so very different about them now? He had killed her parents for money, and she was going to kill him now for love and immortality. Wasn't she better than this?

"No!" she dropped her arm to her side. "I won't kill him!"

She expected McAdams to take his sword and lunge at her, but he didn't move.

Suddenly Hades was at her side holding her hand with the blade to McAdams's throat. "Finish the job!" Hades commanded.

Now Ares was there with McAdams's sword at Therese's throat. "No divine interference!" Ares said through gritted teeth.

All the gods appeared around them. Hades didn't move Therese's blade from McAdams's throat, and Ares didn't move McAdams's blade from her throat. They stood there with the other gods encircling them.

"Ares, she won!" Than demanded. "Put down your blade!"

"There's no victory until death!" Ares said. "No one has won yet. Back away, Hades!"

"Foolish girl!" Hades said, letting go of her hand and retreating to the ring of gods. "Stupid, cowardly girl! You had this won! You can still win! Plunge your blade into this despicable excuse for a human!"

Ares returned McAdams's blade and stepped back to the circle of gods.

"Come on, man!" Ares said. "Don't let yourself get beat by a girl. Stand up and kill her!"

But McAdams didn't move.

"How long should we wait here while this man dies?" Aphrodite asked. "This is clearly a victory for the girl!"

"Hear, hear!" many voices shouted.

Hades moved to the center of the circle. "I swore on the river Styx that she would become a god if she avenged her parents' death. She's failed to do that. McAdams has yet to get his just dessert! This is no victory! This is pathetic and shameful! The girl does not deserve to be a god, especially among the Underworld! What kind of wife to Death would such a one as this make? She can't even end the life of the man who destroyed her parents and brought the worst of human suffering upon her!"

"Kill him!" Artemis pleaded. "You can do it, Therese!"

Than looked at her expectantly. She met his hopeful eyes.

"I'm sorry." Tears fell from her eyes. "I refuse to kill him. I just can't do it. I can't take a life!" She threw her sword down to the canyon floor.

"Kill her, McAdams!" Ares said. "This is your chance!"

Therese looked at the quivering, bloody man who had wet himself, and he looked at her. He didn't move from his spot.

As much as she despised him, she hated herself for her injuries to him. "Apollo," she asked silently in her mind, "Can you heal him?"

He gave her a look of astonishment and then slowly shook his head.

"Oh, this is an outrage!" Hades cried, guessing the meaning of the exchanged looks between her and Apollo. He took up her sword from the canyon floor and plunged it into McAdams's chest.

A collective gasp echoed throughout the canyon. Suddenly Ares had McAdams's sword at her throat and Than stood in front of her protectively.

"Back down, Ares!" Than cried.

"Gods and goddesses of the court," Ares said. "Would you not agree that Hades has broken the rules?"

"At no fault of the girl's!" Athena objected. "Father, she is innocent!"

"Back off, Ares and put down the weapon," Zeus commanded. "Let us think what to do."

Ares took a step back.

Suddenly Hip appeared next to the body of McAdams. He gave Therese a sheepish grin and disappeared with the hazy soul of the man, but the mangled, lifeless body still lay there on the canyon floor.

"Back to court!" Zeus commanded.

Chapter Forty-Three: The Court Decides

Than wrapped his arms around Therese. She leaned into him and closed her eyes with exhaustion. The ground beneath her shifted. When she opened her eyes, she was back on Mount Olympus inside the assembly hall standing—leaning, really, on Than—in the center of the court. Everything had returned to its original luster. The white marble floors were no longer a clearing on a platform above woods with ants burrowing near her feet. The tree stumps had returned to elaborate thrones, and all of the gods were seated on them, except for Than, who held her in his arms.

The mangled body of McAdams was no longer in sight, and through the foyer, Therese could see the golden whale fountain spraying up its heavenly water with its magnificent rainbow on top. Although she couldn't see it, she imagined the battlefield had disappeared and had been replaced with the giant wall of clouds surrounding the palace.

"Fellow gods and goddesses," Zeus said from his position on his throne. "I motion that we take some time to contemplate the decision before us, to rest after so many hours of sitting here watching with anxiety, and to eat the comforting foods we love. Does anyone second my motion?"

"I second it," Aphrodite said.

"All agreed?" Zeus asked.

"Aye."

"All opposed?"

No one, not even Ares, objected. Therese suspected he wanted time to think of some really good punishment for her.

"Good," Zeus said. "We will reconvene in two hours."

The gods and goddesses stood up from their thrones, but unlike the day before, when they had eagerly gathered around her professing their gifts, none but Aphrodite approached her and Than.

"They are all disappointed in me," Therese muttered as she watched them quietly leave the assembly hall.

Than and Aphrodite both looked down to the marble floor.

"And you are disappointed, too," Therese said.

Than tightened his hold on her. "I won't lie and say I'm not disappointed. We could be husband and wife and spending eternity together right this instant." He sighed.

"I should have had Cupid pierce your heart days ago," Aphrodite said to Therese. "You wouldn't have hesitated for the sake of love."

Than swallowed hard. "No. I wouldn't allow it, and even now, as things turned out, I don't regret my decision. I wanted her to love me without Cupid's help."

Therese bit her lip. "You think I don't love you enough? You think that's why I didn't kill him?"

Aphrodite lowered her eyes to give them privacy.

Than pulled Therese against him and kissed away her lines of worry. He kissed her forehead, her eyelids, her cheeks, and her mouth. "No," he finally said. "I know you love me. You wouldn't have chosen to fight otherwise. You could have gone free."

She leaned her head against his chest. "I'm so sorry I couldn't go through with it."

"I'm not," he said, and he kissed the top of her hair. "Your mercy and compassion are part of why I love you so much. You're so different from my father and sisters. They want justice at any price. But you, my sweet Therese, you love and respect life."

"How ironic that she would fall in love with Death," Aphrodite murmured. "Listen, I will leave you two alone, but first I have to do something about Therese's appearance. Just look at yourself."

She pulled a mirror from the air and held it before Therese.

Therese shuddered at her reflection. Twigs and leaves were tangled in her wild hair, her face was smeared with dirt, her bra, which was once white, was a dull gray and stained with sweat, and her jeans were dirty and torn. She looked like a savage.

Instantly Aphrodite made Therese clean and fresh, dressed in a beautiful gown of pale blue silk. Her red curls were swept up in an arrangement on her head, jewels hung from her ears and around her wrist. Her golden locket from Athena sparkled with polish on her throat. Silver sandals adorned her feet.

"Just like Cinderella," she laughed. Then, more seriously, she said, "Thank you, Aphrodite."

The goddess of love smiled and replied, "Although foremost I want you to look spectacular during your final moments with Thanatos, I also suspect the other gods might have more mercy on you looking so angelic."

"You're probably right," Therese said. "Thank you."

Aphrodite turned and left the hall.

"Hungry?" Than asked her when they were alone.

She shook her head. "I just ate a ton of fruit. Can we just sit down for a while?"

"You're tired, I'm sure."

"Yeah. I'm pretty tired, but I'm too nervous to sleep."

"I could take you for a ride on my father's chariot."

"I doubt your father would allow that."

"I won't ask him."

"You think that's wise?"

He shrugged. "I know my father. His mind is made up. Our little ride won't change anything. Besides, I could pop to your house, gather the items you want to give to charity, and pop them back into the chariot. We have two hours. This may be our last chance to get them to the goddesses' charities."

"And that could sway their decision today."

"Possibly."

She laughed.

"What?"

"It just seems odd to use your father's fancy golden chariot to deliver my parents' old clothes to charities."

He gave her a hug.

"Could I see my aunt and uncle?"

Than shook his head. "No. You'll have to remain in the chariot over Mount Olympus. I'll make a few trips back and forth with the bags and boxes while you hang out overhead."

Than and Therese went down the rainbow steps, into the golden-paved plaza, and to the stables to the back stall where Swift and Sure, Hades's black stallions, were boarded. Therese stroked their necks and spoke to them in soft tones. The feel of the animals soothed her.

"They love you already," Than laughed.

Than led Swift and Therese led Sure across the plaza to the chariot shed where Cupid helped them bridle the horses for their journey.

"This is our secret, Cupid," Than said, and Cupid winked in reply.

Hades's golden chariot had a bench seat like Poseidon's, but there was a second bench in back as well. And where Poseidon had trim of waves and ornaments of marine life, Hades's chariot was trimmed with golden flames.

Therese and Than sat beside one another. Than took the reins. Like a shot of lightning, they darted out of the shed and into the sky, high above Mount Olympus. Than put an arm around Therese's shoulders and she curled against him. She wished this moment could last forever, but it seemed to pass by too quickly. Than slowed the chariot down to an easy glide and it hovered, like a hot air balloon, far above the palace.

"I'm so glad to get away for a little while and have a few moments alone with you," Therese said softly. "I have a feeling Ares may insist I be condemned to death, which I really don't mind. I look forward to seeing my parents. But I am so sorry I won't be the same, for your sake."

"I'll love you no matter what," he murmured. "Don't think about that now." He leaned over and kissed her.

She squared herself to him, taking his face in both her hands. Oh, how she would miss these kisses! She moved her fingers over his face—his cheeks, his jaw, his sexy brow. "I won't forget this face. The Lethe River will not make me forget your beautiful face!" She kissed him again.

"I don't think you'll be condemned to death," Than said. "So quit thinking about that now. Just kiss me."

She kissed him, eagerly, but then she pulled back. "You don't think they'll make me a god, do you?"

He shook his head sadly. "No. My father swore an oath on the river Styx. You won't be made a god." He kissed her forehead. "But if they release you, I promise I'll come back for you, not to guide your soul to the dead, but to make you my queen. I don't know how I'll do it, but I swear I'll find a way."

"You think they're going to release me, back to my home in Colorado?" This thought had not occurred to her. It didn't sound like such a terrible option to her anymore. She missed her aunt, and she missed Clifford, Puffy, and Jewels. She missed Jen and her other friends. She missed her cabin across from the lake.

"I shouldn't have told you that. I don't want to build up your hopes in case it goes otherwise. But I don't think Artemis, Apollo, Athena, and Aphrodite will stand for your murder. And Zeus will side with them over the others."

"What about Hades and Ares? They both want me dead now!"

"I don't know. That's our biggest concern. But, please, please shut up and kiss me."

After a long, luscious kiss that set Therese's soul on fire, Than said, "Hold that thought while I get the donations."

"You're going to leave me up here by myself?"

"Swift and Sure will take care of you. And I'll only be gone a few seconds at a time." He kissed her and then vanished.

Instantly he returned with a black yard bag full of her parents' clothes in each hand. He made several such trips until the chariot was overflowing. Then Than took up the reins and told the horses to head for the island of Cyprus.

The rocky shoreline came into view within a matter of seconds. Than pulled the chariot to a stop just above an enormous stone castle. Then, leaving Therese inside the chariot once again to hover in the sky, he disappeared and reappeared several times as he unloaded half of the donations with the society devoted to Aphrodite's annual festival. Then Than returned to the chariot and did the same for Athena's charity in Acropolis.

When they returned to the skies above Mount Olympus, they still had time to cuddle and kiss in the chariot before the court would reconvene.

"Now, where were we?" Than asked with a husky voice as he covered her lips with his.

"Mmm," Therese sighed. "I don't want to ever forget this moment." She was still fairly sure she would be condemned to die and taken on the Lethe River—the river of forgetfulness—to the Elysian Fields. "I won't allow myself to forget how good it feels to be in your arms, to be kissed by you."

A trumpet sounded throughout the air, and Therese immediately thought of her friend Ray, who played the trumpet in her high school band. Next she thought of Todd and his ostentatiously high truck. She thought of Vicki in the wake of her mother's suicide. And she thought of Jen, Bobby, Pete, and Mrs. Holt all doing their best to deal with their fragmented family as it tried to piece itself back together again.

Than pulled the chariot back into the shed and left the horses for Cupid to tend to and then gave Therese his hand and led her from the chariot, past the fountain, up the rainbow steps, and into the assembly hall where all the gods awaited on their thrones.

Hades gave his son a look of admonition as Than led Therese to the center of the court.

Therese felt her whole body quaking. This was it.

Zeus cleared his throat. "The first to speak on the matter at hand shall be Ares."

"Look at her standing there so lovely," Ares said sharply, standing from his throne and walking toward her. "No doubt Aphrodite's doing. Therese Mills, by appearances, could, perhaps, fit in among us gods. But Hades swore an oath on the river Styx, and no oath sworn on that river leading to his kingdom has ever, since the beginning of time, been broken. We must not allow him to make her like us no matter how badly his son desires it. She shall not be made the queen of Death!

"In addition, Hades should be punished for his interference. Who knows what different outcome might have been prevented by his hasty action? Not only shall she not become a god, but Hades must be made to swear that if any of us were ever persuaded to retrieve her from the Underworld," here Ares looked directly at Than, "that Hades would send the Maenads to rip the offending god to shreds once a year, just as they once ripped Orpheus when he stormed back to the Underworld for Eurydice the second time."

A gasp echoed through the court, and all the gods and goddesses looked at one another with solemn eyes as Ares returned to his throne.

Then Zeus said, "Hades, what do you have to say?"

Hades stood up. His eyes looked around the court and fell on his son, standing beside Therese. "It pains me to see my son so unhappy. Therese could have helped us all to avoid this had she done the deed herself. It's true I struck the final blow that killed McAdams, but only because I owed it to my souls, her parents, who deserved to be avenged.

"It is because of her cowardice that we stand here, indecisive. I agree with Ares that she should not become like us. I accept the punishment of sending the Maenads to rip apart any who would drag her from my kingdom. But I wish Ares and the rest of you to consider this: Does this girl, though cowardly, deserve to die? I pride myself on my just ways, and I say to you today, we should send her to her mortal home alive. Believe me, Ares, you who crave victory over me, she will suffer far more alive than in the Elysian Fields frolicking with her parents among the asphodel. You took away her parents, and now we take away her one true love if we condemn her to life, far away from Death. Believe me, Ares, when I say she will suffer." Hades returned to his seat.

Zeus then asked, "Poseidon? Have you any words regarding her? She was your prisoner."

Poseidon stood. "I agree with Hades. Send the girl to her mortal home alive." He returned to his seat.

"Hear, hear!" other gods and goddesses shouted.

"Send her home alive!" Artemis said.

"Send the girl home!" Athena echoed.

"Send the girl home alive!" others shouted.

"Ares?" Zeus asked. "What say you?"

Ares stood from his throne and took a few steps toward Therese. "You made me promise on the river Styx to protect your loved ones if you chose the third option, which you did, and so I do, but I did not promise to protect you! Send her back a mortal girl to her mortal home, as Hades has said. Let her suffer in life without Death."

Applause rang out among the gods.

"On one condition!" Ares shouted.

The Olympians quieted down to listen to Ares's next words.

"I will agree to let her live if everyone here swears on the River Styx not to make this girl like us. She must live as a mortal and die as a mortal and none of us shall change that."

The gods and goddesses stole glances at one another, some content, others outraged.

"Shall Ares be called the king of Olympia now?" Poseidon asked. "How is it your son can make such demands, brother?"

Zeus plunged a thunder bolt down to earth and shouted, "How dare you!"

Therese wasn't sure if Zeus was mad at Ares or Poseidon, but the mystery was solved when Zeus turned his angry face toward his brother.

"Ares has every right to ensure a fair outcome, Poseidon. Do you not see how this girl's life is an affront to him, who was promised that by her hand alone his servant, McAdams, would be destroyed?"

Poseidon gritted his teeth but held his tongue.

"I say we honor my son's request. What say you, Hades?"

Hades clenched his fists at his side and gave Therese a nasty glare. "It's just. I agree with Ares."

"Then it's done," Zeus said. "Let us swear."

"I swear," the Olympian voices rang, Than's among them.

Therese looked at Than with mixed feelings. "I don't want to leave you," she said to him. "Can't you please take me with you?"

"I'll come back for you, somehow some way, I promise. I will never give up. I will spend your whole life finding a way to make you my queen."

"Don't take too long." She reached her lips to his, but before she made contact, he and the assembly hall and all the gods disappeared, and she found herself standing on the gravelly drive to her house.

Chapter Forty-Four: Sleep Returns

Therese stood in front of her log cabin in the dark of night wearing the pale blue gown and silver sandals from Aphrodite. She walked up the drive to the house wondering how long she'd been gone and what kind of trouble she would be in and what she would say about the way she was dressed.

When she opened the front door, she found Carol and Richard curled up on the sofa watching television. They both gave her a look of surprise, and their mouths dropped open.

Oh, boy. I must have been gone a week. Here it comes.

"Wow, you look great," Carol said. "This makeover is a major improvement over the one Jen gave you yesterday. Don't you think, Rich?"

"No contest. That black wig was a little weird. No offense, Therese."

Okay, what were they talking about? "Um, thanks."

"Did you have a good time?" Carol asked. "Jen told us you might sleep over again tonight. I'm so excited you've been having such a good time together, especially with school getting ready to start up again. Sleepovers during the week will have to stop then, you know. So, did you have fun?"

She thought over what she had been doing however many days it had been. "Um, yeah. Great time. I'm going upstairs to call Jen. I stupidly forgot my overnight bag at her house. I'll be back down in a little bit."

Clifford pranced down the stairs and nearly knocked her over. "Clifford!" She squatted down and hugged his neck. Tears flooded her eyes. "Hey, boy! I'm glad to see you, too!"

"You act like you haven't seen him all day!" Carol laughed.

Therese climbed the stairs to her room wondering what in the world had been happening here and how long she'd been gone. She noticed Jewel's lamp was on, so she flipped it off. Fresh lettuce and tomatoes and water had been given to her by someone. Puffy also had a full dispenser of water and fresh food. What had been going on?

She went to the phone to call Jen.

"You're back!" Jen said. "Oh my God, I was wondering when you'd come home. I was so worried. What happened? Are you and Than together now?"

"Sort of. I don't know. He had to, um, he had to go back down…south."

"Oh. I'm sorry. I guess you're pretty bummed out."

"Yeah. Thanks for covering for me, though. How did you do it?"

"I used the crown to sneak around your place to take care of your pets the first day after our sleepover. The second day I dressed up in a wig and a big gaudy dress and told them I was you and that I had given you a makeover. I whipped through the house fast before they noticed anything funny about you. Then today, I used the crown again to feed your pets, and I called them from here to say you might be staying over again."

"So I was only gone for two nights?"

"And three days. Wait, you don't know how long you were gone? Did you guys get drunk or something?"

"Or something." Therese sat on the edge of her bed. Clifford leapt up beside her, and she stroked his fur.

"So give me the details." Then Jen added, "unless you're too bummed."

"I am pretty bummed, and I'm really tired, but maybe we could get together tomorrow. I could come by just before the trail rides, see the horses, and we could visit then."

"That would be great! Plan to have lunch here."

"Sounds good." Then Therese asked, "Did your dad move home?"

"Yeah."

"Everything going okay?"

"I don't know. It's better with the crown. I can't thank you enough."

"Good. See you tomorrow." Then she asked, "Oh, wait. Think we could invite Vicki?"

"That's actually a great idea. I've wanted to call her. This gives me a good excuse. I'll call her now. See you tomorrow."

Therese hung up the phone and looked at herself in her dresser mirror. So she had been gone three days and two nights. Jen had taken care of her pets using the crown. She had also made an appearance yesterday pretending to be Therese. Carol and Richard had no clue she'd been fighting for her life before the gods of Olympus, that she could have won had she not taken pity on the man who had her parents killed, and that she could be a goddess right now with the love of her life for all eternity.

She called Vicki and made arrangements to meet at Jen's tomorrow morning. Then she changed from the gown and hung it up in her closet wondering if she would ever have an occasion to wear it again. Maybe prom. She smiled at the thought of wearing Aphrodite's gown to prom. She put on her nightshirt and lay down on her bed. It wasn't quite as wonderful as Poseidon's, but it sure felt good to be home. Clifford curled against her, and she stroked his fur and kissed the top of his head. At least one of them was immortal.

Although she was tired, she went downstairs to spend some time with Carol and Richard. She curled up with a blanket in her favorite chair near the fireplace, and Clifford joined her on her lap. She stroked his fur as she asked Carol and Richard what they'd been up to.

Carol said, "First of all, I've been waiting to tell you that the lieutenant called. They found the body of the man they believe was responsible for your parents' death. His name was Steven McAdams. Apparently, he was distributing counterfeit drugs all over the world and this had something to do with your mother's work at the college. They also have two men from Pakistan in custody. The men confessed to helping McAdams. They turned themselves in, can you believe it? The lieutenant said something must have scared them into confessing. Anyway, he's closed the case and assures us that we're safe."

Therese smiled. "That's great." She wondered if details about the anthrax antidote were omitted by the lieutenant wanting to spare her aunt, or by her aunt wanting to spare Therese.

Carol looked at Richard, and he gave her a nod.

"Actually," Carol said, "we've wanted to talk to you about something, else, too."

Oh yeah, Therese thought. She remembered now that they had wanted to tell her something important that would affect them all, but right now she didn't think she had the strength to hear it.

Richard piped up, "We really think this would be good for all three of us. We hope you think so, too."

Therese filled with dread.

"Richard and I are getting married," Carol said.

Therese looked at Carol and then at Richard and back at Carol. This was the news? "That's awesome." Is that why Carol might need to leave her?

"You think so?" Carol asked.

Therese nodded and gave her a forced smile.

"And, well," Carol started again, "we were kind of hoping that you would let us adopt you, so that both of us could be your official guardians."

"You don't have to answer right away," Richard said. "You can take some time to think about it. But, as another guardian, I could help your aunt. I could give consent if you needed medical attention and Carol was out of town, or if you needed something simpler, like a permission slip signed. It's okay, though, if you don't like the idea. And we thought we'd all three live here in this house together."

She was so filled with relief to learn that they wanted her—that they both wanted her—that her eyes flooded with tears, and the tears spilled down her cheeks. "I don't know what to say," she said softly. "This is, like, the best news you could give me. The past few days have been so hard. I mean, I had fun with Jen, but I also had to say goodbye to Than. He and his sisters went back…south. And," the tears were turning into sobs, "and, I don't know if you noticed, but we gave Mom and Dad's things away, and, um, and I'm just so relieved that you want me. I was scared that you would leave me, too."

Both Carol and Richard got up from the couch and kneeled on the floor beside her chair. They took her hands in theirs and kissed them. Carol stroked her hair. "Oh, sweetheart," Carol said. "I would never leave you. I'm so sorry you ever even had that thought. I will always be here for you." She kissed her cheek again.

"And I know we're not that close yet," Richard said. "But I will be here for you, too. Did you notice I chopped off that dying branch of the elm outside?"

"You did?" Therese's face lit up. She ran to the window above the kitchen sink to take a look. It was dark outside, but the dim light of the moon showed the elm's new profile. She turned and beamed at Richard across the room.

"And I treated the roots of both elms. I think they're going to make it."

Therese skipped around the kitchen bar and threw her arms around Richard. Then she threw her arms around her aunt. Then she put one around each of them and said, "Thank you. Both of you. Thank you so much."

Clifford lifted his face to hers and licked her tears, making the three humans break their embrace and fall back laughing.

After staying up with Carol and Richard a little while longer, sleep began to take possession of every limb and every muscle on Therese's body. She said goodnight, gave them each one more hug, and dragged herself up the stairs to her bed with Clifford following behind. She crawled beneath her covers, allowing Clifford there, too, and he nestled against her.

He knew, unlike the humans downstairs, that she hadn't been home for three days, and now he wanted nothing more than to stay glued to Therese for as long as she would allow.

She turned off her bedside lamp and lay back on her pillow. It wasn't Artemis's goose feathered pillow, but it would do. Her sheets weren't quite as soft or clean as Athena's had been, but they felt just right. She had no eye mask or silken gown, but she had her dog and her other pets, and she was happy.

And although she couldn't have Than, he said he would come back for her. She had to believe that. She had to have hope. One day he would find a way to make her his queen.

And although it wasn't now, she still had her prayer. She would talk to him, and she knew he would hear. And he would be glad to hear her voice over so many others begging him to stay off his visit or to take them swiftly without pain and suffering. Her prayers would be like a breath of fresh air, as he had once told her himself.

"Oh, Than, I miss you already. I wish I could feel you next to me, holding me, kissing me. But I won't make you sad tonight. I want you to know that I'm happy. My aunt and uncle are getting married, and they're going to adopt me. We're all three going to live here in this house together. Can you believe it?" She continued to tell her stories—of what Jen had done in her absence, including the bit about the black wig, how Clifford was stuck to her like glue, how her uncle-to-be had saved the elm trees in the back of her house. She told him what Jewels and Puffy were doing, how she would be having lunch with Jen and Vicky tomorrow, how she couldn't wait to go for a ride with Todd and Ray in Todd's truck again. Band camp would be starting next week. She really needed to start practicing on her flute. Maybe she and her friends would get together this weekend and play their instruments together. And on and on she went, talking to Death about the life she loved and treasured.

And before she knew it, Therese was standing on a muddy bank. Fog curled around her, so she couldn't see far, but she could tell that the water was flowing in a narrow gorge between two enormous granite mountains. "Mom! Dad!" Her shouts were stifled by the thick fog. She couldn't open her mouth and yell as loudly as she wanted. "Mom! Dad!" She looked around the empty bank. Her bare feet sunk into the mud. Tall blades of grass as high as her knees grew in tufts along the shore. Mosquitoes swarmed over one area of the water. Three large boulders leaned in a cluster on the left side of the shore against the base of steep, massive wall of rock.

She recognized this place.

She leapt into the air and flew her breaststroke above the river. She told the fog to disappear. Down below, she willed Charon to look up at her from his ferry. He was alone rowing toward the bank, perhaps coming for some poor soul.

"Tell my parents I said goodbye, will you?" she cried out to Charon. "Tell them I love them and will miss them and will one day be with them again!"

The old man looked at her and waved.

She took that as a yes. Maybe they wouldn't remember her. But maybe they would.

She turned a few somersaults in the air and then headed back toward the bank. Below she saw two figures, and one of them she could tell, even from this height, was Than. She charged down toward him.

"Hello, my love!" she cried, hovering just in front of him, but without touching the icy water near her feet. Already she could feel herself growing weaker, and she found it more difficult to breathe.

Charon paddled his long stick through the water toward the bank.

"Therese!" Than said beaming. He started to reach out to her, but then thought better of it, and took several steps back. "I love your prayers. Please keep talking to me! But don't linger here another minute, and try to avoid this place. We can't have you die before I figure out how to make you a god! Go! But keep talking to me! I'll come back one day!"

Therese blew him her kiss and, reluctantly, flew away before she felt any weaker.

For all she really knew, he could have been a figment. She might have invented the whole scene. But it didn't matter. She wanted to believe in it, and that was enough for now.

She found herself flying over the San Juan Mountains when Hip came up from behind.

"It's good to be back," he said, flying beside her.

Yes, she thought without speaking. It wasn't bad.

BOOK TWO

Challenge of Hades

Chapter One: Sleep and Death

Therese Mills let out a shrill, gleeful scream. "You're back!" She practically flew into Than's arms, running across the gravelly drive of her Colorado log cabin, the small pebbles working their way between her bare feet and flip-flops. She kept saying, "You're back!" over and over with profound disbelief. The ten months since she had last seen him at Mount Olympus over the dead body of Steve McAdams had seemed an eternity.

"You feel so good," Than murmured as his lips caressed her now-moist skin, hot beneath the summer sun and his even hotter body against her. He stopped, ran his fingers through her short, red curls. "Nice."

"Not too short?"

"I love it. Makes your adorable dimples stand out more." He kissed her again, his hands moving along her bare waist. "On your way for a swim?"

She was wearing the same bikini from last summer, the one she wore shortly after she and Than had met at Jen's ranch down the road. She smiled now at the memory of their swim in the lake. The lake was actually a reservoir tucked in a small valley between the San Juan Mountains. Only five homes, including hers and Jen's, spread apart and wedged in the mountains, shared this spectacular view.

"Care to join me?"

"What about your aunt and uncle?"

"They're inside, working. They won't bother us."

He covered her with more kisses.

They were kissing on her gravelly drive one minute and at the bank the next, holding hands on the jetties, about to jump. A hawk soared over the valley beneath the early morning sun.

"Did we just god travel?" Therese asked Than.

He gave her what seemed an arrogant smirk that said, "Of course."

Before she could ask another question, Than had stripped down to his white boxers and was pulling her into to the frigid water, and she was screaming gleefully again.

"It's so cold!"

"It's awesome," he said. "I've missed you, and all of this, more than you can know."

He held her close, keeping her warm, and was about to kiss her again when they heard the crunch of footsteps along the jetties.

"Pete!" Therese cried, surprised. He had been her rock since last summer, a shoulder to cry on, a friend—maybe more than a friend since Cupid shot his arrow into Pete's heart—to keep her from losing her mind. She pulled back from Than and gave Pete an awkward smile. "Feel like a swim?"

"Hey, Than," Pete said with what seemed like a forced grin. "How's it going?"

"Hey, Pete. How's your family?" Than ran his fingers through his dark wavy hair, maybe in an attempt to appear casual and unaffected by Pete's sudden appearance.

Pete's blond bowl hair cut from last summer had grown out, and he hadn't bothered to cut it. Therese had told him she liked it long. Just now he had it tied back in a ponytail at the nape of his neck. He wore his blue jeans and boots and a long-sleeved shirt open in front, exposing his tanned chest and abdomen. He looked really good, for a mortal.

"The family's okay. Summer is our busy season, you know." Then Pete added, "Need a job?"

"This is a quick visit," Than replied. "But thanks anyway. Tell everybody I said hello."

"You should do it yourself," Pete said. "They'd be happy to see you."

Pete's family—the Holts—ran a trail riding business down the road, and last summer, Than had taken a job as a horse handler when their usual hands had to take time off due to a death in the family. Therese later suspected Than had arranged it all so that they could meet—in the flesh, that is. They had already met when she was in a coma after her parents were killed by one of McAdams's Taliban spies. She had followed her parents to the Underworld, but had assumed it was a dream, and, as she had always been a lucid dreamer and able to manipulate the events of her dreams, she had been especially bossy and flirtatious with the god of death and with his brother, the god of sleep. She couldn't have known then that it had all been real and that the god of death, unused to receiving affection, would fall in love with her and follow her back to the world of the living.

But she was glad. More than glad. She was absolutely thrilled. And now he had finally come back for her. But what would she tell Pete?

She could see the pain in Pete's face.

"Are we still on for the movies tonight?" Pete asked.

Therese could feel the blood leave her face as Than studied it. Surely he, a god, had been aware of her slightly-more-than-friends relationship with Pete. "Umm. I'm not sure, Pete. Can I give you a call?"

Jen stepped up beside Pete with her arms folded across her chest. "Hey, Than. What's up?"

"Hey, Jen. It's good to see you."

Jen, who, like all the people in Therese's life, had remained ignorant of Than's true identity, was pretty steamed that Than hadn't called or written for ten months. Therese also knew Jen wouldn't be too happy that Therese would drop Pete for Than.

"It's been a while," Jen said. "I thought maybe, I don't know, you'd fallen off the face of the earth."

"Not exactly," Than said.

"You might have called," Jen said accusingly.

"It's um, complicated."

"Yeah, right. They don't have phones down south in Texas."

"Jen," Therese said sharply. "Give it a rest."

"We're still going to the movies tonight," Jen insisted. "You and me and Pete and Matthew. I already paid for the tickets online and the movie's sold out."

"Take Bobby," Therese said.

Pete clenched his jaw. "Come on, Jen. We've got work to do."

Pete walked away, and when he was out of sight, Jen, who stood there with her arms crossed, said between gritted teeth, "Don't you dare hurt my brother. Our family has been through enough lately. You should know."

Jen referred to the return of her father after three years of estrangement. Therese didn't know the details, but apparently Mr. Holt had hurt Jen in unmentionable ways while drunk, and after years of therapy and being sober, had returned for a second chance. Therese had loaned Jen her invisibility crown, a gift from Artemis, so she could disappear if her father ever fell off the wagon. But Jen had no idea how the crown worked or how it came to be in Therese's possession.

In fact, it was the existence of the crown from Artemis, the locket from Athena, and the traveling robe and gown from Aphrodite that had assured Therese when she was feeling low that the events of last summer hadn't been imaginary.

Before Therese could reply, Than's sister Meg, one of the Furies, appeared beside Jen. She too had her arms crossed, and her blonde hair, blonder and longer than Jen's and curly where Jen's was straight, blew about her face like a gilded sunburst. "This is wrong, Than!" she roared. Her face was pale and her lips bright red, like fresh blood. "You're screwing with the lives of mortals, not to mention the lives of gods."

Jen's mouth dropped open. "What is she talking about, Therese?"

Therese felt her face go white. Why would Meg expose their identity to Jen?

"Back off, Meg!" Than shouted. "This is none of your business."

"Of course, it is, dear brother! We are all in danger after the oath we took on the River Styx at Ares's command. Do you wish us all to be ripped apart by the maenads?"

Therese cringed at the memory of Mount Olympus. Therese had broken her deal with the Olympians by refusing to kill McAdams, which would avenge the death of her parents. You couldn't refuse the gods and not face consequences, she supposed.

But Meg's words confused Therese. The maenads, women drunk with the wine of Dionysus, could only rip apart someone who dared rescue Therese from the dead. That's not what Than was doing.

What was he doing, anyway?

Now Tizzie, another of the three Furies, stood beside her sister with her hands on her hips. Her dark, serpentine curls hung loose about her shoulders and caressed the chain of emeralds around her neck. Where her sister was pale like the moon, she was dark like midnight. "Let her go, Than. She's been doing fine with the mortal. Let her live a natural life with Peter Holt."

"Therese, you can't hurt Pete!" Jen shouted. "You just can't!"

"You can't hurt Pete!" the two Furies joined in. Their voices became a chant.

Therese took Than's hand. "Get me out of here," she muttered. "Before they kill me."

Suddenly with the sound of an enormous train, the water parted like it must have when Moses commanded the Red Sea.

"What in the world?" Therese stood beside Than, shivering on the rocky bottom.

"Get in!" Poseidon's chariot came out of nowhere, pulled by his three magnificent white steeds, Riptide, Seaquake, and Crest. Poseidon's sun-bleached hair and beard were dry and blowing in the wind against his bronze face, his blue-green eyes scrutinizing them. "What are you waiting for, kids? Get in!"

Than helped Therese into the chariot, and before they had fully sat in the seat beside Poseidon, they were whipped from Lemon Reservoir into the summer sky.

The wind hit Therese's face and stung her now watery eyes. She looked back to see all three Furies following them. Meg and Tizzie were joined by their red-headed sister, Alecto. They were flying through the sky in Hades's chariot, pulled by his two black stallions, Swift and Sure.

Poseidon slapped the backs of his white steeds. "Faster!" he called.

This can't be happening, Therese thought, clinging to Than. The Furies would never reveal themselves to Jen. She gave Than a dubious look. He smiled and kissed her.

Her heart sank in her chest as they soared above the clouds. "Than," she said in his ear. "Tell me this is real!" Despite the threat of the Furies on their tail, she would rather this all be real and her be sitting beside the love of her life than the alternative.

He took her face in his hands and kissed her. She kissed him back longingly. Without letting go of the kiss, she realized the chariot was plummeting, falling back to the earth, to the sea. What sea?

"I wish you'd kiss me like that," Hip, Than's brother, the god of sleep, said beside her. He had taken Poseidon's reins.

Therese looked at Hip. "What happened to Poseidon?"

"You mean the ugly figment you mistook for Poseidon?"

"No, Hip!" Therese shouted. "This isn't a dream!" She wrapped her arms around Than and buried her face in his fine chest.

"You've gotten better and better at believing in them over these last ten months," Hip said.

"What do you care?" Therese hissed.

"You know the answer to that," Hip said.

"Leave us alone," Than said.

"Shut your figment up," Hip said to Therese.

"He's no figment!"

Hip took out a hand-held mirror and put it up to the three of them. Only two faces gazed back. Than's was invisible.

Therese looked at Than with astonishment. He looked real when she wasn't staring at his absent reflection. He smiled at her, but now that Therese knew for certain he was a disgusting figment, she couldn't bring herself to smile back or to lean in at his attempt to kiss her.

"Figment!" she cried. "I command you to show yourself!"

Than disappeared, and in his place was the laughing eel-like creature. It flitted in the air around them and then flew away. She looked back to see the figments that had once been Furies twirl and sail away, laughing at her.

Therese moaned. "When will he come for me, Hip?"

Hip brushed a strand of his blond wavy hair behind his ear and then pulled back on the reins. He looked a lot like his fraternal twin brother: same awesome golden body and gorgeous blue eyes; but whereas Hip's hair was blond, Than's was dark brown, almost black. Therese had been tempted more than once to give in to Hip's jealous demands for affection. Hip was a womanizer who visited many girls at night in their dreams and had his way with them. Therese had managed to keep him at bay in her own dreams, but it wasn't always easy. He was good at seduction.

"I don't think he ever will," Hip said, pulling hard on the reins but unable to slow the steeds. "It's not his place. He's got a job to do."

"It's not fair," she complained.

"Life isn't fair," Hip smiled. "Only death is. Ask my father. That's his favorite line."

Therese wiped the tears from her eyes and choked down a sob. "You could take me to him," she said with an accusing tone as they continued to plummet toward the sea. "You know you could."

"I've promised him I wouldn't," Hip said. "It would kill you. You already know that. In fact, this conversation is beginning to sound like a scratched up CD that skips back to the same spot."

"Just take me for a moment. I'll leave before I get too weak. Take me once and we'll never talk about this again."

"I swore on the River Styx."

Her eyes widened. "You never told me that before. Why didn't you tell me you swore an oath? I'd have given up by now."

"I tell you in every dream, Therese. You choose not to remember. Now wake up and leave me alone. I've grown tired of your company."

Chapter Two: The Search

Than disintegrated and dispatched to several cities throughout the world, collecting the souls of the dead. The more he disintegrated, the more difficult it was for him to focus on his most important task: finding a way to make Therese his queen. Ares had been clever last summer on Mount Olympus when he'd made them all swear on the River Styx not to make her a god like them, nor were they allowed to retrieve her from the Underworld once she died a mortal death. The situation seemed hopeless, but Than was not without hope. He was determined to find a way.

For the past ten months he had traveled from god to god, taking counsel from all those who would give it. Most of them had urged him to give up his dream of making Therese his wife and queen. They told him love was fleeting, and he would learn to forget her. They said she would be dead within the next eighty years, and this amount of time was but a blink of an eye to a god. Even his own father told him to forget her, saying she wasn't worthy. Hades had gone so far as to force Hip to swear on the River Styx, like the gods on Mount Olympus, never to make Therese a god.

But Aphrodite wept for him and understood his pain. They sat together on Mount Olympus in the banquet hall, alone except for Hestia's coming and goings as she set the table for the next meal. Aphrodite took Than's hand into her own and kissed it, something no god save his mother had ever done.

"I'm so sorry for you," she said softly. "You may not believe this, but I know how you feel. I'm not allowed to be with my true love either."

"Hephaestus isn't your true love?"

She pulled her hand away. "Lower your voice." She waited for Hestia to leave the room.

"You knew that, Than. Everyone knows Ares has my heart."

"Then why are you married to Hephaestus?"

"Has it never occurred to you why the most beautiful god would be wed to the only ugly one?"

Than shook his head. "Love is deeper than beauty?"

"God, no." She waved her hand in the air as if to bat such an idea away. "Beauty trumps all, my dear, and Zeus knows that. He feared the people would worship me above him, so he bound me to that hunchback."

"But what good did that do?"

"Beauty also comes from happiness. Some of my beauty faded after my marriage."

"I wouldn't know. I can't imagine you more beautiful."

Aphrodite gave him a smile. "What do you want from me?"

"Can you persuade Ares to change his mind about Therese? Ask him to do it out of love for you?"

"Of course, but that won't help. We've all sworn an oath. Even if Ares sympathizes with your cause, he can't undo what's already been done."

"Does he sympathize?"

"He hates you."

Than was momentarily distracted from the beautiful goddess by the soul of another plant in the hands of a young Indian boy he accompanied to Charon. More and more he was seeing plants evolving souls of their own, like animals and humans. He had been adding these plant souls to his chambers in preparation for the day Therese would join him. He wanted to add as many plants and animals to his chambers as possible for his nature-loving bride-to-be.

Aphrodite touched his hand again and brought his focus back to her. "I'm sorry. Truly. But there's nothing we can do."

"I can't accept that. There's got to be a way. Will you at least think about it, and let me know if an idea comes to you?"

Aphrodite nodded, but her face held no hope.

Then today, months after his conversation with the goddess, Hermes appeared with a summons from Mount Olympus. Aphrodite wished to see him.

Chapter Three: Awake

Therese reached out to Hip but felt something furry in his place. She opened her eyes. She squinted against the bright sun beaming through her bedroom windows. Her eyes gradually adjusted, and she looked around. Her bed covers were thrown across the wooden floor. She lay in her nightshirt, one sock on, one sock off, holding onto her little smooth fox terrier, Clifford. He licked the tears streaming down her cheeks.

"It happened again," she told him. "It seemed so real."

She lay back on her pillow and stared at the ceiling. She noticed a crack that hadn't been there before.

Ten months and not a word from him.

"Than," she whispered. "Thanatos," she said in case his hearing required his full name. "Please do something. Give me a sign you still care about me. I feel so hopeless."

When, once again, nothing earth-shattering happened, she pulled her covers from the floor and lay back down on her bed beneath them. Why get up? What did she have to live for?

"You're so lucky, boy," she said to Clifford. "If only Artemis could have made me immortal when she did it to you. We could be together forever and still have our memories—" Unlike Mom and Dad, she thought, who, because they were dead were forever oblivious to the life they led on earth. They were happy, though, in the Elysian Fields with all of its delusions. It didn't really sound so bad and was maybe a better alternative to this emptiness and longing she felt ever since their death last year—an emptiness and longing that only worsened when Than came into, and then out of, her life.

She wondered if it would have been better not to have met him at all. She shuddered at the thought. No, better to be miserable.

Then she wondered for the millionth time if she could have possibly imagined it all: meeting the gods of sleep and death, falling in love, receiving magical gifts from goddesses, taking a ride with Poseidon, fighting the man responsible for her parents' death on Mount Olympus and then choosing not to kill him, which meant she could not become a god and join Than in the Underworld forever. She had been in the worst state of depression after her parents' death. Could it have all been a delusion?

No, because of the crown and the robe and the blue dress Aphrodite gave her at the end of the battle on Mount Olympus. Because of the locket from Athena she wore around her neck. They were proof.

Clifford did his I-need-to-go-outside dance, so she climbed from the bed. "Okay, boy. Let's go." She tugged off the one sock and skipped down the stairs.

"Good morning, Sleepyhead," Carol said from the granite countertop where she sipped coffee and read the paper. "It's almost time for swim practice."

"I'm not sure I'm going this morning." She slipped on a pair of flip-flops and then followed Clifford out the back door onto the wooden deck. The screen door slammed shut behind her, so she didn't hear whatever her aunt said next. "Come on, Clifford. Let's go for a walk."

She often walked out in the woods in her nightshirt knowing no one would be around to see her. The Melner Cabin was a half mile away toward the dam (just thinking of last summer's guests in the Melner Cabin made her moan), and the Holts lived three-quarters of a mile on the other side. She had only the deer, the chipmunks, the birds, and the occasional wild horse to contend with, and these companions she gladly welcomed. Just now two chipmunks scurried away from her, and a red bird fluttered beneath the feeder on one of two great elms. She made her wish and blew five kisses before the cardinal could make its escape. She doubted the wish would come true, but it didn't hurt to try.

She looked up at the twin elms, which were both healthy now thanks to her uncle, Richard, who had cut off the diseased branch and had treated the roots of both trees to keep the Dutch elm disease away. He and Carol married last Christmas, and in January Richard's adoption of Therese was finalized. They would now celebrate two birthdays for her: April seventh, the day she was born, and January eighth, the day Richard's adoption of her was official. She had two legal guardians who loved her and took care of her. She had friends who loved her, too. And Pete. Why couldn't this be enough?

"Therese?" Carol called from the back door. "Jen's on her way to pick you up. Better get your suit on."

Therese groaned. "Come on, Clifford. Let's go inside."

Clifford rambled down the trail he and she had made over the years, and together they reentered the house.

"You've missed so much practice," Carol said. "You really need to go today. You're not sick, are you?" Carol's straight red hair was pulled up in a high ponytail and rings of mascara had not yet been washed from her face.

Therese shrugged. "I don't think so. Just tired."

"You're a healthy eighteen-year-old. Why are you so tired all the time? Maybe we should go see Dr. Lanford again."

"I don't like Dr. Lanford, and I don't want to go on Prozac again." The Prozac had interfered with the lucidity of her dreams.

"Maybe a therapist, then. I'll do some research. Your parents have been gone a year. This isn't healthy."

Therese sighed. "I'll go get ready."

She trudged up the stairs, with Clifford at her heels. After she changed into her one-piece, she quickly fed and watered her pets. Puffy still didn't look so good. She suspected he had stayed in his plastic tower all night again. His breathing had been labored for over a week. The vet had said it was time. Four years was a long life for a hamster.

Jewels, her tortoise, had nearly doubled in size since last summer and had required a larger tank. The tank stretched across the expanse of Therese's desk, which was no loss to Therese since she always did her homework on her bed. She stroked the tortoise's shell.

She heard the doorbell, so she slipped on some shorts over her suit, grabbed her bag, and skipped downstairs where she slipped her feet into flip-flops.

"Don't you want some breakfast?" Carol asked.

"Not hungry."

When she opened the door, she found Pete instead of Jen.

"Hey, Therese," he said. "Ready?"

"Where's Jen?"

"In the truck. Hers isn't running so well, and there's no way I'm letting her drive my truck."

"See ya, Carol." Therese followed Pete through the screened front porch and down the steps to the gravelly drive where Jen sat in Pete's truck, waiting.

Jen climbed out of the front bench seat so Therese would sit between her and her brother. Therese wished Jen wasn't pulling so hard for her and Pete to get together—though, in Jen's mind, they kind of already had. Therese now noticed that Jen had dark rings beneath her eyes, and they weren't rings of mascara.

"What's wrong?" Therese asked as Pete backed out of the drive.

"Nothing," Jen said in a way that wasn't convincing.

"Dad got drunk last night. Jen didn't sleep a wink."

"Oh no."

"Yeah," Pete said.

"We don't have to go to practice," Therese offered. "Let's go have breakfast."

Jen shook her head. "I need the practice. I need to get my mind off everything."

"His brother died," Pete explained as he passed Lemon Dam. "He and his brother were close when they were young. Last night was a one-time thing." Then he added, "We hope."

Jen shuddered and Therese could see without looking directly at her that she had started to cry.

"Change the subject," Jen choked out.

Pete and Therese spoke at the same time. Therese said, "How's Matthew?" and Pete said something about his band.

"Go ahead," Pete said.

"No, you go," Therese said.

"Okay. My band is playing in a festival at Pagosa Springs this Saturday night. My whole family is going, I think. I'd love it if you'd come, too."

"Sounds like fun. I'll ask my aunt." She turned to Jen. "Is Matthew going?"

"I think so. Todd and Ray, too."

"Todd and Ray? I haven't seen them since school let out."

"You could ask Vicki, too, if you want," Jen added.

Therese nodded. "Yeah. I should, shouldn't I?"

"It's up to you," Jen replied. "Your call."

Vicki had come to Durango High School half way through their sophomore year and had stuck to Therese like glue. She had mousy brown hair and a face that reminded Therese of a Who from Whoville. Therese had tried to be friendly but had felt suffocated by the neediness of the new girl, until the terrible thing happened at the end of the summer: Vicki's mother committed suicide. Therese had made it her mission to get closer to Vicki, and what had started off as charity had gradually grown into a friendship, though still less than equal. Vicki needed Therese and depended on her much more than Therese did Vicki.

"She's coming to the meet," Therese said. "She's coming to support us. She knows how badly I want to beat Lacey Holzmann at breast-stroke."

"You should invite her," Pete said. "She's a nice girl."

"Yeah. If my aunt says I can go, I'll give Vicki a ring tonight."

Pete patted Therese's thigh. "Good call."

A slight tingle pulsed up her leg. Pete's strong hand felt good, and despite her nightly rants to Than, Than hadn't contacted her in over ten months. She smiled up at Pete.

"It's not like you're inviting her to prom." Pete laughed.

Prom. She hadn't thought about that, but her senior prom would be coming up this school year in the spring. She knew Pete would go with her if she asked. Should she? Should she really give up on Than?

In fact, Therese couldn't help but suspect Pete had decided not to go to college so he could remain close to her. If Cupid hadn't shot his arrow in Pete's heart, he might be at Colorado State right now. However, Hip did say the arrow only made stronger a feeling already present. How much of Pete's affection for her was real? And if much of it was because of the interference of the gods, did she owe it to Pete to give in to his desires?

Pete pulled into the Durango High Natatorium where a bunch of other cars were already parked. "I'm gonna run some errands. When do I need to be back?"

"Eleven," Jen said as she climbed from the seat. "But it's no big deal if you run late. We can grab a bite at the Subway next door while we wait."

"I'll just meet y'all at Subway, then," Pete said.

Therese climbed from the seat and said thanks before closing Pete's truck door. Gina Rizzo was climbing from her Mustang convertible at the same time. Her hair was wrapped into a pretty, neat bun at the nape of her neck, blonde ringlets here and there near her face. Even without makeup, Gina was beautiful—until she spoke. Therese lowered her eyes to avoid her, but it was too late. Gina had seen her and had now caught up to her and Jen.

"Hey, Therese. Hey Jen," she said in a friendly voice. "I heard Lacey's breaststroke has improved by over two seconds since last year. Her cousin is friends with my little sister, you know."

"That's great," Jen said. "Lacey will need those seconds if she wants to come in second to Therese."

Therese gave Jen a grateful glance behind Gina's back.

"Dream on," Gina said in her snotty voice.

They went through the glass doors and into the humid building. Gina skipped ahead of them to avoid whatever Jen would say next.

"Chicken shit," Jen muttered.

When they were away from the other teammates in the locker room putting their things in their lockers before practice, Jen said, "Speaking of prom, Matthew and I are definitely going. I haven't gone shopping for the dress, but I've already found the shoes. They're to die for. You are going to ask Pete, aren't you?"

"Jen, it's months away. I haven't given it much thought."

"Well, start giving it some. You can't start shopping too soon."

"Some tomboy you turned out to be."

"Just 'cause I'm good on a horse doesn't mean I can't appreciate pretty stiletto heels."

Therese grabbed her towel from her bag and shut her locker door. "Can you even walk in them?"

"I've been practicing."

Therese smiled at the image and wondered if Jen wore the invisibility crown while she practiced so no one would laugh at her. It had to be funny.

They left the locker room together and went to the poolside, where their coach had gathered the rest of their team. Paul caught Therese's eye and licked his lips in an attempt to be sexy. She shuddered. When would he ever get a clue?

Therese was relieved Jen hadn't asked again about Than. For months, she'd say, "Any word from Than?" and Therese's face would turn the color of tomato soup, she'd stop breathing, and she'd nearly faint. She was glad not to have to admit she still hadn't heard anything from the supposed love of her life. She had wanted to lie to her best friend and say, yes, we email all the time, or, I got a letter this afternoon, or, he texted me from Texas yesterday. But she knew her friend would see right through her and know the truth.

The water actually felt good as she warmed up with freestyle. She hadn't come all week—it was Thursday—and she had forgotten how therapeutic it could be. After two laps of freestyle, she switched to back, and then fly, saving her favorite stroke for last. As she swam, she thought of Poseidon's appearance in her dream. It hadn't really been Poseidon, but still, she thought of him. She recalled the ride he had given her on his dolphin, Arion, last summer when he had reluctantly taken her as his prisoner, and then after, on his really cool chariot. "Oh, Poseidon," she prayed silently. "Why won't Thanatos come for me? Should I just go on with my life?"

As if in answer, when she reached the edge of the pool at the end of her twenty-minute warm up and looked up, she saw Pete gazing down at her. "I finished early and thought I'd hang out." He left the poolside and walked over to the stands a few yards away. He looked good in his jeans. He glanced back and caught her watching. She blushed and turned away, but not before catching his wink.

Luckily, the coach called everyone over and lined them up for drills, and she no longer had the luxury—or curse—of thinking.

Chapter Four: Aphrodite's Message

Y ou can't go like that," Hermes stopped Than before he could god travel to Mount Olympus to answer Aphrodite's summons. "I'm to take your place so you can go in mortal form. She'll meet you at the Café Moulan in Paris near the Louvre. No one's to know of this, not even your father."

Than gave him a grave nod, shook Hermes's hand, and left his position as god of the dead for his rendezvous in Paris, hoping he wouldn't be caught by Hades. His relationship with his father was already strained by the events that took place on Mount Olympus last summer when Therese failed to follow through on her end of the deal she and Hades made with the other gods. Not that Than blamed her. Her compassion for others made her more, not less, desirable to him.

He had forgotten, as he walked the street in Paris, how exhilarating it felt being in mortal form. He could smell the bakery on the corner, feel the sun on his back, and hear the cars passing by and the voices and music carrying out from the shops and cafes with much more intensity than he did as a god, and again he wondered if the lower one went down the animal kingdom, the more intense sensory perceptions became. He wished he could leave his office and join Therese as a man. Life could be so good here on earth with her. But it wasn't to be.

Even in mortal form, Aphrodite was beautiful, though he disagreed that beauty trumped all. As beautiful as Therese was, she couldn't rival a goddess; but it was the whole package that made him love her.

"Please sit," Aphrodite motioned to the chair across from her on the outdoor patio of Café Moulan. She wore a scarf around her head like a hood, whether to protect her face from the afternoon sun or to conceal her identity from others, Than wasn't sure.

"It's good to see you," Than said. "You have some news, I hope?"

"Wine?" She pointed to a glass she had already ordered for him.

Although he had some wine in his rooms, sent to him from Dionysus, he rarely drank. His job required him to have full control of his faculties at all times. He took a sip and closed his eyes.

Aphrodite smiled. "You like?"

"Mmmm." He sipped again. "Yes."

Aphrodite surreptitiously glanced around the patio and then leaned across the table. "Swear on the River Styx you won't tell a soul what I'm about to tell you."

Than returned the glass to the table and lifted his head with surprise. All humor left him as he looked at Aphrodite with wide eyes. "I swear." He felt a mixture of dread and hope as he leaned closer to the goddess to hear what she had to say. Rarely was he asked to take an oath, so he knew this must be important. He hoped it had something to do with a way of making Therese his bride.

"Do you know who's responsible for making wine?"

This question confused Than, not because he didn't know the answer, but because he couldn't fathom how it required such a serious oath. "Dionysus."

"And what do you know of him?"

"He enjoys life. His philosophy is to seize the day and live to the fullest. Wine, good food, dancing, and such are his favorite pastimes, right?"

Aphrodite nodded. "Anything else?"

"He controls the maenads—the wild, frenzied women who tear people's bodies apart. They ripped poor Orpheus to pieces before my eyes. They did leave me a parting gift, though. I have a beautiful sea shell like no other in my room. I also have bottles of his wine, sent to me through Hermes. I've never met him in person, though."

"Do you know nothing more?"

Than shook his head.

"His father?"

"Zeus, I think. Or Hermes? I don't recall."

She took a sip of her wine and then said, "There's a reason you don't."

He leaned closer. "What do you mean?" Had someone put a spell on him?

"The genealogy of Dionysus has been confused for centuries. He is indeed Zeus's son, born of a mortal woman named Semele."

"But how…"

"Not a demigod, I know. Because he was born again of Zeus alone."

"I don't understand."

"Hera got wind of the affair and tricked Semele into asking Zeus to swear to grant her a wish. He swore on the River Styx. But her request was to see him in his full godly form, which as you know, is too bright for human eyes. But he had sworn, so even though he knew it would kill her, he showed himself to her."

"How awful."

"Indeed." She took another sip of her wine. "As Semele died, she gave birth prematurely to Dionysus. Zeus cut a hole in his thigh and placed the unformed infant there, stitching him in until he was ready to be born. Because Dionysus was later born solely to Zeus, immortality was conferred onto him."

"But I thought Dionysus's mother was also immortal. Is that a lie?"

Aphrodite shook her head. "He went back to the Underworld, this was back in Hermes's day, when he used to ferry the dead, when you and Hip were still too young."

"What does all of this have to do with me?"

"Because Dionysus spends his time partying in the mountains with the maenads and the nymphs and the satyrs, many people, and even some gods, think he's this lesser goat-like god who has very little power and authority on Mount Olympus."

"But that's not true?"

"No." Aphrodite glanced around the café. Then her eyes fell on something across the patio. "Oh no."

"What's wrong?"

"It's Ares. He's looking for me. We have an apartment here in Paris. I didn't know where else to meet you. Let's leave before he discovers us talking. There's too many around for god travel. Follow me."

Than followed her from the patio to a lime green Lamborghini parked a block away—not exactly inconspicuous.

"Get in."

He climbed inside behind the wheel.

"Drive!" Aphrodite commanded.

Than gaped. He had no idea how. "I've never driven a car before."

"You're kidding me."

"Tell me when I would have the time. You others have no idea what kind of life I lead."

"Switch places with me." They vanished and reappeared in the opposite seats. Aphrodite turned the key in the ignition and pulled the car away from the curb, causing him to fall back and shriek. "Strap yourself in!"

Than looked around and fumbled with the harness as Aphrodite darted past cars, coming close to crashing several times. He wasn't afraid of death—he was death, after all—but he was afraid of extreme pain, something he'd only experienced a few times in his long life.

"Pull over!" he shouted.

"Hold on!" She made a sharp turn and led him down an alley, where she slowed down the car and came to a stop. "I think I lost him, but we have to make this quick. He'll soon trace my scent."

"You were saying Dionysus is a more formidable god than most realize."

"Exactly. People confuse him with Pan, and rightly so, because Pan doesn't exist."

"What?" Than searched Aphrodite's profile for signs of mockery. "Are you kidding? How can that be?"

"You've heard the rumors he's dead?" She made another sharp turn.

"He's not in the Underworld."

"After Dionysus was born, Zeus put him in Hermes's care to protect him from Hera. When dressing him as a girl didn't keep him from Hera's suspicion, Hermes turned him into a goat and named him Pan and raised him as his own son. The stories of the two became convoluted over time, and intentionally so, to protect Dionysus."

"And this concerns me because…"

"Because unlike all of the other powerful gods of Mount Olympus, he did not swear an oath on the River Styx never to make Therese immortal."

Tears fled to Than's mortal eyes and startled him. As a god, he could shed tears, but as a man, they felt different. He looked into Aphrodite's beautiful face, wanting to kiss her with joy. "Thank you. I can't thank you enough."

"Not so fast," Aphrodite frowned.

"What?"

"In order to ask Dionysus to help you, you will need to win his favor. But first, you will need to make it past the maenads. They'll want to rip you apart."

Chapter Five: Surprise

Friday morning, Jen picked up Therese in her own truck—Pete stayed behind—and before Therese had climbed into the vehicle, Jen said, "My family has a surprise for you. You have to come over today right after practice."

"What is it?" Therese asked.

"It's a surprise. I can't tell you."

All through practice, Therese wondered what the surprise could be. Were they going to offer her a summer job? Had Mrs. Holt made her another jar of tomato jelly (which she loved)? Was Pete going to ask her to prom? Her stomach churned with anticipation.

During the ride back, Therese asked for a hint. "Come on," she begged. "Just a little one?"

"It's bigger than a bread box."

Okay, at least that ruled out a jar of tomato jelly.

When they arrived at the Holts, the first trail rides of the day had already begun, but Mrs. Holt had stayed behind and was waiting near the pen.

It must be a summer job, Therese thought with dread as she walked toward Mrs. Holt. Therese hadn't been on a horse since Dumbo's accident, and she hadn't groomed the horses much since, either.

"Mornin' Therese," Mrs. Holt said. "Well, I guess it's almost noon. You want some lunch?" Her blonde hair was mostly gray and cut like a bowl around her thin, leathery, freckled face.

"No thank you," Therese replied.

"Let's show her the surprise!" Jen said.

"Well Pete and Bobby wanted to be here, too, but I guess Jen can't wait to show you. Let's go inside the barn."

Therese followed Mrs. Holt into the barn, fresh and clean from this morning's chores, to a back stable and pointed to a newborn gray foal in a stall with Sassy.

"That's Sassy's colt," Mrs. Holt explained. "Dumbo was his father."

The foal lay close to his mother, eyeing Therese suspiciously.

"But how? That was over ten months ago." Dumbo was spooked by a snake last summer and broke two legs and had to be put down.

"Horses gestate for eleven months," Mrs. Holt said softly. "Sassy was pregnant before the accident."

Therese looked again at the little gray foal. "What's his name?"

"We're waiting for you to name him," Mrs. Holt said. "This here colt belongs to you, young lady. He's a gift from the family, if you want him, that is."

Therese's mouth dropped open. Just then, Bobby and Pete scrambled in from the pen.

"You've already told her?" Bobby complained. "We wanted to be here, Mama."

Therese couldn't believe how tall Bobby had gotten since school let out three weeks ago. He was almost as tall as Pete now, but, unlike his brother, had kept the boyish bowl haircut, though now it was covered with a white cowboy hat.

"I just told her, Bobby. She hasn't even answered yet. What do you say Therese?"

Jen nudged her friend. "Speechless?"

Therese nodded as the tears rolled down her cheeks. First she hugged Jen, then Mrs. Holt, then Bobby, and finally, Pete, who held onto her longer than the others.

Pete chuckled when he released her. "I think that's a yes," he said.

Therese went over to the newborn colt, which lay in the hay. Sassy stood behind him, her teats full of milk.

"How old is he?" Therese asked.

"Two days," Pete and Jen said together.

"May I pet him?"

Mrs. Holt came up beside her. "He's still getting used to being handled, so for now, use a flat hand at his tail head, just here." Mrs. Holt took Therese's hand and guided it to the top of the colt's tail.

The colt moved his tail closer to Therese.

"I think he likes it," Therese said, smiling. She reached out and stroked the tail head again.

"Now try gently scratching," Mrs. Holt encouraged.

The colt moved closer to Therese, and Sassy put her head nearby to get a better view of what was going on.

"It's okay, Sassy," Pete said, stroking the mare. "It's okay, girl."

"So what are you going to name him?" Bobby asked.

"I'm not sure. He looks like a little gray cloud." Cloudy? Foggy? Tornado? Thundercloud? Thunderhead? Cumulus—is that the scientific name for thunderhead? Hmm, Thunderbolt? Then it came to her. "Stormy. I'll call him Stormy."

"Perfect!" Jen said.

"But is he really mine?"

"Well, Hon', obviously you can't take him home," Mrs. Holt replied. "You'll have to keep him here. But he's yours to take care of, if you want him, and when he's older, you can pay me back for his keep by letting me trail ride him in the summers. I'll cover all his expenses. You just take care of him. You'll have to ride him when he's old enough. It's up to you. It's a big responsibility, so you might want to think about it. You have to come at least twice a week to get him used to you and used to grooming."

Jen put her hand on Therese's shoulder. "Mom thought it might help you want to be with the horses again. You haven't been around them much. They miss you."

The colt nuzzled Therese's hand, and that sealed the deal. "You're so cute, Stormy. Such a cute little fella. I love you so much."

Pete laughed. "I think he loves you, too."

Therese felt the blood rush to her cheeks. Pete might have said, "I think I love you, too," the way her body had responded. But he hadn't. Of course he hadn't. He was talking about Stormy.

"This is such a wonderful gift," Therese said. "I'll have to talk with my aunt and uncle, I suppose."

"I already done cleared it with them, Hon'," Mrs. Holt said. "But you take some time to think on it."

Mr. Holt walked into the barn. "The next group has arrived," he said. Then he noticed Therese with the colt. "So what do you think, Therese? He's perty, ain't he?"

"Very perty," she agreed.

"Named him yet?"

"Stormy," Bobby said. "She's decided to name him Stormy."

"Well that sounds about right," Mr. Holt laughed, "considering the way he came into this world kickin' and a fussin'."

"I wish I could have been there," Therese said.

"None of us were," Pete said. "Dad's just makin' that up."

"No, son, I was here. That was the night I heard the news about Jim. Jim was my brother, Therese. I passed—I mean fell asleep out here in the barn drownin' my sorrows. I locked myself in here so I wouldn't…wake any of you. Stormy here woke me up about four a.m. as he came into the world."

The group fell silent, and Therese continued to scratch Stormy all around his rump. Sassy's snort broke the silence.

"I expect she wants to nurse," Mrs. Holt said. "And the second group is waiting. Better get on it, boys."

As Pete headed toward the barn door, he turned and asked Therese, "You comin' tomorrow night to the festival?"

"Oh, you gotta come!" Bobby said, ahead of his brother.

"I'm planning on it," Therese said.

Pete gave her a smile and then disappeared from the barn.

Saturday morning, during warm up, something strange flickered just below the surface of the water where Therese swam freestyle. Rather than turning at the wall, she stopped, grabbed another breath, and pressed her face down to take a look. Before the image came into view, she thought it was someone's towel that had fallen in by accident, but as the image floated toward her from the depths, she nearly sucked in water because of the shock. It was Poseidon's face—not his whole body— looking up at her. She brought her head up and looked around at the other swimmers. Jen was swimming backstroke in the lane beside her. Carol, Richard, Vicki, and the Holts were up in the stands. Therese dug her finger beneath the swim cap to unclog an ear, grabbed another gulp of air, and thrust her face back down into the water. Poseidon spoke, and, oddly, she could hear him perfectly.

"I have heard your prayers, and although I cannot offer you Thanatos or save your pet, I can help you beat your opponent. As I control all the waters of the Earth, I can command this small pool to make you the winner of your entire swim meet. Do you desire this of me?"

Therese lifted her head from the water, shook it several times to clear the water from her ears. She saw Gina Rizzo swimming butterfly two lanes down. Jen called over from the lane next to her.

"Everything alright?"

Therese nodded. Then she thrust her head back into the water. Poseidon had disappeared.

"No, Poseidon," Therese blubbered into the water, in case she hadn't imagined him. "I want to win this on my own. But thanks, anyway."

His face reappeared. "As you wish." Then he vanished again.

Therese pulled her head up. Gina smirked at her through the water as she came up to breathe during the fly, causing Therese to have second thoughts about her answer to Poseidon.

"What are you doing?" her coach called from above. "Lose something down there?"

Therese blushed as she looked up at her balding coach and his puzzled face.

"I thought I saw a pair of goggles down there, but it's nothing."

"Finish this lap and climb on out," the coach said. "We're about to start."

Despite the humidity and the heat in the high school natatorium, Therese shivered on the bench beneath her towel as she waited with her teammates to swim in her events. Her goggles were perched on her head over her swim cap, and she bounced her knees alternately, full of nerves. She looked around at the banners and decorations that were only up for meets. The natatorium had transformed.

This would be her first meet since her parents' death—the first meet of her life they wouldn't be in attendance, because the swim team at Durango High was part of a summer-only league. Across the pool, she could see her aunt and uncle sitting beside Vicki and the entire Holt clan—including Mr. Holt—in the stands behind them. She could tell from the way they had all been treating her that they knew what she was thinking: My parents aren't here. For the first time in my life, they won't see me race. Pete noticed she was looking his way and gave her a thumbs up. She returned the gesture with a meek, nervous smile.

Why hadn't she accepted Poseidon's help?

Jen, who sat beside Therese, handed over a green sharpie so Therese could record her event, heat, and lane numbers on the top of her thigh rather than trying to memorize them. When she finished copying from the heat sheet, which Jen had held out for her, she handed the sharpie over, and her knees resumed their nervous bouncing.

"Thanks," Therese said.

"You want me to write 'Eat my bubbles' on your back?" Jen asked.

"Sure."

"Do me first."

The night before, Therese had prayed to all the gods except Ares to save Puffy, bring back Thanatos, and help her team win the meet. She hadn't expected anyone to actually materialize and answer her. The appearance of Poseidon had her so distracted that she messed up the words on Jen's back. She had written "Eat my" so big, that there wasn't much room left for "bubbles." Knowing Jen, she'd check herself out in the locker room mirror. Therese decided to draw the bubbles. The finished product actually looked pretty cool.

During the relay, she could hear her family and friends cheering her on as she pulled and kicked, pulled and kicked the breaststroke. When she neared challenge of hades of the lane, she reached out to touch the wall with both hands so Jen could finish with fly. There was something wrong with the wall, though. It had become a spongy mucky mess. Before she had time to think, her hands slipped through the wall of the pool, and her whole body followed.

She found herself in a puddle of mud.

"Climb out and wash off. You're a mess," a voice called.

Therese wiped the mud from her goggles with her fingers and looked up. Above her stood a beautiful young woman with flowing brown hair and high brown suede boots. Therese removed her goggles to get a better look.

"Come on!" the woman urged her. "You're a filthy mess. Take this towel."

"Artemis?" she asked, scrambling to her feet. She took the towel and wiped her face. Immediately the mud left her body and one-piece swimsuit, and she was clean all over. The white towel showed no trace of dirt.

"Of course."

"I'm, I'm supposed to be racing right now."

"It'll wait. No worries. I have something important to tell you." She didn't look back at Therese as she made her way through the woods.

"Where are we going?" Therese followed, slowly because of her bare feet. The dead leaves and twigs scratched at her sensitive skin.

"Just through here."

After another ten feet or so, they came to a small clearing where there were two tree stumps, side by side.

"Sit down," Artemis said as she sat on one of the two stumps.

Therese sat on the other and looked up at Artemis expectantly.

"I've heard your prayers and have decided you need a personal response. First, as to your pet hamster, there's something you need to understand about immortality." The wind gently blew Artemis's brown hair across her green eyes, and she swiped it from her face with a strong hand. "Not all creatures would benefit from it, especially rodents. Your hamster's life consists of feeding, sleeping, and toiling, and that's it. To extend such a life infinitely would be a cruel punishment, not unlike that of Sisyphus, who, at the break of each dawn, rolls the same large rock up the same steep hill. Do you understand?"

Therese thought on it for a moment. Were some lives more valuable than others, or more worthy of living? She wasn't sure of the answer, but she gave Artemis a nod. Maybe Puffy had had enough. "I suppose it would be selfish of me."

Artemis smiled. "Yes. Quite."

Therese shivered. She thought she could see a line of ants marching their way up the stump upon which she sat, and she was cold and worried about the swim meet.

"Immortality would be cruel for most creatures, including most humans. Death in the Elysian Fields is a gift, not a curse, from the gods. Which leads me to another of your prayers—your request for Thanatos."

Therese gave Artemis her full attention, even as another shiver made its way down her back. "Yes. I love him," she said, just above a whisper.

Artemis rolled her eyes and shook her head. "I beseech you to let that go, child. Love is fleeting. And life in the Underworld would be, well, gruesome. It's a place avoided by all gods who can avoid it. Even Persephone…"

"Forgive me, Artemis, but I don't care. I love Thanatos, and I want to be with him forever." A flurry of fear moved through Therese as she watched Artemis's green eyes glare back.

"Then you're doomed to heartbreak until the love wears off, which will happen, I assure you, since Cupid never speared your heart. Why any woman would give her heart away, I know not!"

Therese gave into the shivers overtaking her body. She hugged the towel around her and tucked her chin down to her chest.

"If it weren't for your valiant fighting on Mount Olympus last summer, not to mention your selfless decision to give your friend the invisibility crown, I would call you a stupid, stupid girl. Your decision to let McAdams live was noble in the eyes of some, but your foolish, unrelenting desire to be with the god of death is despicable. Yet you remain a good steward of the earth and its inhabitants, and your good-natured, competitive spirit in the water is admirable. Leave me now with the wisdom I've imparted to you, and know I can answer the last of your three requests: you will win your races today."

Therese resisted the urge to object. She had already angered Artemis enough. Her refusal to accept her help in the swim meet would likely sever their ties completely.

"Thank you," Therese said.

"Go! Go!" Artemis shouted angrily.

Therese was bewildered. She didn't know the way back.

"Go!" Artemis shouted again.

Therese scrambled from the tree stump and stumbled on the dead leaves and twigs back toward the mud puddle. It had been somewhere here, just past this clearing, somewhere here in the thick of the woods. She tripped on a heavy branch and fell.

"Go!" she heard the crowd shouting above her.

She found herself back in the pool, reaching for the wall beneath Jen's feet with both hands. She touched the wall, and Jen dove over her head and swam the butterfly to finish the race.

Her relay team came in first.

Therese won every one of her events.

The Durango Demons were declared the winners of the meet.

After the initial excitement and flood of pride, Therese sat on the bench with her handful of ribbons feeling dissatisfied. Artemis's help had ruined her chances of knowing for certain whether or not she could have outswum Lacey Holzmann on her own. As she watched her teammates congratulating one another with hugs and pats on the back, she fought the frustration clutching at her insides. Then suddenly, the ground below her shifted and she half-expected to come face-to-face with another god.

The building shook, and the crowd of people screamed and began to scatter. She sat there on the bench, stunned as she watched her teammates run for their loved ones. Coolers of water fell over, clip boards dropped from tables, chairs were toppled, and people slipped on the wet deck. A crack ran up the cement wall across from her.

Suddenly someone grabbed her arm and pulled her up and away from the water.

"The locker rooms are safest," Richard said beside her.

"This way," Carol said.

And so Therese followed her aunt and uncle and the rest of the panicked crowd into the locker rooms until the earthquake ended and they were finally able to leave the building and go home.

Chapter Six: Hermes's Advice

Than returned to the Underworld to his private chambers to find Hermes lying on his bed.

"Thank god." Hermes sat up. "I'd forgotten what monotonous work this is. I'm in four thousand different places at once and still bored. Take my hand before I'm forced to disintegrate again."

Than touched his cousin's hand and restored himself as god of death, the transition momentarily jostling the lifeless souls he now stood beside, leading them, his hand paternally on their shoulders, to Charon. He sighed. Hermes was right, but someone had to do it. He turned to his cousin. "Thank you."

"Good news from Aphrodite, I hope?"

"An idea. How well do you know Dionysus?"

"He's like a son to me. Why?"

"What can I do to get on his good side?"

"You can't."

Than took a chair across from Hermes, who remained sitting on the bed and now tucked a pillow under his arm to make himself more comfortable. "Why not?"

"He hates the gods. All of us. He feels cheated. And rightly so. He was hidden away most of his life from Hera. You know the story?"

Than nodded. "But I had nothing to do with it."

"He's got a chip on his shoulder. Don't take it personally."

"There's got to be a way. He's my only hope."

"If he's your only hope, then you have none."

"Is it true he lives on Mount Kithairon?"

"Don't seek him out. The maenads will tear you to pieces."

Than bit his lip, thinking. There had to be a way into Dionysus's heart. Every person was capable of tenderness. As god of the dead, he'd seen even the most powerful weep. "How long does it take to recover from that—being torn to pieces?"

"Trust me when I say nothing is worth that pain. Don't even think of it."

"Too late, Hermes." The pain in his heart was greater; he was sure of it.

"First love. Young love. Believe me, it'll pass."

"Impossible. And I don't want it to pass. You know how monotonous my existence is. Why shouldn't I find happiness? Why should I alone be exempt from it?" He thought of Charon and clenched his jaw. Charon, too, was exempt.

"You have nothing he desires. No leverage. He celebrates life. You are Death. I can think of nothing to help you. And as far as how long it takes to put your pieces back together again? Depends on how badly you're ripped apart. Could take weeks. And you'll need help if you don't want to look like a monster for several years while you heal. Plus, someone else would need to take your job while you're put back together, and it won't be me, cousin." Hermes stood up, as if to leave, but then added. "But there is one among us he respects."

"Who?"

"Your grandmother, Demeter. Maybe she can help." With that, Hermes vanished.

Chapter Seven: Vicki's Idea

But what magnitude are they saying it was?" Richard asked Carol from behind the wheel of his black Maxima. "I don't see any damage anywhere else. It's like it just hit the one building."

"Maybe they don't know yet," Therese said in the backseat with Vicki on their way to Vicki's apartment. Therese had changed from her swimsuit, and, though her hair was still damp, it had been freed from the swim cap and brushed out in the locker room before they left the meet.

"I'm searching," Carol said, bent over her iPhone. "The reception slows down when we get into the pines. Hang on. Okay. Here it is. Five point zero. Wow. Pretty decent."

"Coach said we'll have to use another pool for the rest of the season," Therese said. "I wonder where that'll be."

Richard shook his head. "Five point zero. That is something. Most of the earthquakes in this area hover below three and are rarely felt. I wonder if more will follow. They usually do when they're that big. I wrote an article on earthquakes once."

Therese wondered if Poseidon had been involved. Maybe he was peeved Artemis had helped Therese after Therese had turned down his offer. Surely he knew it hadn't been Therese's fault. Before she had time to think more on it, though, Vicki whispered something cryptic in her ear.

"What?" Therese whispered back.

"I saw my mom last night."

Therese looked at her friend for a moment, wondering what she could mean. Then she asked, "In a dream?"

Vicki gave an even wider smile at Therese's confusion. "Not a dream. Come over for lunch and I'll tell you all about it."

Therese felt wiped out after the meet and the bizarre earthquake, not to mention her unexpected encounters with two gods. She really wanted to go home and take a nap before the festival tonight. But there was something bewildering about Vicki's smile and her apparent certainty that she had seen her mother, who committed suicide a year ago. Therese couldn't resist.

"Hey," she said to her aunt and uncle when there seemed a pause in their conversation about all the seismic occurrences in the history of the planet Earth. "Can I stay at Vicki's for a while?"

Carol turned and looked at Therese. "You don't want to get some rest before tonight?"

"Just a couple of hours," Therese said. "Maybe you could come back for me around three?"

Vicki said, "My dad can bring you home. He won't mind."

"Are you sure?" Carol gave Therese a scrutinizing look. She was aware of the inequity in the relationship between the two girls.

Therese nodded. "Absolutely. Jen's not picking me up until six. I'll have plenty of time to rest."

"What do you think?" Carol asked Richard.

"Fine with me. If Vicki's dad can't bring you home, just give us a call. I've got some errands to run, so I don't mind coming back to town."

Therese hoped Carol wouldn't bring up the fact that Therese was old enough to take driver's education and drive herself, and that her brand new shiny red Honda Civic was waiting in the driveway for her use. Carol had brought it up many times, but Therese hoped she wouldn't in front of Vicki.

The car had been a gift from Carol and Richard last April on her eighteenth birthday, but ever since what happened in her mother's car last summer, Therese could not bring herself to get behind a wheel. At first, Carol and Richard assumed Therese's hesitance had to do with the fact that she didn't want to drive her father's truck. They originally planned for Therese to use it. But when they traded in the truck and bought her a brand-new car, Therese still felt like she wasn't ready to drive.

"Some people take longer than others to feel ready," Therese had said.

That had been three months ago, and today Therese didn't feel any more ready to learn to drive.

Vicki lived on the northern outskirts of Durango in a second story apartment with scenic mountain views. Therese had only visited two other times, both since Mrs. Stern's death, and both times the place had been in disarray. Today was no different. As soon as they entered the apartment and stepped into the living room, Therese recognized the pile of clean laundry that seemed always to occupy the dining room table, and closet doors to the washer and dryer stood open with more laundry, presumably dirty, spilling out from on top of the machines and onto the floor. Therese thought the location of the laundry closet was a major flaw in the design of the apartment, because the position from the dining room table was the only one, except for the balcony, offering the spectacular views that made these apartments worth living in. Their exterior was not quite shabby, but certainly left something to be desired with its dull dirty white siding and lack of nearby garden. The views of the mountains made the apartments, but unfortunately, the views in the Stern apartment were thwarted by the inefficient laundry system overtaking the best square footage. Therese wondered if things had been different when Mrs. Stern was still living here.

On the other side of the laundry heap, Mr. Stern stood stirring something on the stove.

"Hey, Dad," Vicki called as they crossed into the small galley kitchen. "I hope it's okay if Therese stays for lunch. Whatcha cooking?"

"Oh, hi Therese." Mr. Stern was tall and thin, and the thin white muscle shirt showed just how gaunt with the ruffle of ribs pressing through the material. His plaid shorts hung loose and reached down to his knobby knees and bony legs, which seemed less hairy to Therese than her own had been before she had started shaving. Despite the lack of hair on his legs, the mousy brown hair on his head was long and stringy and looked in need of washing. "We're always glad for the company. I'm just making some chicken noodle soup. It's from a box. Hope that's okay with you girls."

"Smells good," Therese said.

Mr. Stern had retired from the Air Force the year the Sterns moved to Durango. He had taken a part-time job at Fort Lewis College teaching computer science and was off for the summer. Therese suspected money was tight in the Stern household. The worn-out furniture and near bare pantry were only a couple of things giving her that impression.

They took their bowls out to the balcony where there was no table, but where there were three Adirondack chairs. Therese wondered if she were sitting in Mrs. Stern's chair as she and Mr. Stern sat on either side of Vicki.

Vicki and Therese told Mr. Stern all about the meet and the earthquake. He said he hadn't felt anything, but he was always interested in earthquakes, so as soon as they finished their soup, he went to the living room and turned on the television to the local news hoping to hear more about the disturbance. He also went to the computer on the small desk near the television and searched the web for news. Therese thanked him for the soup and then followed Vicki to her room.

The girls sat on either side of Vicki's bed—there was no other seating in the room, and only one other piece of furniture: an old, dusty dresser with a mirror hanging over it. Vicki's clothes were scattered on the floor. Therese wondered how she could have enough clothes to overtake the dining room, laundry closet, and the floor of her bedroom. At least the bed was made, which Therese found rather strange. Why make the bed if the rest of the room was so messy?

Therese had just begun to suspect she had been tricked into coming for a visit when Vicki asked, "Have you ever heard of NDE drugs?"

Therese shook her head, disappointed that Vicki was going in a drug direction. Therese had warned Vicki to stay away from the "Demon Druggies" at school, but she had noticed Vicki sometimes talked to them in a friendly way. She dreaded what Vicki might say next.

"Near death experience. The scientific name is ketamine."

Therese's heart rate picked up. "What do you mean 'near death'?"

"Something happens when you take the drug that causes you to die for a few minutes. Then the drug wears off and you come back to life."

"You die for a few minutes? Isn't that risky?"

"Therese, I've been to the other side. I saw my mom."

"You're joking."

"I've never been more serious in my life. Do you want to hear about it or not?"

Therese shifted on the bed. "I'm listening."

"Okay, so last night after my dad went to bed, I injected myself with the ketamine, okay? About five or ten minutes later, I had this awesome feeling of peace. I haven't felt that way since before my mother died. It was so weird, actually, to feel that good, that content. That feeling alone makes me want to do it again."

Therese was growing impatient. "So what happened?"

"Okay, so I'm lying right here on my bed, just like this." Vicki moved over and lay on her pillow on her back. "Then I swear I had this feeling like I was leaving my body. I flew right up there," she pointed to the ceiling in the corner of the room, "and I hovered there for a while—I'm not sure how long. I could literally see myself down here lying on the bed."

"And?"

"Okay, so I'm floating outside of my body, and then it's like the lights go out. I'm somewhere dark, like in a tunnel, and I can see this light at the end. As I go through the tunnel, there's all this fog all around me, and when I get to the end, I see this enormous body of water, like a lake or a river or something."

Therese felt a shudder move down her back. "And then?"

Vicki sat back up. "So then I see this thing like a raft, and on board is this old man. He looks at me all surprised, like he's not expecting me. He doesn't say anything to me. He just stares at me, like he's checking me out. I'm afraid to speak, so I just stand there staring back at him. After a while, I look back behind me, and I can no longer see my room or my body lying on the bed. So I turn back to the old man and say, 'Can you take me across?'

"He doesn't answer, so I wait. Then I just decide to step aboard. The raft man starts pulling us across with this long pole, and I'm so happy and peaceful because I feel sure I'm going to see my mom. It's so strange how I wasn't frightened at all."

Therese's heart was racing. "Then what happened?"

"We floated past these three big black dogs—I think there were three, the fog was so thick I could barely see two feet in front of me. And then there was this huge black iron gate that creaked as it opened. On the other side there was this cavern and inside were three strange-looking people kind of floating just above the surface of the water. They wore long white robes, unlike the filthy red one of my raft man, and they looked clean, but kind of strange, and they pointed the raft man to take me down one of three paths. I could see the light getting brighter and brighter from a river of fire as we wound round the water in through the foggy cavern.

"The raft fell down some rapids, but I wasn't scared—it was fun, actually—and then we went deeper and deeper away from the bright light into darkness. Someone was holding a lantern at the bottom. There were people lying comfortably in a shallow pool of water, like they were sunbathing in the darkness. I saw my mom sprawled out with her eyes closed, and she was still wearing the dress we buried her in. She was beside this really enormously fat dude, but she didn't seem to notice or care about him. Before I could cry out her name, before she could open her eyes to see me, the raft started moving backward. The old raft man looked at me with a threatening glare, like he had known all along I wasn't supposed to be there and his suspicions were now somehow confirmed. There was yelling coming from above. I thought I heard someone yell, 'Grab her!' but then I had left the raft and was flying away from the river back through a dark tunnel. Then I was at my ceiling looking down at my body. All at once I opened my eyes and I was here, again, in my own body, right here on my bed."

Therese stared at her, speechless.

"So what do you think? You believe me, don't you?"

The details of Vicki's tour through the first part of the Underworld were too like what she herself had seen. Therese gave a nod. "I think so. That's so, so weird."

"Yes, it was. Next time I won't wait so long to get on the raft. I think that's why I ran out of time."

"Next time? You mean, you're going to do it again?"

"Of course. Why wouldn't I?"

"Where did you get the drug?"

Vicki's eyes beamed. "Okay, you have to promise not to tell a soul, do you hear me? Not a soul!"

"I promise."

"I swear, if you tell anyone, I'll be so hurt, Therese. It'll be like my mom dying all over again. I won't be able to take it."

"I get it. I promise not to tell."

"Okay, so you know Raleigh Jones?"

"The boy at our school?"

"Yeah. He waits tables at the Ranch House Restaurant down the road from here. My dad and I, we rarely go out to eat, but it would have been my mom's birthday, and we needed a pick-me-up, you know? So a week ago we went, and Raleigh was our waiter, and it turns out it was his birthday, too. Anyway, he was giving away gifts, mostly to the other waiters and waitresses and the bartenders, but he recognized me, and so he brought me one, too, this silly little frog." She held up a frog stuffed animal. "He said it was from the Dollar Store—that all his gifts were—but that's how he celebrated his birthday every year. He bought a bunch of funny stuff from the Dollar Store and handed it out to his friends."

"That's nice."

"That's what I said. I told him he was supposed to receive gifts, not give them away, on his birthday. My dad told him about it being my mom's birthday, and of course he knew what happened—everyone knows—and so that's when he invited me to come to his house later for a party.

"I guess my dad was just glad a boy was showing interest, so he didn't seem bothered by the fact that the party wouldn't start until almost midnight, because that's how long it would take Raleigh to close down his station at the restaurant. Raleigh asked if I wanted to wait at the bar till he got off. I could drink free sodas…"

"Sodas?"

"I mean pop. You all call them pop, I forgot. Anyway, and then he'd take me to the party. He said he'd have me home by two o'clock, if that was alright."

"My aunt says sodas, too. So, your dad let you stay out till two in the morning?"

"My dad was never a stickler with rules. I've never really had a curfew, though up till then, I'd never gone out late. Besides you, well, I haven't made many friends here yet, and after what Mom did, well, I think people are afraid of me or something."

"It just takes time."

"I know. Anyway, so I had a blast at his party. People were smoking pot and taking other stuff, too, but I just drank soda, I mean pop. Then a couple of people came running in from his bedroom—it's just his granny living with him and she's practically deaf. His mom died three years ago and his dad split when he was born. Anyway, this couple runs in, they're seniors, too, one's a football player, I think, and they say they've just come back from the dead. So they tell their story. They've seen their loved ones and stuff. A few days later, I call Raleigh and ask how I can have a near death experience, too. So he gets me the ketamine. And now you know the whole story."

Therese filled with inexplicable excitement. "Do you think he could get me some, too?"

Vicki smiled. "I thought you might be interested. I thought maybe next time I try it, we could do it together, you know?"

Therese nodded. "Yes. Let's do. But isn't it risky? I mean, has anyone actually stayed dead?"

"I did a whole bunch of research before I did it, Therese. Out of the thousands of cases, a few have gone wrong, but the researchers attribute it to something avoidable—like the subject took too much of the drug, or inhaled a powder form rather than injected a liquid, or did consecutive doses, and stuff like that. I think as long as you do the right dose, inject it in liquid form, and wait at least a week in between episodes, it's really safe."

Therese would do her own research, but in the meantime, she'd go ahead and plan this thing with Vicki. Maybe there was a way she could actually see her parents. Certainly she would see Than, wouldn't she? She could plead with him to come back for her, or to at least let her know how much longer he thought it would be before they could be together again. "So next weekend, will you be ready?"

"I'll have to get more from Raleigh. It costs money, though."

"How much?"

"Fifty bucks a pop. Raleigh gave me the first dose for free, but he says he'll have to charge me next time. It's expensive stuff and hard to get. And right now lots of people are into it."

"I can pay for both of ours. I have a lot of money saved up. I'll give you the money tonight at the festival."

"Oh, the festival! That's right! We need to get you home so you can rest. It's almost three." Vicki jumped up and Therese followed her out of the room.

During the car ride home, the two girls talked some about what they were going to wear that night and when Matthew was supposed to be by to pick up Vicki. Matthew was going to drive Vicki, Therese, and Jen. Pete would have to go early in his own truck to set up his equipment with the rest of his band. Mr. and Mrs. Holt would drive Bobby out there in their truck. Todd and Ray would meet them all there, too.

Once the details were worked out and the girls grew quiet, Therese thought about the NDE drug and the possibility of seeing her parents and Than. She was excited, though a little frightened. She would definitely have to do some research first. But so what if she did die? She'd be with him and her parents and untie the lonely knot in her gut. She'd rather go as a god, of course, but the risk seemed worth taking. Besides, Vicki had said only a few had died and the researchers believed the deaths had been avoidable.

Therese went straight to her room after saying hi to Carol and Richard. She checked on her pets. She turned off Jewel's lamp and wished the tortoise a good night. Puffy still didn't look so good. She gingerly took him from his tower—she knew it was selfish of her, for the vet had said to leave him alone and just keep him comfortable, but Therese felt the need to kiss him and tell him she loved him. She wanted to hold him in her hands and feel his soft, furry body. He was breathing so fast now, it wouldn't be long. She returned him to his plastic tower, washed her hands, and crawled under her covers. Clifford curled up beside her.

"I'm so tired, boy," she said. "But I'm not sure I can fall asleep."

She stroked his fur for a while, and he licked her hand, and eventually, she must have drifted off. Not long after, she heard a noise, opened her eyes, and saw Than standing over her bed.

Chapter Eight: Death Comes

Therese stared at him, astonished. She barely noticed the rain falling outside her window. Thump, thump, thump. Was it rain? Or was it the pounding of her heart?

Than looked down at her and smiled. It was a sober smile. It wasn't unfriendly, but it lacked enthusiasm and was sad. He was wearing his loose-fitting trousers and open white shirt and brown leather sandals. His dark hair hadn't grown an inch since she had last seen him and just reached his bright blue eyes.

"Am I dreaming?" She tried to push off into the air but remained solidly on the bed.

"No," he replied.

"Figment!" she nearly shouted. "I command you to show yourself!"

Than stood over her. He hadn't disappeared. "It's me, Therese."

Her mouth dropped open and she jumped to her knees. She twisted the front of her t-shirt in both hands, like she was wringing out a wet rag. She hardly realized what she was doing. In her dreams, she always knew what to do; but now that she was actually looking upon the real Than, she felt speechless and paralyzed.

Clifford stood from where he had been lying beside her and wagged his tail. He gave a playful bark, which brought Therese back to her senses.

"Hi, Clifford," Than said.

"You've come for me, then? Finally? After all these months?" The initial shock wore off. She threw her arms around his neck and immediately felt the cold creeping through her body, the air harder to breathe. But she held him and felt a sense of relief. She wouldn't have to risk her life with Vicki after all.

He gave her one quick kiss and then pushed her back down onto the bed. "I came for Puffy, not for you, Therese. Please stay back so I don't kill you."

As she fell back, she heard his words, took them in, felt their sting. Frustration and disappointment turned into anger. "You're never coming for me, are you? You won't come till I'm dead!"

He frowned. "I've been busy. It's dangerous for you to be close to me while I'm the guide for the dead. I thought you understood." He moved to Puffy's cage.

"If Puffy hadn't died…" she couldn't complete the thought out loud. She felt dizzy and breathless. He hadn't come for her. He was just doing his job. Did he care for her at all? Had he ever loved her? She studied him in profile as he dipped his hand through Puffy's plastic tower and pulled out an orb of light in Puffy's image. Puffy's body remained in the tower curled up in the bedding.

"It's okay, Puffy," he said to the hamster. "I'm here to guide you." Then to Therese, he said, "I didn't have to wake you up and show myself to you. I thought you'd be glad to see me. I guess it was a mistake."

"You're a god, for heaven's sake! If you really loved me, you'd find a way to be with me." She saw the pain in his face, and for a split moment regretted her words. Then he turned from her with Puffy in his hand, and the anger moved swiftly over her again. "Answer me, Than! How much longer?"

The rain fell more heavily and a crash of thunder roared in the distance. The late afternoon thunder showers had come.

"I don't know. Be patient. I need to go before you get too weak, before I kill you." He backed away.

She leapt from the bed and wrapped her arms around him again, desperate and trembling, and now, gasping for air. She held onto his neck and pressed her cheek against his warm, bare chest. Not with her gaping, blue lips, but in prayer, she said, "I'm sorry. I didn't mean to yell. I miss you so much." Her stomach felt like she was going to be sick.

The air felt thick, her efforts at breathing stifled, but she held on. It felt so good to be against him, to feel his body with her own. It felt so wonderful to see him, to squeeze his hand, run fingers through his hair, to know he was real. There were a thousand things she had wanted to ask, but her head was spinning. She couldn't think of what she had wanted to say, and she was frustrated, having longed for this moment for months. Not wanting the moment to end, she clung to him, tried to look into his eyes, and, as he forcefully pried her blue fingers from his neck, fell back into unconsciousness.

When she came to, Than was gone and Puffy had stopped breathing.

She replayed the few minutes Than had been in her room in slow motion. She at first felt the joy of seeing him and the pleasure of being in his presence. Her body felt aroused as she recalled the feel of him against her, her fingers in his hair. But the pleasure turned to pain, and the pain to anger.

She touched Puffy's stiff body without moving him from his plastic tower. Tears rushed from her eyes. "Say hi to Mom and Dad for me." She decided at that moment she hated Than, the god of the dead, and she wished she had never met him. But she would tell him to his face. She would take the NDE drug with Vicki next weekend, she would march to the gates of hell, and she would tell the son of a you-know-what to his face that she never wanted to see him again. Even when she died, she wanted someone else to come for her!

How hard could it be for a god to give her a better indication of what he was doing to try and get her back? Had he worked out a new agreement with his father? Or had he been doing his job with no time for anything but the dead?

Than had said Therese would be unhappy spending eternity in the Underworld. Maybe he hoped she would gradually forget about him. Maybe he was staying away from her because he thought it was best for her.

Then why had he showed himself to her today? Had it been a moment of weakness?

The concept of time was different to the gods, so maybe to Than, ten months was like a snap of the fingers. But hadn't he heard all her desperate prayers? If he had a heart, he'd tell her something more than "I've been busy. Be patient."

She moved to her bed and wept, and after a few moments, Carol knocked at her door.

"Are you okay in there? Can I come in?" Carol opened the door.

"Puffy died," Therese said, sobbing.

"Oh, sweetheart, I'm so sorry." Carol leaned over and gave Therese a hug. The smell of Haiku perfume and Jergen's lotion washed over Therese. It was the same smell of her mother. Carol sat on the bed beside her, and for a moment, Therese thought it was her mother. She almost said, "Mom." Almost. She blinked.

"I know you were expecting this," Carol said, "but even then, it's never easy. Maybe you should stay home tonight."

Therese nodded, still sobbing, all the forces of grief sweeping over her. She felt she might drown even though the rain outside had finally stopped.

"You want me to call the Holts?"

Therese nodded again and then buried her face in her pillow.

Carol kissed the back of Therese's head and closed the door behind her as she left the room.

Therese lay there thinking how much she hated Than. She refused to pray her thoughts to him. She would keep them to herself until she could seek him out and tell him to his face what she thought of him. She knew she was the only one who ever prayed to him in a loving way. He had told her so himself. Except for the desperate pleas of those near death, or from the loved ones beside the deathbed, begging him to change a course he could not change, she was the only voice he heard. Hers was the cheer in his life, he had said. Well, forget that. If he couldn't give her a better explanation, he could feel the same silence she had been feeling on her end.

She finally understood the warning Artemis and Athena had given her about women who loved immortal men and understood why Daphne, a nymph, ran from Apollo and begged her river-father to turn her into a tree.

She tried to recall why she ever thought she loved him and remembered his face turned up to the rain with pleasure. Later he had put his arm around her and comforted her after Dumbo's fatal accident. His face lit up whenever he looked upon the sunset, and his eyes brightened when he moved through the cool water of the lake. A giggle escaped from her throat when she recalled teaching him to waltz, but she quickly sobered at the memory of how he had held her on the dance floor of the Wildhorse Saloon and had touched her like he had never touched a human being. He had relished her lips as much as she had relished his.

She thought of the three sunsets they had visited in one day. The way he had defended her on Mount Olympus. The care he took when he helped her sort through her parents' things.

And he had begged Aphrodite to save Clifford's life because he knew Therese couldn't take another death.

But he had said he would come back for her, and almost a year had passed since he made that promise. Tonight he said he'd been busy. He'd been too busy for her. He hadn't even come to see her. He was only doing his job. Maybe he'd changed his mind. He didn't love her after all.

She hated him. And she couldn't wait to tell him.

She hugged her pillow. If only she had killed McAdams. She'd be with Than now and forever. Why was she blaming him? She was the one who had failed.

But she was only a human. He was a god, for crying out loud. He said he'd come for her and he hadn't. Would she be an old maid before he finally found time in his busy schedule for her?

Therese wasn't sure how much time had passed when another knock came at her door.

"Therese, it's me, Jen. I'm coming in."

Therese didn't get up from the bed. Jen came over and hugged her just as Carol had done. Too much Oscar de la Renta made Therese cough. She noticed Vicki hovering in the doorway as though she was afraid to get too close. Maybe she thought she couldn't encroach on Jen's territory. Jen sat on the bed.

"I'm sorry about Puffy," Jen said.

"Me, too," Vicki said from the doorway.

"Thanks guys. I'm sorry I'm canceling out on you tonight. I hope you understand."

Jen put a hand on each of Therese's shoulders and squared herself to her friend, leaning over her. Therese noticed how pretty Jen looked in makeup, something Jen rarely wore and really didn't need. Her blonde hair fell forward around her face and smelled of hairspray, but the hair itself wasn't stiff. Her pale blue blouse, however, was stiff and wrinkle-free and had probably been starched and ironed. A rhinestone belt buckle showed off her thin waistline. "But lying in bed all evening is the last thing you should do. All this grief is going to build up and eat you alive. I know you, Therese Mills, and you're not just crying over Puffy. I mean, I know you're hurt. I know you loved him. But you're thinking of your parents, too, and probably Dumbo. Am I right?"

The tears gushed from Therese's eyes. Her friend knew her well. "Than…called." Therese hated the lie, but the truth was unbelievable.

Jen stood upright, nearly falling back. "Oh my God! What did he say?"

Therese fought the sobs. "He said he's been busy. He wants me to be patient."

"That jerk!" Jen shouted. Carol and Richard might have heard.

"I hate him, Jen. I hate him so bad. I feel sick!" Therese climbed from her bed and ran to her bathroom where she threw up in the commode.

Jen followed her in and patted Therese, bent over the bowl as she kneeled on the floor, coughing. Jen got her a clean towel from the cabinet. "I hate him, too," Jen said. "And I tell you what. The best thing you can do is go out tonight and dance your butt off with as many guys as you can. Help yourself forget about him. If he calls again, you can tell him you're busy, and you won't be lying!"

The idea didn't sound too bad. "I don't know."

"Matthew's out in the truck and Todd and Ray are in Todd's truck behind us. Todd wanted to follow Matthew. And Bobby will be there, too. You'll have plenty of dance partners to keep your mind off of you know who. And Pete's band won't be playing all night. They're one group of a handful. Pete'll want to dance with you, too. Come on, what do you say?"

Vicki now hovered in the doorway of the bathroom. For the first time, Therese noticed how pretty she looked with her hair pulled away from her face instead of scraggily falling into it. Her brown eyes had been outlined with make up, and her pale cheeks had spots of color. She wore a summer dress and sandals—which would be hard to dance in on the concrete floor at the Pagosa Springs Fairgrounds, but her slight figure and toothpick legs were softened by them. "I think you should go for it. I agree with Jen."

"But I haven't even showered."

Jen helped Therese to her feet. "That's alright. We'll wait for you downstairs. I'll tell the guys to come in. I'll go make some Crystal Light lemonade and some of that spray cheese on crackers. I saw it all out on the counter on the way up. We'll be fine."

Jen and Vicki left the room.

As Therese showered and the warm water fell over her, she caught herself starting to talk to Than. She had been praying to him for ten long months, and it had become a habit. She wasn't always aware she was doing it. He had become her invisible best friend, and cutting off communication with him would be harder than she had at first thought. So maybe she would channel her thoughts to another god. She decided Poseidon might not be the best pick, because she still suspected he might have had something to do with that morning's earthquake. And although she really liked Artemis, the goddess of wild things hadn't been too happy with her at their last encounter. Artemis thought Therese was stupid for loving Than. Athena had said the same last summer. Well, maybe both goddesses would be glad to hear Therese's plan of action. But what if Therese changed her mind? What if she eventually decided she didn't hate Than? Would Artemis and Athena be tolerant of her indecision? What if the goddesses turned on Than?

Now Aphrodite, the goddess of love, understood love's ups and downs, but Aphrodite might not like Therese's plan of going to the Underworld and telling Than off. Aphrodite might try to talk her out of it. Therese didn't want to risk that. She was dead bent on telling off Than to his face.

Persephone and Demeter wouldn't do, either. They were Than's mother and grandmother. Therese couldn't expect them to have an unbiased stance. They'd probably sympathize with Than and thwart Therese's efforts.

Of course Ares was out of the question. The god of war had been behind her parents' death. He wanted to prevent her mother from finding the cure to the mutated Anthrax C. He wanted foreign coups to have a useful store of the mutated Anthrax so a new balance of power could come into the world. Ares wanted to see America fall. Plus, he hated Therese and would take any opportunity to bring her down. He was against her becoming a god because he knew he could never count on her support.

Zeus was just out of her league. She was scared to death of him. Hades, too. Besides, Hades clearly showed his disdain for her when she refused to kill McAdams. And Than's sisters, the Furies, were intimidating to say the least. She couldn't shrug off their description of the way they beat information out of their suspects: blood dripped from their eyes, snakes crawled through their hair, and piercing screams came from their throats. No, Therese didn't think she'd pray to them.

She didn't really know Hestia, Hera, Apollo, or Hephaestus. But Hermes! The messenger of the gods had once been her friend.

Therese rinsed the shampoo from her hair and embraced this new idea of Hermes. He had liked Therese. They played their instruments together and shared laughs together and he had been supportive on Mount Olympus. He had had his share of love affairs and children and so could understand Therese's heartbreak. And yet, Therese had the sense he wouldn't let her hatred of Than ruin his own relationship with the god of the dead. Hermes it was.

She turned off the shower and dried off, and as she put on her blue jeans and green cotton blouse, she attempted her first prayer to him: "Hermes, do you remember me? It's Therese. I hope you don't mind if I talk to you. Thanatos has broken my heart."

She threw on a little makeup and blow-dried her hair. That was enough for now. She would wait and tell Hermes her plans later. Tonight, she was going to have fun and forget all about Than. Around her neck was Athena's locket reminding her that the most common way people give up their power is by believing they have none.

Chapter Nine: The Maenads

Go with food," Demeter had said, "and a belly full of wine." Than's grandmother had no other words of wisdom, tricks, or ideas to help him get on Dionysus's good side except to go into the forest of Mount Kithairon at night emboldened with alcohol and offering food. If he hesitated and showed the slightest insecurity, he would be ripped to pieces.

"They may rip you to pieces anyway," she had said.

So here he was, only yards away from where the god and his followers were said to be, and his confidence waned. He had a bag of food slung over his shoulder—fruits and bread Demeter had given him—but he hadn't taken his grandmother's advice concerning the wine. He wanted to be in control of his actions. He could be merry and bold without alcohol—at least, he hoped he could as he crept through the woods.

Much of the mountain was bare and rocky, but here, in a smattering of thick pines, he could see a campfire in the distance and a hazy line of smoke rising into the night sky. Laughter and singing made the group seem less daunting, but a sudden demonic shriek chilled him and made him hesitate again. Then an idea came to him, hard and fast like a thunderbolt: his sisters. The Furies. Their presence might help his cause. He hadn't asked for help because he didn't want his father to get wind of his plans and try to stop him, but now that he was irrevocably in the middle of them, he disintegrated and dispatched to seek his sisters out. Meanwhile, he slowly stole through the woods, hoping to catch a glimpse of the maenads before they noticed him.

Seeing Therese so angry and hurt this afternoon when he went for the hamster had added a greater sense of urgency to Than's already urgent mission. If his presence wasn't lethal to her, he would have stayed to give a report on his progress, but that was impossible. Hell, he would have swept her in his arms and caressed her face with his lips. He would have…oh, he moaned as he picked through the branches. If she really loved him and had faith in him, she'd wait. Her lot was to wait. His was far worse. His foot cracked a twig and caught the attention of a woman standing ten feet away, on the outskirts of the group.

She looked back at him suspiciously. Her curly brown hair was knotted on her head and ringed with ivy. She wore animal skins around her breasts and hips, but her shoulders and legs were bare, and she held a thyrsus—a staff tipped with a pinecone. "What's this?" She spoke softly to herself. No one else in the group seemed to notice.

"I bring gifts," he said, holding out an orange. "I've come to celebrate, if you'll have me."

His heart raced as he awaited her reply. She narrowed her eyes and took a step closer. "Is it a real orange? They're my favorite, you know."

He tossed it to her. "It's yours. From Demeter, my grandmother."

The woman caught the orange, tore off the peel in less than five seconds, and put the meat to her nose. She smiled and savagely devoured the fruit. She turned to Than with juice dripping down her chin. "Who are you?"

"Someone who has finally found true love." It sounded trite, but it was true, and he thought these women, who danced and loved and drank, would appreciate it. He knew if he revealed himself, he'd disgust her. No one wants Death. "May I join the party?"

At that moment, another woman turned and noticed him. Her curly black hair flowed around her face, which was stained red with blood or wine, Than didn't know which. She held a chalice in one hand and a thyrsus in the other. A panther skin hung over her shoulder, its head still intact at her breast. "Who's this?"

"He says he's found true love," the first maenad said to the other. "For a moment, I thought he meant me."

"We're about to dance," she said. "The flutes and lyres are warmed up. We can't wait for introductions." The woman turned her back to him and began to move her body in a jerky, frenzied movement, not too unlike what Than had seen with epileptics as they fell to their deaths.

The first maenad took his hand and tugged him along the perimeter of the other raving dancers. What began as a soft tap-tap of the drums exploded into a booming, pounding thrash. Than did his best to mimic the movements of the others, feeling foolish but desperate to win their approval. The maenad on the end of his arm shrieked with joy and jerked around like a raving lunatic. Soon he felt himself surrounded by the throng of moving bodies bumping against him. The ecstatic women in the crowd seemed oblivious to his presence and to each other, as though lost in a trance, each singing her own song. The chaos and confusion were overwhelming, making it difficult for Than to feign joy.

This difficulty increased when the maenads fell upon a snake someone had thrown into the dancers. He watched with disgust as they tore the creature to pieces and stuffed chunks of it into their mouths. He disintegrated to escort the snake's soul. Next came a rabbit, flung through the air by someone he could not see and caught in the hands of the mass of women, ripping and tearing the terrified, struggling creature. He disintegrated again. The bodies soon made way for two maenads pulling a thrashing buck by the horns into the center. Its limbs and head were ripped from its body and devoured by the dancers. Another disintegration. Than fragmented constantly, multiple times per second, so often did the living die. A second group fell on the remaining lump of carcass quivering in the grass until it was eaten up, blood dripping down chins.

"Now we are one with nature," one of them said in a bold voice. "Their souls belong to us."

Than decided now would not be a good time to correct her. Their souls had gone on. Instead, he opened his sack and tossed oranges and apples to the crowd. The fruit was gladly received and consumed as savagely as the animals. A ring of dancers formed around Than. They touched his arms and mussed his hair, smiling at him seductively. Then one maenad circled her arms around his waist and kissed him on the lips. As suddenly as she had come to him, she pulled away, screaming.

"Death!" she cried. "Death is among us!"

The joyful faces turned to panic and terror. Than wasn't sure why. They were immortal. He had suspected they wouldn't be too keen to see him if they knew his identity, but he never thought they'd fear him.

"Death is among us!" another shrieked.

At first the maenads scattered from him, leaving him alone in the center of their ring. Then someone yelled, "Kill him! Kill Death, so we can live forever!"

Before Than could say anything, the raving women rushed at him and grabbed a hold of his arms.

"Wait!" He struggled against them, trying not to hurt them as he flung them from his side. "Get back! Get back! Back, I say!"

A maenad grasped his thumb and tore it from his hand, sending shards of pain, deep and intense, through his arm and head. "Ahhh!" He held the hurt hand in the other and once again shouted, "Back!" as he now elbowed the women more forcefully than he dared to before, his blood spurting onto their dresses and skin.

Where were his sisters? He'd been hunting for them in Tartarus and all over the globe. He didn't dare ask his father where they were; Hades would want to know why. Than prayed out to them again and again. "Mount Kithairon! I need you at Mount Kithairon!"

To the maenads, he shouted, "Get back and listen to me! I haven't come to take anyone! I've come to see Dionysus!" His hand throbbed. He spotted the woman with his thumb and he charged at her and took it back, but at the sound of their lord's name, the maenads stopped attacking him. He stood, bewildered by their silence and stillness, searching their faces. Then a youthful god about his own age strolled to the center of the ring to face him. A group of satyrs hovered behind him. His hair was golden, like Hip's, but long and braided in two ropes at the back of his head. He wore nothing but a strap of leather at his loins.

"What does Death want with me?"

"A favor," Than replied.

Dionysus lifted his head and laughed, and the maenads and satyrs did the same.

Than spotted Alecto materialize above him, but he warned her off. "Tell the others I don't need them," he prayed silently to her. "And please, say nothing of this to our father."

She vanished, but he sensed her presence. Dionysus did, too.

"What will you do for me in return, Thanatos?"

"Anything that is within my power." He felt himself losing blood at the wound where his thumb should be. He was in agony but did well to hide it.

Dionysus's merry smile faded and he jutted his chin. "Indeed. Leave us, maenads. Follow the satyrs up the mountain."

The satyrs played a melody on their wooden flutes and led a parade of women further up the mountain. Once they were gone, Than carefully molded his thumb back to his hand and healed it, asking, "Why do they fear me when they're immortal?" The pain continued, but the thumb was back, and though it hurt, he could move it a little. How long it would be before he had full strength in it, he didn't know. He'd never, in his ancient life, sustained an injury such as this. He could only imagine the pain of enduring his entire body ripped this way.

"Only the wine keeps them so. Without me and the fruit of my vines, they would die."

"Tell them I'm your servant."

"There is something I want."

Chapter Ten: The Festival

Therese was surprised by the happiness she felt when she went downstairs to the gallery of friends awaiting her. She hadn't seen Todd and Ray since school let out four weeks ago, and they always managed to lift her spirits.

Ray, a chubby, but tall, Native American with dark eyes and short thick black hair, started things off, as usual. He wore his signature look: an open plaid shirt with a t-shirt underneath, jeans, and sneakers. Unlike Todd, he refused to dress like a cowboy since he wasn't actually a cowboy, and Todd, who also wasn't one, but who looked like one with his tall, wiry frame and Wrangler jeans and boots, was the butt of a lot of Ray's jokes: "You know what the urban cowboy would say…" and so forth. Now, Ray stood up and asked, "Why does it always take girls so long? I mean, what do they do, shave their legs by plucking one hair at a time? Or maybe there's some kind of good luck ritual they have to go through before they even get started."

Jen gave Ray a look that said "Not tonight," but Therese actually laughed.

"You're on to us," Therese said, "on both counts."

The rest of the group stood now, too, and Todd said, "Come see what I've done to my truck." It was a fifty-seven Chevy painted bright yellow and mounted high on a lift kit. They all said goodnight to Carol and Richard and headed outside.

Matthew linked his hand into Jen's as they walked down the steps to the gravelly drive, and Therese felt a stab of pain pierce her chest. She blinked and pushed the pain away, telling herself tonight would be a good time with good friends and nothing else mattered.

"Oh, hold on. I forgot something." Therese ran back inside, up the stairs to her room and into her desk drawer. She had promised to give Vicki the money for the NDE drugs, and she didn't want anything holding up their plans. She ran back out just as the group gathered around Todd's truck. "Okay. So what's new?"

"Check out my chrome. I was so excited when I found this authentic fifty-seven grill. Now my truck matches. Cool, huh?"

"Very cool," Therese said. "It looks so shiny and new. You wouldn't know it was an antique." She enjoyed making a big deal over Todd's truck because she knew how important it was to him. She would have liked to ride with him and Ray, but she knew Vicki would feel like a third wheel riding in Matthew's truck, which had an extended cab, and the two girls couldn't fit in Todd's, which did not. So Therese oooed and awed and then climbed into the backseat of Matthew's truck beside Vicki.

Once they were on the road, Therese silently passed the one hundred dollars over to Vicki, who nodded, folded the bills, and tucked them into her purse.

The Pagosa Springs Fairgrounds were a happening place by the time the two vehicles arrived. They had to drive up and down a dusty dirt parking lot for over fifteen minutes looking for a place to park. They each finally found one a couple of hundred yards away from the entrance. Therese's boots were covered in white dust by the time they paid their cover and entered the grounds.

Carnival rides and game and food booths were scattered across the grassy field that was surrounded by mountains still visible in the summer evening. As the group walked through the lane between the booths, they recognized people they knew and occasionally stopped to talk. Then they continued their way to the dance area where they looked forward to watching Pete's band perform.

Someone came up from behind Therese, tucked his hands beneath her armpits, and lifted her in the air, spinning her around and making her laugh. She could tell before he put her down that she was in Pete's hands. She turned to face him.

"When's your band onstage?"

"About eight." He led the group to a table where the rest of the Holts were already sitting, except for Bobby, who was dancing the two-step on the concrete dance floor with some girl Therese didn't know. "Ready?"

Pete smelled and felt good as he led Therese to the dance floor and took her in his arms. His white cowboy hat brought out the glow in his tanned face and sparkling blue eyes. His nose was sprinkled with a few summer freckles, and when he smiled, his teeth were pearl white. His shoulders were broad and well defined in the starched denim shirt unbuttoned at the very top. His jeans were tight, hugging his backside in a flattering way. Therese wanted to reach out and touch it. She was surprised by how good she felt in his arms, how much she liked him, and now that she was finally giving up on Than, Pete had her undivided attention.

He was a master at dancing—such a good lead that she hardly had to think at all. He twirled her around and past the other dancers in show-off fashion. She squealed a couple of times when he lifted her over his head.

And his voice was as smooth as her father's red wine, which he let her taste when she turned thirteen. She loved to listen to Pete sing the lyrics he knew; and when he didn't know the words to a song, he hummed softly in her ear, sending tingles down her neck and back.

When Todd wanted to cut in after several songs, Pete complained. "I'll have to go on stage soon and you can have her then."

Todd reluctantly backed off the floor and settled for Vicki.

Therese noticed Vicki didn't know how to dance, but Todd was patient with her and took things slow. He kept to a very basic step, talking her through the moves.

The salty taste of sweat made Therese lick her lips. Beads of sweat were pouring down her face and Pete's. They had danced at least a dozen songs—a couple of polkas and swings, several Texas Two Steps, and one slow waltz that had her closing her eyes and imagining a life with Pete. Now Pete asked if she wanted something to drink.

"I need a break before I go on stage," he said.

"A diet coke sounds good."

He walked her to one of the booths on the side of the dance area. "Diet? Why do you drink diet? You sure don't need to watch your weight."

"I just like the taste better. Regular coke tastes too sweet to me."

He gave her a quick and spontaneous peck on the lips. Then with a devilish smile, he asked, "Do I taste too sweet to you?"

She felt the heat rush to her face. "No, definitely not, Peter Holt," was all she could think to say as she turned away toward the booth.

They got in line behind four or five others. "Jen texted me about your hamster. I'm sorry you lost him, but I'm glad you decided to come tonight. My night wouldn't have been the same."

"I'm glad I came, too. You're such a great dancer. I'm having fun."

He blushed and kissed her again with a quick peck on the cheek, which made her blush, again, too. Then it was time for him to get their drinks. He bought himself a Sprite.

"I can pay for my pop," Therese said, but he wouldn't let her. "Then I'll get the next round."

They caught up with the others at the Holts' table when Pete suddenly said, "We gotta ride the octopus."

Therese gave him a doubtful look.

"Come on. It's my favorite ride, and I have a little more time before I go on."

Jen joined in. "Let's all go. What do you think, Matthew?"

"I'm in," Ray said before Matthew replied.

So a whole group of them ran off to get some tickets and get in line for the octopus.

On the ride, Therese sat against Pete, who had his arm around her, as one of the black tentacles whipped them around in the air. She shouted, delirious, not having laughed this hard in a long, long time. Todd and Vicki were in another car, Jen and Matthew in another, and Ray rode alone, with his arms up in the air. When the ride scooped down, Therese buried her face in Pete's chest.

"Oh my God!" she said, her stomach lurching.

Not long after, Pete left her standing near the table by the Holts talking to Ray as they watched Todd and Vicki, Matthew and Jen, and Bobby and his new partner dance to some transitional, pre-recorded music while Pete's band set up. When Pete's smooth voice finally rang out across the Fairgrounds, his crystal eyes and gorgeous smile directed at Therese, she felt surprisingly content. She felt as though he was singing exclusively for her, and she really didn't mind the occasional eyes in the audience who would seek out the object of the singer's attention. For the rest of the evening, Todd and Bobby danced with her, but not without Pete getting in his winks and waves to her. After Pete's band finished its one hour performance and put away the equipment, Pete came back to reclaim her for the evening.

Therese was dizzy with excitement. Pete had not been shy about showing his feelings for her, and she was overwhelmed. But it was a good feeling. She liked the feeling. She had encouraged Pete tonight more than she had all year, and it felt so, so good. By the time the group was ready to go, Pete had convinced Therese to ride back with him. Todd offered to take Vicki home, which took pressure off of her: she didn't have to worry about Vicki feeling like a third wheel with Matthew and Jen.

Pete helped her in on the passenger side, and then went around to the other. When she started to strap herself in near the door, he objected and pulled her over to the middle of the bench seat beside him. She laughed and was delighted by his strength and persistence. He put his hand on her thigh. She covered his hand with hers.

They talked about school—about band and her classes. Then he asked about her plans after high school. She didn't know. Probably college, but not Fort Lewis. It reminded her too much of her mom.

He asked how she was doing with her parents' death, and it felt good to talk about it honestly with someone.

"I still sometimes act a little loony," she said. "I'll be in the mall or at the movies, and I'll see someone with my mom's red hair or my dad's build, and I'll almost call out to them. I guess I still can't accept that they're really gone."

"That's understandable." He squeezed her hand.

She asked if he planned to stay working at the Holt Ranch.

"I'm really happy right now. I work with the horses, get to be around my family, and get to play a few gigs with my band here and there. I feel like I've got everything I want right here. I don't plan to go anywhere." He gave her a wink.

"How's it going with your dad home? Jen doesn't talk about it. I noticed both your parents were drinking pop tonight."

He sighed. "I don't know. I think my dad might be drinking again. Ever since that one night, I guess once you fall off the wagon it's hard to get back on again. It's another reason for me not to go anywhere."

"What makes you think he's drinking again?"

"Well, don't say anything to Jen."

"No, of course not."

"The other day the toilet in our main bathroom wouldn't flush, so I took off the lid of the tank. Inside I found a half-empty bottle of rum. It was a big bottle, leaning in the corner of the tank."

"That's kind of weird. What did you do?"

"I thought about confronting him. I mean, there was a slight chance he had left it there from before."

"Very slight, I would think."

"We hadn't looked in that tank in forever."

"Yeah, you could be right."

"But then I decided to pour it out in the grass and throw the bottle away. If he had put it there recently, it would still send a message someone's on to him."

"But wouldn't he just find better hiding places?"

He shrugged. "I guess I should confront him." He gave her a glance and she nodded.

"I think so. It's the only way to get closure." She was thinking of her own plans to confront Than.

He asked if she would be coming over to groom Stormy tomorrow.

"He's so cute. He'll help me keep my mind off of my hamster."

As they reached Lemon Dam, Pete turned off onto another country road and pulled over. Therese wanted to ask what he was doing, but she already knew.

"There's something I want to tell you, Therese."

She couldn't look at him. She had been so happy to be with him, had felt awesome in his arms, and had been filled with a sincere joy all evening; but now as he was about to say words she already knew, her heart felt gripped with pain and fear. Something wasn't right. Something wasn't right about this at all.

Maybe it was that she hadn't yet told off Than. Maybe she needed to get her feelings off her chest and tell Than where he could go—he was already in hell, anyway—before she could move forward with Pete. Determined that this was the cause of the uneasy feeling, she interrupted Pete and said, "Wait."

Before she could say more, he leaned in and touched his lips to hers. This was no quick peck. His mouth felt warm and good, and something eased up in her chest as she sighed. He put his arms around her and pressed her close to him. His hard chest and strong arms made her feel like she was melting. His kisses moved around her mouth, across her chin, down her neck, toward her throat.

"Wait," she said again, pulling back.

"I'm sorry."

"There's something I have to do," she said. "I haven't officially broken things off with Than. But this weekend, I'm going to do it. I'm going to tell him I don't want to see him again. Once I do that, I'll feel better about this, with you. You know?"

Pete slowly nodded and leaned back. The disappointment was obvious in his face. "I didn't realize you two were still a couple."

"We really haven't been much of one. I just want to be sure. I need closure."

"I understand."

He drove her home, and on the way, he kept both hands on the wheel. They rode in silence, barely touching. When they reached her house she said, "I had a really great time tonight. Thanks for bringing me home."

"My pleasure." He didn't offer her a goodnight kiss, but he gave her a wink to let her know he understood.

She slid from the bench seat and made her way toward her house, shaking like a leaf. She hoped she knew what she was doing.

"Help me, Hermes," she whispered as she lay in bed next to her dog. "Thanatos has broken my heart. I plan to say goodbye to him forever. I need to go on, right? Tell me what to do."

She fell asleep saying her prayers.

Chapter Eleven: Ariadne

Than appeared before the palace ruins of Knossos on the island of Crete under which the ancient labyrinth of the Minotaur lay mostly intact. He'd been here many times to collect the souls of the beast's victims. He had waited till dark so as not to draw attention from tourists as he scoured the ruins for the entrance and its guardian, the beautiful Ariadne and wife of Dionysus. The god of wine agreed to help Than if he could convince Ariadne to return to Mount Kithairon and his side.

No expert when it came to matters of the heart, Than wasn't sure he could succeed, but he had to try. Already, Therese's prayers had become less frequent, and he feared he would lose her heart altogether. In fact, he couldn't recall hearing her lovely voice since he saw her last at Puffy's departure. Her voice had been like food to him, and now he was starving.

A subtle glow appeared beneath a fallen pillar. He immediately sensed another godly presence. He traveled through the rock into a cavern and backed against the wall was a lovely raven-haired goddess he knew must be Ariadne.

"Are you here for a victim of the Minotaur?"

"No."

"Then why?"

"As a favor to Dionysus."

She dropped her eyes and linked her fingers together. "He wouldn't come himself?"

"Too many depend on him. The maenads would die, and they're needed to enforce the oaths."

"He hasn't the power of disintegration afforded to you and your brother."

"Correct. Few of us can be in many places at once."

She looked up at him again. "I did not know you were beautiful. I've seen your brother, and knew of his beauty, but not of yours."

Than blushed. "Most people avoid me because of my job."

She stepped closer to him, her eyes taking him in and making him uneasy. "Few know I was married to Dionysus before I left him for Theseus. I couldn't help myself. Dionysus is beautiful. But Theseus was courageous and honorable. Dionysus cares little for honor."

"It's not honorable to steal away with another man's wife."

"Theseus was unaware."

"But you weren't. You helped him kill the Minotaur and then ran away with him." This was not the way to win her over, he thought. "You must have had your reasons."

"Dionysus is always surrounded by women."

"But none more beautiful than you. Nor more temperate." Of course, that was true of any woman. The maenads weren't hard to beat in temperance.

"What does he want?"

"You by his side. He wants to leave the past in the past. Theseus is in the Underworld now, barely aware of his own history. You have a long life, an immortal one. You could find happiness at Mount Kithairon. Here you're alone."

"You forget the Minotaur, who at no fault of his own, has been imprisoned in this labyrinth. He can't help what his parents did and what he is as a result. Why should he be made to suffer alone, while Dionysus and I drink wine and dance in the woods of Mount Kithairon?"

"You love the Minotaur?"

"I betrayed him once, as you said. I pity him."

"More than you love your husband?"

She stepped closer to Than and searched his eyes, her mouth open and moist. He thought she would kiss him. He stepped back.

"Maybe," she said. "I don't know."

"Go back with me to Mount Kithairon and discover the depth of your love for Dionysus. You can always leave again."

"Why do you care what I do?"

"I love someone."

She stepped closer, her eyes inches from him. "Who?"

"A mortal. I want to make her a god and need your husband's help. He will only consent if you return to his side." Than went down on his knees. "So I beg you, beautiful Ariadne, guardian of the labyrinth. Maybe you could do as my mother does and spend half your time down here and the other half in the woods of Mount Kithairon."

She went down on her knees before him, so her eyes were level with his mouth. "Perhaps if you lie with me, I'll do you this favor."

Than swallowed hard, his throat suddenly dry. No one had ever come on to him like this in the history of his existence. It felt good. Tempting. It occurred to him that if things didn't go right with Therese—no, there could be no one else. Just thinking otherwise broke his heart. "Who wouldn't be flattered by such a proposition? But my heart belongs to another, and I won't betray her. I'll do anything else. Name it."

Ariadne climbed to her feet, her eyes narrowed, and her lips pursed. "Go down into the labyrinth then and find your way out before the Minotaur rips your heart out and devours it, and only then will I go with you to Mount Kithairon."

Chapter Twelve: The NDE Drug

Therese woke up late Sunday morning, unable to recall her dream. She took Clifford out, fed and watered him and Jewels, and then noticed Puffy's body was not in his cage. She ran downstairs again.

"Where's Puffy?"

Richard and Carol had already eaten, but a plate of pancakes waited for her.

"He's right here." Carol pointed to a floral box on the counter by the kitchen sink. "A scented candle came in that box, and it still smells really nice. I put Puffy in there last night so, so you wouldn't have to. I would have cleaned his cage and put it away, but I wasn't sure whether you wanted me to or not."

"Thanks," Therese said. "I want to do it myself."

"I dug a hole," Richard said from the sofa across the room. "Out by one of the elms. We could bury him there, if you'd like."

Therese smiled, her eyes welling, just a little bit. "That would be nice. I'll go get dressed."

She threw on some jeans and a t-shirt and came back down.

The three of them went outside in the back of the house beneath one of two giant elm trees and committed Puffy to the earth. "Ashes to ashes, dust to dust," Therese murmured. Her dad had bought her the hamster four years ago. Puffy's death was one more thing separating her from her parents. She wiped her tears with the back of her hand as her throat constricted, and she felt inexplicably angry at Richard and Carol.

Richard covered the hole up with dirt while Therese and Carol watched on. Then he patted the earth down, leaned the shovel against the tree, and said, "There we go."

The three walked back into the house.

"Did you have fun last night?" Carol asked. She went back to doing something on her laptop.

Therese started on her pancakes. "Yeah, I had fun. We all did."

As she ate her breakfast at the countertop, Therese told her aunt and uncle she was headed over to the Holts to groom Stormy, and Clifford would be going along, too, if that was okay.

With their blessing, she and Clifford walked down the three-quarter-mile path to Jen's house along the dirt road separating the mountain homes from Lemon Reservoir. Clifford stopped to pee on nearly every tree, so Therese had to keep saying, "Come on, boy."

She felt a little nervous about seeing Pete today.

But Pete was as friendly as always and immediately put her at ease. The whole family was already out with the horses. They didn't offer trail rides on Sundays, so they looked forward to finishing up their chores and taking the afternoon off. Jen asked Therese if she wanted to go shopping with her.

"Maybe. What are you shopping for?"

"Nothing. I just want to look at dresses, to get some ideas for prom."

Therese rolled her eyes. "I guess I can go with you, but you do realize prom's like, light-years away from now?"

Jen laughed. "I guess I'm excited, you know?"

Therese stroked Stormy with a soft towel as Jen worked on Sassy. She couldn't believe how big he was getting. He nuzzled her hand.

The whole week went that way. Carol and Richard were supportive, Pete was easy to talk to, Jen asked her to do things with her, and Therese felt surprisingly okay with Puffy's death. She cleaned and put away the cage. She wasn't ready for a new hamster, but she stored the cage in the basement just in case she felt differently one day.

Thursday, Vicki called to say she had the stuff. They made plans to get together Friday night.

Richard drove Therese to Vicki's apartment after supper and helped her carry her sleeping bag to the door. After Richard left, Vicki told Mr. Stern they were going to her room to listen to music. Mr. Stern was half asleep in his recliner in front of the blaring television. The girls didn't have to worry about him interfering in their business.

Vicki injected Therese and then herself using two different sterile needles. There was a slight pinch, and then a little burn, and then nothing. The two girls lay back on Vicki's bed and waited.

"I'm scared," Therese said.

"It's gonna be awesome," Vicki reassured her. "But this time, I'm jumping on the raft as soon as possible."

"Do you think we'll be able to see each other on the other side?" Therese asked.

"I hope so. If I see you, I'll grab your hand."

"Maybe we should hold hands now," Therese suggested.

"Um, sure, if you want."

Therese took Vicki's hand.

"Do you feel anything yet?" Vicki asked.

"I think so. Just a little. Oh."

"What?"

"I feel so peaceful."

"See what I mean? Oh. Now I feel it, too."

Therese could no longer speak, and she could only vaguely feel Vicki's hand in hers. She felt herself float up toward the ceiling, and now she looked down and saw her own body lying beside Vicki's on the bed. This is so weird. Then, right beside her on the ceiling, Vicki appeared holding her hand, but their bodies still lay on the bed. So, so weird, Therese thought again.

She decided to pray to Hermes, to tell him what she was up to. "I'm going to tell him off tonight, Hermes. I'm going to tell him how he broke my heart and how I never want to see him again. I'm going to the Underworld so I can tell him to his face."

She found herself in a dark tunnel. She couldn't see Vicki, but she could vaguely feel her hand in hers. A bright light shone at the end of the tunnel, so she half-walked, half-floated toward it. The walls of the tunnel looked like granite, and she wasn't sure, but she thought there was a very small spring running through the bottom of it. Her feet didn't feel wet, but she thought she could hear herself sloshing through the stream. When she finally reached the end of the tunnel, she recognized the Styx River in front of her. She was at the very same bank she had come to the night her parents were killed.

Fog curled around her, but she recognized the river flowing in a narrow gorge between two huge and creepy granite mountains. Her bare feet sunk into the itchy mud. She held on to Vicki, who stumbled beside her, to try and keep their balance. Tall blades of grass as high as their knees grew in tufts along the shore, tickling her bare legs. She wondered if she should have worn jeans and if it would have made a difference. She seemed to be in the shorts she had worn to Vicki's. Mosquitoes swarmed over one area of the water. Three large boulders leaned in a cluster on the left side of the shore against the base of a steep, massive wall of rock. Where was Charon?

Vicki tugged her across the sticky mud and tall blades of grass to the edge of the river, where Charon and his raft came into view. Without saying a word to the old, stooped man, Vicki jumped on board, pulling Therese with her.

Therese fought the urge to greet Charon by name as he gave them a look of confusion before towing them across.

The fog swirled around them like the tentacles of a gray octopus. Therese was surprised she wasn't cold or nervous. She felt completely at peace and couldn't wait to tell Than what she had come to say.

In fact, she felt so peaceful, that she found it hard to be angry. She had planned to scream her angry words, but the contentment swooned over her like a glittery beam of warm sunshine, and the anger dissipated into the fog.

She recognized Cerberus as they approached the huge black iron gate. She couldn't stop herself from saying sweetly, "Hey, boy. Hi there, Cerberus."

His three huge heads panted happily, and he wagged his long, dragon-like tail.

"You know him?" Vicki whispered.

Charon glared at them, so Therese said nothing.

The big gates creaked open, and Charon hovered just at the entrance.

"What are you waiting for?" Vicki asked the old man.

Then suddenly the contentment vanished from Therese, and she filled with dread as some kind of commotion took place around her. Cerberus's three huge heads barked ferociously. She couldn't quite tell what was happening, but she felt herself lifted away from the raft, and she could make out through the fog Charon leaving. She wondered if the drug could be wearing off so soon. Then someone shouted, "Grab her! Don't let her escape this time!" and big bodies were pushing and pulling Vicki away from her. Another had grabbed Therese and pulled her still further away from the gate. It was Hermes.

"You can't go through the gate," he said, panting from the struggle. "You'll piss off Hades for sure and never win his heart."

His wooly black hair blew in the gentle breeze up here away from the fog, far above the river. His dark eyes and dark beard were barely visible in what seemed to be obscured moonlight. His winged helmet gleamed, though, and so did his white teeth, which were gritted.

"It was foolish of you to come here. What made you think you could get away with this?"

Then she realized Vicki wasn't with them. "Where's my friend?"

Hermes shook his head but made no reply. Panic overcame Therese. She pushed herself free from Hermes and flew down to the gate. She saw Than holding Vicki against her will on the other side of the iron gate, which he was just now closing.

"Vicki!" Therese screamed, trying to push the gate open again. But it slammed shut in her face. "Than! Give me Vicki! She'll die!"

Than held on to Therese's struggling friend. "I'm sorry, Therese. Vicki has to stay here."

"No!" Therese threw herself against the iron bars of the gate, screaming at the top of her lungs. "No! Please! No! I beg you! I'll do anything! Take me instead!" She was tortured by the thought of Mr. Stern losing his only child on the heels of his wife's suicide. "I beg you, Than! If you love me, take me instead!"

"I have no choice. She's angered my father. She came through once before and cheated death. He won't let her do it again."

"But there's got to be a way! You can't let her die! Please! Her father will be so miserable! Please, Than!"

He shook his head again and backed away from the gate.

The anger Therese had felt over Than rekindled in her chest and she gave him a ferocious look. "I hate you, Thanatos! So you've been too busy to worry about me? The other night you were just doing your job? Well, I came down here to tell you to your face that I hate you and I never want to see you again! Stay out of my life! And send someone else to collect me when I'm dead!"

Hermes was there beside her now, trying to calm her down. He took her in his arms and allowed her blows to hit his chest rather than the iron bars of the gate. "I hate him!" she cried. Then she pleaded with Hermes, "Isn't there anything you can do to save my friend?"

"Even gods are limited by the will and actions of others. There's nothing I can do."

She looked through the gate at Than, who backed away, looking miserable. Vicki had stopped struggling, and her face reminded Therese of the blank expressions on her parents' faces the night she saw them in the Underworld. Therese realized Vicki must be dead already, and she wailed as loud as she could in the foggy air.

Than locked eyes with hers, his face contorted with pain. "When I said I'd been busy, I meant…"

But Hermes was pulling her back before she could hear the rest of Than's statement. Back they went from the river, from the muddy bank, through the dark granite tunnel. She floated for a brief moment on the ceiling and then popped back into her body. She opened her eyes and found Vicki lying beside her, dead.

Chapter Thirteen: The Labyrinth

Ariadne vanished, leaving Than alone at the entrance to the cavern, the labyrinth devised by Daedalus for King Minos centuries ago to house the Minotaur. In the old days, the Athenians sent seven warriors and seven maidens to be sacrificed to the Minotaur as payment for killing Minos's son, but once Theseus destroyed the Minotaur, that practice ended.

But the Minotaur was immortal, and he came back.

He had no regular food source, so he must depend on lost travelers for sustenance.

Although Than was immortal, he could be consumed by such a monster. And it would be painful. More threatening, though, was the recovery time. Than wasn't sure how long it would take, and his chances of securing Dionysus's help would be jeopardized. He would never see Therese as his bride.

Though now, as he crept through the winding, rocky maze, he feared he'd already lost her. The anger in her eyes when he kept her friend still haunted him. Why had Therese taken such a risk? Didn't she know she would lose his father's favor, which was already shaky if it existed at all? He was beginning to wonder if he was alone in still wanting this union. She hadn't really meant it when she said she hated him, had she?

Cracks in the rock above him allowed dim points of light to illuminate the passageway, adding to the light cast by his own body. Cables of different colors lay at his feet where others copied Theseus and his ball of yarn. He bent down and held a red colored chord and hoped to use it to find his way back. When he came to a fork in the tunnel, he recalled what Theseus, upon entering the Underworld, told him centuries ago. He said, "One should go straight and down, never right or left." Than went straight and down.

He could easily god travel out of the labyrinth, as Ariadne well knew, but if she discovered it, she would refuse to help him. He could also disintegrate and hover above the labyrinth, making its outer walls transparent so he could guide his other self through, but he didn't want to risk Ariadne catching him at cheating. If he wanted Dionysus's help, he had to do this the hard way.

And since he carried no weapon, he would have to defend himself from the Minotaur with his bare hands.

Chapter Fourteen: Aftermath

Therese touched Vicki's limp body on the bed beside her, still warm. "Vicki?" She shook Vicki's shoulder. "Vicki?" She put her hand to Vicki's throat to feel for a pulse, her ear to Vicki's chest. Both were silent. *This can't be happening. This must be a nightmare.* Therese looked up to the ceiling and let out a blood-curdling scream.

Mr. Stern opened the bedroom door, his face at first bewildered. He might have said something, like "What's going on?" Then his expression changed to terror as he rushed to Vicki's side.

"Ducky? Talk to me, sweetheart!" He put his ear to her chest. "Ducky, love, wake up!"

Vicki did not move.

"Call 9-1-1," he said to Therese as he started CPR. "Now!"

"Oh my God!" she screamed, unable to think. Everything seemed to be happening in slow motion, but still her mind couldn't keep up. She stumbled around the bed for the phone on the nightstand and dialed the numbers, the same numbers she dialed around this same time last year.

She told the person on the other end the Stern's address. "She's not breathing! There's no pulse! Her dad's giving her CPR!" Her own voice kept asking her accusingly, *What have I done?*

"Stay on the line with me until someone arrives," the person on the other end said.

"I'm so sorry!" Therese didn't want to admit what they had done. "This wasn't supposed to happen." *What have I done?*

"Talk to me Therese," Mr. Stern said while he continued to pump Vicki's lifeless chest.

"She wanted to see her mom. She saw her last weekend using this drug. Ketamine. I wanted to see my parents, too. This wasn't supposed to happen." She couldn't breathe. She was hyperventilating. She didn't care. She wanted to die rather than face Mr. Stern.

The woman on the phone asked, "You and your friend took keta-mine? Can you tell me how much and how long ago?"

Tears ran down Mr. Stern's sallow cheeks and some of the determination and hope vanished from his face. He stuck his finger down Vicki's throat. "I need to make her vomit." But Vicki's body would not respond.

Therese knew Hades would not let her return from the Underworld.

"This wasn't supposed to happen," she said again. In her mind, to Than, she said, "How could you?"

Mr. Stern rode in the ambulance with Vicki to the hospital while Carol, Richard, and Therese followed in Richard's car. Therese prayed to Hermes to please, please, please find a way to let Vicki return to the living. She couldn't stop crying and wished she herself could die. If she hadn't provided the money for the drugs, Vicki would be alive.

Carol and Richard weren't talking. They were so upset with her when they discovered what had happened: that Therese had bought the drug, had taken some herself, and not only contributed to the death of her friend but might have died herself.

Therese didn't blame them for being mad at her. She was mad at herself. She wished she, too, would have been taken by Death and forced to stay in the Underworld. The Lethe River was beginning to sound good.

"Hermes," she whispered too softly for the adults up front to hear. "You should have let me die."

Chapter Fifteen: The Minotaur

Straight and down, Than said to himself as he crept through the cave listening and watching for the first sign of the Minotaur. Ariadne had commanded Than to enter and exit the labyrinth, but she hadn't specified how far in he had to go. Couldn't he turn back now, especially since the red chord wound away, in the wrong direction, and he could no longer follow it?

No. He couldn't risk her denying him her help. He could tell she didn't want to go back to her husband, and he didn't want to make it easy for her to refuse him. He would go far into the belly of the beast, down and down, until he couldn't go any deeper. Once the path went uphill again, he'd know he was at its center.

He missed hearing Therese's voice. For ten months, her prayers had been constant, the only joy in his long life. He'd heard his father and other men joke about the tendency for women to talk more than most men, often to the point of annoyance, but Than looked forward to her daily prayers. Sometimes they were full of passion and longing, and his own longing would stir deep within him, nearly unbearable; but often they were clever remarks, funny comments and observations that would have him in stitches even as several thousand fragmented selves somberly escorted the dead. Therese had become the light of his existence. He didn't want to live without her.

But he couldn't hear her anymore. She stopped speaking to him. Hours had passed since he had taken Vicki to Erebus to lie in the pallid pool of the Lethe near her mother. In the interim between now and then, the only words to him from Therese were, "How could you?"

As he came upon a three-way fork in the passage, ignoring those to the left and right, he felt anger move through him. Therese knew he had no choice. It was unfair of her to blame him. Vicki had already gotten away with deceiving Hades once. She couldn't expect to do so twice.

Than had seen others like Vicki come to the gate in their drug-induced trip to jeer at him and Cerberus. Some had even boarded Charon's raft. But none had made it through the gate and gotten out alive save Vicki. It certainly couldn't happen twice. Therese had to know that. He was hurt she didn't seem more sympathetic to his point of view.

"How obtuse of her," he muttered.

No sooner had he made the remark than the Minotaur appeared before him, sprung from some crevice in the side of the rocky cavern. He gave Than no time for words, but shoved him with an unexpected force back against the wall. He hadn't been shoved like that since he and his brother wrestled together in the asphodel before they were old enough to take on their duties. Demigods had sometimes tried to shove him out of their way as they resisted death, but none were his match in strength. This Minotaur gave him pause. He'd forgotten exactly how the beast was immortal, though he sensed immortality was in his blood and not later conferred upon him. He stood up and pushed the monster back.

The Minotaur gasped when his humanoid back hit rock.

"I mean you no harm," Than said. "Let me pass through here, and I won't touch you again."

The beast panted as he pushed himself back to his feet and pointed the horns of his bull head at Than. "Oh, it's you. Why have you come? There are no dead nearby."

"Ariadne sent me."

"She sends only those she wishes to sacrifice to me. She knows how hungry I am. Why would she send a god to taunt my taste buds unless she meant for me to feast upon him?"

"Don't force me to kill you."

The Minotaur lunged for Than, who deftly moved and twisted in a flourish before the Minotaur could blink. The monster was strong, but he was no match in speed to the god of Death. Than pinned the beast's humanoid arms to his sides and again said, "I'm no Theseus, but I will kill you if you give me no choice."

His words seemed to further enrage the monster, who tucked his bull head down and butted Than's head. Than lost his grip on the beast and staggered back. Lighter on his feet, Than skipped past him, uphill and straight.

The path was not well-lit, but Than could see in the darkness and felt confident he would leave the beast in his dust. Then the Minotaur appeared before him and took him by surprise. He either used a shortcut or god traveled. After a moment's hesitation, Than ran into the monster with all his might and fell on him onto the narrow rocky ground of the passageway.

With the creature pinned beneath him, Than asked, "Why do you want to fight me? Are you really that hungry?"

The bull-man bucked Than from his torso, and Than fell on his back. Before the Minotaur could pin him, Than kicked the beast up against the ceiling. The beast and a cart load of rocks tumbled to the ground beside Than's feet. He jumped up and took the monster by the horns. "I hate to do this," he said, and with one twist, he broke the Minotaur's neck.

The body fell beneath Than as the soul emerged. Than put his hand on the beast's shoulder. "Tell me why. Was it really hunger? I could have brought you food."

"You came to take Ariadne."

"You love her?"

Ariadne appeared. "Asterion!" She glared at Than. "You killed him!"

"I had no choice." Than disintegrated so that one self could escort the beast's soul to the Underworld, though it wouldn't stay long.

"Wait!" Ariadne wrapped her arms around the transparent apparition of Asterion's soul. "I'll be waiting for you. I promise." Tears fell from her eyes. "I won't leave you again."

Than left with the soul to Charon while another disintegrated Than confronted the weeping goddess. "You promised you would return to Dionysus with me today."

"That was before you killed my brother."

"Brother?"

She looked up at him. "Our mother is the daughter of the sun-titan. She was tricked into sleeping with a white bull given to my father."

"I know your father. I didn't know you shared the same mother with the beast."

"He can't help what he is. Was."

"Is. As soon as his body regenerates, his soul will return. Though I don't understand how he's immortal if one parent was a bull."

"A magical bull from Poseidon, infused with Poseidon's blood."

"Great. I'm sure I just pissed off the god of the sea." He folded his arms across his chest. "Well, you'll have your brother back."

"Last time that took nearly a week."

"So go with me to Dionysus while you wait."

"Never. I couldn't bear for my brother to wake up here alone. I left him once to go with my husband, and before that, with Theseus, but never again. No one should have to live a life of solitude. It isn't fair."

Than wanted to say what his father had always said, "Life isn't fair, but death is," but he supposed that only applied to mortals. "Come with me now and return tomorrow."

"You know that won't happen. Dionysus has his methods of persuasion. Why do you suppose the maenads and satyrs never leave him? He'll trap me as he has before."

"You never meant to help me. So why did you send me into the maze?"

Ariadne lowered her eyes. "I was hurt when you rejected me. And now my brother suffers. Either comfort me in your arms or leave me before I rip my own eyes out as Oedipus once did."

"Goodbye, Ariadne." Than left her at once and entered his private chamber in the Underworld, not defeated by the Minotaur, but defeated nonetheless.

Chapter Sixteen: Saying Goodbye

Therese didn't want to attend Vicki's funeral, but Carol and Richard forced her to go. She sat between them on a hard wooden pew at St. Francis's Cathedral with a handful of others. The Holts sat in the pew in front of her. Ray and Todd were right behind her. A couple of teachers from Durango High were there. Mr. Stern slouched alone in the front pew. Therese felt the burden of his sadness. She could have stopped Vicki, should have stopped her, but had encouraged her for her own selfish reasons. Therese could meet no one's eyes, especially those of Mr. Stern's. This was mostly her fault. She pondered the bottle of sleeping pills and Prozac in her medicine cabinet. If she took both bottles of pills, would that be enough to kill her?

The funeral mass was the longest service of Therese's life. She could feel the cold, hard, accusing eyes glancing her way. When news spread about what had happened, Therese received a lot of cold looks. Even Jen was outraged, though she had enough heart not to say so. She didn't need to. Therese could see it in her friend's eyes. The only person in Therese's life who showed sympathy instead of judgment was Pete Holt.

At the graveside service, her despair and remorse over everything—the loss of her parents, the loss of Than, the loss of Puffy and Dumbo, and now of Vicki, whom she might have saved had she been responsible enough—shuddered through her body in uncontrollable sobs. She stood behind the metal folding chairs, outside of the canopy, several feet behind Carol and Richard, not wanting to be seen, sunglasses shielding her swollen eyes, when Pete Holt approached from behind and took her hand. He squeezed it, and this small act of kindness sent her into hysterics. He took her in his arms and held her as she wept, allowing herself to collapse in his arms.

After a brief reception at Mr. Stern's apartment, where a few people brought food Mr. Stern would probably never eat, Pete came over and sat with Therese in the swing on her wooden deck where they watched the sunset across Lemon Reservoir. They rocked back and forth, holding hands, saying nothing, and it was nice.

But it wasn't long before Therese's thoughts went to Than. As angry as she was for his role in Vicki's death, and despite her own miserable feelings of guilt, her heart continued to ache for him against her will. She hated herself for that. Why couldn't she love Pete? He was everything she could want in a guy. He was gorgeous, sweet, funny, and smart. And she could tell how much he loved her. Maybe she could learn to love him back.

As if he sensed her thoughts, Pete lifted her chin, looked into her eyes, and said, "Can I kiss you?"

She slowly nodded and closed her eyes.

Pete's warm lips softly swept against hers, but instead of exalting, she filled with dread. This wasn't right. She carried out the kiss and waited for him to end it, but inside, she thought it couldn't end too quickly.

He looked at her with a smile. "That was nice."

"Yes, it was."

He kissed her again, and she bore it, convincing herself it was the right thing to do. How had she ever thought she could marry Death and become a god?

That night, alone in her room, after Carol and Richard had come to talk to her about making good choices—on the heels of her friend's funeral, really?—she took out her flute and played a tribute to Hermes. As she played a piece by Bach, she sang in her mind her prayer to him: "Help me, Hermes. Help me find a way either to fall out of love with Than or to be with him. I can't take this agony. Maybe it's time for me to join my parents. Maybe it's time for me to die, too. Please, Hermes. All my hopes lie with you." She continued to play and to meditate on these thoughts as tears rolled down her cheeks until she was too tired to go on.

Chapter Seventeen: Another Deal with Hades

Than appeared before his father near the flames of the Phlegethon River illuminating the vast private chamber where Hades spent most of his time. Hades sat on a chaise lounge and held a book in his hand, but he wasn't looking at it. He was speaking with Alecto, who stood close by, her python wrapped around her waist and lying over one shoulder. They both looked at Than when he appeared.

"Am I interrupting?"

"We were just discussing you," Hades remarked. "Alecto believes a recent soul taken to Erebus must be vindicated."

"Who?"

"Vicki Stern." Alecto stepped forward and squared herself to her brother. "Your old girlfriend is partly to blame."

"How? She didn't force or persuade the other girl to take the drug."

"She bought the drug." Alecto's eyes turned as red as her hair, and one drop of blood dripped onto her cheek. "She's culpable."

Great. Alecto's charge wouldn't help Than's case. "I came here to tell you of an important decision I've made. Whatever the consequences, I'm determined to make Therese a god."

Alecto gasped.

Hades jumped from his chair. "Are you mad?"

"I guess that means I won't be getting your blessing."

Hades stepped closer. "The maenads will rip you to pieces once a year forever."

Like he didn't already know that. Than resisted the urge to say this sarcastic thought out loud. "I want this."

Hades started to say something, but then didn't. He sat back down in his chair and put his chin in one hand. Than waited quietly for several seconds and was about to speak again, when his father said, "I have an idea."

Alecto moved to her father's side. "You can't be seriously considering a way to…"

"This idea will settle your issues as well."

"I'm listening," Than said.

"We give her five challenges, as penance for her role in the girl's death and as a means for proving she's worthy to become like us. If she succeeds, I'll use all my power to force Dionysus to make her a god. Then you'll be spared the maenads."

"What kind of challenges?" Than's heart sank. This didn't sound good.

"They need to prove she has what it takes. We need to know if she's trustworthy, diplomatic, yet cunning. She has to be strong and brave."

"So we're holding her to higher standards than we do the rest of us."

Hades laughed. "To be sure, though I know you don't include me among those whom you see lacking."

"That goes without saying."

Hades searched Than's face for signs of sarcasm, but Than showed none.

"What do you have in mind, Father?" Alecto asked.

Hades sat silent for a moment, thinking, while his son and daughter waited. Than stared off into the flames of the Phlegethon, silently begging his father to consider his happiness.

Then Hades stood up, and, pacing with excitement, said, "To prove she's trustworthy, we'll have her deliver a black box from Aphrodite to Persephone containing a beauty charm which Therese is not to open. Aphrodite asked this of Cupid's Psyche and countless others, and even though the women were already beautiful, they couldn't resist stealing a little more beauty for themselves. We'll see if Therese can resist what others could not."

Than sighed with relief, feeling confident Therese would not falter. She was anything but vain.

"For her second challenge," Hades said, "to test her skills in diplomacy, she must deliver to Mount Olympus one of Hera's golden apples, guarded in her orchard by the Hesperides and Ladon, the one-hundred-headed dragon."

"How do you expect her to get by the dragon?" Than demanded. "You know it's impossible."

"It wasn't for Hercules."

"She won't be long in finding her way here," Than said. "But not as my bride."

"You have little faith in the girl you love," Alecto sneered.

Than shook his head, his ears thudding with the beat of his heart. His father must not care for him, he thought bitterly. He clenched his jaw and turned away to leave.

"Don't you want to hear what the other three challenges are?" Hades asked.

"To humor you, Father?"

"Indeed."

"I'm listening," he spat angrily.

"The third will test her cunning," Hades said. "For that I want her to negotiate through the Labyrinth."

Both the Minotaur and his sister Ariadne were no friends to Than. If by some miracle Therese made it past the one-hundred-headed dragon, they would kill Therese.

"You are not allowed to intervene," Hades said, as if reading his thoughts. "If you want to train her for battle, you may. You may even offer advice. The actual challenges she must endure alone."

Than glared at his father.

"For strength, she must defeat the Hydra."

Than laughed. "This is ridiculous."

"And for courage, she must descend into the Underworld, find Vicki Stern, and apologize to her."

"Why such an easy task on the heels of the others?" Than asked. "You know she can't defeat the dragon, the Minotaur, and the Hydra, so you throw that last one in there for grins?"

"The last is the most difficult of all," Hades replied. "Because like Orpheus, she won't be allowed to look back."

"She can do that, but it doesn't matter. You've set her up for failure."

Alecto stepped closer to Than, "Don't be too quick to give up."

As much as Than appreciated his sister's encouragement, he said, "Never mind, then, Father. I'll do it without your blessing. I want her alive."

"Wait, brother," Alecto said. "At least give her the choice."

Chapter Eighteen: The Impossible Dream

After Pete left, Therese went straight through the house and up the stairs to her room, hoping neither her aunt nor her uncle would follow. She wanted to be alone. Except for her pets, she didn't want company.

She changed into an old pair of sweats she usually wore in the winter, hoping they would help her body stop trembling. She held Jewels against her neck, the shell warm from its heat lamp. Then she wished the tortoise goodnight, turned off the lamp, and crawled beneath her covers. As exhausted as she was, she lay in bed beside Clifford unable to fall asleep.

"Oh, Clifford," she muttered. "What am I going to do?"

He nudged the palm of her hand with his head, which meant, "Pet me," so she scratched behind his ears and along his back. He rolled over for a belly scratch. Stroking him released some of the anxiety that had built up inside of her. Her neck and shoulders loosened a little, and she sank further into her pillow. She closed her eyes and continued to pet Clifford until she finally drifted off to sleep.

Therese found herself walking through a neighborhood, lost. It was her grandparents' neighborhood, in San Antonio. She used to ride a bike around these blocks during visits, but she'd never gotten lost. Why couldn't she find her way now? She turned a corner and headed up another block. Some of the houses slanted in odd angles to the ground. This is weird, she thought. She'd never seen houses like this before.

She was dreaming.

She kicked off the ground and swam the breast stroke through the air, flying above the treetops. She flipped onto to her back and floated, wondering why her grandparents' old neighborhood had been in her dream and why she had gotten lost in it. Before long, she felt another presence floating near her.

It was a figment disguised as Than. She turned to face it, her body stiff with anger. Even though she knew it was just a stupid figment, she couldn't stop the heat from rising to her skin and the words to her throat. "Get away from me!"

"Therese, please." The figment moved closer, touching a hand to her cheek.

She looked at him with longing, but the fact that he could be this close and not cause her to grow weak with dying proved he was just a stupid figment. She pressed her palms against his bare chest and pushed. "Get away!" she growled.

"No. Not until you've heard me out. If you still want me to go then, I will."

"Figment, I command you to show yourself!"

Than moved closer, taking her hand. "I'm not a figment. It's me."

She jerked back, eyes wide. "What?" Her heart pounded in her ears. She wasn't sure whether she was mad or happy. Maybe a little of both. "What are you doing here? How come I'm not dying?"

He ran a hand through her short hair. "I like your hair this way."

Her mouth went dry, her palms moist. "Why are you here?"

"My father ordered Hip to trade places with me for the night. I need to talk to you."

"And you couldn't manage this months ago?" Her voice came out harsh and bitter. She regretted it as soon as she saw his face.

"I've been trying, believe me. Can we please sit down somewhere and talk?"

She folded her arms across her chest, unsure. Seeing him made her knees weak; she could barely maintain herself in the air because her body felt wobbly, her heart unsteady. Yes, she wanted to sit down, but should she talk to him? After what he did to Vicki? The idea of not talking to him made her stomach ache. "Okay. Where?"

He took her hand and led her down through the clouds, down through tall granite peaks, down into a ravine where a river flowed, down to the gate of the Underworld.

"I thought I wasn't allowed to enter," she said, suddenly terrified. Was he planning to kill her?

"Not through there. I'm taking you around back, to a secret entrance to my rooms. You can only enter through the dream world."

They ran across a field of poppies. Lying amid the flowers on his back with his eyes closed was Than.

"Wait a minute," she said. "Is that you?" She pointed to his sleeping form a few feet away from them.

"That's how I enter the dream world."

"So this isn't the real you?" She touched his chest. It felt good to touch him.

He covered her hand and held it against him. "It's as much the real me as it is the real you. Hard to explain. Just come on."

He led her inside a dome-shaped cavern with high ceilings and a river of fire. A grouping of instruments hung above the flames on one wall. Across from the river was a fireplace, also alight with flames, and arranged in front of it were two leather club chairs. In the center of the room, a table and two chairs looked like they were carved from gold.

"Welcome to my home," he said, his cheeks turning red. "Come, sit down."

Therese looked around in awe, the dome ceiling, curved high above them, reminding her of a cathedral. She took a seat across from him near the fire place in the cozy leather chair. "It's nice."

"You really like it?"

"Yes. I do." She looked up again at the ceiling, where their shadows danced.

Than gave her his adorable smile and leaned toward her, sitting on the edge of his seat. She sat forward, too, so their knees touched, her knees pressed together inside of his. She pressed them together to keep them from shaking. He took one of her hands, holding it on her thigh, hot beneath her sweats.

"I can't believe you're really here," he said. "I've fantasized about this for months."

"Why am I here? What's this all about?" She couldn't keep the resentment from her tone. He should have come for her months ago.

He told her all about his efforts to make her into a god in spite of the oath he and the Olympians took last summer. He told her about Aphrodite, about the maenads, about Dionysus, and about Ariadne and the Minotaur. As he spoke, the iron glove around her heart melted away. She put a hand to her mouth, taking it all in. He hadn't been too busy for her; he'd been busy because of her. She felt like a fool. She closed her eyes to hold in the tears, but they fell down her cheeks anyway.

He smoothed the tears away with his thumbs. "Don't cry."

"I'm so sorry I lost faith in you," she muttered. "I thought you didn't love me anymore. I thought once you returned to your duties, you realized you'd made a mistake, that I wasn't anything special, that you didn't want me."

"No." He stood and pulled her from the chair and into his arms. "No way."

She put her cheek against his chest and let him hold her. Even though she knew this was a dream, she also knew it was real, and it felt real. She could feel the rise and fall of his chest with each breath, could hear his heart pumping against her cheek.

He stroked her hair. "You know I had no choice but to take Vicki, right? You understand that?"

She looked into his eyes. "It was my fault, not yours. Besides, Hades makes no exceptions, does he," she said without inflection. "And you are under his command."

"Exactly."

"Have you ever disobeyed your father?"

He shook his head. "But I will if necessary, to be with you."

"Oh, Than."

He pulled her hard against him and kissed the top of her head, then cupped her chin in his hand and lifted her face to his. She met his eyes, and her body responded to the longing she recognized in them, the longing she knew her eyes also held. Softly, she whispered, "I can't believe this is happening."

"Believe it," he said, just before he covered her mouth with his.

She took his lips in hers, licking, sweeping, tasting. She couldn't resist taking his lower lip between her teeth and gently biting down.

"Mmm," he groaned.

He lifted her up in his arms and carried her from the room into another, following the river of fire, past a stalagmite holding a clock and quill to a round bed beneath a golden sword and shield. Next to the bed was a trickling waterfall cascading over a series of shelves carved from stone and displaying a beautiful shell collection. Three green plants, somewhat transparent, grew in pots beside the waterfall, and though Therese was amazed by the room, and able to take in every detail with the slow motion of a dream, she closed her eyes when Than laid her on his bed and kissed her. He climbed beside her, half on top of her, and cupped her head in his hands, lifting her face to his. The soft, sweeping, gentle kisses became hard and passionate and deep. Therese wrapped her arms around his neck and lifted her body against his.

His hand moved to her cheek, along her chin, down her neck, and gently caressed her collarbone at the top of her sweatshirt.

A moan escaped her lips as she slipped one hand from his neck and circled it around his back, pressing him to her. She tugged his dark wavy hair, pulling his lips harder against hers. Then she stopped, full of panic, and looked, wide-eyed, at Than. Were they going to have sex? She wasn't so sure she was ready for that, even in a dream.

"Therese? What's wrong?"

"I, it's just that, you can't get pregnant from a dream, right?"

His eyes burned with desire. In a low, steady voice, he said, "Right."

"Does that mean you, I mean, are we going to, you know?" She swallowed air, then sucked in her lips.

He smiled down at her. "We're not doing anything you're not ready for."

She hadn't realized she was holding her breath, but she let the air out now.

"Okay?" he asked.

"Okay."

He kissed her again and held her in his arms. "Besides, we still need to talk. I have something serious to discuss with you."

He rolled onto his back with his arm beneath her shoulders. She nestled in the crook of his arm, her cheek against his warm bare chest, her palm against his ripped abdomen. She'd never touched him like this, so freely, probably because she felt less inhibited in the dream world than in the real. She caressed his belly, feeling the muscle tone, every ripple, just above his waistband.

He moaned and stopped her hand, lacing his fingers into hers.

"What are you thinking?" she prayed. "Talk to me."

His answer came to her mind without him uttering it. He said, "I'm going to make you a god so you can come down here and be with me forever. But it's going to hurt. Really bad."

She gasped and prayed, "How did you do that? Communicate with me without talking?"

"This is a dream. The rules are different."

"Oh."

"You know Vicki would have taken the ketamine with or without you, don't you?"

"She didn't have the money. I don't know."

"She would have found a way."

"Maybe."

He stroked her hair and then her cheek. "Would you want to live here with me?"

"Yes."

"My grandmother knows a way. See, only Zeus can confer immortality on a human the normal way on Mount Olympus—where a mortal can drink ambrosia—but without Zeus's power, we have to use a more painful method. I'll understand if you can't do it. To be honest, I've had my doubts about asking you."

"What is it?"

"I'll take you to my grandmother's winter cabin where I'll anoint your body with ambrosia—to drink it without Zeus would kill you. Then I'll light your body on fire."

"What?"

"And your mortal body will burn to death as your immortal body rises from the ashes."

"Are you serious?"

"You don't have to do it. Forget it."

"No. I want to." Therese tried not to let the terror into her thoughts as she wondered if she could allow herself to be set on fire, if she could endure being burnt alive. She shivered at the thought, silently gasping for air, and tears came to her eyes. Though she doubted herself, though she worried at the last moment she would run away from it, she prayed to Than, "I can do it. I'd do anything to be with you. But what about the maenads?"

He put a hand on her cheek and looked into her eyes. "It's like you said: I'd do anything for you. I don't care about that. Once a year, what's that compared to an eternity without you?"

She gave him a sad smile. "Will your father allow this?"

As they lay quietly stroking one another, he told her what his father had proposed. He'd give them his blessing and aid, forcing Dionysus to help, if she proved herself worthy. He described the five challenges.

She sat up and spoke out loud, "You don't think I can do it!"

He sat up, too. "You think you can?"

She hopped off the bed and paced around the room. "No. But I want you to believe I can. Maybe I can. Maybe I can."

"No mortal can. He's giving you a set of impossible tasks to punish you for what you did last summer on Mount Olympus." He moved to the edge of the bed.

"If I fight the dragon, the Minotaur, and the Hydra, you'll be spared. Right? With Dionysus's help, the maenads will leave you alone."

He nodded. "Don't do it, Therese. At least, if we do it ourselves, your life won't be in danger. I can't risk losing you."

"But it's my choice, right? You'll honor my decision?"

He nodded again and took her in his arms. He sat on the bed with his feet on the floor and his legs spread open. She stood between his knees and held his head against her belly while he circled her waist with his arms.

"But please, think seriously about this," he said with his cheek against her sweatshirt. "I promise I can handle the maenads. If you can endure the fire…"

"But that's one time, Than. The maenads will rip you to pieces every year for, like, forever."

He lifted his eyes to hers, his chin against her stomach. "I only told you about the five challenges because Alecto said the choice should be yours, and she's right. But please don't make a hasty decision. You'll break my heart if you die."

She ran her fingers through his hair and kissed his forehead. "I won't let myself die."

He sighed. "Do you know how many times I've heard that right before I've led a soul here?"

"I won't let it happen. I'll think of something. I can feel it. You and I were meant to be together, I know it. I tried to love Pete. I'm sorry, but I did. And it felt so wrong. So wrong. And this, between you and me, it feels like it was always meant to be. So I can't die. I can't."

He stood up and pulled her into him. "I love you."

She looked up at him, feeling brave for the first time in her life, feeling more determined than ever to achieve something she wanted. "I". But before she could utter her thought, she woke up in her bed next to Clifford, and Than was gone.

Tossing and turning and checking her clock every few minutes for over an hour, she couldn't stand the idea that this was her one night with Than and she couldn't get to him because she couldn't fall asleep. "Help me," she finally prayed. "Help me fall asleep."

He appeared beside her, shocking her. She hadn't expected him to come.

"My presence won't kill you," he said, stroking her cheek. "But it will make you . . ."

Before he could complete his sentence, she was back in the dream, only now on the bed beside him.

"Tell me what you were about to say," he whispered.

They lay against one another on his round bed facing each other with the waterfall trickling beside them. The glimmer from the river of fire sparkled in Than's eyes.

"I was going to say, I love you, too."

They held one another in the dream world for the rest of the night, but at dawn, Than kissed her once more and vanished. She found herself floating in the clouds above her grandparents' old neighborhood. Hip appeared beside her.

"He had to go back to guide the dead, but I'll hang out with you, if you'd like."

"Do you know about the five challenges?"

"Yeah. You've got to try, Therese. Don't let the maenads have my brother."

"I'm going to try. I'm going to try my hardest. Your dad said I had to do it alone, but he didn't say I couldn't use the gifts I already have, right? I can use Aphrodite's traveling robe and Artemis's invisibility crown. I wonder where the sword and shield are that Hephaestus made me last summer."

"I'll find out." He moved closer. "Hey, you're waking up."

She opened her eyes to the bright sunlight streaming into her room, and though she was frightened of what lay ahead, she also felt excited to finally have some control over her own destiny.

Chapter Nineteen: Than Prepares

Than should have known Therese would choose to fight for him, but he wasn't going to stand by and let her die. He would hover from a safe distance, so as not to drain her life force, and the moment she was mortally injured, he would carry her off to his grand-mother.

He stood outside the palace at Mount Olympus and said, "Spring, Summer, Winter, and Fall, open the gates of Olympus so I, Thanatos, may enter."

A loud roar carried through the air, and a tunnel of cold wind lifted in front of him. As the wind settled and the rain cloud emptied its contents and dissipated, the giant wall of clouds opened, and Than stepped through. The wall of clouds closed behind him as he crossed the golden-paved plaza and passed the fountain spraying water beneath a rainbow from the spout of a golden whale. He took the rainbow steps, passed the marble columns, and entered the palace.

He was on his way to see Hephaestus to ask after Therese's sword and shield and had put his hand on the knob to the forge when the sound of voices raised in anger coming from the courtroom made him pause.

A movement across the foyer caught his eye, and he turned to see Hestia clearing dishes from the dining room table. She put a finger to her lips and beckoned him inside.

He crossed the foyer, and once beside her, asked, "What's going on in there?"

"Alecto's been here. She told your mother about the five challenges. She also told her about your desire to make Therese a god without Dionysus's help."

"They know I plan to break my oath."

"That's not all. Persephone went to Zeus and begged him to intervene by convincing your father to forget about the challenges. She wants Zeus to force Dionysus to help you. She's so upset with Hades. But Zeus sees no reason to contradict him. Ares got wind of it, and now he's offended that Hades would work in league with Dionysus against him. He's against the challenges, too, but for different reasons than your mother."

For most of his life, Than was spared from the constant conflict among the gods at Mount Olympus, one of the few advantages of dwelling in the Underworld; but now he found himself the center of their attention, and he didn't like it. Why should they control his fate? He was tired of being another cog in the wheel. He wouldn't stand for it. He thanked Hestia and swiftly left the room to confront the other gods.

When Than entered the court, the room became quiet and all eyes turned to him. Every throne was occupied except for those belonging to Hades and Poseidon, who spent their time in their respective palaces beneath the world and sea. Before Than could speak his mind to those present, Zeus spoke in his angry, earth-quaking voice.

"If you break your oath on the River Styx, Thanatos, you will never be allowed to enter these palace walls again. Do you understand?"

So they would exile him. Wasn't he already exiled most of the time? "I understand, Lord Zeus, but my problem could be remedied if Dionysus would do me the favor. He took no oath." Than glanced at Aphrodite, who quickly turned her gaze to the marble floor.

"If Hades hadn't already made this deal with you, I might have intervened, but now I can't risk turning my brother against me over this minor matter."

Than looked across the room at his mother and grandmother, seated on their double throne. His mother was in tears, his grandmother holding her hand and comforting her.

"Can't you just forget this girl?" Artemis suddenly said.

He knew the virgin goddesses would never understand him, so he turned to Aphrodite and Hera, natural enemies most of the time, and silently prayed to them. "Aphrodite, goddess of love, stand by me. Queen Hera, patron of all wives and mothers, feel my aching heart."

Hera's face softened. Than thought she would speak, but it was Hermes who crossed the room to Than's side. "These two lovers won't give up. Therese is willing to fight for Thanatos. I say let her. Thanatos is willing to accept the consequences of breaking his oath. What more is there to say? If he'll withstand the maenads and exile for the rest of eternity, justice will be served."

Persephone stood from her throne. "Justice? I'm so sick of justice! What happened to mercy? Two souls love one another. Why can't we let them be happy?"

Aphrodite stood and said, "Hear, hear!"

The room roared with angry voices until Zeus's thundering growl silenced them. "To answer your question, Persephone, there are too many interests at stake. The girl had her chance to avenge her parents' death last summer. She made her choice. The court agreed on a plan of action. The power of this court would be undermined if we didn't uphold its decisions."

"Hear, hear!" Ares said, mocking Aphrodite with a mischievous smile.

"This discussion is over," Zeus commanded. He stood from his throne and left the room by way of his chamber door, directly behind his throne.

Than went to his mother and grandmother. "Trust me. Don't make any more trouble for me here."

"The thought of my son being torn to pieces every year…"

"Please, Mother." He kissed the top of her head and then crossed the room to Hephaestus.

"Sir, you made a sword and shield for Therese last summer. Do you know what became of them?"

Hephaestus put a hand on Than's shoulder, smiled kindly—his ugly, misshapen face taking on a kind of beauty—and said, "I have them in my forge. I recovered them from the battleground. I don't like to see my handiwork wasted. Listen, I'm sorry for your troubles. And if there's anything I can do to help, I will. I hate that dastardly god of war, for reasons I'm sure you know, and like my wife, I like to see lovers united in marriage."

Than smiled for the first time that day.

Chapter Twenty: The Little Black Box of Beauty

Therese climbed out of bed, recalling the dream. As she turned on Jewels's lamp and headed to her bathroom, she thought it was probably just an ordinary dream—a nice one, the best, but ordinary. It reminded her that her heart belonged to Than no matter how hard she tried to love Pete. But when she climbed beneath the warm water of the shower, the realness of the dream came back to her. Than had come to her in the dream world. They spent the night together in his room. He told her what he'd been doing to get them together again—about the maenads, Dionysus, and the Minotaur. He told her about the five challenges. The determination she felt when she had first awakened returned. It hadn't been an ordinary dream, and she was eager to get started.

She rinsed the shampoo from her hair and prayed to Than, "I miss you already. It won't be long. I promise. I'll start today."

After her shower, she dressed and went downstairs to take Clifford outside. Carol and Richard sat at the granite breakfast bar eating bowls of cereal. Therese had been avoiding them since Vicki's death, but she knew they wanted to talk to her more about what had happened. She hoped it wouldn't be today. She didn't want anything to sour her mood and dampen her determination to face the five challenges. She gave them a smile and said, "Good morning," on her way out the back door.

Once in the woods, she prayed to Aphrodite, asking her to bring her the little black box, or to tell her where she should go to find it. Following Clifford up the trail into the woods behind her house, where the birds chirped and flitted from tree to tree and an occasional chipmunk scrambled across her path, she looked for signs of the goddess.

"Come on, Clifford," she said when he stopped to sniff the grass. "Let's keep going."

She heard a rustle in the brush ahead of her and froze. In her mind, she asked, "Aphrodite?" though she expected to see a deer. She heard the rustle again, and studied the brush in front of her. She could see no signs of an animal but definitely sensed a presence.

"Hello?" Therese said meekly.

A figure appeared before her, but it wasn't Aphrodite; it was Jen. She held the invisibility crown in one hand and wiped tears from her eyes with the back of the other.

"Jen? What's wrong?"

"Same old, same old." Her voice quivered as she spoke.

"Your dad?"

Jen nodded.

Clifford noticed her from across the trail and ambled over to greet her.

Jen leaned down to pet him and gave him a smile. "Hi, Clifford."

"You wanna talk?" Therese asked.

"Sure. Can we go to your room?"

"Come on."

They took the trail down through the forest, past the elms, when Therese noticed a little black box, the size of a Rubik's Cube, on the wooden deck. She picked it up, her heart pounding.

"What's that?" Jen asked.

"I'm not sure."

"Open it."

Therese clamped the lid tight. "Not now. Come on."

They entered the house through the back door, by the kitchen. Carol and Richard stood at the sink rinsing out their breakfast bowls.

"Can Jen come over for a while?" Therese asked.

"What about breakfast?" Carol asked. "Are you hungry, Jen?"

"No thanks."

"I'm not either," Therese added.

Carol glanced up at Richard, who nodded and said, "Let us know when you're hungry, and we'll fix you something, okay?"

"Thanks."

The two girls skipped up the stairs followed by Clifford. Therese put the wooden box in a dresser drawer, hoping Jen would ask no more about it. "So tell me what's going on," she asked as she refilled Clifford's food and water bowls and added more water to Jewels's tank.

Jen sat on the bed, cradling the crown. "My dad won't stop drinking again. My mom keeps threatening to throw him out, but I don't believe her. She likes having him around to help with the ranch. It makes me feel like she loves him more than she does me." Tears poured from Jen's eyes.

Therese sat beside her on the bed, unable to imagine how Jen must feel. Therese's parents would never have hurt her or put her in harm's way. She shivered at their memory, and her longing to be with them resurfaced. Therese shoved it back down and swallowed. "She probably doesn't know what to do. She's human. And humans make mistakes and don't always know the right answers. Have you thought about calling someone, like a social worker?"

"I'm afraid they'll take me and Bobby away. I'd rather stay and use the crown."

"Has it helped then?"

Jen nodded. "I don't know what I'd do without it. I sleep on the floor in my closet with it on every night. I pin it to my hair so it won't fall off. He's only come in my room once, but still. It was terrifying. He acts like he just wants a hug, but when he's drunk, he doesn't know how to stop." Jen shuddered and put on the crown. "Don't look at me."

Therese lowered her gaze to the floor. "I'm so sorry. I don't know what to say except that I'm glad the crown helps."

Jen took it off. "How does it work? Where did you get it?"

"I told you not to ask."

"Please? I've just told you the worst secret ever. Can't you tell me yours?"

Therese considered Jen's question. Could she trust Jen not to tell a soul if she told her everything about Than and the other gods? It would be nice to have someone, someone human, to talk to. "Well," her stomach lurched. She couldn't risk it. She couldn't risk spoiling her chances to be with Than. "There's no real secret, Jen. Someone gave it to me. I think she was my guardian angel. I'm not sure. Maybe my mom."

"You could have kept it for yourself."

"You need it more right now. But I might need to take it back, for a short while."

"Why?"

"Not today. But maybe soon. I'll give it right back."

"You're not going to tell me why?"

"Do I have to?"

Jen shook her head. "You aren't going to take any more drugs, are you?"

"No." Therese's stomach felt sick as she thought of Vicki.

"Why'd you do it?"

"She wanted to see her mom. I wanted to see my parents." Therese bit the inside of her lip.

"That's crazy."

"I know."

Jen looked up at Therese and put a hand on her shoulder. "Thanks for loaning me the crown. I don't know what I'd do without it."

Therese hugged her friend. "You're welcome."

"Now let's open that box," Jen stood up and went to the dresser drawer, opening it.

Therese leapt across the room, her chest tight, her heart pounding. "No!" She reached for the box. For one horrible split second, the box slipped from the hands of both girls and dangerously dropped through the air. Therese gasped and caught it just before it hit the floor.

"You don't know what you almost did." Therese looked at Jen with wide eyes. Her future life with Than would have vanished from the realm of possibility.

"What? What's in there?"

Therese thought quickly. "My parents' ashes."

"I didn't know they were cremated. They fit in that?"

"Yeah."

"Then why were they out on the deck?"

"The box got wet, and I wanted to put it in the sun to dry."

"Then why did you act like you didn't know what it was?"

"I didn't want you to know I like to carry the box around. It makes me feel closer to my parents."

"Oh." Jen sat on the bed. "Don't be embarrassed about that. Okay?"

"Okay. Thanks."

"Are you coming to groom Stormy today?"

"After lunch."

Relief swept over Therese once Jen left. The thought of what had almost happened made her tremble. She set the box on her dresser, afraid to hold it in her quaking hands, moving it to the center, away from the edges, staring at it. Now what was she supposed to do? She silently prayed to Persephone and Aphrodite for further instructions.

Two figures appeared on either side of her. Boys. Twins. They had deep red hair, long and thick like the mane of a lion, and fierce black eyes. They were beautiful, but they frightened her.

She took a step back, sucking in her lips, her heart speeding beneath her ribs. Clifford cowered beside her with his paws over his eyes.

"I'm Phobos," one of them said. "And this is my brother, Deimos."

"We're sons of Aphrodite," Deimos explained.

Clifford started whining.

"Aphrodite?" Therese wanted to be grateful, wanted to believe they were there to help her, but fear choked her and panic gave her the shakes. "I-I-I'm Therese. It's…" She fought the irrational terror taking hold of her. She wanted to attack the boys with her bedside lamp. How crazy was that? "A pleasure to meet you." The air rushed from her body. She clinched her hands together to keep them from trembling and to keep them from flailing out.

The two brothers exchanged looks of surprise and laughed.

"A pleasure to meet us?"

"Us?"

"Y-y-es. I adore your mother." She wanted to flee from the room. She couldn't breathe. In her mind, she screamed, "Help!" to Than, to Hermes, to anyone who'd listen. "Help me, please!"

The boys frowned.

"It's never a pleasure to meet us."

"You're lying."

"Try-trying t-to be p-p-polite!"

"Have you ever taken a good look at yourself in the mirror?" Phobos asked. "You could use a pick-me-up."

"The beauty charm in our mother's box could serve you well, ugly. Think Than wants a plain girl like you at his side?"

Therese backed into the corner of her room. "Go away!" The panic and fear claimed her heart, erratic and mad, adrenaline pumping through every vein in her trembling body. She screamed. The twins laughed. She screamed again.

The door to her room swung open, the twins vanished, and Carol and Richard rushed in.

"Therese!" Carol cried. "What's happening?"

Therese gaped at them.

"Therese?" Richard asked. "You okay?"

"I'm not sure."

"What made you scream?" Carol asked.

"I don't know. I think maybe I was having a nightmare. Maybe I was sleepwalking just now. I don't know."

Carol and Richard exchanged worried glances.

"Why don't you come downstairs and watch a little TV with us, sweetheart?" Carol suggested. "I'll make you some hot tea."

Therese glanced at the black box on her dresser. Carol followed her gaze.

"Oh, what's that?" Carol asked, crossing the room and taking the box in her hands.

"Don't open it!" Therese shouted. "Put it down!"

Carol did not put down the box, but instead looked Therese hard in the eye and asked, "Then tell me what's in it."

"A gift."

"For whom?"

"Uh, I, um, Jen."

"Then why didn't you give it to her earlier?"

Richard took the box from Carol. "This better not be drugs. Are there drugs in here? Were you hallucinating just now?"

"No! No! I promise! I'm not taking drugs."

Richard cupped the bottom of the box in one hand and the lid in the other.

"Don't!"

He pulled the lid from the box.

Therese dropped to her knees. It was over, her life with Than forever out of reach.

Richard and Carol looked inside.

"Oh," Carol said. "A ring. It's lovely. For Jen?"

Therese lifted her eyes and examined her aunt and uncle. They looked unchanged. Why hadn't the beauty charm escaped and transformed them? Not that they weren't already attractive people. "Um..."

Carol plucked the ring from the box and held it up in the light. "Is it silver? Or white gold?"

Therese stared at the thin metal band, wondering if the charm only worked when the ring was placed on a person's finger. "Silver." Please don't put it on, she thought. Please.

Carol closed her eyes for a moment and sighed. When she opened them again, she asked, "Did this belong to your mom?"

Not knowing what else to do, Therese nodded.

"There's nothing wrong with giving it to Jen. Did you think I'd be upset?"

Therese nodded again.

Carol tucked it back inside the box. "I'm sorry we didn't trust you. It's just that, well, after what happened…"

"I know." Therese climbed to her feet.

Richard returned the lid to the box and handed it over. The two of them hugged her, asked again if she was okay, and, after she told them she was, left her alone with her pets and the box.

She returned the box to her dresser, wondering now if it was all over. She had failed to deliver it to Persephone without opening it. Technically, she hadn't opened it. Her uncle had. Did that count?

She asked Than to send her a message. What was she supposed to do?

She looked up from the box to her reflection in the mirror over her dresser. The red-haired twins had called her ugly and plain. She knew she wasn't beautiful, but was she ugly? She studied her features and thought they'd been right. Why had Than chosen her, of all the girls in the world? She was the first to ever kiss him. Was he sure he loved her? Would he always love her? For all eternity? Or would he grow tired of her plain looks?

Maybe she should take a bit of the beauty from the ring. Just a little, so Than wouldn't spend eternity regretting his decision. She could still return the ring to the box. It had already been opened. It had already been touched by her aunt. Who would know if Therese slipped it on her finger?

She put her hand on the lid, her fingers tingling. No. There was still a chance she hadn't failed. She pulled her hand away and flung herself on her bed.

Throughout the day, Therese searched for signs of what she should do with the box, continually praying to Persephone, Aphrodite, and Than, to the point she worried she was either annoying them or had already failed and no god wanted to speak to her again. She sat on her bed with her laptop and researched the five challenges. She read the story about Cupid and Psyche. Aphrodite tested Psyche with the black box of beauty, and Psyche failed.

She researched the golden apples of the Hesperides. Hera was given the orchard as a wedding gift. They were her apples. Maybe Therese could find a way to get a golden apple without having to fight the dragon. Hmm.

It was a relief to leave after lunch, after hiding the box in the bottom drawer of her dresser beneath several pairs of sweats, to groom Stormy at the Holts.

That is, until Pete came into the barn.

He sauntered up to her with a confident smile and took her in his arms. "Afternoon, good-lookin'," he said with his chin on the top of her head. He released her and pecked her nose. "I sure enjoyed last night."

"Me, too." She plucked Stormy's brush from a shelf, trying to keep her hands from shaking. "Isn't Jen coming?"

"I told her I'd groom Sassy today. Hope that's okay." It was Sunday, which meant no trail rides. He stepped to the back of the stall to avoid getting between Stormy and Sassy.

"Sure. I just thought she might want to talk, that's all." Therese sat on a stool at the front of the stall and held the brush out for Stormy to inspect. Then she gently rubbed Stormy's withers. Stormy didn't need to be groomed at such a young age, but the Holts wanted him trained and used to people before he was weaned. "She told me how hard it's been on her with your dad..."

Pete's voice was low and strained when he said, "Let's not talk about that right now."

"I'm sorry."

They brushed in the silence for a while, and then Pete asked, "So how about a movie sometime this week? We could go to dinner, too, if you want."

Therese closed her eyes and took a deep breath.

"You don't seem enthusiastic," Pete said, standing over her.

She looked up at him from her stool, unaware till that moment he could see her face. She opened her mouth to speak, but nothing came out.

"A change of heart already?" he asked softly. He took her hand and lifted her to him, searching her eyes.

The last thing she wanted to do was hurt him. Her stomach clenched into a tight knot and the rest of her body went numb. His eyes were full of hurt. "Pete, I..."

He kissed her, and though she accepted the first gentle kiss, she pulled her lips away. "I'm sorry. I'm confused, Pete. I still have feelings for Than."

He closed his eyes and sighed. Then he squeezed her hand and said, "Let me know when you're over him."

She stood there as he put away Sassy's brush and left the barn with his head down.

After dinner, Therese sat on her bed with Clifford and stared at the little black box on her dresser. Could her chances with Than really be over so soon, on the very first challenge? If Hades cared at all about justice, then no. For the first time since her failure last summer on Mount Olympus, she directed a prayer to Hades. She stood up, stared fiercely at her reflection over the dresser, and said in a low, angry voice, "I have not failed. I have not failed. Send me to Persephone, so I can deliver the box."

She waited. Nothing happened.

She put her hands to her head and pulled her hair. "Then I'm going to Mount Olympus to look for her myself!" It was summer. Persephone should be with her mother, Demeter. Than told her that in fall and winter, when Persephone returned to the Underworld, Demeter left Mount Olympus and shut herself up in a winter cottage on Mount Parnassus. But in spring and summer, both goddesses lived on Mount Olympus.

Therese took the traveling robe from her closet and slipped her arms through each sleeve. Picking up the box, she imagined herself in the middle of the court, and before she could think twice about what she was doing, the invisible plastic wrapped around her, and she was god traveling.

She closed her eyes, afraid to discover where she had landed, when her feet hit solid ground, and afraid to look upon the gods without warning. Last summer, they had protected her from their brightness, but would they today, after she barged into the palace uninvited?

In her mind, she prayed, "Please accept me, please accept me, please accept me."

"Open your eyes, Therese," came a woman's soft voice.

Therese peeked through one half-closed lid to find Persephone before her, her hands on the box.

"Thank you for delivering the box to me. You have completed your first challenge."

Therese opened her other eye and looked around the court. Not all the gods were present today. The virgin goddesses—Athena, Artemis, and Hestia—were absent, as were all the gods save Zeus and Hephaestus. The latter now approached her carrying a sword and shield. Her sword and shield.

"Much luck to you," Hephaestus said, handing them to her. "And congratulations for getting this far."

Therese accepted the weapon and shield from Hephaestus and thanked him with a bow.

His misshapen face crinkled into a grin full of deep lines and hanging flesh, reminding Therese of a French bulldog. Now that she had a good look at him, he didn't seem ugly. He wasn't beautiful, but he wasn't ugly either. He had character. "If there's anything more I can do to help, please let me know," he said.

"Thank you, sir. But I'm not allowed to accept help with the five challenges."

"But you can accept advice."

Therese glanced around the palace courtroom where only a few goddesses remained talking among themselves. No one paid attention to her and Hephaestus. "Yes. Yes, I can."

"So how can I help?"

"Can you tell me how I might get Hera to like me?"

"I'm afraid not. She's my mother, but she has no love for me because I'm ugly."

Therese frowned. "Sir, you're not ugly to me."

He gave her another crinkly smile.

She bowed to him once again and turned toward Hera, her heart picking up speed and pulsing in her throat. She wasn't sure yet what she was going to say, but she had to try something. A hundred heads were too many for anyone, except maybe Hercules, even with the crown of invisibility.

In her mind, she prayed to Hera, "May I approach you?"

Hera turned to her and bid her forward to her throne, Zeus's side still unoccupied. A lucky break, Therese thought.

"What do you ask of me?" Hera said.

Therese had trouble forming a thought much less a string of words. She bowed her head and said, "Hades has given me a set of challenges."

"I'm aware of what goes on in this court."

Okay, not a good start. "I don't want to offend you by taking a golden apple from your orchard without your permission."

"Permission granted, so long as you don't eat the apple. Return it to Mount Olympus intact."

"Could you give it to me, madam? I would be happy to serve you."

"You would serve me even without the favor."

Oh, no. Therese just did what she'd hoped to avoid. She had offended Hera. "Yes, madam."

"Then bring me a fan made of peacock feathers when you deliver the golden apple."

Therese nodded and bowed. "How will I get past the one-hundred-headed dragon?"

"A bit of cake laced with sleeping pills will put Ladon to sleep, but he's not your problem. The Hesperides won't fall for that trick."

She'd read online the Hesperides were three nymphs, daughters of Atlas, but she found nothing more about them. "How can I convince them to let me take an apple?"

"Distract them with your flute. Now leave me. I've other matters to attend to."

Therese meant to ask where Hera's garden was located, but she didn't dare delay the goddess.

Chapter Twenty-One: Than's Objection

Than had hovered above Therese's house watching the sons of Aphrodite and Ares, Fear and Panic, taunt Therese as she held the little black box. He shouldn't have been surprised by her resistance to their powers. Her strong will had amazed him from the beginning. But when the twin gods had finally vanished, and Therese had looked at her reflection with new doubts about her beauty, he wanted to kill the boy lions with his bare hands.

He rushed to his father's chambers to object, his heart pumping fast and loud, like it might burst from his chest. Hades sat at a golden table with Tizzie and Meg, apparently arguing. They all three looked up as Than approached, unable to hide his anger.

"Ares had no right!" Than spat the words out as he crossed the room. "You said no gods could intervene."

"I said help," Hades corrected. "I said no god may help her."

"And I thought you were the god of justice!"

"These are challenges, Thanatos. The more challenging, the better the victory."

"Hah! Admit it. You want her to fail!"

Hades didn't hide the smile creeping across his face as he stood and met Than's eyes, their noses inches apart. "I want her to pay! She was an embarrassment to me last summer. If she's to join us here in my palace, I want her to suffer first."

"The punishment should fit the crime!" Than said.

"Agreed!" Hades bellowed. "I said those very words to your sisters before you arrived. They want to drag on too long the punishment of a murderer in Paris before they bring him here. I think they are motivated by something other than justice."

The Furies stood up, their eyes changing from blue in one and brown in the other to dark red. Blood dripped to their cheeks.

"Who doesn't love Paris?" Tizzie hissed.

"We'll leave you now," Meg snarled.

The Furies vanished.

Hades crossed his arms at his chest. "And you are, too, Thanatos."

"She had compassion for a man who was no longer a threat to her. She refused to kill him in cold blood. How is that a failure?"

"He deserved death. Her parents deserved vengeance. You deserved her to keep her word! She's the one who let you down, son. Not me. She chose to have mercy on that killer over becoming your wife. Doesn't that bother you even a little?"

Than's throat tightened and no words came. He could think of nothing to say. Yes, it had bothered him. It had bothered him a lot. Only her prayers in the aftermath of the battle convinced him of her love. Her prayers, not her actions.

The challenges gave her the opportunity to remedy that. His father was right.

Chapter Twenty-Two: The Golden Apple

Back in her room in Colorado, relieved she succeeded in her first challenge, Therese searched the internet for more information about Hera's golden apple orchard. She sat on her bed with her laptop across her legs and Clifford curled up beside her. Most websites placed the orchard in the Atlas Mountains of Morocco in Northwest Africa. One website described a fabled orchard in Marrakesh on the edge of the Majorelle Garden.

Therese wondered why it was called a fabled garden. If Hades wanted her to pluck an apple and bring it to Mount Olympus, the garden must exist, but wouldn't at least one website verify that? The only logical explanation for the lack of information about the orchard was that it must be invisible to mortals, and if it was invisible, how would Therese be able to find it?

Gods weren't supposed to help her face the challenges, but they could advise her, as Hephaestus pointed out. Therese closed her laptop, knelt on the floor, and pulled her flute case and music stand from beneath her bed. She played a new ballad she learned her junior year as a tribute to Hermes, and as her fingers slipped over the cool metal keys of the instrument, she prayed for his advice.

Not long into the ballad, Hermes appeared in the chair beneath her window, playing his pipe in harmony with her flute. The effect was so beautiful that tears welled in her eyes. She couldn't believe she was contributing to such a perfect sound, the smooth notes reaching high in a trill, only to go low, slow, and long. Her fingers trembled; she didn't want to ruin the beautiful song with a wrong note. When the song finally ended unmarred by her, Therese smiled with both relief and gratitude across the room at the messenger god. "Thank you."

"My pleasure," Hermes said, without getting up. "To answer your question: To see Hera's apple orchard, wear the crown from Artemis.

Only when you're invisible to mortal eyes will you be able to see what mortals cannot see."

Before Therese could ask another question, or thank him for his advice, Hermes disappeared.

Hermes's advice reminded Therese of a fact she'd forgotten: Artemis's crown made her invisible to mortal eyes. The immortal beings could still see her. The crown might help her find the orchard, but it wouldn't protect her from being seen by the Hesperides or the one-hundred-headed dragon, not to mention the Minotaur and the Hydra. She'd been counting on the advantage of invisibility. Even if she were successful in the second challenge, what chance did she have against the two monsters if they could see her?

Therese slumped on her bed, twisting her bedcovers in her hands. This was crazy. She would die. Last summer at Mount Olympus, she was ready to die. She longed for her parents and knew her aunt would be protected by Ares, as part of their deal in her accepting the choice to fight McAdams. But now that she better understood what a life at Than's side would mean, she wanted to live. She didn't want to be like her parents in the Underworld, without free will, without personality, and without much knowledge of the existence of others. She wanted to live.

Though after what happened with Vicki, she would rather die than face her friends when it was time to go back to school. If she could live with Than, she could escape those judging eyes. Poor Vicki. Maybe she could do something for her once she was a god.

But making it through the challenges seemed impossible to her now. Than was right when he said the challenges were designed to punish her. Maybe she shouldn't have accepted them so hastily. Maybe she should have allowed Than to take her directly to Demeter's winter cottage and turn her himself, even though it meant torture forever for him. At least they'd be together.

No. She couldn't stand the thought of him being ripped to pieces every year. Her death was better than his torture. She had to try.

And it was too late to turn back now. She'd already accepted the challenges, and she'd completed the first of them. There was nothing to do but to keep going.

Monday morning, Therese went, for the first time since Vicki's funeral, to swim practice with Jen at the city natatorium, their high school pool still under repair from the earthquake damage. As Jen drove them home afterward, Therese brought up the crown.

"I'll have it back to you tonight," Therese promised, though she worried she might not be able to keep it.

Jen looked at her like a wilted flower, quavering in the wind. She nodded and returned her eyes to the road. Before dropping off Therese, she drove to her own house and got the crown.

"I'll come by later." Therese climbed from the pickup with the crown hidden beneath her towel.

After eating a burger Richard had picked up in town, Therese sat on the living room sofa beside Carol, who had her laptop resting on the coffee table where she worked her pharmaceutical sales. Sometimes Carol had to travel out of town, but she was never gone for more than a few days at a time.

"Everything okay?" Carol asked.

Therese shrugged. She couldn't say how wrong it seemed that she had lived and Vicki had died. She also couldn't tell how she was about to put herself in danger and wanted to sit with Carol awhile in case it was the last time. She wanted to say, "I'm scared," but instead she said, "Yeah."

Carol put an arm around Therese's shoulders and they leaned back on the sofa. Therese crossed her ankles on the coffee table, something her parents allowed and used to do themselves. Carol closed her laptop and did the same.

"Maybe we should do something fun together this week," Carol said. "We could go rafting, or we could take the Silverton train. What sounds good to you?"

Therese shrugged again. "It doesn't matter to me. Whatever you want to do."

"I can take a break now if you want to watch a movie together."

Therese wanted to watch a movie. She wanted to sit quietly beside her aunt, her last remaining blood relative, and feel her close beside her once more before facing the immortal monsters. But if she wanted to start the first challenge today, she didn't have much time before it would be dark in Marrakesh. According to the web, there was a seven-hour time difference between Colorado and Morocco. "How about tonight, after supper?" Hopefully, she'd be alive and back by then.

"Okay, sweetheart."

"I'm going to take a nap." Therese got up from the sofa and went upstairs, Clifford on her heels. She was ready to put on the traveling robe from Aphrodite.

The Majorelle Garden in Marrakesh, Morocco bustled with tourists weaving up and down floral-lined stone paths and over bridges across ponds of lily pads and through antique stone buildings full of paintings. Cobalt blue fountains, railings, and trim unified the otherwise multicolored flowers and foliage. Therese sifted through the crowd and found her way just outside the garden near the trails leading up the Atlas Mountains. A dozen tents and donkeys peppered the valley with the aromas of freshly cooked dinners wafting toward the sky. Picnic tables, scattered across the valley, held tourists eating the food these makeshift restaurants prepared beneath their tents. Therese's belly rumbled at the delicious smells even though back in Durango, she'd just eaten a burger and was full. It was lunchtime back home; here, it was seven in the evening.

She wondered what these people thought of her wearing the silk robe, the golden scabbard at her waist, and the golden shield on her back, carrying a flute in one hand and a crown in the other. Maybe they thought she was an entertainer. It occurred to Therese that, indeed, she was, for Hades.

She wore her purse strapped around her neck and hanging at one hip. It carried a cinnamon roll leftover from breakfast and stuffed with SleepAid caplets and the Prozac she never finished taking. Scouring the landscape for the perfect place to disappear, she trekked past the tents and picnic tables into a copse of pines leading up a mountain. Once she was in the thick of them, she placed the crown on her head as her heart sped up and her fingers twitched.

Immediately, the landscape changed. The pines disappeared, and in their place were fruit trees. She stood between a row of pear and another of orange. Taking a few hesitant steps, she saw no sign of the three nymphs or their dragon. With trembling hands, she put the flute to her bottom lip and played, telling herself that it would be okay if she died. She wouldn't know any better. The Lethe would wipe away her memories and infuse her with a pleasant feeling of contentment for all eternity.

When she reached the end of the rows, she froze. Her fingers would no longer move and all the air rushed out of her body, leaving her nothing to blow across the flute. Three beautiful ladies lounging on the thick, gnarly roots of a giant apple tree looked up at her with their mouths open in surprise and delight, but wrapped around the trunk of the tree was the body of the biggest snake Therese had ever seen, its many green heads looking at her from the branches, blending with the green leaves except for their yellow eyes and flicking tongues. Round, golden apples hung from the branches, but none were within arm's reach from the ground. The ladies all had long black braids and skin the same color of the ashy brown tree trunk. If it weren't for their soft cotton gowns of different colors billowing in the gentle breeze, they would have blended in with the trunk and roots of the tree. Their dark eyes narrowed at Therese suspiciously, so she took in air—though it burned—and blew. The ladies smiled at her again.

One of the three hopped to her feet and took the hand of her sister. Soon all three danced to Therese's melody. She was afraid to stop, playing and playing for hours until the sun began to set, and her fingers felt raw and her throat tight. Worried she'd be too weak to fight if necessary, she stopped playing and decided to speak.

"Hello, Hesperides. My name is Therese. Hera gave me permission to pick an apple from her tree and take it to Mount Olympus."

The three ladies laughed, looking over their shoulder at Ladon's many heads glaring at Therese from the branches.

Therese opened her purse and took out the cinnamon roll. "Hera gave me a gift to give to Ladon." It wasn't exactly true. Technically, Hera hadn't given it to her. But it had been her idea. Too frightened to approach the tree and the nymphs, Therese tossed the roll through the air where it was caught and eaten by one of Ladon's hundred heads.

The middle and tallest nymph stepped toward Therese. "Why would Hera allow you to pick an apple and not one of us, who have been her servants for centuries?"

"She told me I wasn't to eat it, but to bring it to her."

This information made the nymph nod and reconsider Therese, but the other two dashed forward and took Therese by the arms.

"I want to keep her," one of them said.

"Me too," the other said.

Therese tried to pull free but couldn't loosen their hold on her.

"We're so bored," said one.

"We want you to stay and play for us."

Therese looked at the apple tree and noticed Ladon's hundred heads drooping from the branches, all two hundred eyes closed. She wasn't sure how long the drugs would work. She had to get away from the nymphs before the dragon awoke.

"I have an idea," Therese said. "I'll give you my flute and teach you to play if you let me take an apple from the tree while Ladon sleeps."

"He never sleeps."

The nymphs followed Therese's gaze to the tree, then turned to her with ravenous smiles.

"Ha!"

The three rushed to the tree and took several apples each, biting into them with pleasure, moaning and squealing with delight. Therese thought of grabbing one for herself and making a run for it, but she was afraid the nymphs could outrun her, and three to one were difficult odds to overcome. But she had a sword, and they were unarmed.

But they were nymphs and had special powers.

Then she remembered her silver robe. She'd used it to travel from her home in Colorado to the Majorelle Garden in Marrakesh. She'd never used it to travel a few yards at a time. Could she be that precise with god travel? She could dart to one of the upper branches, grab an apple, and then return to her bedroom. She decided to try.

She focused on a thick branch out of the reach of the nymphs. The invisible plastic wrapped around her, and she landed, precariously perched next to one of Ladon's heads. She lifted one leg in the air and leaned forward to maintain her balance and plucked an apple just as one of the nymphs screamed.

Ladon had awakened and had wrapped a neck around each of the nymphs. The head next to Therese's foot opened its eyes and glared at her. She focused on her room in Colorado, but nothing happened. Why couldn't she god travel? She tried again, but the snake pulled back its head, about to strike.

Therese jumped from the high branch and fell to the ground, landing on her hands and knees, pain shooting through her legs and arms and back, the crown tossed to the ground beside her. She could no longer see the garden or the snake as she scrambled to her feet, but the invisible snake grabbed a hold of her legs and yanked her toward the invisible tree. The skin on her arms scraped against the ground. She focused again on her bedroom in Colorado. The invisible plastic wrapped itself around her and she fell to the floor in her room, the golden apple still clutched in her hand.

She did it! She got the apple! She jumped to her feet and looked at her victorious reflection in her dresser mirror.

Then she remembered the crown. What would Jen do without it? She had to go back! But how would she find the orchard without it? She wouldn't be able to see what's invisible to mortal eyes unless she wore the crown. Slumped on her bed, picturing Jen's face, she was overwhelmed by a blend of disappointment and terror. She had to find a way to protect her friend, especially since she hadn't been able to protect Vicki.

The next morning, Jen called to say she wasn't going to swim practice; Therese would have to find another ride.

Therese's eyes squeezed closed as she clutched the phone to her ear. "Are you sick?"

"Sort of."

"What do you mean?"

"Why didn't you call last night? I didn't sleep a wink."

"Did your Dad…"

"No. I stayed in the barn with Stormy and Sassy."

"Jen, I'm…"

"It's not your fault. I'm sorry. It's not your fault I live with a pig."

"Stay with me tonight."

"Can I? That'd be great. Can I have the crown back?"

Therese couldn't think of what to say.

"Therese?"

"Yes. Of course you can."

That afternoon, after a trip with Carol to the craft store in Durango, Therese sat on the wooden floor of her room constructing a fan out of peacock feathers using a hot glue gun. The eight fluffy feathers were long and beautiful. She used the glue to attach them at the base. Then she wound blue yarn tightly around the bottom, gluing it in place, making a handle. She hoped Hera would be pleased. As she cleaned up, she prayed to the gods to inspire her to think of a way to get back the crown. She was surprised when Artemis appeared before her, the crown in her hand.

"The apple for the crown," Artemis said sternly.

"What?"

"You heard me."

"But I told Hera I would deliver the apple to her at Mount Olympus."

"Then I'll keep the crown."

"Wait!" Therese couldn't leave Jen without protection.

"Will it still count? My challenge, I mean? If I give you the apple, will it still count as a victory?"

"You're to deliver an apple to Mount Olympus."

"So that's a no?"

Artemis frowned with impatience.

Therese opened her dresser drawer, found the apple, and handed it over to Artemis.

Artemis gave her the crown and vanished.

Great, Therese thought. She was back at square one. Not wanting to waste any more time, she put her arms through the silver robe and strapped her sword and shield to her body. She doubted the cake of sleeping pills would work a second time, plus she had used all but one of the SleepAid caplets and all of her Prozac. But she had a plan. She would put on the crown and god travel directly to one of the branches of the tree, pick an apple, and disappear before Ladon could react. Now that she'd seen the tree, she should be able to go directly to it.

Just as she was about to god travel, she heard Carol calling up the stairs. "I'm making milkshakes, sweetheart. Want one?"

Therese grinned. Milkshake or dangerous mission to North Africa? Hmm. Tough choice. Then she decided she'd have both. "Sure. I'll be down in a minute." Might as well be an optimist.

She closed her eyes, focused on the golden apple tree, and…nothing. She blinked at her reflection in her dresser mirror. She recalled how she'd been unable to travel from the branch to her bedroom. Maybe something about the tree interfered? She closed her eyes and imagined the orchard. Nothing. Maybe it was the crown. She hadn't made it back to Colorado until the crown had fallen from her head.

She took the crown in one hand, closed her eyes, and focused again on the tree, and was instantly surrounded by invisible plastic. When she opened her eyes, she was standing in the copse of pines on the outskirts of Majorelle Garden.

This must mean she couldn't travel between visible and invisible locations.

She placed the crown on her head and saw the orchard surrounding her. She focused on the treetop and opened her eyes as soon as she felt her foot hit the branch.

One of Ladon's necks wrapped around her ankle as another prepared to strike. Therese pulled out her sword and sliced off the striking head, grabbed an apple, and cut her ankle free. She god traveled to the middle of the orchard, but the snake's long body lurched out at her with at least ten of its heads. Her heart pounded in her ears as she fell to the ground, nearly losing the crown as it slipped from her hair. She grabbed the crown with two fingers from the hand holding the sword, nearly cutting off her ear as she fell among the pines, focusing on her bedroom. The invisible plastic closed around her, and when it released her, she found herself sprawled on all fours on her bed, her sword sticking straight up from her mattress like Excalibur from its rock.

Her mattress might be ruined, and her right ear was bleeding, but at least she had the apple and the crown! She jumped from her bed, never happier, and lifted Clifford into her arms. He barked and wagged his tail excitedly.

It was time to go downstairs and have that milkshake.

Chapter Twenty-Three: Godliness

Than came to Mount Olympus more often in the past year than he had his entire life, and it seemed the other gods were less wary of his presence, which was good. He felt less disconnected from the rest of his kind. He had Therese to thank for that.

He avoided Hera's hard, cold gaze and did not look forward to her treatment of Therese when Therese arrived with the golden apple. Hera was not pleased by the gorging on her fruit by the Hesperides or by the injuries to her pet dragon, but worse was the fact that Artemis possessed one of her precious apples. The garden was a wedding present from Gaia to Hera when she married Zeus. The apples were precious to Hera, and she was stingy with them. They'd only been touched by others a few times, and the one stolen by Eris had been the start of the Trojan War. Eris had thrown the apple into the company of gods and goddesses with a note attached, "For the most beautiful," and three goddesses—Athena, Aphrodite, and Hera—had each claimed the apple belonged to her. They agreed to let a mortal named Paris choose. Hera was not chosen, though secretly Than believed she should have been. He wondered what Artemis planned to do with her apple.

Than knew Ares had just left the city of Paris for Mount Olympus and had timed his own arrival with that of the other god's. After a rendezvous with Aphrodite, Ares might be in a good mood. Than spoke with his mother and grandmother briefly then turned to the god of war, the only god present except for Zeus and Hephaestus.

Ares recoiled in surprise. "What could you possibly want from me, Cousin?"

"It's what you want, Ares."

"I'm listening."

"Which would you enjoy more: a quick slaughter or a more evenly matched battle?"

"You know the answer."

"Then join me tonight in the dream world to give Therese some advice on how best to face the Minotaur. She has no experience with her sword."

"Last summer was a disappointment."

"She'll die at the Minotaur's hands, but with your tips, she may delay her death and entertain you." And give me time to save her, Than thought.

"Tonight then."

Before Than turned to leave, he sensed Therese's presence. All of the gods toned down their brightness to prepare for mortal eyes, and in a split second, Therese appeared before Hera bearing a golden apple and a fan of peacock feathers.

Hera's raging voice made Therese fall to her knees. She set the apple and fan at the goddess's feet.

"What will Artemis do with my apple?" Hera screeched.

"I don't know," Therese said meekly, her eyes to the marble floor. "But it was the only way I could protect my friend. You're the goddess of marriage and children. Surely you understand my friend's need of the crown."

"You shouldn't have dropped it in the first place."

Than was about to speak on Therese's behalf when Zeus beat him to it. "She's only human, dear. Don't be so harsh. I'm pleased she's made it this far."

Therese dipped her head and climbed to her feet. As she turned to leave, she met Than's eyes and rushed to his side.

"I'll come to you tonight, in your dreams." He touched her lips with his and then left the palace before his presence made her weak. He hovered above to watch her from a safe distance.

He was surprised to see her walk across the palace floor to Hephaestus.

"I thought you might feel better knowing Hera doesn't like me either," she said.

"Not to worry," Hephaestus said with a crinkly smile. "Whoever is cursed by Hera is automatically protected by Zeus. You now have the special protection of the king of the gods."

At that moment, Than vowed to himself to help his cousin whenever it was in his power to do so.

Hades had given Than permission to change places with Hip once more because he'd been pleased by Therese's performance. Hip refused to trade until Therese was asleep, wanting to hold off the odious duties of death for as long as possible. So now, Than hovered above her house, waiting.

His heart lightened as he listened in on Therese's conversation with Jen. The two girls lay side by side on the bed with Clifford between them, their heads turned close, their voices low. Jen told stories about her horses, her brother Bobby, and a classmate they both disliked. Therese warmed him with her musical laugh, running her fingers over a hole in the middle of the mattress. He couldn't wait to hold her.

When the girls finally turned off the bedside lamp and said their goodnights, Than met Hip at the field of poppies and entered the world of dreams.

Chapter Twenty-Four: Ares

Therese fell on her knees in a dark alley, the pavement scraping her skin. She climbed to her feet and glanced in all directions. Tall buildings and garbage cans flanked the alley, along with a few cars, but Therese saw no sign of people, no sign of life at all, not even a stray cat or dog.

She was barefoot and wearing her nightshirt, which meant she was dreaming. Before she could kick off the ground and swim through the air to test this theory, someone grabbed her from behind, an arm wrenched around her neck. She couldn't break away.

"You know what they say is true don't you?" a gruff but familiar voice murmured at her ear. "If you die in your dream, you die for real."

The mention of the word dream reminded her that she could do what she wanted. She elbowed the man and god traveled away from him. Who needed a traveling robe in the dream world? She placed herself in her grandparents' old house in San Antonio, not sure why she ended up there so often. Maybe it was a place of comfort. Maybe it was because she associated the place with family. She shook her head. Why am I analyzing my dream now, while I'm still in the middle of it? This is crazy. She willed her grandparents on the living room couch, with Blue, their Blue Merle Australian Shepherd, on the green carpet at their feet.

She sensed a presence outside the front door. A quarter-inch gap appeared around the door, through which bright, ominous light spilled in. Therese pushed her full weight against the door, to keep whatever wanted in out, but the door dissolved, and she fell against the hard chest of Ares, god of war.

This is a dream, this is a dream, she repeated beneath her breath, as she stumbled back. "Figment, I command you to show yourself!"

"I'm no figment, Therese."

Therese god traveled from her grandparents' house to the wooden deck in Colorado.

I'm going to make this a happy dream, she said to herself. She willed a chipmunk to appear on the railing beside her.

"Come here, little fella."

The chipmunk hopped onto her hand and let her pet him. She fed him a handful of seeds. Then she thought of Puffy and turned the chipmunk into him. "Puffy! I miss you so much!" She pressed his soft, furry face against her cheek.

Ares appeared at her side wearing a wry smile. "I see why Hypnos and Thanatos admire you. But this won't help you defeat the Minotaur."

"Why do you care?" Shut up, Therese thought.

Ares laughed.

Than appeared at her side.

"Than? Is that really you?" She wondered if she should repeat her command for figments. She threw her arms around him instead, needing him, even if it was just a stupid figment. She'd take him any way she could get him.

He cupped her face and showered her with kisses, pressing his warm lips to her eyelids, her nose, her cheeks, her forehead, and her mouth. It felt so real. If only she could make Ares disappear. "Make him disappear," she prayed to Than with her eyes closed.

"He's here to help you."

She opened her eyes. "What? Why?"

"Can we please get started?" Ares said impatiently. "I don't have all night."

"He's agreed to teach you how to fight."

"He killed my parents! I don't want his help!"

Her scabbard and shield appeared strapped to her body, startling her.

Than kissed her once more. "Do this for me."

Therese's heart thudded in her ears. She couldn't believe Than was asking her to work with Ares. Her hands shook—out of anger, not fear, and hatred.

"When you face the Minotaur, have your sword drawn," Ares said, drawing his own. "If you wait, you'll be at a disadvantage. Carry it out in the ready position as you make your way through the labyrinth."

Therese drew her sword, narrowing her eyes at him. She wanted to slice off his head.

Ares faced her. "Spread your feet. Wider. You'll lose your balance otherwise. Keep them spread as you walk."

Therese did as he said.

"Bend your knees and lean forward, like this."

She copied his stance.

"Hold the sword closer to your body. If you hold it too far out like this, you make yourself vulnerable to attack. There."

Therese couldn't believe the god of war was being nice to her, and without realizing it, she said the question in the form of a prayer to him. "Why are you being so nice to me?"

He looked down at her, his hand still on hers, adjusting the position of her sword to her body. "I just want to see a good fight."

She lowered her eyes, the blood rushing to her face. She wanted to kill him.

"Keep your elbows in," he said, stepping back from her. "Remember, you want to use the sword, not your arms. If your arm goes out like this, it's easy to get it lobbed off. Repeat to yourself, elbows in. By instinct, you'll want to keep your body as far away as possible from your opponent, forcing you to reach out with your arms, but don't. It's better to get closer, elbows in, so the sword can protect you on your sword side while your shield protects the other. Now, take the shield."

She did as he said.

Ares transformed into a giant beast with the body of a man and the head of a bull. It charged her. She backed away.

"Stay perpendicular to me," Ares's voice shouted through the beast's ferocious mouth. "With your shield side toward me."

She clenched her teeth, accidentally biting hard on her tongue. What had she been thinking when she agreed to fight the Minotaur?

"Feet apart, Therese. Crouch. You want to lower your center of gravity, or he'll knock you right over."

It had been a moment of insanity, she thought, crouching.

"Shift back and forth on your feet. Keep your mind clear. Anticipate my every move."

He lunged for her, and the only thing she could think to do was to will him into a butterfly.

He fluttered his yellow wings twice, a two-inch creature just above her head, before resuming his form as the god of war in front of her. "I'm impressed. But you won't be able to do that when you face the real Minotaur."

She glanced over at Than, the corners of his mouth turned down. "How am I going to do this?" she prayed.

He didn't reply.

Chapter Twenty-Five: A Labyrinthine Dream

Go straight and down, not right or left, Therese reminded herself as she stepped into her silver robe and strapped on her gear. In her purse, beside a ball of yellow yarn, nestled four cinnamon rolls leftover from that morning's breakfast and wrapped in paper towels—two for Ariadne and two for the Minotaur. Therese had baked them for today's purposes. Plus, she knew they were Jen's favorites.

Inside the rolls were crushed sleeping pills Jen had brought the night before, as a favor to Therese, who said she hadn't been sleeping well since Vicki's death, which, although true, wasn't why she wanted them; she needed them for her third challenge. Once she'd realized the crown wouldn't work on immortal beings, she came up with plan B: drug her adversaries. This seemed like her best strategy, since she had little experience with the sword—though her success in defeating Ladon had given her a little more confidence, as had her lessons with Ares.

She closed her eyes and imagined the ancient city of Knossos on the island of Crete, based on photos she viewed on the web. The palace ruins stretched for acres and acres, so she focused on a group of trees between the "Little Palace" and the "Great Palace." The invisible plastic wrapped around her, and moments later she emerged beneath a tree beside a bench where two older ladies sat picnicking. They blinked at her. She gave them a friendly wave.

The two ladies looked at one another over their half-eaten sandwiches and then stared, wide-eyed, back at Therese.

"I was in the tree," Therese said, pointing up awkwardly.

The ladies smiled and nodded, as if to say, "Of course." Therese wondered what they thought of her robe, scabbard, and shield. At least she wasn't carrying her flute and crown, though she did have a headlight clipped to her sun-visor. She waved once more, turned from the ladies, and headed toward the Great Palace.

The last bus back to the modern city of Heraklion would leave in ten minutes, and until then, Therese wandered the grounds, waiting to face the Minotaur alone.

Last night's dream was a whirlwind of a memory to her now, but bits and pieces of her fighting Ares as the Minotaur throughout the night came back to her as she walked through the ruins. Although her favorite part of the dream had been after Ares had left, when she and Than spent the rest of the night together in his rooms, she had to admit fighting Ares had given her a thrill. The adrenaline rush had been incredible.

She followed the steps up to the North Entrance and Pillar Hall, the sunset coating the clouds in a backdrop of pink, purple, and orange. Other tourists ambled along the same path as Therese, but in the opposite direction, down toward the buses and cabs. When she reached the Pillar Hall, she was surprised by the fresco painting of a bull. It was larger than life in deep browns and blacks against the white stone. Two huge horns curled and pointed from each side of its ferocious head.

Did it resemble the Minotaur?

Seeing the image of the bull brought another wave of fear to Therese, so she reminded herself that she had to fight to save Than from an eternity of torment. She had no choice. She couldn't accept his hand otherwise. As Therese watched the last of the tourists taking their photos of the sunset, her thoughts and prayers went to Than. "I can do this," she said over and over in her mind. Then, a half hour later, when dusk had fully settled and the grounds were empty except for her, she said it out loud: "I can do this."

She followed the path past partially fallen stones into the large central court, searching for the Grand Staircase, hoping beyond hope the drugged rolls would work. It would be hard for her to slay the Minotaur as he lay sleeping, because she didn't like taking life, any life, but knowing he was immortal and would come back made Therese think she could follow through with it, unlike last summer with McAdams. Uncertainty and doubt pricked at the back of her neck, with questions like, What if he refused the rolls? What if she had to actually fight him? Through the course of her dream, she'd improved with Ares, but the training had all been mental: her physical body had undergone none of it.

To the south of the central court, she found the stairs—refurbished, reinforced, and beautiful. Therese imagined the ancient civilization that once inhabited these walls. A shudder moved through her as she reached the bottom of the Grand Staircase, anticipating a raven-haired goddess to lead her to the ancient entrance. She drew her sword, as Ares had advised, so she was ready for any surprises. With her other hand, she took out the four cinnamon rolls and laid them by the fallen pillar Than had said marked the entrance. Her hands shook like a starving beggar, and she was suddenly sick. This could be it. Her death. The end of everything.

She took up her shield and waited, sweat forming on her forehead. She chewed on the inside of her mouth. "I can do this," she said again.

A dark-haired woman appeared. Woman was hardly the word. She looked the same age as Therese. Her black wavy hair hung over her shoulders and across a white cotton dress that stopped below the knee. She was barefoot and frowning.

"Who are you?"

"Therese. Hades sent me. I brought cinnamon cakes." Therese tried to keep the tremor from her voice and the quake from her hand as she pointed her sword to the four rolls.

"Why should I trust you when you stand there prepared to kill me?"

Oh, no. Therese sucked in air. What should she do? Ares said to keep the sword in the ready position, but Ariadne wouldn't eat the cakes as long as it was drawn. If she did put the sword away, the Minotaur could sweep down on her out of nowhere, and it would all be over, just like that. Therese returned the sword to its scabbard.

Ariadne picked up one of the rolls. "It smells delicious. You have one first."

This was not going well at all. Now what should she do? She prayed to Than and Ares, like that would do any good. Than couldn't come near her without killing her himself, and Ares wanted her dead. She took the roll. "I baked these for you, Ariadne, and for your brother, Asterion."

Ariadne's eyes lit up. "You're the first to come here and call him by his rightful name. Most only know him as the Minotaur."

"It's not his fault he's what he is," Therese said.

The Minotaur appeared at Ariadne's side. "You seem friendly," he said, "and yet you arrived ready to attack."

"To defend," Therese said. "I just want to negotiate through the labyrinth and prove to Hades I can do it. I don't want to fight you."

"Very well," he said, though she didn't quite trust him. "I'll take your cakes in exchange for your entrance."

"Wait," Ariadne said. "Make her eat one first. They might be poisoned."

Therese put the roll to her lips and took a bite, trying to appear more confident than she was. Maybe a small bite wouldn't affect her. "It's delicious." She said. "Please, have one."

Ariadne took one and gave the other two to her brother. They watched her, waiting for her to take another bite, so she did. Together, the three of them ate the rolls. Therese began to feel sleepy.

"May I enter?" She hoped she wouldn't fall asleep before making it back out. She had no idea how long the maze was, but she needed to get started right away, though now she realized she would likely fall asleep in the middle of it and never escape alive.

"Yes," the Minotaur said, sitting down on a stone ledge. "We'll wait for you here. I think I'll take a nap."

Ariadne narrowed her eyes at Therese. "You wicked girl! You tricked us! You put something in the cakes to make us sleepy!" Ariadne sat on the ledge, fighting sleep.

"I'm sorry!" Therese cried. "I was afraid I couldn't trust you. I'm so sorry!" Therese staggered under the weight of her heavy shield and fell to the ground. She laid her head on her folded arms and went to sleep on the cold stone path, her last thought that the Minotaur would kill her.

Therese ran down a brightly lit hall, someone just ahead of her out of reach. Where was she? Shops lined the empty, narrow corridor that twisted and turned around vendor stands with handbags, toys, cell phones, and other products, creating a maze. She was inside a mall.

"Hey! Stop!" Therese turned a corner. Wait a minute, she thought, slowing down. Who am I chasing? And why? She rested her palms on her knees and caught her breath.

Hip appeared before her. "This is important. If you die in your dream, you die for real."

"Why are you telling me what I already know?"

They both turned their heads toward the sound of slow, heavy footsteps striking the tile floor. Twenty feet away, in front of The Gap, stood the Minotaur.

Hip moved closer to her. "I can't help you fight him, but if you kill him here in the dream world, you won't have to face him in the Upperworld."

"You mean that's not a figment? That's really him?"

"It's him alright."

"He looks mad."

"Yep. He's definitely mad." Hip put a hand on her shoulder. "You of all people have a chance of succeeding. Use your power to kill him here, in the dream world."

"Power?" Therese looked back at Hip to find him gone.

The Minotaur strolled boldly toward her. "That was a mean trick."

"Please forgive me, Asterion. I didn't think you'd let me traipse through your home and come out alive. All the stories paint you as a vicious killer. Can you blame me?"

"Yes. As a matter of fact, I can. People would be better off if they ignored rumors and sought the truth for themselves before passing judgment."

Therese took a step back with feet she could no longer feel as he moved closer. Her heart picked up speed, and she bit the inside of her mouth as she had this revelation: *if I don't kill him here, in this dream, he will kill me when he wakes. I've got to kill him before he kills me. I have no choice.* She braced herself as he bent his horns toward her and prepared to charge.

She turned him into a white rabbit, the kind magicians pull from black top hats, but he immediately returned to his tall, massive form, his eyes a little fiercer. She thought of running away—this was a mall, a labyrinth of another kind—but knew the longer she put off the inevitable, the more likely she would wake and find her chances gone.

In her mind, she said to him, *I'm going to kill you.*

He snarled with a grimace. "You're just a little girl."

His words inspired her to take charge of the dream again. She willed herself into a warrior, modeled after Athena, and then drew her sword. Rather than strike forward, which would make her arm vulnerable, she used a maneuver Ares had shown her: she twirled around, picked up momentum, lifted her arm as she came around, and struck the beast's side.

Although the blade wounded him, blood spilling across his ribs, he did not fall. He lunged at her. She shoved out her shield, her body perpendicular to him, as Ares had shown her, but the sheer force of his weight pushed her back, and she fell on the ground. When he lunged for her again, she turned herself into a snake and slithered between his legs to the back of him, returning to warrior form before he turned around. She took her sword and struck him at the neck, slicing through skin and fur, but again, he did not fall. He turned, and this time found her arm, and with terrifying strength pulled and flung her toward the ground.

Before she fell, she imagined herself as a rubbery, stretchy, malleable warrior, allowing her arm to be pulled past its natural length without causing her to tumble. She stretched her body out, like thick bubble gum, and wrapped herself tightly around him, but he pierced her with his horns, grabbed her arms, and tied them together before flinging her to his feet. She quickly untied her limbs, willed her sword and shield in place, but he caught on to her game and used his own will to manipulate the dream. He made his arm malleable and stretchy, maneuvered it past her sword and shield, and grabbed her by the neck, clutching his long fingers around her throat. Shocked, she looked at him, her mouth agape, unable to catch air. She tried to bring her sword across his arm, but, having learned from her, he bent it in all directions, easily missing her blade.

This is a dream, she reminded herself, and she turned herself into a puddle of water. She changed their landscape to that of a narrow cave, and she filled the cave with her water self, hoping to drown him. He solved the problem by becoming a shark.

I'm running out of time, she thought. We'll wake up, and I'll be screwed. She drained the cave of water in an instant, resuming her tall warrior form, and before the shark turned, brought down her sword. The shark flopped on the dry rocky ground of the cave, and for a mo-ment, she thought she'd won, but before she could blink, the Minotaur was on his feet, ready to charge.

In that split second before he lunged for her, a number of options flew through her mind. She could make herself a bigger Minotaur than he, she could make herself Zeus and perhaps frighten him, or she could make herself fire and try burning him alive. But with each of these ideas came the thought of his counter: he could make himself bigger, he could make himself a Titan, or he could make himself water. At last, a new idea struck her, and before he reached her, she transformed into Ariadne, his sister, and said, "No, Asterion!"

The Minotaur stopped, bewildered, his bull mouth hanging open. Before he came to the realization that he was being tricked, Therese, still in Ariadne's form, drove her sword through the beast's chest, driving it all the way through to the back.

"Ariadne!" the Minotaur cried as he fell back to the rocky ground. He flailed his arms about, like a spider on its back. "You betrayed me. Again."

The real Ariadne must have heard him call out for her, for she appeared in the dream across from Therese, her double. Ariadne looked confused, apparently unaware that she was looking at Therese in disguise.

"What have I done?" Ariadne shrieked. "Oh, Asterion, look at me!" She dropped on her knees at his side. "Please forgive me!"

But her brother was already dead, his thick bull's tongue hanging from his sharp-teethed mouth.

Ariadne shrieked again, her hands on her brother's unmoving chest. Then she stood and pulled the blade from her brother's body. Therese thrust the shield forward, ready to defend herself, but gasped when, instead of attacking Therese, Ariadne drove the blade into her own heart and fell beside her brother.

Therese left the cave and stayed at her grandparents' house with Blue, pretending he wasn't a stupid figment, until the sleeping pills wore off and she awoke at the temple ruins in Knossos beside the dead bodies of the two immortal siblings. She put her hand to her mouth, unable to believe she had killed them. Why didn't she feel victorious, triumphant? Tears formed in her eyes and she clenched her teeth, accidentally cutting into the soft flesh of the tip of her tongue. To the fallen bodies, she whispered, "I'm sorry. I didn't want to do this."

She wasn't finished yet; she still had to make it through the labyrinth, and she had to do it before her victims—is that what they were, her victims?—revived. She pulled the ball of yellow yarn from her purse and unwound it, leaving a long strand at the entrance, and then, flipping on the headlight at her visor, plunged into the dark maze.

Chapter Twenty-Six: Therese's Prayers

Than laid a hand on the shoulders of each of the two siblings, Ariadne and Asterion, as he led their souls from the palace ruins in Knossos, Crete to the Underworld. Relieved and exhilarated by the success of Therese, who still laid sleeping at his feet, and wishing he could sneak a kiss on her cheek without endangering her life, Than made a stupid joke to the Minotaur, for which he was instantly sorry, something like, "At this rate, we'll have to get you a room of your own."

Asterion glared at Than and knocked the god of death's hand from his shoulder.

"Sorry, man. Bull. Bullman." Than inwardly cringed at his horrible lack of tact. He'd never felt so giddy. For the first time since his father issued the five challenges, he actually believed there was a chance—however slight—Therese would succeed. "Sorry. This way."

Not long after, he could hear her praying to him from the labyrinth. Her tone quickly changed from bewildered, "I can't believe I'm still alive," to regretful, "I can't believe I killed them." The more and more she expressed her sorrow over the souls he now helped board Charon's ferry, the less giddy he felt.

"Asterion and Ariadne would have let me through, I bet," Therese prayed. "I tricked them, angered them, and then killed them both. Ariadne may have held the sword, but I'm the one who drove her to use it. I don't want to be this person I'm becoming, Than. I don't want to kill the Hydra. Can't I win your father's approval without having to kill anything?"

He found it interesting that her new fear was not, "The Hydra will kill me," but "I must kill the Hydra and don't want to." Her victory over the Minotaur had given her confidence. Maybe too much.

He left the two immortal souls on the banks of the Lethe River in Erebus and then sought his father.

Than waited for nearly an hour in Hades's empty chamber, passing the time by listening to Therese's constant prayers to him, and was overjoyed to learn she'd navigated her way to safety. Not long after, Hades and Hermes appeared at the golden table, in mid conversation.

"It's a deal," Hermes said, shaking the other god's hand.

Once Hermes left Hades's table and father and son were alone, Than said, "I need clarification."

"Regarding?"

"When you said Therese must defeat the Hydra, did you mean 'kill' or 'overcome'?"

Hades stood from his golden table and crossed the room to his son. "What's this hair-splitting all about?"

"As you know, Therese succeeded in the third challenge. She killed the Minotaur and has just now made it safely through the labyrinth."

"Yes." Hades sat on his chaise lounge and regarded his fingernails. "I'm very pleased."

"She's proved she's capable of overpowering and killing a beast, but it's not her style. She doesn't want to kill the Hydra."

"Honorable trait."

"But you hated that very trait last summer."

"Death was deserved then; the Hydra is innocent and has loyally guarded the underwater entrance for centuries. I do not want her killed."

"Then why challenge Therese to do it?"

Hades gave Than a patronizing look.

"You expect her to fail. You want her to fail."

"I did. I don't anymore." He bit a cuticle and once again regarded his nails.

Than's mouth fell open. A ball of heat arose in his chest. It was hope. A flame of hope. He gripped his hands behind his back and waited for his father's next words.

"If she can make it past the Hydra into the Underworld through that entrance, she will have succeeded in the fourth challenge."

Than rushed to his father's side and took his hand. "Thank you."

Hades jerked his head back with surprise. Than released his father, awkwardly, realizing he hadn't touched him since he was a boy. He studied his father's face, waiting to be mocked, but instead was given the smallest hint of a smile on his father's lips, and for once the smile was not wry.

"I've just convinced Hermes to take your duties for two hours, so you can visit your red-haired girl in the flesh, as a reward for her accomplishment. You can clarify the fourth challenge to her then."

Than found Therese curled up in bed, her wavy red hair a dark gold crown across her pillow, shimmering and dancing as the sobs shook her and her dog, who sat up a moment later, wagging his tail. Therese looked at Clifford, perplexed, and then turned to Than with wide, red-rimmed eyes.

"Am I dreaming?" she asked in the scratchy voice of someone with a cold.

He shook his head, his feet heavy because he, too, could hardly believe they were together. They both gazed at each other for a moment, incredulous. Then she climbed from the covers, wearing her "Durango Demons" t-shirt and very short shorts, and folded herself into him, slinking against him like a cat, her hair slightly damp and smelling of oranges. She tucked her warm face against his neck, her breath tickling his skin. His arms closed around her as her body went limp.

She took in an audible breath. "It's really you."

He ran his hands along the small of her back beneath the thin shirt, having forgotten how soft she felt, how warm, how alive. She slipped her arms around his waist and looked up at him with the most beautiful round green eyes. Her lips parted into a sleepy smile.

"I can't believe it," she said. "How?"

"A gift from my father. To celebrate your victory."

A crease appeared between her brows as she sucked in her lips. Then she asked, "It was a victory, wasn't it?"

"What else would you call it?"

"Tragic." She buried her face in his chest.

He held her, stroking her soft, fine hair.

"I can't get rid of the image of them lying on the ground, dead because of me."

"I know. I'm sorry. They won't be dead forever. In a few days, they'll revive."

She looked up at him. "What about their bodies? What will the tourists think?"

"They're invisible. You could see them because they chose to show themselves to you."

She pressed her cheek against his heart. "Oh, Than. I don't know if I can ever kill again, even to save my life. It's such a horrible feeling. I've been absolutely miserable. But I've got to. I've got to in order to save you. It's crazy."

"You don't have to kill the Hydra."

She stopped sniffling and looked up at him again, her mouth agape. "What?"

"Hades likes that you don't want to kill for no good reason."

She gasped. "Really?"

The gleam in her eyes made his heart swell. "Really." Then he clenched his jaw. "But…"

"What?"

He held onto her, so she couldn't slip from him. He could already feel her lithe body sagging at the word "but." "You have to get past her."

"Her? The Hydra's a she?"

He nodded.

"What do you mean, "past her"?

He sighed and said, without inflection, "Why don't we sit down." He crossed to the chair beneath the window, pulling her into his lap. She curled against him like a newborn fawn—her knees against her chest, feet tucked beneath her bottom, arms around his neck. He wished he could hold her like this all night. Two hours wasn't enough.

"Well?"

He cupped her face in his hands and studied it, not having been this close to her—to the living, breathing, fleshy her—in so long. His fingers weaved into her soft hair of their own accord, and his lips sought hers.

Her next words to him were in prayer, because her lips were too busy kissing his, and he heard them as clearly as if she were speaking. "Oh, Than. I love you so much. I've missed you. I can't believe you're actually here, holding me, kissing me. God. Don't ever leave me again. I'll do anything. Anything."

He felt her tears touch his cheek, and he pulled back to wipe them from her face. "Don't cry."

"I'm so happy. And so sad."

"Me, too."

She stroked his face and gave him a sympathetic smile. Than couldn't recall a single time anyone had ever given him such a sweet look.

"I can't wait to be together like this all the time. Can you imagine? Can you imagine a time when my presence won't kill you, when you don't have to slay monsters and steal heavily protected golden apples just to be with me?"

Therese laughed that musical, lilting laugh that made his heart swell again. "I imagine it constantly."

He touched his forehead to hers, closed his eyes, and said, "We could do it now. Right now. Forget the last challenges."

"But the maenads."

All at once, Than was accosted by an onslaught of panicky prayer cries, "I couldn't be with you like that! I couldn't ask that of you! I'd rather break your heart than put you though a lifetime of such unbearable physical pain!"

He recoiled and searched her face. "What are you saying, Therese? Are you saying you'll refuse me if you fail the last challenges?"

She closed her mouth and pressed her face to his chest. Without speaking, she said, "I don't know. I just don't know."

Than's mouth went dry. He hadn't foreseen this. He'd been feeling afraid for her, afraid of the mortal pain and mental anxiety, but otherwise he'd been confident they'd eventually be together, one way or another. But now…was she really saying she'd refuse him?

"Let's please not think about that. Please let's just get me through these challenges."

"Look at me," he said, pulling her up by her arms, rising to his feet, frantic and angry. "Look at me!"

She lifted her eyes to his.

"You told me you would endure being burned to death to be with me. Isn't that right? Answer me."

She nodded.

"And were you telling the truth? Would you really do it? Suffer the most painful feeling imaginable just to be with me?"

She nodded again.

"And because I love you and respect you, I've agreed. I've agreed to allow you to make that sacrifice, because I believed you when you said you love me."

"I do love you."

"Then why won't you allow me to do the same: to make sacrifices to be with you? Man, Therese! I'm honoring your decision to accept the challenges. I'm honoring your decision to burn to death for me. Can't you honor my choice to face the maenads? Your love is worth so much more to me, and you're killing me!"

"I'm sorry." She shook her head, and he could see in her expression how conflicted she felt, how deep both her love and fear for him was, and he softened. "I'm sorry. It kills me, too. Thinking of that horrible pain every year forever. It kills me."

He pulled her to him and held her. She seemed too small and fragile to be fighting monsters.

"I won't fail," she said. "I will not fail. Tell me what I need to know to make it past the Hydra."

"Put on some warmer clothes and some shoes. And you'll want your traveling robe. I'll take you to her lair tonight so you can see what you're up against."

Chapter Twenty-Seven: The Hydra's Lair

Than held her hand, and together they god traveled, the invisible plastic wrapping itself around her, until she opened her eyes and found herself at the bottom of a massive grassy hill. Over a mile away, at the very top, was a structure she couldn't quite see.

"What's that?"

"It's a castle. Was a castle," Than said. "Nothing but ruins now."

"Where are we?" She used her hand as a visor against the just-rising sun—a strange sight when a few minutes ago, it was nearly midnight.

"Eastern side of the Peloponnesian Peninsula."

She punched his arm. "I suck at world geography. Can you be less specific?"

He laughed. "Greece. And this is Larissa Hill. Ancient Argos once stood here. The modern Argos is there, further down. See it?"

She turned around to discover hundreds of buildings and streets and cars, all modern and bustling with activity in the early dawn. "But where's the water? I thought the Hydra lived underwater."

"She does. Centuries ago, there was a lake here. Lerna. It's all dried up, but, if you look carefully along the base of this hill, you can still find signs of it."

"I don't understand."

"Beneath this hill lies a system of ducts. Most of the tunnels are dry or have a little water, maybe ankle deep. They connect several sinkholes."

"Sinkholes?"

"Little pools formed by underground springs that run from the Aegean Sea."

"Are you saying the Hydra lives beneath this hill?"

"Exactly."

"And the entrance to the Underworld?"

"Also beneath this hill."

She sucked in air and shuddered. "How do we get inside?"

He squeezed her hand and brought it to his lips.

"It's okay," she said. "I can do this. Tell me."

"You could crawl in through a tunnel, but since you have your traveling robe, we'll god travel in. Here's the thing, though: this hill is full of solid rock. You have to focus on a very specific location in order to be successful. That's why I want to take you with me first."

"So far so good."

"But…"

"There's a but?"

"Yeah. 'Fraid so."

She nodded, bracing herself.

"The Hydra could be anywhere. The tunnel I choose could be the very one she's hanging out in."

She lifted her eyebrows. "Great."

"So what I want to practice with you tonight, er," he looked at the sun-filled sky, "this morning, I mean, is split-second travel. I want you to learn how to leave a position before you've arrived."

"Huh?"

"You know that feeling you get when you god travel, that pressure all around you?"

"Like invisible plastic wrap."

"Okay. Plastic wrap? Or more like a thin blanket."

"A tight thin blanket," Therese added.

"Okay. Anyway, just as that blanket begins to release, before you've completely landed, inspect the location."

"You mean open my eyes?"

He took a step back and covered his heart with his free hand. "You've been traveling all this time with your eyes closed? Are you serious? You're lucky to be alive."

"But it's so bright."

"Not too bright. You can handle it. Promise me you'll keep them open from now on."

"I promise."

"Come on. Let's go over by those rocks. Ready?"

She nodded and squeezed his hand.

"Don't close your eyes, okay?"

"Okay."

"Focus."

"I am. Let's go."

The invisible plastic wrapped itself around her and she resisted the urge to close her eyes as brightness surrounded her from every direction. Before the plastic released itself, she saw the boulders coming into focus just as her feet were touching the ground.

"I could see!" she said when they landed. "I saw these rocks before we arrived!"

"Good. Now, what I want you to do is go back where we started, without me, but before you land, return here."

"How do I do that?"

"Just as the pressure gives, and you see that tall weed over there, will yourself back here by my side. You have to focus, okay?"

She nodded, releasing his hand. "Here I go." The pressure and brightness returned, but an image of Clifford on her bed entered her mind and she saw her room materializing around her. Before she landed, she thought of Than and the boulders, and she instantly returned to his side, but felt jolted, lost her balance, and fell on her bottom on the ground at his feet.

He cupped his hands beneath her armpits and helped her to her feet. "Not exactly what I had in mind, but looks like you're getting the idea."

"I went home, on accident." She dusted grass and dirt from the back of her traveling robe and jeans.

"I know. It's okay. If you need to get away from the Hydra, just go there, to your room. Any place is fine. You just want to get away, okay?"

"Okay."

"I want to take you into her lair and show you around. I want you to see the entrance to the Underworld, because if you can god travel straight there, then you might be able to slip inside without ever having to face the Hydra."

"That would be awesome."

"Yeah, but unfortunately, this little practice run of ours will make her angry and more alert. You'll want to wait a few days before you come back and try it on your own. Even if we get lucky and she doesn't spot us, she'll know we've been here by our scent."

"Great."

"Ready?"

"Don't let go." She took his hand, feeling less frightened than excited with him beside her.

The invisible plastic wrapped itself around her as the bright lights came from all directions. Forcing her eyes open, she saw the walls of the cavern come into view, but when they finally landed in a few inches of cold water, they were surrounded by complete darkness.

"I can't see," she whispered, clinging to his arm.

"Oh, I forgot. Humans can't see in the dark."

His body took on a soft glow, illuminating the tunnel a few yards in each direction. He looked amazing, like an angel. She whispered, "Wow."

"What?" he whispered back.

"Nothing." She felt herself blushing. "So, um, can you see in the dark?"

"Yeah. I guess you'll need to bring a light with you when you come on your own."

"Guess so."

"Now look here." He touched a thin column of rock beside him shaped like an hour glass and as tall as Therese. "Focus on this image when you travel here on your own, okay?"

"Got it." They were still whispering, hoping not to be heard by the Hydra.

"If the Hydra's waiting for you, go back to your bedroom before you land and try again another day, okay?"

"Okay."

"On the other side of this column is the sinkhole."

They sloshed through the shallow water to a heart-shaped pool about three yards in diameter.

"That's the entrance there."

"What, you dive in?"

"Yeah. You swim down a few feet and pop up on the other side, right into the Underworld. Ready?"

Something moved just beneath the surface as Therese peered at her and Than's reflections. Before she could speak, that something shot straight up—a long, serpentine neck ringed with scales that sparkled like abalone in Than's glow. At the top of the neck was an enormous dragon head with ferocious eyes and teeth, its mouth open and lunging for her. She stared, frozen and heavy, unable to move. In the next instant, the pressure wrapped around her, and she and Than arrived back inside her bedroom, startling Clifford from his nap on her bed.

Than put his hands on her shoulders and studied her face. "You okay?"

She could tell her eyes were wide, her face pale. Nodding, she asked, "Was that...?"

"Yeah."

"I thought she had nine heads or something."

"Not anymore. Only one was immortal. Hercules slayed and seared the others."

"Oh." Not that it mattered. The one remaining head was big enough to eat her whole.

Than released her to pace the room. "If she's nesting in the sinkhole, you won't make it past her alive."

She couldn't imagine going back and looking over the heart-shaped pool, waiting, only to have that huge head pop out at her again. She'd nearly peed in her pants. "There's no way to tell where she is beforehand?"

"Not that I know of."

"What if I lure her away from the entrance?"

"How?"

"What does she eat?"

"Fish. But she loves cake, too."

"I could put a cake at one end of her lair. When I see her coming for it, I could god-travel to the heart-shaped pool."

He smiled at her as he took her in his arms. "That might just work, you clever girl."

"You'll need to take me in once more. To show me another place to god travel to."

"We'll practice as long as we can, but, first, kiss me."

Chapter Twenty-Eight: A Deadly Accident

Thursday morning after swim practice and lunch with Carol—Richard was out doing an interview—Therese hiked down to Jen's in the warm afternoon sun with Clifford trailing behind her. Stormy might not need to be groomed, but Therese needed to keep busy. Every idle moment added to her anxiety over what lay ahead.

It wasn't just getting past the Hydra, though that certainly would be enough to make anyone anxious. She did, after all, have to time getting in and out of the lair just right, which would be tricky, even after all the practice she and Than did last night. And apologizing to Vicki in the Underworld, well, that was less of a challenge than it was a gift, a gift of closure. Although the last two challenges worried Therese, what really had her stomach in knots was the part about burning to death.

Maybe her body would go into shock, so she wouldn't feel it. Maybe she'd burn quickly, and it would be over before she knew it. She shuddered and tried not to think about her flesh in flames.

Reaching the Holts' gravelly drive, now lined with cars belonging to trail riders, she headed to the barn as Clifford went on to the stream at the back of the house. Pete tapped his hat to her from the pen. She wiggled her fingers to him, and then to Bobby, who also waved. Jen was in the barn brushing Sassy.

Jen looked up as Therese entered. "Hey there."

"Hey. I let Clifford come today. Hope that's alright. He went straight to the stream, as usual."

"Sure. He never gives up, does he? Fishing for trout."

Therese chuckled. "Never." She took Stormy's brush from the shelf and sat on a stool in the front of his stall. He was getting big, though he still wasn't weaned, and he was sometimes skittish even around Therese. "It's okay boy." She stroked his soft gray hide and pressed her cheek against his flank. "Stormy. That's you, boy. You're Stormy. I'm Therese."

"Matt and I are going to the movies this weekend. Maybe you and Pete could join us."

"Hmm. I don't know."

"Think about it."

"Than and I are talking again. I was going to tell you the other day, but…"

"I thought you hated him."

"No. Not anymore. He's been busy trying to find a way for us to be together."

Jen came around from behind Sassy to work her other side. "So, do you really like him? I mean, 'like' like him?"

Therese nodded. "It's bad, Jen. I think I'm in love."

"No way. Y'all haven't even seen that much of each other."

"More than you know."

"What do you mean? He hasn't come up to see you, has he?"

Therese moved her stool, so she could reach the backside of Stormy. "It was a quick trip. He flew in and out in one night. He's done that twice now."

"Is he loaded or something? That's a lot of money."

"I guess so." His father was the god of all precious stones, she supposed.

Just then, Bobby barged into the barn, breathless. "Therese, come quick. It's Clifford."

Therese and Jen exchanged worried glances as they left the stall and followed Bobby. Pete stepped from the pen holding Clifford's limp body in his arms.

"Clifford!" Therese ran to Pete's side.

"He slipped into the pen somehow. The General trampled him."

Clifford's head was a mangled mess, smashed and pouring blood. His little white and brown body twitched.

"He's not dead!" Therese insisted, a lump rising to her throat. "Can you take me to a vet?"

Pete met her eyes. "But..."

"Please?"

He nodded and carried Clifford to his truck. Therese and Jen followed to where it was parked in the garage, Therese no longer able to feel her arms and legs or the rise and fall of her chest.

Mrs. Holt came up alongside the truck as Therese blindly climbed in. "Listen, Honey. No use going to see a vet."

"You don' t understand. He's going to be okay." She said this with a quavering voice, sounding as unsure as she felt.

Bobby came up behind. "It's my fault. I'm sorry! When I opened the gate, Clifford ran past me! It's my fault!"

"No it's not, Bobby," Therese said.

Jen climbed in beside Therese, crying her eyes out. "I'm so sorry. I can't believe it."

"Get me a towel, Mom." Pete held Clifford at the opened passenger side door, blood running down his arms and onto his shirt and jeans.

"Thank you, Pete! Thank you for helping me!" In another life, she would have married him.

Mrs. Holt returned moments later with an old towel, which she wrapped around Clifford. It immediately became soaked with blood. "Ah, hell, let me get another."

"I'm so sorry," Jen said, more of a slobbering mess than Therese.

"It's okay. Clifford will be fine." At least she hoped. Artemis hadn't been angry enough with Therese to undo her gift of immortality, had she?

"Oh, Therese!" Jen cried. "Look at his head. He's not going to be fine!"

Pete lowered his eyes.

"Stop it!" she snapped. "I don't want to hear that." Please, Artemis.

Mrs. Holt returned with another towel, swaddling Clifford like a baby. Then she and Pete lay Clifford in Therese's arms. She cradled him, speaking softly to him, even though she could feel no life left in his body. He wasn't breathing, nor was his heart beating. He felt heavy with death, his stubby tail, usually wagging, stiff. "You'll be alright, soon, Clifford, boy. Hang in there."

Pete climbed behind the wheel and brought his truck to life. Tears streamed from Therese's eyes as she prayed over her best friend, silently. "Please let him be alright. Please, Artemis."

As they neared Therese's house, Carol ran from the gravelly drive, waving her hands for them to stop. Pete rolled down his window. Mrs. Holt must have called her.

"Is there room for me?"

Pete climbed out and helped Carol into the backseat of his truck. Carol leaned over and stroked Therese's hair. "Oh, sweetheart. I'm so, so, sorry."

"He's going to be okay. The vet will know what to do."

Therese sensed Carol and Jen exchange looks.

"Trust me, guys," Therese said as Pete drove across the dam. "Clifford will make it." She cradled his body like a baby as her teeth chattered. "Please hurry, Pete. He's losing so much blood."

She knew what they were all thinking. They were thinking, "Poor Therese. First her parents, then Dumbo, then Puffy, then Vicki, and now Clifford. Poor, poor Therese." But Therese knew Clifford could not die; at least, not forever. At some point, his soul would return to his body, just like Asterion and Ariadne's would. She wasn't sure how long it would take, but she hoped the vet could fix his head so his body would be ready when his soul returned. "Please, Artemis," she whispered, low, so no one could hear over the sound of the engine. "I beg you."

When they reached the emergency vet clinic, Pete dropped everyone off at the door, and Therese rushed Clifford inside. She was immediately led to an operating room, where a technician came in to exam Clifford.

"Let's lay him on the table," the young technician said as she pulled on gloves.

The stainless steel table was cold and hard. Therese kept her arms around Clifford as the technician carefully pulled the bloody towels away from Clifford's body.

"Oh, dear," she said, her eyes wide. She put one end of her stethoscope to her ears and the other to Clifford's blood-matted chest. "Tell me what happened."

"He was trampled by a horse," Therese said. "But he's going to be alright."

Carol shook her head. "Oh, Therese. She lost her parents only a year ago. This is hard for her to accept."

"Stop saying that, Carol!" Therese turned an angry face to her aunt, feeling the blood feverishly flow to her face. "This has nothing to do with my parents! This is totally different! You don't know everything!" Her heart raced fast. She couldn't breathe.

Carol backed away toward the door. The others lowered their eyes.

The technician wiped away some of the blood, gently handling Clifford's head. She pushed his lids down to cover his lifeless eyes. "I'll have Dr. Chenault take a look at him. Why don't you step out into the waiting room, and I'll call you back after she's had a chance to examine him."

"I don't want to leave him," Therese said. "The others can go, but I want to stay here."

Carol put a hand on her shoulder. "Therese, I…"

"Please," Therese said.

"That's fine," the technician said. "But I need the rest of you to clear the room. Thank you."

Carol kissed the top of Therese's head. "Sweetheart, I'm so sorry."

When Therese was left alone with Clifford, she wiped more of the blood away from Clifford's body. He'd stopped bleeding. His head was a clotted mess, and she could see the fractured skull and maybe even some of his brain behind his left ear. At least his eyes hadn't been crushed. She wiped each paw, rinsing one of the towels at the sink and wiping again—wetting, wiping, the whole time praying to Artemis, until, after about three or four minutes, Dr. Chenault entered the room.

The doctor, a thin, petite woman with curly brown hair and glasses, bent over the examining table and looked over Clifford, pressed her stethoscope to his chest, lifted the lids of his eyes and closed them again. "Poor guy didn't have a chance."

"I don't think he's dead. Can you try to revive him?"

The doctor narrowed her eyes at Therese and called her to the other side of the table. "Look here. See how his skull is collapsed? This kind of brain damage means he didn't suffer long. As soon as the hoof hit, this little guy was gone."

Therese wiped her eyes and nose with the back of her hand. "Can you fix him up? I don't care how much it costs. I've got a lot of money. Can you stitch up his head and make him look nice?"

"Do you mean like a taxidermist?"

Therese's mouth dropped open. "No. No, not like that at all." Her shoulders shook as a new wave of sobs constricted her throat and made it impossible to speak.

The doctor put a hand on Therese's arm. "I'm sorry."

One of Clifford's legs twitched. Therese covered her mouth with her hands and held her breath.

The vet saw it, too. "That's normal dear, especially with head injuries. That doesn't mean…"

Clifford blinked open his eyes and began to whine.

"What the…" The vet rushed to Clifford's side and looked at him closely. "He's breathing again. This is unusual. There's a pulse. His heart's beating."

Clifford started writhing and whining, obviously in great pain. Dr. Chenault had to hold him to keep him from falling off the table.

Therese gasped, not sure whether to laugh with glee or to scream in terror at his suffering.

"Call my tech back in here. Her name's Katie."

Therese ran to the door. "Katie! The doctor needs you!"

"You'll need to step out of the room, Therese. I'll update you when I'm done here. This is very unusual."

Therese met the others in the waiting room with a smile on her face. "He's moving around. I think he's coming to."

Jen jumped from her seat. "What?"

Pete crossed to her side and put a hand on her shoulder. "Are you serious?"

"What did the vet say?" Carol asked.

"It's very unusual."

Chapter Twenty-Nine: The Hydra

Dr. Chenault kept Clifford overnight on Thursday and Friday, but Saturday, after a disappointing swim meet, Therese rode with Carol and Richard to pick him up. He wore a hard cast on his head, covering all but his eyes and snout and would have to be fed a liquid diet with a turkey baster for a while. Therese suspected his skull would heal faster than most patients. After waiting a few more days for Clifford to get settled at home, she decided it was time to bake a cake for the Hydra.

She perused the pantry for a cake mix. Let's see, she thought. Chocolate, white, and yellow. Which would a monster like best? Chocolate was poisonous to dogs, but could it hurt a dragon-headed sea snake? She decided on her favorite—white cake with white icing—so if things went wrong, she could die eating it.

"What's the special occasion?" Carol asked when Therese slid the two round cake pans full of batter into the oven.

Therese had already prepared her answer: "I never properly thanked the Holts for Stormy." She realized then that she should bake a cake for the Holts, and she promised herself she would, if she succeeded in her fourth challenge.

Later that evening after dinner, she carried the cake up to her room, under the pretense of wanting to decorate it privately (which sounded weird and got her a funny look from her aunt), donned her sneakers, jeans, and traveling robe, along with her sword, shield, and visor with headlight, and god traveled to the foot of Larissa Hill near Argos, Greece. It was three in the morning there and dark, for the city was far below, like strands of white Christmas tree lights spread across an enormous field, and though the stars and waning moon shone brightly, the hill was in shadows.

"I can do this," she said to the wind. She shivered in the cold. It was warmer when she came with Than at dawn several days ago. The night air chilled her to the bone. She should have worn a coat over the traveling robe. She could pop back and get one, but she decided to move on. "Let's get this over with," she said to no one in particular, or to any gods who might be watching.

She drew the sword, balancing the two-layers of cake in her left hand. Then, keeping her eyes open as she had practiced, she imagined the decoy zone located on the opposite side of the hill from the heart-shaped pool.

The invisible plastic wrapped around her, and the bright light shined from all directions. She recognized the fork in the tunnel with its peculiar anvil-shaped dividing wall. Since the Hydra was nowhere in sight, Therese landed at the fork, flipped on her headlight, set the cake on a rock near the ground, and then took several steps away from it to wait.

Her heart thudded in her ears as she ferociously bit the inside of her lips. The Hydra could come from any one of three directions—from either of the two tunnels that forked from the anvil-shaped wall, or from the main tunnel feeding into them, currently at her back. She sloshed around in the three-inches of ice-cold water, constantly turning to shine her light down each of the three ducts, both wanting and not wanting the monster to come.

She wondered if any of the gods were watching her crouched and shivering in the dark tunnel, her teeth now chattering uncontrollably as she held her breath, her limbs stiff, frozen with both cold and fear. She felt small beneath the massive hill and the ancient ruins, a tiny dot in the larger scheme of things. Realizing the gods would see her as nothing but a little frightened girl, she pulled her shoulders back, jutted out her chin, gritted her teeth, and narrowed her eyes. She was a warrior, and she would fight.

That is, if the Hydra would ever come.

As the minutes wore on, and the cold crept deeper into her bones, and the shivering made her feel like a victim of Parkinson's disease, she pondered the idea of calling out to the monster. She had tried and failed to study the petroglyphs carved into the rock throughout the tunnels. She had tried and failed to observe the tiny fish swimming near her feet. She had tried and failed to appreciate the stalactites, hanging like icicles from the ceiling. When she thought she could no longer take the cold, that she'd have to either pop back home for a coat or give up for another day, in a moment of insanity or delirium or both, she muttered, "Here Hydra, Hydra. Here Hydra, Hydra."

In less than a second, the water moved like the tide coming in across her calves, and a scream, like a train screeching to a halt, echoed throughout the tunnels. Therese couldn't tell from which direction the monster was coming. She spun around and around, dizzy and panting, telling herself to go, to leave, to get the hell out of there. But she couldn't focus. She couldn't imagine her destination, and this made god travel impossible.

Think, Therese! Focus!

In her spot of light, Therese saw the scaly beast, its huge dragon head bobbing up and down on the end of its long, serpentine neck. She also saw claws and legs and realized it wasn't a sea snake after all as it half slithered and half tromped through the water toward her. Eight other necks, four on each side of the base of the center one, hung seared and lifeless, flopping like wings. Therese stood with leaden feet, watching in terror wherever her light fell, her mouth agape and her mind blank and stunned. The great mouth opened, exposing rows and rows of sharply pointed teeth, and lunged toward her, its head now within inches of her. Therese closed her eyes and thought of her room and Clifford nestled on her bed, but she didn't leave as the monster's snapping jaw grazed her nose before rearing back to strike again. Stupefied, Therese looked around in all directions, in full panic, swinging her sword madly, blindly, and hitting nothing. She leapt away from the path of the Hydra and fell on her hands and knees, her traveling robe ripped from her in shreds, hooked on the claws of the beast.

Therese sprang to her feet and retrieved her fallen sword as the monster discovered the cake and devoured it, making a noise sounding something like glee. Without stopping to look, Therese ran in the direction from which the Hydra had come, with only the circle of light to guide her. She stumbled once and fell, but scrambled to her feet, her eyes locked on the path before her. All she could do was run for her life. Even if she prayed, the gods couldn't help her.

At a fork in the tunnel, she went to the right, because the water seemed to get deeper the other way, and she knew the tunnel leading to the heart-shaped pool was shallow. The Hydra must have finished licking the icing from her mouth, for Therese heard the ground shaking again. She ran on, at full speed, but could hear the monster closing in on her, getting closer and closer to the shield on her back.

Another fork made her pause, and that was her undoing. If she'd flung herself one way or the other, she might have avoided being plucked up by the shield and lifted into the air. Therese threw her sword at the Hydra's head, slipped her arms from the shield, and jumped toward the rock wall. Scraping her hands and knees and elbows, she scuttled into a small cavity in the upper side of the wall, barely able to maneuver herself because it was a tight squeeze. She wriggled as far in as she could, flat on her stomach and elbows, until she hit up against solid rock. The Hydra screamed in frustration, chipping at the rock with her sharp teeth. Therese had nowhere to go and nothing to do but lie there.

"I will not freak out," she said aloud. "I will not freak out." She lay there, panting, trying to catch her breath, stuck like an insect in a spider's web, the walls closing in on her, like a cocoon, weaving tighter and tighter around her. The Hydra continued to scream and chip as Therese shouted, "Think!"

Using her hands and elbows, she rolled over onto her back to inspect her nook more fully, wincing with the realization that her back had been scratched by the claw of the Hydra. It stung and throbbed with pain now that she was aware of it. Up above her was another hole. She propped herself up, sticking her head into it, shaking so badly that her head repeatedly bumped into the rock. The light on her visor revealed another tunnel, so, like a termite, Therese pulled herself up till she was standing on her feet, cringing at the loud wails of the Hydra and the pounding against the rock near her. She unbelted her scabbard, useless now that her sword was lost, and let it drop to her feet. Then she grasped on to the rocks above her and found lodgments for her feet as she inched her way further up.

Therese rejoiced when she noticed the tunnel widening, allowing her to breathe and hold her arms out to each side. Eventually, she had to choose one side to scale, no longer able to stand astride the opening. She chose the side which was furthest from the wailing beast.

The wall became easier to scale, no longer upright, but slanting now into the steep slope of a hill, and the air became fresher, crisper. A few more strides, and Therese found herself safely out of the hill, staring up at the star-filled sky over Greece!

She emerged from the caverns and lifted her arms toward the moon, happy to be alive. She had been face to face with the monster and had lived!

Her elation quickly turned to dread as the pain throbbed in her back and she had this realization: if she left the hill now, she'd never have another chance to complete the fifth challenge. She had no traveling robe, and she had no way of getting another. She wasn't allowed to ask the gods for help, and they weren't allowed to help her, except to give advice. If she was going to make it through the entrance to the Underworld, she'd have to do it tonight. Besides, how would she get home without the robe? She might make it down to the city of Argos and ask for help, inventing some story about being abducted and taken to Greece. Then she wouldn't have to climb back into the cold and narrow lair and risk her life again. But that would mean no life with Than. He might insist on changing her anyway, but how could she live with herself knowing that her cowardice was the cause of his eternal torment?

She must succeed or die trying.

She took in another breath of the crisp, chilly air and then turned back to the hill, descending down the steep slope of the tunnel toward the Hydra.

As she bent her knees and hiked into the musty cavern, the quiet, still air made her shudder. The thrashing and wailing had stopped, and the beast could be anywhere. Therese turned her head in all directions, shining her light around the tunnel, not wanting to return the same direction she came. To her right, above a boulder wedged in the rocky slope, she spotted another opening. She inched over to it and discovered it was more gradual in its descent. Crouched low, she crept along as quietly as she could, following its curves as it spiraled down. When she reached a fork, she sat on her bottom and looked down both ways. If only one of the gods could give her a sign. This was worse than the labyrinth. She would never find the heart-shaped pool; she might as well find a needle in a haystack. Tears pricked her eyes, and she gave into the tears as they slid down her face.

Then she spotted water in the tunnel to her left, so she took it. Not long into the tunnel, Therese could stand, and a few yards further, the walls opened up into a massive cavern, at least a hundred feet wide and twenty or more feet high. Shining her light all over the walls and ceiling, she lost her footing and fell into a body of water. She scrambled back to the bank, crawling on her hands and knees, and pointed her light on the water. It wasn't the heart-shaped pool. As she sat there catching her breath, she noticed something moving beneath the water, and the craziest idea struck her: the only way she'd ever find the heart-shaped pool was by having the beast lead her to it. If the Hydra nested there, she might return to it. So, without allowing herself to think twice, Therese climbed to her feet, and when the Hydra emerged from the water and slithered across the bank, Therese ran toward, rather than away, from her.

"Ahhhh!" Therese screamed as she ran, summoning the courage by burning her throat with the loudest sound she could muster. "Ahhhh!" she shouted again, and, surprisingly, the monster paused.

Therese leapt from the ground onto the scaly neck and wrapped her arms and legs tightly around her. "Don't hurt me, don't hurt me, don't hurt me!" She closed her eyes, pressing her face against the slimy scales. The Hydra swung her neck back and forth, trying to buck her off, and, for a second, Therese compared the feeling to riding the octopus at the Pagosa Springs Fair.

Time for a new tactic, she thought in a lucid moment. "It's okay girl," Therese said softly. "There, there. I'm not here to hurt you."

The Hydra screamed back in reply and dipped down into the water. Therese held her breath and closed her eyes. When they resurfaced, Therese's light was gone, and she found herself in complete darkness.

Down into the ice-cold water they plunged, only to come up again. Down and up. Down and up. Therese shivered but clung to the neck, her ankles crossed, her right hand holding tightly to her left wrist. Apparently, the Hydra hoped to wash Therese from her neck by continuously dunking her underwater, but Therese fiercely held on. Then like the fastest rollercoaster ride ever, they streamed through the air, turning one way and then another, Therese gritting her teeth and clamping shut her eyes. Before she had a chance to take a breath, they plunged down into the water again.

The Hydra rolled round and round beneath the water, like an alligator, but Therese clung to the beast's neck with her arms and legs. Her neck and shoulders ached, and she trembled with cold, and now, she felt like she couldn't hold her breath much longer. She opened her eyes with panic and noticed a light glowing across from her. The memory of the night her parents died flashed through her. There had been a light then, too. But this light was different. It was a boy. A glowing boy. Was it Than? No, it was Hip, and he was swimming toward her!

She dived away from the Hydra and power kicked the dolphin kick to Hip. He wrapped his arms around her, and in the next instant, she was enveloped by sleep.

Chapter Thirty: Apollo

Than hovered helplessly above the Argos underwater entrance, ready to intervene and take Therese to his grandmother's winter cabin the moment she became mortally wounded. When her traveling robe got hooked on the claw of the Hydra, he cursed himself for not anticipating that possibility. Without god travel, she was doomed. But when she crawled from the hill, safe in the Grecian moonlight, he couldn't be happier, until he saw her turn back. She wanted to face the monster to spare him the maenads. His heart clenched with dread and love.

He couldn't believe his eyes when he saw her leap to the Hydra's neck and hold on. What was she thinking? Was she actually trying to befriend the beast? Was she cooing, "There, there"? This was crazy. He couldn't believe it. The Hydra could not be tamed. He wanted to reach down into the lair and shake Therese. Then he recoiled from the thought as he watched in horror: the Hydra thrashed Therese around like a loose, live wire.

He'd never seen the monster in such a panic. He couldn't recall anyone ever clinging to her neck like that. The beast flailed her head like a huge whip, but Therese held on, even underwater. The Hydra became more and more terrified the longer Therese held on, submerging herself again and again, hoping to free herself of Therese. Then she did the only other thing she could think of: she ran to her nest.

At last, Than realized Therese's plan, and, though he hadn't thought it possible, his esteem for her grew. He disintegrated and dispatched to the dream world to get his brother's help.

Than wished he could have been the one to meet Therese at the underwater entrance, but he couldn't risk weakening her further. Better for her to fall asleep anyway after sustaining so many injuries. When Hip took her in his arms and carried her to his field of poppies, Than saw the wound on her back and winced. He fragmented and dispatched to Mount Olympus to beg Apollo for help.

"He's not here," Artemis, Apollo's sister said, after Than addressed those present.

"Do you know where I can find him? It's an emergency."

"He's in Dallas with his boyfriend, who's running in a marathon today," Artemis replied.

Than thanked her and dispatched to Dallas, hovering above the city where the sun was now rising, until his eyes spotted a street filled with runners. Among them in mortal form was Apollo, running alongside another man. Than traveled to a copse of trees on the edge of the road, waiting. When the runners caught up, he fell in line beside the two runners, not in mortal form—he couldn't disintegrate and be in many places at once if he changed—but as a dimly lit god in a hooded track suit, hoping he wouldn't be noticed by the runners whose faces turned forward, focused on the road ahead.

"Can you be bothered, Cousin?" Than asked.

"For a price." Apollo's face gleamed with sweat in the light of dawn.

"Name it."

The next words by Apollo were prayed rather than spoken: "When this lover of mine perishes, hopefully many decades from now, give me time with him before you take him to the Underworld, and speak on his behalf to the three judges. He's a good man, deserving of the Elysian Fields."

"I swear," Than prayed back.

Apollo then turned to his lover. "Marvin, this is my cousin, Than."

The blond, trim man beside Apollo saluted Than, who dipped his head in reply.

"We've got a family emergency to attend to," Apollo continued. "Sorry to have to back out of the race. I'll see you at Monica's later."

"Sounds good," Marvin said.

Than and Apollo veered from the road and into more trees, Than saying, "My chambers," and together god-traveled to the Underworld.

On Than's bed, on her side, sound asleep, lay Therese, with Hip beside her. Than left as soon as he arrived to watch from a distance, so as not to endanger her life.

"The Hydra," Hip explained to Apollo.

The god of healing, and of music, and of many other things, hesitated. "My healing her won't implicate me in anyway, will it? Do we have your father's blessing?"

Hades appeared beside them. "Yes. She fought well and is deserving of your help."

Apollo laid his fingertips gently on Therese's wounds. The torn skin sought and found where it had once been joined and reunited into a seamless organ. He found other wounds on her legs and arms and healed them, too.

"She's a beautiful girl," he said when he had finished. "She'll make a lovely goddess."

Than felt his heart heat up like a spark ignited from stones. The hardest parts of the challenge were behind her, and now that she was healed, the excitement kicked in: soon, Dionysus would change her and they would spend eternity together. No more would he be forced to look at her from a distance. No more would he have to steal moments with her in her dreams. Never again would he have to beg and bargain to have his brother or Hermes take his place so he could be at her side. Soon, he would have unlimited access to her. They would spend all their days together. It occurred to him that though she must live with him in the Underworld, there was no reason why they couldn't travel the world together. Unlike his father, Than could disintegrate and be at many places at once, so while Persephone was forced to remain at Hades's side in the gloomy Underworld for six months out of the year, Therese could accompany Than anywhere. Why hadn't he thought of this before? Only now, had the possibility of her being his wife seemed real enough for him to fully contemplate. He'd never felt happier.

Of course, there was the problem of finding her a purpose. All gods and goddesses must perform a service, a duty to either humanity or to the world. If they were to be accepted on Mount Olympus, and if the transformation to immortality were to be permanent, Therese must find a purpose. He'd have to help her.

Before Apollo left, Than thanked the god of healing and music and assured him that he would keep his promise. Then he hovered above his chambers and took great pleasure in watching his future wife sleep.

Chapter Thirty-One: Preparations

Before Therese opened her eyes, she smelled him. Than's scent surrounded her as she stretched and yawned and hugged his pillow to her chest. In her mind, she prayed to him, "It won't be long now. One more challenge to go."

As she enjoyed the soft sound of the water cascading down the shelves of stone beside her, she wondered if she was supposed to begin the last of her challenges now. Could she find her way to Erebus on her own? There were two doors to Than's room: one led from his sitting room. The second must lead out to other parts of the Underworld. She walked across the room and to the second door, reaching out her hand. Strangely, her hand moved through the wooden door as though it were a curtain of light.

"This is odd," she muttered, but dismissed the anomaly as a typical occurrence in the Underworld and pressed the rest of her body through the door.

Light from the river of fire illuminated a narrow passageway, reminding her of the tunnels beneath Larissa Hill in Argos and the palace ruins in Crete. Just what she needed, she thought: another labyrinth. She followed the flaming river along the passageway, twisting and turning first to the right and then to the left and again to the right, the shadows on the walls and ceilings creeping her out and making her flinch more than once. Up ahead, she thought she saw someone turn a corner. She quickened her pace to catch up.

"Hello?" she called.

When no one replied, Therese moved onward, mentally sending out prayers to Than, Hip, and the Furies for help and guidance. "What am I supposed to do?" she asked. "How can I succeed in the last challenge without directions?"

It was like trying to solve a puzzle with too many missing pieces, or to write with an inkless pen. This was crazy. This was ridiculous. But she pushed on through the tunnel, hoping for inspiration.

Therese turned another corner to find the path opened up to a large body of water, very much resembling the pool of water beneath Larissa Hill where she had leaped onto the Hydra's neck. A movement beneath the surface made her take several steps back. What appeared was not the Hydra, but Meg. Her blonde hair wasn't wet, as it should be, but long and curly, and blowing about her fiercely beautiful face, though no current moved through the cavern. A falcon rested on her shoulder, his feathers also dry. He stretched his wings with two quick motions, and then resumed his statue-like position at attention.

"Hello, Therese." Meg strolled across the surface of the water toward her. "I've been meaning to tell you how sorry I am that I was reluctant to accept you into our family. I'm afraid I wasn't very nice to you in Colorado. But I've been truly pleased with your performance and look forward to the day when I can call you my sister."

Therese clamped her mouth shut to keep it from hanging open and blinked several times to prevent her eyes from widening with surprise. Instead, she clasped her hands nervously behind her back. "Thanks, Meg. That's nice of you to say."

"As a token of my apology, I've brought you a gift."

"Have you come to tell me how to find Erebus?"

"No. Better." On either side of Meg, Therese's parents appeared, standing on top of the water, and smiling at Therese.

"Mom? Dad?" Therese stood in shock, her mouth agape without restraint. After a moment, she stumbled to the edge of the water, reaching out toward them, beyond excited by their presence. "It it really you?"

"Therese!" her mother cried out as she dashed to the bank and took her daughter in her arms.

Therese's father was close behind, enveloping the two of them in his warm embrace. "We've missed you so much."

Tears of joy sprang from Therese's eyes. "I didn't get to say good-bye. I've missed you like crazy. Does this mean I'm allowed to be with you again? When I complete the challenges, will we be together again?"

"I think so," her mother said. "But listen. There's something I need to tell you."

Therese looked at her mother with longing, breathing in her scent of Jergen's lotion and Haiku perfume. It lingered on her still. Therese was incredulous, absolutely in disbelief that her mother's arms held her again. And she felt warm, supple, alive—not cold, not lifeless. Her body felt like it always had when her mother had held her, rocked her as a child, sang to her on nights she couldn't sleep.

Her mother stroked Therese's hair. "We once told you we didn't want any more children, but that wasn't true."

"Really? I don't understand. If you wanted more kids, why didn't you…"

"We tried," her father said. "We tried and couldn't. So we were in the process of adopting. We were going to surprise you."

"Oh my gosh. I almost had a little brother or sister?"

"Almost, sweetie pie," her mother said. "And when we died, we wished more than ever that we hadn't left you alone."

"But I've had Carol."

"Of course. Thank goodness for her," her father said.

Her father's face looked exactly as it always had, his brown eyes warm, his smile gentle. She leaned in and smelled him, the musk of his cologne. The blankets on his bed and the clothes in her parents' closet had held that smell for months. Oh, how she missed it.

"I just wanted you to know." Her mother squeezed her tight. "I wanted you to know that we did try. Your father knew what it was like to be an only child, and it was important to him to give you pets and to keep trying."

"It's so nice to be with you again," her father said.

"You have your complete memory back, then?" First she took her father's face in her hands and examined it. "You remember everything about your past, the accident, me?"

"Why wouldn't I?" he said. "You're the best thing that ever happened to me."

Therese then took her mother's face between her hands and studied her mother's expression, felt her warm breath against her face. "Mom? You, too? You remember everything about our lives?"

"Oh, Therese! How could I forget? You're my most precious little girl!"

Therese wrapped an arm around each of her parent's waists and huddled there between them. "Once I marry Than, I'll spend every day with you. We'll be together again, like we used to be. Even Clifford can come. I can't wait! I can't wait to be with you like we used to be. Oh, Mom! Dad!" Tears fell rapidly down her cheeks and she thought she would burst with joy.

As she glanced back at Meg to thank her, something strange happened: Therese's hand fell from her arm and plopped onto the bank of the water. Then her ear slipped off the side of her face. "What's happening to me?" She screamed in terror. "I'm falling apart!"

Her parents picked up her hand and her ear and tried desperately to reattach them to her body, but they couldn't. Then the other ear slipped from her head, and she could no longer hear anything. "I'm falling to pieces," she said, just as a few teeth loosened in her mouth, and she had to spit to keep from choking on them. Holding tightly to her parents, she dreaded the new realization coming over her.

"No!" she screamed. "No! This isn't a dream! It can't be!" She wrenched her arms more tightly around her parents, even though a part of her knew they were silly, stupid figments.

She opened her eyes to find herself on Than's bed, and sitting on a golden chair looking at her was Hades, god of the Underworld.

"The human mind is an interesting thing," he said. "You not only reconstructed your original family, making it intact once again, but you also added an addition, so that the next time around—there really isn't a next time around, but humor me, will you?—so that the next time around you wouldn't be left alone. Your mind wants to correct what you perceive to be your parents' mistake: they should have given you a sibling, so when they died, you wouldn't be left alone."

"But I have Carol…and Richard. And there's Clifford and Jewels."

"Yes, yes, well. Good for you. But your mind longs for a more intimate connection to your parents, am I right?"

Therese sat up and stared blankly at the god, not sure if he was mocking her or sympathizing. "I suppose."

"You might find it interesting to know that they were not interested in having more children. In fact, though they loved and treasured you, they conceived you by mistake. Immediately after your birth, your mother had her tubes tied. She and your father never intended to have children because they worried their careers would take too much time away from parental responsibilities."

Therese felt her face go pale, her stomach queasy.

"They loved you dearly, of course, and never regretted having you. I'm giving you this information because I want you to understand why they didn't have more children."

"Because they never intended to have any."

"But they loved you. Remember that."

She nodded, wishing he hadn't told her she'd been a mistake.

"Listen to me, Therese, because I've said this many, many times to many, many mortals, and it always seems to go in one ear and out the other—hence your ears being among the first parts of your body to fall off in your dream. Interesting symbolism. Wouldn't you agree?"

She frowned.

"I've lost count of how many times I've said this. Even the gods don't know how many. Once a mortal dies, he or she cannot come back, though there have been rare exceptions. This means that, should you succeed in the fifth challenge—and we're all rooting for you now, dear girl, really, we are. You're performance has been impressive. A pleasant surprise. So, should you succeed in the fifth challenge, you will not be reunited with your parents as you dreamed. They are happy in the Fields of Elysium, but believe me when I tell you they do not remember you. Their memories have left them and cannot be restored. Look at me, Therese."

Therese, who had looked away to fight tears, forced herself to meet his eyes. She was surprised to see kindness, compassion, and acceptance. As he tugged his curly, black beard, his dark eyes bore into hers like those of her swim team coach, of her spelling bee sponsor, of her own mother and father—of every adult who had ever advised or counseled her. He wanted her to succeed.

"I want to warn you about a few characters whose paths you may cross on your journey to Erebus. Each of the five rivers is inhabited by at least one nymph, and they are mischievous creatures who will try to distract you. Pay them no mind, but be polite. If offended, they can impede you."

"Okay. Thanks."

"In addition to the nymphs, there are other daemons that dwell here. You've met my daughters, the Furies. The Fates are also here, though they will not likely try to speak with you. Usually mortals wish to seek them out to bribe them into changing their destinies."

"Can they do that?"

"Not without a price that's usually too difficult to pay."

Therese swallowed hard.

"I also have a vulture, Euronymus, who flies though the tunnels coming and going. He strips the flesh from the uneaten human corpses. He won't bother you, but he may screech by and bulldoze you down— he's as big as you are—so be on the lookout. Ascalaphus, my owl, may also screech or hoot as he flies about the caverns. He's friendly. No worries there. And, of course, there are other creatures that lurk here—bats, spiders, snakes, and such.”

“I'm not afraid of them.” She was elated by how obvious it was that he really did hope she would succeed, but she didn't dare smile. He frightened her still.

“One more thing, Therese. Every mortal whom I have ever allowed to descend down here to speak with the dead has been told to return to the land of the living without looking back. I ask this of them as a sign of trust. Orpheus, above them all, seemed the most likely to succeed. Of them all, I thought he had a chance. But at the last minute, he, like everyone before and after him, suspected me of cheating him, of tricking him in some way. He looked back to make sure I was keeping my end of the bargain. Believe me when I tell you I was disappointed. Crushed, really. I loved Orpheus. His music filled me with happiness. I tell you this because you and Than seem confident that the challenges are essentially over. All you have to do is journey down to Erebus and apologize to Vicki Stern. Then you must turn back to the gates, board Charon's raft, and allow him to return you to the Upperworld. That all sounds easy, but here's the rub: You shall not look back. Do you hear me? Ares will try to trick you, do you understand? I can do nothing to prevent his interference. You must not look back. In case I'm not being clear, let me say once more: YOU MUST NOT LOOK BACK. Do you understand?”

Therese nodded dumbly.

Hades rolled his eyes. “I doubt this little talk of ours has done any good. I can only hope. If I could take back the challenge I would, dear girl. But you must complete it. Are you ready?”

“Now? Right now?”

“There's no better time than the present, as they say.”

“Yes. Yes, I'm ready.”

“Follow the Phlegethon—that's the river of flames—until it crosses the Lethe. At that junction, turn right and follow the Lethe down to the edge of a deep cavern. If Charon comes by on his raft, you may ask him to take you into Erebus; otherwise, you will have to scale down the walls yourself. But you can do it. I've seen you climb. Once you apologize to Vicki, you can either catch the raft back, or, if you don't want to wait for Charon, you'll have to climb back up. Don't come back this way, though. Follow the Lethe in the opposite direction, toward the Styx. Turn right at the Styx. It will take you to the main gate, where Cerberus sits on guard. Wait on the bank for Charon. He'll take you on the raft by way of the Acheron. Although you'll come out at what will look like the middle of a desert, don't worry. If you succeed, I will fetch you myself and take you to Dionysus."

"And if I fail?"

"If you fail because of mortal injury, you will stay here. The judges will determine precisely where. If you look back—and, please, Therese, don't look back—then Hip will carry you home to Colorado, as you sleep."

"I won't look back."

Chapter Thirty-Two: The Final Challenge

As Therese stepped through the wooden door of Than's room—opening it, for it was solid, unlike it had been in her dream—she wished again Hades hadn't told her the truth about her parents. She hated the idea that she'd been an inconvenience to them, a burden, even if, later, they loved her. Therese emerged into a tunnel similar to the one in her dream, and for a moment she worried, actually wished, it was another dream. If she were dreaming, then what Hades had said about her being an accident might not be true. She pushed off the ground with her feet but landed squarely on her sneakers. Pinching herself brought no change. As far as she could tell, she wasn't dreaming.

The tunnel opened onto a larger cavern, and as soon as Therese stepped inside, a coven of bats was disturbed and rushed in a whirlwind around her before making its escape through a tight opening above. The coven consisted of thousands, perhaps even hundreds of thousands, of small fruit bats similar to some she had seen once with her parents and grandparents at an abandoned train tunnel near San Antonio.

Hades had warned her there were creatures, but hundreds of thousands? Maybe Ares had multiplied them in an attempt to scare her. *You'll have to do better than that, Ares,* she thought.

Had that been a thought or a prayer? What was the difference between the two, especially when one addressed a god? Hoping Ares had no privy to the thought, Therese hiked on along the river of fire. The last thing she needed was for the god of war to feel challenged.

As she hiked, she thought again of her parents and their plan not to have children. Had the accident not occurred she wouldn't exist. At all? Not even here, or in heaven, or somewhere else? How strange her existence, her whole being, depended on one unplanned act.

People say things happen for a reason and things are meant to be, so maybe she came along in spite of her parents' wishes. She was destined to live, to meet Than, and to be here, right now, at this moment. Or, maybe life consisted mostly of accidents and there was no plan, no destiny. Maybe you had to make your own destiny.

Hades said her parents had no regret about having her. How could he be sure? What if there were moments when her parents wished they didn't have to compromise their careers in order to take care of her?

She wondered if it would be possible to see them, even though they wouldn't recognize her. The dream had seemed so real and had felt so awesome. Maybe she would pass by the Elysian Fields and catch a glimpse of them on her way to Erebus. Maybe.

The passageway turned sharply to the right, and as she followed it, a swarm of rats ran down the ceiling and onto her. They weren't biting, so she didn't panic. She had often wanted rats for pets because she had learned, after her parents got her Puffy, that hamsters were generally antisocial, whereas rats loved human company. She had played with rats at the pet store in town and had tried to convince Jen to get some—you should never get just one, because they get lonely and need companionship, the pet store worker had said. Now, as the rats crawled up her arms and legs, along her shoulders and the front and back of her neck, she giggled.

"That tickles." She lifted one with both hands—you should never lift a rat by the tail, she recalled, because you could injure its spine—and looked into its beady eyes. They were red because of the reflection of the river of fire. She imagined they were black otherwise. "Hello there," she said to it.

One rat made its way beneath the leg of her jeans, so she bent over and grabbed it with her other hand. "Oh no you don't, mister." Meanwhile, several were burrowing in her hair and licking her earlobe. "I have to get going guys. Are you coming with me?" She set the two in her hands down on her shoulders.

Carefully, so as not to step on any of them, she moved forward. Most ran from her limbs and hair, but a few lingered on her shoulders and the back of her neck, their tails clinging to her face for balance. She spit when one of the tails moved across her lips. Otherwise, their company wasn't so bad.

Jen would freak, she thought.

All but the two perched on her shoulders eventually scurried away. She was glad for their company, especially as she neared the junction where the river of fire met the Lethe, and before she could turn right, away from the flames, a beautiful woman with long green hair and flowing robes of the same hue emerged to the surface of the river and smiled at her.

Therese smiled back, unsure whether she should stop or keep going. Recalling Hades's warning to be polite, she stopped and said, "Hello."

"Hello. Who are you?"

"Therese. And you?"

"Lethe."

"I thought Lethe was a river."

"Indeed. It's named for me. Why are you passing this way?"

Therese wasn't sure whether she should tell the whole story, but when she considered that it might win the woman's sympathy, she decided to tell all. "Thanatos and I are in love and want to marry, but in order to be accepted by Hades, I have to complete one last challenge of five."

"Oh? Why would such a young lady wish to join the daemons of the Underworld?"

Therese looked about her. "It's actually pretty fascinating down here. And, as I said, I love Than."

Lethe asked her more about her life, about the challenges, about how she came to know Thanatos. When she seemed satisfied with Therese's answers, she asked one more.

"Do you miss your parents?"

"Of course."

The woman floated on the river with only her head above the water, and her long green hair streamed behind her like fishing line carried by the current. "It hurts, doesn't it," she said without inflection.

"Yes. Very much."

"I can help you with that pain."

"How?"

"I can help you forget. Think how much happier you'd be as Than's wife if you didn't have to be burdened by that feeling of loss for all eternity. Wouldn't you rather be happy?" Lethe floated right up to Therese, her face only a foot away, and smiled. "We'd all like to be happy. Happy forever, Therese. Wouldn't you like that?"

It sounded lovely to Therese just then, and she felt her body relaxing. She could forget how badly she had let Vicki down, how she should have died, too. She could forget about her parents' death, about all her losses. Lethe began humming a soft melody, soothing Therese, making her shoulders relax for the first time in months. The rats on her shoulders sat very still as the peace beckoned her.

"Don't you want to be happy? Forever?" Lethe asked again, smoothly. "All you have to do is take a sip of the river; or, better still, take a swim with me and feel its refreshing current move through you, giving you a new life."

"A new life?"

"That's right, Therese. Doesn't that sound nice?"

Therese nodded. The shame over Vicki and the longing for her parents could be erased with one small sip, or one restful dip. Then she could marry Than and live happily ever after.

But would she remember Than? Or would a sip from the Lethe wash away all her memories?

And did she really want to forget her parents altogether, as though they had never existed?

The thought of losing all recollection of her parents made her throat tighten and her shoulders tense. The two rats fled down her arms and legs and disappeared.

"Thanks, Lethe, but I don't want to forget."

The goddess rose from the river, a giant, as tall as Todd's truck, and looked down at her. "Come with me, Therese. Only I will make you happy!"

Therese turned from the goddess and ran, following the river, which flushed white in ripples, like bursting pipes, as she passed it. As she ran away from the river of flames, the cavern became darker, and if she hadn't slowed because of the darkness, she would have plunged into the canyon below. As it was, she teetered on the edge, struggling to regain her balance. She plopped on her bottom, panting and gritting her teeth, hoping this was all nearly over. Please, she prayed. Please let this be over soon. She stared down the canyon wall and sighed with relief when she recognized Erebus in its purple glow.

Although the canyon was deep and narrow, it spread out near the bottom where hundreds of souls lay around with half-closed eyes in a shallow pool of the Lethe, which trickled down the canyon wall like water from a faucet that hasn't been properly closed. Hades had said she could scale down to the bottom to look for Vicki, but she was worried about falling into the water and erasing her memory. She sat with her legs dangling over the edge, watching for Charon and his raft.

In the next instant, she felt something tickle the back of her neck. Thinking it was one of the rats, she reached back to pick it up when her hand wrapped around the slimy body of a snake. She threw the snake across the cavern, unsure whether it was poisonous, and climbed to her feet. The snake, which had landed only a few yards away and which looked to be about four feet long, curled into a tight coil and lifted its round head to look at her. She studied its black opened mouth and grey scales, trying to identify it, slowly backing away from its head, now recoiled as though about to strike.

Within seconds, the grey monster leapt into the air toward her face. Therese jumped back, the snake barely missing her as it fell to the ground. As the snake coiled and lifted its head for another go, Therese careened through the air, her knees suddenly wobbly. She looked all about and discovered she was standing beside Charon on his raft sailing through the air toward Erebus in a downward spiral.

She couldn't be happier to see the old god, his bright bald head and slender, bowed frame. He held his long pole in both hands, circling it to their left, the center of their spiral. Soon they hovered above the shallow pool, unnoticed by those lying in it. Charon pointed one long bony finger across the canyon. Therese turned in the direction he pointed to see Vicki on the edge of the pool only a few yards away.

Vicki sat on the edge of the pool surrounded by others, but Mrs. Stern wasn't one of them. Her face was mostly expressionless except for a hint of sadness in her eyes, which stared off in a daze. Tears streamed down Therese's own eyes as she again wished it had been her instead of her friend who'd died. She couldn't stand the thought of Mr. Stern being all alone, heart-broken, for the rest of his life.

Therese looked once more at Charon, whose face remained impassive. Afraid to step from the raft, she cupped her hands around her mouth and shouted, "Vicki! Vicki Stern!"

Nothing happened. No one even looked in her direction.

Did Vicki even remember her own name? How could Therese apologize for something her friend no longer remembered? Maybe this apology wasn't about Vicki. Maybe it was the only way Therese could come to terms with what happened—to accept responsibility for her part. Maybe she'd feel better after. Maybe she'd prove to Hades she'd learned a lesson.

While she was pondering these thoughts, the three Furies appeared floating above the pool of water between Therese and Vicki. "Apologize!" they shouted, blood pouring from their eyes. Their hair lifted up into coils of slithering snakes as they grew closer to her. "Apologize!"

"Um…"

Blood dripped from their lips. Alecto's hands reached for Therese's neck, wrapping cold fingers around her throat. "Apologize!"

"I'm sorry!" Therese cried, her voice only a squeak beneath the pressure of Alecto's fingers. "I shouldn't have bought the drug! I hate that I'm still alive and you're not! I hate what I did and wish I could take it all back! Oh, Vicki! Look at me!"

To her surprise, Vicki sat up and turned to look at her.

"I'm so sorry!"

Vicki first bent her brows; then she smiled and waved. "It's nice to see a friendly face."

"Do you remember me?"

"Should I?"

"Are you okay?"

Vicki shrugged. "I felt sad for a long time, but I'm feeling much better. They say around here that I'm due to leave this place soon. Supposedly there's a much prettier place. Are you going there?"

"One day, maybe."

The Furies disappeared and the raft spiraled upward. Therese fell to her knees, aghast by what had just happened, bewildered by the Furies' treatment of her, relieved by Vicki's smile, and dizzy from the circling movement of the raft. She silently thanked Hades as they sailed above Erebus and then swiftly turned down the Lethe in the opposite direction from where she came. Water jumped up at her from the river, threatening to touch her, and in so doing, wipe away some of her past. They sailed so quickly that the underground scenery was a whirlwind. Therese prayed to Hades, to Than, to Hip, and to all the gods to help her even though she knew they weren't allowed to come to her aid. The raft swiftly turned again, and now they flew along the blackest of the rivers—the Styx. Therese thought she saw a pair of eyes in the water looking up at her alongside the raft, following them, but before she could bend closer to the water, they stopped at the black iron gate, just on the inside, where Charon pointed to the bank and waited.

"I'm to get off here?"

He continued to point, though his face remained without expression or reply.

Therese climbed from the raft and waited near the gate, careful not to look back, but relieved she had made it to the end. She could see Cerberus just on the other side as Charon passed him.

"Therese!" someone called from behind her. It sounded like the voice of her father. "Therese, don't look back. Just listen to me! Hades has sent us as a gift."

"Sweetheart!" This was the voice of her mother. "We've been allowed to hug and kiss you, but that's all. Be careful not to look at us."

"What? Is that really you, guys? You can remember me?"

A hand touched her shoulder.

"We couldn't for the longest time, but Hades has given you this gift. You're allowed one moment to be with us again."

She felt arms wrap around her waist from behind, and a kiss was planted on the top of her head. "We love you so much," the voice of her father said. "It's so good to be close to you again."

"I miss you, sweetheart."

Therese's teeth began to chatter, and her knees felt weak. "That can't be you, can it?" She wanted to turn to look at them so badly. What if Hades really did wish to reward her with this gift? "I miss you, too," she said feebly.

"We can't wait to see you again," her father's voice came behind her. "You've grown so much, in just a year. How are those chipmunks doing? Are you remembering to feed them the seeds I bought?"

She wanted to turn to see her father's face, to touch her mother's cheek!

"No!" she shouted without turning, shutting her eyes closed. "Whoever you are, you aren't my parents! I'm not falling for it!"

"You can take us with you," her father said more gently. "Hades even admitted that there have been rare exceptions to the rule that mortals can't return from the Underworld. Why can't we be one of those exceptions? Thanatos loves you, for heaven's sake! Who better to be granted an exception?"

Therese paused. That was true. If any exception could be made to the rule that mortals could not return, why couldn't one be made for her parents? If Than loved her, what stopped him from demanding this favor of Hades?

But this had to be a trap. Ares was trying to get her to look back. She wouldn't fall for it. "Leave me alone! If you are my parents, leave me alone, and, if it's possible, I'll come back for you once I'm a god."

"We understand," her mother's voice cried. "Don't look at me, but come and give me one last kiss."

Therese fixed her eyes on the gate and shouted, "Figments, I command you to show yourselves!"

A fluttering of wings sounded behind her, but she dared not turn to see what it was. After a moment, she heard only the sound of the river lapping against the bank.

Up ahead, Charon circled across the Acheron where she could see Than boarding with two others. They sailed back to the Styx and past Cerberus. The great gate groaned open as the raft came toward her. She waved to Than and called out his name. The look he gave her puzzled her. Here she was at the end of her final challenge, and his expression was more apprehensive than ever. What was wrong?

She watched him sail past her, and then, without thinking, she turned and followed him with her eyes as he sailed into the Underworld.

Her hand flew to her mouth, and she immediately turned back toward the gate, hoping no one had seen, but knowing they must have. Of course they'd seen! She dropped to her knees, begging any god who'd listen to have mercy on her.

Then Than appeared. "Do you want to do this thing?"

"You mean burn to death?"

"Yes."

"But the maenads." She felt herself losing consciousness.

"Forget the maenads. Will you burn?"

"Yes."

Chapter Thirty-Three: Demeter's Winter Cabin

Than fragmented and flew to Therese, and, with her consent, scooped her in his arms, and traveled to his grandmother's winter cottage in a heavily wooded area near the base of Mount Kronos. As soon as he arrived, he laid Therese on a bed and left the house so as not to further endanger Therese's life. Once he was a safe distance away, he hovered above the cabin ready to explode with frustration. Therese had almost succeeded. If only she hadn't spotted him, she would have left through the gate and become his queen, accepted by the other gods, rather than exiled from Mount Olympus for all eternity. He'd tried to issue her a look of warning, to remind her of Hades's one command—do not look back—but his expression had only bewildered her into watching him. He bellowed out his frustration, shaking the woods below. Birds darted from their nests, rabbits dashed into holes, and even humans turned their heads up to the sky, looking for thunderclouds. The tears gathering in his eyes fell like rain on a few treetops. He bit his tongue so hard it bled. So close. She had been so close.

Demeter and Persephone arrived moments later, also full of tears, but not for Therese. They flew to where he hovered above the cabin and threw their arms around him.

"They'll rip you to pieces," his mother said through thick sobs.

"And not just once," his grandmother added. "But every year."

His mother cupped his face in her hands. "Please don't do this, Thanatos. I beg you, as the mother who gave life to you. I beg you with all my heart. Your pain will be unbearable, but so will mine when I hear your cries each year forever."

"Please, Thanatos," his grandmother added. "Heed your mother's words. Those who love you will suffer for all eternity. Love is fleeting. Punishment for broken oaths is not."

Thanatos pulled back from their suffocating embraces. He loved them, but this was hard enough without them reminding him every minute of every day. Having his one thumb ripped from his body had hurt like hell. Multiply that by a thousand. He shuddered. Yes, he knew what they were saying made sense, but he had to have Therese. "You don't understand. Without her, I have no life. If you don't want to suffer over my pain, then stop trying to talk me out of this thing. If I don't do it, I'll be miserable. With Therese at my side, you may hear my cries once a year; without her, they'll be constant. If you love me, give it to me now."

Demeter pulled a vial from the folds of her robe and reluctantly handed it over to Than. "The more you rub over her, the faster she'll burn. Use it all to ensure a speedy death."

"And son, you can't take her soul from her body. If you do, the process is ruined."

Than's mouth dropped open. "But all along I planned to take her before I set fire to her body."

Demeter lowered her eyes. "I'm sorry. It won't work if you do."

"Maybe now you'll change your mind?"

Than chewed his bottom lip, which, like his tongue, trickled with blood from his own doing. "Therese must decide. Please go and put the question to her."

Chapter Thirty-Four: Burned Alive

Therese awoke in a strange room, feeling dazed. Her throat was tight and dry, and she was overcome with a desperate thirst.

"Water," she muttered to anyone who might hear. "I need water."

Demeter appeared beside her, her long corn-blonde hair in two braids wrapped in buns on each side of her head, a little too high to resemble those of Princess Lea from Star Wars. The goddess handed Therese a golden goblet. Therese sat up and drank greedily.

Once satisfied, she looked around the room. The cabin was rustic and quaint, with windows on three sides and a kitchen and table across from her where she sat on the only bed in the room. Two closed doors might have led to other rooms.

Therese took another swallow of the fresh, cold water, and then gave the goblet back to Demeter. "Thank you."

"You're welcome." Demeter laid the cup on the table and turned back to Therese. "It seems you have a very important decision to make, young lady."

"I do?"

Demeter took a seat in a chair at the table across from the bed and narrowed her eyes at Therese. "Yes. The lives of many others will be affected by your choice, so choose wisely."

"Yes, ma'am."

"As you know, you failed the last challenge set to you by Hades."

Therese lowered her eyes. She'd been so stupid. After fighting the urge to look at her precious parents, she lost her mind and forgot what she was doing for a split second as she watched Than enter the Underworld. "I can't believe it." Tears welled in her eyes and she sniffled. "I'm so sorry. I was so stupid."

"You were set up to fail."

Therese lifted her head and searched Demeter's face. "What? How?"

"When Ares's plan of luring you with the voices of your parents failed, he sent his sons, Fear and Panic, to arouse your worry over Than."

Therese jumped to her feet. "But that's not fair!"

"Life rarely is."

Therese stared back, her mouth agape, letting it all sink in. Deflated, she muttered, "But death is," and sank back down on the bed.

"You know what will happen if Thanatos follows through with his plan to give you immortality."

Therese had tried so hard. She'd given each challenge her all. She risked her life to spare Than. The tears of frustration overwhelmed her as she covered her face with her hands. "I did everything I could! I tried so hard! I got past the Hydra, for crying out loud! Can't I have another chance? Can't I do something else to show I'm worthy?"

"Hades knows you're worthy, but, as he would say, 'A deal is a deal.' The laws of the challenge are immutable, and now, you must deal with the consequences."

"Why is it that so many exceptions have been made throughout history and none can be made for me?"

"Even those exceptions required a terrible price. Nothing in life is free."

Therese absently rubbed her tired legs as she muttered, "I can't let Than suffer for all time."

Persephone appeared beside them. "Thank you, dear girl. I'll take you home when you're ready."

"Wait," Demeter ordered. Looking at Therese, she said, "If you don't accept Than's gift of immortality, he may suffer just as horribly as he would if you do. Perhaps more."

"But," Persephone objected, "he may not. Maybe he will for a year or two, and what are they to a god? There's a good chance he'll get over Therese and move on with his life and never suffer again."

Than's voice boomed throughout the house: "Can you hear me Therese?"

She climbed to her feet and turned her face toward the ceiling. "Than? Where are you?"

"I'm close. Listen to me."

She nodded, shifting her weight nervously from one foot to the other, again and again.

"I love you more than I know how to say, and, more than anything, I want you at my side. But…"

She laughed nervously. "There's a but?"

"Originally, when I agreed to make you into a god, I thought, since I'm Death, I could take your soul just before I set you aflame, sparing you the pain of burning alive. But my mother and grandmother have just informed me doing so will ruin the transformation. This means that, if I were to go through with this, you would have to endure unimaginable pain. So, my question is, do you still choose to join me under those conditions."

Therese pulled at her hands, looked briefly at each of the goddesses in the room with her, and then turned her face back up to the ceiling. "Than, I already expected to feel the pain, so that changes nothing for me; what does affect my decision is the cost of my failure to you."

"Do you promise that is your only hesitation?"

"Yes. Absolutely. Definitely."

"Leave us!" Than's voice boomed. In the next instant, the two goddesses vanished, and she was alone in the cabin with him. He looked into her eyes, cupped her head with his hands, and pressed his lips to hers.

Her knees gave out, and he lifted her in his arms and laid her on the bed.

"I'll try to make this quick," he whispered at her ear, his breath warm and sweet.

He tugged off each of her sneakers, letting them drop to the floor. He unrolled her socks, quickly, and tossed them down with her shoes. Then he unbuttoned and unzipped her jeans.

"What are you doing?" she asked weakly, trembling with fear, her entire body erect with goose bumps.

"I have to undress you, in order to anoint you with the ambrosia."

"Oh."

He leaned over her and pressed his mouth against her cheek, feverishly working his mouth down her throat as he unbuttoned her shirt. She helped him by pulling her arms from the sleeves, unable to hide her trembling as he tossed her shirt in a heap on the floor with her other things. She lay on the bed in nothing but her bra and underwear.

"You're so beautiful," he whispered. "I'm so sorry for what I'm about to do."

She felt weak—whether from his presence, so lethal to her, or because of the tremendous fear she felt, she didn't know. She managed to mutter, "It's nothing compared to what you'll have to go through. Oh, please. Let's just get this over with. I'm thinking of us together. Forever." Her teeth began to chatter on that last word, and her body jerked and twitched, as though it were freezing.

He took a vial from his pocket and opened it. He poured the smooth liquid onto his hands. It reminded Therese of Jergen's lotion, and she thought of her mother, and then of her aunt Carol. She wondered if she'd ever see her aunt again, and this thought made her cry again.

Than rubbed the ambrosia first on her legs and feet. Therese tried vainly to pretend she was having a body massage, like she and her mother had done a few times in town, but nothing she thought of could help her body to relax and stop its fretful twitching and jerking and chattering.

Next, he rubbed the ambrosia on her arms and hands. As he did so, he said again and again how much he loved her and how grateful he was to know her. In spite of her fear and weakness, and now a shortness of breath and tightening of throat, Therese actually felt the pleasant pulse of desire and arousal when his hands moved to her shoulders and collarbone. He swept his hands quickly along her stomach, then her face. Then beneath her, along her back, his hands swept in long, gentle strokes. She found herself distracted by a desire for him to touch her in other places, too. She closed her eyes and actually sighed with pleasure when he finally did. She knew he couldn't linger anywhere because her life was already extinguishing due to his presence, but his soft touch, however rushed, gave her a taste of something to look forward to and something to think about other than burning alive.

When he'd finished, he carried her nearly naked body from the cabin and onto an altar beneath the bright blue sky. Though she was weak and short of breath and trembling with fear, she noticed the birds flying overhead and the sun setting behind the mountain. The wind blew, not too hard, but not gently, and Therese had this sickening thought: the wind would help her burn quickly.

She gritted her teeth and prayed, "Oh, god, oh god," repeatedly to anyone and everyone who might be listening.

Then Than lit a match.

"I love you, Therese," he cried as he put the flame to her hair. "May you go quickly."

Then, as she watched her hair light up in thick, hot flames around her face, she was surprised to see Than pour kerosene over his head and entire body and then lay beside her on the altar and throw his arms around her.

He was going to burn with her!

"I love you!" he cried again.

The flames reached her scalp, and sharp, intense pain spread across her skin. In the next instant, Than's entire body was a flurry of flames. She resisted the urge to struggle away from him and held on, feeling fainter and fainter as the fire licked across their bodies. She buried her flaming head into his flaming chest to muffle her cries, and all went dark.

BOOK THREE

A New Goddess

Chapter One: From the Ashes

The smell of ash permeated the air, and the cry of birds echoed over the valley. Therese's mouth was dry, her lips parched. She opened her sleepy eyes, her lashes momentarily sticking together, and found her face pressed against Than's chest. The pain had finally stopped. She knew exactly where she was.

She wasn't sure how long she'd been asleep on the altar beside Than beneath the Grecian skies at the base of Mount Kronos outside of Demeter's winter cabin, but her last memory was of the pungent scent of burning flesh, and that had been replaced by the fresh smell of morning dew. Blinking her dry eyes to produce tears, she wondered at the gray papery flakes of ash covering the two of them like dirty snow, which, when she flicked it from her arm, lifted in the air and floated before drifting to the ground. She shuddered, realizing she was brushing away bits of her old self.

Than met her bewildered gaze and gave her a hesitant smile.

"You okay?" he asked.

"We're glowing. Like embers."

"Like gods." He leaned in and kissed her forehead. "My grandmother's method worked. The transformation was a success. You should see how beautiful you look." He propped himself up on his elbows, gazing lazily at her.

"What?"

He pulled a mirror from thin air and handed it to her. She gasped at her own reflection. Her eyes were brighter, her hair shinier, gleaming like the sun. Even her skin and teeth were impeccable, in spite of the flakes of ash peppering her face.

She was also much brighter than humans. Humans. It felt weird not to be included in that category anymore. And she was drop-dead gorgeous. Every one of her features was in better harmony with all the others. She looked airbrushed. Then she had this thought: "I look like my mother." She blinked her eyes several times. Tears formed but didn't fall. She was a goddess.

Her mouth dropped open. "Does this mean…?"

He smiled and nodded, a soft chuckle playing from his throat.

She jumped to her feet and brushed more of the ash from her arms, her legs. What was she wearing? The short white tunic was the only part of her not covered in the gray flakes. When she touched the silk, her dusty hand tainted it.

"I put that on you, just before you woke up," Than explained.

Blood rushed to her cheeks. Other than the locket from Athena, which had survived the flames, the tunic was the only thing on her. Did that mean he saw her naked?

The soft chuckle played from his throat once more. "Your modesty is…"

"What?" She hadn't meant that defensive edge in her voice.

"Sweet."

She relaxed a bit and smiled back at him, handing over the mirror, which immediately vanished. "I can't believe this. Am I dreaming?" She pushed off the ground and soared above Than, not quite reaching the treetops surrounding them. Disappointment quaked through her as she landed on her feet in front of the altar. "Are you a figment?"

"You're not dreaming, and I'm not a figment. That little test of yours won't work anymore, now that you can really fly."

"Now that I can…what? Are you saying I can fly?"

"You don't have very high expectations for what it means to be a god."

"I can fly? While I'm awake?" She jumped up into the air, turning somersaults just above Than's head. "I can fly! Woohoo!" Images from Peter Pan rushed to her, and, though she laughed at herself, she didn't stop twirling in the air.

Than shook his head. "Come back down here, you crazy girl."

She continued to turn and glide across the sky, daring to go higher, above the trees. "Whoa," she cried when she wobbled and dropped a few feet. Then, confident again, she soared up to the clouds. "Wheeee!!!" Slowly, she descended, feet first, back to the ground, but before she landed, another idea struck her. She took off running up the mountain and was halfway there in seconds. "Look how fast I can run!" Spotting a boulder wedged in the mountainside, she stopped, tugged at it, easily loosening it from the surrounding earth, and lifted it above her head. "Look how strong I am!" Her voice echoed throughout the valley.

"So I can finally kiss you without killing you, and you'd rather fly and lift heavy rocks?"

She giggled and flew to the altar and lay beside him, propping her head on an elbow. "Sorry. I'm all yours." Then, as Than's face moved near hers, she frowned.

"What's wrong?"

"Can we take a shower somewhere? We're both covered in ash." She shuddered again. Yuck. Her own dead body. She'd like to get clean of it as soon as possible.

Than snapped his fingers and a black cloud appeared above them. The cloud opened and dropped cool, refreshing rain.

"Mmm." Therese lifted her face to it and allowed it to cascade down her cheeks, neck, shoulders. "Can I do that, too? Make it rain?"

He swept her wet hair out of her eyes. "Do you really want an education on what it means to be a god? Right now?" With each word, he moved his lips nearer to hers.

"No." She looked at his mouth. "No, not really."

He reached his lips towards her, but she stopped him once again.

"Now what?"

"You burned, too. I saw you pour the kerosene all over yourself. Why?"

He cupped her chin. "I didn't want you to go through that alone."

"Wow. That's so…"

He covered her lips with his as the exhilarating rain softly washed away their ashes and reinvigorated her. She slipped her arms around his neck and pressed her body against his. He pushed her hip down onto the altar and lay half on top of her, crushing her, but she didn't mind, wanting to be as close to him as possible, making every part of her touch every part of him. She curled a leg over his and reveled at the sound of a moan escaping from his lips.

"Oh, Than. I can't believe it. We're finally together."

He snapped his fingers, and the rain stopped, and the morning sunshine warmed and dried them as they kissed, caressed, and stroked one another on Demeter's altar.

Memories of Than anointing her body—every inch of it—with ambrosia, his hands stroking her, quickly but lovingly, filled her with desire.

"Maybe we should go somewhere more private," Than whispered.

Therese nodded, but asked, nearly breathless, "What happened to your mom and grandma?"

Than stopped and sat up. "That's a good question."

Therese sat up, too. "Are you worried?"

"They gave me the vial of ambrosia. They could be in trouble."

"We need to find out."

"I've just disintegrated and dispatched to Mount Olympus to look for them."

"How do you do that?"

"Comes with the job."

"Can I do it?"

"I don't think so, but, ultimately, it'll depend on your purpose."

Just then Therese heard her aunt's voice calling to her, as though she were right there with them. "Oh my god."

"What's wrong?"

"Nothing." She tried to ignore it. "What purpose?"

He leaned back once again on his elbows. "Every god and goddess must serve humankind or the world in some way. We have to find a purpose for you, or this transformation won't last."

Therese hopped from the altar to her feet. "You never mentioned that." It seemed like pretty important information, too. "My god, how much time do I have?"

"I'm not sure, but don't worry."

She frowned, unhappy with his vague answer. She didn't think she had it in her to go through the transformation process again. The anticipation of burning to death had been horrible; the actual pain of burning alive had been worse. "I need a better answer than that. I didn't just burn to death for nothing."

"My grandmother will know. I'm looking for her, so be patient. Hephaestus just told me he hasn't seen her, but that I'm not allowed in the palace. He's going in to ask for me."

Therese heard her aunt again: "Please, Therese, wherever you are. Please come home."

She covered her face with her hands. The voice, full of desperation, seemed so close; her aunt's mouth might have been at her ear.

Than god traveled to her side. "What's wrong?"

"I didn't think about how I would be able to hear my aunt. She's talking to me, begging me to come home. How long have I been gone?"

"A few days."

Therese sat on the ground and covered her face again. "She's in full panic. I knew this would be hard—leaving her and everything—but I didn't know I would hear her crying for me. I can't bear it."

"It's worse than I thought."

Therese lifted her head. "What?"

"My mom and grandmother are being held prisoners at Mount Olympus and are awaiting trial, which we thought could happen, but..." He pulled Therese up to her feet.

"But what?"

"They're coming for us."

"Now? What'll we do?"

He shook his head.

She grabbed his hand and pointed to the top of the mountain. "Let's run and hide. Come on. There could be a cave." What was she thinking? They could go anywhere. "Let's go to China!"

"I'm disintegrated in thousands of places. There's no way I can hide. But you could."

"I'm not leaving you."

Therese wrapped her arms around his waist and pressed her cheek to his chest, the pure joy she felt moments ago vanishing. She hadn't thought completely through the consequences, and they didn't look good. His mother and grandmother were being tried in court. Her aunt and uncle were worried sick, her aunt crying out to her. And now the other gods were coming for them.

Just then roots from the ground at their feet shot up and coiled themselves around Than and Therese's legs, climbing higher and higher, cold and abrasive, ensnaring them in a net of plant. Therese screamed and Than pulled at the roots, to no avail, and soon they were encased in a kind of cocoon. Therese clung to Than, her new heart pounding, her new blood coursing through her limbs. Although she was stronger than she'd ever been in her life, it wasn't enough to break free of the trap. Then she felt the invisible plastic wrap itself around them, recognized the feeling of god travel, and the next instant, she and Than were standing in the middle of the court surrounded by the gods of Mount Olympus.

Chapter Two: Prisoners at Mount Olympus

Than could feel Therese's body trembling against him as they faced his family, the final note of Apollo's lyre lingering in the air before dead silence overtook the palace. Everyone, including his father, was there. The last time they were all together had been nearly a year ago, when Therese chose to fight McAdams, her parents' killer. Most years went by like the blink of an eye, but this past year had seemed longer than any in his life. He finally understood human longing and suffering and the dragging by of time.

Last June, while in a coma, Therese flew to him, wrapped her arms around him, and told him he was lovely. She thought she was dreaming, ignorant that she was at the junction of the dream and under worlds. In the long history of his ancient existence, no one had ever shown him such affection, and no one had made his heart race and his lips quiver with excitement like this girl, who had literally dropped from the sky.

Than needed to remind himself that his father was on his side at first. Hades had, after all, allowed Than to go to the upperworld as a mortal to try and win Therese's heart, forcing Than's brother, Hypnos, to take his place as god of the dead. In order to become a god, though, Hades required Therese to avenge her parents' murder. Therese fought valiantly on Mount Olympus against McAdams, but she refused to take his life once he was incapacitated and no longer a threat. Her compassion and her value on human life cost them their eternity together, and all the gods at Mount Olympus swore an oath on the River Styx never to make Therese a god or to retrieve her from the Underworld.

He and Therese were given another chance when Hades agreed to force Dionysus, who was not at Mount Olympus and so swore no oath, to make her a god if she could complete five challenges. Hades set her up for failure, disgusted by her decision not to kill McAdams, but when he witnessed her determination to be with Than and her cunning, strength, and bravery, somewhere along the way, Hades, too was wooed by her. Than could feel it. His father wanted Therese to succeed, even when he knew she wouldn't.

In the end, her concern for Than was her undoing. She looked back. And Than was forced to take matters into his own hands.

He was forced to break his oath.

Now, his mother and grandmother, their blond hair mussed about their lovely faces like savages, were wrapped together in a similar cocoon of roots, which was damp and possessing the rich smell of tilled earth. Hestia and Hephaestus looked away in polite sympathy, while Aphrodite stared with her hands over her mouth. Athena and Artemis looked on with skepticism, especially the latter whose forest green eyes were narrowed into an accusation. Ares wore a smirk on his red-bearded face, Hermes fear, and Apollo concern, though not as pronounced as Aphrodite's. Poseidon's eyes were on Zeus, and he looked as though he was in a hurry, impatient for this meeting to adjourn. Zeus had already told Than he would be exiled and subject to an annual visit by the maenads, so why had they been brought here?

He looked again at his mother and grandmother, their corn-blond hair pointing in all directions, their worried brown eyes meeting his. He never meant to drag them down with him. This was all wrong. Why wasn't his father helping them? He sat on his throne tugging his beard, eyes glazed like he was deep in thought.

Zeus asked for silence and then said, "Hades, you need to get your house in order. How do you propose to punish these offenders for their crimes against the rest of us?"

Hades looked up without letting go of his beard. "Well, now, it seems to me Thanatos's punishment has already been mandated by you, brother. In addition to the maenads playing havoc with his body, you've decided to exile him from Mount Olympus."

"Do you object?"

"No. The punishment is fair."

Than narrowed his eyes. Would his father do nothing to help him, then?

"But no more punishment is necessary," Hades added.

"Prevent him from marrying the girl," Ares said.

A wave of nausea overcame Than, and he bent over, holding his stomach. Therese sucked in a sharp, audible gasp. They couldn't let that happen, not after all they'd been through to be together. If it weren't for the cocoon of roots, he would punch Ares. Yes, he would very much like to punch Ares.

"No!" Aphrodite objected.

"What say you, then?" Ares quipped to the goddess of love.

"I object to these silly cocoons, first of all. Demeter and Persephone don't deserve to be treated this way. Than and Therese aren't going anywhere, besides."

The cocoons vanished, and Than felt a sense of relief to have someone stand up for him and his women.

"But something must be done," Zeus complained.

"Watching Than ripped to pieces each year is punishment enough," Hades said.

Many of the other gods and goddesses nodded their heads and muttered their agreements. Than closed his eyes for a moment, silently thanking them. Maybe his father was on his side after all.

"What of the girl?" Zeus asked.

"She fought bravely against the Hydra," Athena said. "Be merciful, father."

Than met Athena's sharp grey eyes. She liked Therese and had even given her a locket with an inscription that had helped Therese face the challenges: The most common way people give up their power is by believing they have none. Those words may have been more powerful than any of the gifts Therese received, including the crown of invisibility from Artemis and the traveling robe from Aphrodite.

Than pulled Therese more closely to him and asked, "Permission to speak?"

Zeus nodded.

"She committed no crime. Why should she be punished?"

"By assenting, she is guilty," Zeus replied.

Than looked around at the others present and then turned to his father, who said, "Yes, but she broke no oath and so shouldn't be subjected to the maenads."

Thank the gods for that, Than thought.

Therese shivered in his arms.

He prayed to her, "It'll be okay. You'll see." He didn't want her to know how he really felt. One never knew what to expect from the gods.

In fact, Zeus once sentenced Apollo to Tartarus for killing the Cyclops that made the thunderbolt Zeus used to strike one of Apollo's sons. The son, a demigod and not immortal, was brazen and irreverent and deserving of his punishment, but sentencing Apollo, one of the great gods, to Tartarus? That was harsh. Fortunately for Apollo, his mother stepped in and got the sentence reduced to a year of hard labor. Than could only imagine what Zeus had in store for Therese.

"Someone will need to stand in for Thanatos while he recovers," Zeus said. "That should be her punishment. No one else wants that burden."

Yet another consequence Than hadn't thought through when deciding to make Therese a god. Surely Zeus didn't expect this life-loving, inexperienced girl to handle every dead being on the planet. Plus, she had no concept of disintegration. How could she be in hundreds of thousands of places at once?

Therese's eyes widened. Than patted her back and gave her a half smile.

"That's not your call," Hades bellowed.

"But it's only fair," Hermes said. "Someone must take his place, and it won't be me."

Hades stood from his throne and moved closer to Than and Therese. "She has no experience. Knows nothing."

"Than will train her before his punishment is carried out," Zeus said.

Another lucky break, Than thought. "For how long?" he asked.

Zeus turned to the god of the Underworld. "Hades?"

"At least a week."

"Two days, then," Zeus said.

Than squeezed Therese's hand when tears flooded her eyes. "We can do this."

Her lips were close to him when she said, "I can barely look at a dead animal in the road."

He felt his throat tighten as he watched the fear darken her pretty face. He had to protect her, no matter what. The last thing he wanted was to see her suffer.

Zeus stood from his throne, spittle spraying from his brown-bearded lips as he spoke. "Furthermore, unless she fails to find a purpose and reverses her transformation, I recommend that she be forced to replace Thanatos every year during his incapacitation. No other god should be punished for a choice made by these two."

Therese's mouth fell open as she met Than's eyes. He clenched his jaw and said nothing.

"Hear, hear," the other gods said, some forlornly.

Only Hades refused his assent. Than knew his father resented being told how to run his domain. He hoped he wouldn't take his anger out on Therese.

Zeus commanded, "Take your leave, Thanatos. And you, too, Therese. Never again shall either of you set foot on Mount Olympus."

A chill moved down Than's spine.

"No!" Persephone ran to Than and circled his arm with both of hers. "Please, Zeus! Have mercy!"

"Thanatos knew the consequences," Zeus said. "He chose his path, not I."

His mother kissed his hand and then his cheek. "I know I'll see you in the Underworld, but the idea of exile from this good place forever saddens me beyond grief."

"It's okay, Mother. I rarely come here anyway. I need you to be happy for me, not sad."

She shook her head. "Oh, son. I hope you won't regret this choice you've made."

He didn't hesitate. "Never."

Chapter Three: A New Plan

Therese followed Than using god travel to his sitting room in the Underworld. Despite the cozy fire from the Phlegethon and the fireplace, she was overcome with anxiety. As if the ordeal on Mount Olympus weren't enough, her aunt was crying out to her, afraid she'd been abducted.

Therese paced the room as soon as they arrived. "I have to get a message to my family. They're worried sick!"

"What will you tell them?"

"I don't know. But I've got to tell them something. That I ran away? That would break their hearts." She continued to pace and to beat one palm with a fist.

"Tell them you took the bus to come see me. Tell them you're on your way home and you're sorry."

She flung around to face him. "You want me to lie to them? To lead them into thinking I'm coming home? That would kill them!"

"No."

"Than, what are you saying? You want me to leave you?" Her stomach felt sick.

"No. God, Therese. Would you calm down?" He tried to take her hands, but she pulled them away.

"Calm down? Calm down?" Everything was crumbling to pieces before her eyes, and he wanted her to calm down?

"Listen to me, please? Will you sit down?" He pointed to one of two leather club chairs in front of the fireplace.

She sat, but on the edge of her seat on top of her hands, clenched in tight balls beneath her thighs. She wanted to kick something. To punch something. She'd never felt this anxious. Hearing her aunt's suffering was too much. How did the gods do it?

He sat across from her, his hands on her knees. "You'll call her on the phone. You'll tell her you were upset about Vicki and wanted to see me, but you knew she and your uncle would say no. You'll tell her how sorry you are that you worried them, but you're coming home in a few days by bus and should arrive in a week's time."

"They'll insist I come home immediately." Her fingers curled around the locket from Athena. Even as a god, she felt powerless.

"Tell them you can't."

"I suppose I can say my ticket is non-refundable or something." She pulled at her fingers and jumped to her feet to pace some more. "I don't want to leave you right after, you know. I want to be here for you."

"We'll have eternity together. This way you can ease their minds."

"And tell them what? That I'm leaving again?" She fell into the club chair and put her face in her hands.

"What if…"

She looked up at him. "What? Just say it."

"What if you tell them you want to marry me?"

"They won't go for that. I'm only eighteen."

He gave her a hurt look. "You do want to though."

"Yes. Eventually. After I…" She was about to say after she graduated, but was that really necessary anymore? She was a god, for crying out loud. What was she thinking?

"After what?"

"I was going to say after I graduate high school, but I guess that's not important anymore."

"Wait. No. That's a good idea." He jumped to his feet and paced around as she had done moments before.

"What are you talking about?"

"After I'm recovered, go back to your family, in mortal form. Go back to school and graduate."

"But how? And why? I'm probably too far behind, anyway. I need to talk to a counselor."

"So? Talk to one."

"Why does it matter? I don't need a high school diploma to be a god."

"No, but if you graduate, your aunt and uncle will be less likely to object to our marriage. Don't you want their blessing?"

Yes. The idea of leaving them in a state of pain—either because they'd think she was dead or that she'd run away—had burdened her from the beginning. If she could make them think she'd left them to get married, and if she could win their blessing, they wouldn't have to suffer. She stood from her chair, feeling hopeful as she bit on her lower lip.

Than put his hands on her shoulders. "Problem solved?"

"If I can graduate on time. And even if I can, it means being away from you for almost a year. If I can't, it'll be two years."

"We're gods. I can visit you every day. We don't have to worry about my presence killing you."

"Really?"

"Really." He moved closer to her, so their faces were inches apart.

"Every day?"

"Every day." He leaned in and kissed her.

"Oh, Than!" More tears pricked her eyes. She couldn't get enough of him and didn't want to leave, ever. But her happiness wasn't the only thing important to her. "So how do we call my aunt and uncle?"

He handed her a cell phone.

"A cell phone? Really? Don't tell me you get reception down here." She half-laughed, sniffling at the same time.

"It's magic but works like one of yours. Try it."

Her hands trembled as she punched in her home number. "They're going to kill me," she whispered nervously.

Than smiled at her, his eyes mocking. "Like that's possible."

"It's an expression. Wait. Shh." How strange. She could sense her aunt answering the phone before she answered it. Now she could see her, too, standing in the kitchen, elbows on the granite bar, a hand rubbing her forehead, her straight red hair in a ponytail.

"Hello?"

"Carol, it's me."

"Therese? My God! Where are you? What happened? Are you alright?"

Therese could see Carol stand upright and turn to Richard, who was sitting on the sofa with black rings beneath dark, bloodshot eyes, but who now stood, too, his mouth agape.

"I, I'm okay."

"Thank God! Where are you? What's going on?"

"I was upset. About Vicki. I wanted to see Than. But I'm coming back. I'm sorry I didn't tell you. I was afraid you'd say no."

"My God, Therese. Do you know what we've been through the past three days? Three days! You should have called before now. The police are…"

"The police? You called the police?"

"Of course, we called the police. What did you think we'd do? You disappeared. We thought you were stolen."

Therese could see her aunt sink into Richard's arms. He led her to the sofa, and they both collapsed into it.

"You better call Jen, too."

"I'm so sorry."

"Where are you?"

"At Than's. But I'm taking the bus home in a few days. I'll be home in a week, I think."

"A week? You get on that bus today, Therese. Do you hear me?"

"I can't. The return ticket is nonrefundable."

"I'll buy you a new one. Better yet, I'll fly down and get you."

"No. Please. I need time."

"You and Than haven't…"

"What?"

"Are you being safe?"

"Oh my God! Nothing to worry about. I just needed to see him." Yuck. Her aunt was asking about sex?

"Does he live with his parents or alone?"

"His parents."

"And they're there?"

Therese looked up at Than. "Yes. They're here. Well, his dad is. His mom's, um, visiting his grandmother."

"Let me speak to his dad."

"You can't. He's working right now."

"Call me tonight, when his father returns, so I can speak with him, and call me every night till you're home safe, to let me know you're still okay."

"Okay."

"You promise?"

"I promise."

"I still can't believe you did this to me."

"I'm so sorry."

As she hung up the phone, she closed her eyes and sighed, wondering if her aunt and uncle would ever forgive her. Then her stomach balled up in a knot at the thought of having to ask Hades to talk to her aunt.

Than kissed the top of her head. She wrapped her arms around his neck and relished his comforting squeeze. "We'll get through this," he said.

She nodded, pulling back and brushing tears from her cheeks. They felt different. Less wet. Almost as though her cheeks were numb.

Next she called Jen. As she punched in the number, she could see Jen with her bright blond hair in two braids in the barn talking to a girl their age she'd never met before. The girl was shorter than Jen with long brown hair and a thin frame. Jen answered the phone in the barn.

"It's me," Therese said.

Jen stopped, rigid. "Are you okay? Where are you?"

"With Than. I'm coming home. I just freaked, you know? I'm sorry I scared everyone."

"Have you called your aunt?"

"Yeah."

"Why didn't you tell me? I could have kept your secret and come up with a cover so your aunt and Pete and everybody wouldn't go all nut-so."

"Pete?"

"When will you be back?"

"In a week or so. I'm taking the bus."

"Call me or text me, okay?"

"I will. Who's that with you?"

"What? How did you know someone was with me?" Jen glanced in all directions, as though searching for Therese.

"I thought I heard another voice."

"That's weird. She didn't say anything. Anyway, it's Vicki's cousin, Courtney."

"Vicki's cousin?"

"Yeah. She and her mom are visiting Mr. Stern for the rest of the summer. Her mom is Mr. Stern's sister."

"I didn't know he had a sister. That's good." Therese was glad for Vicki's dad. She'd been worried about him being alone after Vicki died, only a year after her mother took her life. Hopefully having family around for the summer would ease his pain.

"Yeah. He called your aunt and my mom to see if we'd spend some time with Courtney, so she wouldn't get bored. Turns out she knows a lot about horses. Her mom grew up around them. They're from…hang on, did you say North Carolina?"

"North Dakota," the girl named Courtney corrected.

"North Dakota," Jen said into the phone.

"Cool. I'm looking forward to meeting her." Therese felt slightly jealous that Jen was having fun with a friend. She hadn't seemed all that worried about Therese's disappearance. "Later, Jen."

When she hung up, she internally reprimanded herself for thinking that way.

"What's wrong?" Than asked.

"Nothing. I'm an idiot, that's all."

Than looked back at her, his mood suddenly dark.

"What?" she asked.

"You regret…"

"No. Absolutely not. How can you think that? No. I have no regrets." She hugged him, feeling his mood lighten and his body relax. Then she added, "Things are a mess, though. I need to fix them."

"First things first." He touched the tip of her nose and brushed a stray tear from her cheek. "I have to train you."

Chapter Four: Goddess of Death
in Training

Of all the places Than had to be today, this death seemed the gentlest for Therese's first time. He didn't want to throw her in the middle of a tough one. He needed to help her gradually get used to people dying all around them.

Therese stood beside him in a hospital room near the bed of an old woman, whose eyes were closed, breathing erratic. Two middle-aged women sat on either side of the old one, holding her hands and praying. Therese said, without speaking, "I can hear them."

"Please let her go easy," one prayed.

"Take Mama to heaven," the other prayed.

"She's almost ready." Than wrinkled his nose at the pungent smells of urine, perspiration, and body odor, not uncommon in his line of work, but desensitized he was not. "When her body stops, you have to reach in and put your hand on her soul. She won't know what to do. We'll guide her, okay?"

Therese nodded, looking apprehensive but determined. That's what he loved most about her: her determination.

"Say hi to Daddy," one of the women said, sensing the end. "Tell him we love him!"

In the next instant, the old woman's eyes flashed open, and she looked directly at Therese. Her mouth opened wide, and she gasped.

"Can she see us?"

"Yes. Tell her it's okay."

"It's okay, Madeline. I'm here to help." She looked at Than. "How do I know her name?"

"It's like that with everyone. You'll see."

The old woman collapsed against her pillow, her eyes fixed and unblinking. Her breathing stopped.

"Mama?"

"She's gone! Call the nurse!"

Than led Therese closer to the bed. "Now reach in, just at her shoulders."

"Into her body?"

Than took Therese's hand, and together they penetrated the old woman's shoulders and fell upon the airy, feathery feel of something not quite solid, but palpable.

"Help her out."

Together they helped the soul emerge from the woman's body and out into the room.

"It's going to be okay, Madeline," Than said to the woman. He kept a hand on her shoulder.

Therese did the same, and together they left the bustle of nurses, machines, and departed loved ones to god travel with the woman to the banks of the Acheron where Charon waited on his raft. As they neared Cerberus, Therese gave the three-headed dog a friendly wave, and he wagged his dragon tail as his three tongues hung from his three mouths. Cerberus loved her almost as much as Than did.

They passed Cerberus and entered the iron gate. Then Charon delivered them to the judges, who declared the woman destined to the Fields of Elysium. Once they saw her safely there, Therese and Than returned to his rooms.

Therese sank into the leather club chair by the fire. "That wasn't so bad." Although she was a bit drained looking, something in her eyes appeared radiant, triumphant even. "I didn't think I could handle it, but I could. It felt good. Like I was helping."

"Yes. Those are the best cases—when they're ready to go and their loved ones have accepted it."

"I guess most cases aren't so easy, huh?"

Than shook his head. She had so much more in store, so much pain and agony. He wished he hadn't put her in this position. He wished he could spare her from it all. Her willingness to suffer for him made him love her all the more.

"I keep telling myself it's temporary—their pain and sadness, I mean."

"That's right. That's a good girl." He leaned in and kissed her cheek. "Ready?"

"Already?"

Than frowned. "This job is never-ending. That's your first big lesson. Remember, I'm all over the world right now. You'll have to be, too."

He helped her from the chair and into his arms. "Hold me close," he whispered. "This won't be easy."

She gave him a brave smile, which made him proud. "By the way," he said. "Demeter says you have three months to find your purpose."

"Three months?" He watched her count on her fingers. She was so cute. "October. What's today?"

"July third in some places. The fourth in others."

"October third. I have to figure this out by October third."

The room was small and stuffy, the stringent smell of anesthetic and cleaner overpowering the lesser one of urine. The thirty-six-year-old woman, bald and sallow, lay in a morphine-induced sleep in a hospice bed with her older brother collapsed and sleeping in a nearby chair in the dim circle of light from a bedside lamp. The dying woman's six-year-old twin sons and eleven-year-old daughter had already said their good-byes the night before. Her ex-husband and his new wife and children had also come and gone. The only one left was her lifelong friend, her brother, and, knowing her time was close, he had refused to leave her side. Than usually took it upon himself to wake such a dedicated loved one just before or after the body expired so the soul could whisper goodbye in passing.

Therese held his hand with a tight grip. He could hear her thoughts, aimed at him, "Poor woman! Poor woman! She's so young, her children not ready. This doesn't seem fair."

"Life isn't fair," came his automatic reply. He wished he didn't have to put Therese through this.

"I can feel how hard she fought," Therese said. "And I can sense the pain she was in before the medication took over. The cancer started in her breasts but spread throughout her body. I can feel it in her liver and in her kidneys. It's eating her alive from the inside."

Than gave her a solemn nod. "We're here to end her pain."

"But her children."

"They have their father and a stepmother who love them. Not all left behind are as fortunate."

"Fortunate?"

"Sorry. Poor choice of words."

"I can feel her dying," Therese said. "I feel it all around my body, especially my chest. It's weird how I can sense her every breath, her every movement."

"It's time to reach inside for her soul. I'll just nudge her brother awake."

"Why not let him sleep?"

"He'll feel good tomorrow knowing he had the chance to say goodbye."

Therese gave him a loving smile that made his heart fill up with joy even in the midst of this overwhelming sadness. Together they reached into the woman's body for that feathery part of her still alive.

"This way, Tamara," Than said.

Her brother opened his eyes and looked at her, instantly aware that she was no longer breathing. He grabbed her hand. "Sis?"

The brother seemed to look directly at his sister's soul, as though he could see it. "I love you," he said. "Wait for me."

Tamara was at first confused, but when she heard her brother's words, she turned and touched his face. "I love you, too."

Then Therese and Than swept her off to the banks of the Acheron and onto Charon's raft. After they left her in the Elysian Fields, they returned to Than's room so Therese could collect herself. She was trembling, her cheeks wet with tears.

"This isn't easy," she whispered.

"No," he said. "No, it's not." He took her in his arms and held her. "It gets much worse." He kissed her wet lips tenderly and looked into her eyes. "Ready?"

She held him tightly for many seconds. Then she wiped her eyes and cheeks and gave him a brave nod. He could not be prouder.

Chapter Five: The Trapped Boy

Therese stood beside Than near a mountain of rubble and debris where hundreds of people in various uniforms and civilian clothing, of multiple nationalities and ethnicities, dug with shovels and combed the site with metal detectors and, unfortunately, carried bodies, most of them dead, off to the nearby ambulances awaiting them.

Other people—old men and women and children—huddled along the perimeter, weeping and praying. Some of their prayers, she could hear.

"Let my grandson be alive."

"Help the rescue workers find my baby boy."

The prayers weren't in English, but Therese could understand them. Adding to their anxiety was the fact that dusk was settling, and darkness wouldn't be far behind. As she looked over the scene, she felt a pang of sorrow for Than, whose entire existence was filled with scenes exactly like it. More than ever, she wanted to add joy to his life. She wondered if her love for him could be enough to tip the scales of the balance of his life toward happiness.

"Where are we?" she asked Than.

"In a Turkish town near the border of Iran. These are earthquake victims. A building, several stories high, collapsed earlier in the week. I've taken over two hundred souls to the Underworld. Men, women, and children of all ages. This was a building of department stores among other businesses."

"Oh my god." She covered her mouth.

"There's one more boy here about to die. It won't be easy, so brace yourself. He's young, only four years old, and has been trapped beneath this rubble for five days. The others trapped with him have already died. He's the last of them."

Tears rushed to Therese's eyes. "Okay. I'm ready."

Now she could hear the prayers of the boy. "I want my mother and grandmother. I want my mother and grandmother." Over and over, his prayer was the same. She could sense his desperate thirst and hunger, but his only prayer was for his mother and grandmother. "Ahn-neh! Ba-ba-ahn-neh!"

"How do you do this every day, all day?" she asked as they stepped closer to the rubble above the boy.

"You're about to find out."

"But you do it all the time, forever. How do you avoid depression?"

"Until I met you, I was depressed—mainly because my life never varied. But look around you."

"What do you mean?"

"See how they all work together, helping one another?"

Therese surveyed the multitudes digging, sweeping, praying, carting, reviving. "It is heartwarming to see people working in harmony for a common cause." She held her eyes on Than for a moment longer, realizing the thing she loved most about him: He always managed to see the good in things and to make the most out of each circumstance.

"Some of them are enemies, but to save the victims, they put aside their differences." He took her hand. "It's almost time for the boy. Let's go to him."

She squeezed his hand and nodded. He softly kissed her forehead.

Therese cringed as they passed lifeless bodies. Some of their eyes and mouths were still open; they died gasping for their last breaths. Others were crushed and had likely died instantly. All were covered in dirt. The boy, Sahin, cried dry tears and muttered soundless words: "Ahn-neh! Ba-ba-ahn-neh!" His hair was white with powdered concrete. Rings of caked mud circled each eye where pre-hydration tears must have gathered on his light brown skin. His brows were knitted together, his eyes half closed with fatigue and dread. He sat on the ground with his knees pressed against his growling stomach, all but his head hidden in the wedge between two collapsed walls. His parched lips moved their soundless cries. "Ahn-neh! Ba-ba-ahn-neh!"

"Can you see me?" Therese asked the boy.

The boy nodded, sucking in his lips, and for a moment his prayers halted.

"I'm here to help you," Therese added. "Are you in pain?"

He said the words for thirsty and scared. Then he continued his chant of "Ahn-neh! Ba-ba-ahn-neh!"

Therese glanced at Than, wishing the boy's torment would end. How much longer did they have to wait?

Clutched in Sahin's hand was a yellow toy the size of his fist. He held it out to her, above the block of cement trapping the rest of his body, so she took it. It was a miniature dump truck.

"For Mother," he whispered in his language. "Please give it to her."

Above their heads, a thick concrete beam lay across other broken walls, creating a small space that allowed air to circulate. This had surely kept the boy alive. Otherwise, he would have expired days ago with the others. Therese could sense the rescue workers above them, digging the rubble on top of the beam overhead. They were so close. She wished she could hasten their work and help them find the boy, but she knew she wasn't to interfere. Than had told her again and again it was not his place; nor was it hers. The earth could not support a human population that never died. But she wished people didn't have to die so young and in such tragic ways, with their mothers and grandmothers praying for their lives. She wished all people could live to old age and then die a peaceful death. Why did things have to be this way? Now that she was a god, could she change them?

Maybe that could be her purpose—her service to humankind. She could be the goddess of those too young to die. She could save people from dying before old age.

Than knew her thoughts before she spoke them. She hadn't realized she'd been sharing them with him this entire time.

"We tried that once before," he said. "It was a terrible time in human history. We thought we were adding value to human life, but we were actually diminishing it."

"What happened?"

"People stopped caring."

She looked up again toward the sound of digging and scraping. They were so close! "So there's nothing we can do to save this boy?" she asked.

The boy looked at her as though he could hear and understand her. "Ahn-neh! Ba-ba-ahn-neh!" He pressed his little legs against the concrete wall for what must have been the hundredth time. He squirmed against his trap, like a butterfly in a jar.

Therese held out her hand to comfort him. "I'll give your toy to your mother. I promise."

The multitude of prayers above them was overwhelming, but even louder were the fervent sounds of digging and scraping. The rescuers were closer, about to break through. They would miss the boy by minutes!

The boy lifted his now empty hand above his concrete trap and circled his fingers around Therese's index finger. He looked at her as though he knew it was time. She gave him a sad smile and kissed his little hand, which seemed to hasten his death. But just as his eyes widened and he sucked in what should have been his last breath, a shovel struck through the rubble above, and a hand reached down and grabbed the boy by his arm.

Sahin flew up from his trap and into the hands of a rescue worker. A storm of activity followed. Therese and Than left the heap to watch as the boy was rushed, oxygen mask to his face, across the debris to an ambulance. The mother and grandmother lifted their faces as though they knew who he was before seeing the child's face. Other parents, too, looked on with hope.

"What just happened?" Therese asked Than, full of excitement. "I could feel him die. I could sense his death with my whole being, like a pressure, like god travel. My heart knew he was dead one instant, but then he was alive the next. Does that happen often? Is he going to live?"

"Hold on." Than took her hand and together they returned the toy dump truck to the boy's hand. "You can give this to your mother," Than whispered just before he and Therese left the back of the ambulance and the doors were closed and the engine roared to life.

He took Therese to his sitting room and held her on his lap. "Someone intervened." He ran a hand through his hair. "It was Athena. Only gods of Mount Olympus can, and they do so rarely. Someone must have moved her with their prayers. Perhaps a soldier, since she is their special patron."

Therese buried her face in Than's neck. She was happy for the boy and his family, but sad for all the others who, for whatever reason, had not moved Athena. She held back her tears, though, and gritted her teeth, because she had to be strong for Than. This was only the beginning of her training, and she had to make him feel secure about leaving his duties in her hands. She was death, and death, though sad for those left behind, was a gift to those who suffered and was inevitable to all.

Than's strong arms wrapped more tightly around her, and a sigh escaped her lips. She peeked up at his hooded eyes, his bottom lip between his teeth. The sight of his beauty, so close to her, made her shiver. Despite the gloomy training, she was grateful to be with him.

She bent her face to his and said, "So what's next?"

He pushed a strand of hair behind her ear. "You need to learn to disintegrate."

"Yeah, what exactly is that, anyway?" She shifted in his lap so she could better face him. "I mean, how does it work?"

He bit his lower lip, drawing her attention to his mouth again. She couldn't believe she was really here with him, and she wasn't ready to give him up to the maenads. Two days wasn't long enough. She suddenly felt giddy after all the depressing events.

"Let me see if I can think of an analogy," he said.

As he gazed up at the shadows on the ceiling of his room, she couldn't resist taking a quick nibble of his lower lip.

He squeezed each of her upper arms, laughing. "Holy moly."

"Holy moly? Who says that anymore? Holy moly!"

"At one time it was a very popular expression." He tickled her sides. "Now quit making fun of me and pay attention."

"Yes, sir." She smirked.

He tickled her again.

"Stop! Stop and tell me your analogy."

"Okay. Imagine a shower head."

She pulled her head back and bent her brows. "A shower head? Okay?"

"Dozens of individual streams pour through the openings of the shower head, and all of those streams are water—not part water, but fully, wholly H20, correct?"

"Correct."

"Both the overall flow coming from the shower head and the independent streams consist of one hundred percent water."

"Correct."

"And yet the streams are all part of the flow of water even as they are complete in and of themselves."

"What a philosopher you are." She playfully punched his arm.

"That's disintegration. You are one hundred percent you, but you are simultaneously in many places, and in each place you occupy, you are still one hundred percent you."

"I think I get it. Piece of cake. Let's do this thing."

"But it can be overwhelming, processing all the stimuli. Because even as you disintegrate into multiple selves, each self knows what every other self is experiencing. You are inundated with sights, sounds, smells, etc."

She jumped from his lap. "Well, I'm as ready as I'll ever be. Beam me up, Scotty."

He laughed. "That saying's almost as old as holy moly."

"I don't think so."

"Let's see…of the two of us, who's been around longer?"

"Oh, shut up."

"So, here we go. We'll stay here, in my room, but we'll also go see Hip in the field of poppies, okay?"

"Okay."

"Ready?"

"Ready."

For a moment she thought it was interesting he'd used water to describe disintegration, because she felt, at that instant, as though water—cold water—was running across her back. She even reached over her shoulder, half expecting to find herself wet. She now had four arms and two backs, and her peripheral vision was like looking through a kaleidoscope at a bunch of distorted, but patterned, images. When Than spoke, she heard an echo, as though he used a microphone and loudspeaker.

"Are-are-you-you-okay-okay?"

Slowly, like when you can hear an echo of yourself on your cell phone, she said, "I-feel-dizzy."

"I-I-want-want-one-one-of-of-you-you-to-to-sleep-sleep-and-and-the-the-other-other-of-of-you-you-to-to-stay-stay-awake-awake."

"Hu-uh?"

He pulled her onto his lap in one of the club chairs in front of the fireplace, and, simultaneously, led her across the field of poppy. She felt sleepy and wanted to lie down.

"Over-over-here-here."

They lay together among the flowers, and she closed her eyes, but she could still see him, holding her in the club chair, leaning in for a kiss.

Hip appeared, and she was simultaneously kissing Than and trying to hear what Hip had to say. She couldn't understand a word.

"What?"

"You look like you've been drinking," Hip repeated.

"I'm dizzy and confused."

"Well, what I was trying to tell you is that I think I'm in love with your friend Jen."

"You stay away from her."

He put his hands on his slim hips. "Just because you're a god now doesn't mean you get to tell me what to do. Besides, she needs me."

"She doesn't need you."

"She's heartbroken, and I make her feel better."

"What do you mean she's heartbroken?"

"Some friend you are. Didn't you know Matthew broke up with her?"

Therese realized she was hovering above the poppies, above where her body slept. Than was beside her. She glared at Hip. "How do you know they broke up?"

"At night, she begs me to come, to help her forget. She calls me Mr. Sandman."

Therese muttered the familiar lyric, "Mr. Sandman, bring me a dream."

"Exactly. I've been comforting her for three days now."

Therese turned to Than. "Matthew must have broken up with her the day I left to face the hydra. She didn't say anything to me on the phone."

Than put an arm around her. "She'll be okay."

"She needs me. Hip's right. I haven't been a very good friend."

"Courtney's with her."

Therese's stomach felt sick. Courtney. Would Courtney replace her as Jen's new best friend? She should be glad that Jen wouldn't be alone when Therese left to live in the Underworld, but she wasn't. Even when

Courtney returned to North Dakota, they could email and text. The thought of it made her sad and hurt. Could she email and text from the Underworld?

"And after that we'll try a dozen," Than said.

"Yes. Three, six, twelve. That's a good plan," Therese said, suddenly aware that she'd been having two conversations simultaneously, and was able to follow both.

"You're doing good," Than said. "I'm sorry about Jen."

She and Than hung out in the dream world with Hip, lounged on the club chairs and made out, and disintegrated once more, dispatching to Tartarus to visit Tizzie.

"Hey." Tizzie, her dark, serpentine curls hiding her face, spoke without looking up from the soul she tortured, a young man whom Therese sensed had been there a few years. He lay on a marble slab bound at the wrists and ankles to leather straps connected to chains on a pulley. Tizzie cranked the pulley, which pulled at the straps and stretched the soul.

"Can souls feel pain?" Therese asked, sensing this one could.

"It's more psychological than physical," Tizze said. "But, yes."

The soul looked at them warily, tears slipping from the corners of his transparent eyes.

"You do realize the oath-breakers are brought here while their bodies heal?" Tizzie's black, serpentine curls momentarily parted as she looked up from her victim. The emerald choker around her neck and the silver halter top gleamed with the light cast by the Phlegethon. Her wolf paced a few yards away, ready to serve her.

"Are you going to stretch me as well?" Than asked.

Tizzie glanced up at the jug carriers, drenched from their leaking vessels as they walked across a narrow bridge above the bottomless pit. "I may require you to fill a bath to wash away your sins, like those women."

"But their jugs are leaking faster than they can carry them," Therese noted.

"Exactly."

"Or should I help poor Sisyphus by taking over his rock?" Than offered.

Tizzie abruptly turned to face them, her eyes dripping with blood. "You can't take over the punishment of another."

"Relax, I was only joking."

Tizzie's eyes returned to their usual black discs. "You deserve no additional punishment, brother. You have a kind heart, and the maenads are punishment enough."

"So what will you have me do? Twiddle my thumbs?"

"You won't be here long."

"If Apollo…"

"He won't touch you, I don't think. Not with Ares against it."

"In that case," Than said. "I've seen gods require days, weeks to heal."

"You can take over my job while I take a holiday in Paris."

"Oh, yay," Than said with sarcasm. "Can't wait."

"So why are you really here, if it's not to admire my work?"

"Therese is practicing disintegration. We're in two other places together. We're going to watch you for a while, if that's okay, while we disintegrate and dispatch to other locations to retrieve the dead."

"Watch away. Let's see how far I can stretch him before he breaks."

Chapter Six: Time's Up

Than couldn't stop laughing. In the presence of the dead, he was somber and melancholy, and he was making sure Therese could handle each horrific scene they visited, but here in his room in front of the fireplace with Therese in his lap, he was having the time of his life. He was testing her ability to concentrate on her duties in other places while he distracted her here.

And he was enjoying the hell out of his distraction techniques.

The brightness of her green eyes framed by her long, dark lashes undid him every time she looked at him. There was something in her expression, too. Even if he hadn't been able to hear her prayers of love and longing, her sweet eyes said it all. He wondered if his eyes held the same message for her.

"Yes." She touched her forehead to his. "They do."

Had he directed those thoughts to her? Had he been praying to her?

"I guess so. If I can hear them." She looked at his mouth. "Now where were we?"

"Here." He kissed her neck. He'd been kissing every inch of her skin, starting with her forehead and working his way around her face.

She moaned as his lips worked their way down from below her chin, behind her ear, and to her throat. "Oh my."

Now he followed a shoulder and kissed down the length of her smooth, soft arm. "Put your hand on Melvin's shoulder, Therese. Stay aware in all locations."

She closed her eyes. "Oh my heaven. Don't stop."

He sucked each of her fingers.

"Patricia's going to miss the raft if you don't keep her steady."

"Sweet heaven. I've got her. Don't stop."

He laughed. "I'm going to make this even more interesting."

Her eyes shot open and she gave him a playful grin. "How?"

"Let's disintegrate and dispatch to Demeter's winter cabin. We can make out there while we make out here." He leaned in and licked her bottom lip before smiling and adding, "That is, if you think you can handle it."

"Where's Demeter?"

"Mount Olympus. The cabin's empty."

She tucked in her chin and looked up at him through her dark lashes. "Bring it on."

They disintegrated and landed with a thud on the bed in his grandmother's guest bedroom. For a moment, he worried he'd crushed her, but her laughter told him otherwise.

"I hit my head!"

"Oops. Sorry." He shifted his weight so he wasn't fully on top of her.

He broke out in laughter again when he felt her arms at his torso tugging him back on. "I'm a god now, remember? You can't hurt me that easily."

He climbed back on.

"Wait."

He met her eyes, which looked full of mischief. They were beautiful.

"This isn't sacrilegious is it? Making out here and in your room while we're escorting souls to the underworld?"

"It's good practice for you," he insisted. "It's important."

"Important."

"Necessary."

"Necessary." She gave him a smile that showed she didn't quite believe him.

"Now, back to your lessons." He ran his mouth along her jawline.

"In that case, do what you're doing back in your room. The same thing, but in the other ear. I want to see how that feels."

He liked the way she was thinking and moved his mouth to her ear.

She gasped and whispered, "Oh. My. God."

Just then the door crashed open, and Than immediately sensed the presence of two gods—Hermes and Dionysus. He and Therese flew to their feet, holding one another as they faced the two intruders.

"What the hell do you want, cousins?" Than asked.

"Sorry to be the one to tell you," Hermes said. "But it's time."

"Zeus said two days!" Therese moved her body in front of Than.

Dionysus stepped toward her and twirled a strand of her hair between his fingers. His own golden hair hung in the same two long braids at the back of his head Than remembered from their last encounter, and his half-naked body gleamed in the sunlight pouring in from the windows. "That may well be, but Zeus has apparently changed his mind."

Than pulled Therese into his arms and away from the clutches of Dionysus.

She searched Than's face, her brows nearly touching. "Can he do that?"

Than held her face in his hands and forcefully pressed his lips to hers. "I love you. Remember that. Now go and do your duty in my place."

"But I'm not ready. I haven't even disintegrated to more than twenty places. How can I manage hundreds of thousands?"

"Thanatos has no choice but to go with us," Dionysus said grimly.

"Sorry, Therese," Hermes added. "But you'll get the hang of it. And Than will be back to himself soon."

Than's throat constricted as he anticipated the pain he was about to endure. He recalled the sharp sting of his thumb being ripped from his hand and shuddered. "It won't be long. I promise."

"No! Don't take him! He doesn't deserve this!" She turned to Dionysus, and for a moment Than thought her eyes would bleed like the eyes of his sisters. "This is your fault! If you'd only helped us, he wouldn't have had to break his oath!"

"So I forced him to go against his word?" the god of the vine mocked.

"You selfish bastard! You could have helped us!" Therese beat at the god of wine's chest.

Than's mouth dropped open at Therese's choice of words, and he held her back, back in his arms. Dionysus was a bastard, in all its connotations, and the fact that he had a chip on his shoulder and hated all the other gods for his isolation meant he probably didn't appreciate being reminded of it.

Dionysus narrowed his eyes. "I'm going to enjoy this now, thanks to you, missy! I'll be sure to instruct the maenads to take their time."

Therese turned her wide eyes to Than. "What have I done?"

Before Than could stop her, Therese threw herself on the ground, prostrate before the wine god. "I beg you with all my heart to forgive me. I'm your servant. If there's any way you can minimize Than's pain and suffering, I'll be your servant for all eternity."

"Therese!" Than cried, his blood rushing to his face in a pool of heat. "You don't know what you're doing! You can't swear yourself to him and live a life with me." He plucked her from the ground and turned her to face him. "What are you saying? You'll be with him?"

Her face flushed now, too. "No. That's not what I meant."

"That's how he'll take it."

Therese glanced at the golden braids, the tan face. Than hated that he wore only the loin cloth. Exhibitionist bastard.

"I only meant I'd do his bidding, any time he needed help."

"When a woman says that to a man…" Than couldn't finish.

Dionysus and Hermes were overcome with laughter. Than gritted his teeth.

Before Than could speak, Hermes put a hand on his shoulder and said, "Sorry, ol' cousin. Truly. But you should see the looks on each of your faces." He busted out in laughter again.

Dionysus clapped a hand against Than's back. "No worries, Thanatos. My heart belongs to Ariadne."

Nevertheless, Than noticed the once over Dionysus gave Therese.

"She is tempting though."

Than pulled back his fist, ready to launch it at Dionysus, but Hermes and Therese held him back.

Dionysus laughed again.

Hermes grew somber, running a hand through his curly black hair. "You're like a little brother to me. I hate to do this."

Roots shot up from the ground and curled themselves around Than's ankles, legs, and body as they'd done less than twenty-four hours ago when he and Therese had been taken to Mount Olympus.

"Touch my hand," he said to Therese. "It's time for you to take over."

Her fingers trembled when she reached through the web of roots and put her hand in his. He hoped and prayed to all the gods that Therese could manage without him.

"Don't worry," she said bravely. "I've got this. And I'm coming with you."

"No. I don't want you to."

"How can I not?"

"I don't want you to see me suffer."

"I have to be there for you. I can't let you go through it alone."

He didn't want to tell her what he was really thinking: he was embarrassed by the thought of how he would behave. Would he cry and scream like a baby? He didn't want her to see him like that.

"You need to concentrate on your duty."

"My duty is first and foremost to you."

She reached her pretty face in through the webbing and kissed him once more. She kissed him like a mortal saying goodbye, as though she didn't really believe he'd be back.

Chapter Seven: The Maenads

Therese was instantly overwhelmed by the souls from all over the world calling to her. She disintegrated thousands of times and dispatched to all walks of life. Despite her initial disorientation, she resolved to regain focus, finding that if she used her instinct more than her mind, she could work more efficiently. She went with the natural flow of it, trying not to think, but to stay in the zone like a seasoned athlete, letting her body—bodies—do the work.

But one of her remained with Than as they god traveled from Demeter's winter cabin with Hermes and Dionysus to a pine forest on Mount Kithairon. She chewed ferociously at the inside of her lips as sweat beaded on her face. If only she had succeeded in the fifth challenge. She wished she could trade places with Than. Maybe she could.

As she followed the gods up the hill toward a large throng of dancers and music makers, she cried, "Wait!" Her voice echoed through the valley. She'd forgotten how powerful she was now that she, too, was a god.

The other gods stopped and turned. Even the music stopped in the distance.

"This isn't fair!" She clenched her fists at them. "Than had no choice but to take that oath. He was forced into it. It shouldn't count."

"You should have made your case at Mount Olympus," Dionysus said. "It's too late now." He and the others turned to go on, up the hill.

"Can't I take his place?"

They stopped to look back at her again.

"What are you talking about, Therese?" Than snapped.

"Didn't Admetus once get his wife to take his place in the Underworld? Can't we ask for a similar deal?"

"No!" Than practically burst from his webbing as he ripped and snarled at her like a caged animal. "Stop this! Are you mad?"

"I could look into it," Hermes said.

"I won't allow it!" Than growled. "Now stop, Therese, or I swear!"

"Swear what? It's my fault! I should be the one to suffer the maenads."

Dionysus turned to Than. "You lucky rogue."

Than said between gritted teeth, "She won't be taking my place."

The god of wine grabbed Therese by the elbow too roughly for her comfort.

"What are you doing?" she asked as he pulled her closer to him. His mostly naked body unsettled her.

He looked deeply into her eyes, studying them. "You would lay at the hands of the maenads for him? Tell me the truth. Do you mean what you say?"

She glared at him. "Absolutely."

"Damn you, Dionysus!" Than growled. "Let her go! I won't let her do it!"

Dionysus ignored Than's shouts. "Has Cupid pierced your heart with one of his arrows?"

Therese shook her head. She thought of Pete.

"Can you teach me to win Ariadne's heart?"

Therese flinched with surprise. "I don't know."

"What's the secret to love?"

"Shouldn't you ask Aphrodite?"

"I'm asking you."

Therese combed her mind for the best answer, studying Than's pained expression as he struggled against the net of roots. "Sacrifice. You win someone's love by making sacrifices."

Dionysus pushed her away from him with disgust. "I don't believe in making sacrifices. I believe in living life to the fullest every moment of the day!"

Therese stumbled, but caught herself before she fell. She stood tall and proud, remembering that she was a god, too. "That's why you're alone."

He narrowed his eyes at her as though they were weapons.

"Let me take his place," she said again.

"No."

Before she could speak another word, he god traveled with Than to the throng of people up the mountain. She and Hermes followed close behind.

She fought against the one or two hundred women crowding around Dionysus and the cocoon of roots still encasing Than. Their bodies writhed against her, their long hair thrashing across her face. She reached through the roots and took his hand, praying that she'd remain at his side for as long as she could.

The music roared to life through the lyres and flutes of at least a dozen satyrs, and the women around her flailed their arms in the air and jerked their bodies in a state of madness as the roots slowly fell away from Than.

He turned to her with a hint of panic in his eyes. "It's okay. Do your job."

She was shoved aside as the women clamored toward Than, grabbing his limbs from all directions. Therese hoped he would expire quickly so he wouldn't suffer long.

Wait. He had said, "Do your job." Now that she was the god of death, she could take his soul any time, couldn't she? She reached into his body and pulled, but his soul would not come free. What the…?

"That only works with humans," he said through gritted teeth. He turned up toward the clouds, opened his mouth, and cried out in pain as his left arm was ripped from his torso. His scream echoed across the valley, over the sounds of the music makers. Birds scattered from the treetops. Blood spilled from his body, and the severed flesh of his arm pit hung grotesquely. It was his body being torn apart, but it felt like her heart.

Panic gripped her. "No! How long do I have to wait before I can take you?" She wrenched her fingers around the feathery, ethereal mass that was his soul, ready to take him as soon as she could pull him free. Her tears poured down her face and into her mouth and mixed with his blood.

He couldn't reply.

The maenads ripped his leg at the knee and he howled across the mountainside.

"Hermes! Help me preserve him!" she cried. She disintegrated into three more and collected Than's bloody limbs, still warm and twitching in her hands, blood running down her arms.

A hand, an arm, the other leg—as soon as they were ripped from his torso, she bounded to retrieve them, sometimes fighting off a maenad wishing to eat the flesh. Hermes helped, his face grim.

Then the maenads ripped off Than's head, and his soul came free. One of her found his precious head, closed her eyes, and cringed as she added it to the rest of her collection. She couldn't look; she just couldn't look. Another of her wrenched what was left of his torso free from the wild women and dispatched in multiples to Demeter's cabin to find Demeter and Persephone waiting with Apollo.

"Apollo?" She burst into tears, grateful to see the god of healing and traumatized by the fact that she was holding the bits of her true love. Her three fragmented selves lovingly lay Than's parts on the altar without quite looking at them, and then she fell onto the floor, shuddering and sobbing, allowing the trauma and grief to consume her.

As she led his bewildered soul to Charon, she told him how sorry she was, realizing she, too, was in shock and unable to think clearly.

He seemed more confused than she. "Where are we going?"

"Tartarus. You know that. Are you okay?"

"Who am I?"

Her heart cramped in one painful knot. "What? Than? Thanatos?"

He blinked his ethereal eyes. "Therese? What a nightmare."

Tears of relief and regret rushed to her eyes, and in all two hundred thousand places she now journeyed with souls across the lands, she wept. She wept for Than, for what he'd endured. She wept for herself, wishing no one had to witness such an atrocious sight. And she wept with relief for the great fact that he was free for a whole year. The worse was over, for a while, anyway. As soon as she could graduate from high school, they'd be together. And although they'd have to go through this every year, she wouldn't think on that now.

"Therese?" Than whispered. "You okay?"

He'd just been ripped to pieces and he was worried about her? "Yes, Baby. Everything's going to be okay."

And everything would be okay, wouldn't it? As long as she could find her purpose.

When she and Than stepped onto Charon's raft, Ariadne and Asterion were stepping off to leave. They both gave her hateful looks. Her face went hot with embarrassment, but she didn't lower her gaze. Instead, she went closer to them and said, "I'm sorry. What I did to you was wrong. I promise to spend eternity trying to find a way to make it up to you."

Brother and sister looked at one another and then back at Therese with parted lips.

"I mean it," Therese assured them. "I can sense you're good, and I feel bad about wronging you. I will think of something, I promise."

Asterion and Ariadne looked back at her skeptically as Charon carried them off to the land of the living.

Than took her hand and said, "I love you." He bent his ethereal face down to hers and produced a barely perceptible kiss. She missed his body, his warm lips, but his soul would do for now.

Chapter Eight: Return Home

Therese disintegrated to lie beside Than's body while it awaited its soul, but it was so cold and so morbidly still that it gave her the creeps. So she kept Than's soul company in Tartarus while she disintegrated into hundreds of thousands to escort the dead. They mostly visited with Tizzie and Meg, and occasionally Alecto, who was usually hunting, until, on the third day, Than felt his body beckoning to him. Overjoyed, Therese guided him back to his chambers where he lay on his bed. His body was instantly warm and glowing once again: the union was complete.

Than sat up, but before he could stand, Therese pressed him back down with her enthusiastic embrace, lying partly on top of him as she covered his face with kisses. Now that the warmth and vitality had returned, she clung to his body, caressed it, moved her lips across his throat.

"I'm so glad you're okay," she murmured in between kisses.

"Sweet homecoming."

She felt the transference of duty from her to him, and her hundreds of thousands of selves reintegrated into the one. It was nice to be one again.

They played in bed for many hours, caressing, petting, kissing, until Therese felt the familiar pull of responsibility.

"I have to go back," she said.

"I know."

"Can't you come with me?"

"I'll come by later, okay? First talk to your family."

She'd been keeping a watchful eye over Clifford and Jewels, grateful to see her aunt and uncle taking such good care of them but looked forward to being with them. After one last kiss, she god traveled to her bedroom in the middle of the night, gave her pets hours of love, surprised to discover she could understand them perfectly. They didn't communicate in words, but in ideas and emotions. Her Russian tortoise had missed her but had gotten to business by saying she had hoped for more lettuce and less carrots. She also hoped for more hibiscus petals and leaves, if possible. Clifford, her brown and white fox terrier, also had requests. His biggest demand was that she never, ever, leave him for so many days in a row again. He hadn't stopped trembling since she had left. And Carol and Richard were nice, but they didn't like going for long walks in the forest, nor did they remember to give him rawhide to chew on in the evenings. Plus, they wouldn't sleep with him, and he preferred a warm body to snuggle against.

Therese changed into a comfy pair of sweats and curled on the bed with Clifford, even though she didn't sleep. Having been a goddess for five whole days, she had learned that, although gods do sleep, it's not often. Than had said he slept once a month at most.

Clifford still wore a bandage on his head, which he scratched at when he wasn't licking Therese. When she asked if she could remove it, he panted with happiness. She tugged it off. He was healed, good as new, except for a little redness from where he'd been scratching.

No, she didn't sleep as she snuggled with Clifford, but she did do a lot of thinking. Foremost in her mind was what she would say to Carol and Richard. She hoped she could make it up to them in some way, but how?

Before she could come up with answers, she sensed Carol climbing the stairs and couldn't decide whether she should stay or disappear. The indecision was painful for fifteen seconds as she sat there, frozen, listening to Carol's footsteps. She had to face this sooner or later, so she may as well now. She quickly dimmed herself to mortal form and turned on a lamp, which she hadn't needed, able now to see in the dark.

"Therese?" Carol stood in the doorway, her hands at her mouth in shock. "When…how…"

"I didn't want to wake you." Therese moved to the edge of the bed and sat with her feet on the floor, not sure if she should hug Carol or stay put. "My bus arrived a while ago. I, uh, took a cab home."

Carol stood with her mouth agape.

"I'm sorry I left without telling you." Therese pulled at her hands, nearly ripping her own fingers off. She had to get used to her incredible strength. "I wanted to go someplace where people wouldn't look at me like I killed Vicki." Therese had been the one who paid for the ketamine, and everyone knew it. What had been meant as a near death experience in order to visit loved ones had turned into a disaster that was mostly her fault. "It's been hard enough without the cold stares, you know?"

Carol frowned. "You scared me to death. How could you hurt me like that?"

Therese dropped her head.

Carol rushed to her and put her arms around her, falling to her knees beside the bed. "You had me and Richard so worried. Than's dad didn't reassure me much."

Yeah, that conversation hadn't gone well, Therese recalled. What had Hades said? Kids will be kids? What can you do? Thanks, Hades. Thanks a lot.

Hades voice pierced her thoughts: "At least I spoke to her. Be thankful for that."

Oops. "Thank you, Hades."

"What?" Carol pulled back to look at her.

Had she said that out loud? "I mean, can you forgive me?"

Carol's face turned white and she rushed to Therese's bathroom and retched into the commode. Had she made her aunt sick with worry? Therese chewed on the inside of her bottom lip.

She followed her aunt to the bathroom. "Carol, I...I don't know what to say. It was stupid of me."

Carol wiped her face with a towel and turned to Therese. "What?"

"I didn't realize how worried you'd be. I didn't think."

Carol stood up. "Oh, sweetheart." She washed her hands and patted her face with cool water. "There's something I need to tell you. Let's sit down."

Therese returned to her bed. Carol sat on the edge of it, beside her.

"I was going to wait to tell you with Richard, but he's sleeping so soundly for the first time in days, so I won't wake him."

"Carol, what's going on?" Had they decided they couldn't handle her? After the drugs she'd done with Vicki and now running away, maybe they couldn't take having a teenager. She pulled Clifford into her lap. She'd be okay, right? She'd just go to Than, but the thought of them giving up on her broke her heart. Tears formed in her eyes, and she blinked them away.

"I'm pregnant."

Now it was Therese's turn to gape.

"I was going to tell you yesterday. Richard and I had planned something special for July fourth." Tears rushed from Carol's eyes.

That's right. It was Independence Day.

"We were going to take you to the park, to watch the fireworks. Then we were going to give you a gift from the baby." She wiped her face with the back of her hand. "These damn hormones."

"I'm having a baby cousin?"

Carol frowned. "Cousin and sibling. We adopted you, so, at least in the eyes of the law, this baby will be your brother or sister. Didn't you say you always wished you had one?"

Therese nodded, unable to stop the tears from streaming down her face. Yes. She'd always wanted a brother or sister. And now that she was getting one, she was leaving to join Than in the Underworld. She threw her arms around Carol, sadness gripping her heart. "I'm so happy."

The following day, Therese changed into jeans and boots and walked down to the Holts' place beneath a canopy of dark clouds to groom

Stormy. She was surprised to find Courtney and Jen already there, doing her work.

"Hey," Therese said awkwardly.

The two girls turned in her direction.

"You're back!" Jen bounced from Sassy's side and threw her arms around Therese. "It's about time. Stormy's missed you."

With Courtney sitting on the stool in the stall, nuzzling the foal's nose, Therese felt doubtful, but she ignored her feelings of insecurity and gently reached out to stroke her horse—her horse. "Hey, boy. I've missed you, too."

Stormy met her eyes and neighed. Therese was shocked that she could understand him. "Where have you been?"

She ran her fingers through his mane. "I had to help out a friend. He knew your mother."

The petite brunette politely moved out of the way. "I'm Courtney, by the way."

Therese found it hard to meet her eyes, wondering if she blamed Therese for her cousin's death. When she did finally look, she found her dark eyes to be beautiful, reminding her of a famous French model she'd seen in her favorite magazines. "Hey."

Just then, Pete walked in, his blond hair framing his face down to his strong jaw. His blue eyes were full of relief. "I thought I saw you walking over. You're finally back."

Therese returned his smile. Dang, he was good looking for a mortal, and even by god standards. When he spread his arms for a hug, his flannel shirt slipped open, and sticking through his t-shirt was what, an arrow? "What's that sticking out of your chest?" She crossed the barn but stopped short of the hug.

"Huh?" Pete looked over his t-shirt.

Therese realized it was Cupid's arrow. Mortal eyes must be blind to it. She stepped closer, pretending to brush away a piece of straw. "Been rolling around in the hay or something?"

Pete laughed and threw his arms around her. "I wish."

She felt the blood rush to her face and wondered, as he held her, if she could pull the arrow out. She wrapped her hand around it. Yes, it was partially tangible. She tightened her grip. Would it hurt him? What if it killed him? She decided to leave it for now, after she had a chance to ask Than. Maybe she could pull the arrow out of Pete's heart and spare him from suffering from a broken heart.

She stepped back from his embrace and patted his shoulder, nearly knocking him over.

"Whoa. Been working out?"

She blushed again. "A little." She had to learn to control her strength.

"Have you met Courtney?" Pete asked.

Therese nodded, but not without noticing Courtney's face light up when Pete said her name. Things just keep getting more and more awkward, she thought.

Later, after taking a shower and changing into clean jeans and a light sweater, Therese sat at the wooden table on the deck with Carol and Richard with a pair of binoculars in one hand. Dusk was settling, the perfect time to spot wild horses and other animals in the mountains across the reservoir. Plus, she was hoping she wouldn't have to talk too much about why she'd left. They already told her they expected her to swim in the championship meet tomorrow, even though she hadn't been to practice in over a week. The heat sheets were probably finalized anyway, so she wasn't sure she could swim in it even if she wanted to.

"Believe me," Carol had said. "The coach wants his top swimmer in this meet. He'll find a way."

Now, as Carol brought out a pan of brownies, she presented Therese with a gift bag.

"It's from the baby," Richard said. "I told Carol it was kind of corny, but you know your aunt."

Therese pulled away the tissue to find a multi-colored Coach handbag inside. "It's beautiful." Jen would kill for this, she thought. Therese liked it just fine but wasn't into designer accessories as much as her friend.

"Look inside," Carol said.

Therese opened the purse to find a matching wallet. "Thank you."

"Keep going," Richard said. "Open the wallet."

Surely the baby wasn't giving her money, she thought as she unsnapped the button and unfolded the fabric. Inside were dozens of clear plastic photo holders. Most were empty, but four of them held photos. The first was of her with her mom and dad, taken when she was six. She fingered their images, tears springing to her eyes. She'd forgotten how long her mom's hair once was, before she started keeping it short. And her dad's had never looked shorter. She gazed at his deep, brown eyes and warm smile, missing his arms around her.

Move on, Therese, she thought, biting her lip.

The second was a photo taken at her grandma and grandpa's in San Antonio. They were all in this one: her grandparents, mom and dad, Carol and Richard, Therese, and even Clifford and Blue. Her mom's mouth was open in this shot, like she was saying something to the photographer. Therese recalled that expression. She wished her mother was here, calling to her from the kitchen window with that same look on her face.

The third was from Carol and Richard's wedding last fall with Therese in between them. The fourth was a black and white blurry photo of...what?

"That's the baby," Carol explained. "That's a copy of the sonogram. That's how we were going to tell you."

More tears clouded Therese's view of the photos in the wallet, and she blinked them away, looking over the images again and again, not knowing what to say.

"We'll take more and add them in as time goes on," Richard said. "By the time you go to college, you'll have every one of those plastic slots full of your family."

Therese closed her eyes to fight the tears from turning into outright sobs. The idea of sharing her life with them and her new brother or sister sounded pleasant just then. She pictured the family vacations they might share, her little brother or sister always in her arms. Then later, when the baby was older, they could hike, canoe, bike, fish—all the things she'd always longed to share with a sibling. But it wasn't to be. Her place was with Than now. Neither the family photos nor the going off to college would become a reality.

"Thank you both. I guess I don't really deserve this."

"Enough talk like that," Carol said. "Let's put that behind us."

Therese nodded, desperately wanting to change the subject. "Speaking of school, I may have to attend summer school to graduate on time."

"Why?" Richard asked before shoving a brownie into his mouth.

"I got behind. And there's no way I'm redoing my senior year. Summer school is embarrassing enough."

"If you really feel that way, why not attend school online?" Carol asked.

"What?"

"I don't know, Carol. Should we encourage her to run away from her fears?"

"I finished my last two years of high school and my entire master's degree program online." Then she added with a wrinkled nose, "Don't like working in large groups."

Therese studied Richard's face for disapproval, but he appeared to be coming around to the idea.

"Really?" Therese asked. "You would let me do that?"

"Don't think it's easier," Carol warned. "The nice thing is it's competency based, so you work at your own pace. But the hard part is you have to be self-motivated."

Oh, she was definitely motivated. She jumped up from the table and hugged first Carol and then Richard. "This is the answer to my prayers."

"Hold on one minute," Richard said, taking her hand in his. "I want to make a deal with you first."

He sounded like Hades. She cocked her head to the side and waited.

"We'll let you enroll in an online school if, and only if, driver's education is part of your curriculum. We need you to learn to drive, Therese. We can't take you everywhere you need to go forever."

Drive? But she could god travel now. Too bad she couldn't explain that to them.

Therese glanced at Carol, who nodded. "Sounds fair to me. No more stalling, okay, sweetheart?"

Ever since her mother's car had plunged into Huck Finn Pond last summer with her and her parents inside…ever since she had to watch them drown before her, trapped in the car underwater…the idea of being in control of her own vehicle frightened her beyond reason. She reminded herself that she had sneaked past Ladon, outwitted the Minotaur, and faced the Hydra. She was a god now, for heaven's sake. But that didn't matter. She could still kill others. She hadn't been able to save her parents, and somewhere, deep down, she still felt responsible. She had killed her parents. She had killed Dumbo. She had killed Vicki. She could kill others from behind the wheel. Is that what she was afraid of? She didn't know, but she was definitely afraid.

Chapter Nine: Sweet Nothings

Than was waiting for Therese when she came upstairs after dinner. He wished he could have joined her and her aunt and uncle, but although he was no longer a threat to Therese, he continued to be to mortals. He envied Pete's ability to freely interact with Therese's friends and family. He'd watched them in the months since he left last summer. What made matters worse was the fact that everyone liked Pete, including Than.

"What's wrong?" he asked Therese as she plopped into the chair beneath her window without so much as a hug or kiss in his direction.

"Where do I start?" She folded her arms. "My aunt and uncle expect me to swim in the championship meet tomorrow, and I'm nowhere near ready. I haven't been to practice in ages. I'll probably let the whole team down."

Unbelievable. He lifted his palms up. "You're forgetting something."

"What?" She snapped.

"Wait for it."

A light in her eyes turned on. "Oh, yeah. I'm a god."

"Feel better?"

"Guess there's no doubt I'll beat Lacey Holzmann this time."

"Problem solved."

"But they're also making me learn to drive. I don't need to drive. But they don't know that. I can't very well tell them I can travel from here to China in a snap."

"What's the big deal?"

She frowned, obviously fighting off tears.

"Therese?" He scooped her into his arms and carried her to her bed. "Talk to me."

She stroked his hair, making him want to purr like a cat. "I don't know exactly."

"I have an idea." He touched the tip of his nose to hers. "And it's gonna be fun."

"What?"

"First kiss me."

Her lips tasted salty as he pressed his mouth to hers, her body warm against him. He missed the feel of mortal skin against mortal skin, but this was quite nice, too.

She ran her fingers through his hair, sending heat down his neck, his shoulders, his back. He rolled on top of her, keeping his weight off, then remembering she was no longer fragile. He sank against her.

"Oh my," she whispered, making him want her.

The phone rang. Therese looked at him. "I should get that. It's Pete. If I don't, Carol or Richard will just come up here."

He nodded and rolled off her. Of course, it was Pete.

With his keen sense of hearing, he followed their conversation, which was yet another of the cowboy's attempt to get Therese out on a date. He didn't call it a date, of course. A group was going to the movies tomorrow night to celebrate the end of their swimming season.

"Yeah, sounds good," Therese said, to Than's surprise.

What?

She hung up the phone.

"You're going?"

"Why not?"

"Because Pete's in love with you."

"So? I can't help that. Talk to Cupid. Which reminds me. I can see the arrow sticking from his chest. Can I pull it out without hurting him?"

"That's weird. I don't see an arrow. You see an actual arrow?"

Her eyes narrowed. "You don't?"

"No."

"What does that mean?"

"I'll find out. Meanwhile, why string him along by going with him to the movies?"

"Jealous?"

He wrapped a hand around her narrow waist and pulled her to him, side by side, face to face on the bed. "Damn right."

She bit his lip.

He bit back and then gave her a deeper kiss.

"Mmm," she moaned. "You have nothing to be jealous of. I just want to spend time with my friends before I leave them all, you know?"

He cupped her cheek. "Yeah. I get it."

"Besides, I haven't told you the worst news of all. The worst and the best."

"I'm listening."

"Carol's pregnant."

He sat up in the bed, confused. "How is that bad news? That's wonderful news." Then he added, "You don't feel like you're being replaced, do you? Because that's ridiculous."

"I hadn't thought of that, thank you." She got up and sat in the chair across the room.

Great. They were right back where they started: on opposite sides of the room. "Then what?"

"It's just, well…it's going to be even harder now to say goodbye."

He studied her sweet, worried face as a lump rose to his throat. So she was having second thoughts? After all they'd been through together? He didn't know what to say. Finally, he asked, "What are you thinking?"

"I'm thinking that on top of everything else, I have no idea what my purpose should be. Didn't you say it had to be unique? I can't be the goddess of animals, because that's Artemis. What about the goddess of friendship?"

"That's Philotes."

"Who?"

"She's one of the primeval gods, before Zeus and the other Olympians. Even before the Titans."

"There's nothing left for me, Than. How can I make this transformation stick if I never figure out my purpose?"

"You will." He tried to hide how unsure he felt.

They sat together in the silence for a while, Clifford moving from the bed to Therese's lap. She stroked Clifford, but Than could tell her mind was someplace else. He cleared his throat and said, "Let's get out of here."

"Where are we going?"

"You'll see."

Chapter Ten: Driving with Gods

Than took her hand and together they god traveled to an enormous building made of glass and filled with cars. Although the building was well-lit, both from the indoor lights and the outdoor floodlights in the predawn darkness, it was quiet and empty of people.

"Where are we?" Therese stood with Than on the ground floor gazing up at yet another level, visible from the open staircase, displaying the sexiest cars she'd ever seen.

"Sant A'gata Bolognese, Italy. The Lamborghini Museum." Than took her hand and led her around the cars. "Aphrodite drives a green one just like that one over there."

She followed his finger. "It's beautiful." She skipped ahead of him, pulling him along. "Look at this one. It's like the Batmobile. Rad, huh?"

"You prefer the Aventador to the Gallador?"

"I guess. Love the deep orange. How do you know so much about them?" They walked on, touring the gallery.

"I don't, but recently Aphrodite got me thinking. I took a brief ride in hers."

"Thinking about getting one of your own?"

"Our own."

Therese liked the sound of that. "As long as you're the one driving."

He squeezed her hand. "No, m'am. It's time for you to learn."

Just then, a flash of orange sprang from beneath the car nearest them.

"A cat," Therese said. "A tabby."

"It's frightened. Can you hear her?"

Therese nodded. She lunged to her knees and held her hands. "Hey, kitty. We won't hurt you."

Therese could sense the cat beneath the car, could hear her purring a frightened message: "I'm lost. I'm scared. I don't know where my boy is."

"We'll help you find your boy," Therese said. "Come out and talk to us."

The tabby poked her head from beneath a candy-apple red convertible. Tentatively, she padded a little closer to Therese, who sat back on her heels with her hands held out, Than standing close behind her.

"What's your boy's name?" Therese asked.

"Luis. He brought me here this afternoon and left without me."

"I bet he's looking for you." Than said. "The museum's closed tonight, but I bet he'll come back in the morning."

"I'm hungry, and thirsty, and scared."

Therese glanced up at Than. "Maybe we can find Luis."

Without warning, the tabby leapt into Therese's arms and then rubbed her face against Therese. She stroked the cat. "What's your name?"

"Belle."

Therese stood with Belle in her lap. "I have an idea." She turned to Than. "Listen to your human prayers. I bet a boy is praying that Belle isn't dead."

Than stared into space, apparently sifting through the multitude of prayers. At last he nodded. "You're right. I hear him. I know where he is."

Than took Therese's hand, and together with Belle, they traveled to a dilapidated townhouse in the historic district barely illuminated by one crooked streetlamp. Belle recognized the place and scampered from Therese's arms.

The two gods watched on as Belle pawed at the front door, and the surprised, gleeful boy who opened the door swept her up.

"Belle! You're back!"

A woman in a tattered nightgown stepped from the stoop and hollered, "I told you to get rid of that flea-infested parasite! What's she doing back?"

"I don't know," the boy replied. "Please let her stay. I'll keep her in a box outside."

"So long as she doesn't set foot in our house."

The tabby glanced back at the two gods just before Than took Therese's hand and led her back to the Lamborghini museum.

"Poor thing," Therese said, not feeling all that confident that the cat would be well cared for. "Maybe we should have kept her."

"The boy will make sure she's fed."

"Now that I'm a god, I can look in on her. I won't let her starve."

"Now, where were we?" Than asked.

She grinned. "So you're going to teach me how to drive, huh?"

"He's not." Hermes appeared like a flash between them. "I am."

Therese's eyes widened. "Hermes? Where did you come from?"

"Than disintegrated and persuaded me to meet you here."

Therese glanced at Than. Really? "You can't be serious."

"Why not?" Hermes quipped. "I am, after all, the god of travelers."

"I thought you were the messenger god."

"I am. And also of language, persuasion, animal husbandry, astronomy, commerce, and theft, among other things."

"Commerce and theft? Isn't that a conflict of interest or something?"

"Or something." Hermes put his fists on his hips.

Therese tipped her head back. "So you're to blame for the economy."

"Humans have free will, remember?" Hermes raised one wiry eyebrow. "Now do you want to learn to drive or not?"

"In one of these?" she asked. "Are we stealing one, then?"

"Just borrowing." Hermes winked. He turned and pointed to a long silver beauty. "That one. The Estoque. It's a four-seater."

Than opened the driver's door and motioned for Therese to climb in. "Ladies first."

"Um, that's okay. You go ahead."

"I insist."

Biting her lower lip, she climbed behind the wheel, reminding herself that they were gods, they couldn't be injured—at least not mortally—and they weren't on the road where others could be hurt. However, as soon as they were all comfortably seated and strapped inside, Hermes in the passenger's seat and Than behind him in the back, the landscape changed.

The sun was rising in a blue sky across rolling fields lined with rows of wheat. Cows grazed on other fields to their left from where they sat in the middle of a country road on the top of a hill.

"Don't just sit there," Hermes said impatiently. "Start the engine."

She felt for a key in the ignition, but there was none. "Uh…"

"Oh, for heaven's sake." Hermes rolled his eyes and the engine roared to life.

Therese clutched the steering wheel with both hands, her heart racing. With her right foot, she placed a slight pressure on the accelerator. The engine sped, but, otherwise, nothing happened. She looked at Hermes.

"Put her in drive first." More eye rolling.

"Sorry." She looked around the steering column and dashboard, only to have Hermes show her the gearshift on the console between them. She grabbed the end of it and tried to move it, but it wouldn't budge. She wrestled with it, breaking it off completely. "Oh, no!"

"You've been in this car less than two minutes and you've already broken it?" Hermes took the broken gear shift. "Where's Hephaestus when you need him?"

Warm blood rushed to Therese's face. "Look, I didn't ask you to do this."

Than's squeezed her shoulder. "I did."

"Yeah, but why?"

"Because I don't know how to drive either."

She studied his reflection in the rearview mirror. He seemed serious. Hadn't he done anything but escort the souls of the dead?

"Just so you know next time," Hermes said, holding the knob in front of her face, "you have to push this button in before shifting."

She turned to him sharply. "I'll remember that next time I'm driving a Lamborghini."

Hermes sighed. "That's true of most cars, Therese."

"Oh."

Hermes manipulated the shiny steel nub from which the stick had broken. "There. She's in drive. Now let's get started."

She eased on the accelerator again. When nothing happened, she pressed harder, gunning the engine.

"Parking brake?" Hermes asked with an impatient tone.

Therese lifted her foot as she looked around the dash. "Where is it?"

Hermes pointed to the knob. "Pull it. Keep your right foot on the brake. Then gently ease your foot onto the accelerator."

Therese did as he said and finally got the car in motion. She sped up to twenty miles an hour, feeling jittery.

"Take her up to fifty," Hermes said. "Looks like you've got the road all to yourself."

She eased on the pedal, unable to believe she was actually driving. "So where are we anyway?"

"Derbyshire, not too far from Ashbourne, one of my favorite towns. Hecate and I used to go fishing together there. So many good memories."

She glanced at the speedometer. "I'm at fifty. Now what?"

"Just get the hang of driving straight. Follow the road."

The road turned downward and then up as they passed sheep and more wheat. This wasn't so bad, she thought. Smiling for the first time since she'd climbed into the car, she let out the breath she hadn't realized she'd been holding. Her hands hurt from clamping the wheel, so she loosened her grip. Not too bad, she thought again, feeling like an adult. Up ahead, she noticed a sign indicating a deer crossing. "Why is the sign on the left side of the road?"

"Huh?" Hermes looked at the sign. "Oh, dear."

Before Therese could ask what was wrong, a big farm truck came into view heading straight for them. Why was it in her lane?

"What's going on? What should I do?" This was exactly what she was afraid of: killing someone. Her heart throbbed in her ears.

"Bloody hell!" Hermes shrieked, turning the wheel to the left.

The truck whizzed by them as Therese caught her breath and pressed on the brake, bringing the car to a choppy stop. All three plunged forward and then back in their seats.

"Forgot we're in England." Hermes gave her a sheepish grin. "They drive on the left side here. My mistake."

She looked at him with her mouth open. "That was close."

Another car came up behind them, sounding the horn and making her jump in her seat. Luckily it went around them, but not without giving them a furious glance.

"Get us off the road, Therese. Maybe we'll give Than a turn."

A little too slowly, she eased off into the tall grass on the side of the road. As she was about to climb out, Hermes grabbed her arm.

"You can god travel now, remember?"

"Oh, yeah."

She and Than switched in a flash, Therese falling back in the seat more abruptly than she had planned, having forgotten to keep her eyes open again. How long would it take for her to get used to her new abilities?

The landscape changed again, to a palm and papaya tree-lined street, narrower than the one in Derbyshire, and, here, the sun was at high noon. A volcano loomed on the horizon past fields of high grass where caribou were feeding.

"Take her over to the right lane," Hermes said. "We're on one of the Philippine Islands, where people drive on the right."

From the backseat, Therese watched Than maneuver the vehicle like a pro. "You sure this is your first time?"

"Positive."

"Why haven't you driven before? My god, you can disintegrate and do whatever you want. You never wanted to take a drive someplace?"

"Why, when I can god travel?"

She sat back in her seat. "I guess."

"And I have no problem driving my father's chariot."

"That's true."

"But you're right. There's a lot I haven't done."

"We can do it together."

"Have you chosen a purpose then?" Hermes asked.

"Not yet. Too bad you can't give me one of yours. You have a bajillion purposes."

Hermes chuckled. "Yeah. I used to have more before Thanatos and Hypnos were born. I used to do their jobs as well. Imagine that."

"I can't," Than said. "Don't know how you did it."

Than came upon a stop sign but pushed on the brake too hard and too fast, throwing Therese and Hermes forward and back.

"Sorry," Than said.

"Take a right here," Hermes said. "You know how to use the blinker?"

Than found it and made the turn. Then the car sped from thirty to seventy in a matter of seconds.

"Slow her down," Hermes said.

"I can't. Something's gone wrong."

Therese watched helplessly from the backseat as Than pumped the brake. The car turned a sharp left, just missing a group of people walking along the side of the road.

"Than, what's happening?" Therese cried.

Suddenly, gusty winds made the tall trees sway like hula dancers, and someone's hat flew past them.

"I don't know!" He continued to pump the brake and to wrench the steering wheel with both hands. "The Lamborghini's moving on its own. Let's god travel out of here."

"The car might hurt someone!"

"She's right," Hermes added. "We can't just abandon it. I sense another god at work."

They took another sharp turn to the left toward the sea. As they zoomed past little huts and a rickshaw toward a sandy beach, Therese was overwhelmed by a flashback of the evening her mom's car flew into Huck Finn Pond. She recalled the way her father, trapped by the steering shaft, had writhed and her mother, paralyzed by the bullet shot in her neck, had closed her eyes and yielded to the water overtaking them. She had been able to do nothing to save them.

The Lamborghini lifted up off the road, flew ten feet in the air over the sandy beach, and then plunged into the sea.

"Ahh!" Therese cried as the cold water rushed into the car.

"We're bound to the car!" Hermes said. "No god traveling out of this mess!"

Than reached back for Therese. "You okay?"

Before the car submerged, she felt herself being lifted at lightning speed up from the water, the Lamborghini falling away in a hazy mist. She rubbed her eyes and blinked, shivering in the cold wind. Sitting beside her was Poseidon.

Chapter Eleven: Poseidon's Warning

Than and Hermes sat in the seat just behind her as Poseidon held the reins of his chariot, drawn by Riptide, Seaquake, and Crest—three white stallions who flew across the water's surface at amazing speeds.

"Poseidon?" she asked. "What's happening?"

Hermes and Than leaned forward in their seats, Hermes shouting, "What in the world is going on, Uncle?"

"I'll explain when we get down to my palace." His long, sun-bleached hair, longer than hers, whipped in the wind, and his sunburnt face was set hard and unyielding.

They zipped high in the air above a volcano, Therese's stomach turning a flip-flop as she clutched on to the side of the chariot, her fingers cold, her knuckles white. Hair whipped in her face as she glanced back at Than, and her teeth chattered as she recalled the last time Poseidon had taken her for a ride. It had been as his prisoner to Mount Olympus. Maybe he never got over the fact that Artemis helped her win her meet earlier in the summer after Therese had turned down his offer. Maybe he'd been responsible for the earthquake that had damaged her school natatorium after all. The chariot flew in a chasm between two volcanoes and then out into the open sea. Therese glanced back again at Than to see his look of alarm, though his prayer to her was, "It's going to be okay."

In the next instant, the chariot submerged into the ocean depths. Therese was amazed to find she could breathe, and although she was cold, she wasn't freezing. Her body, like those of the other three gods, glowed in the darkness, creating a halo of light in which she could see the marvels of the sea around her. She could see beyond their glow as well, further into the darkness all the way down to the ocean floor. Though she passed by at nearly lightning speed, her goddess eyes could easily detect everything—the colorful fish, coral, and shells, in addition to two curious nymphs astride dolphins who followed them, one on each side of the chariot. One of the dolphins was Arion, the dolphin on whose back she had ridden last summer. She waved, and he gave her a nod.

"Hello, again," he clicked.

She gasped, forgetting that she could now communicate with all beings, including dolphins.

"Hello!"

Up ahead, she could see Poseidon's palace. Worried as she was for his motives for bringing them here, she was nevertheless delighted to see it again. Bright golden lights came from the bottom of the ocean, illuminating the amazing transparent structure, its clear crystal walls making her think of an aquarium. Through the walls, she could see many figures inside of it—merfolk with tails and other, more human-like, people sitting among the furniture, eating at tables on golden chairs, and lounging on beds clustered in curtains of seaweed growing up from the ocean floor. At the back of the palace, the walls were no longer transparent and were made of shiny mother-of-pearl.

The three white steeds slowed and came to a stop inside a crystal chamber on the bottom level of the magnificent structure where three merfolk immediately swam over to unbridle the horses and lead them away. The dolphin-riding nymphs stopped outside the chamber and swam off, out of sight. Now that they were no longer in motion, Therese and the others floated up from their seats, and she had to continually pull her sweater down to keep herself covered. Despite this struggle with her top, Therese felt like she was in her element, having loved the water all her life. She'd started swimming at an early age, and her parents used to joke that she must have been a dolphin in a previous life. They didn't believe in reincarnation—at least not her mother. Therese had never been able to get a straight answer from her father.

Poseidon led them from what must have been the chariot garage, and they followed, swimming in their own fashion. Therese and Than swam breaststroke. Hermes, ahead of them, swam like a dog, paddling his arms and cycling his feet. Therese had the urge to laugh, and couldn't help it when she thought, "I don't want to make waves." The pun was corny, but she was nervous and excited and couldn't stop from giggling.

They entered a lounge with four couches facing one another in a square. Therese couldn't see how they would be able to sit on them, since all four gods floated on top near the crystal ceiling. But that problem was soon remedied when long tentacles reached out to them and handed them each a heavy boulder, save Poseidon, who was given his trident by a merman, and this kept him from floating. Therese followed the arms of the tentacles with her eyes to see the octopus on the floor between dancing rows of seaweed. She took the boulder he offered her and immediately sank to the floor with the others. She manipulated herself over to the couch next to Than and sat beside him. The couch was surprisingly comfortable and spongy, reminding her of a Temperpedic bed.

"You have our attention," Hermes said to Poseidon. His voice was clear underwater, as though he were speaking into Therese's ear through an earbud. "So tell us. What's the meaning of this?"

Poseidon sat on the couch directly across from Hermes. Than and Therese sat close together on a couch to themselves. "I've brought you here to warn you. I wanted to be safe within these palace walls with all my allies and servants at the ready. I couldn't speak of this anywhere else."

"Warn us?" Than asked. "Sounds serious."

Poseidon grimaced. "If you consider a plot by Ares to lock Therese into the depths of Tartarus with Cronus and his ilk serious, then yes."

Therese gasped, which made her gag on a bit of water. Than patted her back. She looked at him and asked, "Why? What could he gain by that? Does he hate me so much?" Tears sprang to her eyes.

"Not hate. Fear," Poseidon said. "He actually admires your loyalty and determination. He fears you as his enemy."

"But, but I still don't get why? How am I a threat to him?"

Than curled his arms around her more possessively. "It's not like we can vote on Mount Olympus. We're banished. We're out of the way. Tartarus? Really?"

"He doesn't want to see your union take place," Poseidon explained.

"That's ridiculous!" Therese said. "He just doesn't want me to be happy. Is that it? He wants to see me suffer!" The boulder rolled from her lap, and she started to float up again, but Than held her down. She took up her rock with both hands and returned it to her lap.

"He's not like that," Poseidon said. "He may love war and conflict, but he has no need for personal vengeance."

"Then why?" Than demanded.

"Gods beget gods," Poseidon said. "You may be banished from Mount Olympus, but your future children might one day skew the balance of power against him."

"Ah," Hermes said. "Now I understand."

Therese felt her face go white. She hadn't even thought of having children. That seemed so far away in the future.

"Can't we promise never to have children?" Therese wasn't sure she wanted to make such a promise, but it sure beat living eternity in fear of being captured. It sure beat remaining trapped at the bottom of Tartarus.

Hermes actually guffawed.

"What's so funny?" she asked with narrowed eyes.

Than turned to her with an awkward smile. "Um. Gods don't have birth control."

She almost said, "So?" but she caught herself. Oh. She could feel her cheeks turn bright pink. If they promised never to have children, they would essentially be swearing abstinence. No wonder Hermes laughed. What kind of marriage would that be?

"No more god travel," Poseidon warned. "It makes you vulnerable to abduction. Have you ever wondered why I prefer my chariot? Well, that's why. Most gods with something to lose prefer chariot travel. It's safer."

"What a pickle," Hermes muttered.

Therese swallowed more water, breaking into another fit of coughing as Than patted her back. When she'd gotten the water out of her windpipe, she asked, "Any idea how Ares plans to capture me?"

Poseidon frowned. "No. The only reason I know of his plan is that he asked me to do it. When I refused, he said no more."

Therese looked again at Than, wondering what they should do, but was only further worried by the expression on his face. His brows bent together, forming a v, his eyes were narrowed, and his mouth pressed into a tight line. She could see his jaw clenching against his cheeks near his temples. He looked like he was going to punch something.

"We'll get through this," she said to him, her turn to be the reassuring one. "It's going to be okay."

He stood up with his rock and paced. "Ares isn't getting away with this. I'll have my father block every entrance to Tartarus. My sisters will be on watch day and night. He can't control us like this. I won't let him. Damn him."

"We've got to find a weakness of his to exploit," Hermes said. "It's the only way. Even if he can't get her to Tartarus, there are other places to hold a victim."

"What weakness?" Therese asked.

"There's only one for Ares," Poseidon said.

They all looked at him.

"Aphrodite."

Chapter Twelve: Café Moulan

Than waited for Aphrodite in Paris on the patio at Café Moulan beneath the striped umbrella erected from the center of the round table. He was pissed that she could think of nowhere else to meet him when Ares could be right around the corner, where the two gods frequently rendezvoused. He supposed he'd rather Ares be in Paris than in Colorado hunting Therese. After Poseidon had delivered them in his chariot to Therese's house in the wee hours of the morning, Than hadn't wanted to say goodbye, but she had to compete in her championship swim meet today to maintain the illusion of being human. It was important that they keep Carol and Richard on their side. Therese would be unhappy otherwise.

Than clenched his jaw when Aphrodite finally pulled up in her lime-green Lamborghini half an hour late. He watched her graceful figure move through the tables on the patio, all eyes drawn to her, even though a scarf concealed her face. She exuded beauty in every feminine curve of her body, in the long golden tresses of hair gliding down her back. Than hid his frustration as she sat down across from him. As angry as he felt, he doubted he could carry out the backup plan Poseidon had suggested if Aphrodite could not help them: capture her in exchange for an oath from Ares to never interfere with Therese and Than's happiness again. Than didn't want to play that card if he could avoid it. Aphrodite had become his favorite aunt, and he didn't want to spend eternity on her bad side. He bit down his anger and frustration and said, "I ordered you a glass of wine."

"Wonderful." She took the glass and sipped. Then she sat back in her chair, crossed one leg over the other, swirling the wine in the glass between sips. "Why are we here?"

"I need your help."

She closed her eyes and sighed. "This has to do with Ares?"

Than nodded.

She gave him an exasperated look. "What's he done now?"

"He plans to capture Therese and lock her away."

"I thought as much. He doesn't like being out-numbered."

Than swallowed hard, embarrassed by what he was about to say. "If I promise not to touch her…"

Aphrodite's eyes widened.

Than felt the blood rush to his cheeks. "I love her. I'd do anything to keep her safe."

"Ares won't believe you. You're an oath breaker."

His lips twitched into a frown.

Aphrodite leaned forward, awkwardly averting her eyes. "Than, have you considered that maybe she'd be better off human?"

"Isn't it a bit late for that?" he growled.

"Not if she can't discover her purpose."

Than folded his arms across his chest, trying to suppress the mix of anger and frustration boiling inside of him. "So you want us to give up? After all we've gone through?"

"In time, she could be happy with the mortal struck by Cupid."

The anger blazed through him as he imagined Therese in Pete's arms. Then he recalled Therese's question about the arrow. "That reminds me. Therese can see the arrow in his chest and wants to know what would happen if she pulled it out."

Aphrodite pressed both hands against the table and leaned even closer. "She can see the arrow?"

Than lifted his chin. "So?"

"This is good news for you. Only a descendant of Cupid can see his arrows once they've pierced a heart."

"She was a demigod?"

"Not demigod. But she had some godly blood in her. Once the transformation took place, the sight of Eros came to her."

Than marveled at this revelation. He'd been impressed with her control over her dreams and her abilities with animals. "That explains a lot." He wondered again if they'd been fated to find one another. Had they always been meant to be together? Then he realized something else. "That means she comes from you and Ares."

Aphrodite flipped her long blonde hair from her shoulder and smiled. "I knew there was something special about her."

"Ares wouldn't hurt her knowing this, would he?"

She frowned. "She's too far down the blood line to matter to him. Many humans have some residual godly blood."

"But you just said she was special."

"Special because she comes from me." She leaned across the table. "Look, Ares was responsible for her parents' death. He can never trust Therese or her progeny not to retaliate against him."

"Then how is her relationship to Cupid a good thing for us?"

"There may yet be some undiscovered talents. And as to Peter Holt's arrow, she can't pull it out, but she might be able to shoot another in, to neutralize it."

"That would comfort her." And it was no lie it would put him more at ease as well.

"It could backfire and make him despise her."

Than sucked in his lips. He supposed hate was a better alternative to love.

"I'll speak with Cupid," Aphrodite promised.

"Meanwhile, you can do nothing about Ares?"

Aphrodite frowned. "There is one possibility."

"What is it?" A flicker of hope brought him to the edge of his seat.

"Ares once made a golden girdle for his daughter Hippolyta."

"The Amazon? I know. So?"

"Well, in addition to giving her the highest status among the Amazons, it also protected her from male attention. Whereas my magic girdle attracts men, hers protected her chastity."

"So you're saying he could make another girdle for Therese?"

"No. I don't think he would. It wasn't easy to make." She swallowed another sip of wine. "You could find Hippolyta's. It's been lost ever since Hercules took it from her as part of his labors."

"And once I find it?"

"Offer to have it permanently fitted to Therese."

Than sighed. To spend an eternity longing to make love to his wife would be a worse torment than the one imposed by the maenads, but if it was the only way to secure Therese's safety while allowing them to be together, well, he'd have to do it.

"Any idea where it might be?"

Aphrodite shrugged. "It was last seen during the war in Athens with the Amazons. Maybe Athena can help."

Chapter Thirteen: The Championship Meet

Therese stood in the locker room before warm-up showing Jen the new Coach purse and wallet Carol and Richard had given her. She flipped through the photos, lingering on the first one, the one of her and her parents.

"That was a sweet idea." Jen tugged off a pair of sweats and stuffed them in her locker with her flip-flops so that only her red Durango Demon swim team suit remained. "Just don't ditch me if it's a girl."

Therese tucked the wallet back into the purse and set it in her locker. "What are you talking about? I'd never ditch you." Guilt flooded through her, because that's exactly what she'd be doing once she graduated and married Than.

"You're my sister, too." Jen poked Therese's shoulder hard with her finger. "And don't you forget it." Jen walked away, ready to warm up.

Therese pulled her t-shirt off and over her head and folded it before laying it on top of her purse. Then she tugged her red swim cap over her head. Her face felt warm and her eyes moist. She was really going to miss Jen.

Lined up for relay, Therese glanced up to the stands once more and caught Carol and Richard's gaze. They waved again. She waved back. Pete, Bobby, and Mr. and Mrs. Holt were there, too, all looking down at the pool deck where she and Jen stood on opposite sides of the pool with the rest of their relay team.

The buzzer sounded throughout the indoor pool. Therese's teammate dove in for butterfly and maintained a hand's width distance behind the A-team swimmers for Pagosa Springs—Lacey's group. The backstroke swimmer widened the gap, leaving Therese's teammate in her wake. Therese was so distraught over this unexpected gap, that she forgot herself when she dove in for breast. She jumped off the platform with so much force and shot out across the pool with such speed, that by the time she landed in the water, she was only a few feet from the other side. Jen looked down at her from the deck in shock, gaping.

Someone yelled, "Go! Go, Jen! Go!"

Jen dove over Therese and took off, easily coming in first.

Throughout the rest of the meet, Therese struggled to keep a low profile, making sure to come in second and third for the rest of her races. Jen didn't mention the freakish dive throughout the meet, but everyone else couldn't stop talking about it. The coach said the word "Olympics" at least a dozen times.

Once they were alone in the locker room and changed out of their wet suits, Jen slipped on her sweats and flip-flops and turned to Therese.

"It has something to do with the crown, doesn't it?" Jen asked.

"What?"

"The dive."

Therese nodded, opening her locker for her t-shirt. That's when she discovered her purse was missing. Before she could respond, a voice called from across the locker room.

"Therese! What in the world?" The voice belonged to a teammate named Stephanie. "Look what I found in the trash can!"

Therese and Jen crossed the room and found Stephanie holding the photo of Therese and her parents.

Tears flooded Therese's eyes and anger clutched the back of her throat. "Who would do this?" She looked in the trash to see the other photos crumpled inside as well, even the sonogram. Had a god done this, or a human?

Later that afternoon while Carol and Richard were at a doctor's appointment for the baby, having another sonogram—this time to find out the gender—Therese was sitting on the couch in front of the television half-watching and half-thinking about the stolen purse when Than appeared beside her.

She threw her arms around his neck. "Hey, you," she said.

"I'm sorry about what happened today."

"At least I got the pictures back."

"Do Carol and Richard know?"

"No. It would break their hearts. I've got to try and keep it from them."

"Maybe I can find a replacement. Then they'll never know."

She popped up into an upright position, feeling perkier. She hadn't thought of that. "Aren't you clever?"

He took her back into his arms and kissed her. Then he said, "Listen. I've got some good news, some bad news, and some semi-good news."

"You met with Aphrodite?" She squared herself to him.

"She said only the descendants of Cupid can see his arrows."

"But we know that's not true because I can see it." Then she added, "I even felt it. It wasn't completely solid, but I could wrap my hand around it. Did you find out what would happen if I were to pull it free?"

"Therese. Stop talking and listen to me."

She rolled her eyes. "Than. I am listening to you."

"Only the descendants of Cupid can see his arrows."

"Like I said…wait." Did this mean what she thought it meant? "Are you saying…hang on, are you saying that I must be Cupid's descendant?"

"And Aphrodite and Ares's as well."

She jumped to her feet and waved her arms in the air, emitting a joyous whoop. This would let them off the hook, then, right? As much as she loathed Ares, he couldn't possibly want to capture her if he was her own ancestor.

"Wait." Than pulled her back down to the sofa beside him. "Aphrodite doubts this will change Ares's position, but what it does mean is that you can help Pete. You might even possess some talent we haven't discovered yet, something akin to your lucid dreaming and your ability to communicate with animals while you were still mortal."

She wasn't sure how to take this news. "Help Pete how?"

He explained what Aphrodite had told him.

"He could hate me?"

"Maybe. Maybe not. But it's better than letting him pine away for you, don't you think?"

"Better for whom?" she asked suspiciously.

"Him, of course."

He was right. Pete could move on with his life. She wouldn't be around anyway, so why did she feel sick at the thought of him hating her? "I suppose I'll need some practice first." She crossed her arms. "What's the rest of your news?"

She watched the blood drain from his face. Oh, no. More bad news? Her back stiffened. "Tell me." She braced herself.

"You remember how you said we could promise Ares we'd never have children?"

"Of course I remember. I got laughed at." Why did he have to bring it up? She felt her own blood drain from her cheeks in mortification.

"Well, there is a way."

Her heart sank. He was willing to give that up? "You mean abstinence."

He nodded. "Not my first choice, but, yeah." He told her about Hippolyta's golden girdle. "Aphrodite says we could have it put on you permanently, guaranteeing we could never…"

"I get it." She stood up and crossed the room. So she would live eternity like one of the virgin goddesses. "This is so unfair. You don't deserve this." She turned off the television, the annoying commercial making it even more difficult to hide her frustration.

"Neither do you. But I don't want to live in fear of your safety."

"It's so unfair."

"Life isn't fair."

Chapter Fourteen: The Parthenon

While Than gave Therese archery lessons in the afternoon in Colorado, he disintegrated and dispatched to Athens, where it was dusk, to meet Athena, who'd been summoned for him by Hermes, at the Parthenon. The ruins were no longer littered with tourists, so Than waited, alone, by the old statue of Athena.

Once Athena appeared, her raven hair barely visible beneath her silver helmet, her grey eyes brighter than the metal gleam above them, he told her about his plan to find the girdle.

"So Therese will join the ranks of the virgin goddesses," Athena said with an approving tone.

"If it's the only way we can be together without fear of Ares."

"Do you see those sacred caves across the acropolis from here?" She pointed to the west.

Than saw them. "I sense something dangerous dwells there."

"Yes. Do you remember Medusa?"

"Of course. Perseus cut off her head. It's there now, on your shield."

She lifted the shield proudly. "You know why I wanted it, don't you?"

"She and Poseidon met here at your temple."

"And soiled it with their love-making."

Than knew the story. Perseus himself had told it to him when he came to the Underworld. When Perseus cut off Medusa's head, their children, Pegasus and Chrysaor, sprang free. "Is it the giant dwelling in the caves?"

"Not Chrysaor, but another of her offspring formed from spilled drops of her blood. She's a serpent called Amphisbaena. She has a dragon head on each end. I brought her from the desert to dwell in the caves to protect my temple from further dereliction."

"What's this got to do with Hippolyta's girdle?"

"Amphisbaena is a seer of lost objects. The two heads don't always agree, but much insight can be gained from her. She might be able to tell you where the girdle can be found, especially if it exists somewhere in this region."

"Is she amiable?"

"No. But if you tell her I sent you, you might get her to cooperate."

"And if she doesn't?"

"You'll have to bind her two heads together and give her an elixir from Apollo. It will force the truth from her lips."

With his special power for summoning gods and delivering messages, Hermes located Apollo for Than more quickly than Than would have been able to find the god of truth on his own. Apollo lingered before a painting at an art gallery in Dallas standing beside his lover. In a black tuxedo, a fedora pulled over his eyes, a white scarf wrapped around his face, and dimmed to his lowest light possible, Than crossed the room, all the while sending his silent prayer to Apollo.

Apollo replied in like form that he was only too pleased to hand over the elixir, hoping for a speedy end to the conflict with Ares. As Than approached, he noticed how many of the patrons in the gallery allowed their eyes to linger on Apollo. Men and women alike couldn't stop looking at him and admiring his beauty. Even now, with his lover beside him, Apollo was greeted by two women competing against one another for his attention. Than wondered if he would have a similar effect on the living if he weren't Death.

"Absolutely," Apollo said to him silently. "You are quite stunning, you know."

"Thank you," Than replied, also in silence, as he grew closer to the god of light.

"But it can become dreary, attracting the attention of so many," Apollo said. "I try to avoid public places, but Marvin loves this artist. The painting is quite good, is it not?"

Than looked over the abstract movement of colors. He was surprised to find it reminding him of a melody, the way it lifted and seemed to sway one way and then another. "Yes, it is."

As Than reached him, Apollo took a vial tied to leather string from the inside pocket of his tuxedo and handed it to Than, turning his back on the ogling women. "Here you are, cousin." Then Apollo put a hand on his lover's shoulder. "You remember Marvin, don't you?"

"Sure. How are you?"

"Great. Thanks for asking. And you?"

"Not too bad, but I'm in a bit of a hurry." Than tipped his hat to the both of them. "Thanks again, cousin."

Now, armed with his sword and shield, a coil of rope around one arm, and the elixir on a leather string around his neck, Than returned to Athens to face Amphisbaena.

Chapter Fifteen: Piercing Pete

Therese reminded herself that no one else could see the arrow as she tucked it into the back pocket of her jeans and looked over her hair and makeup in her bathroom mirror. Jen and Pete were on their way to pick her up.

Carol and Richard still weren't back from their appointment and shopping in town. Therese had tried to call them on their cell phones but had gotten no reply. Rather than freak out, she decided buying a crib and stuff for the nursery was probably taking longer than planned.

Than had shown her how to hold the bow and arrow, and though Therese had carried off a perfect shot on the first try, and many more since, she was nervous something would go wrong tonight when she tried to pierce Pete's heart with the special arrow from Cupid. After adding fresh water to Jewels's and Clifford's bowls, she folded the collapsible bow into her purse and headed downstairs.

"Wanna go outside, Clifford?"

He followed her to the back door and out onto the deck. She immediately sensed another presence.

"Who's there?"

She felt fear and panic gripping her chest, and this time she knew Ares's twin sons were close.

"Back inside, Clifford."

Clifford whined and followed her indoors, though a locked door would be no protection from the twins. "Than!" she cried.

Immediately he appeared in the kitchen beside her.

"Deimos and Phobos," she said. "They're right outside."

"I sense them, too."

The front doorbell rang. It was Jen.

"What do we do?" Therese asked.

"The twins won't touch you as long as you're in the company of mortals. They wouldn't risk Zeus's wrath."

"Therese?" Jen walked inside, looking around. "Hey, there you are."

Than had disappeared.

"Hey. I was just locking up." She checked the lock on the back door, grabbed her purse, and followed Jen out the front, hoping the twins wouldn't think of hurting her pets while she was gone. If they touched one hair on Clifford's body or one scale on Jewels's shell, she'd find a way to torment them.

As they walked to the truck, Jen said, "Matthew and I broke up."

Therese stopped and turned to her. "Oh, Jen. When?" Therese pretended like she didn't already know.

"Last week. The day you left. I didn't want to talk about it yesterday in the barn with Courtney there, though she knows. And I especially didn't want to say anything at the meet. Afraid I'd lose my focus."

"I'm sorry I haven't been there for you." She gave Jen a hug. "You doing okay?"

"I'll be alright." She pulled away. "We better get in the truck before Pete honks at us."

Todd, Ray, and Courtney met them outside the movie theater in the ticket line. Ray looked like he had a thing for Courtney. She hoped Courtney would give him a chance, though she seemed to prefer Pete. If she had the right arrow, could she play matchmaker like Cupid?

As they waited in line, they chatted and watched the people walking up and down the street, Therese still paranoid by the appearance of the twins. Deimos and Phobos wouldn't dare take her from a crowd of movie-going mortals would they? What about from a dark theater? She shuddered. Across from them was a café, and further over, a grocer, both well-lit and bustling with activity. The afternoon shower had left behind a residual coolness to the air, and Jen crowded close to her, warming herself with Therese's body heat. She heard Jen direct a prayer her way: "I'm so cold, Therese. Keep me warm."

Therese flinched, wondering if her friend knew she was communicating with her. Surely not, she thought, putting an arm around her, happy to have contact with a mortal. "Cold?"

Jen nodded.

A man walked by with his dog, a golden boxer with a brown head. Therese noticed them because the dog was muttering, "So unfair. So unfair."

Therese wondered what the dog meant. Testing her new abilities to communicate with animals, she sent a thought out toward the dog. "What's not fair?"

He looked at her with surprise, stopping in his tracks, and gave one short, desperate yelp. Therese understood it to mean, "My man beats me."

Therese gasped.

"What's wrong?" Jen asked.

"Look at that dog. He looks so sad."

Just then the man holding the leash jerked the dog, saying in a gruff voice, "Come on, you idiot. What are you stopping for?"

Jen and Therese exchanged looks of concern.

"He's a jerk," Jen said.

Therese watched the dog and his man continue down the street, wishing she could shoot an arrow into the man's heart and make him love his dog.

In the darkened theater in the middle of the center row, Therese sat between Jen and Pete, pretending to be interested in the bucket of popcorn in her lap, which the three of them were sharing. Courtney sat on the other side of Jen, with Ray and then Todd on the end. At first, Therese was disappointed she wasn't closer to Ray and Todd, since she hadn't seen them much this summer, but she realized not far into the movie that it didn't matter where she was sitting. All she could think about was piercing Pete. Her arrow of hate should neutralize Cupid's arrow of love so that when Pete looked at her, he would feel indifference. There was a chance the hate would be stronger than the love, since it would be the fresher wound. She fidgeted in her chair and mopped the sweat from her forehead with the back of her sleeve.

Her plan was to ask him to walk her to her door and then, when they were alone, she'd shoot him at such a high speed that mortal eyes couldn't detect it. Then she'd tell him she was getting back with Than and wait for his response. Hopefully he'd shrug and walk away.

When the time finally came and Pete was pulling into her gravelly drive, she said, "Pete, would you mind walking me to the door?"

"I'll walk you," Jen offered.

"Thanks, Jen, but I need to talk to Pete. Call me later. Maybe you can sleep over tomorrow."

Jen wrinkled her brow. "O-kay." Her tone carried a hint of sarcasm.

Pete turned off his truck and followed Therese to the base of the wooden steps leading up to her screened porch.

"Pete, I…" before she could say another word, he took her in his arms.

"Oh, Therese. I knew you'd come around." He showered her with kisses.

She pulled back, a bit too forcefully, forgetting her god-strength.

"Whoa," he said, stumbling back.

"I'm so sorry. I just want to talk." She whipped out the invisible, collapsible bow from her purse and cocked it in position. "There's something I need to tell you."

"What are you doing?"

Therese took the arrow from her back pocket and fitted it into the bow in less time that it took to take a breath. As she released the arrow into his chest, afraid of the finality of whatever consequences lay ahead, Jen ran up from behind him.

"Pete!"

"No!" Therese cried.

Pete turned toward Jen as soon as the invisible arrow struck, his eyes falling upon his sister.

"What do you want?" he growled at Jen. "You're interrupting!"

Jen stopped in her tracks and looked at Pete, bewildered. "What? Mom's been trying to get a hold of me. I've got a ton of missed calls from her."

"All our problems would be solved if you'd just go away."

Therese staggered forward. "Wait." Now what would she do? She couldn't have Pete hating his own sister. And she couldn't pierce him with a love arrow in Jen's presence and risk him desiring her. Her father was bad enough. Oh, god! She prayed to Than and to Cupid as the two siblings yelled at one another. What have I done?

"Take another arrow," Than prayed back. Then he appeared beside her, invisible to the others. "Tell Jen to wait for you in your room upstairs and pierce him again as he looks upon you." He disappeared, leaving her with the arrow in her trembling hand.

"Jen, Pete's upset."

"No shit, Sherlock," Jen snapped.

"Leave him alone for now. Wait for me in my room."

"He's never talked to me like that before. God, Pete. How can you say that to me?"

"Please," Therese begged. "Go to my room so we can talk. I'll be right there."

"Get out of here, Jen!" Pete hollered. "I can't stand the sight of you."

Jen wiped tears from her red cheeks as she ran up the porch steps. "Shut up already!"

Therese waited until Jen was out of sight. Then she fitted the new arrow to the bow and shot Pete once more. "Look at me, Pete!"

He wore a sneer, like a hungry wolf.

"Than and I are together again. It's for good this time. I just wanted you to know that."

Pete stomped toward his truck, snarling as he passed her, "Why don't you two bitches stay out of my life, okay? I'm sick of all the drama."

He drove off, leaving Therese stunned in the dark night. At least he no longer loved her. She heard a twig snap in the forest and rushed inside. The house was dark except for the small light over the kitchen sink. Carol and Richard must have already gone to bed. She went down the basement stairs to the garage to make sure Richard's car was back. Yep. Thank goodness they were alright. She headed up the stairs to her room, thinking it was good she wouldn't be alone tonight. She and Jen both needed one another's company but for different reasons.

Jen sat slumped on Therese's bed with a wad of tissues in her hand. Her eyes were swollen, her nose red. "Can you believe he said those things to me?"

Therese sat on the bed across from her. She couldn't let Jen think her brother hated her. Then she recalled what Hip had once told her: people have free will. The arrows only make stronger a feeling already present. Maybe Pete really did blame Jen for their family problems. If so, he was a jerk.

No. He couldn't have meant what he'd said. Therese knew Pete. "He didn't mean it. He was just mad and taking it out on you."

Jen wrapped her arms around herself, shivering like a wet cat. "He's never talked to me like that. He's been plenty mad before. What did you say to him?"

"That Than and I are back together for good. I thought he needed to hear it from me."

Jen sighed. "I need to call my mom. Can I sleep over?"

"Of course." It would mean Than would have to stay away, but she was probably safer with Jen, anyway. Deimos and Phobos wouldn't take her in the dead of night if she were lying by a mortal, would they? She doubted she would sleep.

"Broken heart or not, he shouldn't have said those things to me." Jen kicked off her boots and piled them in the corner of the room.

"I'm so sorry, Jen. There's something else you need to know."

Chapter Sixteen: Amphisbaena

The cool chill of night in Athens lingered in the air and wrapped its long fingers around Than, as though wanting to deter him from visiting Amphisbaena. The sacred caves in the underbelly of the acropolis smelled acrid and dank, and for once Than was glad his immortal senses weren't as sensitive to stimuli as mortal ones. With heavy boots, he trudged into the first of the caves searching for signs of the serpent dragon.

He could sense her presence but couldn't pinpoint her exact location as he stole silently over the rocky cavern floor. A thin ribbon of water, stagnant and foul, divided the ground in half. Than straddled it as he followed it to the back of the cave. The first chamber opened onto a second, larger one, the size of an auditorium. He unsheathed his sword as he glanced around the cliff edges above him, feeling the serpent close. A billow of fire shot across the top of the cavern, and the residue of smoke lingering behind spelled, "I see you, Thanatos."

"Amphisbaena? I just want to talk," he said into the darkness.

Another flash of fire illuminated the cavern ceiling, and this time the smoke remaining spelled out, "Drop your sword."

Than gripped the hilt, fearing a trap. If he didn't drop it, he'd have to take her by force. "Can I trust you?"

The fire shot in a blaze above him, and the smoke read, "One says yes. Two says no."

"What is that supposed to mean?"

He waited for the fire, but when none came, he put down the sword. His fingers had barely left the hilt when the serpent darted from her lair and wrapped her thick, slimy body, at least a foot in diameter, around him, binding his arms to his sides. No matter how hard he pressed his arms against her, he couldn't get free of her ever-tightening grip. He disintegrated and grabbed his sword and was about to slice the serpent in two when a spider, the size of his skull, jumped on the end of the sword and spun a cocoon around him, trapping him. He disintegrated once more, in time to see the spider leap in all directions, from one side of the cavern wall to the next, weaving a web around the serpent. The moment he realized the spider was Athena, the web was cinched and the two heads of the serpent drawn tightly together. Fire spewed through the air from both dragon heads.

Athena transformed from the spider and commanded, "Release Thanatos."

Amphisbaena loosened her coiling body, and Than god traveled out while his third self cut his second self free of the cocoon. Then he integrated and faced Athena, sword in hand.

"I don't want her slain," Athena explained. "I've grown fond of her, and her screams would torment me."

"She's immortal, though, yes?"

"Yes. Unlike her mother," Athena replied. "Nevertheless, I intervened to protect her, not you. But I will help you get your answer."

"Why? Do you need something from me?"

"No. I only want peace among the gods. Hand me Apollo's elixir."

Than tugged at the leather strap around his neck and tossed the vial to Athena, who caught it and poured it into one of Amphisbaena's mouths.

"Ask your question," Athena said.

Than took a step toward the serpent. "Amphisbaena, do you know where Hippolyta's golden girdle is?"

Fire shot from both heads. The smoke on the right side read, "One says yes." The smoke from the left read, "Two says yes."

"Good. That's great," Than said. "Where? Where is it?"

The fire came again. The smoke on the right read, "One says Crimea." The smoke from the left read, "Two says Samsun."

Than narrowed his eyes. "But those cities are in two different re-gions. Crimea is part of the Ukraine. Samsun is on the northern tip of Turkey. Which is it, Amphisbaena?"

When the fire cleared, the smoke repeated the same message: "One says Crimea. Two says Samsun."

Than scratched his chin. "Is the girdle in someone's possession?"

The smoke that lingered read, "One says no. Two says no."

"Is it underground, lost among ruins?"

"One says water. Two says water."

"The golden girdle is underwater?"

"One says yes. Two says yes."

Than looked at Athena. "So the girdle is underwater near the shore of either Crimea or Samsun? That narrows it down, I suppose."

"Perhaps Poseidon can help."

"Yes. Good idea."

Chapter Seventeen: Mr. Holt

Before Therese could tell Jen what was on her mind, Carol burst through the door.

"It's a girl! You're going to have a sister!"

Therese jumped from her bed, a surge of joy sweeping over her. "A sister?"

Carol took her in her arms and gave her a squeeze. Then she pulled back, holding onto one of Therese's hands. "A sister. Are you happy?"

"Yes." She would have been happy either way. "A sister."

Richard could be heard ambling up the stairs, and in a moment, he popped inside. "Oh, hi, Jen. Are you sleeping over?"

"Is that alright?" Therese asked.

"As long as it's okay with her parents," Carol said.

"I was just about to call them," Jen said. "Congratulations."

"What do you think, munchkin?" Richard said to Therese, using one of many terms of endearment he'd called her over the past several months. "A sister sound good to you? You can teach her how to paint her nails and put on makeup and all that girl jazz."

Carol laughed. "Well, maybe not right away."

Therese laughed, too, adding, "I promise not to turn her into a diva."

"That's my area of expertise," Jen said.

"Some tomboy you turned out to be," Therese told her for the millionth time.

"Come down and see what we've been doing." Carol turned to the door, motioning for the girls to follow.

Richard, taking up the rear, said, "Don't you think we ought to warn her first?"

Carol stopped on the bottom stair and looked up. Therese stopped, too, wondering what the new look on her aunt's face could mean.

"Richard and I have moved into the master bedroom to make room in the guest room for a nursery. I'm sure your parents would have wanted that."

Therese's knees weakened, and heat rose to her skin. Of course her parents would want this. She knew it was the right thing to do. Nevertheless, her knees felt weak and she needed to sit down.

Jen caught her before she fell. "You okay?"

"Yeah. I'm fine," she lied.

They continued down the stairs to the guest room where Carol and Richard had been living all year. The walls had been painted a soft pale pink. Lacey cream window treatments matched the cushions on a corner rocking chair and the cream and pink striped bedding on the new crib. Over the crib, a brown teddy and block letters spelling "Lynn" adorned two low floating shelves.

"You're going to name her Lynn?" Therese asked.

"It's what I called your mother," Carol said. "I rarely called her Linda. So it seemed right to name the baby Lynn."

Tears filled Therese's eyes and she found herself unable to speak. She felt happy and sad at the same time.

Jen threw her arms around her. "That's so sweet."

Therese leaned on Jen, happy to have someone holding her up. Her knees still quavered. She cleared her throat, trying to rid herself of the lump lodged there. She tried again. "This room is beautiful."

Richard laughed. "So much for going gender neutral."

"That was the original plan," Carol explained. "But today, when we heard the news, well, I just went pink crazy."

"It's a pretty pink," Jen said, releasing Therese. "Not too bright."

"I like it, too," Therese added.

Just then the phone rang. Richard went to the kitchen and answered it.

"Oh, no. Of course. Absolutely. Sure. We'll be praying for him."

Therese followed Jen into the main room, with Carol close behind.

"It's my dad, isn't it?" Jen said without inflection.

Richard hung up the phone. "He's in the hospital. Your mother and brothers are with him. The doctors think he had a stroke and are running tests on him now."

"Oh my God!" Jen staggered to the sofa.

Therese sat beside her. "I'm so sorry."

Richard sat in the chair across from them. "Your mother wants you to stay here with us. She says there's no reason to go up to the hospital tonight. You wouldn't be able to see him anyway."

Jen put her face in her hands and wept, which surprised Therese. She thought Jen hated her father.

Carol sat on the couch on the other side of Jen and put an arm around her. "Is there anything I can get you? Do you want some water or anything?"

Jen shook her head. "I just want to go upstairs."

Clifford put his paws on Jen's knees. She scooped him up in her arms and kissed his head. "Thank you, boy."

She carried the dog upstairs. Therese followed, secretly thanking Clifford, too.

Once they were alone together in her room, Therese couldn't decide whether she should explain about Pete's arrow. Jen had accepted the invisibility crown without probing too hard into its origins; maybe she would accept the mystery of the arrow, too. But if Jen did press for more information, what would Therese tell her? Could she confide everything to her friend? Could she admit she was a god?

No. It would just freak her out, especially now, with her worried about her dad. Plus, knowing Therese would be leaving soon for good would only make Jen more upset. Therese also needed to consider the possibility that Jen would ask her to use her powers in ways that would make the gods of Olympus angry, like to heal her father. Just telling a mortal might bring repercussions. But she couldn't let Jen think Pete hated her. She had to think of something.

How could she be a god and still feel so helpless?

Chapter Eighteen: Dione

From inside the horse drawn carriage, Than gazed out at the raging Black Sea and the rocky shoreline rolling by as the driver above headed toward the northern city of Turkey known as Samsun. Because Amphisbaena's second head had been right about whether he should trust the serpent, he had decided he would try its prediction of the whereabouts of the golden girdle first. He crossed his arms, tired of waiting, wondering if Poseidon would stand him up, when, finally, the god of the sea appeared.

"Thank you for meeting me," Than said, before the other god had fully materialized.

"Don't thank me yet."

"Why not?" Than shifted in his seat and frowned.

"I cannot help you, Thanatos. I've already risked too much. Ares has been an ally of mine for many decades, and I can't afford to lose him."

"But I hope to appease Ares."

"Zeus also frowns upon any dealings with one of the banished. I won't get further involved. The sea is full of Oceanids, and if you call upon them, they may be able to give you the answers you seek."

Before Than could say another word, the god of the sea vanished.

He punched his fist against his seat. There was no way Than would allow Therese to be taken from him after they had sacrificed so much to be together. He would find a way without Poseidon's help.

When the carriage reached the outskirts of town, Than used the hilt of his sword to tap on the ceiling. The carriage stopped, and Than climbed out, thanking and paying the driver.

"How will you get back, sir?" the driver asked.

"I'll walk."

Than turned grimly toward the sea, the rising whitecaps reflecting his angry mood. At least the wind off the shoreline offered him some relief from the humidity and heat. He hadn't dealt with many Oceanids in his life. In fact, he could count them all on one hand. He'd met Calypso when she tried to kill herself after losing Odysseus. Amphitrite, Poseidon's wife and the weaver of his golden nets, had come to Than once, demanding the return of a pod of dolphins which had died from being trapped in a fisherman's net. He couldn't help her, so he doubted she would want to help him. There were also his mother's three friends, the Sirens, whose deathly songs had brought him many souls, but he didn't trust anyone who lured innocent people into traps for their own entertainment. There were thousands of other Oceanids he did not know. Where to begin?

He hiked over boulders and sand to the end of a point where foam clung in white rings, took up a rock, and hurled it into the sea. The ocean was vast and deep. The girdle was the size of a woman's waist. He could disintegrate into a thousand parts and still spend years searching for it.

From the bottom of his heart, he asked the sea, "Is there anyone there who can help me?"

The pleasant face of a woman appeared in the foam near his boots. Silver hair and eyes shimmered against the rocks as she smiled up at him and said in a sing-song voice, "True love. So heartwarming."

"And heartbreaking," Than added. "With whom do I have the good fortune of speaking?"

"I am Dione. I'd know you anywhere, Thanatos. You, too, have broken many hearts by separating lovers with death."

"But I have no say in the matter."

"Who decides such things, then?"

"Usually, Tyche, the goddess of chance, an Oceanid and sister of yours, I believe. I've never had the pleasure of meeting her."

"You give her too much credit I think."

"Perhaps." He didn't want to displease a nymph who'd possibly come to help him. "How is it you know so much about broken hearts?"

"My daughter is the goddess of love."

Of course. He'd heard of Dione. Few gods on Mount Olympus acknowledged her role in Aphrodite's existence, wanting to subjugate the daughters of the Titans. Both Aphrodite, daughter of Dione, and Athena, daughter of Metis, had had their histories rewritten with sole credit of their parentage attributed to Zeus. Only Hades, least happy with his lot and most concerned with justice, had mentioned their names on rare occasions.

"I recognize your name now," Than said, bending to one knee. "My father has spoken of you. He prefers you to some of your sisters."

Dione smiled at that. "You speak of the Sirens."

"Yes."

"And yet they add souls to his kingdom."

"In ways unjust and that cannot be avenged."

"Ah."

"My father often says that life isn't fair, but death is."

"How noble."

Than didn't know if justice was nobler than compassion, but he kept the thought to himself. Plus, he may have detected a touch of sarcasm in the nymph's tone. "I'm looking for Hippolyta's lost golden girdle. The serpent seer, Amphisbaena, believed it to be underwater either off of this coast or that of Crimea. Do you have any knowledge of its whereabouts?"

"No."

Than sighed and closed his eyes.

"But I can ask around. Maybe someone else has seen it."

Than smiled at the nymph in the foam and thanked her.

"But why do you care for an old girdle?" she asked.

He explained his problem with Ares.

"I'm saddened to hear that. One of the surest ways to weaken true love is to have your true love wear it."

Than climbed to his feet. "I hope she'll never have to cast eyes on it, but I'm desperate to have her in my life any way I can."

"I see. If I learn anything about the girdle's whereabouts, I'll send my courtier to find you."

He followed her eyes to the sky and saw a white gull, her courtier, flying overhead. Before Than could reply, Dione disappeared from the foam.

Chapter Nineteen: Baby Lynn

Therese spent the next several days with Jen visiting Mr. Holt in the hospital and grooming Stormy and Sassy. She avoided Pete, who continued to snap at Jen about the most trivial things—like who woke up earlier or ate the most food. His attitude toward Therese seemed to settle on indifference. This was what Therese had wanted, but it still hurt. Carol helped Therese enroll in an online high school, and she had already completed her first assignments. She was amazed by how quickly she absorbed information. By no means omnipotent, she nevertheless understood and memorized concepts and facts so quickly that she was flying through her courses. Than stayed with her at night, keeping her updated on his progress in his search for what she had come to call the item of doom. Since she didn't need as much sleep as she had as a mortal, she had a lot of extra time to worry about her future, like what her unique purpose would be. Would she ever figure it out?

And she constantly looked over her shoulder for the twin sons of Ares.

After a week's time, Mr. Holt was placed into an assisted living center in Durango because his stroke had left him paralyzed on one side of his body, and he needed more care than Mrs. Holt and her kids could give him. Therese thought Jen would be relieved, even thrilled, with this, but, instead, she was depressed, saying that her mother and Bobby would now be miserable. Somehow Jen blamed herself for her father's condition, which made no sense to Therese. Maybe Therese didn't have all the information she needed to understand Jen's feelings, but whenever she asked Jen about it, her friend clamped up.

On top of feeling guilty for her father's condition, Jen was depressed about her breakup with Matthew. Worst of all was her treatment from Pete, the big brother who had always stood up for her in the house when no one else would. So even though Therese was burdened by her own fears and concerns, she had to be strong for Jen.

She distracted Jen over the next several weeks by inviting her to do things with her. Part of Therese's new curriculum required her to accumulate service hours, so she convinced Jen to go with her to the animal shelter they used to volunteer at back when they were in the Girl Scouts in the fourth and fifth grades. Even though Therese hadn't gone to the animal shelter regularly since then, she had continued to volunteer there a few times a year, and the employees remembered her. They also volunteered at Mr. Holt's assisted living center on Sundays, running games like Bingo and Jeopardy. After their third visit, Therese had an idea.

The idea came from a paper she was writing for one of her classes on the use of animals in therapy. The therapy ranged from children with autism to the elderly. Therese shared her idea with Jen, and together, they convinced both the assisted living center and the animal shelter to allow them to take two well-behaved dogs, Bo and Meatball, to visit the elderly at the center every Sunday. They developed a routine in which they worked at the animal shelter on Saturday and took animals to the assisted living center on Sundays. Jen led Bingo or Jeopardy while Therese supervised the pet therapy, and then during the week Therese worked on her studies and groomed Stormy. At night, she and Than spent time together. Some evenings, she and Jen went to the movies with Ray, Todd, and Courtney.

Pete no longer joined them and their friends on their outings.

Besides looking for the item of doom, Than was also helping her to figure out how to reverse the effects of the arrow on Pete's attitude toward Jen. Cupid had no answers and Aphrodite was looking into it.

She also discovered, weeks after Than had found her a replacement Coach bag and wallet, who had stolen her purse. It had been a mortal after all. In late August, when marching band camp began, Jen recognized the purse on Gina Rizzo's shoulder. She called Therese that night.

"Maybe Gina bought one like it, but it looks just like the one you had. I thought you should know."

She thanked her and hung up but was surprised to find she wasn't angry. If Gina really wanted that bag, let her have it. She was hurt that her precious photos had been so carelessly thrown away, but thankfully, she had them back. She saw no reason to confront Gina. Jen tried to change her mind, offering to help, but Therese wasn't interested. She laughed a little at herself over this. Here she was a powerful goddess finally able to kick some ass, and she no longer wanted to.

Her mood was further lifted by the fact that she had saved a two-year-old yellow lab from being euthanized by convincing Todd that his yellow truck would look even better with a yellow dog. Ray and Todd had come to the shelter to take a look at Chuck while she and Jen were there volunteering.

"Chuck is short for Chuckles," Therese had said. "We call him that because he's always happy."

Then just about the time when Therese thought things might be getting better, they got worse. She was home cooking dinner for Carol and Richard. She wore her favorite t-shirt and faded pair of jeans with holes in the knees, which reminded her of her father. Than, supposedly guarding her from the evil twins, was a distraction with his flirtatious kisses and booty slapping as she bent over the oven to check on her spinach lasagna. When they heard Richard's vehicle pulling up on the gravelly drive, Than gave her one last kiss goodbye with promises of seeing her later that night. Therese hummed cheerily as she mixed the salad and got out the dinner plates. But when Carol and Richard walked in, she could tell by their tear-stained cheeks and red-rimmed eyes that something was wrong.

"What's happened?" Therese asked, nearly dropping the plate in her hand. What could possibly be wrong now?

"Come and sit down." Richard helped Carol to the couch. "We need to talk."

Had they learned Therese's secret? Were they mortified to discover she would soon be joining the god of death in the Underworld? What else could have them so fragile-looking and defeated?

Therese emptied her hands and moved to the living area to sit across from them, pulling her knees up to her chest and hugging them.

"We have some bad news," Richard said.

Carol hadn't even looked at her yet. Oh, God. This was not good.

"There's something wrong with the baby," Richard said in a broken voice.

Therese dropped her feet to the floor and sat up. "What? What's wrong? Is everything going to be okay?"

Carol shook her head. Without looking up, she choked out, "No. I'm afraid not."

Therese felt her chest tighten and her hands and feet go numb. Was there a ringing in her ears? "Why? I don't understand."

"It has to do with Carol's placenta. Apparently, the baby isn't getting enough nutrients and isn't growing properly. The doctor said odds are Lynn…won't make it."

Therese sat quietly, dazed and unable to believe. She felt like she was looking down at herself from the ceiling and recognizing how helpless she looked. But she was a god now. There was bound to be something she could do, some other god she could bribe. Athena had saved Sahin. Someone must be able to save Lynn. Hera was the goddess of marriage, family, and unborn children. She would go to Hera.

She jumped to her feet. "I won't let this happen."

Carol crumpled into a ball of shaking sobs in Richard's arms at Therese's defiant tone.

Therese stroked her arm. "I'll think of something. There must be something we can do."

"Calm down, pumpkin," Richard said. "Just take a breath and calm down. This won't help your aunt. You've got to be strong. All we can do is wait and see."

Therese dropped to her knees at Carol's feet and took one of her hands. "I'm going to think of some way to save Lynn, Carol. I promise you."

Carol gave her a half-smile, with quavering, wet lips. "Oh, sweetheart. There's nothing you can do but pray." She kissed Therese's hand before breaking down into more tears.

Therese hugged them both, stood up, and said, "I know you probably don't feel like eating, but maybe you should try, for Lynn. Everything's on the table. I've already eaten." That last part was a lie, but she wouldn't be able to eat now. She had to figure out a way to help her sister. "I'm going upstairs."

Than was waiting for her in her room with open arms. "I'm so sorry."

She sank against him and wept harder than she had since the day Than was ripped by the maenads. He held her close, caressing her hair. He kissed her forehead, her cheek, and the top of her head. Then she stood up, wiped her eyes, and said, "I'm going to see Hera. I don't care how mad she is at us, I'm going."

"You can't go to Mount Olympus."

"Oh yes I can." She clenched her fists and lifted her chin, feeling the power rising inside her.

Than's eyes widened at her resolve. "Well, at least let me take you in my father's chariot so you don't risk god travel."

"I'll wait for you outside."

"Are you sure about this?"

"Absolutely. Please hurry."

"I'll be right back."

Chapter Twenty: Hades

Than entered his father's chamber, having decided to ask for, rather than take, the chariot. He and Therese were already going to be in so much trouble when they showed their faces on Mount Olympus. He didn't need to add to their problems by stealing a chariot, too.

He knew his father was in his worst mood at this time of year after having been bereft of Persephone's company for five long months. On September 21st, she would finally return, but until then, Hades would be irritable.

His father sat at his table across from Meg in a whispered conversation when Than arrived. The two of them stopped talking and glared up at him.

"Sorry to interrupt."

"Then don't," Hades said.

"Therese and I are going to Mount Olympus tonight."

Hades narrowed his eyes. "Good luck with that."

"I need to borrow your chariot."

"Take it. It's yours."

Than looked from his father to Meg, her blonde hair usually up in a knot now spilling down her shoulders. He asked, "Is everything alright, Father?"

"Nothing's been alright since you first laid eyes on that girl."

"What's going on? It concerns me, doesn't it?"

Meg averted her eyes, but Hades climbed to his feet. "It seems Ares never intended to take Therese to Tartarus. That was a decoy. We've been monitoring the pit every minute of every day, wasting valuable resources when he's been hatching another plan."

"What plan?" He looked at his sister. "Tell me." He wondered if Poseidon had been duped by Ares or had been working with him to throw them off the real plan.

Meg stood now, too. "We don't yet know."

"But trust no one."

"Do you think it's unwise, going to Mount Olympus?"

"It's the safest place for you. Ares would never take her in front of the other gods."

"Even though we disobey Zeus in going?"

Hades tugged at his beard. Then he put a hand on Than's shoulder. "I'm no seer, son. I don't know how Zeus will react." He lowered his voice, "So you're finally standing up for yourself? I'm glad."

Than glanced again at his sister, but her expression told him nothing. "It's Therese. She wants to ask Hera for help."

"She's got some nerve," Meg said.

"I like it," Hades added. "Take the chariot and go."

Than bridled Swift and Sure to the golden chariot, wondering over his father's reaction. He really wanted Than to stand up to Zeus? In what way exactly?

Chapter Twenty-One: Storming Mount Olympus

Although the chariot was invisible to mortal eyes, they had to fly it high in the Colorado skies to avoid the tree-covered mountains. The air was crisp and the stars bright and the moon only a sliver, like the shiny hilt of a sword. Therese wished she hadn't lost hers at Lerma with the Hydra—not that she would have used it to attack. She clutched the locket from Athena at her throat. She was a god, and she could do this.

"What's the plan?" Than asked.

"I don't know yet. I'll make it up as I go." What more could the gods do to her? Turn her over to the maenads? She'd do anything to save her sister.

She was glad Than hadn't tried to talk her out of this, hadn't forced her to articulate her motives and expectations. She was thankful he sat beside her with the reins, supporting her in silence as they sailed across the night sky. If only she could think of her purpose before facing them, then she'd feel less temporary, less transient. What could she do? Hermes had so many purposes and Artemis had all Therese's favorites. She loved music, but Apollo had that covered. Even her ability to maneuver through the water was outdone by Poseidon. What talent did she possess that could possibly add anything new to the roster of gods and goddesses?

"Help me think of my purpose," she said. "There's got to be something I can do."

"Only you can discover it."

"You've got to have some ideas. Anything?"

"Your gift with animals is remarkable."

"But Artemis has animals."

Than leaned over and kissed her nose. "You don't have to figure this out right now. Quit being so hard on yourself."

Than was such a good person. The gods were wrong to keep him from Mount Olympus. He may have broken an oath, but they were wrong to make him take it. They hadn't asked him to swear on the River Styx never to make her a god; they had told him he must. There was a difference. And their demand was simply not fair.

She decided not to tell Than about her second reason for facing the other gods. She wanted to save her sister, but she wanted to save Than, too.

If it could only be as easy as saving Chuck, the yellow lab. Wait a minute, she thought. She looked at Than, her mouth and eyes wide open. Saving animals. Not wild animals, because that was Artemis. Saving animal companions.

"What?"

"I know what my purpose is!" She waved her fists through the air, full of excitement. "I know what I'm meant to do!" She jumped to her feet.

Than pulled her back down in her seat. "You're going to fall out of this thing. Now sit down and tell me."

She spread her arms wide. "Meet the goddess of animal companions."

"The what?"

"You know how Cupid shoots arrows into people to make them fall in love?"

"Yeah?"

"Well, I'll shoot arrows into humans and their animal friends to make them love one another. I'll help save rescue animals by piercing the hearts of visitors when they come into the shelters. Don't you see?"

"You'll rescue pets. That's you to a tee."

"And I'll stop animal abuse by piercing the hearts of the abusive owner!"

"Like that man you told me about and his pit bull."

"Boxer."

"That's right."

"And I'll help reunite lost pets with their humans."

"Like we did with the tabby."

"Oh, Than! I know this is what I'm meant to do! I just know it! Artemis shouldn't object. She's the goddess of wild animals. That's totally different!"

Than dropped the reins, took her face in both hands, and pressed his mouth hard against hers. The chariot took a sudden dive toward the land, so he snatched the reins back up, laughing. "You're so great, Therese. I knew you'd figure it out. I can feel your power emanating from you. The transformation is complete!"

"Zeus has got to listen to me now. He's got to!"

When they reached the summit of Mount Olympus, Than guided the chariot to the outer gates and said, "Spring, Summer, Winter, and Fall, open the gates of Olympus so Therese and I, Thanatos, may enter."

A face appeared in a gray cloud, female and beautiful with black-lined eyes and an equally black-lined mouth. She blinked long lashes and smiled upon them. "I'm afraid we cannot open the gates for you, Thanatos."

Therese stood up in the chariot. "Listen. We need to speak with Zeus and Hera. I want to explain why they were wrong to banish us, but I can't do that if you don't let us inside."

"Sure you can," the cloud replied. "Through prayer."

"You want to explain what?" Than interrupted. "I thought we were here to save your sister."

Therese turned inward, to her mind, and directed a prayer to Zeus. "I need to talk to you in person. We've traveled a long way. Please let me make my case to you and to your queen, Hera. Plus, I need to claim my purpose!"

The cloud moved from the gate, saying, "You may enter, Therese, but Thanatos must remain outside the gates."

"I go everywhere she goes," Than insisted, standing.

The cloud returned to the center of the gates. "Goodbye then."

"Wait!" Therese squeezed Than's hand and looked up at him. "I know you want to protect me, but I'm a god now, too. Let me go alone."

"You don't know what Zeus is capable of, what he's done to other gods in the past."

"I need to do this. Trust me. Please."

He took both her hands in his. "You're sure?"

"Never surer."

She kissed him hard on the mouth and then stepped from the chariot and walked through the gates and across the courtyard to the steps of the palace. When she entered the court, all gods were present, including Hades and Poseidon, who were usually in their respective palaces. She hadn't expected a full audience. Even Ares was there. She glared at him wishing she could hurl something at his smug face. Now was not the time to pick a fight. She'd take on Ares another day.

Her throat felt dry as she walked to the center of the ring of gods and faced the double throne where Zeus and Hera sat, but she swallowed hard and said, "I've come here for three reasons. Please hear me out."

"Speak," Zeus said, his manner and look reminding her of Hermes. His curly hair and beard were darker than those of his brother Hades but exactly the same as the god of both commerce and theft.

"First, I've found my purpose. I'm the goddess of animal companions." She turned to face Artemis. "Not of wild animals. Not of the hunt. I'm talking about tamed animals meant to live with humans. As a descendent of Cupid, I've shown I can use a bow and arrow. My job will be to pierce the hearts of humans to make them love their pets, and vice versa, and also to help them when they've lost one another."

"Bravo," Artemis said. "Well done!"

"Congratulations!" said Athena.

"Wonderful news!"

"Congratulations!"

Therese turned slowly around the circle to meet the eyes and congratulations from each of the gods. She filled with pride, the corners of her mouth spread wide. All but Ares seemed happy.

"Thank you." Therese felt confident and more powerful than ever. "Now for my second purpose for coming here tonight. The only reason Than swore an oath on the River Styx was because you made him do it. He had no choice."

"He most certainly did," Zeus objected.

"Not a real choice. When you hold a gun at someone's head and tell them to do something or you'll shoot, is that someone truly free? No. When you tell a woman give me all your money or I will kill your child, does she freely give it? No. You coerced him by giving him horrible consequences if he refused: My death. That's no choice, Zeus, and you know it."

"Now just one minute, Therese, goddess of animal companions," demanded Zeus.

"Please let me speak. I have more to say." Therese widened her stance, setting her feet firmly on the marble floor. "Than is a good person. He has served all of you and humanity for centuries without a single complaint. He has the most loathsome job of all of you." She looked upon each of the gods surrounding her. "Would any of you say otherwise?"

No one replied.

"I thought so. I've been taking classes lately, and I've had the opportunity to study what humankind knows of you. I've learned that all of you have done things you aren't proud of, except maybe Hestia, who lives her life serving the rest of you."

Hera gasped.

"I won't allow such insolence!" Zeus shouted. A crack of thunder sounded above them. "You may be one of us, but no one comes to court pointing an accusing finger at me."

Therese felt her knees weaken, and she thought, Oh, crap! What have I done? Now they're all against me! But she clenched her fists and kept her stance.

Before she could speak, Hades was at her side. "I say we hear her out. Isn't her fierce ability to stand up for someone she cares about something we gods value?"

"Hear, hear!" Persephone cried, and a smile was exchanged between husband and wife.

Zeus looked down his nose at Therese and pressed his lips tightly together. He stared at her with an expression that said he was not pleased. She held her breath, wondering if she had just made the biggest mistake ever. Maybe she should have come on her knees begging for mercy.

No. She knew she was right.

She didn't wait for an invitation to continue. "Like I said, nearly all of you have done something you're not proud of. I'm not here to accuse, but merely to point out that this is the first time Than has done anything that might be considered wrong.

"And think about it. He did it because he wanted what everyone wants: Someone to hold his hand. Someone to love him forever, no matter what. We all want that."

"What are you asking us to do?" Zeus demanded.

She took a breath and said, "He broke no real oath. He deserves no punishment. No maenads. No banishment. What he went through with the maenads already is more punishment than he deserves. I want you and the court to reconsider your decision."

"Impossible!" Ares objected.

The gods broke out into quarrelling among themselves, some nodding, others shaking their heads, and all Therese could think was, Crap, crap, crap! This isn't going the way I envisioned!

"Quiet!" Zeus commanded. The voices stopped and all looked at the king of the gods. "I'll discuss this matter with the others once you leave, but I make no promises of another outcome."

"Thank you." Therese turned to Hera. "I came for one final reason. I want to offer my services to Hera in return for a favor. My aunt is pregnant and the baby, my sister, is in jeopardy. Hera, can you save her? I'll do anything you ask of me."

All eyes were now on Hera. She glanced around the room, apparently delighted by the attention. "There is something I want. If you can get me this thing, I will save the baby."

Therese's heart burst with joy. "Name it."

"I want my golden apple back from Artemis!"

Therese couldn't help but think how petty this queen of the gods could be. She would demand an apple when she had hundreds? Therese hid her distaste.

Now all eyes turned to the goddess of the hunt.

Artemis pushed a stray brown hair back from her face and crossed her arms. "Well, I…I'm not giving it back."

Again, Therese was filled with disgust over the pettiness of these gods. She resolved to never become like them, heartless and selfish. Her baby sister's life was in danger and these two were quibbling over an apple?

As if Artemis read her mind, the goddess said, "Thousands of humans die each day, Therese. You must understand that the birth or death of one more baby doesn't move me enough to give up an apple that has the power to transform whoever eats it."

"Name your price," Therese said, her heart pounding against her ribs. "One thing I've learned from Thanatos is that everyone longs for something. What do you long for, Artemis? I'll do anything."

"What I want, you can't give."

"Try me. Tell me what it is."

The goddess of wild animals walked across the marble floor to the center of the court and faced Therese. "Not here." Then Artemis prayed, so the other gods couldn't hear her, "Maybe you can help me. And if so, I will give up the apple. But what I want must remain a secret between you and me. I'll come to you soon in the forest by your home."

Chapter Twenty-Two: Artemis's Tale

When Therese turned to leave the palace on Mount Olympus, she felt something press against her back. She reached over her shoulder and found a quiver full of arrows.

"I don't understand." She glanced at the gods around the room. "Is this a gift?"

"No." Hades took her elbow and ushered her to the door. "The quiver and arrows magically appeared when you declared yourself."

"They aren't from Cupid?" They descended the rainbow steps.

"No. They came from you." He led her past the whale fountain and out the gates to Than.

Than helped her into the chariot. "What a relief. What happened in there?"

"You should be proud of her, Thanatos."

"I am, but perhaps you should tell me why."

"As the poet John Donne once wrote, rarely can a man find a woman both true and fair. Therese is as loyal as she is beautiful." He kissed her hand. "I'll be glad to one day call her daughter." Hades disappeared.

Therese turned, open-mouthed, to Than. "Can you believe that? He kissed me."

"I knew it wouldn't take long for everyone to see you as I do."

She circled her arms around his neck. "Take me home."

He kissed her cheek and stroked her hair. "Let's go, but tell me what happened on the way."

Over the next several days, Therese spent much of her time walking through the woods behind her house, begging Artemis to show herself. Without mortal company, she was no longer safe from Deimos and Phobos, but she had to risk facing them if she was to meet Artemis and save her sister. She carried the collapsible bow given to her by Cupid, and slung across one shoulder was the quiver of arrows, feeling as natural there to Therese as if they had grown from her body. They must be meant to serve in her new purpose as goddess of animal companions, but she didn't know if they could protect her from enemies. If the twins appeared, she'd find out.

She conveyed these thoughts to Artemis in the form of prayer, pleading with her to appear and share her secret. Therese didn't know how long the baby had to live, so every minute was precious. "Please, Artemis. I'm here." She stole up the path, paying special attention to the surrounding cypresses, since those were the hunter goddess's favorite trees. But each day and night, Artemis did not come.

During this time, Therese was also inundated with prayers from people around the world who had lost their pets or who were worried about their pets' health or behavior. She prayed to Zeus to grant her the power of disintegration so she could more efficiently respond to these prayers, and he prayed back that he would consider her request. Meanwhile, she'd sworn to Than, Poseidon, and Hermes that she wouldn't god travel, so the only thing she could think to do was to inspire them by planting ideas in their psyches. "Look in your neighbor's shed," she whispered to one regarding a lost puppy, and, "Don't feed him gluten," she whispered to another whose cat had allergies. She was pleased when people took her inspiration to heart and solved their problems but was frustrated when others didn't seem to hear her.

She also sped through her online courses, passing exams with perfect scores. At this rate, she would have her degree in less than a year.

During the day, because Carol was on bed rest, Therese did most of the cooking and cleaning around the house. Although Richard helped out, his job as a freelance reporter sometimes required him to leave to conduct research, including interviews. The solemn mood in the house was oppressive, so Therese didn't mind stealing away to pick through the forest with Clifford. Most of the time, they went at night, before or after a visit from Than, while Carol and Richard slept.

One night, well past midnight, in her sneakers, black jeans, black t-shirt, and black winter cap pulled low over her head, she crept past the twin elms and climbed up the path through the pines and cypresses with Clifford, when a sinking feeling came over her as it occurred to her that Artemis's instructions to meet her in the forest might be a trap. Could it be a coincidence that the goddess of wild things chose the very woods in which Ares's twin sons had been stalking her for weeks? She pressed her back against the trunk of a tree and took a deep breath. Clifford sat on his haunches near her feet. Focus, she told herself. Use your new senses. She closed her eyes and reached out with her consciousness, feeling for the pressure created by the presence of other beings. She felt the chipmunks in the trees, the deer yards away in the shrubs, the birds in nests overhead, and the insects in the wood and earth. Further up the mountains, she sensed a family of bears, but, like every night since she left Mount Olympus, she sensed no other god.

Then the ground beneath her opened up and she fell into the crack. Although she landed firmly on her feet, she winced in surprise. Her head was level with Clifford, who barked ferociously beside her. She followed Clifford's gaze to see the twins standing over her with their fists on their hips and smiles on their faces.

"What a foolish girl you are," Deimos said.

"She decided to make this easy for us," added Phobos.

Fear and panic threatened her, but not as overwhelmingly as when she was mortal. She took an arrow and fitted it to her bow.

The twins looked at one another and guffawed.

"Should we feel threatened?" Phobos mocked.

Deimos laughed so hard that Therese could see tears forming in his eyes. "Maybe we should run for our lives, brother."

"That's right. She looks so frightening."

They held their bellies and continued to laugh at her.

She took aim and shot Deimos in the heart. Without pause, she fitted another arrow and shot his brother. Upon penetration, both gods turned into miniature dachshunds. She fitted another arrow, just in case they transformed back into their original forms. Clifford growled, baring his teeth, and the two dachshunds whined. Clifford sprang for them, but the twin dogs vanished.

"Bravo," came Artemis's voice from a nearby tree. "Nicely done."

Therese aimed her arrow at the shimmering cypress. "So you didn't come to trap me?"

"I came to tell you the most important story of my life." The tree fluttered, and in the next instant Artemis stood above her, her leather boots level with Therese's eyes. "The saddest story of my life." She waved her hand over the ground and a stump emerged. "Have a seat."

Therese returned the unused arrow, noticing others remained in the quiver, as though she hadn't already spent two. Realizing they must regenerate, like skin cells, she leaped from the crack in the earth to stand on solid ground beside her dog. "We made a good team, Clifford. You deserve praise as well." She scratched his back. Then she sat on the stump and patted her thighs. Clifford jumped onto her lap. She was grateful for his warm body and friendly face as she wrapped her arms around him, her heart returning to its normal steady rhythm after its panicky flutter during her encounter with the twins and listened to the goddess's tale.

"Centuries ago, I met my one, true love. Her name was Callisto, one of many nymphs who kept company with me, hunting in the woods, running foot races, picnicking beneath trees. We began as friends, but, over time, we grew to love one another, and we swore we would remain pure and true to each other forever."

Therese knew precisely what it felt like to swear your heart to another and wondered what could have happened to have made the two lovers part. She kissed the top of Clifford's head.

"But one day while we were bathing together in a warm spring with a handful of other nymphs, I noticed she was with child. Can you imagine my horror, my heartbreak, my rage?"

Therese would have crawled inside a hole to die, but goddesses don't die. "What did you do?"

"I made her leave my company and all our friends. I told her to go away and to never return." She tucked a strand of her brown hair back up into its knot and wiped a tear from her cheek.

"So you never saw her again?"

"No." Artemis's voice cracked. "Soon after, I learned Zeus had tricked Callisto into having relations with him."

"Tricked her? How?"

A single tear slipped down Artemis's cheek from a forest-green eye. "He disguised himself as...me."

Therese widened her eyes in surprise. Zeus had raped Callisto. Once again, her shock and disappointment over the behavior of the gods gave her the resolve to be better than they. "Callisto was innocent. She never broke her vow to you."

"No."

"So what did you do?"

"I went everywhere looking for her, but after weeks of searching high and low, I learned Hera, full of jealousy, had turned Callisto into a bear."

"A bear? But it wasn't Callisto's fault. Hera should have turned Zeus into a bear!"

"Sshh. Lower your voice. We can't be overheard."

"Sorry." She nestled her chin against Clifford's head. "Go on."

"I continued to look for Callisto, but I was no longer sure what she looked like. I couldn't sense her. And I was scared a hunter would kill her."

"Is that what happened to her?"

Artemis folded her arms and shook her head. "The son she bore almost killed her by mistake when he was sixteen and out hunting, but Zeus intervened and turned him into a bear as well. Then he flung them both high into the heavens where they became Big Bear and Little Bear, or Ursa Major and Ursa Minor."

"The constellations?"

"That's right. They possess asterisms more commonly known as the Big Dipper and the Little Dipper."

"And Callisto's there still?" She wasn't sure how that could be, since the stars were light years away.

"Yes. For all these centuries. A day hasn't gone by that I haven't longed for her company, or a night that I haven't stood gazing up at her, begging her to forgive me. If I'd given her a chance to explain, I might have protected her from Hera."

Therese didn't know what to say. Artemis was right.

"That's why I took Hera's apple. I tried to use it as a bargaining tool to force Hera to give me back Callisto, but she claims she can't. I've also heard the apple can return a person back to his or her original state, but I have not been able to figure out how to get her from the sky without upsetting the universe."

It would be impossible, Therese thought. "That is a sad story, Artemis. I'm really sorry for you. But I don't understand what you would have me do."

"The Big Bear is one of the circumpolar constellations in the northern hemisphere, meaning it rotates around the North Star. For centuries, it was the only of these constellations to never reach the horizon."

"I still don't see…"

"Just listen. You've heard the tilting of the earth on its axis has changed over time, haven't you?"

"Yes?"

"So in more recent years, Callisto's feet have touched the Aegean Sea, especially in autumn."

"And this is important because…"

"In order to have the apple, you must reunite me with my Big Bear now that she can reach the earth."

"How do you propose I do such a thing? You yourself haven't been able to, and you're more powerful than I am."

"Perhaps as the goddess of animal companions, you will find a way. That is for you to determine. But tell no one. I can't risk Hera getting wind of it." Artemis vanished.

Chapter Twenty-Three: Goddess of Animal Companions

For the rest of the night, Therese researched the Ursa Major constellation on the internet and considered how she could possibly take Big Bear out of the sky. She sat on her bed with her laptop across her legs and Clifford curled up beside her, asleep. The prayers of pet owners everywhere distracted her from her research, and she took time to inspire as many of them as she could, but knowing Baby Lynn could die any day forced her to make Artemis's quest a priority.

Than seemed hurt when she asked him not to come tonight, but he said he understood. As promised to Artemis, she did not tell him the details, only that she didn't know if she could succeed, but that she had to try.

She learned the Big Dipper was used for centuries to find the North Star and to help nighttime travelers find their way. If she pulled it from the sky, how would they find their way and what would people think? Maybe they would assume the end of the world was on its way, as they had when the Mayan calendar ran out on December 21, 2012. Worse than their confusion would be the impact on the universe and the gravitational pull between the planets, stars, and other space matter. Big Bear couldn't just disappear from the northern skies without repercussions.

Damn Hera for requiring her apple, and damn Artemis for not freely giving it. She swore to herself once more that she would never allow herself to become the kind of goddess who put her needs before everyone else's.

But wasn't that what she was doing? Pet owners everywhere were praying to her for help, and her top priority was saving her sister. Was she no better than the other gods? A bead of sweat formed on her forehead. She closed her laptop and sighed.

Why shouldn't she help herself first? Was it a god's responsibility to serve others foremost? She had the power to help, but did she also have the obligation to make helping others her number one priority?

Before she could answer her questions, she heard a scream. She brushed her laptop to the bed and jumped to her feet. Faster than the time it took a human to blink, she grabbed her bow and quiver and was at the foot of the stairs searching for Carol. The scream came again, and this time, she realized it wasn't Carol, but Jen, and the scream wasn't coming from inside Therese's house, but through Jen's agonizing prayer.

"Should I call you, Therese? What am I going to do?" Jen's fervent prayer was followed by another wail.

The early dawn light streamed in through the kitchen window. Carol and Richard were likely asleep. Therese scribbled a note for them, leaving it on the kitchen bar, and then ran at her full speed to the Holts' place. She arrived within seconds.

Not sure whether she should knock at the door, storm inside, or fly up to Jen's window, Therese paused on the front porch. The scream came again, but louder, blood-curdling. She stormed through the door.

The chaotic scene unfolded. In less than a second, she took it all in: kitchen chairs overturned, dishes smashed all over the tiled floor, a red stain splattered on the wallpaper in the breakfast nook, the light fixture over the table still swinging as though something had hit it minutes earlier, and sprawled on the kitchen floor, blood spilling from his arm, was Pete. He looked at her without speaking, apparently in shock, flat on his back, breathing like a runner. On the other side of the room, Jen stood with a pistol in her trembling hands, lowered and pointing to her feet. Tears streamed down her face.

"I had no choice," Jen said through labored breaths. She was a blubbering mess. "He was going to kill me."

"Where's your mom? And Bobby?" Therese crossed the room and took the gun from her friend's quavering hands.

"On the way to see Dad. After they left, Pete attacked me."

Therese helped her to a chair. "I'll take care of him." She put the gun in her back pocket and rushed to Pete's side. He was losing blood fast. "You're going to be okay."

He turned his crystal blue eyes toward her but did not speak.

"I'm so sorry this happened." She kissed his forehead. "It's all my fault." She prayed to Apollo as she took a dish cloth and wrapped it around Pete's arm. Apollo replied that he was tied up and could not come. She prayed to Than, but he reminded her that his presence would only ensure Pete's death. Then she had an idea.

She stood up and fitted an arrow to her bow. As the arrow shot, Jen jumped from her chair and screamed, "What are you doing for God's sake?"

The arrow struck Pete in the chest, alongside the other two, and he transformed into a beautiful golden retriever. Jen looked at Therese with wide eyes, started to say something, and then fainted across her chair.

"Good," Therese muttered. She didn't need Jen in her way. She knelt beside the injured dog and unwrapped the towel from the wound. She focused her energy on healing him. Maybe her powers as goddess of animal companions would extend to healing.

"What's happening?" Pete asked though his new dog mouth.

At first nothing happened, but then she noticed the bleeding stopped. She applied more pressure to the wound with her towel. When she lifted the towel, the wound remained, but it looked less serious. She stroked the dog's belly and said, "You're going to be okay." She stood over him with another arrow.

Jen opened her eyes and stumbled toward her. "What are you doing? Where's Pete?"

"I need you to trust me. Can you do that? I gave you the crown, didn't I? Can you trust me?"

Jen stared back dumbly and nodded.

"Come stand in front of me. I need Pete to see you first."

"What? Where is he?"

"I'm right here!" he growled, but Jen couldn't understand him.

"Come over here Jen, so the dog can see you."

The dog whimpered as Jen approached.

"It's okay, boy," Therese said, taking aim. "Stay still, Jen. My timing has to be just right." Therese released the arrow, and in the split second before it struck, she ran out the front door so the only person Pete could lay eyes on was his sister.

Therese paused outside the house for a moment before returning to Jen's side. The dog had climbed to his feet and was now licking Jen's hand.

"Where did he come from?" Jen asked, unable to see the arrows sticking out from the dog's chest. "And what happened to Pete? Did an ambulance come?"

Therese's shoulders relaxed with relief. "Yes. Pete's at the hospital. I called 9-1-1 while you were passed out. The paramedic told me to tell you to get plenty of rest."

"Am I in trouble?"

"No. I told him it was an accident. Now go upstairs and get some rest. I'll find out if this dog strayed from the Melner Cabin or something."

"What about my morning chores? The horses?"

"I'll help you with them later. Go back to bed."

Jen padded across the room to the stairs, still somewhat shaky, and climbed up to her room while Therese kept Pete from following her.

"It's okay, Pete," Therese whispered. "You'll see her in a minute. And I'll get you back to normal as soon as I can."

"I'm so confused. I'm not sure who I am anymore."

"You're going to be okay." She knew her arrow hadn't infected him with desire, because her arrows were meant to bond human and animal companions with platonic affection. But she couldn't leave him as a dog, and if she could transform him back into a person—and she hoped beyond hope she could—she worried over what his feelings would be for Jen. She also wondered if he'd recall what Therese had done to him.

She stroked his fur for many more minutes, giving Jen time to get in bed and fall asleep. Then, after a half hour had passed, during which she continued to inspire pet owners who prayed to her, she fitted another arrow into her bow, wished he'd become human, and shot him.

Nothing happened. The golden retriever looked back at her, as though he hadn't felt the arrow penetrate. Then he turned from her and trotted up the stairs, limping on his left front leg, which though better, wasn't healed. Therese followed. The dog went directly to Jen's bedroom and curled beside her sleeping form. Jen started awake and saw first the dog beside her and then Therese bending over them.

"What's going on?" Jen asked.

"Can he stay with you awhile, just until I find his owner? He seems to like you an awful lot."

"Sure." She smiled sleepily and pet Pete.

"I'll call your mom and tell her about the accident and let her know everything's okay. I'll tell her Pete cut himself real bad."

"But she'll find out you lied."

"Not if Pete goes along with it, which he'll do after the way he's been treating you." Therese met the golden retriever's eyes, daring him to say differently. "I'll clean up, too. You just go back to sleep now. I'll see you later."

Therese returned downstairs to call Mrs. Holt and clean up the mess. She also tucked the pistol away in a kitchen drawer. Then, at a speed approaching that of light, she cleaned the barn and groomed the horses, including Stormy, speaking to them in soft tones so as not to spook them with her inhuman movement.

She could sense Carol and Richard were awake, so she flew to her bedroom window. Than was waiting for her.

"I couldn't change him back!" she cried as he swept her into his arms. "I really thought I'd be able to do it. How stupid could I be?"

He pushed a strand of her hair behind her ear. "At least he no longer wants to kill her."

She pulled back, gripping his shoulders with both hands. "But he's a dog!"

"Calm down. I know a way."

"You do?" She wrapped her arms around his neck and kissed him. "Thank god! Tell me."

"Hera's apple. It's been used before to transform a beast that was originally human."

That's right. Artemis had said as much. "Should I try to take another from the garden of the Hesperides?"

Than crossed his arms and sucked in his lips, thinking. He shook his head. "Hera won't save Lynn if you do."

Then she realized something else. She dropped her arms to her side and lowered her eyes, feeling hopeless. More tears fell on her cheeks. "Hera won't give me an apple. And if I succeed in Artemis's quest and then get the apple from her, I can't transform Pete and save Lynn. I'll have to choose."

"Maybe Pete and Jen are better off…"

She snapped her head up, eyes wide. "I can't leave him in the body of a dog! It's my fault. I changed him! I've got to change him back. It was the only way I could think of healing him and reversing his hate for Jen. I knew I could help animal companions and make them love their humans. That's why I did it. But I truly expected to be able to change him back. Ugh!" She opened one of her bedroom windows and leapt out.

Chapter Twenty-Four: Vanished

Than followed her out the window. "Wait up!"

He used his keen vision to scan the perimeter but could not find her. "She better not have god traveled." He reached out with his consciousness but could not sense her. He prayed to her, "Where are you?"

She replied, "I don't know!"

His body stiffened where he stood on the ground outside her house. "What happened?"

She did not reply.

"Therese?"

Nothing.

He god traveled directly to the gates of Mount Olympus demanding to be let inside.

The gray cloud refused him.

He pounded against the golden gates and screamed in frustration. "Zeus! Let me in! Ares has taken Therese! Let me in, or you can find someone else to guide the dead!"

The gray cloud floated up in fear, but the gates did not move. Than disintegrated into the hundreds of thousands and, as one huge mass, charged the gates. They barely budged, but the tiny gap he created was large enough for one to slip though. The hundreds of thousands of Thans pressed against the gates while the one entered. He reintegrated and charged across the courtyard and up the rainbow steps.

Hephaestus worked in his forge and Hestia in her kitchen. Hades and Persephone were absent—autumn having arrived because his mother had returned to the Underworld. Artemis was also gone, and Demeter had returned to her winter cabin. But the others were seated on their thrones visiting among one another, Poseidon with Apollo and Hermes, Hera with Zeus and Ares, and Aphrodite with Cupid, who had come in from tending the stables. They all looked up when Than entered like a bull from its gate. He ran at Ares and wrapped his hands around his throat.

Ares laughed.

Than disintegrated into five and surrounded the god of war, each taking a limb and disabling him. "Tell me where she is, you coward."

"Or what?" he asked. "You'll rip me apart as the maenads did you?"

"Good idea."

Zeus stood before them in his full form and bellowed, "Release my son!"

"Not until he tells me where he's taken Therese!"

"How dare you speak to me in this manner, Thanatos!" Zeus roared.

Zeus's army of three Cyclopes, larger and stockier than any among them, entered the palace, ambling across the marble floor in their slow, ungraceful gait. One by one, Arges, Brontes, and Steropes peeled each Than from Ares and threw him to the ground. Than responded by continually disintegrating, despite the painful blows. Like a colony of ants from its hill, he kept multiplying until the Cyclopes wailed in anger and frustration. Than had never turned against the gods before, and now he realized his special power of disintegration gave him a unique advantage. He would never attempt to use it to overthrow the Olympians, but he would fight for Therese.

"Enough!" Zeus shouted.

The other gods looked on, some with concern and others with amusement.

The Cyclopes stopped and ambled from the palace.

Than integrated into five and maintained his hold on Ares, who was no longer laughing.

"Get this repulsive god away from me!" Ares wailed.

Than took great satisfaction in having bested the god of war, if for even a little while. "Tell me what you've done with Therese!"

"She's not been harmed, only taken," Ares growled.

"Return her you mother f…" Than looked up at Hera and thought better of his words. "You weasel!"

Ares strained against him but could not break free. "On one condition."

"Name it."

"You find Hippolyta's girdle and let me fit it to Therese."

Than wanted to strangle the god, and he tightened his grip around Ares's neck. "What have I ever done to you?"

"Besides threaten to break my neck?" Ares mocked.

"Tell me where to find the girdle."

"I've been looking for it, but with no luck."

"Let her go. I promise to search for it. I promise not to touch her. Please." Than released Ares and integrated. He stood before him.

Ares rubbed his neck and gave Than a hateful glare. "You find the girdle and I'll set her free."

Than glanced at each of the gods present in a circle around him. "Will no one help me?"

All but Zeus lowered their eyes, even Hermes, whom he loved like a big brother.

"You're an oath breaker, Thanatos," Zeus said. "You've lost our respect."

Than looked at Aphrodite, whose face was pink and whose mouth was turned into a frown, but she did not look back. Cupid, too, avoided his eyes. These were Therese's ancestors. Didn't they care for her safety? And Ares, also from the same blood, was to blame for all of this! He glared up at Zeus. None of this was fair.

Just as he was about to give up on all of them, Athena stepped forward. "I will help you, Thanatos."

"As will I." Hephaestus came up from behind and put a hand on Than's shoulder.

Chapter Twenty-Five: The Amazonian Pit

Therese's arms were bound behind her back. She was blindfolded and sat on a surface that felt like dirt and rock. Something blocked her from being able to stretch out her consciousness to see beyond the blindfold, to god travel, and to pray. She could hear Than's frantic prayers to her, but clearly he could not hear hers to him.

If it weren't for his voice raging through her head, she'd feel utterly alone.

Tears of frustration rolled down her cheeks. Her throat was sore and her voice hoarse from screaming. She didn't have time for this! Baby Lynn could die any day. And Pete! What would Mrs. Holt and Bobby think when they returned home and Pete wasn't back from the hospital, as Therese had promised? Would they get rid of the golden retriever?

She screamed again. "Let me out of here!" Her throat stung with pain. "Let me out of here!"

Feeling along the floor with her hands, she recognized fine sand mixed with pebbles. She scooted on her hands and bottom, trying to get a sense for how large a space her prison was. As she scooted along, her hands fumbled against a larger rock with a sharp point. Hopeful, she snatched it up and rubbed the point against the binding at her wrists, over and over, sawing as fast as she could, approaching the speed of light and creating so much heat she nearly produced a flame. At last, the binding broke and her arms were freed. She removed her blindfold and looked around.

"What on earth?"

She found herself in a pit about ten feet deep and twelve feet in diameter. The walls of the pit were made of smooth incandescent stone, which cast a purplish glow throughout the prison and emanated a low buzzing sound reminding her of the extra freezer back home in the basement. Above was an opening, three feet in diameter with a metal grate over it, also aglow.

"Hello!" She called out toward the opening. "Anyone there?"

When no one answered, she felt along the incandescent walls, hoping to find a hidden door. The walls seared her hands. "Ouch!" Fanning her burnt hands in the air, she studied the walls, finding the bright glow wasn't too hard on her eyes, but there was no crack or crevice, no hidden door.

The floor! She crouched on her hands and knees, her black jeans and top nearly white now from the dust, examining every inch of the dirt and pebble-covered ground, hoping for a trap door. Unlike the smooth walls, the ground did not emanate heat or purple light. She found her collapsible bow and slung it over her shoulder with her quiver. Then she had the idea of shooting an arrow through the opening, to see if anything would happen. She fitted the arrow and released it perfectly. It incinerated as soon as it broached the grate.

Discouraged but not without hope, she retrieved her sharp-pointed rock and struck the ground with it, her burnt hand, nearly healed, stinging from the contact. In spite of the pain, she found she could dig a hole in seconds with her godly strength. Full of renewed hope, she eagerly crawled next to the wall and started digging with the idea that she would tunnel below the incandescent wall, behind it, and up toward the surface.

Perhaps it was because her mind was so singularly focused, but however it happened, as she dug beneath the incandescent wall, she realized how she would get Callisto from the sky without upsetting the universe. She would find another bear to take her place. If she could switch the bears at the speed of light, she might be able to avoid any repercussions to both the universe and the notice of humankind. She didn't know exactly how the bear held the stars, light-years away from one another, together in their constellation, but if one bear could do it, another could.

She would see to it, but she needed a bear. There were plenty in the woods near her house.

She didn't want to force one against its will. That would make her no better than the other gods who used people and animals for their own selfish purposes. No, she had to find a way to convince a bear to volunteer. First, she had to get out of this pit.

She hadn't yet decided whether she would feed the apple to Pete or return it to Hera. If she fed it to Pete, she would likely lose Hera's favor forever, and worse, Baby Lynn would die. But she remembered reading that Artemis, too, was sometimes called upon to help the unborn because immediately after her own birth, she helped her mother travel to a safer island away from Hera's wrath to give birth to Apollo. Maybe Therese could feed the apple to Pete and then ask Artemis to save Lynn. A shiver worked its way down her spine as she realized she had nothing to give the goddess of the hunt in exchange for the favor. Could Artemis be trusted to give another gift out of the kindness of her heart? The goddess was generous to Therese when she was human, but things seemed different between them now.

Therese could return the apple to Hera, and then ask her to save both Lynn and Pete. She bashed the rock against the earth, again and again, frustrated by the thought that, Hera, too, would have no reason to help her beyond her original promise.

Although she had successfully dug beneath the incandescent wall, she hadn't made much progress tunneling up toward the surface when something fell from the opening above with a thud. Turning, she saw it was a man. He held a spear in his hands and wore torn trousers and no shirt on his muscled torso. His sky-blue eyes glared at her warily through blond messy bangs, and his strong jaw lifted in defiance as he climbed to his feet and crouched with the spear pointed at her.

"Who are you?" She stood up and backed away.

"Leif Anders, from Norway. Who are you?"

"You don't know? I thought I was your prisoner."

"Am I not yours?" Leif looked to be in his early twenties and was tall, broad, and strong, but was clearly just a man. Despite his size and weight, she felt confident she could defend herself against him if he attacked.

"You're the one with the spear."

He narrowed his eyes, as though he didn't trust her. "It's hard to see you in this purple haze."

"I'm Therese Mills from the U.S. Where are we?"

"Amazon territory."

"The rainforest?"

He shook his head. "I don't know our exact location. It's kept secret. You don't want to know either. I've heard they kill anyone who discovers it."

"They?"

"The Amazons."

"What? The Amazons? Why?" She paced around him, and he turned defensively with his spear keeping himself square to her. "What would the Amazons want with me?"

"To reproduce for them. That's what they want with me. If it's a girl, they let us go. If it's a boy, they kill him and make us start again."

Her jaw dropped open. "What?"

"They're a tribe of women. They capture men for reproduction."

"They can't find anyone willing?"

"What man wants his son murdered? And it's not like the Amazons are desirable. Their faces are beautiful, but they cauterize their right breasts as infants."

"What? Why would any woman mutilate her young like that?"

"They believe it makes them better warriors with the spear."

"That's so…antiquated and morbid, especially when we have automatic assault weapons."

"They're loyal to their traditions. Another reason why I'm here instead of a sample from a sperm bank."

"So they're really going to force you to have sex with them?"

"That's what they said just before they tossed me down here. I think I'm meant to have sex with you."

The blood rushed to her face. "No. No, not me."

"So you aren't going to rape me?"

"God, no. I want to get us out of here." She crossed her arms at her chest, trying to think why the Amazons would take her prisoner. Then she remembered that the first Amazons were daughters of Ares. He must have solicited their help in keeping her away from Than. How ironic that Leif was here to be forced to reproduce while she was here to be kept from it—unless they meant for her to become impregnated by a man as a way to prevent her from conceiving a god's child. Was the god of war buying himself some time? Nine months to be exact? A demigod would be no threat to him if she was raised among the Amazons. Her heart sped up and pounded against her ribs as she returned to her digging. "I think I've found a way out."

He dropped his spear. "They'll kill us if we try to escape."

"We can't let them catch us then."

He surprised her from behind, shoving her to her bottom. "Stop digging! They'll kill us!"

She pushed him away, but not with her full strength so as not to hurt him. "It's okay. I'll protect you."

"You'll protect me? Yeah, right. Now let's get this over with. They won't bring us food or water till the deed is done."

He came at her again, and this time she forced him to the ground. "Give it up! I'm stronger than you."

"I didn't believe them when they told me you'd be." He took a vial from his trouser pocket and removed the cork. "Didn't drink their damn elixir, sure it was a sleeping potion." He swallowed its contents and tossed the vial to the ground. "Didn't quench my thirst, but they said it would give me strength. I'm so thirsty. I've been their prisoner for days without food or water. Now come on. Please. Let's get this over with. I promise to be gentle."

Chapter Twenty-Six: Interrogation with the Furies

You have your methods," Tizzie growled at Than, her dark serpentine curls coming alive, like the hair of Medusa.

"And we have ours." Blood dripped from Meg's eyes as she bent over the former Queen of the Amazons.

"But she says she doesn't know where it is," Than objected. "This is a waste of time."

The two Furies had Hippolyta connected to their stretcher in the upper pit of Tartarus, not far from where Tantalus lay with water dripping on his forehead and grapes dangling just out of his reach. Even though Hippolyta was as transparent as all souls in the Underworld, her raven hair sparkled, as did the metal trim on her boots and armor. Her dark eyes were wide with fright and her teeth clenched with pain. Than fought the impulse to rescue her from his sisters, who were trying to help him.

Tizzie cranked the stretcher. "You'd be surprised what souls can remember with a little help from this machine."

Hippolyta shrieked. "I told you, I gave the girdle to Hercules!"

Meg leapt on top of the table, her blond hair flying like golden flames, the falcon on her shoulder, ready to peck. Meg straddled the Amazon, allowing the blood from her eyes to spill onto Hippolyta's face. "That's not what he says. He says he stole it from you and then gave it back, after his labor was complete."

Hippolyta pressed her mouth and eyes closed to avoid the blood and then screamed, "Liar!"

"Why aren't you interrogating Hercules?" Than insisted.

Tizzie cranked the stretcher. "He's next."

Hippolyta said in a frantic, pleading voice, "I gave it to Hercules! He wanted everyone to think he bested me, for the sake of his labor, but I fell in love with him and gave it to him as we sailed together to Athens. But, but then he betrayed me!" Tears flowed from the corners of her eyes and down to her ears.

"Betrayed you, how?" Meg demanded.

"Hera wanted him to fail," Hippolyta said through gritted teeth. "She spread a rumor that he abducted me. My sister Antiope believed it and led an army of Amazons to attack Athens. Hercules…" Hippolyta stopped, fighting off sobs.

"Speak!" Tizzie hissed, echoed by the serpent curls. "Speak!"

"Hercules gave me back, refused me!" Hippolyta said as she wept. "His men were more important to him!"

"And the girdle?" Meg demanded.

"I think Hercules gave it to Theseus, but I'm not certain."

"Aha!" Tizzie loosened the stretch machine and turned to Meg. "I'll fetch Theseus while you take her to Erebus to purge her pain."

"What about Hercules?" Than said. "I thought you said he was next."

"Come with me, brother," Tizzie said. "If you want him so badly, I'll let you interrogate him."

Unlike his former arrogant self, Hercules was docile where he sat in the Elysium Fields. He didn't resist when Than beckoned him to follow, but the moment he was strapped to the stretcher, he became aware. Pain was the great tool of awakening.

Tizzie strapped Theseus on a second machine so that the two fallen heroes lay side by side, their armor mirror reflections of each other. Only the color of their hair—Hercules blond and Theseus black—kept them distinct from a distance. Meg returned from Erebus and leapt onto Theseus, frightening him with the blood from her eyes and the falcon at her shoulders, threatening to peck his face.

Than bent over Hercules. "What do you know of Hippolyta's girdle?"

"I returned it to Hippolyta when I gave her back to the Amazons."

"Lies!" Tizzie hissed, and her serpent hair echoed. "Lies!"

In the distance, Tizzie's wolf howled while she cranked the stretcher.

Hercules grunted. "Theseus, old friend! I'm sorry!"

"So you did give the girdle to him!" Than said.

"No one was to know, but yes. Now get me down!" Hercules cried.

"Why was no one to know?" Than demanded. "Tell me!"

Tizzie pulled the crank as Meg brought her falcon down to Theseus's face.

"What became of Hippolyta's girdle!" Meg shrieked.

Hercules panted as sweat poured from his skin. "Tell them, Theseus!"

"I gave it to Antiope, to woo her!" Theseus cried with pain.

"Hippolyta's sister?" Than asked.

"She fell in love with me and turned against her own people after they attacked us. She fought alongside me and protected me from her own sisters."

"Keep going!" Meg prodded, blood dripping from her face to his throat.

"She believed me when I told her of Hera's lie, but she couldn't convince the other Amazons of our innocence, so she killed for me. But…"

"But what?" Than said, rushing to Theseus's side. "Get to the point!"

"When I gave the girdle to Antiope, she was horrified. She thought Hercules and I had killed Hippolyta, even though Hippolyta died at the hands of her own people. The Amazons didn't recognize her when they killed her."

"Did you tell Antiope this?" Meg asked.

"Of course, but she wouldn't believe me. She took her own life and broke my heart. I lied about her death in our treaty with the Amazons, claiming they had killed her along with her sister. I also lied about the girdle, worried they'd jump to the same conclusions as Antiope."

"What became of the girdle?" Than's urgent voice echoed throughout Tartarus.

"The sea nymph Dione promised me safe passage back to Athens if I gave it to her, so I did."

Than's mouth dropped open. "Dione?"

Theseus nodded.

"Are you speaking the truth?" Than asked.

Tizzie cranked the machine.

"I swear! I swear! I gave the golden girdle to Dione!"

Chapter Twenty-Seven: Tunnel Vision

Leif! No!" Therese jumped to her feet and pushed against the Norwegian, but he clung to her.

He crushed her in his arms and kissed along her neck. "Can't we make this pleasant?" he murmured. "Mmm. You smell nice." He clutched her hair and lifted her face to his. "And fortunately for me, you're beautiful." He covered her mouth with gentle lips.

She spat at him. "I promised myself to someone else!"

He wiped his mouth on her black shirt, over her right breast.

"Stop!"

His sky-blue eyes pleaded with her. "You'll never get out of here alive unless you bear them a girl. I've heard the stories. Please. Let's make the best of it." He kissed her again.

She bit down on his lip.

"Ah!" He loosened his hold on her.

She stepped back and kicked him in the chest. He staggered back.

"Fine!" He raised both hands in the air. "I give up. Dig your tunnel."

She watched him warily as she found her rock and returned to her digging. "Nothing against you. I'm in love with someone else. We're going to get married."

"Keep dreaming," the Norwegian said. "Even if you do tunnel all the way out, they'll only capture you again. This place is heavily guarded."

"I told you, I'll find a way."

For another hour, she worked, tunneling up the other side of the incandescent wall. The loose dirt and rock fell in her hair, mouth, and eyes, making her cough and spit and blink, but she kept going, desperate to escape. She resented the Norwegian, who'd made himself comfortable in the middle of the pit, lying on his back, sometimes watching her, sometimes closing his eyes. She could no longer see him now that she could stand on her feet and crouch in the three-foot tunnel she'd made.

Every fifteen minutes or so, she had to stop digging to push the fallen debris into the pit and out of her way.

"Oh, Than," she prayed. "If only you could hear me."

"Therese?"

"Than? You can hear me?"

"Yes! But I can't sense you! Where are you?"

"I don't know! The Amazons have me in some kind of enchanted pit. I'm trying to dig myself out."

Before she could explain more, the Norwegian grabbed her by her sneakers and pulled her from her tunnel, her head and arms hitting and scraping against the rock. He tugged her into the middle of the pit and climbed on top of her.

"Worn out yet?" His body was flush on top of hers, but he lifted his head to look at her, elbows propped on the ground on either side of her. He pushed her hair out of her eyes. "I'm starving and dying of thirst down here. Forgive me for what I'm about to do."

He pinned her down with his body as he ripped open her black jeans and tugged them past her hips.

"Stop!" she screamed. "Please!"

When he lifted himself to undo his own trousers, she reached back for an arrow from her quiver and stabbed him in the chest. He immediately transformed into a yellow canary, fluttering above her.

"What's happened to me?" he chirped.

"I didn't know what else to do."

"Change me back!"

"I can't. I'm sorry."

"Then I'm getting out of here!" He flew toward the grate above them.

"No! You'll get fried!"

He ignored her and flew up. Like her arrow, as soon as he broached the grate, he disappeared in a puff of smoke.

"Leif!" Therese covered her face and wept. "I had no choice," she said again, this time to herself. "I had no choice."

A few minutes later, she wiped her eyes with the back of her hands, fastened her jeans back at her waist, and found her rock.

Then it came to her. It came so fast she squealed with surprise, clutching the locket near her throat. If Than could hear her prayers while she was in the tunnel, maybe she could god travel, too. With her bow and quiver slung over her shoulder, she crawled beneath the incandescent wall and into the three-foot tunnel she'd made on the other side. As soon as she focused on Than's chambers, she was there, safe in his room. Hades appeared a moment later.

"Well played," he said.

"You knew where I was?" Therese asked with astonishment.

"Not in time to do anything about it." Hades scratched his beard. "The Amazonian Pit is the only territory underground I cannot control. Even Poseidon's sea caves are subject to me and my power." He narrowed his eyes. "Are you hurt?"

She shook her head. "I'm fine. Where's Than?"

"He must be well distracted not to sense your presence here." He crossed the room and sat in one of the club chairs in front of the fireplace, crackling with flames and wood.

"I thought he'd be here."

"He's in Tartarus, among other places, torturing souls." He steepled his fingers and smiled, as though delighted by the idea.

"What?"

"He needs information to help you."

"Never mind. He can't come with me, anyway. I need to go."

"Go? Where?"

"On a quest."

He motioned for her to sit in the chair opposite him.

"I don't have time. My sister's life is in jeopardy. Artemis gave me a quest in exchange for her help."

"What would the huntress have you do?"

"It's a secret."

"Ah, a secret quest. Wonderful. As soon as you leave my kingdom, Ares will hurl you back into the Amazonian Pit. This time, free of sharp rocks for digging."

She sank into the chair opposite him. "What can I do to protect myself? Artemis made it very clear that I can't involve Than."

"Hmm." He tugged at his beard. "Take the Furies with you."

"Thanks, but I promised I would go alone."

"Alone? With Ares after you? Impossible."

"I have to try." She stood up to leave.

"Then wear this." Something appeared in Hades's hand. A golden helmet? "My helm of invisibility."

"But…"

"Even the gods can't sense you while you're wearing it."

She sat back down on the edge of her chair. "Are you serious?"

"Quite. Though Zeus and Poseidon can sometimes become suspicious if you travel by sky or sea." He brought the helm to his face to inspect it carefully. "I've never been able to figure out what gives me away to them." He stood up and took her hand, helping her to her feet. "In any case, if you stick to the land, you'll be safe."

The sky and the sea were the two places she must go to complete her quest. She hid her fear and gave Hades a grateful smile.

Hades added, "And don't god travel. The helm won't protect you if you do. Now, come. I'll take you home in my chariot. Persephone's home. She can mind the store."

"I don't know how to thank you." She followed him from the room, presumably toward the garage.

"Oh, don't worry," he said, turning back to her with an unnerving smile. "I'm sure I'll think of a way."

Chapter Twenty-Eight: A Bear in the Woods

Wearing Hades's helm of invisibility, which wobbled uncomfortably, being a bit large for her head, Therese checked in on Carol and Richard to find Richard on the deck feverishly typing on his laptop and Carol eating a bowl of soup in front of the television, sobbing to some soap opera, rubbing her swollen belly. Therese couldn't tell if it was the knowledge that the baby was dying or the drama on the television or both that was making her weep. She wondered for a moment what it must feel like, carrying a baby you could not protect, knowing your own body was killing her. Hope kept Carol from terminating the pregnancy. Although the doctor warned her that she would likely have to suffer through a stillborn birth, Carol hoped he was wrong.

Therese took consolation in the fact that neither was concerned with her whereabouts, even though she'd been gone for seven hours. Given the note she left them on the bar, they must think she was at Jen's.

Not that the chariot ride with Hades had taken much time. Swift and Sure flew from a chasm of the Underworld and up into the bright afternoon skies of Colorado faster than Therese could swallow. At least she didn't have the burden of making small talk.

Next, she checked in on the Holts. Their trail ride season had ended the weekend after Labor Day, and today was the end of September, but the horses still had to be exercised on Saturday and Sunday now that Jen and Bobby were back at school during the week. Nevertheless, Therese was surprised to see Jen and Bobby riding even though Pete was missing. He wasn't missing, of course, for Therese saw him, still in the form of a golden retriever, sitting forlornly by the pasture gate licking his wound and waiting for Jen to return. Therese entered the house under the helm of invisibility to find Mrs. Holt on the phone, a pen and a cigarette in each hand, and a list of nearby hospitals written on a pad at her elbow. All but three were crossed out.

"Can I leave my number in case he's there and you just don't know it?" Mrs. Holt said into the phone.

Therese watched on, feeling terrible, as Mrs. Holt relayed her contact information to the woman on the other end. Mrs. Holt then hung up, sucked at her cigarette, and ran her hand through her gray-blonde, bowl-cut hair.

"Maybe I should try Therese again." She punched the numbers on her phone. "Maybe this time someone will answer."

What? Therese pulled at her hands, trying to think of what to do. If Mrs. Holt called her aunt and uncle, they would know she was missing and become concerned. What to do? What to do?

"Hello, Carol?" Mrs. Holt said. "I'm sorry to bother you, but I was wondering if I could speak with Therese."

Therese stepped outside through the exterior wall, removed her helmet, and knocked on the back door before entering. "Mrs. Holt? Jen asked me to…oh, sorry. Didn't know you were on the phone."

"Never mind, Carol. Therese is here. Sorry. Yeah, I didn't realize. Thanks anyway. I'll tell her." She hung up the phone and looked at Therese. "Thanks for all the work you did for us in the barn and with the horses this morning. That must have taken you hours."

"Not really."

"I didn't realize you were still here. I'm going crazy trying to find Pete. What hospital did the ambulance take him to?"

"Um, gosh, they didn't say. But I bet he's left by now. The cut wasn't that bad. I think the blood just freaked us all out. You know Jen."

"I've called a dozen different places and none of them claim to have seen him. And he's not answering his cell phone."

Therese knew the longer she went without the helm, the more vulnerable she'd be to Ares finding her.

"What's that in your hand?" Mrs. Holt asked.

"Oh, um, this?" What could she say? "This is part of a costume, for larping. You know, live action role play? Heard of it?"

Mrs. Holt shook her head and stood from the kitchen chair. "No, but I better get to work. Maybe you're right and Pete called a friend to come get him. Maybe he's milking his wound to get out of working today."

"Maybe." She headed for the back door. "Listen, would you mind if the golden retriever hangs out here for a while until I find him a home? Pretty please?"

"Oh, sure. One more animal won't make a difference on this ranch. I like him. He's fond of Jen, isn't he? Maybe we'll keep him."

Great. Therese gave Mrs. Holt a forced smile. "Well, I have to um, join Jen." She needed Mrs. Holt to think she was hanging out at their ranch in case Carol called.

"Sure thing." Then she added, "Didn't you say Jen wanted you to tell me something?"

"Oh." Therese stopped at the back door, hand on the knob. "I can't remember what it was. Sorry." She bolted out, put on the helmet, and ran back to her own house, to the woods behind it.

Once she caught her breath, she reached out her consciousness to sense the beings inhabiting the national forest up the mountain. "Than?" she felt him nearby.

"Where are you?" he prayed.

"In the forest. Where are you?"

"What a relief! In your room. I can't sense you."

"I'm wearing your father's helm." She jogged down the path toward her house.

"Really? He never lets anyone borrow it."

"Meet me on the back deck."

"Okay. But watch out for your uncle."

"I see him."

When she spotted Than, she threw her arms around his neck. "Thank God!"

He reached for her, but his arms moved through her. "I can't feel you. I can't sense you at all. I can only hear your prayer."

She removed the helm for just a moment and pressed her lips to his. They both remained invisible to mortal eyes, their words inaudible to mortal ears, which was necessary since her uncle was typing on his laptop less than twenty feet away.

"Mmm. Thank goodness," he moaned, pulling her close against him.

She kissed him back, but quickly returned the helm. "I've got to go."

"Where?"

"Artemis's quest. I promised her I'd keep it a secret. It's the only way she'll help me."

"I don't like this. Take me with you."

"Goodbye, Than." She backed away from him.

"Wait! Therese! Please! I want to protect you! Come back!"

She ran up the path despite his pleas for her to return, blocking his prayers as best she could as she wiped the tears from her cheeks and scrambled toward the top of the mountain, where she could sense the bears.

It felt cruel, leaving Than like this, but she had no choice. Lynn's life—and Pete's—hung in the balance. For now, getting the apple from Artemis seemed her only hope of saving either of them. Than would understand, but that didn't mean her heart wasn't aching to have him by her side.

It wasn't long before she saw them—a mother and two cubs. The cubs were walking toward her across a log ten yards away while the mother looked warily from the mouth of a cave partially shrouded by chokecherry bushes. The mother lifted her black head and snorted.

Although Therese was a god and completely invisible, old habit made her tremble with mortal fear. She slowly backed away.

The mother bear took three strides from her den and called to her cubs, as though she sensed Therese's presence.

The cubs were older and would probably go on their own in the spring, but Therese needed a bear that could leave now. This mother bear was not for her. She turned and ran around to the other side of the mountain.

She sensed other mothers with their cubs and a few solitary males, but none she thought would be willing to spend eternity in the sky. She kept searching, feeling frantic and foolish. What was she thinking, running around the mountainside? Was she crazy?

The warm scent of pine lingered in the forest air as the gray clouds gathered above for their typical afternoon shower. Birds sang or cried. Chipmunks jumped from tree to tree.

Further up the mountain, she sensed an old female bear, alone, fishing in the spring that fed into the Holts' pasture miles below. Less agile, less quick, and with patches of fur missing along her back and flanks, this bear was exactly what Therese was looking for.

"Hello!" Therese called out to her from ten feet away.

The bear turned in Therese's direction, and, seeing and hearing nothing, resumed her fishing in the stream.

"How would you like to live forever?"

The bear moaned something incoherent and trudged further up the stream.

As Therese was about to speak again, the old bear growled and ran toward a young female fishing several yards away.

"My territory!" the old bear roared.

"Huh?" came a snort of surprise from the younger female. When she saw the old bear running toward her, she wailed, "Wait! My mother drove me away. I have no place to go!"

The old bear hurled herself at the younger. "Leave!"

A cacophony of growling followed, along with threatening looks and gestures from both bears. Therese stood still, wondering how she could grab the old bear and carry her off.

Before Therese could intervene, the older bear struck the younger, and as the two bears fell against the banks of the stream, Therese heard the snap of the brittle spine of the old female, and then its body lay limp on the wet rocks.

"No!" If only Therese had been quicker. She ran to the side of the unmoving bulk on the bank as the younger bear moved away, downstream. Therese lifted the old bear's head and gently stroked its mouth as it panted and moaned. "You're alive. I may be able to save you. Tell me, old bear. Do you want to live forever in the sky?"

Chapter Twenty-Nine: Dione Revisited

While Meg and Tizzie escorted the two demigods to Erebus, Than communicated his new knowledge to Athena and Hephaestus, who'd been flying above the seas combing their depths for the lost girdle. He also shared Dione's earlier deception and his bewilderment over her motive. The three gods met on the northern shore of Turkey, at the banks of the Black Sea, where Than last spoke to the deceitful Oceanid.

"Therese escaped," Than said. "I just spoke to her. But until we find that girdle, I fear for her safety."

"Surely she's safe in the Underworld," said Athena.

Than frowned. "She's off on a quest for Artemis, hoping to save her sister's life."

"Honorable but foolish under these circumstances." Hephaestus scooped up a handful of sand and carefully sifted through it.

"Hades gave her his helm." Than turned to face the breeze off the water. It felt good after so much stress, but there was no time to rest.

Athena arched a brow. "He must like her a great deal."

"I sense Dione nearby." Hephaestus clapped his hands together to clean them of sand. "I think I know why she deceived you."

"Is that so, Hephaestus?" Dione's silver hair and eyes shimmered in the foam clinging to the rocks at their feet.

"You are my mother-in-law, after all," the god of the forge replied. "I've loved you more than I do my own mother."

Dione smiled. "Then you understand why I've hidden Ares's monstrous contraption?"

So, she admitted it, Than thought.

"I still recall the day you asked me to make its opposite for your daughter."

"You're a good god, Hephaestus. A good husband to have done so, even at the cost of your own happiness. Passions of the heart are meant to be fed, not stifled."

"Passions are best subdued." Athena widened her stance and lifted her chin defiantly. "I'm afraid we have different philosophies, Dione."

Than was about to move the focus back to saving Therese, when Dione replied, "Indeed, virgin goddess. You, Hestia, and Artemis see the purpose of existence quite differently than I."

"Don't put me in the same category as Artemis. Her passions are tempered only by the absence of her heart's true love."

"Who's that?" Than asked, wondering if the answer might be related to Therese's quest.

"Callisto, of course," Athena replied. "Big Bear."

Than absorbed and processed Athena's words. What quest could have anything to do with Callisto?

"But you remain chaste by your own free choice," Dione objected. "Hippolyta's golden girdle offers no freedom. Once it's fitted, a woman is held prisoner by it. No woman should give up the rights to her own body."

"Agreed." Than stepped closer to Dione and gazed down at her. "But the girdle can be fitted temporarily, can it not? Hippolyta had the power to remove it and give it to Hercules."

"Yes," Dione agreed. "But if you expect Ares to leave Therese alone, he will want to fit it to her himself. Then only he can remove it."

Than looked up at Athena and Hephaestus, but they made no comment. "Until Therese and I can find a better way to protect ourselves from Ares, the golden girdle is our best solution."

"A temporary solution, Mother," Hephaestus echoed.

Dione scoffed. "What makes you so certain Ares will ever agree to remove it once he's fitted it to her?"

"Everyone wants something," Than replied. "I just need to find out what Ares wants, more than our chastity."

"And you can't keep her in the Underworld under your father's protection?"

"That would be another kind of prison," Than replied. "She needs to be able to visit her family." He didn't want her to be trapped in the Underworld. He wanted her to be free. "Plus, she's the goddess of animal companions and wouldn't be able to serve from the Underworld. Her transformation wouldn't hold in that case."

"If I hand over Hippolyta's girdle, what shall I get in return? One of you will owe me. And the girdle must be returned to me the moment Therese no longer requires it."

The other two gods on the bank stared at Than, waiting for his reply.

Chapter Thirty: Out in the Open Sea

Therese crouched on the bank of the stream with the old bear's head in her hands. If Than came to collect the bear's soul, neither he nor Therese could do anything to prevent the bear from dying. Her powers as goddess of animal companions did not extend to healing. If they did, she would have been able to heal Pete once he transformed into a golden retriever.

She wondered if she could ask Than to hold off taking the bear's soul, to give Therese time, but then she would have to betray her promise to Artemis.

As goddess of wild animals and as one of the Olympians, Artemis did have the power to save the old bear's life, but Therese worried Artemis might take the bear and complete the quest on her own, keep the apple, and leave Therese with no leverage to seek Hera's aid in saving Lynn.

Therese had to do this on her own if she had any hope of saving Lynn and Pete, though she still had no idea how she would save both. Her face flushed as she realized she was putting her own needs ahead of those of the old bear.

I'm exactly like the other gods.

Not wanting to waste another moment, Therese grabbed the bear's front legs, and hefted the furry beast onto her back, careful to shift the quiver of arrows to one side. The bear moaned in protest.

"I'm going to help you," Therese assured her. "Just hold on a while longer." She hesitated, wondering if she should let the old bear die and find a younger, stronger bear for her journey, like the younger bear downstream, but the younger bear had her whole life ahead of her, and flinging her into the sky for all eternity might seem more a punishment to her. This bear would die otherwise; plus, Therese didn't want to waste any more time.

Without god travel or a chariot, she had no choice but to traverse land and water in what her senses told her was a bee-line to the Aegean Sea, where Artemis said Big Bear's feet touched the horizon at night. She was tempted to take her chances and god travel, but if Ares caught her again, she'd never save Lynn and Pete. So, with the helm of invisibility on her head, her quiver and bow over her left shoulder, and the old bear slumped across her back, its back paws almost grazing the ground, Therese clung to the bear's forelegs at her neck and ran down the mountainside as fast as she could manage. She ran through the San Juan Mountains and National Forest past the Great Sand Dunes, and over the last of the Rocky Mountains, moving southeast across grassland into Kansas. It took an hour to reach the river, where she laid the bear down to rest, giving her water and consoling her as best she could. Above her, in the late afternoon sky, buzzards swirled over them, sensing the old bear's demise, so she put her hands on the bear again to extend the helm's powers to her, and the vultures eventually flew away.

Then she followed the Cimarron National Grasslands northeast into Missouri, avoiding heavily populated cities as much as possible—not because she or the bear could be seen, since everything she touched was also protected by the helm, but because the city landscape slowed her down. In some areas, she risked being sensed by Zeus and took flight, but only when it was unavoidable. At one point, when she was flying into the Ozarks over Branson, a flock of geese followed her, and it felt more than coincidental. Therese worried they were working for Zeus. When she veered to her left, so did they. When she veered to the right, they followed. Trying not to panic, she landed near a lake in the Ozarks and decided to stick to the ground from then on.

She found her way through the Ozarks, stopping briefly in the Bald Knob Wilderness of southern Illinois to catch her breath and give water to the bear. She used a clam shell to scoop water from the river and drizzle it into the panting bear's mouth. In another hour, dusk would come, but the bear would not survive if Therese didn't give her opportunities to rest. She dipped the clam into the river, when suddenly a water moccasin sunk its fangs into the top of her hand. Painful poison surged through her veins. She pulled her hand away and dragged the bear from the bank, sure Poseidon or another sea deity must recognize her presence. She decided she would continue to follow the river but would be more careful about touching it for the rest of her journey.

Without stopping, she trailed the Ohio River along the Indiana and Ohio borders, and then crossed through the Glades of West Virginia to the Virginia coast.

She was a god and was strong, but not invincible. Her hand and arms still burned from the snake's venom, and her feet, knees, and back ached, but she trod on. The old bear looked as though she might expire at any moment. Night was falling, and because she was moving east, she was losing time. To make matter worse, she had to find a way across the Atlantic and the Mediterranean to the Aegean Sea without losing the bear and without being discovered by Poseidon. If a deity had sensed her near the river in a small patch of land in Illinois, it would have a field day with her swimming, without an escape route, in the middle of the wide open sea.

"No more," the bear moaned as Therese looked out across the Atlantic, deciding on her next move. "I can't take anymore."

"Hold on," Therese urged. "Wouldn't you like to live forever in the sky?"

"And never die?"

"That's right."

"You can…really make that…happen?"

"If you want me to."

The bear panted a barely audible, "Yes," before passing out and losing consciousness.

"No!"

Therese pressed her hand against the old bear's chest and felt a fragile heartbeat and wondered if Lynn's heartbeat was also weak. What if

Therese was too late? She bit her lip, wiped her eyes, heaved the beast onto her back, and dove into the sea.

She was able to help the bear to breathe and remain somewhat warm underwater. Because she had to use her hands to hold the bear's forelegs around her neck, Therese had no choice but to rely on her legs, and this slowed her down. She alternated between using the dolphin kick, breast kick, and flutter until she found the dolphin kick was the most efficient. She thought, mockingly, Mental note: if you ever have to swim across the ocean with a bear on your back, the dolphin kick is best.

She hadn't been in the water long when a school of sharks surrounded her. There were six of them circling her not ten feet away, baring their teeth. One by one, she shot them with her arrows, and as soon as they were pierced, they sidled up to her and nuzzled her hand. She asked them if they would escort her through the sea. The biggest and strongest offered her his back, but as she climbed on, holding the bear with one hand, a golden net fell over her, cinched her and the bear into a heap, and dragged them down, down, to the darkest depths of the sea.

Therese wrapped her arms around the bear, trying with all her might to keep the beast as comfortable as possible as they were mercilessly dragged through all manner of sea life and over rocky landforms, bouncing around as if they were tied to a trailer hitch and were being dragged through the Rocky Mountains by an SUV with four-wheel drive. Therese used her own body to shelter the blows to the bear, encasing the bear like the yolk of an egg. Her skin stung where coral, rock, and shell dug into her as she passed. Both fear and relief came over her when the brightly lit palace that belonged to Poseidon came into view.

The net stopped in the middle of a courtyard just outside of the palace walls. Poseidon swam toward them with his trident, and in a booming voice that blasted her eardrums like an IPod turned up to full volume, Poseidon demanded, "You thought you could sneak around my domain unnoticed? Exactly what is the meaning of this? Show yourself, Hades!"

Therese removed the helm to expose both herself and the bear, still in the net, floating but tethered.

"Therese?" Poseidon asked, sounding genuinely surprised. "It's you."

"I'm sorry I tried to be sneaky," Therese said. "I'm on a secret quest for Artemis."

"Why must you travel through my domain for Artemis?"

"It has nothing to do with your domain. I promise. I'm just passing through."

"It's hard to trust an oath breaker."

"Please let me pass. I'll do anything you ask."

The golden net disappeared, and a group of merfolk swam to the aid of both Therese and the bear, keeping them from floating away while guiding them toward Poseidon. The bear was still unconscious, its tongue hanging from its mouth, its eyes closed, and its heart barely beating. The school of sharks remained faithfully behind, wagging their tails like dogs.

"I'm running out of time, Poseidon. If I don't finish my quest before this bear dies, I won't be able to save my baby sister or my friend."

"I can't afford to have Ares against me," Poseidon said. "You must understand how complicated the relationships between the gods can be."

"I'm getting the idea."

Poseidon placed his trident on the bear's back, and a bright light emanated from its prongs and over the bear and throughout the water in rings that lit the sea for miles. "I just bought you some time. Now come inside and tell me why I should let you cross."

Therese was pleased to see the bear open her eyes. But once the old animal saw she was underwater among gods and merfolk, she flailed her legs in a panic and fainted with confusion. The fact that her heart beat strong and steadily was reassuring to Therese, but this feeling did not last, for when she entered the palace doors, the god of war was there to greet her.

Chapter Thirty-One: Hippolyta's Golden Girdle

The golden girdle had not been in Than's possession long when Hermes arrived at his chambers in the Underworld to summon him to Poseidon's palace.

"What's this about?" Than asked.

"Ares has Therese. Everything's in chaos. If you come now, you can keep Therese from the Amazonian Pit."

"Ares has Therese?" He grabbed the golden girdle from his sideboard and followed Hermes.

Together they god traveled directly to Poseidon's palace, where Poseidon was on one side of the large foyer with Therese, a sleeping bear, eight merfolk, and a school of happy sharks. Ares was on the other side red-faced and yelling, his voice so much louder underwater than on land.

"Enough trifling!" Ares growled. "Hand her over!"

"Enough indeed!" Than tossed Hippolyta's girdle through the water to Ares, who caught it like a Frisbee. "This should lay your fears to rest!" Then he mumbled, "Along with my dreams."

Than prayed to Therese and made eye contact with her, "Are you okay?"

"I'm running out of time," she prayed back.

Ares inspected the belt with a smile. "Yes, Thanatos. I haven't seen this for centuries. Where did you find it?"

"Does it matter?" Than spat. "You have it now and should have no more reason to whine and moan about my future marriage."

"You agree to allow me to fit it to her?"

"Yes. I'd rather have her in chastity than not at all. Though it seems perfect bliss is a faraway dream."

"I learned that lesson years ago," said Ares. "The day Aphrodite was given to Hephaestus."

Than pounded his fist into his hand. "One day, I'll find a way to make you remove that girdle from Therese, and then our love and happiness will finally be complete."

"Good luck with that," Ares mocked.

"I'm a patient god." Than moved close to the god of war. "I will find your weakness, and I will exploit it until you have no choice. That's a promise."

"We shall see," Ares scoffed. "Meanwhile, let's get this over with. Poseidon?"

Poseidon moved away from Therese, but to Than's surprise, Therese did not look happy.

"Are you pleased with yourselves for having so happily determined my fate?" she snapped. "Well, I am not a child. I'm a god, like you, and I determine my own destiny, and I will not allow anyone to tell me what I can and cannot do with my own body!"

Before Than, or anyone, could reply, Therese was surrounded by a school of sharks, and with them and the sleeping bear, she god traveled from the palace. Ares looked about to follow, but Dione appeared in her full glory, large and beautiful with silver eyes and hair shimmering in the glow of her skin. She occupied most of the foyer, pressing against all present. In her sing-song voice, she said, "That's my girl! My own descendant! I couldn't be more proud! God of war, just try to interfere, just try to get past me, and I will suck you down into the darkest, deepest abyss beneath the sea!" She turned to Poseidon. "Will you fight me?"

"This is not my fight," Poseidon replied.

Dione then turned back to Ares. "If you want Aphrodite to continue to have anything to do with you, give me back that golden girdle!"

Than turned to Ares and was amused by the sight of the war god's mouth hanging so wide open that a minnow could find a comfortable home inside.

Chapter Thirty-Two: Betrayal

In the dark of night, Therese and her entourage of sharks arrived with the bear on the surface of the Aegean Sea beneath a blanket of stars. Therese combed the sky for the Big Dipper, and once she recognized its shape, was able to trace the Ursa Major constellation down to Big Bear's paws.

"Therese, talk to me," Than prayed.

"Let me finish this quest."

"Are you angry with me?" he asked.

She hadn't liked the way he'd assumed she would wear the girdle, but she knew he was trying to protect her. "We'll talk when I'm done."

"Okay." She could hear the hurt in his voice. "Be safe."

Oh, Than. She didn't want him to feel hurt. She couldn't wait to return to his arms. "I love you. I'll come to your rooms when I'm done."

"I'll be waiting."

She knew what she was about to do shouldn't be possible, but she closed her eyes and believed. Balanced on the backs of two sharks so as to avoid being detected by Zeus in the sky, she reached her hand up until she felt the palpable fur of a foreleg. Then, as she heaved the Big Bear down from the sky she hefted her old bear up in one counter-clockwise motion.

"Good-bye, old bear! I hope you enjoy your view of the world!"

"Thank you!" the old bear said.

Big Bear, larger and more powerful than the old bear, fell on Therese, plunging them both into the water. The sharks, unsure how to serve Therese, scattered but circled nervously around them. Therese bid them farewell as, gripping the bear, she god traveled back to the woods behind her home in Colorado, where the sun was just now beginning to set.

She hadn't yet removed her helm when Callisto asked, "What's happening to me?"

Therese showed herself, wet and coughing up sea water. When she could, she said, "My name is Therese. I'm the goddess of animal companions. Artemis asked me to reunite the two of you."

"Did it not occur to you to ask me what I wanted?" The bear stood up on her hind legs and stretched a foot taller than Therese.

Therese laced her hands together at her chest, feeling like the biggest hypocrite in the world. She had just yelled at a palace full of gods for making a decision on her behalf, and here she was doing the same thing to Callisto. Tears of frustration stung her eyes. "I'm sorry. I'll take you back."

Callisto came down on all fours. "No, I don't want to go back. I'm just angry at Artemis for not trusting me. I did nothing to deserve the punishment I served for so many centuries. It's hard to get over it."

Therese reached out with her hand, hesitant at first, but then continued when Callisto did not recoil or attack and stroked the fur on the bear's back. Realizing this was not a gesture Therese would make if the bear were in her true form, she felt awkward and not sure at all how best to behave. "What do you want to do?"

"It's crazy, but I still love Artemis," she said. "Her prayers to me all these years have made life bearable. Where is she?"

"I am here," Artemis said from a shimmering cypress. She leapt from the tree and threw her arms around the bear's neck. Her voice cracked from the tears caught in her throat. "I never thought this day would come! I can't believe you're in my arms! Is this really happening?"

"I wish I could hold you properly," Callisto said. "A bear's body is so clumsy."

"I have a way to change you back." Artemis made the golden apple appear in her hand. "Eat this, and then we can be as we once were."

Trembling with disbelief over this betrayal, Therese fitted an arrow to her bow. "Stop! You promised that apple to me! I need it to save my sister!"

Artemis turned to face Therese. "I'm sorry, but this is the only way we can be together."

"But you promised!"

"Didn't Than break an oath to all of the gods of Mount Olympus so that he could be with you? And he swore on the River Styx."

"Artemis, please!" Therese cried.

"You don't need this apple to save your unborn sister," Artemis said. "I can save her, and then both of us can be happy."

"But what will Hera do when I don't return her apple?"

"What she always does. Listen, Therese, you can never get on Hera's good side. Even if you were to return the apple to her, she might not save your sister. You didn't require her to swear on the River Styx."

Therese considered this for a moment. "Would it be possible to share the apple?"

"No. Once the apple is defiled by a single bite, it's drained of all its power." Artemis turned back to Callisto. "Now eat, Callisto, before anything happens to this apple."

Therese raised her bow again. "Wait! I can pierce her heart with an arrow of hate before she swallows. If you don't want that, I need you to promise on the River Styx to save my sister's life!" It was a bluff. She had no more arrows of hate from Cupid.

A moment of clarity helped Therese to see the similarity between this situation and the one in which Than was forced to swear never to turn her into a god. She realized in that moment that she would never succeed in freeing Than of his annual visit by the maenads.

"I swear on the River Styx," Artemis said.

Therese lowered her bow, and Artemis fed the golden apple to the bear. Within seconds of her first bite, Callisto transformed into a beautiful nymph, strong and tall like Artemis with black hair and black eyes and bronze skin that gleamed in the starlight. She was breathtaking.

The two goddesses embraced. Therese said her goodbyes and then god traveled to Than's chambers to return Hades's helm and to tell Than about her next quest. She had to face Ladon and the Hesperides again. It was the only way to save Pete.

Chapter Thirty-Three: Therese's Return

Than took Therese in his arms and held her. "Let me go with you this time. I can help."

"That would be so awesome!" She circled her arms around his neck.

He noticed streaks of red when she rested her arms on his shoulders. "Look at your skin."

"I got a little scraped when Poseidon dragged me along the ocean floor."

"He what?" Than couldn't imagine Poseidon being cruel for no apparent reason.

"He thought I was your father sneaking into his domain."

"Are you okay?" He scanned her all over. "Your jeans are ripped. Are your legs okay?" He opened the holes in the back of her jeans to inspect her legs. "Looks like you're healing quickly enough."

"Yeah. It stung pretty badly while it was happening, but I'm fine." She wrapped her arms around him once more. "I wish we could stay."

He kissed her. It wasn't nearly as long as he'd wished. "Then let's stay." He ran his hands through her hair. "It's curlier than usual. I like it."

"Sea water and no blow dryer." She immediately looked self-conscious as she combed through her red curls with her fingers.

He grabbed her wrists and returned her hands behind his neck. "You look beautiful. Now where were we?"

"Can I use your magic phone again?"

He lifted his brow.

"Carol and Richard and Mrs. Holt are probably worried about me and Pete. What am I gonna say?"

"Let's see. It's seven o'clock at night there. Can you say you and Pete went somewhere together?"

"Well, his truck is still at home. How did we get there?"

He couldn't resist saying, "God travel?"

"Yeah, right." She paced the room. "Wait. I'll say I asked his friend Eric to come pick me up to look for Pete and when we found him with some other friends, we all went to hang out." She started dialing. "I'll say we needed to talk, to get things cleared up between us."

"You don't have to tell me the details." He didn't like the images she was conjuring.

When she hung up, she had a smile on her face.

"So?" he asked.

"They both said they wish we would have called and to come home immediately."

"I don't understand. Then why the smile?"

"Carol said Lynn is moving around a lot, like a healthy baby."

The corners of his mouth stretched of their own accord. "Artemis has already made good on her promise." He took her hands in his and kissed her.

"I made a difference. I can't believe it." She spun around on one foot to rest in his arms again.

"So how are you going to get Pete home immediately?"

"I told them we'd already bought movie tickets and convinced them to let us come home by midnight."

"So you bought yourself more time."

"Would you give this back to your father for me, and tell him thank you?" She took the helm from the sideboard where she had laid it when she had first arrived and handed it over to Than.

"Don't you need it?"

"No. I'm tired of hiding from Ares. Plus, we're going to god travel, and this won't protect me anyway."

Than felt blood rush to his face. "What do you mean you're tired of hiding from Ares? You do realize he will capture you again, don't you? And this time, you won't escape."

"But…"

"Listen. I know you're a god now, too. You've reminded me many times. And I know you're powerful and determined. I know you can take care of yourself. But Ares isn't someone to be taken lightly. Of all the gods, he's the cruelest and the most exacting. Even my father has more mercy than Ares."

"Than, calm down."

"Calm down?" How could he possibly calm down? It was like she was looking to get caught again. "Do you want to go back to the Amazonian Pit?"

"Of course not. But I have an idea."

He crossed his arms at his chest. "Well? What is it?"

"I want to offer him a truce."

"Oh." His shoulders sagged, and his throat constricted. "Then I guess that means you've decided to wear the girdle."

"No. I'll never wear that thing."

"I'm confused. What do you have to offer?"

"Well, since I've already pissed off Hera by failing to return the apple from Artemis, I may as well steal as many apples from her garden as I can."

He pressed his palms through the air. "Hold on. This does not sound good."

She put her hands on his hips and playfully shook him. "How many kids do you want to have?"

He jerked back his head. Hip once told him that the conversational style of females was very different from that of males, but this was the first time Therese had changed topics so quickly and radically. "Um, I'm not following you."

She laughed. "How many kids do you want to have? Take Ares out of the equation."

He tapped his chin with three fingers. "I suppose if Ares couldn't threaten to separate us for all eternity…, I would want two or three.

And by the way, I had to promise Dione we would name a daughter after her."

"Okay. I like that name. So let's say two."

"Why are we talking about this right now? Isn't Pete's life hanging in the balance? I mean, I'm happy for us to stay here all night and dream of the future kids we'll never get to have, but I don't understand why you've had a change of heart."

"I haven't." Her smile was contagious.

Maybe his father had been right the time he said gods and men would never understand goddesses and women.

"Oh, Baby, listen." Her smile was even brighter, which made him happy and confused at once. "Ares is hung up about us having kids because he doesn't want the balance of power skewed against him. Right?"

"Right. So?"

"So, in addition to taking a golden apple from Hera's garden to transform Pete, I'm going to take two more and offer them to Ares."

"Hera won't like that."

"Who would you rather have against us, Hera or Ares?"

"Good point, but how will that keep Ares from being against us?"

"I'll tell Ares that for each child I bear, he should use an apple to create his own immortal ally, to keep the power among the gods balanced."

"And if we have more than two children?"

"We'll cross that bridge when we get there." Her faced turned a little red.

"What's wrong?"

"Nothing. It's just that…well…. Goddesses don't get pregnant every time they have sex, right? Otherwise Ares and Aphrodite would have a ton of kids."

Desire flared in Than's heart. Her blushing cheeks and the awkward way she lowered her eyes made him want to sweep her into his bed. "Right." He cleared his throat, feeling the blood rush to his face. His cheeks were probably as pink as hers. "When a god and a mortal get together, a pregnancy always results. Between two gods, it's less often, but one can't predict when it will happen. They say only the Fates know."

Therese's eyes widened with a spark that meant she had an idea.

Just what he needed: another idea. "What?" he asked warily.

"The Fates live here, in the Underworld, right?"

"Right."

"Are they related to you?"

"They're my great-aunts, but I rarely see them because they're heavily guarded. Especially since that one time Apollo got them drunk to help his friend Admetus. You remember, the story I told you about…"

"Yeah, I remember. He's the one that asked his wife to die in his place."

"Yeah. Anyway, I don't think I've even been to their chambers. Our paths usually cross out there."

"Out there?"

"When I'm collecting souls. See, they also have the power of disintegration."

"Why? Why would they need to be at more than one place at a time?"

"They visit each person on his or her seventh day, when they weave, measure, and cut out the thread of life for that person."

Therese put her fists on her hips. "I don't believe that they get to decide how people live their lives. People have free will. Your brother said so, too."

"That's true."

"Then how can the Fates already know what a person's going to do?"

Than sat in one of the leather chairs in front of the fireplace and beckoned Therese to his lap. "I'm going to give you an analogy."

"Like the shower head?"

"Yes. Like the shower head. But this time, imagine you go see a fortune teller, and she says your shoelace is going to break. Then your shoelace breaks later that day. Just because she foresaw it, doesn't mean she caused it. Understand?"

"So you're saying the Fates see what we are going to do with our lives, but we still have the power to make our lives what we want them to be?"

"Not complete power, not total freedom, but yes."

"Why not total freedom?"

"Well, you don't get to choose your parents or the other circumstances of your birth, like what economic class you're born into, religion, culture, and so forth. If you're born a king, you are limited and free in different ways than if you're born a slave."

"Okay, I see. But within certain parameters, people are free to make their own destinies."

"Yes. Within limited parameters."

"So when can you take me to them?"

He seriously doubted it was possible. "Both gods and people have tried to manipulate the Fates. Like I said, they're heavily guarded."

"But if the Fates don't cause your destiny."

"Well, they do weave part of it. Those things outside of your control. And then the goddess of chance comes into play. But people, especially demigods, have come seeking my aunts under the misguided notion that the Fates can change anything. They can't. Once a thread is woven it's immutable."

"Immutable?"

"Can't be changed."

"But can't you just explain that we don't want to change anything? We just want to know how many kids we're going to have."

He shook his head. "Nothing good ever comes from knowing what the future holds."

"But our case is different." She jumped from his lap. "We need to know so we can get Ares to cooperate."

He crossed the room and grasped her shoulders, looking hard into her eyes. "And what if we don't like what we hear?"

"Like what? That we won't have any kids?"

He nodded, but he worried there could be other information they wouldn't want to know, like her being captured by Ares and kept for all eternity in the Amazonian Pit, Than helpless to save her.

"Well…, that would be disappointing…, but then we could tell Ares with confidence that he has nothing to worry about. Don't you get it?" She pulled away to pace around his room again. "If we can find out for sure how many kids we're going to have, even if it's none, we can bring back the right number of apples and have more credibility when we make our proposition to Ares."

"The Fates are never wrong."

"Exactly." She turned to him and put her hands on his chest. "So how can we arrange to meet with them tonight?"

Chapter Thirty-Four: The Fates

The chamber belonging to the Fates resembled a Las Vegas casino. It was alight with blinking colors from slot machines crammed together with archaic pinball machines along the Phlegethon, which also illuminated the room as it flowed in a circle around the perimeter of the cave through a haze of thick cigarette smoke. Two tables occupied the middle of the room. The bigger and more central was a roulette wheel that emanated a barely audible melody reminding Therese of circus music. On the right side of the roulette wheel was a much smaller table with three chairs and stacks of playing cards. Sitting in each chair was a petite wrinkled old lady holding a cigarette. They didn't look up from their cards when Than and Therese entered.

"Is it already time for their visit?" said one in a raspy, throaty voice as she picked up a card. Half of her gray hair sat in a bun on the crown of her head, and the other half lay in straight lines along her back and shoulders, across her pink velvet pantsuit. "Hit me one more time."

"Are you sure?" The sister dealing was plumper than the others but as small in stature and throaty in voice. Her gray hair was short and curly and she wore a bright blue shawl over a blue velvet dress.

"Of course not, but hit me anyway." She looked at the card. "Damn. I'm busted." She tossed the card on the table and took a drag from her cigarette.

"Hit me," said the third, who wore her white hair in a bob with bangs that curled under, reaching the top of her black-rimmed spectacles. She took the card from the dealing sister and turned all three cards over. "Twenty-one. I'm on a roll tonight."

"I think I'll hit the slots for a while," the one in the pink velvet pantsuit said.

Her sister, who wore a lavender jacket and a denim skirt, pointed to Therese. "But what about our guests, Clotho?"

"You deal with them," Clotho replied. "I need to be amazed."

"Do you want me to bring that magician from the fifth century in again?" the one who had dealt offered.

Clotho sat down before one of the blinking machines, her back to Therese and Than. "No thanks, Lachesis. He was a little too predictable for my taste." She pulled the lever.

Lachesis stacked the cards back into a full deck and said, without looking up, "You may as well have a seat." She pointed to her own as she left the table to spin the roulette wheel. "Call out a number between one and a hundred."

Therese, taking Clotho's seat, glanced at Than.

"Fifty," Than said.

The one in the lavender jacket, who was the only sister seated at the table, said, "Don't you remember? He doesn't get it right."

"I'd forgotten, Atropos. But thank you for spoiling it for me," Lachesis, the dealer, complained before returning to the table. "Please, honey, take my seat," she said to Than. "I'd ask you how you've been, but I already know. And I'd ask you why you're here, but I know that, too. I don't know how you feel, so, tell me, Thanatos, how are you feeling?"

"Anxious," Than replied. "I've witnessed only bad consequences when people seek answers from you. By the way, you know Therese. Therese, these are my great-aunts. Clotho, across the room, is the spinner. Lachesis here is the measurer. Atropos is the cutter."

"Nice to meet you," Therese said, repeating their names in her head so she wouldn't forget them: Clotho, Lachesis, and Atropos.

"I wish that were true," Lachesis said. "But it won't be nice, dearie."

"What do you mean?" Therese asked.

Atropos of the spectacles and lavender jacket blew cigarette smoke from her mouth. "Only that it's best not to know what lies ahead. But, despite this warning, you will still ask your question, so proceed."

"We wouldn't ask it if we could think of any other way to be together," Therese said.

"Blah, blah, blah," Clotho said in her pink pantsuit from across the room. "Just get on with it. Ask your question. I'm ready for a game of roulette."

"Why do you play if you already know the outcome?" Therese asked.

"It's your turn, Atropos," Clotho said. "I answered it the last time it was asked."

"But that was two centuries ago," Atropos complained.

"It still counts," Clotho said.

Atropos sighed. "The threads of gods are woven, but they are neither measured nor cut like they are for the mortals. The threads belonging to us three Fates remain unwoven, for the sake of our sanity. We do not know the details of our own futures."

"Except for those moments when we cross paths with others," Lachesis added. "Such as this visit. That's how Atropos knew what number you'd call out, Than, dearie."

Atropos exhaled more cigarette smoke and said, "We are weary of always knowing what was, what is, and what will be. These games of chance in isolation from others divert us from our otherwise dreary existence."

"But each time a new person is born, you weave, measure, and cut a new thread," Therese said. "Each one is different, right?"

Clotho waved her hand through the air. "There's nothing new under the stars, dearie. One person's life in a given culture and context is very much like another."

Lachesis came around the table next to Therese and put a wrinkled hand on her shoulder. "Occasionally someone different comes along, but it's quite rare. You, for example. Your thread was a delightful surprise."

Therese smiled. "Thank you."

Atropos looked at Therese over her spectacles and from beneath her curled white bangs. "That doesn't mean you'll like the answer to your question."

"Ask already," the impatient Clotho said again.

Therese glanced at Than, who appeared as nervous and worried as she felt. Why wouldn't she like the answer? "Okay. How many children will Than and I have?"

"Two, but none immortal," Atropos said.

"What does that mean?" Therese asked.

"Are you sure you want to ask more questions, dearie?" Lachesis asked.

"If I remember correctly," Atropos began. "They ask one more."

"Yes, you remember correctly." Therese climbed from her chair to stand beside Than. "What does that mean, none immortal?"

Atropos rolled her eyes. "I mean you produce mortal children."

"Don't ask more," Than cautioned Therese. "We have enough information to satisfy Ares."

"But…" Therese wanted a better explanation.

Than shook his head and gave her an urgent stare. "Let's go," he said. "Thanks for your help, ladies."

"Oh, good," Clotho said jumping from her seat. "Time for roulette."

"Yes, thank you," Therese added.

"Our pleasure." Lachesis gave her a friendly nod.

Clotho shook her head as she crossed the room toward the roulette wheel. "I knew she would ask it, but I still hoped she wouldn't. Why? Why do I bother?"

Therese and Than god traveled back to Than's room.

"We need to see Ares immediately," Than said. "This will put his fears to rest."

"But what does it mean, no immortal children?"

He took her in his arms. "I don't know. I don't want to know."

"But I do. What if I can't remain a god?"

"They said we have children together. There's no way I could sire children by you if you return to being a mortal."

"Unless for some reason you, too, become mortal."

Than pulled away and faced the fire crackling in his fireplace. "I knew we shouldn't have gone."

"But at least we'll get Ares off our backs." She went to him and hugged him from behind, burying her face in his strong back.

"Can you be happy with me, knowing what you know? Can you just let the future be and enjoy the present?"

She nodded against him. "Yes. I'll trust that whatever happens, as long as you and I are together, we'll be happy."

He turned around and kissed her. "Mmm. That's my girl. Now, we need to see Ares."

"How do we manage that? I don't know if they'll let us in at Mount Olympus."

"Hermes can arrange a meeting."

Chapter Thirty-Five: Conference in Paris

Than thanked Hermes for summoning the others, and then he and Therese god traveled from his chambers to Paris. He had asked Hermes to invite Apollo, so the god of truth could vouch for the veracity of Than's statements to Ares, and for Aphrodite, so her presence would put Ares in a good mood. Alecto would also be present, in case Ares tried anything, like abducting Therese again.

Aphrodite and Ares were already seated beside one another at the table on the patio of Café Moulan when Than and Therese arrived with Alecto on their heels. They had barely sat down when Apollo appeared and joined them beneath the striped umbrella that stood erect through the center of their table.

"Thank you for meeting us," Than said to the others.

Apollo eyed the snake around Alecto's neck with disdain, reminding Than how much the gods of Olympus were revolted by members of Than's family. Only Hip and Persephone seemed immune to the negative bias against which the other members of the Underworld suffered.

"Hermes said you had important news for me." Ares took a sip from his wine.

"Yes, and I've asked Apollo to come since he can recognize a lie when he hears it. I want you to know I speak the truth."

"And Alecto?" Aphrodite asked with a forced smile.

Than could see through her attempt to be polite, and his ears became hot with anger.

Alecto licked her lips in a way that resembled the darting tongue of her snake and said, "For moral support."

"Go on," Ares said.

Therese jumped into the conversation. "We went to see the Fates."

"Oh?" Ares asked. "And what did they have to say?"

Than could see the blood rush to Therese's face. She said, "They see no immortal children in our future."

"No immortal children?" Aphrodite asked.

Than cleared his throat. "For reasons we don't yet know, Therese and I have two mortal children. We share this information with you, Ares, hoping this will alleviate your need to sabotage our marriage."

"Indeed," the god of war replied. "This is good news."

Therese narrowed her eyes. "I'm glad you're satisfied. Now you can leave me alone."

After a suspicious glance toward Apollo, Ares said, "Yes, I can."

Aphrodite reached across the table and took Therese's hands in hers. "I'm so glad we have this chance to talk, Therese, because I've wanted to tell you how proud I am of you."

"Thank you," Therese said, her face turning from red to pink.

"Do you know how much of who you are comes from your godly family?"

Therese shook her head.

"Before you became like us, you already possessed gifts. You could fly in your dreams, and that helped you to control them. Your ability to fly with such zest comes from Zeus, whose blood runs in me, to Cupid, and down the line to you."

"I hadn't thought of that. I love to fly, especially now that I can do it while I'm awake." She glanced in Ares's direction before turning back to the goddess of love. "That is, when I'm not being hunted down and kidnapped."

Aphrodite smiled politely. "Your talent for swimming comes from my mother, Dione, who's quite impressed with you, by the way. She will be an advocate of yours for all time."

Therese frowned. "Have I met her?"

"She's the silver lady who stopped Ares from following you when you left Poseidon's palace with the bear," Than explained.

"Silver lady?" Therese shook her head. "I didn't see her. I was so focused on finishing the quest, I suppose."

"I think she arrived after you'd left," Ares said.

Therese glared at him. Than stifled a giggle. She was so cute when she was angry.

"And your courage comes from Ares," Aphrodite continued. "Like it or not, his blood runs through you, too."

Therese averted her eyes.

"Of course, your talent with the bow and arrow comes from Cupid." Aphrodite took a sip of her wine. "And another of your gifts is your love for others, which is quite profound, is it not, Ares?"

Ares nodded. "Yes. Quite profound, and a thorn in my side, I might add."

"But, darling, she gets that from me."

Than and Alecto exchanged amused smiles.

Ares stroked Aphrodite's long blond hair. "Yes, I know."

"And it's her most important quality," Aphrodite said defensively. "She couldn't fulfill her purpose as goddess of animal companions without it."

"Indeed," Ares said.

"A happy family reunion," Apollo interrupted. "But I'm afraid I've no time for it." He stood to go.

"Thank you for coming," Therese said, standing with the god of truth and shaking his hand. "Thank you so very much."

Apollo gave Than a silent prayer, "I don't believe you are rid of Ares."

Than prayed back as he stood and shook Apollo's hand, "Why?"

"Good bye, all." Apollo vanished.

Therese and Than remained standing.

Alecto joined them, "I, too, must get back to my work." The Fury vanished.

"Are you leaving so soon?" Aphrodite's question was directed at Therese.

"I have something I have to do," Therese replied. "A friend of mine needs help."

"Oh?" Aphrodite looked concerned.

"You remember Pete Holt? The one Cupid shot to make fall in love with me?" Therese turned a scowl in Ares's direction, and Than again stifled a smile at how cute she could be.

Aphrodite nodded.

"Well, I shot him with an arrow of hate, hoping to neutralize it, but he looked upon his sister first."

"That's terrible! Jen, the one whose father…?"

"Yes," Therese said. "So I transformed Pete into a dog and shot him with one of my companion arrows, which was great and all, but I thought I would be able to change him back, and I couldn't. So I'm going to find a way to do that."

"How?" Aphrodite asked.

"She's going on a secret quest," Than interrupted. The last thing they needed was for Hera to learn of Therese's plan before it was enacted. "And it's time sensitive. We need to go. Thanks again for meeting with us."

Than took Therese's hand and together they returned to his rooms. He sent a prayer of thanks to his sister before turning to Therese.

"You said too much," he told her.

"What do you mean? They wouldn't tell Hera, would they?"

He pushed her hair out of her eyes and gently kissed her cheek. "Probably not. But it's best to keep this adventure to ourselves." He decided not to share Apollo's warning with her. No need to make her any more anxious than she already was. "I'll get my sword and shield."

"And we should hop over to my room and grab my flute."

He kissed her again. "Sounds like a plan."

Chapter Thirty-Six: Atlas

After checking on Clifford and Jewels, Therese grabbed her flute case from beneath her bed, opened it, and assembled its three silver pieces.

"Ready?" Than asked.

"Outside the Marjorelle Garden, right?" she asked.

"Right."

Together they god traveled to Marrakesh, Morocco to pluck two apples from Hera's garden, but before the pines at the base of the Atlas Mountains came into view, an unexpected embrace pulled Therese away from her destination, and before she could blink, she was standing on a mountain peak on the tallest mountain for miles. More startling than her location was the proximity of the giant standing in front of her, looking down at her with a creepy smile and intense black eyes. The giant wore a white sarong at his hips, golden sandals, and nothing else but his curly black hair and beard. His arms were lifted up to the heavens, as though he were holding a bank of clouds. Then Therese realized who he was.

"Atlas?"

"Ah, you know my name," he said in a voice that was deep and loud enough to echo throughout the mountains. "Now tell me yours."

"Therese." She straightened her back and lifted her chin. "I'm the goddess of animal companions."

"Have you come to play your flute for me?"

She lifted her flute to study it, having forgotten it was in her hand. "No. I was actually on my way to play it for the Hesperides."

"My lovely daughters. How nice." He narrowed his intense black eyes. "But you must have another reason for visiting them. You must hope to pluck an apple."

Therese wasn't sure if she should admit this to the father of the Hesperides, so she said nothing, her throat suddenly tight.

"If you play for me on your flute, I'll get the apples for you," the Titan offered.

"Really?" She screwed her face up at him, not at all sure of his trustworthiness. She thought she recalled a story in which Atlas had tricked someone by making a similar offer.

"Yes. Can you imagine how boring it is to stand here day after day with no one to talk to, no music, no laughter? I receive very few visitors."

Therese thought it couldn't hurt to play a brief song, but she would then be on her way. She put the flute to her chin and blew across the hole, fingering a soft ballad she remembered from her junior year. Tears flooded the Titan's eyes and his creepy smile softened into a grateful one.

"That was beautiful," he said when she had finished.

"Thank you. And thanks for your offer, but I better be going now."

"Wait. Didn't you visit my daughters last summer and deceive them with that very flute?"

Therese's mouth fell open. She tried to god travel away, but her feet stayed glued to the ground. "Am I your prisoner?"

"Not his. Mine." Ares appeared beside her.

She dropped her flute and fitted an arrow to her bow, but Ares vanished before she could release it. He appeared again at her other side. She took aim again, but again, he vanished. He came up behind her, his hands pinning her arms to her side. She clutched her bow in one hand and the arrow in the other, but she could not lift her arms, nor could she god travel away.

"Why are you doing this?" she asked through gritted teeth. "You heard what the Fates said."

"As relieved as I am that you'll have no immortal children, I can't help but suspect it's because of what I'm about to do."

"Yeah? And what's that?"

He used his superior strength to force her to stand beside Atlas. Then he squeezed her wrists until she dropped her bow and arrow, and lifted her arms toward the bank of clouds.

"You'll be taking Atlas's place for a while." He nodded to the giant. "Ready?"

The Titan nodded back and slowly lowered the bank of clouds onto Therese's hands.

"No! Help! Than! Thanatos!" The clouds were heavier than they looked and she labored beneath them.

Atlas turned his intense eyes to her. "I'm sorry to leave you with this burden. Long ago, I was made to keep Uranus, the Sky, from mating with Gaia, the Earth. Now it's your turn."

"Wait! How do you know I won't drop Uranus and let him and Gaia have at it?" She lowered the clouds to her shoulders, her arms trembling from the weight.

Ares gave her a sardonic smile. "Because the first thing the Titans will do if they overpower the Olympians will be to destroy humankind, and you wouldn't want that on your back."

He and the Titan vanished, leaving her alone with the sky in her hands.

"No! Please! I have to help Pete! Please!" Why couldn't Than hear her cries, her prayers?

Chapter Thirty-Seven: The Garden

Than arrived outside of the Majorelle Garden in Marrakesh, Morocco where, unlike in Colorado where it was seven hours behind, the sun was rising above the Atlas Mountains. But where was Therese? They had just left her room in Colorado moments ago. He disintegrated to go back and look for her, but his other self went on, feeling for the entrance to the garden of the Hesperides, which was invisible to mortal eyes. The scent of pine was soon replaced with that of citrus, and the long rows of fruit trees came into view. With each step he took through the garden, Than disintegrated, so that by the time he saw the huge sprawling apple tree with its gnarly roots and branches, he was equal in number to Ladon's hundred heads.

The three daughters of Atlas awoke from where they lay curled between the roots, their beautiful figures so matched in color to the dark gray bark of the tree that they at first appeared to be nothing but gowns billowing in the breeze. Their eyes widened at the army Than had amassed, and they quickly sprang from the tree and disappeared.

Ladon, who had also been sleeping, opened his two hundred eyes and lifted his one hundred heads from where they'd been dripping from the branches like tree sap.

"I don't want to hurt you," Than warned, preferring a peaceful relinquishing of the apples to a slaughter. The beast was immortal and would return to his body in a few days, but if there were another way, he'd take it.

In case peace was not an option, he raised his one hundred swords. "I need two apples from the tree."

Ladon's heads struck in less time than it took to breathe, but Than spun out of reach and then brought his sword around. He managed to slice off a good third of the heads, but a moment's hesitation as he realized Therese was not at home in Colorado or at his rooms in the Underworld made him vulnerable. Ladon's fangs pierced through his trousers. Even though it was one bite, pain seared through all three hundred thousand of him everywhere he was in the world as the hot poison burned through his veins. He managed to slice off another third of the heads before his vision became blurry and he was struck again.

He multiplied himself into the billions, and like insects swarming its prey, he surrounded Ladon and the tree, crawling up the gnarly trunk to the highest branches. Though he could barely see, he climbed and swung, climbed and swung, an explosion of his disintegrated selves, all mercilessly attacking, long after, he soon realized, the dragon lay still.

He integrated into one at the garden, though he continued to carry out his duties for hundreds of thousands of souls. His vision was nearly gone, but he managed, so keen were his other senses and so familiar was his path through the Underworld. The Hesperides screamed from a distance as he looked with the last of his sight over the chopped bits of Ladon and at the blood dripping from the leaves and bark, and pooling on the grass near his feet. His vision became weaker and weaker as he escorted Ladon's soul to the Underworld. Than felt sorry for the beast, who was only doing his job, but he said nothing as he led him to Charon. The one Than at the garden amid the screams of the Hesperides quickly plucked two golden apples from the tree and returned to the safety of his chambers. Once the apples were well hidden, he asked Alecto to help him hunt for Therese.

Before he could set out on his journey, he found himself blind to the point that he could no longer find the souls calling to him.

In the next instant, he felt the transference of his duties as death to another, and he fell in a heap on his bed, feeling useless and afraid.

Chapter Thirty-Eight: The Goddess of Sleep

Therese struggled under the weight of the sky as the sun continued to climb over the Atlas Mountains, when suddenly the souls of the dying beckoned to her from all over the world, and she found herself disintegrating and dispatching to aid the dead. This could only mean one thing.

"Than!"

One of her dispatched to the garden of the Hesperides to look for him. Meanwhile, the one on the mountain summit multiplied into the twenties to better distribute the weight of the sky and ease her burden. Then she had the idea of stacking rocks to form pillars to take her place entirely. She disintegrated into thirty workers, each pulling out boulders from the sides of the mountain, cracking them by hitting them together to make flat edges, and stacking them up to equal her height. She built four columns along the peak of the mountain and then carefully lifted the sky from her shoulders and balanced the bank of clouds on the pillars of rock.

Back at Hera's garden, Therese was mortified by what she saw: Ladon chopped to bits, blood draping from the branches, and the three Hesperides weeping beneath the gnarly apple tree. The three nymphs looked up at her with their sad faces, their tears glinting in the morning sun, and before they could say a word, Therese took up her flute and played them a ballad to comfort them. Doing so wasted no time. She felt it was the least she could do. While she played, she disintegrated and dispatched to the Underworld.

As she neared the Underworld, she sensed Than in his bedroom and god traveled directly there. Relieved to find him all in one piece, she rushed to his side.

"Than? What's happened? Are you okay?" She leaned over where he lay on the bed, placed her hands gently on his chest, and looked into his face. That's when she noticed his eyes moving around in their sockets, apparently unable to focus on her. "You can't see!"

"Ladon's poison."

She brought her hand to her mouth to stifle a gasp. "How long will this last?"

"I don't know. Maybe forever. I need Apollo. But first, tell me. Where have you been? Are you alright?"

Therese shuddered. Forever? He could be blind forever? So in trying to save Pete, she'd ruined Than's life. She sank on the bed beside him resting her elbows on her knees, her face in her hands. "I can't believe this."

Than sat up on the edge of the bed beside her. "When I arrived in Morocco, you weren't there."

"Ares intercepted me and took me to Atlas. He forced me to take the Titan's place."

"What? Why? Are you still there now?"

"Yes, but I'm constructing pillars to hold the sky. I'm nearly done. Where can I find Apollo?"

"Damn that Ares! Damn him forever!" Than took a deep breath and blew it out. "First take the apple to Pete."

She jumped from the bed. "You got an apple?"

"Two. An extra to offer to Ares, like we planned." He told her where she could find them.

Therese took one and left the other hidden. "How can I give Pete the apple without killing him?"

"That's right. He'll die in your presence. Damn that Ares!" Then he turned his face up to the ceiling. "Hip we need you! It's urgent!"

"What can he do?" Therese asked, pacing.

"He can switch with you."

Hip appeared. "Why would I switch with her?"

Therese hadn't seen him in a while, and she'd forgotten how much he resembled his brother, even though they weren't identical: same height and build, same strong jaw and dark brows, and same sweet blue eyes, but where Than's hair was dark brown—nearly black—Hip's was golden.

"Please help us!" Therese said frantically. "Than's blind!"

"Blind?" Hip went to his brother's side and studied his face. "How?"

"Ladon's poison. Look, can you switch with Therese and be Death one more time so she can save her friend? I'll owe you another."

"Are we talking about Pete Holt?"

"How'd you know?" Therese asked.

"His sister, Jen. We've become quite close in her dreams. In fact, she's my favorite right now." He gave her his radiant smile and flirtatious wink.

"She's fragile, Hip," Therese said. "Please don't toy with her."

"Toy? I'm in love."

"Hip," Than interrupted. "We don't have time for this. Will you please just switch with her?"

"Will you get me a date with Jen?" he asked.

Therese rolled her eyes. "Are you serious? You want to break my friend's heart?"

"No. I want her to fall in love with me. Than, you, of all people, should understand. Why can't I find a partner, too?"

"You can't be serious," Than said. "You're not the type to settle down."

"People change."

"Look, whatever," Therese said with exasperation. "I'll get you the date. Now switch with me."

Hip took her hand and the transference of duty was immediate. Therese continued to disintegrate, but now, instead of guiding the souls of the dead, she was monitoring, and in some cases participating in, the dreams of hundreds of thousands of people all over the world. She disintegrated again and dispatched to the Holt place with the apple.

The Therese that remained behind stood before Hip with her mouth wide open. "This is so…surreal."

"Tell me about it," Hip said, laughing. "Now you know why I hate switching. Than definitely got the worse lot."

"You can leave now," Than said.

"Fine." Hip disappeared.

Therese turned to Than. "Tell me how I find Apollo. I can help Pete and look for Apollo at the same time."

"Hermes is best at finding gods in a hurry, and my father can summon Hermes in a flash."

Hades appeared near the stalagmite that held Than's clock and quill. "You called?" He took a closer look at Than. "Dear god, what happened to you?"

Than explained what happened in Hera's garden. In the next instant, Hermes arrived, followed by Persephone, who swooned over Than in a high-pitched, frantic voice.

"How can this be? How could this happen?"

"We need Apollo," Hades said. "The longer Ladon's poison runs through Thanatos's blood system, the worse are his chances for recovery."

"Yes, Lord Hades." Hermes disappeared.

Back at the Holt place, Therese hovered outside Jen's window to scope out the situation before entering. Jen and the golden retriever lay side by side in Jen's bed, sound asleep. Therese flew inside, picked up the dog, whose sleep was deepened by her presence, and god traveled to Pete's room. Then she entered Pete's dream, a bit frazzled to find him making out with Vicki's cousin Courtney in the hay in the barn with Stormy and Sassy looking on. It wasn't really Courtney, of course; it was a figment. Stormy and Sassy were also figments. Therese commanded them to show themselves. They transformed into three scaly eels, which swirled about the barn with hilarious laughter before flying away.

Pete sat up in the hay and looked at Therese, dumbfounded. "Therese?"

"Listen to me, Pete. I need you to eat this golden apple."

"But I'm not hungry." He stood up and wiped the hay from the back of his jeans. "I'd rather make out with you."

"But we're just friends, remember?"

"Can't we be friends with benefits?" He took her in his arms.

She held him back at arm's length, but gave him a smile. "So you're not in love with me anymore, right?"

"Love? Well, more like a little crush. Now are you gonna kiss me?"

"I'm with Than, remember?"

He frowned. "So that's a done deal? You sure? What do you know about him, anyway?"

"Quite a lot, actually. Now will you please try a bite of this apple?"

In the dream, she handed it to him, and he took a bite. In the awake world, Therese fed the apple to the sleeping dog. As soon as a single bite was swallowed, the golden retriever changed back into Pete Holt, the man.

"Oh, thank goodness," Therese whispered as she tucked Pete into bed. Tears flooded her eyes, and she batted them away with the back of her hands. She kissed Pete on the forehead. In the dream world, she hugged him, too, and told him she was sorry.

"Why are you sorry?" he asked.

"I just am." She pulled away. "Still friends?"

"Always." He winked.

Therese snapped her fingers and a figment obediently appeared in the form of Courtney. "I'm glad you two found each other."

"It's nothing serious," Pete said. "I've already told her I'm not ready for a relationship. Still too burned by you." He smiled, to let her know he would be alright.

More relief swept over Therese and, even in the dream world, her eyes filled with tears.

"See ya," she said, waving.

"See ya."

Therese decided to enter Jen's dream, too, to check on her. To her horror, she found a vicious cycle reeling round and round without end of Pete screaming hateful words to Jen, knocking over chairs. Then Pete's hands were at Jen's throat. Jen wriggled free, grabbed a gun, shot. Over and over, these same events occurred. Jen was stuck in the hellish cycle.

Therese intervened by appearing in the dream. First, she commanded the figment disguised as Pete to show itself and leave. Then she took the gun from Jen and told her everything was going to be okay.

Without transition, Jen was a little girl, maybe five or six, wearing a short simple dress and a pair of boots and milking a goat tied to the back of the house. Therese looked on from above, no longer in Jen's view. Mr. Holt, much younger and much handsomer, ambled from the barn.

"Where's your mama?" he asked her cheerfully.

"Store."

"And your brothers?"

"Out to pasture."

"Then why don't you come sit on Daddy's lap and let me tell you a story?"

Little Jen squealed with pleasure. She picked up the bucket of milk and skipped inside the house behind her father. Therese looked on, overcome with anxiety.

"Will you tickle me again?" Jen asked, pulling off her dress.

"I'll tickle you if you tickle me."

"Deal!"

Therese covered her mouth in horror as she watched the father molest the daughter in a way that made the daughter think it was fun, normal, and acceptable behavior. Five-year-old Jen enjoyed herself, laughing and smiling as though it were all a game. More tears fell from Therese's eyes as she realized now why Jen blamed herself. She'd been taught to enjoy her father's abuse and so felt responsible. Therese felt sorry for her friend, and helpless, too, until she had an idea.

"Figment, I command you to show yourself!" she said to the vision of Mr. Holt.

The eel-like creature whisked about the room, giggling before flying away.

Therese took on the form of Mr. Holt and approached Jen, whom Therese had transformed into her seventeen-year-old self wearing her favorite t-shirt and blue jeans. "Jen, I need to tell you something."

"Dad?"

"None of this was your fault. You were just a baby girl, and I was a messed up man, and I'm so sorry for hurting you."

Jen's face contorted into an expression of pain and misery. "I, I…"

"You don't have to say a thing, baby girl. You are a good girl. You've done nothing wrong. I'm entirely to blame. I can't apologize enough."

Therese could barely watch as Jen's body shook, her mouth open and gasping for air, her face white, then red, then white again. She cried and cried.

Therese went to pat her on the arm, but Jen cringed beneath the touch. That's when Therese decided to change back to her own form and comfort her friend.

"Therese?"

"It's going to be okay, Jen."

Jen threw her arms around Therese, and Therese held her for as long as it took.

At the same time Therese comforted Jen, she appeared before Carol, who had waited up on the couch in front of an old movie.

"I'm sorry I'm home so late." Even though Therese was in mortal form, her presence made it difficult for Carol to fight sleep.

"I'm…" yawn, "just…glad…you're…home." Carol's head fell back on the pillow tucked in the corner of the couch.

Therese pushed Carol's legs up in a comfortable position and rearranged the quilt over her. Then she turned off the television and went to check on her pets. Jewels's lamp had been turned off and Clifford's water bowl was still full. She stroked her sleeping pets and returned to the Underworld, where Apollo had arrived and was busy concocting a liquid remedy on an elaborate structure recently erected on Than's sideboard.

Apollo had already explained that he was using the venom from Python—a snake he defeated centuries ago and whose venom he preserved and has often used—to create an antidote that should work on Ladon's poison, since the two serpent dragons shared the same mother. Steam boiled up from a purple liquid bubbling in a glass beaker. Apollo took a glass syringe the size of a turkey baster and siphoned some of the purple liquid into a test tube, which he then added in gradations to another beaker filled with dark red syrup. When the syrup turned orange, he handed the beaker to Than and told him to drink all of it.

Therese was momentarily startled from the scene in the Underworld by her aunt's dream, which unexpectedly pulled her in. A big winding staircase made of solid oak floated from the floor of what appeared to be her home in Colorado, except each room was decorated slightly differently, and there were extra rooms, too, which Therese had never seen before. She knew the man and woman on either side of her aunt were figments, but they looked so much like her mom and dad that she hung in midair at the base of the hovering stairs and watched, dumbstruck, as they ascended with Carol to the next level.

Therese crept up the stairs and looked around. On every level, there were toddlers sitting on the wooden floors playing with toys and laughing. One grabbed a rope and swung through the air, over the staircase, and landed in a net, like the ones used at the circus for the trapeze artists and tight-rope performers. Then she saw Richard in the kitchen downstairs at the kitchen sink, his hands covered in raw meat and seasonings.

"Where's the olive oil?" he asked.

"Second cabinet to the right of the sink!" Carol called from above.

Therese caught up to her aunt and the figments and watched silently from behind.

"This is the conservatory," Carol was saying. "And over here is the library."

"You've added quite a few books to our collection," her father, or rather the figment, said.

"Here's the gymnasium," Carol said. "And across from it is the indoor pool where Therese practices her strokes."

"Does she miss us?" her mother asked.

Therese stopped dead in her tracks, which somehow attracted Carol's attention.

Carol turned to her. "Therese?"

"I do miss you, Mom," Therese whispered, her voice caught in her throat. "I miss you, too, Dad."

"I'm just showing them around," Carol said. "The nursery for Lynn is right this way."

Babies and toddlers swung by on the rope and bounced up in the air from the net below. Richard called up to locate other spices and household items, and Carol continued to point out one extravagant room after another—a game room, a sitting room, a sewing and craft room, a sculpture room—but Therese could only stare at the backs of the figments beside her, feeling the old familiar longing for her parents.

"Therese?" Than said, taking her face in his hands. "Are you okay?"

Persephone stood beside her son with an arm draped over his shoulders.

"Can you see?" Therese asked, pulling her thoughts away from the dream.

"Yes! Well, it's still a bit blurry."

"It may take a few days for your vision to return to normal," Apollo explained.

Therese turned to the god of light and gave him a beaming smile. "Thank you! I can't thank you enough!"

"Perhaps some time when things settle down around here, you can play your flute with me while I play my lyre."

"I'd like that very much," Therese said.

"So would I," Hades said. "We haven't had music down here in many years. I look forward to having a musician living among us."

Therese felt her cheeks get hot. She couldn't wait to be with Than, but her aunt's dream pulled her away again.

"Mom and Dad?" They turned briefly to look down at her from the steps of the staircase and to give her smiles, and then they continued toward the top with Carol.

"And this is the puzzle room, where we like to have tea…"

Hip appeared and took Therese's hand. The dream vanished, and she was immediately integrated into one. She was no longer the goddess of sleep. And she was no longer the goddess of death. Hip and Than had resumed their respective offices.

Chapter Thirty-Nine: Halloween Night

Therese stayed with Than for a few more hours and then returned home where she slept for the first time since becoming a goddess. She tried to manipulate her dreams, searching for her mom and dad, but nothing went right, and she woke to the sun streaming through her windows.

Maybe she would visit them in the Underworld. The idea had occurred to her before, but she'd been afraid. She knew they wouldn't recognize her, and she was afraid she wouldn't be able to handle the blank look in their eyes. Even now, she wasn't sure she could do it.

Over the next few weeks, while Hermes attempted to secure a safe and secret meeting for her with Ares, Therese took more tests online and groomed Stormy, pleased to find the Holts relatively back to normal. Therese also practiced driving with her uncle Richard. In fact, she fell into a comfortable routine: morning walks with Clifford, breakfast with Carol and Richard, and grooming Stormy and visits with the Holts until noon. Then it was lunch back home with Carol, online tests and papers in the afternoon, and driving with Richard until dinner. She spent dinner and evenings with Carol and Richard, and then nights in her room with Than. Since god travel made her vulnerable, Than preferred to come to her room rather than she to his just in case Ares had something else up his sleeve.

Throughout the day, Therese also continued to answer the prayers related to animal companions and to inspire people and animals as often as she could. She looked forward to a day when she could freely god travel so she could use her bow and arrow to help people and animals more fully love one another.

Carol's most recent doctor's appointment showed promising test results and healthy progress for the baby, which, though not wholly unexpected by Therese was nevertheless a surprise. The mood around the house was positive and hopeful, and Carol's doctor even allowed her to get off bed rest. With her due date in early November—a few short weeks away—she kept herself busy shopping for the baby.

Hermes chose Halloween night for the meeting, because the other gods would be distracted by the festivities. According to Hermes, just about every god and goddess, from the most powerful Olympian to the smallest nymph, liked to dress up in costume and roam the cities in playful camaraderie with humans.

While it was still nighttime on Therese's side of the world, the people on the eastern half of the globe were already well into the first day of November, so Hermes chose The Philippine Islands for the meeting place—specifically, Boracay, on a dinner boat not far from the island.

Hermes joined Than and Therese at a round table covered in a white linen cloth and set for four. A bottle of wine had been brought and poured in glasses for all three by a beautiful sea nymph already familiar with Hermes. The nymph had radiant caramel skin, long black hair, and black eyes framed with lush lashes.

Therese took a sip of wine and waited, clutching Hera's apple in a blue velvet pouch in her lap. Ares was late.

Than squeezed her free hand on his thigh beneath the table. He was trying to reassure her, but she could tell he was nervous, too. She gave him a smile. He smiled back. Hermes cleared his throat and tried to make small talk.

"The fishing off this island is supposed to be the best in the world."

"I don't doubt it," Than said.

"Maybe you and I should go sometime," Hermes said.

"Why, cousin!" Than said with surprise. "You've never invited me before. What's changed?"

Hermes frowned and took a sip of wine. "You always kept to yourself. Therese has brought you out, so to speak."

Than nodded and cleared his throat, unable to deny the truth in what his cousin said. He had kept to himself, but he had done so partly because he did not feel accepted by the other gods. He supposed he should have tried harder to help them get to know him, to show them that he wasn't as gloomy as his office.

Than distracted himself from the anxiety he felt by gazing at Therese. She looked beautiful in her white sundress beneath the afternoon sun, her green eyes sparkling from the gleam off the sea. The gentle breeze lifted her hair around her face like bronze flames. He couldn't resist reaching out and touching it. She met his eyes and gave him her nervous smile. He wished their meeting with Ares was behind them, and then they could enjoy the breathtaking scenery, the delicious food about to be served, the wine, and each other.

As the salad plates heaped with cold greens and tomatoes were brought out, Ares appeared in the empty seat at their table. The nymph, used to such things, did not flinch.

"I was beginning to think you wouldn't show," Hermes complained.

"You said you'd make it worth my while," Ares replied. "I find that hard to believe, unless your plan is to betray these two and turn the girl over to me."

"I'm not a girl," Therese said with narrowed eyes. "I'm a god, and I won't have you talk about me like I'm not here."

Than's throat tightened. He was proud of her, but he was also afraid. He squeezed her hand in his lap. She squeezed back.

Ares ignored Therese's remark and took a bite of the salad. "Delicious. Good choice, Hermes. I like this boat, this view of the island, and its beach. I see beautiful women not far away. The pristine sky stretches for miles. Maybe I'll bring Aphrodite here some time. I think she's grown tired of Paris."

The others ate their salads, too. They were anxious to get the meeting over with but were afraid to begin.

Plates of grilled fish smothered in white sauce and rice were brought out next. Therese found it difficult to enjoy her food. As good as it tasted, her stomach was churning with fear and dread. Would Ares accept the apple? Could they finally call a truce and live their lives in peace?

Hermes and Ares spoke of water sports and volcanos and other topics which seemed to put Ares in a good mood. Therese began to relax a little too. She managed to finish most of her plate just as the dessert was brought out.

She took another sip of wine, feeling as though she would not be able to eat another bite. She watched Ares scoop the chocolate covered strawberries and cream into his mouth. He occasionally ran a hand through his red hair. She realized then that his hair and hers were the same shade. She wondered if his blood ran through her from her father or mother. She had never thought to ask.

As he finished his dessert, she could wait no more. "We've asked you here to offer a truce."

"And how do you propose to leverage it?" Ares dabbed his chin and lips with his white linen napkin.

Therese took her hand from Than's grasp and opened the blue velvet pouch to reveal Hera's golden apple of immortality.

Ares's mouth dropped open. "I thought the mission was a failure."

"And now you see you were wrong," she replied.

Ares looked first at Hermes, then at Than, and back again to Therese. "Is it authentic?"

"Absolutely," Than said. "Do you need us to bring in Apollo?"

"No. I can tell with my own eyes. I just find it hard to believe you managed to get this apple without Hera's knowledge."

"I'm sure she knows," Than said. "I have felt her watching me ever since I took it."

"And if I take it from you, I will incur her wrath."

"She did nothing to Artemis," Hermes said. "What could she do to you that she couldn't to Artemis?"

"As her son, I often make alliances with her. Artemis has never cared for Hera."

Therese and Than exchanged worried glances.

Than asked, "Do you reject our offer?"

Ares seemed to consider it for a moment. Therese returned her hand to Than's and gripped it tightly.

The boat pitched to one side, knocking over the glasses on the table, except for the one belonging to Ares, as he held it in his hand. Red wine soaked into the white table cloth. Ares wore a smile on his face where the others looked confused. Across the horizon, Zeus's chariot led by four horses dropped from the sky and glided across the waves toward their boat. The four black stallions stampeded from the sky, their manes lifting in the wind behind them like dark flames. The air filled with the sound of a loud train. As the chariot neared, Therese saw Hera held the reins in one hand and a whip in the other. Her golden crown sat firmly on her head, her red hair fastened in a bun. A gold silk gown billowed at the sleeves against the wind. She was coming for her apple.

Therese knew that if Hera took her apple back, Therese would have nothing left to bargain for her safety. She glanced at Hermes and Than, wondering how the three of them would fare against Queen Hera and the god of war. She took a second glance at Hermes, unsure if she could count on his support, since he often favored neutral ground. Wishing she had her sword and shield, she sent a distress prayer to Hephaestus. To her surprise, the god of the forge appeared in person, bearing not only her weapons, but Than's and his own. Then Athena appeared beside Than, her sword drawn at the ready. Ares's smile faded.

Although Therese firmly held the apple, it left her hand and appeared across the table on Ares's empty dessert plate. Before she or Than could retrieve it, Ares took it up. The boat leveled as Hera approached. Then a massive wave arose from the sea, and a silver hand snatched the apple from Ares's fist. The apple floated on the wave in the silver hand twenty feet above them before Dione showed herself, emerging from the wave as a giant silver gleam. In another moment, a second chariot appeared on the opposite horizon, and by the time Dione's wave settled itself back into the sea like a soft blanket and she returned to her original size, Poseidon drew his chariot beside her and brandished his sword, pointing it directly at Ares.

"So much for our secret meeting," Hermes muttered.

"Give me back my apple!" Hera commanded from her chariot, which was alongside the boat.

"I will keep it with me, thank you," Dione said in her sing-song voice. "It deserves to rest beside Hippolyta's golden girdle in the bottom of the sea, safeguarded from all who would use it unwisely."

Therese glanced anxiously at Than. If Dione kept the apple, how would Therese protect herself from Ares?

As if the silver lady read her mind, Dione said, "Ares, I know you wish for balance among the gods as well as the people of the world so that one power will not dominate over another but will always be in conflict. I swear on the River Styx to keep this apple in neutral territory until it is needed to restore balance."

Ares stood up, and pointed at Therese. "Her very presence among us unsettled the balance."

"That's where you're wrong," Than said, also standing.

All eyes turned to him.

"You witnessed Therese face off against her parents' murderer two summers ago. We all did. If she carried vengeance in her heart, we would have seen it then. You have nothing to fear by her presence."

Ares scrutinized Therese and then Than. He opened his mouth to speak, and then didn't.

Hephaestus put a hand on Than's shoulder. "The boy speaks the truth."

"You need to let it go, Ares," Athena said. "There's nothing more to fight about."

"I don't want vengeance!" Therese said. "I just want to be happy with Than. I swear!"

"You're an oath breaker," Ares said, scowling.

"She broke no oath," Athena said. "You have nothing to fear from her."

"Fear?" Ares scoffed. "She's just a girl. I don't fear her."

"Then we're done here," Than said.

"I want my apple!" Hera screamed.

Ares rolled his eyes. "Shut up, Mother!"

Before Hera could object, Ares climbed into her chariot and took the reins, leading them back into the sky across the horizon.

Therese turned to Than and the others, and they exchanged the smiles of victors.

Chapter Forty: Goddess at Large

Therese hovered above a dilapidated townhouse on a pock-marked street corner in Sant A'gata Bolognese, Italy with an arrow fitted to her bow. The tabby cat named Belle, from the Lamborghini Museum, sat on the front stoop lapping up milk the boy Luis had given her while his mother was away. Therese spotted the woman with her meager groceries walking on the sidewalk among the other people. The woman stopped at a corner to wait for the traffic to clear, and then continued on her way. As soon as she reached the front of her house and spotted the tabby, Therese let the arrow fly. It pierced the woman's heart.

"Well, hello, kitty," the woman said cheerfully to Belle in her native tongue. "Are you cold out here? Come inside and I'll make a fire."

Luis opened the door with his mouth agape, having heard his mother's voice. He watched in silent bewilderment as the tabby followed his mother inside the house.

Therese later found the boxer whose owner beat him. The man returned home from work one day in his tiny sports car, and as he parked in his garage and carried his briefcase indoors, Therese hovered, invisible, in the kitchen above the dog, who lay forlornly with his head on his paws near an empty bowl. When his human entered the house, his tail, which had once wagged excitedly at this time of day, tucked under him as he shivered and whined. Therese took aim and shot the man before he had opened his mouth to complain about the noise, and what came out was a surprise to the dog.

"Are you hungry, Butch? Come here and let me have a hug."

Tears sprang to Therese's eyes as she watched the boxer lift his head and dare to approach his human. When the man wrapped his arms around the dog, the tail, for the first time in months, began to wag.

Zeus had denied Therese the power of disintegration, apparently still troubled by Than's reaction to the Cyclopes and worried another office with such power might prove a threat. But he did revoke his decision to banish the two of them from Mount Olympus, though Than's annual punishment at the hands of the maenads would stand.

Ten days after the confrontation with Ares on the dinner boat off Boracay, Lynn was born at eight pounds, four ounces, twenty inches long, with wisps of red hair and blue-green eyes. She was healthy in every way, and the joy in Therese's Colorado home carried the other three members through the adjustments necessary to accommodate a new little addition to the household. Therese helped with nighttime feedings, since she rarely slept, and after she obtained her driver's license, was able to run errands into Durango for more diapers and formula. Soon, she was doing most of the grocery shopping for the family, which she didn't mind, since it took her very little time to locate the items on Carol's list. She also found she enjoyed driving the red Honda Civic Carol and Richard had bought her a year ago, and she would often take Jen, and sometimes even Bobby, into town with her.

Though Therese was also busy finishing her coursework, grooming Stormy, and working at her new job at the animal rescue shelter, the freedom to god travel made it easy for her to respond to prayers from both humans and animals all over the world. And she always found special time every day of the week to be with Than.

In April, when Lynn was nearly six months old, Therese's nineteenth birthday arrived, and Than surprised her by getting Hip to take his place so Than could attend her party with her family. Carol and Richard hadn't seen Than since the summer before last, and it filled Therese with happiness to have him there, her family complete. The Holts also came—all except Mr. Holt, of course, who now lived permanently at the assisted living center—and Ray and Todd and a few other friends from Therese's swim team.

After Richard's grilled burgers and Carol's homemade fries were served and eaten and the Happy Birthday song sung and the cake cut, and while the guests sat around a fire pit on the deck beneath the countless stars, finishing off their cake and ice cream, Than asked if he could have everyone's attention. Even Baby Lynn was silent.

He stood in the middle of the group near the fire pit with Therese beside him. "All of you already know what a special person Therese is. She'd do anything for her friends and family and pets. She also helps others when she can. Her compassion seems boundless. Most of you also know I fell in love with Therese two summers ago when I visited the Melner Cabin next door and took a job as a horse handler for the Holts. Therese and I have grown close in the nearly two years we've known each other." He looked at her and smiled.

She smiled back, a bit nervous, wondering what all this speech-making was about and beginning to suspect the reason.

When he went down on one knee and pulled out a tiny black box from his trouser pocket, her heart stopped.

He opened the box to reveal a beautiful tear-drop diamond ring on a delicate gold band. "Therese, I love you with all my heart. I knew the moment we met that you were the one. Will you marry me?"

Her family and friends remained silent for a moment as she gazed back at Than with her mouth open, speechless. Finally, some of her friends whooped and hollered and someone said, "Answer him!"

Therese went down on her knee beside him, took his hand in hers, and said, "It would be impossible for someone to love another more than I love you. I want to spend eternity with you."

Everyone around them applauded. Someone whistled—Jen, Therese realized. Therese's aunt and uncle appeared happy but concerned. Than took Therese by the arm and helped her to her feet.

"Just so you don't freak, Carol and Richard, I promise to wait another year. This time next year, when I turn twenty, we'll be married, and all of you are invited."

Than gave her a quizzical look, but she kissed him before he could say anything.

Later that night, when they were alone in her room after he had received his office back from Hip, Than wanted to know why she wanted to wait a year.

"A year to us is nothing," she said, sitting beside him on her bed. "And I can spend time with Lynn before I move out. They need me right now."

"But what about our plans to travel the world together?"

"We can do that while I'm planning our wedding. Believe me, my aunt and uncle are going to expect a traditional wedding. Do you suppose the Olympians will come?"

"They'd be too curious to miss."

"So you're okay with waiting?" she asked. "Because if it bothers you, I'll marry you now. I don't want to disappoint you, Than."

"You could never disappoint me." He kissed her gently on the lips. "And, as you said, you should spend Lynn's first year here at home, bonding with her. She's your sister, after all."

Therese circled her arms around Than's neck and pressed her lips hard against his. "I love you so much! Sometimes it hurts and feels good all at the same time!"

"I know exactly what you mean." He kissed her back, and in between kisses he said, "That's how I felt when the maenads ripped me apart. It hurt like hell, but knowing it meant being with you forever made it feel good, too."

Therese found herself spending more and more time in the Underworld, preparing Than's rooms for her official move in date. The two rats that perched on her shoulders during her final challenge last summer found her again, and they sometimes flew with her on her missions to help humans and animals to better love one another. This gave her the idea of inviting along Clifford, who at first found flight and god travel disconcerting, but who eventually adjusted and even came to enjoy their missions together. A few weeks before the wedding, Therese shot an arrow into Jewels and gave her the gift of immortality. Therese set up her tank in their chambers in the Underworld to help her adjust to her new quarters. She'd been gradually moving more and more of her things from Colorado into her new rooms, and on occasion solicited Charon's assistance with some of her bulkier items. Luckily, Cerberus took an immediate liking to Clifford, and the two of them sometimes played together outside of the gates while Therese organized and decorated her rooms. Than surprised her by bringing in the souls of plants he'd been collecting and by giving her the idea of bringing Stormy.

"What?" Mrs. Holt asked Therese where they stood in the barn by Stormy's stall. It was late March, two short months before the wedding.

"I want to take Stormy to Texas," she said. "I promise to take excellent care of him."

Mrs. Holt looked from Pete to Jen to Bobby and back again to Therese. "Well, I must say I never expected this. When we gave him to you, I thought he'd stay here with us."

"But we did give him to her," Pete said. "Didn't we? Or did you do it in name only."

Mrs. Holt shook her head. "No. Stormy belongs to Therese, and if she wants to take him to Texas, she can."

"He's almost two, after all," Jen said. "Old enough to leave Sassy."

Therese couldn't explain that she planned to visit Sassy often, via god travel. She also had to lie and say Than would drive up to Texas with a trailer to transport Stormy, when in reality, she'd shoot him with an arrow before taking him directly to the Underworld. Although most mortal horses weren't strong enough to ride until they were four, as an immortal being, Stormy could handle Therese, especially since most of the time they'd be in the air.

Before the night that she took Stormy, Therese switched duties with Hip once more so he could go as a mortal to the upper world and take

Jen on a date. Jen was pleased to meet Than's twin brother. Therese could tell Jen recognized him from her dreams.

"I saw him coming," Jen told Therese one spring afternoon as they kayaked together on the Lemon reservoir. "I've been dreaming about Hip for months."

"Long distance relationships can be difficult," Therese warned, afraid for her friend. If Hip broke Therese's heart, she'd punch him, and now that she was a god, she knew it would hurt.

"Well, it was just one date," Jen said. "But you never know, do you?"

One day while she was moving more things into the Underworld, her rats jumped from her shoulders and ran along the Phlegethon through winding chambers toward the Lethe. They didn't beckon Therese, like they sometimes did, to show her something new down there she hadn't seen before, but, she followed them anyway, curious. Long before the rats joined their friends in some dark crevice, Therese noticed the Fields of Elysium and the multitudes of souls sharing their common illusions. With her keen goddess eyesight, she spotted the souls of her parents picnicking beneath a tree. Her father scribbled notes inside a book, and her mother pinched a flower between her fingers, breaking off petals. Therese knew they would not recognize her, but she decided it was time to say goodbye. Without touching the Lethe streams, lest she lose her memory as well, Therese flew to their tree and said hello.

"Hello," her mother said.

"Would you like to hear a poem?" her father asked.

Therese smiled. "Yes."

Her father read from where he had written in his book:

A constellation of three

Hung in the sky

Sparkling happily

Ever nigh.

Their light shone

For years and years

Long after time
Had taken the spheres.
Look in the sky
And see all three
Sparkling happily.

Her father looked up from his book. "What do you think?"

Tears flooded her eyes and rolled down her cheeks. "It's beautiful."

"I think you made her cry," her mother said to her father.

Therese batted the tears with the back of her hands. "That's okay. It was lovely. And these are happy tears."

Her father returned to his scribbling and her mother to breaking apart her flower. Therese whispered goodbye and floated away.

Two weeks before the wedding, Therese had completely moved everything she was taking with her to her chambers in the Underworld. She flew through the air on Stormy's back with her rats on her shoulders, Clifford in the saddle in front of her, and her quiver and bow over her shoulder. She looked down at her aunt and uncle preparing for dinner with Lynn scooting around in her walker cooing "Terry!" her name for Therese. Then she turned and looked through the earth and into the Underworld, where Than lit candles at their golden table, opened a bottle of wine, and turned on the CD player Therese had given him as a present. Jewels listened from her tank. Therese couldn't be happier about the family she was leaving (though she would often visit) and the one she would soon be making with the love of her life. She sailed through the air as the sun set in the west and rose in the east, both which she could see at once.

THE END

The House of Hades, Chapter One: Under Attack

Please enjoy this excerpt from the fourth book in the series, *The House of Hades:*

Therese stood in the doorway, twirling a strand of her red hair round and round her index finger. There was only one bed in the center of Hecate's room. That could be a problem, even though Therese only slept about once a week.

"Maybe this wasn't such a good idea." Therese took a step back, knocking her quiver and bow against the cold stone wall.

"It will be fine." Hecate skipped forward and snatched up Therese's bag. "You can unpack your things in my closet." When she spun around toward the back of the room, her black and white hair fanned out around her slim shoulders.

Hecate didn't look like a witch or a hag or the dozens of other descriptions Therese had found on Google while visiting her family and friends in Colorado a month ago. She was an inch taller than Therese, and, in spite of the white streaks in her hair, she looked young, closer to Hermes's age, mid-twenties, with a delicate nose and thin lips. Therese knew Hecate was ancient—older than Than—but one thing she'd learned since becoming the goddess of animal companions was that immortal beings aged at different rates from humans and from one another.

"You aren't what I was expecting," Therese said with a smile.

"Mortals get me confused with Than's sister, Melinoe. That's probably it. Were you expecting someone more terrifying?"

Therese pulled her eyebrows together in confusion. "Do you mean Megaera?"

Hecate's face broke into a grin. "Those two are nothing alike." Then, in a somber voice, Hecate added, "I'm not surprised Than never mentioned Melinoe."

"Well that makes one of us," Therese said. How could he omit such an important detail? She'd told Than everything about herself and her family. Why wouldn't he have ever mentioned Melinoe? "Does she live down here, too?"

"She used to, until Hades banished her a few centuries ago. Now she lives on the outskirts of the Underworld in a cave on Cape Matapan."

"And that is…"

"On the southernmost tip of Greece." Hecate stepped forward. "Where are my manners? Meg will scold me later. Please come on inside. It's so nice to have company. I get lonely here when Persie moves in with Hades." Hecate slipped Therese's bag behind a wooden door, as though she wished to give Therese no opportunity to change her mind. "In the springs and summers on Mount Olympus, Persie and I share rooms with Demeter. Down here, I have a lot of time to myself."

Therese looked around the chamber for the first time, its dome ceiling high and covered with dancing shadows, cast by the light of the Phlegethon, the river of fire. A stream ran from an upper crevice down a series of rocks and pooled in a six-foot-wide basin before thinning and disappearing behind another smooth boulder.

"That's where I wash," Hecate explained. "The spring is fresh and good enough to drink."

Beside the basin and curled on a pillow was a small animal, a cute brown fur ball Therese had never seen. "Who's this?"

"Galin, my polecat. This is the time when she likes to sleep."

"I won't disturb her, then."

"My dog is awake and around here somewhere." Hecate glanced about the room. "Cubie? Where are you?"

A black Doberman pinscher with tall ears and a long tail crawled out from beneath the one big bed.

"There she is." Hecate reached over and patted the dog on the head. "Were you spying on us?"

"Absolutely," the dog answered.

Hecate laughed. "Cubie, this is Therese."

"Pleasure," the dog said.

"Likewise." Therese stroked Cubie's back, wishing Clifford had taken her seriously when she'd announced that she was moving out of Than's rooms. Instead, he'd given her an unconcerned stare as she had said goodbye and I mean it this time. "I have a dog, too. Maybe you would like to meet him."

"Is he intelligent?" Cubie asked.

"He's pretty smart." As the goddess of animal companions, Therese had met quite a lot of dogs, and she felt positive that Clifford was as smart as any of them.

"But probably not as smart as Cubie," Hecate said. "She was once the Queen of Troy."

Before Therese could ask why a former Queen of Troy was now a dog, the floor trembled beneath their feet, followed by a loud boom.

Therese clutched the wall as Hecate fell back on the bed and shouted, "Ahhh!"

"What was that?" Therese asked when the floor stabilized.

"I don't know." Hecate's voice was frantic. "I can't get a prayer through to Hades or to Persie."

Therese tried, too, but sensed no response. Blood pounded in her head as the ground began to quake again. She clutched the locket at her throat and prayed to Athena but got no answer.

"Will these walls hold?" She glanced up at the ceiling, a host of scenarios playing through her mind. If the walls of the Underworld were to crumble, what would happen to its billions of inhabitants, including the souls of her mom and dad?

"Where are they—Hades and Persephone?" Therese asked.

Hecate winced as another boom sounded throughout the chamber. "Mount Olympus."

Just then, a crack ran across the ground, up the wall, and through the dome ceiling.

"It's going to collapse!" Therese shouted.

Small chunks of the ceiling fell on the bed, on the golden table by the hearth, and in the water basin, causing Galin to leap from her pillow and into Hecate's arms.

"Clifford and Jewels!" Therese cried. "They're in Than's rooms." Her stomach balled into a knot when she imagined them harmed.

"I'll go with you." Hecate set Galin down on the bed and spoke to the shivering weasel. "You and Cubie go to Demeter's winter cabin and wait for me there. Okay?"

More rocks crumbled down the walls as a series of booms sounded throughout the chamber. The stream, which once ran gently down the wall, shot out, spraying in all directions.

"I'm not leaving you!" Galin returned to her mistress's arms.

"Nor I!" Cubie declared.

Soaked and trembling, the four of them rushed down the winding path along the Phlegethon, dodging the falling rocks. Cracks chased them all across the walls, and loud booms shuddered through the air. Therese was afraid to pray to Than, worried he'd god travel straight into danger. Even in her limited experience, she knew that if you arrived at a point occupied by solid mass, such as a large boulder, your body composition would momentarily meld with it. She'd discovered this problem when she once arrived in a brick wall. It had taken over an hour to recover, and the pain had been excruciating.

She found Clifford barking nervously by the hearth. "Come on, boy! We've got to get Stormy!"

Therese carried Jewels like a football in the crook of one arm as the group scurried down the narrow passageways toward the stables. She wondered if Than would be angry with her for not calling to him right away. He was already angry with her, and she didn't want to put another rift between them.

As they passed by the intersection of the Lethe and the Styx, deities cried out, and, although Therese and Hecate slowed down and searched the waters, they could not find the source of the cries. Cubie said she'd stay behind and keep searching.

When Therese rounded a corner, a colony of bats whirred up from a crevice below and fluttered past them, and then out climbed Tizzie, up from Tartarus with blood dripping down one arm.

"What is happening?" Tizzie demanded, her black serpentine curls covered in dust.

"We don't know," Therese replied.

"Well that's just great," Tizzie said, waving her hands. "The souls are in chaos. And if the pit ruptures, the Titans will be unleashed. Where the devil is my father?"

"Mount Olympus," Hecate said, dodging a falling rock that landed with a clack beside her.

Sensing Stormy's danger, Therese sent a prayer to Tizzie as she hustled toward the stables, explaining why she was on the run instead of god traveling to the gate.

I'll meet you at Cerberus, Therese added.

The three judges floated by her in their long robes headed in the opposite direction, toward the gate. Perhaps their demigod status kept them from god travel, she thought. Hecate was no longer behind her as Therese reached the stables with Clifford and Jewels. When she opened the wooden door, she found the walls had completely collapsed, and Stormy lay on his side crushed beneath the rubble with blood pouring from his flanks.

   ***

Among the weeping women and children, Than pulled the soul of the Chinese man from the limp body on the bed. As sorry as he felt for those left behind, Than's own troubles distracted him beyond measure. He tried to put the doubts out of his mind, but with no success. They appeared, against his will: Therese had used him so she could become a god. She had never loved him as he loved her. The death of her parents, and so many after, had motivated her to find a way around her own mortality.

He ushered the soul across the heavens and then down through the deep chasm, where hundreds of his disintegrated selves led other souls from different parts of the world. Like a great machine—the greatest conveyor belt imaginable—he swept along, an automatic cog in the wheel of life. And there below him on his raft, long pole in hand, was his fellow cog, Charon, ready to carry the souls to their judgment.

For centuries, he'd done this same work, longing for a change, and now that he'd finally found his wish, he was only more miserable.

Therese never meant to marry him. He'd been a fool.

In the weeks since she moved in, her twentieth birthday and their wedding date had come and gone. Therese had said she wasn't ready, postponing their marriage indefinitely. When he asked her why, she had repeated, "I'm not ready."

Than was a patient god. Although disappointed, he could wait for as many years as Therese needed. But it wasn't her spoken objection that had his stomach in knots and his emotions unstable; it was the physical distance she put between them of late that made him shiver and regret the day he'd met her.

How could the same touch of his hands on her that had once made her smile and cling to him cause her to avert her eyes and pull away? If she once loved him, it was clear she did no longer.

Aphrodite had warned him this might happen.

As he neared Charon, he noticed Cerberus whining, and beside him stood his sister Tizzie. Then he saw a great explosion beyond the gates, and red and orange sparks flew through the sky. Rocks tumbled down the walls of the chasm, like the beginning of an avalanche. In all the centuries Than had lived in the Underworld, he'd never witnessed anything like this before.

"Charon," Than said. "What's happening?"

"I believe the Underworld is under attack," the old man replied in his husky, gravelly voice.

At that moment, Than sensed Stormy's death in the stables, and he disintegrated and dispatched where he found Therese, with Jewels clutched to her chest and Clifford barking hysterically at the crushed body that belonged to Stormy.

"What in the hell is going on?" Than asked.

"I don't know! We can't reach your parents. We've got to get out of here."

Before Than could respond, a thick black boulder loosened from the ceiling and landed squarely on Therese's head, knocking her and the tortoise to the floor. The tortoise slid across the ground, spinning on its back, and stopped several feet away, safe from harm, but Than heard the crunch and thud of Therese's body beneath the weight of the massive rock. His heart stopped beating as he held his breath and stared in shock.

"Father!" he shouted into the falling debris surrounding him. He felt like a helpless, desperate child. "Father!"

***

Hypnos lifted the saddle onto the beast and tightened the tack. He still wasn't used to the sharp smell of hay and feces, stirred about by the brushing by humans of the other beasts surrounding him. It wasn't a bad smell, really. Having spent most of his life in the Dreamworld, where sensory perceptions were dulled by a degree of separation between the mind and the body, he rather liked the pungent assault on all of his senses, not just the olfactory ones. Besides, his eyes were continually pleased by the prettiest girl he'd ever seen who was now bent over in front of him. The corners of his mouth twitched, and he fought the urge to slap her on the rump. Instead, he patted Hershey, the horse in his charge, and told him what a good boy he was, as he'd often heard the other humans say to their beasts.

Hip was grateful to the old Holt woman for taking him on as a horse handler yesterday when he'd shown up, unannounced. He'd finally won his father's permission to follow in Than's footsteps to journey to the Upperworld as a mortal in pursuit of a queen. Whether Hip would actually marry her was a different story. Hip realized that his brother had the right idea in finding a way to spend time in the Upperworld, and Hip wanted his turn. All these years of visiting girls in the Dreamworld didn't compare to the feeling of being in the physical presence of one.

Centuries ago, he'd come close to marrying one of Aphrodite's youngest Graces, Pasithea, but she overwhelmed him with her neediness, and he finally broke off their relationship. Since then, he'd been content playing with mortals in their dreams, but his brother's recent love affair, he had to admit, had made him jealous. He couldn't help but wonder what real girls were like and if they'd be as eager to put their arms around him in the Upperworld as they were in their dreams.

Hip hoped to soon have a taste of Jen's pretty lips. Maybe he'd get lucky and taste all of her.

Mrs. Holt looked at him now from behind the big stallion they called The General.

"You're as handy as your brother," Mrs. Holt said. "Too bad he couldn't come with you."

Jen stood up and brushed her mare's mane. "He's too busy with the wedding plans, I bet."

Hip couldn't stop the smile from crossing his face every time Jen looked at him through narrowed eyes. She recognized him, he was sure of it, but she was having trouble admitting to herself that she knew him from her dreams.

"I doubt that," Hip said with a shrug.

Jen whipped around to face him with her hands on her hips, her pretty mouth making a perfect "O." Then she said, "He better not make her do everything by herself. Damn your brother if he does."

This tickled Hip beyond control, and he couldn't stop himself from busting out laughing. What mortal had the gall to damn the god of death? Of course, this girl had no idea what she was saying.

"Language," Mrs. Holt said from the back of the barn.

Jen ignored her mother. "What's so funny?" She moved closer, her brown eyes glaring up at Hip from beneath her pretty blonde bangs and equally blond lashes. "Don't tell me you're a chauvinistic pig."

"Jen!" Mrs. Holt scolded from behind her beast. "Don't talk to Hip like that."

Jen kept her eyes blazing on Hip, but spoke to her mother. "I have the right to talk like that to anyone who laughs at me, Mama."

"My apologies," Hip said, reining in his chuckles. "But you misunderstood. Than's not busy with the wedding because, last I heard, Therese called it off."

Jen's mouth dropped open. Then, after staring incredulously at Hip for an uncomfortable amount of time, she threw her hands up in the air and presented him with a smile he hadn't earned. "Allelujah, praise the Lord! It's about time she came to her senses."

Was she praising him? Had he become her lord? Somehow he doubted it, but he was amused by how quickly Jen's demeanor changed from attack mode. She looked about to hug him. He liked being the bearer of good news.

"When's she coming home?" Jen asked him.

Hip shook his head. "I don't think she is. I, I…" He wished he'd kept his mouth shut. It wasn't his job to explain why a goddess couldn't live among her mortal friends and family.

Jen stepped between the horses and planted her feet inches from his. He wanted to reach out and touch her to see if she felt as good as she did in the Dreamworld. Her eyes narrowed and then widened, and for a moment, he thought she had figured out who he was. But then she said, "Don't tell me she's going to stay in Texas."

"Why would she…" Hip stopped himself. "Maybe you should talk to her yourself." He turned his back to her and continued to brush the horse. This conversation was over. He'd never had to make explanations to mortals, and he wasn't about to start doing it now.

But Jen moved close behind him, so close, he could feel the heat from her body. He could smell her sweat and something else. Something fruity and sweet.

"I can't get a hold of her," Jen said in a desperate voice. "She hasn't returned any of my texts and calls in over a month. I don't know if she has her new email yet. She's not on Facebook anymore, or Instagram. Nothing. It's like she's disappeared off the face of the earth."

She has, he wanted to say. That's exactly what's happened. But, of course, he wouldn't.

Jen put her hand on his shoulder, and he felt every part of him come to attention.

"Please," she said softly. "Please help me get in touch with her."

He turned and saw tears welling in her eyes. "I'll do what I can."

***

Jen was surprised by the sudden tenderness in the new handler's voice. It reminded her of something from a dream. She closed her eyes and shook her head.

"What?" Hip asked, his face close.

She took a step back. "I need to get back to work."

As she brushed Satellite, Jen stole glances at Hip. He'd taken her out to a movie over a year ago when his brother had introduced them, but then he'd never called her again after that. He'd said he'd never been to this part of the world, as though he were from another country. But he was from Texas. He spoke as if Texas were in a different part of the world.

Well, maybe all Texans thought that way.

Now he had the gall to show his face and ask for a job. He could have called her just to say, "Hey."

She glanced at him once more, and this time she noticed a look of worry come over his face, even horror.

"You alright?" she asked. He was freaking her out.

He turned to Jen's mother and said, "I'm sorry, Mrs. Holt, but I have to go."

"What is it?" Jen's mom asked, also noticing the obvious look of horror on their new handler's face.

"I can't explain," he said. "Something's not right. I need to go immediately. My apologies."

"Do you need a ride anywhere?" Pete asked, having just walked in from the pen and having overheard the last bit of their conversation.

"Um, no thanks," Hip said. "Thanks anyway, man."

Jen's mouth dropped open. This made absolutely no sense. She followed Hip from the barn and stood at the gate, where he let himself out of the pen.

"Are you coming back tomorrow?" she asked.

"I don't know. I hope so." He didn't even look at Jen, which hurt after the tenderness between them moments ago. She'd begun to forgive him. And now he was leaving?

"Will I ever see you again?" she cried out as he jogged down the gravel drive from her house to the road.

"I hope so," he repeated, but again without turning and meeting her eyes.

Overcome with a sudden feeling of dread, Jen opened the gate and followed him down the path. She watched him turn past a line of oak trees. When she rounded the corner, her throat pinched closed by the shock. He had disappeared.

She looked all around the one-mile stretch of road from her house to the Melner Cabin, where he was staying. Panting for breath and trembling, she knocked on the door of the cabin and got no answer.

"Hip? Are you there?" she called again and again, but the boy had vanished.

779

Eva Pohler is a *USA Today* bestselling author of over thirty novels in multiple genres, including mysteries, thrillers, and young adult paranormal romance based on Greek mythology. Her books have been described as "addictive" and "sure to thrill"—*Kirkus Reviews*.

To learn more about Eva and her books, and to sign up to hear about new releases, and sales, please visit her website at www.evapohler.com.

www.ingramcontent.com/pod-product-compliance
Lightning Source LLC
Chambersburg PA
CBHW070541310726
48982CB00010B/1427/J